The Second Nathaniel Drinkwater Omnibus

The Bomb Vessel
The Corvette
1805

RICHARD WOODMAN

A *Time Warner* Paperback

This edition first published in Great Britain by Warner Books in 2000
Reprinted by Time Warner Paperbacks in 2004

Previously published separately:

The Bomb Vessel
first published in Great Britain in 1984 by John Murray (Publishers) Ltd
Published by Sphere Books Ltd 1985
Reprinted 1987 (twice), 1989, 1991
Reprinted by Warner Books 1994
Reprinted 1995

The Corvette
first published in Great Britain in 1985 by John Murray (Publishers) Ltd
Published by Sphere Books Ltd 1986
Reprinted 1987, 1988, 1990, 1991
Reprinted by Warner Books 1996
Reprinted 1995 (twice), 1997

1805
first published in Great Britain in 1985 by John Murray (Publishers) Ltd
Published by Sphere Books Ltd 1987
Reprinted by Warner Books 1995
Reprinted 1999

A CIP catalogue record for this book is available from the British Library.

ISBN 0 7515 3108 1

Typeset in Palatino by M Rules
Printed and bound in Great Britain by Clays Ltd, St Ives plc

Time Warner Paperbacks
An imprint of
Time Warner Book Group UK
Brettenham House
Lancaster Place
London WC2E 7EN

www.twbg.co.uk

The Bomb Vessel

For
OSYTH LEESTON
with many thanks

Contents

Author's Note

The part played by Nathaniel Drinkwater in the Copenhagen campaign is not entirely fiction. Extensive surveying and buoy-laying were carried out prior to the battle, mainly by anonymous officers. It seems not unreasonable to assume that Drinkwater was among them.

Drinkwater's bomb vessel is not listed as being part of Parker's fleet but as she was nominally a tender this is to be expected. When ships of the line are engaged historians are apt to overlook the smaller fry, even, as occurred at Copenhagen, when it was the continuing presence of the bomb vessels left before the city after Nelson withdrew, that finally persuaded the Danes to abandon their intransigence. It has also been suggested that Nelson's success was not so much due to his battleships, which were in some difficulties at the time fighting an enemy who refused to capitulate, but to the effect of the bombs, throwing their shells into the capital itself.*

The presence of the Royal Artillery aboard bomb vessels is not generally known and it was 1847 before the three surviving artillerymen received recognition with the Naval General Service Medal and the clasp 'Copenhagen', confirmation of that famous regimental motto 'Ubique'.

Evidence suggests only four bombs got into station though contemporary illustrations show all seven. Quite possibly one of the four was *Virago*.

The hoisting of the contentious signal No 39 by Sir Hyde Parker has been the subject of controversy which has been clouded by myth. Given Parker's vacillating nature, his extreme caution and the subsequent apotheosis of Nelson, I have tried to put the matter in contemporary perspective.

As to the landing of Edward Drinkwater, the 'Berlingske Tidende' of 27th March 1802 stated that British seamen landed near Elsinore the day before 'for water' without committing any excesses. This landing does not appear to be corroborated elsewhere.

* See Journal of the Royal Artillery. Vol LXXVI Part 4, 1949, October, pages 285–294.

PART ONE

Tsar Paul

'Whenever I see a man who knows how to govern, my heart goes out to him. I write to you of my feelings about England, the country that . . . is ruled by greed and selfishness. I wish to ally myself with you in order to end that Government's injustices.'

TSAR PAUL TO BONAPARTE, 1800

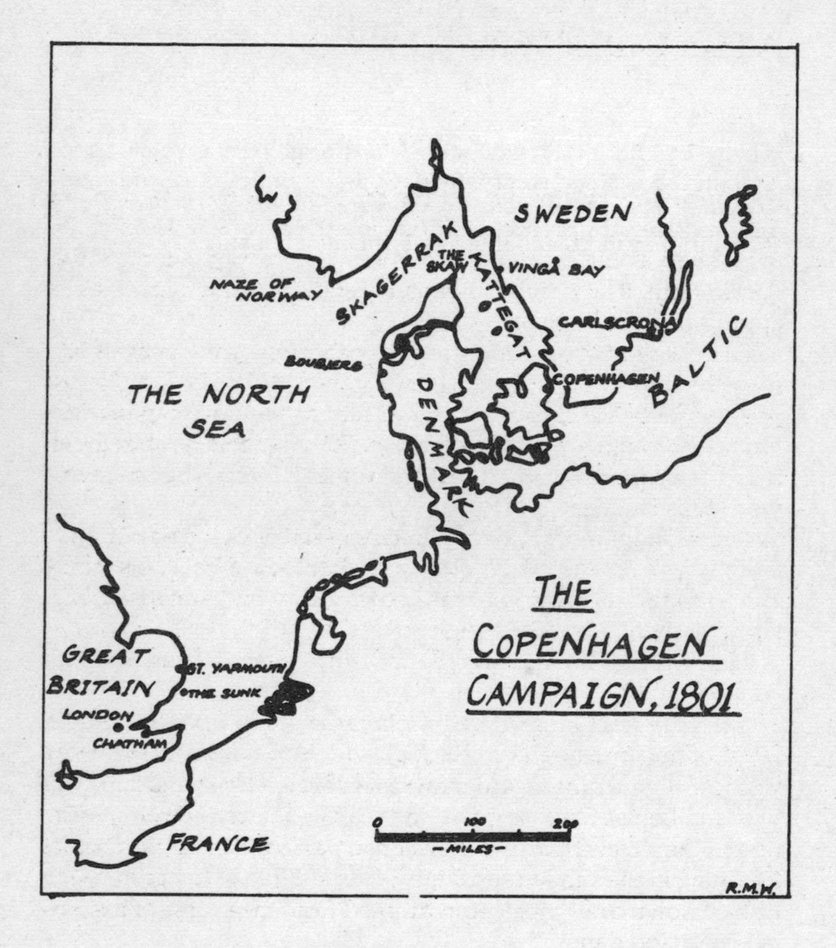
SWEDEN
NAZE OF NORWAY
SKAGERRAK
THE SKAW
KATTEGAT
VINGÅ BAY
CARLSCRONA
BOUBJERG
THE NORTH SEA
DENMARK
COPENHAGEN
BALTIC
GREAT BRITAIN
ST. YARMOUTH
THE SUNK
LONDON
CHATHAM
FRANCE
THE COPENHAGEN CAMPAIGN, 1801
0
100
200
MILES
R.M.W.

Chapter One *September 1800*

A Fish Out of Water

Nathaniel Drinkwater did not see the carriage. He was standing disconsolate and preoccupied outside the bow windows of the dress-shop as the coach entered Petersfield from the direction of Portsmouth. The coachman was whipping up his horses as he approached the Red Lion.

Drinkwater was suddenly aware of the jingle and creak of harness, the stink of horse-sweat, then a spinning of wheels, a glimpse of armorial bearings and shower of filth as the hurrying carriage lurched through a puddle at his feet. For a second he stared outraged at his plum coloured coat and ruined breeches before giving vent to his feelings.

'Hey! Goddamn you, you whoreson knave! Can you not drive on the crown of the road?' The coachman looked back, his ruddy face cracking into a grin, though the bellow had surprised him, particularly in Petersfield High Street.

Drinkwater did not see the face that peered from the rear window of the coach.

'God's bones,' he muttered, feeling the damp upon his thighs. He shot an uneasy glance through the shop window. He had a vague feeling that the incident was retribution for abandoning his wife and Louise Quilhampton, and seeking the invigorating freshness of the street where the shower had passed, leaving the cobbles gleaming in the sudden sunshine. Water still ran in the gutters and tinkled down drainpipes. And dripped from the points of his new tail-coat, God damn it!

He brushed the stained breeches ineffectually, fervently wishing he could exchange the stiff high collar for the soft lapels of a sea-officer's undress uniform. He regarded his muddied hands with distaste.

'Nathaniel!' He looked up. Forty yards away the carriage had pulled up. The passenger had waved the coach on and was walking back towards him. Drinkwater frowned uncertainly. The man was older than himself, wore bottle-green velvet over silk breeches with a cream cravat at his throat and his elegance redoubled Drinkwater's annoyance at the spoiling of his own finery. He was about to open his mouth intemperately for the second time that morning when he recognised the engaging smile and penetrating hazel eyes of Lord Dungarth, former first lieutenant of the frigate *Cyclops* and a man currently engaged in certain government operations of a clandestine nature. The earl approached, his hand extended.

'My dear fellow, I am most fearfully sorry . . .' he indicated Drinkwater's state.

Drinkwater flushed, then clasped the outstretched hand. 'It's of no account, my lord.'

Dungarth laughed. 'Ha! You lie most damnably. Come with me to the Red Lion and allow me to make amends over a glass while my horses are changed.'

Drinkwater cast a final look at the women in the shop. They seemed not to have noticed the events outside, or were ignoring his brutish outburst. He fell gratefully into step beside the earl.

'You are bound for London, my lord?'

Dungarth nodded. 'Aye, the Admiralty to wait upon Spencer. But what of you? I learned of the death of old Griffiths. Your report found its way onto my desk along with papers from Wrinch at Mocha. I was delighted to hear *Antigone* had been purchased into the Service, though more than sorry you lost Santhonax. You got your swab?'

Drinkwater shook his head. 'The epaulette went to our old friend Morris, my lord. He turned up like a bad penny in the Red Sea . . .' he paused, then added resignedly, 'I left Commander Morris in a hospital bed at the Cape, but it seems his letters poisoned their Lordships against further application for a ship by your humble servant.'

'Ahhh. Letters to his sister, no doubt, a venomous bitch who still wields influence through the ghost of Jemmy Twitcher.' They walked on in silence, turning into the yard of the Red Lion where the landlord, apprised of his lordship's imminent arrival by the emblazoned coach, ushered them into a private room.

'A jug of kill-devil, I think landlord, and look lively if you please. Well, Nathaniel, you are a shade darker from the Arabian sun, but otherwise unchanged. You will be interested to know that Santhonax has arrived back in Paris. A report reached me that he had been appointed lieutenant-colonel in a regiment of marines. Bonaparte is busy papering over the cracks of his oriental fiasco.'

Drinkwater gave a bitter laugh. 'He is fortunate to find employment . . .' He stopped and looked sharply at the earl, wondering if he might not have been unintentionally importunate. Colouring he hurried on: 'Truth to tell, my lord, I'm confounded irked to be without a ship. Living here astride the Portsmouth Road I see the johnnies daily posting down to their frigates. Damn it all, my lord,' he blundered on, too far advanced for retreat, 'it is against my nature to solicit interest, but surely there must be a cutter somewhere . . .'

Dungarth smiled. 'You wouldn't sail on a frigate or a line of battleship?'

Drinkwater grinned with relief. 'I'd sail in a bath-tub if it mounted a carronade, but I fear I lack the youth for a frigate or the polish for a battleship. An unrated vessel would at least give me an opportunity.'

Dungarth looked shrewdly at Drinkwater. It was a pity such a promising officer had not yet received a commander's commission. He recognised Drinkwater's desire for an unrated ship as a symptom of his dilemma. He wanted his own vessel, a lieutenant's command. It offered him his only real chance to distinguish himself. But passed-over lieutenants grew old in charge of transports, cutters and gun-brigs, involved in the tedious routines of convoy escort or murderous little skirmishes unknown to the public. Drinkwater seemed to have all the makings of such a man. There was a touch of grey at the temples of the mop of brown hair that was scraped back from the high forehead into a queue. His left eyelid bore powder burns like random ink-spots and the dead tissue of an old scar ran down his left cheek. It was the face of a man accustomed to hard duty and disappointment. Dungarth, occupied with the business of prosecuting an increasingly unpopular war, recognised its talents were wasted in Petersfield.

The rum arrived. 'You are a fish out of water, Nathaniel. What would you say to a gun-brig?' He watched for reaction in the grey eyes of the younger man. They kindled immediately, banishing the rigidity of the face and reminding Dungarth of the eager midshipman Drinkwater had once been.

'I'd say that I would be eternally in your debt, my lord.'

Dungarth swallowed his kill-devil and waved Drinkwater's gratitude aside.

'I make no promises, but you'll have heard of the *Freya* affair, eh? The Danes have had their ruffled feathers smoothed, but the Tsar has taken offence at the force of Lord Whitworth's embassy to Copenhagen to sort the matter out. He resented the entry of British men of war into the Baltic. I tell you this in confidence Nathaniel, recalling you to your assurances when you served aboard *Kestrel* . . .'

Drinkwater nodded, feeling his pulse quicken. 'I understand, my lord.'

'Vaubois had surrendered Malta to us. Pitt is of the opinion that Mahon is a sufficient base for the Mediterranean but many of us do not agree. We will hold Malta.' Dungarth raised a significant eyebrow. 'The Tsar covets the island, so too does Ferdinand of the Two Sicilies, but Tsar Paul is Grand Master of the Order of St John and his claim has a specious validity. At the present moment the Coalition against France threatens to burst like a rotten apple: Austria has not fired a shot since her defeat at Marengo in April. In short the Tsar has it in his power to break the whole alliance with ease. He is unstable enough to put his wounded pride before political sense.' He paused to toss off the rum. 'You will recollect at our last *contre-temps* with His Imperial Majesty, he offered to settle the differences between our two nations in single combat with the King!' Dungarth laughed. 'This time he has settled for merely confiscating all British property in Russia.'

Drinkwater's eyes widened in comprehension.

'I see you follow me,' went on Dungarth. 'For a change we are remarkably well informed of developments both at St Petersburg and at Copenhagen.' He smiled with an ironic touch of self-congratulation. 'Despite the massive subsidies being paid him the Tsar feigns solicitude for Denmark. A predatory concern, but that is the Danes' affair. To be specific, my dear fellow, the pertinent consequence of this lunatic's phobia is to revive the old Armed Neutrality of the Baltic States, moribund since the American War. The combination is already known to us and means the northern allies have an overwhelming force available for operations in concert with the French and Batavian fleets in the North Sea. I have no idea how to reconcile mad Paul with First Consul Bonaparte, but they are said to have a secret understanding. After your own experiences with the Dutch I have no need to conjure to your imagination the consequences of such a combined fleet upon our doorstep.'

Drinkwater shook his head. 'Indeed not.'

'So whatever the outcome . . .' A knock at the door was accompanied by an announcement that the fresh horses had been put-to. Dungarth picked up his hat. 'Whatever the outcome we must strike with pre-emptive swiftness.' He held out his hand. 'Good-bye, Nathaniel. You may rely on my finding something for you.'

'I am most grateful, my lord. And for the confidences.' He stood, lost in thought as the carriage clattered out of the yard. Less than half an hour had passed since the same coach had soiled his clothes. Already he felt a mounting excitement. The Baltic was comparatively shallow; a theatre for small ships; a war for lieutenants in gun-brigs. His mind raced. He thought of his wife with guilty disloyalty, then of Louise Quilhampton, abandoned in the dressshop with Elizabeth, whose son he had brought home from the Red Sea with an iron hook in place of his left hand.

Drinkwater's mind skipped to thoughts of James Quilhampton, Mr Q as he had been known to the officers of the brig *Hellebore*. He too was unemployed and eager for a new appointment.

He picked up his hat and swore under his breath. There was also Charlotte Amelia, now nearly two years of age. Drinkwater would miss her sorely if he returned to duty. He thought of her bouncing upon Susan Tregembo's knee as they had left the house an hour earlier. And there was Tregembo, too, silently fretful on his own account at his master's idleness.

The old disease gnawed at him, tugging him two ways: Elizabeth and the trusting brown eyes of his daughter, the comforts and ease of domestic life. And against it the hard fulfilment of a sea-officer's duty. Always the tug of one when the other was to hand.

Elizabeth found him emerging from the Red Lion, noting both his dirtied clothes and the carriage drawing steadily up Sheet Hill.

'Nathaniel?'

'Eh? Ah. Yes, my dear?' Guilt drove him to over-played solicitude. 'Did you satisfy your requirements, eh? Where is Louise?'

'Taken offence, I shouldn't wonder. Nathaniel, you are cozening me. That coach . . .?'

'Coach, my dear?'

'Coach, Nathaniel, emblazoned three ravens sable upon a field azure, among other quarterings. Lord Dungarth's arms if I mistake not.' She slipped an arm through his while he smiled lopsidedly down at her. She was as lovely as when he had first seen her in a vicarage garden in Falmouth years earlier. Her wide mouth mocked him gently.

'I smell gunpowder, Nathaniel.'

'You have disarmed me, madam.'

'It is not very difficult,' she squeezed his arm, 'you are a poor dissembler.'

He sighed. 'That was Dungarth. It seems likely that we will shortly be at war with the Northern Powers.'

'Russia?'

'You are very perceptive.' He warmed to her and the conversation ran on like a single train of thought.

'Oh, I am not as scatter-brained as some of my sex.'

'And infinitely more beautiful.'

'La, kind sir, I was not fishing for compliments, merely facts. But you should not judge Louise too harshly though she runs on so. She is a good soul and true friend, though I know you prefer the company of her son,' Elizabeth concluded with dry emphasis.

'Mr Q's conversation is merely more to my liking, certainly . . .'

'Pah!' interrupted Elizabeth, 'he talks of nothing but your confounded profession. Come, sir, I still smell gunpowder, Nathaniel,' and added warningly, 'do not tack ship.'

He took a deep breath and explained the gist of Dungarth's news without betraying the details.

'So it is to be *Britannia contra mundum*,' she said at last.

'Yes.'

Elizabeth was silent for a moment. 'The country is weary of war, Nathaniel.'

'Do not exempt me from that, but . . .' he bit his lip, annoyed that the last word had slipped out.

'*But*, Nathaniel, *but*? But while there is fighting to be done it cannot be brought to a satisfactory conclusion without my husband's indispensable presence, is that it?'

He looked sharply at her, aware that she had great reason for bitterness. But she hid it, as only she could, and resorted to a gentle mockery that veiled her inner feelings. 'And Lord Dungarth promised you a ship?'

'As I said, my dear, you are very perceptive.'

He did not notice the tears in her eyes, though she saw the anticipation in his.

Chapter Two *October–November 1800*

A Knight Errant

'Drinkwater!'

Drinkwater turned, caught urgently by the arm at the very moment of passing through the screen-wall of the Admiralty into the raucous bedlam of Whitehall. Recognition was hampered by the shoving that the two naval officers were subjected to, together with the haggard appearance of the newcomer.

'Sam? Samuel Rogers, by all that's holy! Where the deuce did you spring from?'

'I've spent the last two months haunting the bloody waiting room of their exalted Lordships, bribing those bastard clerks to put my name forward. It was as much as the scum could do to take their feet out of their chair-drawers in acknowledgement . . .' Rogers looked down. His clothes were rumpled and soiled, his stock grubby and it was clear that it was he, and not the notorious clerks, that were at fault.

'I must have missed you when I tarried there this morning.' Drinkwater fell silent, embarrassed at his former shipmate's penury. All around them the noise of the crowds, the peddlers, hucksters, the groans of a loaded dray and the leathery creak of a carriage combined with the ostentatious commands of a sergeant of foot-guards to his platoon seemed to emphasise the silence between the two men.

'You've a ship then,' Rogers blurted desperately. It was not a question. The man nodded towards the brown envelope tucked beneath Drinkwater's elbow.

Drinkwater feigned a laugh. 'Hardly, I was promised a gun-brig but I've something called a bomb-tender. Named *Virago*.'

'Your own command, eh?' Rogers snapped with a predatory eagerness, leaning forward so that Drinkwater smelt breath that betrayed an empty belly. Rogers seemed about to speak, then twisted his mouth in violent suppression. Drinkwater watched him master his temper, horrified at the sudden brightness in his eyes.

'My dear fellow . . . come . . .' Taking Rogers's elbow, Drinkwater steered him through the throng and turned him into the first coffee house in the Strand. When he had called for refreshment he watched Rogers fall on a meat pie and turned an idea over in his mind, weighing the likely consequences of what he was about to say.

'You cannot get a ship?'

Rogers shook his head, swallowing heavily and washing the last of the pie down with the small beer that Drinkwater had bought him. 'I have no interest and the story of *Hellebore's* loss is too well known to recommend me.'

Drinkwater frowned. The brig's loss had been sufficiently circumstantial to have Rogers exonerated in all but a mild admonishment from the Court of Enquiry held at Mocha the previous year. Only those who knew him well realised that his intemperate nature could have contributed to the grounding on Daedalus Reef. Drinkwater himself had failed to detect the abnormal refraction that had made the reckoning in their latitude erroneous. Rogers had not been wholly to blame.

'How was it so "well known", Sam?'

Rogers shrugged, eyeing Drinkwater suspiciously. He had been a cantankerous shipmate, at odds with most of the officers including Drinkwater himself. It was clear that he still nursed grievances, although Drinkwater had felt they had patched up their differences by bringing home the *Antigone*.

'You know well enough. Gossip, scuttlebutt, call it what you will. One man has the ear of another, he the ears of a dozen . . .'

'Wait a minute Sam. Appleby was a gossip but he's in Australia. Griffiths is dead. I'll lay a sovereign to a farthing that the poison comes from Morris!' Rogers continued to look suspiciously at Drinkwater, suspecting him still, of buying the pie and beer to ease his own conscience. Drinkwater shook his head.

'It was not me, Sam.' Drinkwater held the other's gaze till it finally fell. 'Come, what d'you say to serving as my first lieutenant?'

Rogers's jaw dropped. Suddenly he averted his face and leaned forward to grasp Drinkwater's hand across the table. His mouth groped speechlessly for words and Drinkwater sought relief from his embarrassment in questions.

'Brace up, brace up. You surely cannot be that desperate. Why your prize money . . . whatever happened to reduce you to this indigent state?'

Rogers mastered himself at last, shrugging with something of his old arrogance. 'The tables, a wench or two . . .' He trailed off, shamefaced and Drinkwater had no trouble in imagining the kind of debauch Samuel Rogers had indulged in with his prize money and two years celibacy to inflame his tempestuous nature. Drinkwater gave him a smile, recollecting Rogers's strenuous efforts in times of extreme difficulty, of his personal bravery and savage courage.

'Empty bellies make desperate fellows,' he said, watching Rogers, who nodded grimly. Drinkwater called for coffee and sat back. He considered that Rogers's chastening might not be such a bad thing, just as in battle his violent nature was such an asset.

'It is not exactly a plum command, Samuel, but of one thing I am certain . . .'

'And that is?'

'That we both need to make something of it, eh?'

Drinkwater lent Rogers ten pounds so that he might make himself more presentable. Their ship lay above Chatham and Rogers had been instructed to join Drinkwater at his lodgings the following morning. In the meantime Drinkwater had to visit the Navy Office and he left the latter place as the evening approached, his mind a whirl of instructions, admonitions and humiliation at being one of the lowest forms of naval life, a lieutenant in command, permitted into those portals of perfidy and corruption. It was then he had the second encounter of the day.

Returning west along the Strand he came upon a small but vicious mob who had pulled a coachman from his box. It was almost dark and the shouts of disorder were mixed with the high-pitched screams of a woman. Elbowing the indifferent onlookers aside Drinkwater pressed forward, aware of a pale face at the carriage window. He heard a woman in the crowd say, 'Serve 'im bleedin' right for takin' 'is whip to 'em!'

Drinkwater broke through the cordon round the coach to where a large grinning man in working clothes held the tossing heads of the lead-horses. The whites of their eyes were vivid with terror. Rolling almost beneath the stamping hooves, the triplecaped bundle of a bald-headed coachman rolled in the gutter while three men, one with a lacerated cheek, beat him with sticks.

The offending whip lay on the road and the coachman's huge tricorne was being rescued and appropriated by a ragged youth, to the whoops of amusement of his fellows. Several hags roared their approval in shrill voices, while a couple of drabs taunted the woman in the coach.

Drinkwater took in the situation at a glance. A momentary sympathy for the man who had been whipped faded in his angry reaction to disorder. The noise of riot was anathema to him. As a naval officer his senses were finely tuned to any hint of it. London had been wearing him down all day. This final scene only triggered a supressed reaction in him.

Still in full dress he threw back his cloak and drew his hanger. His teeth were set and he felt a sudden savage joy as he shoved his heel into the buttocks of the nearer assailant. A cry of mixed anger and encouragement went up from the mob. The man fell beneath the pawing hooves and rolled away, roaring abuse. The other two men paused panting, their staves ready to rebuff their attacker. Drinkwater stepped astride the coachman, who moaned distressingly, and brought his sword point up to the throat of the man with the whipped face. With his left hand he felt in his pocket.

'Come now,' Drinkwater snapped, 'you've had your sport. Let the lady proceed.'

The man raised his stave as though about to strike. Drinkwater dropped the coin onto the back of the coachman. The glint of the half-crown caught the man's eye and he bent to pick it up, but Drinkwater's sword point caught the back of his neck.

'You will let the fellow go, eh? And set him upon his box if you please . . .' He could feel the man's indignation. 'I'm busy manning a King's ship, cully. Do you take the money and set the fellow up again.' Drinkwater sensed the man acquiesce, stepped back and put up his sword. Threat of the press worked better than the silver, but Drinkwater did not begrudge the money, disliking the arrogant use of corporal punishment for such trivialities.

The man rose and jerked his head at his accomplice. The coachman was hauled to his feet and bodily thrown onto the box. His hat had disappeared and he put his face into his hands as the crowd taunted him and cheered. Drinkwater turned to the window.

'Would you like me to accompany you, ma'am?' The face was pale and round in the gloom. He could not hear her whispered reply but the door swung open and he climbed in.

'Drive on!' he commanded as he closed the door. When he had pulled the blinds he sat opposite the occupant. She was little more than a child, still in her teens. The yellow carriage lights showed a plain face that seemed somehow familiar. He removed his hat.

'You are not hurt?' She shook her head and cleared her throat.

'I . . . I am most grateful, sir.'

'It was nothing. I think, ma'am, you should tell your coachman to be less eager to use his whip.'

She nodded.

'Are you travelling far?' he went on

'To Lothian's hotel in Albemarle Street. Will that take you far out of your way? If so, I shall have poor Matthew drive you wherever you wish.' She began to recover her composure.

Drinkwater grinned. 'I think that inadvisable. My lodgings are off the Strand. I can return thither on foot. Please do not trouble yourself further.'

'You are very kind, sir. I see that you are a sea-officer. May I enquire your name?'

'Drinkwater, ma'am, Lieutenant Nathaniel Drinkwater. May I know whom I had the honour of assisting?'

'My name is Onslow, Lieutenant, Frances Onslow.'

'Your servant, Miss Onslow.' They smiled at each other and Drinkwater recognised the reason for her apparent familiarity. 'Forgive my curiosity but are you related to Admiral Sir Richard Onslow?'

'His daughter, Mr Drinkwater. You are acquainted with my father?'

'I had the honour to serve under him during the Camperdown campaign.' But Drinkwater was thinking he knew something else about Miss Onslow, something more keenly concerning herself, but he could not recollect it and a minute or two later the carriage turned off Piccadilly and drew to a halt in Albemarle Street.

After handing the young lady down he refused her invitation to reacquaint himself with the admiral.

'I regret I have pressing matters to attend to, Miss Onslow. It is enough that I have been of service to you. ' He bent over her hand.

'I shall not forget it, Mr Drinkwater.'

Drinkwater forgot the encounter in the next few days. He became immersed in the countless details of preparing his ship for sea. He visited the Navy Board again, bribed clerks in the Victualling Office, wrote to the Regulating Captain in charge of the Impress Service at Chatham. He accrued a collection of books and ledgers; Muster books, Sick and Hurt books, Account books, Order books, orders directives. He had many masters; the Admiralty, the Navy Board, the Victualling Board, Greenwich hospital, even the Master-General of the Ordnance at Woolwich. Towards the end of November, he paid his reckoning, complaining about the exhorbitant charge for the candles he had burned in their Lordships' service. In company with a sprightlier Lieutenant Rogers he caught the Dover stage from the George at Southwark at four in the morning and set out for Chatham.

As the stage crossed the bridge at Rochester and he glimpsed the steel-grey Medway, cold beneath a lowering sky, he recalled the contents of a letter sent to his lodgings by Lord Dungarth. The earl had concluded, . . . *I realise, my dear Nathaniel, that she is not what you supposed would be in my power to obtain for you, nevertheless the particular nature of the service upon which you are to be employed would lend itself more readily to your purpose of advancement were you in a bomb.* Virago *is a bomb in fact, though not in name. I leave it to your ingenuity to alter the matter . . .*

Drinkwater frowned over the recollection. It might be a palliative, though it was unlike Dungarth to waste words or to have gone to any effort to further the career of a nobody. What interested Drinkwater was the hint underlying the encouragement. *Virago* had been built as a bomb vessel, though her present job was to act as a mere tender to the other bomb ships. That degrading of her made her a lieutenant's command, though she ought really to have a commander upon her quarterdeck. He could not resist a thrill of anticipation as the stage rolled to a halt outside the main, red-brick gateway of Chatham Dockyard. As they descended, catching the eye of the marine sentry, the wind brought them the scent of familiar things, of tar and hemp cordage, of stored canvas and coal-fired forges and the unmistakable, invigorating smell of saltings uncovered by the tide.

Despatching Rogers with their sea chests and a covey of urchins to lug them to an inn, Drinkwater was compelled to kick his heels for over an hour in the waiting room of the Commissioner's house, a circumstance that negated their early departure from the George and reminded Drinkwater that his belly was empty. In the end he was granted ten minutes by a supercilious secretary who clearly objected to rubbing shoulders with lieutenants, whether or not they were in command.

'She is one of several tenders preparing to serve the bombs,' he drawled in the languid and increasingly fashionable manner of the *ton*. 'As you may know your vessel was constructed as a bomb in '59 whereas the other tenders are requisitioned colliers. Your spars are allocated, your carpenter's and gunner's stores in hand. The Victualling Yard is acquainted with your needs. You have, lieutenant, merely to inform the Commissioner when your vessel is ready to proceed in order to receive your orders to load the combustibles, carcases, powder and so on and so forth from the Arsenal . . .' he waved a handkerchief negligently about, sitting back in his chair and crossing his legs. Drinkwater withdrew in search of Rogers, aware that if all had been prepared as the man said, then the dockyard was uncommonly efficient.

Fifteen minutes later, with Rogers beside him, he sat at the helm of a dockyard boat feeling the tiller kick gently under his elbow. The wind was keen on the water, kicking up sharp grey wavelets and whipping the droplets from the oar blades. The sun was already well down in the western sky.

'She's the inboard end of the western trot,' said the boatman curtly as he pulled upstream. Drinkwater and Rogers regarded the line of ships moored two and three abreast between the buoys. The flood tide gurgled round their bluff bows. Two huge ninety-eights rode high out of the water without their guns or stores, laid up in ordinary with only their lower masts stepped. Astern of them lay four frigates wanting men, partially rigged but with neglected paintwork, odd gun-ports opened for ventilation or the emergence of temporary chimneys. Upper decks were untidy with lines of washing which told of wives living on board with the 'standing officers', the warrant gunners, the masters, carpenters and boatswains. Drinkwater recognised two battered and decrepit

Dutch prizes from Camperdown and remembered laying *Cyclops* up here in '83. There had been many more ships then, a whole fleet of them becoming idle at the end of the American War. The boatman interrupted his reverie.

'Put the helm over now, sir, if'ee please. She be beyond this'n.'

Drinkwater craned his neck. They began to turn under the stern of a shot-scarred sloop. The tide caught the boat and the two oarsmen pulled with increased vigour as they stemmed it. Drinkwater watched anxiously for the stern of *Virago*.

Chapter Three *November–December 1800*

The Bomb Tender

The richness of the carved decoration on her stern amazed him. It was cracked and bare of paint or gilt, but its presence gave him a pleasurable surprise. The glow of candles flickered through the stern windows. The boat bumped alongside and Drinkwater reached for the manropes and hauled himself on deck.

It was deserted. There were no masts, no guns. The paint on the mortar hatches was flaking; tatty canvas covers flapped over the two companionways. In the autumnal dusk it was a depressing sight. He heard Rogers cluck his tongue behind him as he came over the rail and for a moment the two officers stood staring about them, their boat cloaks flapping in the breeze.

'There's a deal of work to be done, Mr Rogers.'

'Yes, sir.'

Drinkwater strode aft, mounted the low poop and flung back the companion cover. The smell of food and unwashed humanity rose, together with a babble of conversation. Drinkwater descended the steep ladder, turned aft in the stygian gloom of an unlit lobby and flung open the door of the after cabin. Rogers followed him into the room.

The effect of their entrance was instantaneous. The occupants of the cabin froze with surprise. If Drinkwater had felt a twinge of irritation at the sight of candles burning in his cabin, the scene that now presented itself was a cause for anger. He took in the table with its greasy cloth, the disorder of the plates and pots, the remnants of a meal, the knocked over and empty bottles. His glance rolled over the diners. In the centre lolled a small, rotund fellow in a well-cut coat and ruffled shirt. He had been interrupted in fondling a loosely-stayed woman who lay half across him, her red mouth opened in a grimace as the laughter died on her lips. Two other men also sprawled about the table, their dress in various states of disorder, each with a bare-shouldered woman giggling on his lap. There was a woman's shoe lodged in the cruet and several ankles were visible from yards of grubby petticoats.

The oldest of the women who sat on the round, well-dressed man's knee, was the first to recover. She hove herself upright, shrugged her shoulders in a clearly practised gesture and her bosom subsided from view.

'Who are you gentlemen then?' The other women followed her example, there was a rustling of cotton and the shoe disappeared.

'Lieutenants Drinkwater and Rogers, madam. And you, pray?' Drinkwater's voice was icily polite.

'Mrs Jex,' she said, setting off giggles on either side of her, 'just married to 'Ector Jex, here . . . my 'usband,' she added to more giggles. 'My 'usband is purser of this ship.' There was a certain proprietory hauteur in her voice. Mr Jex remained silent behind the voluptuous bulk of his wife.

'And these others?'

'Mr Matchett, boatswain and Mr Mason, master's mate.'

'And the ladies?' Drinkwater asked with ironic emphasis, eyeing their professional status.

'Friends of mine,' replied Mrs Jex with the sharp certainty of possession.

'I see. Mr Matchett!'

Matchett pulled himself together. 'Sir?'

'Where are the remainder of the standing warrant officers?'

'H'hm. There is no gunner appointed, nor a master.'

'How many men have we?'

'Not including the warrant officer's mates, who number four men, we have eighteen seamen. All are over sixty years of age. That is all . . .'

'Well, gentlemen, I shall be in command of the *Virago*. Mr Rogers will be first lieutenant. I shall return aboard tomorrow morning to take command. I shall expect you to be at your duty.' He swept them with a long stare then turned on his heel and clattered up the ladder. He heard Rogers say something behind him as he regained the cold freshness of the darkened deck.

As they made for the ladder and the waiting dockyard boat a figure appeared wearing an apron, huge arms in shirtsleeves despite the chill wind. He touched his forehead.

'Beg pardon, sir. Willerton, carpenter. You've seen that pack of whores aft sir? Don't hold with it sir. 'Tis the wages of sin they have coming to 'em. There's nowt wrong with the ship, sir, she's as fine today as when they built her, she'll take two thirteen inch mortars and not crack a batten . . . nowt wrong with her at all . . .'

Slightly taken aback at this encounter Drinkwater thanked the man, reflecting, as he took his seat in the boat, that there were clearly factions at work on the *Virago* with which he would become better acquainted in the days ahead.

'You are required and directed without delay to take command of His Majesty's Bomb Tender *Virago*, which vessel you are to prepare for sea with all despatch . . .'

He read on in the biting wind, the commission flapping in his hands. When he had finished he looked at the small semi-circle of transformed warrant officers standing with their hats off. The sober blue of their coats seemed the only patches of colour against the flaked paintwork and bare timbers of the ship. They had clearly been at some pains to correct the impression their new commander had received the previous evening. They should be given some credit for that, Drinkwater thought.

'Good morning gentlemen. I am glad to see the adventures of the night have not prevented you attending to your duty.' He looked round. Matchett's eighteen seamen, barefoot and shivering in cotton shirts and loose trousers, were standing holding their holystones in one hand, their stockingette hats in the other. Drinkwater addressed them in an old formula. He tried to make it sound as though he meant it though there was a boiling anger welling up in him again.

'Do your duty men. You have nothing to fear.' He strode aft.

The cabin had been cleared. All that remained from the previous night were the table and chairs. Rogers followed him in. Drinkwater heard him sigh.

'There is a great deal to do, Sam.'

'Yes,' said Rogers flatly. From an adjacent cabin the sound of a cough was hurriedly muted and the air was still heavy with a mixture of sweat and lavender water.

Drinkwater returned to the lobby and threw open the door of the adjacent cabin. It was empty of people though a sea-chest, bedding and cocked hat case showed it was occupied. He tried the door on the opposite cabin. It gave. Mrs Jex was dressing. She feigned a decorous surprise then made a small, suggestive gesture to him. Her charms were very obvious and in the silence he heard Rogers behind him swallow. He closed the door and turned on the first lieutenant.

'Pass word for Mr Jex, Mr Rogers. Then make rounds of the ship. I want a detailed report on her condition, wants and supplied state. Come back in an hour.'

He went into the cabin and sat down. He looked round at the bare space, feeling the draughts whistling in through the unoccupied gunports. The thrill of first command was withering. The amount of work to be done was daunting. The brief hope of raising the status of *Virago* as Lord Dungarth suggested seemed, at that moment, to be utterly impossible. Then he remembered the odd encounter with Mr Willerton, that vestigial loyalty to his ship. Almost childlike in its pathetic way and yet as potent to the carpenter as the delights of the flesh had been to last night's revellers. Drinkwater took encouragement from the recollection and with the lifting of his spirits the draught around his feet seemed a little less noticeable, the cabin a little less inhospitable.

Mr Jex knocked on the cabin door and entered. 'Ah, Mr Jex, pray sit down.'

Jex's uniform coat was smartly cut and a gold ring flashed on his finger. His hands had a puffy quality and his cheeks were marred by the high colour of the bibulous. The Jexes, it seemed, were sybaritic in their way of life. Money, Nathaniel observed, was not in short supply.

'When I was at the Navy Board, Mr Jex, they did not tell me that you were appointed purser to this ship. Might I enquire as to how long you have held the post?'

'One month, sir.' Mr Jex spoke for the first time. His voice had the bland tone of the utterly confident.

'Your wife is still on board, Mr Jex . . .'

'It is customary . . .'

'It is customary to ask permission.'

'But I have, sir.' Jex stared levelly at Drinkwater.

'From whom, may I ask?'

'My kinsman, the Commissioner of the Dockyard offered me the appointment. I served as assistant purser on the *Conquistador,* Admiral Roddam's flagship, sir, the whole of the American War.' Drinkwater suppressed a smile. Mr Jex's transparent attempt to threaten him with his kindred was set at nought by the latter revelation.

'How interesting, Mr Jex. If I recollect aright, *Conquistador* remained guardship at the Nore for several years. Your experience in dealing with the shore must, therefore, be quite considerable.' Drinkwater marked the slightest tightening of the lips. 'I do not expect to see seamen on deck without proper clothing, Mr Jex. An officer of your experience should have attended to that.' Jex opened his mouth to protest. 'If you can see to the matter for me and, tomorrow morning, bring me a list of all the stores on board we may discuss your future aboard this ship.' Indignation now blazed clearly from Jex's eyes, but Drinkwater was not yet finished with him. In as pleasant a voice as he could muster he added:

'In the meantime I shall be delighted to allow you to retain your wife on board. Perhaps she will dine with all of the officers. It will give us the opportunity to discuss the progress of commissioning the ship, and the presence of a lady is always stimulating.' Jex's eyes narrowed abruptly to slits. Drinkwater had laid no special emphasis on the word 'lady' but there was about Mrs Jex's behaviour something suspicious.

'That will be all, Mr Jex. And be so kind as to pass word for Mr Willerton.'

Several days passed and Drinkwater kept Jex in a state of uncertainty over his future. The men appeared in guernseys and greygoes so that it was clear Jex had some influence over the dockyard suppliers. Drinkwater was pleased by his first victory.

He listened in silence as Rogers told of the usual dockyard delays, the unkept promises, the lack of energy, the bribery, the venality. He listened while Rogers hinted tactfully that he lacked the funds to expedite matters, that there were few seamen available for such an unimportant vessel and those drafted to them were the cast-offs from elsewhere. Drinkwater was dominated by the two problems of want of cash and men. He had already spent more of his precious capital than he intended and as yet obtained little more than a smartened first lieutenant, a few documents necessary to commission his ship, only obtained by bribing the issuing clerks, and victuals enough for the cabin for a week. Apart from the imposition of further bribing dockyard officials for the common necessities needed by a man of war, he had yet to purchase proper slops for his men, just a little paint that his command might not entirely disgrace him, a quantity of powder for practice, and a few comforts for his own consumption: a dozen live pullets, a laying hen, a case or two of blackstrap. He sighed, listening again to Rogers and his catalogue of a first lieutenant's woes. As he finished Drinkwater poured him a glass of the cheap port sold in Chatham as blackstrap.

'Press on Samuel, we do make progress.' He indicated the litter of papers on the table. Rogers nodded then, in a low voice and leaning forward confidentially he said, 'I, er, have found a little out about our friend Jex.'

'Oh?'

'More of his wife actually. It seems that after the last war Jex went off slaving. As purser he made a deal of money and accustomed himself to a fine time.' There was a touch of malice in Rogers as he sipped the wine, he was contemplating the fate of another brought low by excess. 'I gather he invested a good bit of it unwisely and lost heavily. Now, after some time in straightened circumstances, he is attempting to recoup his finances from the perquisites of a purser's berth and marriage to his lady wife.' Rogers managed a sneer. 'Though not precisely a trollop she did run a discreet little house off Dock Road. Quite a remunerative place, I am led to believe.'

'And a berth in a King's ship purchases *Madame* Jex a measure of respectability. Yes, I had noticed an assumption of airs by her ladyship,' concluded Drinkwater, grinning as an idea occurred to him. Making up his mind he slapped his hand on the table. 'Yes, I have it, it will do very nicely. Be so good as to ask Mr Jex to step this way.'

Jex arrived and was asked to sit. His air of confidence had sagged a little and was replaced by pugnacity. The purser's arms were crossed over his belly and he peered at his commander through narrowed eyes.

'I have come to a decision regarding you and your future.' Drinkwater spoke clearly, aware of the silence from the adjoining cabin. Mrs Jex would hear with ease through the thin bulkhead.

'Your influence with the dockyard does you credit, Mr Jex. I would be foolish not to take advantage of your skill and interest in that direction . . .' Drinkwater noted with satisfaction that Jex was relaxing. 'I require that you do not sleep out of the ship until you have completed victualling for eighty souls for three months. Your wife may live on board with you. You will be allowed the customary eighth on your stores, but a personal profit exceeding twelve and one half per cent will not be tolerated. You will put up the usual bond with the Navy Board and receive seven pounds per month whilst on the ship's books. Until the ship is fully manned you may claim a man's pay for your wife but she shall keep the cabin clean until my servant arrives. You will ensure that the stores from the Victualling Yard are good, not old, nor in split casks. You may at your own expense purchase tobacco and slops for the men. You will, as part of this charge, purchase one hundred new greygoes, one hundred pairs of mittens, a quantity of woollen stockings and woollen caps, together with some cured sheepskins from any source known to you. You will in short, supply the ship with warm clothes for her entire company. Do you understand?'

Jex's jaw hung. In the preceeding minutes his expression had undergone several dramatic changes but the post of purser in even the meanest of His Britannic Majesty's ships was sought after as a source of steady wealth and steadier opportunity. Drinkwater had not yet finished with the unfortunate man.

'We have not, of course, mentioned the fee customarily paid to the captain of a warship for your post. Shall we say one hundred? Come now, what do you say to my terms?'

'Ninety.'

'Guineas, my last offer, Mr Jex.'

Drinkwater watched the purser's face twist slowly as he calculated. He knew he could never stop the corruption in the dockyards, nor in the matter of the purser's eighth, but he might put the system to some advantage. There was a kind of rough justice in Drinkwater's plan. Mrs Jex's wealth came from the brief sexual excesses of a multitude of unfortunate seamen. It was time a little was returned in kind.

Virago presented something of a more ordered state a day or two later. Both Matchett and Mason, despite their unprepossessing introduction a few days earlier, turned out to be diligent workers. With a third of Jex's ninety guineas Drinkwater was able to 'acquire' a supply of paint, tar, turpentine, oakum, rosin and pitch to put the hull in good shape. He also acquired some gilt paint and had Rogers rig staging over the stern to revive the cracked-acanthus leaves that roved over the transom.

While Drinkwater sat in his cloak in the cabin, the table littered with lists, orders, requisitions and indents, driving his pen and dispatching Mason daily to the dockyard or post-office on ship's business, Rogers stormed about the upper deck or terrorised the dockyard foremen with torrents of foul-mouthed invective that forced reaction from even their stone-walling tactics. Storemen and clerks who complained about his bullying abuse usually obliged Drinkwater to make apologies for him. So he developed an ingratiating politeness that disguised his contempt for these jobbers. With a little greasing of palms he could often reverse the offended clerk's mind and thus obtain whatever the ship required.

Drinkwater made daily rounds of the ship. Forward of the officers' accommodation under the low poop stretched one huge space. It was at once hold and berthing place for the hammocks of her crew. Gratings decked over the lower section into which the casks of pork, peas, flour, oatmeal, fish and water were stowed. Here too, like huge black snakes, lay the vessel's four cables. Extending down from deck to keelson in the spaces between the two masts were two massive mortar beds. These vast structures were of heavy crossed timbers, bolted and squeezed together with shock-absorbent hemp poked between each beam. Drinkwater suspected he was supposed to dismantle them, but no one had given him a specific order to do so and he knew that the empty shells, or carcases, stowed in the gaps between the timbers. He would retain those shell rooms, and therefore the mortar beds, for without them, opportunity or not, *Virago* would be useless as anything but a cargo vessel. Store rooms, a carpenter's workshop and cabin each for Matchett and Willerton were fitted under the fo'c's'le whilst beneath the officers' accommodation aft were the shot rooms, spirit room, fuse room and bread room. Beneath Drinkwater's own cabin lay the magazine space, reached through a hatchway for which he had the only key.

It was not long before Drinkwater had made arrangements to warp *Virago* alongside the Gun Wharf, but he was desperate for want of men to undertake the labour of hoisting and mounting the eight 24-pounder carronades and two 6-pounder long guns that would be *Virago's* armament. They received a small draft from the Guardship at the Nore and another from the Impress service but still remained thirty men short of their complement. By dint of great effort, by the second week in December, the carronades were all on their slides, the light swivels in their mountings and the two long guns at their stern ports in Drinkwater's cabin. The appearance of the two cold black barrels upon which condensation never ceased to form, brought reality to both Mrs Jex and to Drinkwater himself. To Mrs Jex they disturbed the domestic symmetry of the place, to Drinkwater they reminded him that a bomb vessel was likely to be chased, not do the chasing.

Virago had been built as one of a number of bomb ships constructed at the beginning of the Seven Years War. She was immensely strong, with futtocks the size of a battleship. Though only 110 feet long she displaced 380 tons. She would sit deep in the water when loaded and, Drinkwater realised, would be a marked contrast to the nimble cutter *Kestrel* or the handy brig *Hellebore*. She was reduced to a tender by the building of a newer class of bomb vessel completed during the American War. Normally employed on the routine duties of sloops, the bomb vessels only carried their two mortars when intended for a bombardment. For this purpose they loaded the mortars, powder, carcases and shells from the Royal Artillery Arsenal at Woolwich, together with a subaltern and a detachment of artillerymen. The mortars threw their shells, or bombs (from which the ships took their colloquial name) from the massive wooden beds Drinkwater had left in place on *Virago*. The beds were capable of traversing, a development which had revolutionised the rig of bomb vessels. As of 1759 the ketch rig had been dispensed with. It was no longer necessary not to have a foremast, nor to throw the shells over the bow, training their aim with a spring to the anchor cable. Now greater accuracy could be obtained from the traversing bed and greater sailing qualities from the three-masted ship-rig.

Even so, Drinkwater thought as he made one of his daily inspections, he knew them to be unpopular commands. *Virago* had fired her last mortar at Le Havre in the year of her building. And convoy protection in a heavily built and sluggish craft designed to protect herself when running away was as popular as picket duty on a wet night. So although the intrusion of the stern chasers into the cabin marked a step towards commissioning, they also indicated the severe limitations of Drinkwater's command.

However he cheered himself up with the reflection that *Virago* would be sailing in company with a fleet, the fleet destined for the 'secret expedition' mentioned in every newspaper, and for the 'unknown destination' that was equally certain to be the Baltic.

Even as Mr Matchett belayed the breechings of the intrusive six-pounders, muttering about the necessity of a warrant gunner, Drinkwater learned of the collapse of the Coalition. The Franco-Austrian armistice had ended, hostilities had resumed and the Austrians had been smashed at Hohenlinden. Suddenly the Baltic had become a powder keg.

Although Bonaparte, now first consul and calling himself Napoleon, was triumphant throughout Europe, it was to the other despot that all looked. Sadistic, perverted and unbalanced, Tsar Paul was the cynosure for all eyes. The thwarting of his ambitions towards Malta had led to mistrust of Britain, despite the quarter of a million pounds paid him to which a monthly addition of £75,000 was paid to keep 45,000 Russian soldiers in the field. When Napoleon generously repatriated, at French expense, 5,000 Russian prisoners of war after Britain had refused to ransom them, Tsar Paul abandoned his allies.

The Tsar's influence in the Baltic was immense. Russia had smashed the Swedish empire at Poltava a century earlier, and Denmark was too vulnerable not to bend to a wind from the east. Her own king was insane, her Crown Prince, Frederick, a young man dominated by his ministers.

When the Tsar revived the Armed Neutrality he insisted that the Royal Navy should no longer be able to search neutral ships, particularly for naval stores, those exports from the Baltic shores that both Britain and France needed. The Baltic states wanted to trade with whomsoever they wished and under the double-headed eagle of the Romanovs they would be able to do so; the British naval blockade would be rendered impotent and France, controlling all the markets of Europe, triumphant. With one head of the Russian eagle ready tensed to stretch out a talon to cripple impotent Turkey, the effect of the other's influence in the Baltic would finish Britain at a stroke.

So, inferred Drinkwater, argued Count Bernstorff, Minister to Crown Prince Frederick. And though Russia was the real enemy it was clear that the Royal Navy could not go into the Baltic leaving a hostile Denmark in its rear.

Drinkwater coughed as clouds of smoke erupted into the cabin from the bogey stove.

'I beg you, Mrs Jex, to desist. I would rather sit in my cloak than be suffocated by that thing.' He leant helplessly on the table, covered, as was usual, with papers.

''Twill not draw, Mr Drinkwater, 'tis the wind. For shame I will perish with the marsh ague if I do not freeze first.' She sniffed and snuffed with a streaming cold.

'Perhaps madam, if you wore more clothes . . .' offered Drinkwater drily.

She gave him a cold look. Her early attempt to flirt with him had ceased when she learned of the bargain he had driven with her husband. He bent once more to the tedious task of the inventory, almost welcoming the interruption of a knock at the door, though the blast of icy air made him swear quietly as it blew papers from his desk.

'Beg pardon, sir . . .'

'Mr Willerton, come in, come in, and shut that door. What can I do for you?'

'We needs a leddy, sir.'

'A leddy? Ah, a *lady*, a figurehead, d'you mean?'

'Aye sir.'

Drinkwater frowned. It was an irrelevance, an expensive irrelevance too, one that he would have to pay for himself since he had spent the rest of Mr Jex's contribution on barrels of sauerkraut. He shook his head. 'I'm afraid that ain't possible, Mr Willerton. We have a handsome scroll and, in accordance with regulations, as I have no doubt you well know, ships below the third rate are not permitted individual figureheads. Most make do with a lion, we have a handsome scroll . . .' He tailed off, aware that Mr Willerton was not merely stubborn, but felt strongly enough to oppose his commander. Mr Willerton's almost bald head was shaking.

'Won't do sir. Bad luck to have a ship without a figurehead, sir. I was in the *Brunswick* at the First of June, sir. Damned Frogs shot the duke's hat off. We lashed a laced one on and sent the *Vengeur* to the bottom, sir. Ships without figureheads are like dukes without hats.'

Drinkwater met the old man's level gaze. There was not a trace of humour in his eyes. Mr Willerton spoke with the authority of holy writ.

'Well, Mr Willerton, if you feel that strongly . . .'

'I do, sir, and so does the men. We've raised a subscription of fifteen shillings.'

'Upon my soul!' Drinkwater's astonishment was unfeigned. Together with the realisation that his financial preoccupations were making him mean, came the reflection that the carpenter's request and the response of his motley little crew somehow reflected credit on the ship. He suddenly felt a pang of self-reproach for his tightfistedness. If that shivering huddle of men he had seen on deck the morning he had read his commission at the gangway had enough esprit-de-corps to raise a subscription for a figurehead, the least he could do was encourage it. He tried to suppress any too obvious emotion, but the brief silence had not gone unnoticed. Mr Willerton pressed his advantage. 'I have ascertained, sir, that a virago is a bad tempered, shrewish woman what spits fire.' Drinkwater watched a slight movement of his eyes to Mrs Jex, who sat huddled in sooty disarray over the smoking stove. As the former madame of a brothel she would have had a choice phrase or two to exchange with the men in one of her less ladylike moods.

'I believe that is correct, Mr Willerton,' replied Drinkwater gravely, mastering sudden laughter.

'I have my eye on a piece of pine, sir, but it cost eight shilling. Then there is paint, sir.'

'Very well, Mr Willerton.' Drinkwater reached into his pocket and laid a guinea on the table. 'The balance against your craftsmanship, but be careful how you pick your model.'

For a second their eyes met. Willerton's were a candid and disarming blue, as innocent as a child's.

Chapter Four *December 1800–January 1801*

A Matter of Family

Lieutenant Drinkwater was in ill humour. It was occasioned by exasperation at the delays and prevarications of the dockyard and aggravated by petty frustrations, financial worries and domestic disappointment.

The latter he felt keenly for, as Christmas approached, he had promised himself a day or two ashore in lodgings in the company of his wife. Elizabeth was to have travelled to Chatham with Tregembo and his own sea-kit, but now she wrote to say she was unwell and that her new pregnancy troubled her. She had miscarried before and Drinkwater wrote back urging her not to risk losing the child, to stay with Charlotte Amelia and Susan Tregembo in the security of their home.

Tregembo was expected daily. The topman who had, years ago, attached himself to young Midshipman Drinkwater, was now both servant and confidant. Also expected was Mr Midshipman Quilhampton. Out of consideration for Louise, Drinkwater had left her son at home when he himself went to London. Later he had written off instructions to the young man to recruit hands for *Virago*. Now Drinkwater waited impatiently for those extra men.

But it was not merely men that Drinkwater needed. As Christmas approached, the dockyard became increasingly supine. He wanted masts and spars, for without them *Virago* was as immobile as a log, condemned to await the dockyard's pleasure. And Drinkwater was by no means sure that Mr Jex was not having his revenge through the influence of his kinsman, the Commissioner. As the days passed in idleness Drinkwater became more splenetic, less tolerant of Mrs Jex, less affable to Rogers. He worried over the possibilities of desertion by his men and fretted over their absence every time a wooding party went to search the tideline for driftwood. Unable to leave his ship by Admiralty order he sat morosely in his cloak, staring gloomily out over the dull, frosty marshes.

His misgivings over his first lieutenant increased. Rogers's irascibility was irritating the warrant officers and Drinkwater's own doubts about selecting Rogers grew. They had already argued over the matter of a flogging, Drinkwater ruling the laxer discipline that customarily prevailed on warships in port mitigated the man's offence to mere impudence. The knock at the door brought him out of himself.

'Come in!'

'Reporting aboard, sir.'

'James! By God, I'm damned glad to see you. You've men? And news of my wife?'

James Quilhampton warmed himself over the smoking stove. He was a tall, spare youth, growing out of his uniform coat, with spindle-shanked legs and a slight stoop. Any who thought him a slightly ridiculous adolescent were swiftly silenced when they saw the heavy iron hook he wore in place of a left hand.

'Aye sir, I have fifteen men, a letter from your wife and a surgeon.' He stood aside, pulling a letter from his breast. Taking the letter Drinkwater looked up to see a second figure enter his cabin.

'Lettsom, sir, surgeon; my warrant and appointment.' Drinkwater glanced at the proffered papers. Mr Lettsom was elderly, small and fastidious looking, with a large nose and a pair of tolerant eyes. His uniform coat was clean, though shiny and with overlarge, bulging pockets.

'Ah, I see you served under Richard White, Mr Lettsom, he speaks highly of you.'

'You are acquainted with Captain White, Lieutenant Drinkwater?'

'I am indeed, we were midshipmen together in the *Cyclops*, I saw him last at the Cape when he commanded the *Telemachus*.'

'I served with him in the *Roisterer*, brig. He was soon after posted to *Telemachus*.'

'I have no doubt we shall get along, Mr Lettsom.' Drinkwater riffled through the papers on his table. 'I have some standing orders here for you. You will find the men in reasonable shape. I have had their clothes replaced and we may thus contain the ship-fever. As to diet I have obliged the purser to buy in a quantity of sauerkraut. Its stink is unpopular, but I am persuaded it is effective against the scurvy.' Lettsom nodded and glanced at the documents.

'You are a disciple of Lind, Mr Drinkwater, I congratulate you.'

'I am of the opinion that much of the suffering of seamen in general is unnecessary.'

Lettsom smiled wryly at the earnest Drinkwater. 'I'll do my best, sir, but mostly it depends upon the condition of the men:

> When people's ill, they come to I,
> I physics, bleeds and sweat's 'em;
> Sometimes they live, sometimes they die,
> What's that to I? I let's 'em.'

For a second Drinkwater was taken aback, then he perceived the pun and began to laugh.

'A verse my cousin uses as his own, sir,' Lettsom explained, 'he is a physician of some note among the fashionable, but of insufficient integrity not to claim the verse as his own. I regret that he plagiarised it from your humble servant.' Lettsom made a mock bow.

'Very well, Mr Lettsom, I think we shall get along . . . Now gentlemen, if you will excuse me . . . '

He slit open Elizabeth's letter impatiently and began to read, lost for a while to the cares of the ship.

> *My Dearest Husband,*
> *It is with great sadness that I write to say I shall not see you at Christmastide. I am much troubled by sickness and anxious for the child whom, from the trouble he causes, I know to be a boy. Charlotte chatters incessantly . . .*

There was a page of his daughter's exploits and a curl of her hair. He learned that the lateness of Tregembo's departure was caused by a delay in the preparation of his Christmas gift and that Louise Quilhampton was having her portrait painted by Gaston Bruilhac, a paroled French *sous-officier*, captured by Drinkwater in the Red Sea who had executed a much admired likeness of his captor during the homeward voyage. There was town gossip and Elizabeth's disapproval of Mr Quilhampton's recruiting methods. Then, saved in Elizabeth's reserved manner for a position of importance in the penultimate paragraph, an oddly disquieting sentence:

On Tuesday last I received an odd visitor, your brother Edward whom I have not seen these five or six years. He was in company with a lively and pretty French woman, some fugitive from the sans culottes. He spoke excellent French to her and was most anxious to see you on some private business. I explained your whereabouts but he would vouchsafe me no further confidences. I confess his manner made me uneasy . . .

Drinkwater looked up frowning only to find Quilhampton still in the cabin.

'You wish to see me, Mr Q?'

'Beg pardon, sir, but I am rather out of pocket. The expense of bringing the men, sir . . .'

Drinkwater sighed. 'Yes, yes, of course. How much?'

'Four pounds, seventeen shillings and four pence ha'penny, sir. I kept a strict account . . .'

The problem of the ship closed round him again, driving all thoughts of his brother from his mind.

Mr Easton, the sailing master, with a brand new certificate from the Trinity House and an equally new warrant from the Navy Board joined them on the last day of the old century. Six days later Drinkwater welcomed his final warrant officer aboard. They had served together before. Mr Trussel was wizened, stoop-shouldered and yellow-skinned. Lank hair fell to his shoulders from the sides and back of his head, though his crown was bald.

'Reporting for duty, Mr Drinkwater.' A smile split his face from ear to ear.

'God bless my soul, Mr Trussel, I had despaired of your arrival, but you are just in time. Pray help yourself to a glass of black-strap.' He indicated the decanter that sat on its tray at the end of the table, remembering Trussel's legendary thirst which he attributed to a lifelong proximity to gunpowder.

'The roads were dreadful, sir,' said Trussel, helping himself to the cheap, dark wine. 'I gather we are a tender, sir, servicing bombs.'

'Exactly so, Mr Trussel, and as such most desperately in want of a gunner. I shall rely most heavily upon you. As soon as we are rigged we are ordered to Blackstakes to load ammunition and ordnance stores. You will of course have finished your preparations of the magazines by then. Willerton, the carpenter, has a quantity of tongued deals on board and has made a start on them. I've no need to impress upon your mind that not a nail's to be driven once we've a grain of powder on board.'

'I understand, sir.' He paused. 'I saw Mr Rogers on deck.' The statement of fact held just the faintest hint of surprise. Trussel had been gunner of the brig *Hellebore* when Rogers wrecked her in the Red Sea.

'Mr Rogers is proving a most efficient first lieutenant Mr Trussel.' Drinkwater paused, watching Trussel's face remain studiously wooden. 'Well, I'd be obliged if you would be about your business without delay; time is of the very essence.'

Trussel rose. 'One other thing, sir.'

'Yes, what is that?'

'Are we to embark a detachment of artillerymen?'

Drinkwater nodded. 'I have received notice to that effect. It is customary to do so when ordnance stores are loaded.'

'Then we are for the Baltic, sir?'

Drinkwater smiled. 'You may conjecture as you see fit. I have no orders beyond those to load powder at Blackstakes.' Trussel grinned comprehendingly back.

'I hear Lord Nelson is to be employed upon a secret expedition. The papers had it as I came through London.' He smiled again, aware that the news had come as a surprise to the lieutenant.

'Lord Nelson . . .' mused Drinkwater, and it was some moments before he bent again to his work.

'I congratulate you, Mr Willerton.' Drinkwater regarded the brilliantly painted figurehead that perched on *Virago*'s tiny fo'c's'le. The product of Willerton's skill with mallet and gouge was the usual mixture of crude suggestion and mild obscenity. The half bust showed a ferociously staring woman with her head thrown back. A far too beautiful mouth gaped violently revealing a protruding scarlet tongue, like the tongue of flame that must once have issued from *Virago*'s mortars.

To the face of this harpy Mr Willerton's artistry had added the pert, up-tilted breasts of a virgin, too large for nature but erotic enough to satisfy the prurience of his shipmates. But it was the right arm that attested to Mr Willerton's true genius. While the left trailed astern the right crooked under an exaggerated breast, its nagging forefinger erect in the universally recognisable position of the scold. The 'leddy' was both termagant wanton and nagging wife, a spitfire virago eminently suitable to a bomb vessel. It was a pity, thought Drinkwater as he nodded his approval, that they were not so commissioned.

The handful of men detailed by Lieutenant Rogers to assist Willerton in fitting the figurehead grinned appreciatively, while Willerton sucked his teeth with a peculiar whistling noise.

'Worthy of a first rate, Mr Willerton. A true virago. I am glad you heeded my advice,' he added in a lower voice.

Willerton grinned, showing a blackened row of caried teeth. 'The right hand, sir, mind the right hand.' His blue eyes twinkled wickedly.

Drinkwater regarded the nagging finger. Perhaps there was some suggestion of Mrs Jex there, but it was not readily recognisable to him. He gave Willerton formal permission to fit the figurehead and turned aft.

A keen easterly wind canted *Virago*'s tub-like hull across the river as she lay to her anchor clear of the sheer hulk. The three lower masts had been stepped and their rigging, already made up ashore and 'lumped' for hoisting aboard, had been fitted over the caps and hove tight to the channels by deadeyes and lanyards. The double hemp lines of fore, main and mizzen stays had been swigged forward and tightened. Rogers and Matchett were at that moment hoisting up the maintopmast, its heel-rope leading down to the barrel windlass at the break of the fo'c's'le, the pawls clicking satisfactorily as the topmast inched aloft.

Drinkwater began to walk aft, past the sweating gangs of sea and landsmen being bullied and sworn at by the bosun's mates, round the heaps and casks being counted by Mr Jex, and ascended the three steps to the low poop. He cast a glance across the river where Mr Quilhampton brought the cutter out from the dockyard, towing the mainyard from the mast pond. Over the poop with its huge tiller, a mark of *Virago*'s age, fluttered the ensign. In its upper hoist canton it bore the new Union flag with St Patrick's saltire added after the recent Act of Union with Ireland. For a second he regarded it curiously, seeing a fundamental change in something he had come to regard as almost holy, something to fight and perhaps to die under. Of the Act and its implication he thought little, though it seemed to make sense to his ordered mind as did Pitt's attempt to emancipate the Roman Catholics of that unfortunate island.

He descended the companionway into his cabin. Mrs Jex had been evicted. On 27th January the Admiralty had ordered a squadron of bombs and their tenders to assemble at Sheerness. The dockyard had woken to its responsibilities. All was now of the utmost urgency before their Lordships started asking questions of the Commissioner.

Tregembo was hanging Elizabeth's gift, the cause of his delay in joining. Drinkwater watched, oddly moved. Bruilhac's skill as a portraitist showed Elizabeth cool and smiling with Charlotte Amelia chubby and serious. He was suddenly filled with an immense pride and tenderness. From his position at the table his two loved ones looked down at him, illuminated by the light that entered the cabin from the stern windows behind him, the moving light that, even on a dull day, did not enter his cabin without reflecting from the sea.

Mr Quilhampton interrupted his reverie. 'Mainyard's alongside, sir, and I've a letter left for you at the main gate.' He handed the paper over and Drinkwater slit the wafer.

My Dear Nathaniel,

I'd be obliged if you would meet me at the sign of the Blue Fox this evening.

Your brother, Edward

He looked up. 'Mr Q. Be so good as to ask the first lieutenant to have a boat for me at four bells.'

The Blue Fox was in a back street, well off the Dock Road and in an alley probably better known for its brothels than its reputable inns. But the place seemed clean enough and the landlord civil, evincing no surprise when Drinkwater asked for his brother. The man ushered Drinkwater to a private room on the upper floor.

Edward Drinkwater rose to meet him. He was of similar height to Nathaniel, with a heavier build and higher colour. His clothes were fashionably cut, and though not foppish, tended to the extremes of colour and decoration then *de rigeur*.

'Nathaniel! My dear fellow, my dear fellow, you are most kind to come.'

'Edward. It has been a very long time.' They shook hands.

'Too long, too long . . . here I have some claret mulling, by heaven damned if it ain't colder here than in London . . . there, a glass will warm you. Your ship is nearly ready then?'

Nathaniel nodded as he sipped the hot wine.

'Then it seems I am just in time, just in time.'

'Forgive me, Edward, but why all the mysterious urgency?'

Edward ran a finger round his stock with evident embarrassment. He avoided his brother's eyes and appeared to be choosing his words with difficulty. Several times he raised his head to speak, then thought better of it.

'Damn it Ned,' broke in Drinkwater impatiently, "tis a woman or 'tis money, confound it, no man could haver like this for ought else.'

'Both Nat, both.' Edward seized on the opportunity and the words began to tumble from him. 'It is a long story, Nat, one that goes back ten or more years. You recollect after mother died and you married, I went off to Enfield to work for an India merchant, with his horses. I learned a deal about horses, father was good with 'em too. After a while I left the nabob's employ and was offered work at Newmarket, still with horses. I was too big to race 'em but I backed 'em and over a long period made enough money to put by. I was lucky. Very lucky. I had a sizeable wager on one occasion and made enough in a single bet to live like a gentleman for a year, maybe two if I was careful.' He sighed and passed a hand over his sweating face.

'After the revolution in France, when the aristos started coming over there were pickings of all sorts. I ran with a set of blades. We took fencing lessons from an impoverished marquis, advanced an old dowager some money on her jewels, claimed the debt . . . well, in short, my luck held.

'Then I met Pascale, she was of the minor nobility, but penniless. She became my mistress.' He paused to drink and Drinkwater watching him thought what a different life from his own. There were common threads, perceptible if you knew how to identify them. Their boyhood had been dominated by their mother's impecunious gentility, widowed after their drunken father had been flung from a horse. Nathaniel was careful of money, neither unwilling to loot a few gold coins from an American prize when a half-starved midshipman, nor to lean a little on the well-heeled

Mr Jex. But where he had inherited his mother's shrewdness Edward had been bequeathed his father's improvidence as he now went on to relate.

'Things went well for a while. I continued to gamble and, with modest lodgings and Pascale to keep me company, managed to cut a dash. Then my luck changed. For no apparent reason. I began to lose. It was uncanny. I lost confidence, friends, everything.

'Nathaniel, I have twenty pounds between me and penury. Pascale threatens to leave me since she has received an offer to better herself . . .' He fell silent.

'As another man's mistress?'

Edward's silence was eloquent.

'I see.' Drinkwater felt a low anger building up in him. It was not enough that he should have spent a great deal of money in fitting out His Britannic bloody Majesty's bomb tender *Virago*. It was not enough that the exigencies of the service demanded his constant presence on board until sailing, but that this good-for-nothing killbuck of a brother must turn up to prey on his better nature.

'How much do you want?'

'Five hundred would . . .'

'Five hundred! God's bones, Edward, where in the name of Almighty God d'you think I can lay my hands on five hundred pounds?'

'I heard you did well from prize money . . .'

'Prize money? God, Ned, but you've a damned nerve. D'you know how many scars I've got for that damned prize money, how many sleepless nights, hours of worry . . .? No, of course you don't. You've been cutting a dash, gaming and whoring like the rest of this country's so-called gentry while your sea-officers and seamen are rotting in their wooden coffins. God damn it, Ned, but I've a wife and family to be looked to first.' His temper began to ebb. Without looking up Edward muttered:

'I heard too, that you received a bequest.'

'Where the hell d'you learn that?' A low fury came into his voice.

'Oh, I learned it in Petersfield.' That would not be difficult. There were enough gossips in any town to know the business of others. It was true that he had received a sizeable bequest from the estate of his former captain, Madoc Griffiths. 'They say it was three thousand pounds.'

'They may say what the hell they like. It is no longer mine. Most is in trust for my children, the remainder made over to my wife.' He paused again and Edward looked up, disappointed yet irritatingly unrepentant.

It suddenly occurred to Drinkwater that the expenses incurred in the fitting out of a ship, even a minor one like *Virago*, were inconceivable to Edward. He began to repent of his unbrotherly temper; to hold himself mean, still reproved in his conscience for the trick he had played on Jex, no matter how many barrels of sauerkraut it had bought.

'Listen, Ned, I am more than two hundred pounds out of pocket in fitting out my ship. That is why we receive prize money, that and for the wounds we endure in an uncaring country's service. You talk of fencing lessons but you've never known what it is to cut a man down before he kills you. You regard my uniform as some talisman opening the salons of the *ton* to me when I am nothing but a dog of a sailor, lieutenant or not. Why, Ned, I am not fit to crawl beneath the bootsoles of a twelve-year-old ensign of horse whose commission costs him two thousand pounds.' All the bitterness of his profession rose to the surface, replacing his anger with the gall of experience.

Edward remained silent, pouring them both another drink. After several moments Nathaniel rose and went to a small table. From the tail pocket of his coat he drew a small tablet and a pencil. He began to write, calling for wax and a candle.

After sealing the letter he handed it to his brother. 'That is all I can, in all conscience, manage.'

Then he left, picking up his hat without another word, leaving Edward to wonder over the amount and without waiting for thanks.

He was too preoccupied to notice Mr Jex drinking in the taproom as he made his way through to the street.

Chapter Five *January–February 1801*

The Pyroballogist

Drinkwater raised the speaking trumpet. 'A trifle more in on that foretack, if you please Mr Matchett.' He transferred his attention to the waist where the master attended the main braces. 'You may belay the main braces Mr Easton.'

'Aye, aye, sir.'

Virago slid downstream leaving the dockyard to starboard and the ships laid up in ordinary to larboard. 'Full and bye.'

'Full an' bye, zur.' Tregembo answered from the tiller. Drinkwater, short of men still, had rated the Cornishman quartermaster.

They cleared the end of the trot, slipping beneath the wooded hill at Upnor.

'Up helm!' *Virago* swung, turning slowly before the wind. Drinkwater nodded to Rogers. 'Square the yards.' Rogers bawled at the men at the braces as *Virago* brought the wind astern, speeding downstream with the ebb tide under her, her forecourse, three topsails and foretopmast staysail set. The latter flapped now, masked by the forecourse.

They swung south east out of Cockham Reach, the river widening, its north bank falling astern, displaced by the low line of Hoo Island. They passed the line of prison hulks, disfigured old ships, broken, black and sinister. The hands swung the yards as the ship made each turn in the channel, the officers attentive during this first passage of the elderly vessel. They rounded the fort on Darnetness.

'Give her the main course, Mr Rogers.'

'Aye, aye, sir. Main yard there! Let fall! Let fall! Mind tacks and sheets there, you blasted lubbers! Look lively there! Watch, God damn it, there's a kink in the starboard clew garnet! It'll snag in the lead block, Mr Quil-bloody-hampton!'

Virago gathered speed, the tide giving Drinkwater a brief illusion of commanding something other than a tub of a ship. He smiled to himself. Though slow, *Virago* was heavy enough to carry her way and would probably handle well enough in a seaway. She had a ponderous certainty about her that might become an endearing quality, Drinkwater thought. He swung her down Kethole Reach and Rogers braced the yards up again as the wind veered a point towards the north. To the west the sky was clearing and almost horizontal beams of sunlight began to slant through the overcast, shining ahead of them to where the fort at Garrison Point and the Sheerness Dockyard gleamed dully against the monotones of marsh and islands.

'Clew up the courses as we square away in Saltpan Reach, Mr Rogers.' He levelled his glass ahead. Half a dozen squat hulled shapes were riding at anchor off Deadman's Island, a mile up stream from Sheerness. They were bomb vessels anchored close to the powder hulks at Blackstakes.

A chattering had broken out amidships. 'Silence there!' snapped Rogers. Drinkwater watched the line of bombs grow larger. 'Up courses if you please.'

Rogers bawled, Quilhampton piped and Matchett shouted. The heavy flog of resisting canvas rose above Drinkwater's head as he studied the bombs through his glass, selecting a place to bring *Virago* to her anchor.

They were abeam the upstream vessel, a knot of curious officers visible on her deck. There was a gap between the fourth and fifth bomb vessel, sufficient for *Virago* to swing. Drinkwater felt a thrill of pure excitement. He could go downstream and anchor in perfect safety at the seaward end of the line; but that gap beckoned.

'Stand by the braces, Mr Rogers! Down helm!'

'Down helm, zur!' *Virago* turned to starboard, her yards creaking round in their parrels, the forestaysail filling with a crack.

'Brace sharp up there, damn it!' he snapped, then to the helm, 'Full and bye!'

'Full an' bye, zur,' replied the impassive Tregembo.

Drinkwater sailed *Virago* as close to the wind as possible as the ebb pushed her remorselessly downstream. If he made a misjudgement he would crash on board the bomb vessel next astern. He could see a group of people forward on her, no doubt equally alerted to the possibility. He watched the relative bearing of the other vessel's foremast. It drew slowly astern: he could do it.

'Anchor's ready, sir,' muttered Rogers.

'Very well.' They were suddenly level with the bow of the other ship.

'Down helm!' *Virago* turned to starboard again, her sails about to shiver, then to flog. She carried her way, the water chuckling under her bow as she crept over the tide, leaving the anxious watchers astern and edging up on the ship next ahead.

Drinkwater watched the shore, saw its motion cease. 'All aback now! Let go!'

He felt the hull buck as the anchor fell from the cathead and watched the cable rumble along the deck, saw it catch an inexperienced landsman on the ankle and fling him down while the seamen laughed.

'Give her sixty fathoms, Mr Matchett, and bring her up to it.'

He nodded to Rogers. 'Clew up and stow.'

Mr Easton went below to plot their anchorage on the chart and when the vessel was reported brought to her cable Drinkwater joined him. Looking at the chart Drinkwater felt satisfied that neither ship nor crew had let him down.

His satisfaction was short-lived. An hour later he stood before Captain Martin, Master and Commander of His Majesty's bomb vessel *Explosion*, senior officer of the bomb ships assembled at Sheerness. Captain Martin was clearly intolerant of any of his subordinates who showed the least inclination to further their careers by acts of conspicuousness.

'Not only, lieutenant, was your manoeuvre one that endangered your own ship but it also endangered mine. It was, sir, an act of wanton irresponsibility. Such behaviour is not to be tolerated and speaks volumes on your character. I am surprised you have been entrusted with such a command, Mr Drinkwater. A man responsible for carrying quantities of powder upon a special service must needs be steady, constantly thoughtful, and never, ever hazard his ship.'

Drinkwater felt the blood mounting to his cheeks as Martin went on. 'Furthermore you have been most dilatory in the matter of commissioning your ship. I had reason to expect you to join the bombs under my command some days ago.'

Martin looked up at Drinkwater from a pair of watery blue eyes that stared out of a thin, parchment coloured face. Drinkwater fought down his sense of injustice and wounded pride. Feeling like a whipped midshipman he applied the resilience of the orlop, learned years ago.

'If my conduct displeased you I apologise, sir. I had no intention of causing you any concern. As to the manner of my commissioning I can only say that I exerted every effort to hasten the matter. I was prevented from so doing by the officials of the dockyard.'

'The dockyard officers have their own job to attend to, Mr Drinkwater, you cannot expect them to give priority to a bomb tender . . .' Aware that he had offended (Martin was probably related to some jobber in the dockyard), Drinkwater could not resist the opening.

'Precisely my point, sir,' he said drily. Martin's upper lip curled slightly, a mark of obvious displeasure, and Drinkwater added hastily, 'I mean no offence, sir.'

He stared down the commander who eventually said, 'Now, to your orders for the next week . . .'

'Your sport was most profitable, Mr Q,' said Drinkwater laying down his knife and fork upon an empty plate.

'Thank you sir. Did you favour the widgeon or the teal?'

'I fancy the teal had the edge. Mr Jex, would you convey my appreciation to the cook.'

Jex nodded, his mouth still full. Drinkwater looked round the table. It was a cramped gathering, sharing his small cabin with the officers were the two stern chasers and two 24-pound carronades in the aftermost side ports.

The cloth was drawn and the decanter of blackstrap placed in front of Drinkwater. They drank the loyal toast at their seats then scraped their chairs back. A cigar or two appeared, Trussel brought out a long churchwarden pipe and Willerton slipped a surreptitious quid of tobacco into his mouth. Lettsom took snuff and Drinkwater reflected that apart from himself and Rogers and Mr Quilhampton all those present, which excepted Mr Mason on deck, were well over forty-five, possibly over fifty. The preponderance of warrant officers carried by *Virago* ensured this, but it sometimes made Drinkwater feel old before his time, condemned to spend his life in the society of elderly men. He sighed, remembering the attitude of Captain Martin. Then he remembered something else, something he had been saving for this moment. 'By the way gentlemen, when I was aboard *Explosion* this morning I learned some news from London that will affect us all. Has anyone else learned of it?'

'We know that Admiral Ganteaume got out of Brest with seven of the line,' said Rogers.

'Aye, these damned easterlies, but I heard that Collingwood's gone in pursuit,' added Matchett. Drinkwater shook his head.

'You mean, sir, that it is intended to defend the Thames by dropping stone blocks into it?' asked Quilhampton ingenuously.

'No, young shaver, I do not.' He looked round. No one seemed to have any idea. 'I mean that Billy Pitt's resigned and that Mr Speaker Addington is to form a new government . . .' Exclamations of surprise and dismay met the news.

'Well, 'twill be of no account, Addington's Pitt's mouthpiece . . .'

'No wonder there are no orders for us . . .'

'So the King would not stomach emancipating the papists.'

'Damned good thing too . . .'

'Come Mr Rogers, you surely cannot truly think that?'

'Aye, Mr Lettsom, I most certainly do, God damn them . . .'

'Gentlemen please!' Drinkwater banged his hand on the table. The meal was intended to unite them. 'Perhaps you would like to know who is to head the Admiralty?' Their faces turned towards him. 'St Vincent, with Markham and Troubridge.'

'Who is to replace St Vincent in the Channel, sir?'

'Lord Cornwallis.'

'Ah, Billy Blue, well I think that is good news,' offered Lettsom, 'and I hear St Vincent will be at Sir Bloody Andrew Snape Hammond's throat. He has sworn reform and Hammond is an infernal jobber. Pray heaven they start at Chatham, eh?'

'I'll drink to that, Mr Lettsom,' said Drinkwater smiling.

'What d'you say Jex?' said the surgeon turning to the purser, 'got your dirty work done just in time, eh?' There was a rumble of laughter round the table. Jex flushed.

'I protest . . . sir . . .'

'I rule that unfair, Mr Lettsom,' said Drinkwater still smiling. 'Consider that Mr Jex paid for the sauerkraut.'

'The hands'll not thank you for that sir, however good an anti-scorbutic it is.'

Drinkwater ignored Jex's look of startled horror. He did not see it subside into an expression of resentment. 'What about the other members of the cabinet?' asked Lettsom.

'I forget, Mr Lettsom. Only that that blade Vansittart is to be Joint Secretary to the Treasury or something. That is all I recollect . . .'

'Well the damned politicians forget us; why the hell should we remember them?' Rogers's flushed face expressed approval at his own jest.

'I have it!' said Lettsom suddenly, snapping his fingers as the laughter died away.

'Have what sir?' asked Quilhampton in precocious mock horror, 'The lues? The yaws?'

'An epigram, gentlemen, an epigram!' He cleared his throat while several banged the table for silence. Lettsom struck a pose:

> 'If blocks can from danger deliver,
> Two places are safe from the French,
> The first is the mouth of the river,
> The second the Treasury Bench.'

'Bravo! Bravo!' They cheered, banged the table and were unaware of the strange face that appeared round the doorway. Drinkwater saw it first, together with that of Mason behind. He called for silence. 'What is it Mr Mason?'

The assembled officers turned to stare at the newcomer. He wore a royal blue tail coat turned back to reveal scarlet facings. His breeches were white and a cocked hat was tucked underneath his arm. His face was round and red, covered by peppery hair that grew out along his cheekbones, though his chin was shaved yet it had the appearance of being constantly rasped raw as if to keep down its beard. The man's head sat low upon his shoulders, like a 12-pound shot in the garlands.

'God damn my eyes, it's a bloody lobster,' said Rogers offensively and even though the man wore the blue uniform of the Royal Artillery his apoplectic countenance lent the welcome an amusing aptness.

'Lieutenant Tumilty of the artillery, sir,' said Mason filling the silence while the artillery officer stared aggressively round his new surroundings.

Drinkwater rose. 'Good day, lieutenant, pray sit down. Mr

Tumility, make way there. You are to join us then?' He passed the decanter down the table and the messman produced a glass. The other occupants of the cabin eyed the stranger with ill-disguised curiosity.

Tumilty filled his glass, downed it and refilled it. Then he fixed Drinkwater with a tiny, fiery eye.

'I'm after asking if you're in command of the ship?' The accent was pugnaciously Irish.

'That is correct, Mr Tumilty.'

'It's true then! God save me but 'tis true, so it is.' He swallowed again, heavily.

'What exactly is true, Mr Tumilty?' asked Drinkwater, beginning to feel exasperated by the artilleryman's circumlocution.

'Despite appearances to the contrary, and begging your pardon, but you being but a lieutenant, then this ain't a bomb vessel, sir. Is that, or is that not the truth of the matter?'

Drinkwater flushed. Tumilty had touched a raw nerve. '*Virago* was built as a bomb vessel, but at present she is commissioned only as a tender . . .'

'Though there's nothing wrong with her structure,' growled the hitherto silent Willerton.

'Does that answer your question?' added Drinkwater, ignoring the interruption.

Tumilty nodded. 'Aye, God save me, so it does. And I'll not pretend I like it lieutenant, not at all.' He suddenly struck his hat violently upon the table.

'Devil take 'em, do they not know the waste; that I'm the finest artilleryman to be employed upon the service?' He seemed about to burst into tears, looking round the astonished faces for agreement. Drinkwater was inclined to forgive him his behaviour; clearly Mr Tumilty was acting as a consequence of some incident at Woolwich and cursing his superiors at the Royal Arsenal.

'Gentlemen, pity me, I beg you. I'm condemned to hand powder like any of your barefoot powder-monkeys. A fetcher and carrier, me!'

'It seems, Mr Tumilty, that, to coin a phrase, we are all here present in the same boat.' A rumble of agreement followed Drinkwater's soothing words.

'But me, sir. For sure I'm the finest pyroballogist in the whole damned artillery!'

Chapter Six *February 1801*

Powder and Shot

'Pyroballogy, Lieutenant Drinkwater, is the art of throwing fire. 'Tis both scientific and alchemical, and that is why officers in my profession cannot purchase their commissions like the rest of the army, so it is.'

Drinkwater and Tumilty stood at the break of the poop watching the labours of the hands as they manned the yardarm tackles, hoisting barrel after barrel of powder out of the hoy alongside. They had loaded their ordinary powder and shot, naval gunner's stores for their carronades and long guns, from the powder hulk at Blackstakes. Now they loaded the ordnance stores, sent round from Woolwich on the Thames. From time to time Tumilty broke off his monologue to shout instructions at his sergeant and bombadier who, with *Virago*'s men, were toiling to get the stores aboard before the wind freshened further.

'No sir, our commissions are all issued by the Master-General himself and a captain of artillery may have more experience than a field officer, to be sure. I'm not after asking if that's a fair system, Mr Drinkwater, but I'm telling you that a man can be an expert at his work and still be no more than a lieutenant.'

Drinkwater smiled. 'And I'd not be wanting to argue with you Mr Tumilty,' he said drily.

''Tis an ancient art, this pyroballogy. Archimedes himself founded it at the siege of Syracuse and the Greeks had their own ballistic fireballs. Now tell me, Mr Drinkwater, would I be right in thinking you'd like to be doing a bit of the fire-throwing yourself?'

Drinkwater looked at the short Irishman alongside him. He was growing accustomed to his almost orientally roundabout way of saying something.

'I think perhaps we both suffer from a sense of frustration, Mr Tumilty.'

'And the carpenter assures me the ship's timbers are sound enough.' Drinkwater nodded and Tumilty added, "Tis not to be underestimated, sir, a thirteen-inch mortar has a chamber with a capacity of thirty-two pounds. Yet a charge in excess of twenty will shake the timbers of a mortar bed to pieces in a very short time and may cause the mortar to explode.'

'But we do not have a mortar, Mr Tumilty.'

'True, true, but you've not dismantled the beds Mr Drinkwater. Now why, I'm asking myself, would that be?'

Drinkwater shrugged. 'I was aware that they contained the shell rooms, I assumed they were to remain in place . . .'

'And nobody told you to take them to pieces, eh?'

'That is correct.'

'Well now that's very fortunate, Mr Drinkwater, very fortunate indeed, for the both of us. What would you say if I was to ship a couple of mortars on those beds?'

Drinkwater frowned at Tumilty who peered at him with a sly look.

'I don't think I quite understand.'

'Well look,' Tumilty pointed at the hoy. The last sling of fine grain cylinder powder with its scarlet barrel markings rose out of the hoy's hold, following the restoved and mealed powder into the magazine of *Virago*. The hoy's crew were folding another section of the tarpaulin back and lifting off the hatchboards to reveal two huge black shapes. 'Mortars, Mr Drinkwater, one thirteen-inch weighing eighty-two hundredweights, one ten-inch weighing forty-one hundredweights. Why don't we ship them on the beds, eh?'

'I take it they're spares.' Tumilty nodded. Drinkwater knew the other bomb vessels already had their own mortars fitted for he had examined those on the *Explosion*. There seemed no very good argument against fitting them in the beds even if they were supposed to be struck down into the hold. After all *Virago* had been fitted to carry them. He wondered what Martin would say if he knew, as doubtless he would in due course.

'By damn, Mr Tumilty, it is getting dark. Let us have those beauties swung aboard as you suggest. We may carry 'em in their beds safer than rolling about in the hold.'

'That's the spirit, Mr Drinkwater, that's the spirit to be sure.'

'Mr Rogers! A word with you if you please.' Rogers ascended the ladder.

'Sir?'

'We have two mortars to load, spares for the squadron. I intend to lower them on the beds. D'you understand Sam? If we've two mortars fitted we may yet get a chance to do more than fetch and carry . . .'

The gleam of enthusiasm kindled in Rogers's eye. 'I like the idea, damned if I don't.' He shot a glance at Tumilty, still suspicious of the artilleryman who seemed to occupy a position of a questionable nature aboard a King's ship. The Irishman was gazing abstractedly to windward.

'Now, 'twill be ticklish with this wind increasing but it will likely drop after sunset. Brace the three lower yards and rig preventers on 'em, then rig three-fold purchases as yard and stay tackles over both beds. Get Willerton to open the hatches and oil the capsquares. Top all three yards well up and put two burtons on each and frap the whole lot together. That should serve.'

'What weights, sir?'

'Eighty-two hundred weights to come in on the after bed and . . .'

'Forty-one on the forward . . .'

'Forrard, Mr Tumilty.'

'I'm sure I'm begging your pardon, Mr Rogers.' Rogers hurried away shouting for Matchett and Willerton. 'Why he's a touchy one, Mr Drinkwater.'

'We're agreed on a number of things, Mr Tumilty, not least that we'd both like to add 'Captain' to our name, but I believe there was much bad blood between the artillery and the navy the last time an operation like this took place.'

'Sure, I'd not be knowing about that sir,' replied Tumilty, all injured innocence again.

Virago creaked and leaned to starboard as the weight came on the tackles. The sun had already set and in the long twilight the hands laboured on. The black mass of the ten-inch mortar, a little under five feet in length, hung above the lightened hoy.

At the windlass Mr Matchett supervised the men on the bars. Yard and stay tackles had been rigged with their hauling parts wound on in contrary directions so that as the weight was eased on the yard arms it was taken up on the stay tackles. The doubled-up mainstay sagged under the weight and Rogers lowered the mortar as quickly as possible. Mr Willerton's party with handspikes eased the huge iron gun into its housing and snapped over the capsquares. *Virago* was upright again, though trimming several inches by the head.

'Throw off all turns, clear away the foretackles, rig the after tackles!'

It was as Drinkwater had said. The wind had died and the first mortar had come aboard without fuss. Mr Tumilty had left the pure seamanship to the navy and gone to closet himself with his sergeant and Mr Trussel, while they inspected the powder stowage and locked all the shell rooms, powder rooms, fuse rooms and filling rooms that Willerton had lined with the deal boards supplied by Chatham Dockyard.

The tackles suspended from the main and crossjack yards were overhauled and hooked onto the carefully fitted slings round the thirteen-inch mortar. Next the two centreline tackles were hooked on. To cope with the additional weight of the larger mortar Drinkwater had ordered these be rigged from the main and mizzen tops, arguing the mizzen forestay was insufficient for the task.

Again the hauling parts were led forward and the slack taken up. There were some ominous creakings but after half an hour the trunnions settled on the bed and Mr Willerton secured the second set of capsquares. The sliding section of the mortar hatches were pulled over and the tarpaulins battened down. The last of the daylight disappeared from the riot of cloud to the west and the hands, grumbling or chattering according to their inclination, were piped below.

For the first time since the days of disillusion that followed his joining the ship, Nathaniel Drinkwater felt he was again, at least in part, master of his own destiny.

'Well, Mr Tumilty, perhaps you would itemise the ordnance stores on board.'

'Sure, and I will. We have two hundred of the thirteen-inch shell carcases, two hundred ten-inch, one hundred and forty round, five-vented carcases for the thirteens, forty oblong carcases for the tens. Five thousand one pound round shot, the same as you have for your swivels . . .'

'What do you want them for?' asked Rogers.

'Well now, Mr Rogers,' said Tumilty, tolerantly lowering his list, 'if you choke up the chamber of a thirteen inch mortar with a couple of hundred of they little devils, they fall like iron rain on trenches, or open works without casemates, or beaches, or anywhere else you want to clear of an enemy. Now to continue, we have loaded two hundred barrels of powder, an assortment as you know of fine cylinder, restoved and mealed powder. I have three cases of flints, five of fuses, six rolls of worsted quick-match, a quantity of rosin, turpentine, sulphur, antimony, saltpetre, spirits of wine, isinglass and red orpiment for Bengal lights, blue fires and fire balls. To be sure, Mr Rogers, you're sitting on a mortal large bang.'

'And you've everything you want?' Tumilty nodded. 'Are you happy with things, Mr Trussel?'

'Aye, sir, though I'd like Mr Willerton to make a new powder box. Ours is leaky and if you're thinking that . . . well, maybe we might fire a mortar or two ourselves, then you'll need one to carry powder up to the guns.'

'Mr Trussel's right, Mr Drinkwater. The slightest leak in a powder box lays a trail from the guns to the filling room in no time at all. If the train fires the explosion'll be even quicker!' They laughed at Tumilty's diabolical humour; the siting of those ugly mortars had intoxicated them all a little.

'Very well, gentlemen. We'll look at her for trim in the morning and hope that Martin does not say anything.'

'Let us hope Captain Martin'll be looking after his own mortars and not overcharging them so that we haven't to give up ours,' said Tumilty, blowing his red nose. He went on:

'And who had you in mind to be throwing the shells at, Mr Drinkwater?'

'Well it's no secret that the Baltic is the likely destination, gentlemen,' he looked round at their faces, expectant in the gently swinging light from the lamp. From the notebooks he had inherited from old Blackmore, sailing master of the frigate *Cyclops*, he had learned a great deal about the Baltic. Blackmore had commanded a snow engaged in the timber trade. 'If the Tsar leagues the navies of the north, we'll have the Danes and Swedes to deal with, as well as the Russians. If he doesn't, we've still the Russians left. They're based at Revel and Cronstadt; iced up now, but Revel unfreezes in April. As to the Swedes at Carlscrona, I confess I know little of them. Of the Danes at Copenhagen,' he shrugged, 'I do not think we want to leave 'em in our rear.'

'It's nearly the end of February now,' said Trussel, 'if we are to fight the Danes before the Russkies get out of the ice, we shall have to move soon.'

'Aye, and with that dilatory old bastard Hyde Parker to command us, we may yet be too late,' added Rogers.

'Yes, I'm after thinking it's the Russkies.' Tumilty nodded, tugging at the hairs on his cheeks.

'Well, they say Hyde Parker's marrying some young doxy, so I still say we'll be too late.' Rogers scratched the side of his nose gloomily.

'They say she's young enough to be his daughter,' grinned Trussel.

'Dirty old devil.'

'Lucky old sod.'

''Tis what comes of commanding in the West Indies and taking your admiral's eighth from the richest station in the service,' added the hitherto silent Easton.

'Well well, gentlemen, 'tis of no importance to us whom Admiral Parker marries,' said Drinkwater, 'I understand it is likely that Nelson will second him and *he* will brook no delay.'

'Perhaps, perhaps, sir, but I'd be willing to lay money on it,' concluded Rogers standing up, taking his cue from Drinkwater and terminating the meeting.

'Let us hope we have orders to proceed to the rendezvous at Yarmouth very soon, gentlemen. And now I wish you all a good night.'

Chapter Seven *February 1801*

Action off the Sunk

Lieutenant Drinkwater hunched himself lower into his boat cloak, shivering from the effects of the low fever that made his head and eyes ache intolerably. The westerly wind had thrown a lowering overcast across the sky and then whipped itself into a gale, driving rain squalls across the track of the squadron as it struggled out of the Thames Estuary into the North Sea.

Their visible horizon was circumscribed by one such squall which hissed across the wave-caps and made *Virago* lean further to leeward as she leapt forward under its impetus. A roil of water foamed along the lee scuppers, squirting inboard through the closed gunports and Drinkwater could hear the grunts of the helmsmen as they leaned against the cant of the deck and the kicking resistance of the big tiller. A clicking of blocks told where the quartermaster took up the slack on the relieving tackles. Drinkwater shivered again, marvelling at the chill in his spine which was at odds with the burning of his head.

He knew it could be typhus, the ship-fever, brought aboard by the lousy draft of pressed men, but he was fastidious in the matter of bodily cleanliness and had not recently discovered lice or fleas upon his person. He had already endured the symptoms for five days without the appearance of the dreaded 'eruption'. Lettsom had fussed over him, forcing him to drink infusions of bark without committing himself to a diagnosis. The non-appearance of a sore had led Drinkwater to conclude he might have contracted the marsh-ague from the mists of the Medway. God knew he had exposed himself to chills and exhaustion as he had striven to prepare his ship, and his cabin stove had been removed with Mrs Jex, prior to the loading of powder.

He thought of the admonition he had received from Martin and the recollection made him search ahead, under the curved foot of the forecourse to where *Explosion* led the bomb vessels and three tenders to the north eastward. What he saw only served to unsettle him further.

'Mr Easton!' he shouted with sudden asperity, 'do you not see the commodore's signalling?' Martin, the epitome of prudence tending to timidity, was reducing sail, brailing up his courses and snugging down to double reefed topsails and a staysail forward. Drinkwater left Easton to similarly reduce *Virago*'s canvas and repeat the signal to the vessels astern. He fulminated silently to himself, having already decided that Martin was a cross they were all going to have to bear. As senior officer he had been most insistent upon being addressed as 'commodore' for the short passage from Sheerness to Yarmouth. Drinkwater found that sort of pedantry a cause for contempt and irritation. He was aware, too, that Martin was not simply a fussy senior officer. It was clear that whatever advancement Drinkwater expected to wring out of his present appointment was going to have to be despite Captain Martin, who seemed to wish to thwart the lieutenant. Drinkwater threw off his gloomy thoughts, the professional melancholy known as 'the blue devils', and watched a herring gull glide alongside *Virago*, riding the turbulent air disturbed by the passage of the ship. With an almost imperceptible closing of its wings it suddenly sideslipped and curved away into the low trough of a wave lifting on *Virago*'s larboard quarter.

'Sail reduced sir.'

'Very well, Mr Easton. Be so good as to keep a sharp watch on the commodore, particularly in this visibility.'

Easton bit his lip. 'Aye, aye, sir.'

'When will we be abeam the Gunfleet beacon?'

''Bout an hour, sir.'

'Thank you.'

Easton turned away and Drinkwater looked over the ship. His earlier premonition had been correct. She had an immensely solid feel about her, despite her lack of overall size. Her massive scantlings gave her this, but she was also positive to handle and gave him a feeling of confident satisfaction as his first true command.

He looked astern at the remainder of the squadron. *Terror*, *Sulphur*, *Zebra* and *Hecla* could just be made out. *Discovery* and the other two tenders, both Geordie colliers, were lost in the rain to the south westward. The remaining bomb, *Volcano*, was somewhere ahead of *Explosion*.

He saw one of the tenders emerge from the rain astern of *Hecla*. She was a barque rigged collier called the *Anne Reed*, requisitioned by the Ordnance Board and fitted up as an accommodation vessel for the Royal Artillery detachment, some eight officers and eighty men who, in addition to half a dozen ordnance carpenters from the Tower of London, would work the mortars when the time came. Lieutenant Tumilty was somewhere aboard her, no doubt engaged in furious and bucolic debate with his fellow 'pyroballogists' over the more abstruse aspects of fire-throwing.

Drinkwater smiled to himself, missing the man's company. Doubtless there would be time for that later, when they reached Yarmouth and again when they entered the Baltic.

A stronger gust of wind dashed the spray of a breaking wave and whipped it over *Virago*'s quarter. A cold trickle wormed its way down Drinkwater's neck, reminding him that he need not stand on deck all day. Already the Swin had opened to become the King's Channel, now that too merged with the Barrow Deep. Easton lifted his glass and stared to the north. The rain would prevent them seeing the Naze and its tower. Drinkwater fumbled in his tail pocket and brought out his own glass. He scanned the same arc of the horizon, seeing it become indistinct, grey and blurred as yet another rain squall obscured it. He waited patiently for it to pass, then looked again. This time Easton beat him to it.

'A point forrard of the beam, sir.'

Drinkwater hesitated. Then he saw it, a pole surmounted by a wooden cage over which he could just make out a faint, horizontal blur. The blur was, he knew, a huge wooden fish.

'Very well, Mr Easton, a bearing if you please and note in your log.'

A quarter of an hour later the Gunfleet beacon was obliterated astern by more rain and as night came on the wind increased.

By midnight the gale was at its height and the squadron scattered. Drinkwater had brought *Virago* to an anchor, veering away two full cables secured end to end. For although they were clear of the longshoals that run into the mouth of the Thames they had yet to negotiate the Gabbards and the Galloper and the Shipwash banks, out in the howling blackness to leeward.

The fatigue and anxiety of the night seemed heightened by his fever and he seemed possessed of a remarkable energy that he knew he would pay dearly for later, but he hounded his officers and took frequent casts of the lead to see whether their anchor was dragging. At six bells in the middle watch the atmosphere cleared and they were rewarded by a glimpse of the lights of the floating alarm vessel* at the Sunk. With relief he went below, collapsing across his cot in his wet boat cloak, his feet stuck out behind him still in their shoes. Only his hat rolled off his head and into a damp corner beneath a carronade slide.

Lieutenant Rogers relieved Mr Trussel at four in the morning.

'Wind's abating, sir,' added Trussel after handing the deck over to the lieutenant.

'Yes.'

'And veering a touch. Captain said to call him if it veered, sir.'

'Very well.' Rogers wiped his mouth with the back of his hand and slipped the pewter mug that was now empty of coffee into the bottom shelf of the binnacle. He looked up at the dark streamer of the masthead pendant, then down at the oscillating compass. The wind was indeed veering.

'Mr Q!'

'Sir?'

'Pass word to the Captain that the wind's veering, north west a half west and easing a touch, I fancy.'

'Aye, aye, sir.'

The cloud was clearing to windward and a few stars were visible. Rogers crossed the deck to look at the traverse board then hailed the masthead to see if anything was visible from there.

Drinkwater arrived on deck five minutes later. It had taken him a great effort to urge his aching and stiffened limbs to obey him.

'Morning sir.'

'Mornin',' Drinkwater grunted, 'any sign of the commodore or the Sunk alarm vessel?'

'No sign of the commodore but the Sunk's still in sight. She's held to her anchor.'

'Very well. Wind's easing ain't it?'

'Aye, 'tis dropping all the time.'

'Turn the hands up then, we'll prepare to weigh.'

Drinkwater walked aft and placed his hands on the caned taffrail, drawing gulps of fresh air into his lungs and seeking in

* Early light vessel with fixed lights; that at the Sunk was established in 1799.

vain some invigoration from the dawn. Around him the ship came to life. The flog of topsails being cast loose and sheeted home, the dull thud of windlass bars being shipped. There was no fiddler aboard *Virago* and the men set up a low chant as they began to heave the barrels round to a clunking of pawls. The cable came in very slowly.

They had anchored north east of the Sunk, under the partial shelter of the Shipwash Sand and *Virago* rolled as her head was pulled round to her anchor. Already a faint lightening of the sky was perceptible to the east. Drinkwater shook the last of the sleep from him and turned forward.

'Forrard there, how does she lead?'

'Two points to larboard, sir, and coming to it.' Matchett's voice came back to him from the fo'c's'le. Drinkwater drummed his fingers on the poop rail.

'Up and down, sir.'

'Anchor's aweigh!'

'Topsail halliards, away lively there . . . haul away larboard braces, lively now! Ease away that starboard mainbrace damn you . . .!' The backed topsails filled with wind even before their yards had reached their proper elevation. *Virago* began to make a stern board.

'Foretopmast staysail, aback to larboard Mr Matchett.' The ship began to swing. 'Helm a-lee!'

'Hellum's a-leek, zur.'

'Larboard tack, Mr Rogers, course nor' nor' east.'

He left Rogers to haul the yards again and steady *Virago* on her new course. They would be safely anchored in Yarmouth Roads before another midnight had passed. Around him the noises of the ship, the clatter of blocks, the grind of the rudder, the flog of canvas and creak of parrels, told him Rogers was steadying *Virago* on her northward course. He wondered how the other members of the squadron had fared during the night and considered that 'commodore' Martin might be an anxious and exasperated man this morning. The thought amused him, although it was immediately countered by the image of Martin and the other ships sitting in Yarmouth Roads awaiting the arrival of *Virago*.

The ship heeled and beneath him the wake began to bubble out from under her stern as she gathered headway. Instinctively he threw his weight on one hip, then turned and began pacing the windward side of the poop. The afterguard padded aft and slackened the spanker brails, four men swigging the clew out to the end of the long boom by the double outhauls.

'Course, nor' nor' east, sir.'

'Very well, Sam. You have the deck, carry on.'

Rogers called Matchett to pipe up hammocks. The routine of *Virago*'s day had begun in earnest. Drinkwater walked forward again and halted by the larboard mizzen rigging at the break of the poop. He searched for a glimpse of Orfordness lighthouse but his attention was suddenly attracted by something else, an irregularity in the almost indistinguishable meeting of sea and sky to the north of them. He fished in his tail pocket for the Dolland glass.

'Mr Rogers!'

'Sir?'

'What d'you make of those sails,' said Drinkwater without lowering his glass, 'there, half a point on the larboard bow?'

Rogers lifted his own glass and was silent for a moment. 'High peaks,' he muttered, 'could be bawleys out of Harwich, but not one of the squadron, if that's what you're thinking.'

'That ain't what I'm thinking Sam. Take another look, a good long look.'

Rogers whistled. One of the approaching sails had altered course, slightly more to the east and they were both growing larger by the second.

'Luggers, by God!'

'And if I'm not mistaken they're in chase, Sam. French *chasse-marées* taking us for a fat wallowing merchantman. I'll wager they've been lying under the Ness all night.'

'They'll eat the logline off this tub, God damn it, and be chock full of men.'

'And as handy as yachts', added Drinkwater, remembering the two stern chasers in his cabin and his untried crew. He would be compelled to fight for he could not outrun such swift enemies.

'Wear ship, Sam, upon the instant. Don't be silly man, we're no match for two Dunkirkers, we'll make the tail of the bank and beat up for Harwich.'

Rogers shut his gaping mouth and turned to bawl abusively at the hands milling in the waist as they carried the hammocks up and stowed them in the nettings. The first lieutenant scattered them like a fox among chickens.

Drinkwater considered his situation. To stand on would invite being out-manoeuvred, while by running he would not only have his longest range guns bearing on the enemy, but might entice the luggers close enough to pound them with his carronades. If he could outrun them long enough to make up for the Sunk and Harwich they might abandon the chase, privateers were unwilling to fight if the odds were too great and there was a guardship in Harwich harbour.

The spanker was brailed up again as *Virago*'s stern passed through the wind. Drinkwater tried to conceal the trembling of his hand, which was as much due to his fever as his apprehension, while he tried to hold the images of the approaching luggers in the circle of the glass. Thanks to the twilight they had been close enough when first spotted. They were scarcely a mile distant as Rogers shrieked at topmen too tardily loosing the topgallants for his liking.

'Look lively you damned scabs, you've a French hulk awaiting you if you don't stop frigging about . . .'

'Beg pardon, sir.'

Drinkwater bumped into a crouching seaman scattering sand on the deck. He abandoned a further study of the enemy and looked to the trim of the sails. Easton was at the con now, still rubbing the sleep out of his eyes.

'We'll make up for Harwich as soon as we're clear of the Shipwash Sand, Mr Easton. Do you attend to the bearing of the alarm vessel.'

'Aye, aye, sir.'

Daylight was increasing by the minute and Drinkwater looked astern again. He could see the long, low hulls, the oddly raked masts and the huge spread of canvas set by the luggers. He was by no means confident of the outcome, and both of the pursuing sea-wolves were coming up fast.

Drinkwater walked forward again. Rogers reported the ship cleared for action.

'Very well. Mr Rogers, you are to command the two chasers in the cabin. We will do what damage we can before they close on us. They will likely take a quarter each and try to board.' Rogers and Easton nodded.

'Mr Easton, you have the con. From time to time I may desire you to ease away a little or to luff half a point to enable Mr Rogers to point better.'

'Aye, sir, I understand.'

'Mr Mason the larboard battery, Mr Q the starboard. Rapid fire as soon as you've loosed your first broadside. For that await the command. Mr Rogers you may fire at will.'

'And the sooner the better.'

Drinkwater ignored Rogers's interruption. 'Is that clear gentlemen?'

There was a succession of 'ayes' and nods and nervous grins.

Drinkwater stood at the break of the low poop. The waisters were grouped amidships, the gun crews kneeling at their carronades. They all looked expectantly aft. They had had little practice at gunnery since leaving Chatham and Drinkwater was acutely conscious of their unpreparedness. He looked now at the experienced men to do their best.

'My lads, there are two French privateers coming up astern hand over fist. They've the heels of us. Give 'em as much iron as they can stomach before they close us. A Frog with a bellyful of iron can't jump a ditch . . .' He paused and was gratified by a dutiful ripple of nervous laughter at the poor jest. 'But if they do board I want to see you busy with those pikes and cutlasses . . .' He broke off and gave them what he thought was a confident, bloodthirsty grin. He was again relieved to see a few leers and hear the beginnings of a feeble cheer.

He nodded. 'Do your duty, lads.' He turned to the officers, 'Take post gentlemen.'

It suddenly occurred to him that he was unarmed. 'Tregembo, my sword and pistols from the cabin if you please.'

He looked aft and with a sudden shock saw the two luggers were very much closer. The nearer was making for *Virago*'s lee quarter, the larboard.

'God's bones,' muttered Drinkwater to himself, trying to fend off a violent spasm of shivering that he did not want to be taken for fear.

'Here zur,' Tregembo held out the battered French hanger and Drinkwater unhooked the boat cloak from his throat and draped it over Tregembo's outstretched arm. He buckled on the sword then took the pistols.

'I've looked to the priming, zur, and put a new flint in that 'un, zur.'

'Thank you, Tregembo. And good luck.'

'Aye, zur.' The man hurried away with the cloak and re-appeared on deck at the tiller almost at once.

A fountain of water sprung up alongside them, another rose ahead.

'In range, sir,' said Easton beside him, 'they'll be good long nines, then.'

'Yes,' said Drinkwater shortly, aware that his tenure of command might be very short indeed, his investment in *Virago* a wasted one. An uncomfortable vision of the fortresses of Verdun and Bitche rose unbidden into his mind's eye. He swore again softly, cursing his luck, his fever and the waiting.

Beneath his feet he felt a faint rumble as Rogers had the chaser crews run the 6-pounders through the stern ports. He thought briefly of the two portraits hanging on the forward bulkhead and then forgot all about them as the roar of *Virago*'s cannon rang in his ears.

He missed the fall of shot, and that of the second gun. At least Samuel Rogers would do his utmost, of that Drinkwater was certain.

At the fourth shot a hole appeared in the nearer lugger's mizen. Beside Drinkwater Easton ground his right fist into the palm of his left hand with satisfaction.

'Mind you attend to the con, Mr Easton,' Drinkwater said and caught the crest-fallen look as Easton turned to swear at the helmsmen.

The nearer lugger was overhauling them rapidly, her relative bearing opening out broader on the quarter with perceptible speed. 'Luff her a point Mr Easton!'

'Aye, aye, sir.'

Virago's heel eased a little and Rogers's two guns fired in quick succession.

Drinkwater watched intently. He fancied he saw a shower of splinters somewhere amidships on the Frenchman then Mason was alongside him.

'Beg pardon sir, but I can get the aftermost larboard guns to bear on that fellow, sir.' The enemy opened fire at that very moment and a buzz filled the air together with a whooshing noise as double shotted ball and canister scoured *Virago*'s deck. Drinkwater heard cries of agony and the bright gout of blood appeared as his eye sought out the damage to his ship.

'Very well, Mr Mason . . .' But Mason was gone, he lay on the deck silently kicking, his face contorted with pain.

'You there! Get Mr Mason below. Pass word to Mr Q to open fire with both batteries. Independent fire . . .'

His last words were lost in a crack from aloft and the roar of gunfire from the enemy. The mainyard had been shot through and was sprung, whipping like a broomstick.

'Mains'l Mr Easton! And get the tops'l off her at once . . .' Men were already starting the tacks and sheets. Matchett's rattan rose and fell as he shoved the waisters towards the clew and buntlines, pouring out a rich and expressive stream of abuse. Even as the carronades opened fire *Virago* slowed and suddenly the leeward lugger was upon them.

Lining her rail a hedge of pikes and sword blades appeared.

'Boarders!' Drinkwater roared as the two vessels ground together. A grapnel struck the rail and Drinkwater drew his hanger and sliced the line attached to it.

He saw the men carrying Mason drop him halfway down the poop ladder as they raced for cutlasses.

'God's bones!' Drinkwater screamed with sudden fury as the Frenchmen poured over the rail. His hanger slashed left and right and he seemed to have half a dozen enemies in his front. He pulled out a pistol and shot one through the forehead, then he was only aware of the swish of blades hacking perilously close to his face and the bite and jar in his mangled arm muscles as steel met steel.

The breath rasped in his throat and the fever fogged him with the first red madness of bloodlust longer than was usual. The cool fighting clarity that came out of some chilling primeval past revived him at last. The long fearful wait for action was over and the realisation that he was unscathed in those first dreadful seconds left him with a detachment that seemed divorced from the grim realities of hand to hand fighting. He was filled with an extraordinary nervous energy that could only have owed its origins to his fevered state. He seemed wonderfully possessed of demonic powers, the sword blade sang in his hand and he felt an overwhelming and savagely furious joy in his butchery.

He was not aware of Tregembo and Easton rallying on him. He was oblivious to James Quilhampton a deck below still pouring shot after shot into the French lugger's hull at point blank range with two 24-pounder carronades. Neither did he see Rogers emerge on deck with the starboard gun crews who had succeeded in dismasting the other lugger at a sufficient distance, nor that Quilhampton had so persistently hulled their closer adversary that her commander realised he had caught a Tartar and decided to withdraw.

He did not know that the Viragos were inspired by the sight of their hatless captain, one foot on the rail, hacking murderously at the privateersmen like a devil incarnate.

Drinkwater was only aware that it was over when there were no more Frenchmen to be killed and beneath him a widening gulf between the two hulls. He looked, panting, at his reeking hands; his right arm was blood-soaked to the elbow. He was sodden from the perspiration of fever and exertion. He watched their adversary drop astern, her sails flogging. She was low in the water, sinking fast. Several men swam round her, the last to leave *Virago* he presumed. Staggering as though drunk, he looked for the second lugger. Her foremast was gone and her crew were sweeping her up to the assistance of her foundering consort.

Drinkwater was aware of a cheer around him. Men were shouting and grinning, all bloody among the wounded and the dead. Rogers was coming towards him, his face cracked into a grin of pure delight. Then there was another cheer out to starboard and *Virago* surged past the anchored red bulk of the Sunk alarm vessel, her crew waving from the rail, her big Trinity House ensign at the dip.

'They bastards've bin 'anging round three days 'n' more,' he heard her master shout in the Essex dialect as they passed.

'I fancy we fooled the sods then, God damn 'em,' said Rogers as the cheers died away. Drinkwater's head cleared to the realisation that he was shivering violently. He managed a thin smile. Ship and company had passed their first test; they were blooded together but now there was a half-clewed main course to furl, a topsail to secure and a mainyard to fish.

'Do you wish to put about and secure a prize, sir?' asked the ever hopeful Rogers.

'No Sam, Captain Martin would never approve of such a foolhardy act. Do you put about for Yarmouth, we must take the Shipway now. Those luggers'll not harm the alarm vessel and have problems enough of their own. Mr Easton, a course to clear Orfordness if you please. See word is passed to Willerton to fish that bloody yard before it springs further, and for Christ's sake somebody get that poor fellow Mason below to the surgeon.'

Drinkwater was holding the poop rail to prevent himself keeling over. He was filled with an overwhelming desire to go below but there was one last thing to do.

'Mr Q!'

'Sir?'

'Do you bring me the butcher's bill in my cabin directly.'

PART TWO

Sir Hyde Parker

'If you were here just to look at us! I had heard of manoeuvres off Ushant, but ours beat all ever seen. Would it were over, I am really sick of it!'

NELSON, March 1801

Chapter Eight *February–March 1801*

An Unlawful Obligation

'Hold him!' Lettsom snapped at his two mates as they struggled to hold Mason down on the cabin table. A cluster of lanterns illuminated the scene as Lettsom, stripped to the shirt-sleeves, his apron stained dark with blood, bent again over his task.

Despite a dose of laudanum Mason still twitched as the surgeon probed the wound in his lower belly. The bruised flesh gaped bloodily, the jagged opening in the groin where the splinter had penetrated welled with blood.

Drinkwater stood back, against the bulkhead. Since the action with the luggers that morning he had slept for five hours and fortified himself against his fever with half a bottle of blackstrap. *Virago* was now safely anchored in Yarmouth Roads in company with a growing assembly of ships, partly the preparing Baltic fleet, partly elements of Admiral Dickson's Texel squadron. Drinkwater was feeling better and the absence of *Explosion* had further encouraged him.

Mason was the last of the three serious casualties to receive Lettsom's attention. One seaman had lost an arm. Another, like Mason, had received severe splinter wounds. An additional eight men had received superficial wounds and there were four of their own people dead. The seven French corpses left on board had been thrown overboard off Lowestoft without ceremony.

Lettsom had left Mason until *Virago* reached the relative tranquility of the anchorage. He knew that the long oak sliver that had run into Mason's body could only be extracted successfully under such conditions.

Drinkwater watched anxiously. He knew Lettsom was having difficulties. The nature of the splinter was to throw out tiny fibres of wood that acted like barbs. As these carried fragments of clothing into the wound the likelihood of a clean excision was remote.

The set of Lettsom's jaw and the perspiration on his forehead were evidence of his concern.

Lettsom withdrew the probe, inserted thin forceps and drew out a sliver of wood with a sigh. He held it up to the light and studied it intently. Drinkwater saw him swallow and his eyes closed for a moment. He had been unsuccessful. He rubbed his hand over his mouth in a gesture of near despair, leaving a smear of blood across his face. Then his shoulders sagged in defeat.

'Put him in my cot,' said Drinkwater, realising that to move Mason further than was absolutely necessary would kill him. Lettsom caught his eye and the surgeon shook his head. The two men remained motionless while the surgeon's mates bound absorbent pledgets over the wound and eased Mason into the box-like swinging bed. Lettsom rinsed his hands and dropped his reeking apron on the tablecloth while his mates cleaned the table and cleared Drinkwater's cabin of the gruesome instrument chest. Drinkwater poured two glasses of rum and handed one to the surgeon who slumped in a chair and drained it at a swallow.

'The splinter broke,' Lettsom said at last. 'It had run in between the external iliac vein and artery. They were both intact. That gave me a chance to save him . . .' He paused, looked at Drinkwater, then lowered his eyes again. 'That was a small miracle, Mr Drinkwater, and I should have succeeded, but I bungled it. No don't contradict me, I beg you. I bungled it. The splinter broke with its end lodged in the obturator vein, the haemorrage was dark and veinous. When he turns in his sleep he will move it and puncture his bladder. Part of his breeches and under garments will have been carried into the body.'

'You did your utmost, Mr Lettsom. None of us can do more.'

Lettsom looked up. His eyes blazed with sudden anger. 'It was not enough, Mr Drinkwater. God damn it, it simply was not enough.'

Drinkwater thought of the flippant quatrain with which Lettsom had introduced himself. The poor man was drinking a cup of bitterness now. He leaned across and refilled Lettsom's glass. Drinkwater was a little drunk himself and felt the need of company.

'You did your duty . . .'

'Bah, duty! Poppycock, sir! We may all conceal our pathetic inadequacies behind our "duty". The fact of the matter is I bungled it. Perhaps I should still be probing in the poor fellow's guts until he dies under my hands.'

'You cannot achieve the impossible, Mr Lettsom.'

'No, perhaps not. But I wished that I might have done more. He will die anyway and might at least have the opportunity to regain his senses long enough to make his peace with the world.'

Drinkwater nodded, looking at the hump lying inert in his own bed. He felt a faint ringing in his ears. The fever did not trouble him tonight but he seemed to float an inch above his chair.

'I don't believe a man must shrive his soul with a canting priest, Mr Drinkwater,' Lettsom went on, helping himself to the bottle. 'I barely know whether there is an Omnipotent Being. A man is only guts sewn up in a hide bag. No anatomist has discovered the soul and the divine spark is barely perceptible in most.' He nodded at the gently swinging cot. 'See how easily it is extinguished. How much of the Almighty d'you think he contains to be snuffed like this?' he added with sudden vehemence.

'You were not responsible for Mason's wound, Mr Lettsom,' Drinkwater said with an effort, 'those luggers . . .'

'Those luggers, sir, were simply a symptom of the malignity of mankind. What the hell is this bloody war about, eh? The king of Denmark's mad, Gustav of Sweden's mad, Tsar Paul is a dangerous and criminal lunatic and each of these maniacs is setting his people against us. And what in God's name are we doing going off to punish Danes and Swedes and Russians for the crazy ambitions of their kings? Why, Mr Drinkwater, it is even rumoured that our very own beloved George is not all that he should be in the matter of knowing what's what.' Lettsom tapped his head significantly.

'We are swept up like chaff in the wind. Mason is hit by the flail and I bungle his excision like a student. That's all there is to it, Mr Drinkwater. One may philosophise over providence, or what you will, as long as you have a belly empty of splinters, but that *is* all there is to it . . .'

He fell silent and Drinkwater said nothing. His own belief in fate was a faith that drew its own strength from such misgivings as Lettsom expressed. But he could not himself accept the cold calculations of the scientific mind, could not agree with Lettsom's assumption of ultimate purposelessness.

They were both drunk, but at that brief and peculiarly lucid state of drunkenness that it is impossible to maintain and is gone as soon as attained. In this moment of clarity Drinkwater thought himself the greater coward.

'Perhaps,' said Lettsom at last, 'the French did themselves a service by executing King Louis, much as we did the first Charles. Pity of the matter is we replaced a republic by a monarchy and subjected ourselves voluntarily to the humbug of parliamentary politics . . .'

'You are an admirer of the American rebels, Mr Lettsom?'

The surgeon focussed a shrewd eye on his younger commander. 'Would you not welcome a world where ability elevated a man quicker than birth or influence, Mr Drinkwater?'

'Now you sound like a leveller. You know, you quacks stand in a unique position in relationship to the rest of us. Wielding the knife confers a huge moral advantage upon you. Like priests you are apt to resort to pontification . . .'

'Moral superiority is conferred on *any* man with a glass in his hand . . .'

'Aye, Mr Lettsom, and when we rise tomorrow morning the world will be as it is tonight. Imperfect in all its aspects, yet oddly beautiful and full of hidden wonders, cruel and harsh with battles to be fought and gales endured. There is more honesty at a cannon's mouth than may be found elsewhere. Kings and their ambition are but a manifestation of the world's turbulence. As a scientist I would have expected you to acknowledge Newton's third law. It governs the entire travail of humanity Mr Lettsom, and is not indicative of tranquil existence.'

Lettsom looked at Drinkwater with surprise. 'I had no idea I was commanded by such a philosopher, Mr Drinkwater.'

'I learnt the art from a surgeon, Mr Lettsom,' replied Drinkwater drily.

'Your journals, Mr Q.' Drinkwater held out his hand for the bound notebooks. He opened the first and turned over the pages. The handwriting was large and blotchy, the pages wrinkled from damp.

'They were rescued from the wreck of the *Hellebore*, sir,' offered the midshipman.

Drinkwater nodded without looking up, stifling the images that rose in his mind. He took up a later book. The calligraphy had matured, the entries were briefer, less lyrical and more professional.

A drawing appeared here and there: *The arrangement of yards upon a vessel going into mourning*. Drinkwater smiled approvingly, discovering a half-finished note about mortars.

'You did not complete this, Mr Q?'

'No sir. Mr Tumilty left us before I had finished catechising him.'

'I see. How would you stow barrels, Mr Q?'

'Bung up and bilge free, sir.'

'A ship is north of the equator. To find the latitude, given the sun's declination is south and the altitude on the meridian is reduced to give a correct zenith distance, how do you apply that zenith distance to the declination?'

'The declination is subtracted from the zenith distance, sir, to give the latitude.'

'A vessel is close hauled on the larboard tack, wind southwesterly and weather thick. You have the deck and notice the air clearing with blue sky to windward. Of what would you beware and what steps would you take?'

'That the ship might be thrown aback, the wind veering into the north west. I would order the quartermaster to keep the vessel's head off the wind a point more than was necessary by the wind.'

'Under what circumstances would you not do this?'

Quilhampton's face puckered into a frown and he caught his lip in his teeth.

'Well, Mr Q? You are almost aback, sir.'

'I . . . er.'

'Come now. Under what circumstances might you not be able to let the vessel's head pay off? Come, summon your imagination.'

'If you had a danger under the lee bow, sir,' said Quilhampton with sudden relief.

'Then what would you do?'

'Tack ship, sir.'

'You have left it too late, sir, the ship's head is in irons . . .' Drinkwater looked at the sheen of sweat on the midshipman's brow. There was enough evidence in the books beneath Drinkwater's hands of Quilhampton's imagination and he was even now beset by anxiety on his imaginary quarterdeck.

'Pass word for the captain, sir?' Quilhampton suggested hopefully.

'The captain is incapacitated and you are first lieutenant, Mr Q, you cannot expect to be extricated from this mess.'

'Make a stern board and hope to throw the ship upon the starboard tack, sir.'

'Anything else?' Drinkwater looked fixedly at the midshipman. 'What if you fail in the sternboard?'

'Anchor, sir.'

'At last! Never neglect the properties of anchors, Mr Q. You may lose an anchor and not submit your actions to a court-martial, but it is quite otherwise if you lose the ship. A prudent man, knowing he might be embayed, would have prepared to club-haul his ship with the larboard anchor. Do you know how to club-haul a ship?'

Quilhampton swallowed, his prominent Adam's apple bobbing round his grubby stock.

'Only in general principle, sir.'

'Make it your business to discover the matter in detail. Now, how is a topmast stuns'l set?'

'The boom is rigged out and the gear bent. Pull up the halliards and tack, keeping fast the end of the deck sheet. The stops are cut by a man on the lower yard. The tack is hauled out and the halliards hove. The short sheet is rove round the boom heel and secured in the top.'

Drinkwater smiled, recognising the words. 'Very well, Mr Q. Consequent upon the death of Mr Mason I am rating you acting master's mate. You will take over Mason's duties. Please take your journals with you.'

He waved aside Quilhampton's thanks. 'You will not thank me when the duty becomes arduous or I am dissatisfied with your conduct. Go and look up how to club-haul in that excellent primer of yours.'

Drinkwater picked up his pen and returned to the task he had deliberately interrupted by summoning Quilhampton.

Dear Sir, he began to write, *It is with great regret that my painful duty compels me to inform you of the death of your son . . .*

Explosion and the rest of the squadron came into Yarmouth Roads during the next two days to join the growing number of British men of war anchored there. Most of the other bomb vessels had been blown to leeward and Martin merely nodded when Drinkwater presented his report. The fleet was reduced to waiting while the officers eagerly seized on the newspapers to learn anything about the intentions of the government in respect of the Baltic crisis.

A number of British officers serving with the Russian navy returned to Britain. One in particular arrived in Yarmouth: a Captain Nicholas Tomlinson, who had been reduced to half-pay after the American War and served with the Russians at the same period as the American John Paul Jones. He volunteered his services to the commander-in-chief. Admiral Parker, comfortably ensconced at the Wrestler's Inn with his young bride, refused to see Tomlinson.

No orders emanated from either Parker or London. It was a matter that preoccupied the officers of *Virago* as they dined in their captain's absence.

'Lieutenant Drinkwater is endeavouring to discover some news of our intentions either from Martin or anyone else who knows,' explained Rogers as he took his place at the head of the cabin table and nodded to the messman.

'I hear the King caught a severe chill at the National Fast and Humiliation,' said Mr Jex in his fussy way, 'upon the thirteenth of last month.'

'National Farce,' corrected Rogers, sarcastically.

'I heard he caught a cold *in the head*,' put in the surgeon with heavy emphasis.

'At all events we must wait until either Addington's kissed hands or Parker has got out of his bed,' offered Easton.

'At Parker's age he'll be a deuced long time getting up with a young bride in his bed,' added Lettsom with a grin, sniping at the more accessible admiral in the absence of a king.

'At Parker's age he'll be a deuced long time getting *it* up, you mean Mr Lettsom,' grunted Rogers coarsely.

'Yes, I wonder who exhausts whom, for it is fearful unequal combat to pit eighteen years against sixty-four.'

'Experience against enthusiasm, eh?'

'More like impotence against ignorance, but wait, I have the muse upon me,' Lettsom paused. 'I am uncertain on whom to lay the greater blame for our woes.

'Why here is a thing to raise liberal hopes;
Government can't do as it pleases,
While the entire fleet 'waits the order to strike
Addington awaits the King's sneezes.'

A cheer greeted this doggerel but Lettsom shook his head with dissatisfaction.

'It don't scan to my liking. I think the admiral the better inspiration:

> "Tis not for his slowness in firing his shot
> That our admiral is known every night,
> But his laxness in heaving his anchor aweigh
> Must dub him a most tardy knight.'

There were more cheers for the surgeon and it was generally accepted that the second verse was much better than the first.

'But the lady's no fool, Mr Lettsom, and I'll not subscribe to her ignorance,' Rogers said as the laughter died away. 'Parker flew his flag in the West Indies. He's the richest admiral on the list. His fortune is supposed to be worth a hundred thousand and all she has to put up with is a few years of the old pig grunting about the sheets before the lot'll fall into her lap. Why 'tis a capital match and I'll drink to Lady Parker. There's many a man as would marry for the same reason, eh Mr Jex?' Rogers leered towards the purser.

Jex shot a venomous look at the first lieutenant. His conduct during the fight with the luggers had not been exactly valorous and he had dreaded this exposure as the butt of the officers' jests.

'Ah, Mr Jex has seen victory betwixt the sheets and is accustomed to seek it between the sails, eh?' There was another roar of laughter. At the end of the action off the Sunk Jex had been discovered hiding in the spare sails below decks.

'You are being uncharitable towards Mr Jex, Mr Rogers. I have it on good authority he was looking for his honour,' Lettsom said as Jex stormed from the cabin the colour of a beetroot.

'Come in. Yes Mr Q, what is it?' Drinkwater's voice was weary.

'Beg pardon, sir, but the vice-admiral's entering the anchorage.' Drinkwater looked up. There was a light in the young man's eyes. 'Lord Nelson, sir,' he added excitedly. Drinkwater could not resist Quilhampton's infectious enthusiasm.

'Thank you, Mr Q,' he said smiling. The hero of the Nile had a strange way of affecting the demeanour of his juniors. Drinkwater remembered their brief meeting at Syracuse and that same infectious enthusiasm that had seemed to imbue Nelson's entire fleet, despite their vain manoeuvrings in chase of Bonaparte. What a shame the same spirit was absent from the present assembly of ships. Drinkwater sighed. The subsequent scandal with Hamilton's wife and the vainglorious progress through Europe that followed the victory at Aboukir Bay, had curled the lip of many of Nelson's equals, but Drinkwater had no more appetite for his paper-work and he found himself pulling a muffler round his neck under his boat cloak to join the men at *Virago*'s rail cheering the little admiral as the *St George* stood through the gatway into Yarmouth Roads.

The battleship with her three yellow strakes flew a blue flag at her foremasthead and came in with two other warships. Hardly had her sheet anchor dropped from her bow than her cannon boomed out in salute to Parker's flag, flying nominally at the main-masthead of the 64-gun *Ardent* until the arrival of Parker's proper flagship. The flag's owner was still accommodated at the Wrestler's Inn and this fact must have been early acquainted to Nelson for his barge was shortly afterwards seen making for the landing jetty. It was later rumoured that, although he received a cordial enough welcome from the commander-in-chief, Parker refused to discuss arrangements for the fleet on their first meeting.

Although a man who appeared to have lost both head and heart to Emma Hamilton, Nelson had never let love interfere with duty. It was soon common knowledge in the fleet that his criticisms of Parker were frank, scatological and scathing. Nelson's dissatisfaction spread like wildfire, and ribald jests were everywhere heard, particularly among the hands on the ships that waited in the chill winds and shivered in their draughty gun decks while Sir Hyde banked the bedroom fire in the Wrestler's Inn. In addition to Lettsom's doggerel there were other ribaldries, mostly puns upon the name of the hostelry where Parker lodged and all of them enjoyed with relish in gunrooms as on gun decks, in cockpits and in staterooms. Nelson had given a dinner the evening of his arrival and expressed his fears on the consequences of a delay. His impatience did not improve as day succeeded day.

The final preparations for the departure of the expedition were completed. Nearly eight hundred men of the 49th Foot with a company of rifles had been embarked under Colonel Stewart. Eleven masters of Baltic trading ships and all members of the Trinity House of Kingston-upon-Hull had joined for the purpose of piloting the fleet through the dangers of the Baltic Sea. On Monday 9th

March Parker's flagship the *London* arrived and his flag was ceremoniously shifted aboard her at eight o'clock the next morning. The admiral remained ashore.

Later that day an Admiralty messenger arrived in Yarmouth with an order for Parker to sail, but still he prevaricated. His wife had arranged a ball for the coming Friday and, to indulge his Fanny, Parker postponed the fleet's departure until after the event.

That evening Lieutenant Drinkwater also received a message, scribbled on a piece of grubby paper:

Nathaniel

I beg you come ashore at eight of the clock tonight. I must see you on a matter of the utmost urgency.
I beg you not to ignore this plea and I will await you on the west side of the Yare ferry.

Ned

The word *must* was underlined heavily. Drinkwater looked up at the longshoreman who had brought the note and had refused to relinquish it to Mr Quilhampton who now stood protectively suspicious behind the ragged boatman.

'The man was insistent I give it to you personal, sir,' he said in the lilting Norfolk accent.

'What manner of man was it gave you this note?'

'Why, I'd say he were a serving man, sir. Not a gentleman like you sir, though he was gen'rous with his master's money . . .' The implication was plain enough without looking at the man's face. Drinkwater drew a coin from his pocket.

'Here,' he passed it to the boatman, frowning down at the note. He dismissed the man. 'Mr Q.'

'Sir?'

'A boat, please, in an hour's time.'

'Aye, aye, sir.'

'And Mr Q, not a word of this to anyone if you please.' He fixed Quilhampton with a baleful glance. If Edward was reduced to penury in a matter of weeks he did not want the world to know of it.

A bitter easterly wind blew across the low land south of the town. The village of Gorleston exhibited a few lights on the opposite bank as he descended into the ferry. Darkness had come early and the fresh wind had led him to order his boat off until the following morning. To the half guinea the note had cost him it now looked as though he would have to add the charge of a night's lodging ashore. Brotherly love was becoming an expensive luxury which he could ill afford. And now, he mused as the ferryman held out a fist, there was an added penny for the damned ferry.

Clambering up the far bank he allowed the other passengers to pass ahead of him. He could see no one waiting, then a shadow detached itself from a large bush growing on the river bank.

'God damn it, Ned. Is that you?'

'Ssh, for the love of Christ . . .'

'What the devil are you playing at?'

'I must talk to you . . .' Edward loomed out of the shadows, standing up suddenly in front of Drinkwater. Beneath a dark cloak Drinkwater could see the pale gleam of a shirt. Edward's hair was undressed and loosely blowing round his face. Even in the gloom Drinkwater could see he was in a dishevelled state. He was the longshoreman's 'serving man'.

'What in God's name . . .?'

'Walk slowly, Nat, and for heaven's sake spare me further comment. I'm deep in trouble. Terrible trouble . . .' Edward shivered, though whether from cold or terror his brother could not be sure.

'Well come on, man, what's amiss? I have not got all night . . .' But of course he had. 'Is it about the money, Edward?'

He heard the faint chink of gold in a purse. 'No, I have the remains of that here. It is not a great deal . . . Nat, I am ruined . . .'

Drinkwater was appalled: 'D'you mean you have lost that two hundred and fifty . . .? My God, you'll have no more!'

'God, Nat, it isn't money that I want.'

'Well what the devil is it?'

'Can you take me on your ship? Hide me? Land me wherever you are going. I speak French. Like a German they say. For God's sake, Nat you are my only hope, I beg you.'

Drinkwater stopped and turned to his brother. 'What the hell is this all about, Ned?'

'I am a fugitive from the law. From the extremity of the law, Nat. If I am taken I . . .' he broke off. 'Nat, when I heard your ships were assembling at Yarmouth and arrived to find *Virago* anchored off the shore I . . . I hoped . . .'

'What are you guilty of?' asked Drinkwater, a cold certainty settling round his heart.

'Murder.'

There was a long silence between the brothers. At last Drinkwater said, 'Tell me what happened.'

'I told you of the girl? Pascale?'

'Aye, you did.'

'I found her abed with her God damned marquis.'

'And whom did you murder?'

'Both of them.'

'God's bones!' Drinkwater took a few paces away from his brother, his brain a turmoil. Like at that moment in the Strand, his instinct for order reeled at the prospect of consigning his brother to the gallows. He remembered his mother, then his wife and child in a bewildering succession of images that drove from his mind the necessity of making a decision and only further confused him. Edward was guilty of Edward's crimes and should suffer the penalty of the law; yet Edward was his brother. But protecting Edward would make him an accessory, while Edward's execution would ensure his own professional oblivion.

He swore beneath his breath. In his passion Edward had murdered a worthless French aristocrat and his whore. How many Frenchmen had Nathaniel murdered as part of his duty? Lettsom's words about duty came back to him and he swore again.

But those were moral judgements of an unrecognised morality, a morality that might appeal to Lettsom and his Paine-like religion of humanity. In the harsher light of English justice he had no choice: Edward was a criminal.

The vain pontifications of the other night, as he and Lettsom had exchanged sallies over the dying body of Mason, came back to confront him now like some monstrous ironic joke. He felt like a drowning man. What would Elizabeth think of him if he assisted his brother up the steps of the scaffold? Would she understand his quixoticism if he helped Edward escape? Was his duty to Edward of greater significance than that he owed his wife?

'Nat, I beg you . . .'

'I do not condone what you have done. You confront me with an unlawful obligation.'

A thought occurred to him. At first it was no more than a half-considered plan and owed its inception to a sudden vicious consideration that it might cost this wastrel brother his life. Edward would have to submit to the harsh judgement of fate.

'How much money have you left?'

'Forty-four pounds.'

'You must return it to me. You have no need of money.' He heard the sigh of relief. 'You will accompany me back to the ship and will be entered on the books as Edward Waters, a landsman volunteer. Tell your messmates you are a bigamist, that you have seduced a young girl while being married yourself, any such story will suffice and guarantee they understand your morose silences. You will make no approach to me, nor speak to me unless I speak to you. If you transgress the regulations that obtain on board you will not be immune from the cat. As far as I am concerned you importuned me whilst ashore and asked to volunteer. Being short of men I accepted your offer. Do you understand?'

'Yes, Nat. And thank you, thank you . . .'

'I think you will have little to thank me for, Ned. God knows I do not do this entirely for you.'

Chapter Nine *Tuesday, 10 March 1801*

Batter Pudding

Drinkwater woke in the pre-dawn chill. By an inexplicable reflex of the human brain he had fallen instantly asleep the night before, but now he awoke, his mind restlessly active, his body in a lather of sweat, not of fever, but of fear.

His first reaction was that something was terribly wrong. It took him a minute to separate fact from fancied dreaming, but when he realised the extent of reality he was appalled at his own conduct. He got out of his cot, dragged his blankets across the deck and slumped in the battered carver he had inherited as cabin furniture in the *Virago*.

Staring unseeing into the darkness it was some time before he had stopped cursing himself for a fool and accepted the events of the previous evening as accomplished facts. The residual effects of his fever sharpened his imagination so that, for a while, his isolation threatened to prevent him thinking logically. After a little he steadied himself and began to examine his actions in returning to the ship.

The first point in his favour was that he and Edward had returned in a hired beach boat picked up in the River Yare. The boatmen had got a good price for the passage out through the breakwaters and Edward a soaking by way of an introduction to the sea-service. Drinkwater had insisted on his brother leaving the cloak on the bank of the Yare, thinking the more indigent he looked the better. The fugitive had been frozen, wet and dishevelled enough not to excite any comment as to there being any connection between the two men. Indeed the silence between them had been taken for disdain on Drinkwater's part to the extent of one of the longshoremen offering a scrap of tarpaulin to the shuddering Edward. And, now that he recollected it, he had heard a muttered comment about 'fucking officers' from the older of the two boatmen as he had agilely scrambled up *Virago*'s welcome tumble-home.

He wondered if he had over-played his hand in arriving upon the deck, for in the darkness the officer on watch, already expecting the captain to remain ashore until the morning, had not manned the side properly. Trussel's embarrassment was obvious and Drinkwater pitied the quartermaster who had not spotted the boat in time.

Trussel's apologies had been profuse and Drinkwater had excused them abruptly.

''Tis no matter, Mr Trussel, I went upon a fool's errand and am glad to be back.' Drinkwater turned aft and had one foot on the poop ladder when he appeared to recollect something. 'Oh, Mr Trussel,' he looked back at the rail over which the sopping figure of Edward was clambering. He had clearly been sluiced by the sea as he jumped from the boat and even in the gloom the dark stain of water was visible around his feet. He stood shivering, pathetically uncertain.

'This fellow importuned me ashore. Damned if he didn't volunteer; on the run from some jade's jealous husband I don't wonder. See he's wrapped up for the night and brought before Lettsom and the first lieutenant in the morning.'

He heard Trussel acknowledge the order and knew Edward's reception would be cruel. Trussel would not welcome the necessity of turning out blankets and hammock at that late hour and Jex, the issuing officer, would be abusive at being turned from his cot to oblige the gunner. Trussel's own irritation at being found wanting in his duty on deck only added to the likelihood of Edward becoming a scapegoat. Now, in the cold morning air, Drinkwater hoped that his play-acted unconcern had sounded more genuine to Trussel and the other members of the anchor watch than to his own ears.

He made to find his flint to light a lantern, then realised that it would not do to let the morning anchor watch know he was awake by the glow in the skylight. He continued to sit until the wintry dawn threw its cold pale light through the cabin windows, gleaming almost imperceptibly on the black breeches of the two stern chasers. Then he roused himself and passed word for hot water. Already the hands were turning up to scrub decks. After he had shaved and dressed his mind was more composed. He had formulated a plan to save Edward's neck and his own honour. By the time he was ready to put it into practice there was enough light in the cabin by which to write.

The easterly wind had died in the night and the morning proved to be one of light airs and sunshine, picking out the details of the fleet with great clarity, lending to the bright colours of the ensigns, jacks, command flags and signals the quality of a country fair; quite the reverse of their stern military purpose. Had Drinkwater been less preoccupied by his dilemma he might have remarked on the irony of the situation, for the Baltic enterprise seemed to be in abeyance while preparations were made for Lady Parker's ball. Around *St George* there congregated an early assortment of captain's gigs; water beetles collecting round the core of disapproval at the frivolous attitude of the fleet's commander-in-chief.

Pacing his tiny poop Drinkwater resisted the frequent impulse to touch the sealed letter in his breast pocket. He should have called his own boat away half an hour ago but morbid curiosity kept him on deck to see what his brother would make of his first forenoon in the Royal Navy. Edward had one powerful incentive to keep his mouth shut and Drinkwater had advised him of it just before he hailed the boatman on the beach the previous night.

'If the people ever learn they've their captain's brother among them they will make your life so hellish you'd wish you'd not asked for my protection.'

If Edward had doubted his brother then, he had little cause to this morning. Graham, bosun's mate of the larboard watch, was giving him a taste of the starter as he hustled the new recruit aft to where Mr Lettsom sat on the breech of a gun waiting to give the newcomer his medical examination.

Drinkwater stopped his pacing at the poop rail. 'Is that our new man, Mr Lettsom?'

'Aye sir.' Lettsom looked up at his commander. Drinkwater studiously ignored his brother although he felt Edward's eyes upon him.

'I don't want that fellow bringing the ship-fever aboard. God knows what hole he's out of, but if he wants a berth aboard *Virago* he must formerly have been quartered in a kennel.'

Lettsom grinned with such complicity that Drinkwater thought his own performance must be credible. With an assumed lofty indifference he resumed his pacing as Lettsom commanded 'Strip!'

As Drinkwater paced up and down he caught glimpses of his unfortunate brother. First shivering naked, then being doused by a washdeck hose pumped enthusiastically by grinning seamen, and finally bent double while Lettsom examined him for lice.

'Well, Mr Lettsom?'

'No clap, pox or crabs, sir. Teeth fair, no hernias, though a little choleric about the gills. Good pulse, no fever. Sound in wind and limb. Washed from truck to keel in the German Ocean and fit for service in His Britannic Majesty's Navy.'

'Very well. Ah, Mr Rogers . . .' Drinkwater touched his hat in acknowledgement of Rogers's salute.

'Good morning sir.'

'I have a new hand for you. Volunteered last night and I knew you were still short of men. God knows what induces voluntary service but a mad husband or a nagging wife may drive a man to extremes.'

'Not a damned felon are you, cully?' Rogers asked in a loud voice that started the sweat prickling along Drinkwater's spine.

Already ashamed of his nakedness Edward did not raise his eyes. 'N . . . No . . .'

Graham's starter sliced his buttocks and the bosun's mate growled 'No *sir*.'

'No sir.'

Drinkwater had had enough. 'Take him forward, Graham, the fellow's cold. Volunteers are rare enough without neglecting 'em. See he washes the traps he wore aboard and is issued with slops from the purser, including a greygoe. Oh, and Graham, get that hair cut.'

'Aye, aye, sir.'

Graham hustled Edward forward. Drinkwater had one last thought. Afterwards he thought the timing capped the whole performance. 'By the way, what's your name?'

'Waters, sir . . . Edward Waters.'

'Very well Waters, do your duty and you have nothing to fear.' The old formula had a new meaning and the two brothers looked at each other for a moment then Drinkwater nodded his dismissal and Graham led 'Waters' away.

Drinkwater resumed his pacing, aware that he was shaking with relief. When he had calmed himself he called for his gig.

*

Great Yarmouth is a town built on the grid pattern, squeezed into the narrow isthmus between the North Sea and the River Yare that flows southwards, parallel to the sea from the tidal Broadlands, then turns abruptly, as if suddenly giving up its independence and surrendering to the ocean. More than once in its history the mouth had moved and the population turned out to dig a cut to preserve the river mouth that ensured their prosperity.

The walled section of the old town had streets running from north to south between the quays lining the Yare and a sea road contiguous with the beach. At right angles to the streets, alleys cut east to west, from sea to river, and Drinkwater was hopelessly lost in these before he eventually discovered the Wrestler's Arms in the market place.

He walked past it three or four times before making up his mind to carry out his plan. The metaphor to be hung for a sheep as a lamb crossed his mind with disquieting persistence, but he entered the coffee room and called for a pot of coffee. It was brought by a pleasant looking girl with soft brown hair and a smile that was pretty enough to distract him. He relaxed.

'Be that all, sir?' she asked, her lilting accent rising on the last syllable.

'No, my dear. Have you pen, paper and ink, and would you oblige me by finding out if Lady Parker is at present in her rooms?'

The girl nodded. 'Oh, yes sir. Her ladyship's in sir, her dress-maker's expected in half an hour sir and she's making preparations for a gala ball on Friday, sir . . .'

'Thank you,' Drinkwater cut in abruptly, 'but the paper, if you please . . .'

The girl flushed and bobbed a curtsey, hurrying away while Drinkwater sipped the coffee and found it surprisingly delicious.

When the girl returned he asked her to wait while he scribbled a note requesting permission for Lieutenant Drinkwater to wait upon her ladyship at her convenience, somewhat annoyed at having to use such a tone to an eighteen-year-old girl, but equally anxious that the gala would not turn her ladyship's mind from remembering her deliverer in the Strand.

Giving the girl the note and a shilling he watched her bob away, her head full of God knew what misconceptions. She returned after a few minutes with the welcome invitation that Lady Parker would be pleased to see Lieutenant Drinkwater at once.

He found her ladyship in an extravagant silk morning dress that would not have disgraced Elizabeth at the Portsmouth Assembly Rooms. The girl's plain face was not enhanced by the lace cap that she wore. Drinkwater much preferred the French fashion of uncovered hair, and he could not but agree with Lord St Vincent's nickname for her: *Batter Pudding*. But somehow her very plainness made his present task easier. Her new social rank had made her expect deference and her inexperience could not yet distinguish sincerity from flattery.

Drinkwater bent over her hand. 'It is most kind of your ladyship to receive me.' He paused and looked significantly at a door which communicated with an adjacent room and from which the low tone of male voices could be heard. 'I do hope I am not disturbing you . . .'

'Not at all. Thank you Annie, you may go.' The girl withdrew and Lady Parker seated herself at a table. There was a stiffness about her, as though she were very conscious of her deportment. He felt suddenly sorry for her and wondered if she had yet learned to regret being unable to behave like any eighteen-year-old.

'Would you join me in a cup of chocolate, Lieutenant?'

He felt it would be churlish to refuse despite his recent coffee. 'That would be most kind of you.'

'Please sit down.' She motioned to the chair opposite and turned to the tray with its elegant silver pot and delicate china cups.

'May I congratulate you, Lady Parker. At our last meeting I had not connected your name with Admiral Parker's. You must forgive me.'

She smiled and Drinkwater noticed that her eyes lit up rather prettily.

'I had hoped, sir, that you had come to see me as a friend and were not calling upon me as your admiral's wife . . .'

The blow was quite sweetly delivered and Drinkwater recognised a certain worldly shrewdness in her that he had not thought her capable of. It further reassured him in his purpose.

'Nothing was further from my mind, ma'am. I came indeed to see you and the matter has no direct connection with your husband. I come not so much as a friend but as a supplicant.'

'No direct *connection*, Mr Drinkwater? And a *supplicant*? I will willingly do anything in my power for you but I am not sure I understand.'

'Lady Parker forgive me. I should not have importuned you like this and I do indeed rely heavily upon having been able to render you assistance. The truth of the matter is that I have a message I wish delivered in London. It is both private and public in that the matter must remain private, but it is in the public interest.'

She lowered her cup and Drinkwater knew from the light in her eyes that her natural curiosity was aroused. He went on: 'I know I can rely upon your discretion, ma'am, but I have been employed upon special services. That is a fact your own father could verify, though I doubt your husband knows of it. In any event please confirm the matter with the recipient of this letter before you deliver it, if you so wish.' He drew out the heavily sealed letter from his coat and held it out. She hesitated.

'It is addressed to Lord Dungarth at his private address . . .'

'And the matter *is* in the public interest?'

'I believe it to be.' His armpits were sodden but she took the letter and Drinkwater was about to relax when the sound of raised voices came from the other room. He saw her eyes flicker anxiously to the door then return to his face. She frowned.

'Lieutenant Drinkwater, I hope this is not a matter of spoiling my ball.'

'I am sorry ma'am, I do not understand.'

'Certain gentlemen are of the opinion that it would be in the public interest if I were not to hold a ball on Friday, they are urging Sir Hyde to sail at once, even threatening to write to London about it.'

'Good heavens, ma'am, my letter has no connection with the fleet. I would not be so presumptuous . . .' He had appeased her, it seemed. 'The matter is related to affairs abroad,' he added with mysterious significance, 'I am sorry I cannot elaborate further.'

'No, no, of course not. And you simply wish me to deliver this to his lordship?'

'Aye, ma'am, I should consider myself under a great obligation if you would.'

She smiled and again her eyes lit attractively. 'You will be under no obligation Mr Drinkwater, provided you will promise to come to my ball.'

'It will give me the greatest pleasure, ma'am, and may I hope for a dance?'

'Of course, Lieutenant.' He stood. The noises from the other room sounded hostile and he wished to leave before the door opened. 'It would be better if no one knew of the letter, your ladyship,' he indicated the sealed paper on the table.

'My dressmaker comes soon . . .' She reached for her reticule and hid the letter just as the door burst open. As Drinkwater picked up his hat he came face to face with a short florid man in a grey coat. He was shaking his head at someone behind him.

'No, damn it, no . . . Ah, Fanny, my dear,' he saw Drinkwater, 'who the deuce is this?'

'May I present Lieutenant Drinkwater, Hyde dear.' Drinkwater bowed.

'Of which ship, sir?' Parker's eyes were hostile.

'*Virago*, bomb-tender, sir. I took the liberty . . .'

'Lieutenant Drinkwater took no liberties, my dear, it was he who rescued me from the mob in the Strand last October. The least I could do was present him to you.'

Parker seemed to deflate slightly. He half faced towards the man in the other room, whose identity was still unknown to Drinkwater, then turned again to the lieutenant.

'Obliged, I'm sure, Lieutenant, and now, if you'll excuse me . . .'

'Of course sir. I was just leaving . . .' But Lady Parker had a twinkle in her eye and Drinkwater, grateful and surprised at the skill of her intervention, suspected her of enjoying herself.

'Lieutenant Drinkwater served under father at Camperdown, Hyde, I am sure he is worthy of your notice.'

Parker shot him another unfriendly glance and Drinkwater wondered if the admiral thought he had put his wife up to this currying of favour. Clearly the other man was forming some such notion for he appeared disapprovingly in the doorway. The shock of recognition hit Drinkwater like a blow. If he thought Parker saw him in a poor light it was clear Lord Nelson saw him in a worse.

'If you want your dance, Sir Hyde, and your wife wants her *amusements*, then the fleet and I'll go hang. But I tell you time, time is everything; five minutes makes the difference between a victory and a defeat.'

Chapter Ten *10–11 March 1801*

Truth in Masquerade

Drinkwater began Tuesday afternoon pacing his poop as the sky clouded over and the wind worked round to the west. The encounter with Lord Nelson had made him resentful and angry. He paced off his fury at being taken by his lordship for one of Lady Parker's *amusements*. The sight of the little admiral, his sleeve pinned across his gold-laced coat, his oddly mobile mouth in its pale, prematurely worn face, with the light of contempt in his one good eye had had an effect on Lieutenant Drinkwater that he was still trying to analyse. It had, he concluded, been like receiving raking fire, so devastating was Nelson's disapproval. The second and more powerful emotion which succeeded in driving from his mind all thoughts of his brother, was the despair he felt at having earned Nelson's poor opinion.

He found Sir Hyde Parker's assurance of 'taking notice of the Lieutenant's conduct to please my wife', which ordinarily ought to have been a matter for self-congratulation, brought him no comfort at all. Nelson had cut him as they both left the Wrestler's Inn and Drinkwater felt the slight almost as intensely as a physical wound.

Drinkwater began to realise the nature of Nelson's magic. He had glimpsed it two years earlier at Syracuse animating a weary fleet that had been beaten by bad luck, bad weather and compounded the break-out of the French through their blockade of Toulon by an over-zealous pursuit that had made them overtake the enemy without knowing it. Yet Nelson had led them back east to smash Brueys in Aboukir Bay in the victory that was now known as The Nile. Now Drinkwater stood condemned as the epitome of all that Nelson despised in Parker and Parker's type.

And because it was unjust he burned with a fury to correct Nelson's misconception.

As he paced up and down he realised the hopelessness of his

case. He began to regret asking Dungarth for his own command. What hope had he of distinguishing himself in the old tub that *Virago* really was? Those two mortars that Tumilty had so slyly placed in their beds were no more than a charade. There would be no 'opportunity' in this expedition, only drudgery, probable mismanagement and a glorious débâcle to amuse Europe. No fleet orders had been issued to the ships, no order of sailing. All was confusion with a few of Nelson's intimates forming a cabal within the hierarchy of the fleet which threatened to overset the whole enterprise.

Added to the demoralisation of the officers were the chills, fevers, agues and rheumatism being experienced by many of the seamen. The much publicised Baltic Fleet had the constitution of an organism in an advanced state of rot. Drinkwater's own condition was merely a symptom of that decay.

Only that morning on his return from the shore Rogers had brought a man aft for spitting on the deck. Although Drinkwater suspected the fellow had fallen into an uncontrollable fit of violent coughing he had ordered the grating rigged and the man given a dozen lashes. It was only hours later that he felt ashamed, unconsoled by the reflection that many captains would have ordered three dozen, and only recognising the unpleasant fact that events of the last few days had brutalised him. He had watched Edward's face as Cottrell had been flogged. Only once had his brother looked up. Nathaniel realised now that he had flogged Cottrell as an example to Edward, and he cursed the rottenness of a world that penned men in such traps.

But Lieutenant Drinkwater's wallow in the mire of self-pity did not last long. It was an unavoidable concomitant of the isolation of command and the antidote, when it came in the person of a midshipman from *Explosion*, was most welcome. He was invited to dine on the bomb vessel within the hour. The thought of company among equals, even equals as bilious-eyed as Martin, was preferable to his own morbid society.

It proved to be a surprisingly jolly affair. After a sherry or two he relaxed enough to cast off the 'blue-devils'. If they were going to war he might as well enjoy himself. In a month he might be dead. If they ever did sail of course, and it was this subject that formed the conversation as the officers of the bomb vessels gossiped. The fleet was buzzing with a rumour that delighted both the naval and the artillery officers crowded into Martin's after cabin. Lord Nelson, it was said, had written direct to Earl St Vincent, the First Lord. Lady Parker's ball and the delay it was causing was believed to be the subject of his lordship's letter. Among the assembly an atmosphere of almost school-boy glee prevailed. They waited eagerly for the outcome, arguing on whether it would be the supercession of Parker by Nelson or an order to sail.

Drinkwater exchanged remarks with two white-haired lieutenants who were in command of the other tenders and normally employed by the Transport Board. They were both over sixty and he soon gravitated towards Tumilty and the other artillery officers who were more his own age. The merry-eyed Lieutenant English, attached to *Explosion*, sympathised with him over Martin's apparent animosity and cursed his own ill-luck in being appointed to the ship. Fitzmayer of the *Terror* and Jones of the *Volcano* seemed intent on insulting Admiral Parker and had embarked on a witty exchange of military *double entendres* designed to throw doubts on the admiral's ability to be a proper husband to his bride. The joke was becoming rather stale. From Captain-Lieutenant Peter Fyers of *Sulphur* he learned something of the defences of Copenhagen where Fyers had served the previous year in a bomb vessel sent as part of Lord Whitworth's embassy. Captain-Lieutenant Lawson, attached to *Zebra*, was expatiating on the more scandalous excesses and perverted pastimes of the late Empress Catherine and the even less attractive sadism of her son Tsar Paul, 'the author', as he put it, 'of our present misfortune, God-rot his Most Imperial Majesty.'

'There seems a deal of hostility to kings among these king's officers,' remarked Drinkwater to Tumilty, thinking of the regicide tendencies of his own surgeon.

'Ah,' explained Tumilty with inescapable Irish logic, 'but we're not exactly *king's* officers, my dear Nat'aniel, no we're not. As I told you our commissions are from the Master General of the Ordnance, d'you see. Professional men like yourself, so we are.' He paused to drink off his glass. 'We're pyroballogists that'll fire shot and shell into heaven itself if the devil's wearing a general's tail coat. Motivated by science we are, Nat'aniel, and damn the politics. Fighting men to be sure.'

Drinkwater was not sure if that was true of all the artillery officers mustered in *Explosion*'s stuffy cabin, but it was certainly true of

Lieutenant Thomas Tumilty whose desire to be throwing explosive shells at anyone unwise enough to provoke him, seemed to consume him with passion so that he sputtered like one of his own fuses.

'And I've some news for you personal like. Our friend Captain Martin has heard that our mortars are mounted. I'd not be surprised if he were to mention it to you . . .' Tumilty's eyes narrowed to slits and the hair on his cheeks bristled as he sucked in his cheeks in mock disapproval. He took another glass from the passing messman and turned away with an obvious wink as Captain Martin approached.

The commander's appearance as though on cue was uncanny, but Drinkwater dismissed the suspicion that Tumilty intended anything more than a warning.

'Well, Mr Drinkwater, itching to try your mortars at the enemy are you?'

'Given the opportunity I should wish to render you every possible assistance in my power, sir,' he said diplomatically.

'Were you not ordered to strike those mortars into your hold, Mr Drinkwater?' asked Martin, an expression of extreme dislike crossing his pale face.

'No sir,' replied Drinkwater with perfect candour, 'the existence of the mortar beds led me to suppose that the mortars might be shipped therein with perfect safety. The vessel would not become excessively stiff and they are readily available should they be required by any other ship. Struck into the hold they might have become overstowed by other . . .'

'Very well, Mr Drinkwater,' Martin snapped, 'you have made your point.' He seemed about to turn away, riled by Drinkwater's glib replies but recollected something and suddenly asked, 'How the devil did you get command of *Virago*?'

'I was appointed by the Admiralty, sir . . .'

'I mean, Mr Drinkwater,' said Martin with heavy emphasis, 'by whose influence was your application preferred?'

Drinkwater flushed with sudden anger. He appreciated Martin's own professional disappointments might be very great, but he himself hardly represented the meteoric rise of an admiral's élève.

'I do not believe I am anybody's protégé, sir,' he said with icy formality, 'though I have rendered certain service to their Lordships of a rather unusual nature.'

Drinkwater was aware that he was bluffing but he saw Martin deflate slightly, as though he had found the justification for his dislike in Drinkwater's reply.

'And what nature did that service take, Mr Drinkwater?' Martin's tone was sarcastic.

'Special service, sir, I am not at liberty to discuss it.' Martin's eyes opened a little wider, though whether it was at Drinkwater's effrontery or whether he was impressed, was impossible to determine. At all events Drinkwater did not need to explain that the special service had been as mate of the cutter *Kestrel* dragging the occasional spy off a French beach and no more exciting than the nightly activities on a score of British beaches in connection with the 'free trade'.

'Special service? You mean *secret* service, Mr Drinkwater,' Martin paused as though making up his mind. 'For Lord Dungarth's department, perhaps?'

'Perhaps, sir,' temporised Drinkwater, aware that this might prove a timely raising of his lordship's name and be turned to some advantage in his plan for Edward.

Real anger was mounting into Martin's cheeks.

'I am quite well aware of his lordship's activities, Drinkwater, I am not so passed over that . . .' he broke off, aware that his own voice had risen and that he had revealed more of himself than he had intended. Martin looked round but the other officers were absorbed in their own chatter. He coughed with embarrassment. 'You are well acquainted with his lordship?' Martin asked almost conversationally.

'Aye sir,' replied Drinkwater, relieved that the squall seemed to have passed. 'We sailed together on the *Cyclops*, frigate, in the American War.' Drinkwater sensed the need to be conciliatory, particularly as the problem of Edward weighed heavily upon him. 'I beg your pardon for being evasive, sir. I was not aware that his lordship's activities were known to you.'

Martin nodded. 'You were not the only officer to serve in his clandestine operations, Mr Drinkwater.'

'Nor, perhaps,' Drinkwater said in a low voice, the sherry making him bold, 'the only one to be disappointed.' He watched Martin's eyes narrow as the commander digested the implication of Drinkwater's remark. Then Drinkwater added, 'You would not therefore blame me for mounting those mortars, sir?'

For a second Drinkwater was uncertain of the result of his

importunity. Then he saw the ghost of a smile appear on Martin's face. 'And you are yet known to Lord Dungarth?'

Drinkwater nodded. The knowledge that the lieutenant still commanded interest with the peer was beginning to put him in a different light in Martin's disappointed eyes.

'Very well, Mr Drinkwater.' Martin turned away.

Drinkwater heaved a sigh of relief. The antagonism of Martin would have made any plan for Edward's future doubly hazardous. Now, perhaps, Martin was less hostile to him. He caught Tumilty's eye over the rim of the Irishman's glass. It winked shamelessly. Drinkwater mastered a desire to laugh, but it was not the mirth of pure amusement. It had the edge of hysteria about it. Elizabeth had been right: he was no dissembler and the strain of it was beginning to tell.

Drinkwater returned to *Virago* a little drunk. The dinner had been surprisingly good and during it Drinkwater learned that it had been provided largely by the generosity of the artillery officers who had had the good sense to humour their naval counterparts. It was only later, slumped in his carver and staring at his sword hanging on a hook, that the irrelevant thought crossed his mind that it had not been cleaned after the fight with the French luggers. He sent for Tregembo.

When the quartermaster returned twenty minutes later with the old French sword honed to a biting edge on Willerton's grindstone he seemed to want to talk.

'Beg pardon, zur, but have 'ee looked at they pistol flints?'

'No, Tregembo,' Drinkwater shook his head to clear it of the effects of the wine. 'Do so if you please. I fancy you can re-knap 'em without replacing 'em.'

'There are plenty of flints aboard here, zur,' said Tregembo reproachfully.

Drinkwater managed a laugh. 'Ah yes, I was forgettin' we're a floating arsenal. Do as you please then.'

Tregembo had brought two new flints with him and took out the pull-through. He began fiddling with the brace of flintlocks. 'Do 'ee think we'll sail soon, zur?'

'I hope so, Tregembo, I hope so.'

'They say no one knows where we're going, zur, though scuttlebutt is that we're going to fight the Russians.' He paused. 'It's kind of confusing, zur, but they were our allies off the Texel in '97.'

'Well they ain't our allies now, Tregembo. They locked British seamen up. As to sailing, I have received no orders. I imagine the government are still negotiating with the Baltic powers.'

Drinkwater sighed as Tregembo sniffed in disbelief.

'They say Lord Nelson's had no word of the fleet's intentions.'

'*They say* a great deal, much of it nonsense, Tregembo, you should know that.'

'Aye zur,' Tregembo said flatly in an acknowledgement that Drinkwater had spoken, not that he believed a word of what he had said. There followed a silence as Tregembo lowered the first pistol into the green baize-lined box.

'That volunteer, zur, the one you brought aboard t'other night. Have I seen him afore?'

Drinkwater's blood froze and his brain swam from its haze of wine and over-eating. He had not considered being discovered by Tregembo of all people. He looked at the man but he was nestling the second pistol in its recess. 'His face was kind of familiar, zur.'

Suddenly Drinkwater cursed himself for a fool. What was it Corneille had said about needing a good memory after lying? Tregembo had not left Petersfield when Edward called upon Elizabeth. It was quite likely that he had seen Edward, even that he had let him into the house. And it was almost certain that either he or his wife Susan would have learned that their mistress's visitor was the master's brother.

'Familiar, in what way?' he asked, buying time.

'I don't know, zur, but I seen him afore somewhere . . .' Drinkwater looked shrewdly at Tregembo. Edward's present appearance was drastically altered. Clothes and manners maketh the man and Edward had been shorn of his hair along with his self respect. He was also losing weight due to the paucity of the food and the unaccustomed labour. It was quite possible that Tregembo was disturbed by no more than curiosity. He might think he had seen Edward in a score of places, the frigate *Cyclops*, the cutter *Kestrel*, before he connected him with Petersfield. On the other hand he might remember exactly who Edward was and be mystified as to why the man had turned up before the mast aboard Drinkwater's own ship.

It struck Drinkwater that if the authorities got wind of what he had done he might only have Tregembo to rely on. Except Quilhampton, perhaps, and, with a pang, he recollected James Quilhampton was a party to the little mystery of Edward's note.

Drinkwater was sweating and aware that he had been staring at Tregembo for far too long not to make some sort of confession. He swallowed, deciding on a confidence in which truth might masquerade. 'You may have seen him before, Tregembo. Have you mentioned this to anyone else?'

Tregembo shook his head. 'No zur.'

'You recollect Major Brown and our duties aboard *Kestrel*?' Tregembo nodded. 'Well Waters is not unconnected with the same sort of business. I do not know any details.'

'But I saw him at Petersfield, zur. I remember now.'

'Ah, I see.' Drinkwater wondered again if Elizabeth had revealed Edward's relationship. 'His arrival doubtless perturbed my wife, eh? Well I don't doubt it, he was not expecting to find me absent.' Drinkwater paused; that much was true. '*Whatever* you have heard about this man Tregembo I beg you to forget it. Do you understand?'

'Aye zur.'

'If you can avoid any reference to him I'd be obliged.' Then he added as an afterthought, 'So would Lord Dungarth.'

'And that's why he is turned forrard, eh zur?'

Drinkwater nodded. 'Exactly.'

Tregembo smiled. 'Thank 'ee zur. You'll be a commander afore this business is over, zur, mark my words.'

Then he turned and left the cabin and Drinkwater was unaccountably moved.

Drinkwater turned in early. The effects of his dinner had returned and made him drowsy. He longed for the oblivion of sleep. A little after midnight he was aware of someone calling him from a great distance.

He woke slowly to find Quilhampton shining a lantern into his face.

'Sir! Sir! Bengal fires and three guns from the *London*, sir! Repeated by *St George*. The signal to weigh, sir, the signal to weigh . . . !'

'Eh, what's that?'

'Bengal fires and three guns . . .'

'I heard you, God damn it. What's the signal?'

'To weigh, sir.' Quilhampton's enthusiasm was wasted at this hour.

'Return on deck, Mr Q, and read the night orders again for God's sake.'

'Aye, aye, sir,' the crestfallen Quilhampton withdrew and Drinkwater rose to wash the foulness out of his mouth. It was not Quilhampton's fault. No-one in the fleet had had a chance to study the admiral's special signals and it boded ill for the general management of the expedition. Drinkwater spat disgustedly into the bowl set in the top of his sea chest. A respectful knock announced the return of the mate. 'Well?'

'The signal to unmoor, sir.'

'Made for . . .?'

'The line of battleships with two anchors down.'

'And how many anchors have we?'

'One sir.'

'One sir. The signal to weigh will be given at dawn. Call all hands an hour before. Have your watch rig the windlass bars, have the topsails loose in their buntlines ready for hoisting and the stops off the heads'ls.'

'Aye, aye, sir.'

Drinkwater retired to sleep. There was an old saying in the service. He prayed God it was true: all debts were paid when the topsails were sheeted home.

He did not know that an Admiralty messenger had exhausted three horses to bring Parker St Vincent's direct command to sail, nor that Lady Parker would return to London earlier than expected.

Chapter Eleven *11–18 March 1801*

Nadir

'What a God damn spectacle!' said Rogers happily as he watched the big ships weigh. The misfortunes of others always delighted him. It was one of his less likeable traits. Drinkwater shivered in his cloak, wondering whether his blood would ever thicken after his service in the Red Sea and how much longer they would have to wait. It was nine o'clock and the Viragos had been at their stations since daylight, awaiting their turn to weigh and proceed to sea through the St Nicholas Gat.

The signal to weigh had caused some confusion as no one was certain what the order of sailing was. Towards the northern end of the anchorage two battleships had run foul of each other, but already the handful of frigates and sloops had got away smartly, led out by the handsome *Amazon*, commanded by Edward Riou. Following them south east through the gatway and round the Scroby Sands, went the former East Indiaman *Glatton*, her single deck armed with the carronades which had so astonished a French squadron with their power, that she had defeated them all. Her odd appearance was belied by the supreme seamanship of the man who now commanded her. 'Bounty' Bligh turned her through the anchorage with an almost visible contempt for his reputation. Drinkwater had met Bligh and served with him at Camperdown. Another veteran of Camperdown, the old 50-gun *Isis* ran down in company with the incomparable *Agamemnon*, Nelson's old sixty-four. The order of sailing had gone by the board as the big ships made the best of their way to seaward of the sands. The 98-gun *St George*, with Nelson's blue vice-admiral's flag at the foremasthead was already setting her topgallants, her jacks swinging aloft like monkeys, a band playing on her poop. The strains of *Rule Britannia* floated over the water.

Despite himself Drinkwater felt an involuntary thrill run down his spine as Nelson passed, unable to resist the man's genius despite the cloud he was personally under. Even Rogers was silent while Quilhampton's eyes were shining like a girl's.

'Here the buggers come,' said Rogers as the other seventy-fours stood through the road; *Ganges*, *Bellona*, *Polyphemus*. Then came *Monarch*, Batter Pudding's father's flagship at Camperdown, and the rest, all setting their topgallants, their big courses in the bunt-lines ready to set when the intricacies of St Nicholas's Gat had been safely negotiated.

'*Invincible*'s going north sir,' observed Easton pointing to the Caister end of the anchorage where the cutters and gun brigs were leaving by the Cockle Gat.

'I hope he has a pilot on board,' said Drinkwater thinking of the treacherous passage and driving *Kestrel* through it years ago.

'Some of the storeships goin' that way too,' offered Quilhampton, aping Drinkwater's clipped mannerism.

'Yes, Mr Q. Do you watch for *Explosion*'s signal now.'

'Aye, aye, sir.'

'Martin's still playing at bloody commodore,' said Rogers to Easton in a stage whisper. The master sniggered. 'Hey look, someone's lost a jib-boom . . .' They could not make out the ship as she was masked by another but almost last to leave was Parker's *London*.

'The old bastard had trouble getting his flukes out of the mud,' laughed Rogers making an onomatopoeic sucking plop that sent a burst of ribald laughter round *Virago*'s poop.

'I hope, Mr Rogers, that is positively the last joke we hear about the subject of the admiral's nuptials,' said Drinkwater, remembering the plain-faced girl on whom he so relied. He might at least defend her honour on his own deck.

'In fact,' he added with sudden asperity, 'I forbid further levity on the subject now we are at sea under Sir Hyde's orders.'

Drinkwater put his glass to his eye and ignored Rogers who made an exaggerated face at Easton behind his back. Quilhampton laughed, thus missing the executive signal from *Explosion*.

Drinkwater had seen the bunting flutter down from the topgallant yardarm where the wind spread it for the bombs to see.

'Heave up, Mr Matchett. Hoist foretopmast stays'l!'

The anchor was already hove short and it was the work of only a few minutes to heave it underfoot and trip it. 'Anchor's aweigh, sir!'

'Tops'l halliards, Mr Rogers! Lee braces, there!' He turned to Mr Quilhampton who had flushed at missing the signal from *Explosion*. 'See those weather braces run, Mr Q.'

'Aye, aye, sir,' the boy ran forward to vindicate himself.

'Starboard stays'l sheet there! Look lively, God damn it!'

'Anchor's sighted clear, sir.'

Aloft the topsail parrels creaked against the greased topmasts as the yards rose. The canvas flogged, then filled with great dull crumps, flogged and filled again as the yards were trimmed. Drinkwater looked with satisfaction at the replaced mainyard.

'Steady as you go.'

'Steady as you go, zur.' *Virago* gathered way and caught up on *Zebra* which had not yet tripped her anchor.

'Port your helm,' Drinkwater looked round to see the order was obeyed. The big tiller was pushed over to larboard and *Virago* began to turn to starboard her bowsprit no longer pointing at *Zebra*.

'Trim that foreyard, Graham, God rot you! Don't you know your business?' bawled Rogers as the petty officers directed the stamping, panting gangs of men. Matchett was leaning outboard fishing for the anchor with the cat tackle.

'Course south east a half south.' Drinkwater looked to starboard and raised his hat. Aboard the *Anne Reed* he saw Tumilty acknowledge his greeting.

'Course south east a half south, zur,' reported Tregembo.

'Course south east a half south, sir,' repeated Easton, the sailing master. Drinkwater suppressed a smile. He almost felt happy. It was good to be under way at last, and upon his own deck at that. He did not want to look astern at the roofs and church towers of Great Yarmouth with their reminders of the rule of Law, which he so much admired yet had so recently disregarded.

The reflection made him search for his brother as the hands secured the deck and adjusted the sails to Rogers's exacting direction. He found him at last, in duck trousers and a check shirt, hauling upon the anchor crown tackle, a labour for unskilled muscles, supervised by Mr Matchett in the starboard forechains. The heaving waisters brought the inboard fluke of the sheet anchor in against its bill board and able seamen leapt contemptuously outboard to pass the lashings.

'You had better cast the lead as we pass the Gatway, Mr Easton, the tide will set us on the Corton side else, and I've no wish to go aground today.'

'Aye, aye, sir. Snape! Get your arse into the main chains with a lead!'

'Give her the forecourse, Mr Rogers. And you may have Quilhampton set the spanker when we come on the wind off the Scroby Sands.'

Drinkwater looked at his watch. It was eleven o'clock. A ship was coming up from the south and Drinkwater checked her number against the private signals. She was the *Edgar*, Captain George Murray, joining the fleet. He remembered Murray as the frustrated captain of the sluggish frigate *La Nymphe*, unable to get into action during the fight of St George's Day off the Brittany coast. With a shock Drinkwater realised that had been seven years earlier. It had been his first action in charge of a ship, the cutter *Kestrel* whose commander, Lieutenant Madoc Griffiths, lay sweating out the effects of malaria in his cabin.

At noon Drinkwater checked Easton's entry on the slate and stood down the watch below. Despite the confusion in the fleet Martin's little squadron was keeping tolerably good station. It was clear Martin wanted a post-captaincy out of this expedition.

'What course for the passage, sir?' asked Easton formally.

Drinkwater smiled wanly. The fleet was tired of uncertainty. 'I have only orders to stand towards the Naze of Norway, Mr Easton, as I told you yesterday.'

'Mushrooms, Mr Easton,' said Rogers cheerfully, 'that is all we are, mushrooms . . .'

'Mushrooms, Mr Rogers?' said Easton, frowning.

'Aye, mushrooms, Mr Easton. Kept in the dark and fed with bullshit.'

'But I tell you I am right, Bones.' The smell of rum hung in the heavy air.

Mr Jex had drawn the surgeon into the stygian gloom of *Virago*'s hold on the pretext of examining the quality of a barrel of sauerkraut. The familiar tone he used in addressing Lettsom only emphasised the purser's misjudgement of the surgeon's character. Listening to the exaggeratedly flippant remarks which Lettsom customarily used, Jex had assumed the surgeon might prove an ally. Part of Jex's desire to find a confidant was due to his isolation after the discovery of his conduct in the affair off the Sunk. Lettsom avowed an abhorrence of war and the machinations of Admiralty, a common attitude among the better sort of surgeon and a product of keeping educated men in a state of social limbo, mere warrant officers among compeers of far lesser intellect.

Jex had decided that since he could not escape the taint of cowardice he might as well assume a spurious conscientious objection. The rehabilitation of himself thus being complete in his own eyes, if in no-one else's, he now began to search for a means of furthering his own ends. But Jex's mind was expert in calculating, and the readiness and facility with which he did this was apt to blind him to his limitations in other fields. He was a man who considered himself clever when he was not. He was, therefore, a dangerous person to thwart, and Drinkwater had crossed him.

Mr Jex's stupidity now led him to believe that certain facts that had come his way were a providential sign that his new, Quakerish philosophy had divine approval, and that his deductive powers used in reaching his conclusion merely proved that he was a man of equal intellect with the surgeon, hence the familiar contraction of the old cognomen, 'Sawbones'.

It was unfortunate that a mind skilled in feathering its own nest and dividing the rations of unfortunate seamen to an eighth part (for himself) was a mind that delighted in nosing into the affairs of others. He had nursed a grievance against Lieutenant Drinkwater since he had been out-manoeuvred in the matter of his appointment. Drinkwater had intimidated him as well as humiliated him in his own eyes. Jex had not expected fate to be so kind as to put into his hands such weapons as he now possessed, but now that he had them it seemed that it was one more confirmation of his superior abilities.

It had started when he had been turned from his cot at one in the morning by an angry Mr Trussel. The gunner had brought a new recruit and Jex had let the dripping wretch know exactly what he thought of being roused to attend to the wants of waterborne scum. So vehement had he become that he had shoved his lantern in the face of the newcomer. Jex was incapable of analysing the precise nature of the expression he found there, but the man was not afraid as he should have been, only cold and shivering. Jex's suspicions were roused because the man did not quail before him.

Jex had seen the man immediately he came aboard, before his

hair was cut and he had lost weight, while he was still dressed in a gentlemen's breeches. At that moment Jex did not recognise Edward, merely took note of him. And because Jex had taken note of him he continued to observe 'Waters'. Rogers had quartered Edward Drinkwater among the 'firemen', an action station for the most inept and inexperienced waisters whose duty was to pump water into the firehoses deployed by the purser.

There might have been no more to it had Jex not gone ashore for cabin stores at Yarmouth shortly before the order to sail. Being idly curious he had bought a newspaper, an extravagance he was well able to afford. Had he not purchased the paper he might never have made the connection between the new 'landsman volunteer' and the man he had seen in the Blue Fox, a man who had come into the taproom immediately Lieutenant Drinkwater had left the Inn.

The *Yarmouth Courier* reported: 'A foul double murder, which heinous crime had lately been perpetrated upon an emigrant French nobleman, the Marquis de la Roche-Jagu, and his pretty young mistress, Mlle Pascale Eugenie Vrignaud. The despicable act had been carried out in the marquis's lodgings at Newmarket. He had died from a sword cut in the right side of the neck which severed the trapezius muscle, the carotid artery and the jugular vein. Mlle Vrignaud had been despatched by a cut on the left temple which had rendered her instantly senseless and resulted in severe haemorrhage into the cranial cavity. Doctor Ezekiel Cotton of Newmarket was of the opinion that a single blow had killed both parties . . .'

Jex rightly concluded that the two lovers had been taken in the sexual act and that the murderer had struck a single impassioned blow. But it was the last paragraph that filled Mr Jex's heart with righteous indignation: 'A certain Edward Drinkwater had earlier been in the company of Mlle Vrignaud and has since disappeared. He is described as a man of middle height and thick figure, having a florid complexion and wearing his own brown hair, unpowdered.'

Mr Jex had embraced this news with interest, his curiosity and cunning were aroused and he remembered the man in the Blue Fox.

'I tell you I *am* right,' Jex repeated.

Lettsom looked up from the opened cask. 'There is nothing

wrong with this sauerkraut, it always smells foul when new opened.'

Lettsom straightened up.

> 'To save 'em from scurvy
> Our captain did shout,
> You shall feed 'em fresh cabbage
> And old sauerkraut.

'Make 'em eat it, Mr Jex, Mr Drinkwater's right . . .'

'No, no, Mr Lettsom. Damme but you haven't been listening. I mean this report in the paper here.' He thrust the *Yarmouth Courier* under Lettsom's nose. Lettsom took it impatiently and beckoned the lantern closer. When he had finished he looked up at the purser. Jex's porcine eyes glittered.

'You are linking our commander with the reported missing man?'

'Exactly. You see my point, then.'

'No, I do not. Do you think I am some kind of hierophant that I read men's minds.'

Jex was undeterred by the uncomprehended snub.

'Suppose that the murderer . . .'

'Even that scurrilous rag does not allege that the missing man actually carried out murder.' The legal nicety was lost on Jex.

'Well suppose that he *was* the murderer, and *was* related to the captain.'

'Good heavens Mr Jex, I had no idea you had such a lively imagination.' Lettsom made to leave but Jex held him.

'And suppose that the captain got him aboard here under cover of night . . .'

'What precisely do you mean?' Lettsom looked again at the sly features of the purser.

'Why else would Lieutenant Drinkwater turn his own brother forrard? Eh? I'm telling you that the man Edward Waters is the man wanted for this murder at Newmarket.' He slapped the paper with the back of his hand. Lettsom was silent for a while and Jex pressed his advantage. Lettsom did not know that Drinkwater's acquisition of Jex's funds had poisoned the purser against his commander. Jex had writhed under this extortion, ignoring the fact that his own perquisites were equally immoral.

'Well, will you help me, then?' asked Jex revealing to Lettsom the reason for this trip into the hold and the extent of Jex's stupidity.

'I? No sir, I will not.' Lettsom was indignant. He made again to leave the hold and again Jex restrained him.

'If I am right and you have refused to help me you would have obstructed the course of justice . . .'

'Jex, listen to me very carefully,' said Lettsom, 'if you plot against the captain of a ship of war you are guilty of mutiny for which you will surely hang.'

Lettsom retired to his cabin and pulled out his flute. He had not played it for many weeks and instantly regretted his lack of practice. His was not a great talent and he rarely played in any company other than that of his wife. He essayed a scale or two before launching into a low air of his own composition, during which his mind was able to concentrate upon its present preoccupation.

Mr Lettsom was a man of superficial frivolity and apparent indifference which he had adopted early in his naval life as a rampart against the cruelty in the service. He had found it kept people at a distance and, with the exceptions of his wife and three daughters, he liked it that way. The experience of living as a surgeon's mate through the American War had strangled any inherent feeling he had for the sufferings of humanity. In the main he had found his mess mates ignorant, bigotted and insufferably self-seeking; his superiors proud, haughty and incompetent and his inferiors brutalised into similar sub-divisions according to their own internal hierarchy.

To his patients Lettsom had applied the dispassionate results of his growing experience. He was known as a good surgeon because he had an average success rate and did not drink to excess. His frivolous indifference did not encourage deep friendship and he was usually left to his own devices, although his versifying brought him popular acclaim at mess dinners. He had rarely made any friends, most of his professional relationships were of the kind he presently enjoyed with Rogers, a kind of mutual regard based on respect overlaying dislike.

But Mr Lettsom's true nature was something else. His deeper passions were known only to his family. His wife well understood his own despair at the total inadequacy of his abilities, his resentment at the inferiority of surgery to 'medicine', his fury at the quackery of socially superior physicians. A long observation of humanity's conceit had taught him of its real ignorance.

In a sense his was a simple mind. He believed that humanity was essentially good, that it was merely the institutions and divisions that man imposed upon man that corrupted the metal. It was his belief that mankind could be redeemed by a few wise men, that the dissenting tradition of his grandfather's day had paved the way for the unleashing of the irresistible forces of the French Revolution.

Drinkwater had been right, Lettsom was a Leveller and a lover of Tom Paine. He did not share Drinkwater's widely held belief that the aggression and excesses of the revolution put it beyond acceptance, holding that man's own nature made such things inevitable just as the Royal Navy's vaunted maintenance of the principles of law, order and liberty were at the expense of the lash, impressment and a thousand petty tyrannies imposed upon the individual. A few good men . . .

He stopped playing his flute, lost in thought. If Jex had discovered the truth, Lettsom feared for Drinkwater. Despite their political differences the surgeon admired the younger lieutenant, seeing him as a man with humanist qualities to whom command came as a responsibility rather than an opportunity. Jex's evidence, if it was accurate, appeared to Lettsom as a kind of quixotic heroism in defiance of the established law. Drinkwater had hazarded his whole future to assist his brother and Lettsom found it endearing, as though it revealed the lieutenant's secret sympathy with his own ideals. With the wisdom of age Lettsom conduded that Drinkwater's subconscious sympathies lay exposed to him and he felt his admiration for the younger man increase.

He took up the flute again and began to play as another thought struck him. If the new landsman-volunteer was indeed Drinkwater's brother then Lettsom would not interfere and to hell with Jex. He did not find it difficult to condone such a crime of passion, particularly when it disposed of a marquis, one of those arrogant parasites that had brought the wrath of the hungry upon themselves and destroyed the peace of the world.

'Flag's signalling, sir.'

'Very well.'

'Number 107, sir.' There was a pause while Quilhampton strove to read the signal book as the wind tore at the pages.

'Close round the admiral, as near as the state of the weather and other circumstances will permit.'

'Very well.' The circumstances would permit little more than a token obedience to Parker's order. Since the early hours of Monday, 16 March, a ferocious gale had been blowing from the west south west. It had been snowing since dawn and become very cold. The big ships had reduced to storm canvas and struck their topgallant masts. At about nine o'clock the fireship *Alecto* had reported a leak and been detached with the lugger *Rover* as an escort.

Drinkwater ordered an issue of the warm clothing he had prudently laid in at Chatham as Lettsom reported most of the men afflicted with coughs, colds or quinsies. His own anxiety was chiefly in not running foul of another ship in the snow squalls that frequently blinded them. The fleet began to fire minute guns.

'Do you wish to reduce sail, sir?' asked Easton anxiously, shouting into his ear.

Drinkwater shook his head. 'She stands up well, Mr Easton, the advantage of a heavy hull.'

'Aye, aye, sir.'

Virago was a fine sea-keeper, bluff and buoyant. Though she rolled deeply it was an easy motion and Drinkwater never entertained any apprehension for her spars. Although at every plunge of her bowsprit much of it immersed she hardly strained a ropeyarn.

'She bruises the grey sea in a most collier-like style, Mr Easton, how was she doing at the last streaming of the log?'

'Six and a half, sir.'

'Tolerably good.'

'Yes sir.'

Two hours later the wisdom of not reducing sail was borne out. In a gap in the snow showers the *London* was again visible flying Number 89.

'Ships astern, or in the rear of the fleet, make more sail!'

'Aye, very well. We've no need of that but I wonder if those in the rear can see it. ' Half an hour later Parker gave up the struggle.

'Number 106, sir, "Wear, the sternmost and leewardmost first and come to the wind on the other tack".'

'Oh, my God,' said Rogers coming on deck to relieve Easton, 'that'll set the cat among the pigeons.'

'That'll do Mr Rogers,' said Drinkwater quickly. 'At least the admiral's had the foresight to do it at the change of watch when all hands should be on deck.'

And so the British fleet stood away from the Danish coast in the early darkness and the biting cold, uncertain of their precise whereabouts and still with no specific orders for the Baltic.

The cold weather continued into the next day while Parker fretted over his reckoning and hove-to for frequent soundings.

'I'll bet those damned pilots aboard *London* are all arguing like the devil as to where the hell we are,' laughed Rogers as he handed the deck over to Trussel who as senior warrant officer after the master kept a deck watch. It was eight in the morning and the gale showed little sign of abating, though the wind had veered a point. It was colder than the previous day and cracked skin and salt water boils were already appearing.

'Hullo, that's a new arrival ain't it Mr Rogers?' asked Drinkwater coming on deck. He indicated a seventy-four, looming out of the murk flying her private number and with a white flag at her mizen. Rogers had not noticed that the ship was not part of the fleet as they stood north east again under easy sail, the ships moving like wraiths through the showers.

'Er, ah . . . yes, sir,' he said flushing.

'*Defiance*, sir,' volunteered Quilhampton hurriedly, 'Rear Admiral Graves, sir, Captain Richard Retalick.'

'Thank you Mr Q.' Quilhampton avoided the glare Rogers threw at him and knew the first lieutenant would later demand an explanation why, if he was such a damned clever little wart, he had not informed the officer of the watch of the sighting.

The forenoon wore on, livened only by the piping of 'Up spirits', the miserable file of men huddled in their greygoes, their cracked lips, red-rimmed eyes and running noses proof that the conditions were abysmal. The only fire permitted aboard a vessel loaded with powder was the galley range and the heat that it dissipated about the ship was soon blown away by the draughts. The officers fared little better, their only real advantage being the ability to drink more heavily and thus fortify themselves against the cold. Mr Jex, whose duties rarely brought him on deck at all, took particular advantage of this privilege.

Edward Drinkwater had received an issue of the heavy-weather clothing that his brother had had the foresight to lay in against service in this northern climate. He had found it surprisingly easy to adapt to life below decks. A heavily built man who could afford to lose weight, his physique had stood up well in the few days he had been on board. His natural sociability and previous experience at living on his wits inclined him to make the best of his circumstances, while his connections with the turf and the stud had made him familiar with the lower orders of contemporary society as well as 'the fancy'. The guilt he felt for what he had done had not yet affected him and although he was periodically swept by grief for Pascale it was swiftly lost in that last image of her in life, her face ecstatic beneath her lover. He relived that second's reaction a hundred times a day, snatching up the sword and hacking it down in ungovernable fury in the turmoil of his imagination.

The rigorous demands of his duties combined with the need to be vigilant against exposing his brother, and hence himself, had left him little time to ponder upon moral issues. When turned below, his physical exhaustion swiftly overcame him and the fear of the law that had motivated his flight to Yarmouth evaporated on board the *Virago*. From his messmates he learned of the numbers of criminals sheltering in the navy, and that the service did not readily give up these living dead, could not afford to if it was to maintain its wooden ramparts against the pernicious influence of Republican France. Edward had relied upon his brother with the simple trust of the irresponsible and Nathaniel had not let him down. He did not know the extent to which Drinkwater had risked his career, his family, even his life. From what Edward had seen of the Royal Navy, the captain of a man of war was a law unto himself. He was fortunate in having a brother in such a position, and delivered his fate into Nathaniel's capable hands.

As to his altered circumstances, Edward was enough of a gambler to accept them as a temporary inconvenience. He was certain they would not last forever and from that sense of impermanence he was able to derive a certain satisfaction. His messmates took no notice of the quiet man amongst them, they lived cheek by jowl with greater eccentricities than his. But the gestures did not go unnoticed by Mr Jex.

'Come man, lively with that cask, damn it.' Mr Jex stood over the three toiling landsmen as they manoeuvred the cask clear of the stow, sweating with the effort of controlling it as the ship pitched and rolled. Mr Jex's rotund figure condescended to hold up a lantern for them as they finally succeeded in up-ending it.

'Open it up then, open it up,' he ordered impatiently, motioning one of the men to pick up the cold chisel lent by Mr Willerton. He watched Waters bend down to take the tool and dismissed the other two with a jerk of his head. Things were working out better than he had supposed. Waters grunted as he levered the inner hoop of the lid and Jex held the lantern closer to read the number branded into the top of the cask.

'Get the damn thing open then,' Jex was sweating himself now, suddenly worried at the notion of being alone in the hold with a murderer. He had to force himself to recover his fugitive mood of moral ascendancy. Circumstances again seemed to come to his aid. Waters staggered back appalled at the smell that rose from the cask of salt pork. Jex's familiarity with the stench ensured he reasserted himself.

'Not used to the stink eh? Too used to comfortable quarters,' Jex paused for emphasis, 'comfortable quarters *like the Blue Fox, eh, Mister Drinkzvater*?' Jex's tiny eyes glittered in the lamplight, searching Edward's face for the reaction of guilt brought on by his accusation.

But the purser was to be disappointed. That slight, emphatic pause had alerted Edward to be on his guard. The quick instinct that in him was a gambler's intuition, while in his brother showed as swift intelligence, caused him to look up in sharp surprise.

'You're mistaken, sir,' he said in the rural Middlesex accent of his youth, 'my name is Waters,' he grinned, 'I'm no relation to the cap'n, Mr Jex.' He shook his head as if in simple wonderment at the mistake and looked down at the mess inside the cask as though swiftly dismissing the matter from his mind.

Jex was non-plussed, suddenly unsure of himself, and yet . . .

Waters looked up. Jex was still staring at him. He shrugged. 'As for the Blue Fox, was that what you said? I don't know anything about such a place. Tavern is it? Strewth, if I could afford to live in a tavern I'd not be aboard here, sir.'

That much was true, thought Edward, as he strove to maintain a matter-of-fact tone in his voice though inwardly alarmed that he had been discovered.

But Jex was not satisfied. 'Landsman volunteer aren't you?'

'That's right, sir.'

'What did you volunteer for?'

'Woman trouble, Mr Jex, woman trouble.'

'I know,' began Jex, a sudden vicious desire spurring him to provoke this man to some act of insubordination that would have him at the gratings to be flogged by his own brother. But his intentions were disturbed by the arrival of Mr Quilhampton with a message that the purser was to report to Lieutenant Rogers without delay. He had lost his chance, and Edward was doubly vigilant to avoid the purser as much as possible, and even, if necessary, take matters into his own hands.

Drinkwater watched the brig beating up from the east with the alarm signal flying from her foremasthead. She reminded him of *Hellebore* and would pass close under *Virago*'s stern as she made for *London* to speak with the admiral.

'The *Cruizer*, sir, eighteen-gun brig, same as our old *Hellebore*.'

'I was just thinking that, Mr Trussel.' The two men watched her approach, saw her captain jump into the main chains with a speaking trumpet. Drinkwater had met James Brisbane in Yarmouth and raised his hat in salutation.

'Afternoon Drinkwater!' Brisbane yelled as his ship surged past. 'We sighted land around Boubjerg. We must be twenty leagues south of our reckoning!' He waved, then jumped inboard as his brig covered the last two miles to the flagship.

'God's bones!' Drinkwater muttered. Sixty miles! A degree of latitude, but it was no wonder, since they had seen neither sun, moon nor stars since leaving Yarmouth. It was equally surprising that the bulk of the fleet was still together.

A little later the flagship signalled, firing guns to emphasise the importance of the order. The fleet tacked to the north west and once more clawed its way offshore.

The following day the battleship *Elephant* arrived with the news that the *Invincible*, which they had last seen leaving Yarmouth Roads by way of the Cockle Gat, had been wrecked on the Haisbro Sand with the loss of most of her crew. As this intelligence permeated the fleet Drinkwater was overwhelmed with a sense of impending doom, that the whole enterprise was imperilled by the omens. And his fears for Edward and himself only seemed to lend potency to these misgivings.

*

That evening the weather showed signs of moderating. Shortly after dark as he sat writing up his journal by the light of a swaying lantern Drinkwater was disturbed by a knock at his cabin door. 'Yes?'

Mr Jex entered. He was flushed and smelt of rum. He held what appeared to be a newspaper in his hand.

'Yes, Mr Jex? What is it?' Jex made no reply but held out the paper to Drinkwater. Unsatisfied with the replies of Waters, Jex sensed the landsman's cunning was more than a match for him. And the purser was nervous of a man he suspected of murder. To himself he disguised this fear in the argument that it was really Lieutenant Drinkwater who was the target for his desire to settle a score. The rum served to restore his resolve to act.

Drinkwater bent over the print. As he read he felt as though a cold hand was squeezing his guts. The colour drained from his face and the perspiration appeared upon his forehead. He tried in vain to dismiss the image the description called to mind.

From somewhere above him came Jex's voice, filled with the righteous zeal of an archangel. 'I know the man you brought aboard in Yarmouth is your brother. And that he is wanted for this murder.'

Chapter Twelve *19–23 March 1801*

A Turbot Bright

The cabin filled with a silence only emphasised by the creak of *Virago*'s fabric as she worked in the seaway. The rudder stock ground in the trunking that ran up the centre of the transom between the windows and stern chasers.

Drinkwater crossed his arms to conceal the shaking of his hands and leaned back in his chair, still staring down at the newspaper on the table. Its contents exposed the whole matter and Jex, of all people, knew everything. He looked up at Jex and was made suddenly angry by the smug look of satisfaction on the purser's pig-like features. His resentment at having been forced into such a false position by both Edward and this unpleasant little man before him combined with his weariness at trying to argue a way out of an untenable position. His anger boiled over, made worse by his awareness of the need to bluff.

'God damn it, sir, you are drunk! What the devil d'you think you are about, making such outrageous suggestions? Eh? Come, what are these allegations again?'

'The man Waters is your brother . . .'

'For God's sake, Mr Jex, what on earth makes you think that?'

'I saw you together in the Blue Fox, a house in which I have an interest.'

A piece of the jig-saw as to how Jex had discovered his deception was now revealed to Drinkwater. Even as he strove to think of some way out of the mess he continued to attack the purser's certainty. He barked a short, humourless and forced laugh.

'Hah! And d'you think I'd turn my brother forward, eh? To be started by Matchett and his mates?'

'If he had committed murder.' Jex nodded to the paper that lay between them.

Drinkwater leaned forward and put both hands on the *Yarmouth*

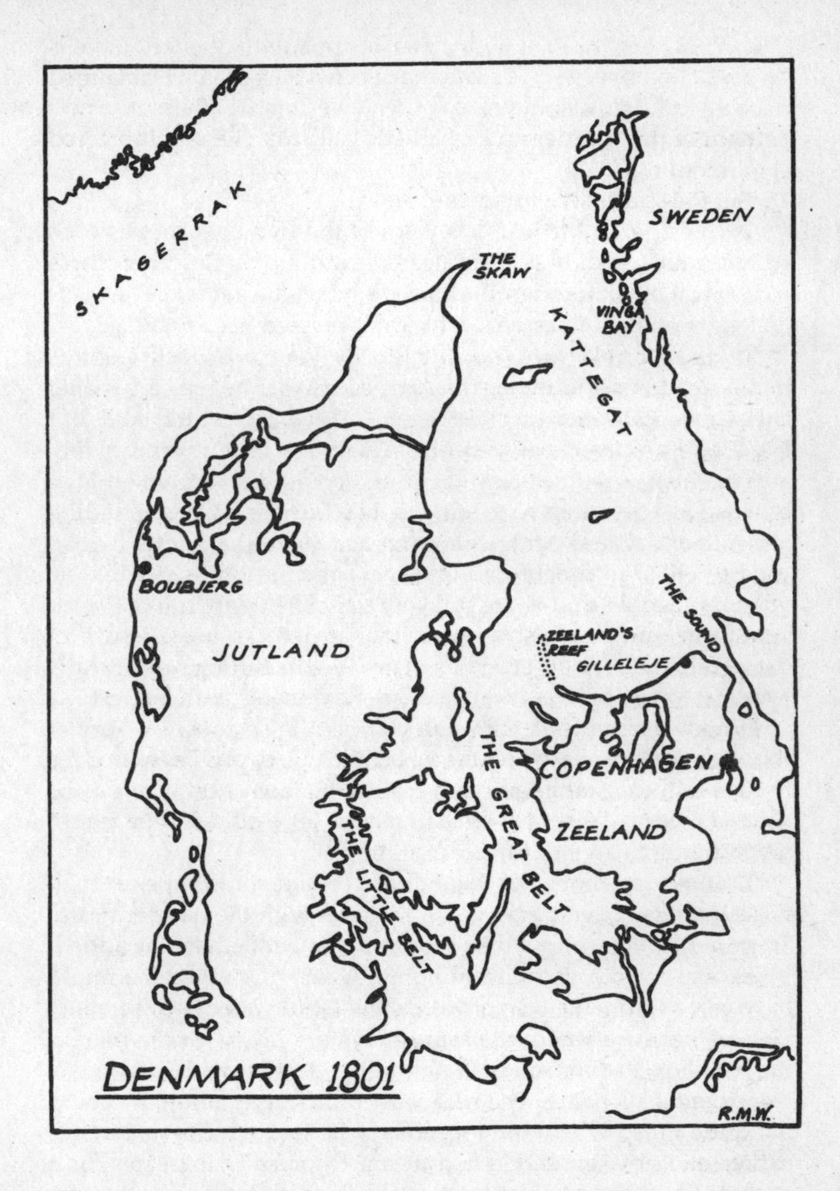
SKAGERRAK
THE SKAW
SWEDEN
VINGA BAY
KATTEGAT
BOUBJERG
JUTLAND
THE SOUND
ZEELAND'S REEF
GILLELEJE
THE GREAT BELT
COPENHAGEN
ZEELAND
THE LITTLE BELT
DENMARK 1801
R.M.W.

Courier. 'Mr Jex,' he said with an air of apparent patience, 'there is no possible connection you can make between a man who claimed to be my brother whom you saw in a tavern in Chatham, the perpetrator of this murder and a pathetic landsman who volunteered at Yarmouth.'

'But the similarity of names . . .'

'A coincidence Mr Jex.' The eyes of the two men met as each searched for a weakness. Drinkwater saw doubt in the other man's face, saw it break through the alcohol-induced confidence. Jex was no longer on the offensive. Drinkwater pressed his advantage.

'I will be frank with you, Mr Jex, for your misconstruction is highly seditious and under the Articles of War,' he paused, seeing a dawning realisation cross Jex's mind. 'I see you understand. But I will be frank as far as I can be. There is a little mystery hereabouts,' he was deliberately vague and could see a frown on Jex's brow now. 'I do not have to tell you that the liberal Corresponding Societies of England, Mr Jex, those organisations that Mr Chauvelin tried to enlist in ninety-one to foment revolution here while he was French ambassador, are still very active. They are full of French spies and you can rest assured that a fleet as big as ours in Yarmouth has been observed by many eyes including some hostile eyes that have doubtless watched our movements with interest . . .'

Drinkwater smiled to himself. Jex was a false patriot, a Tory of the worst kind. A place-seeking jobber, jealous of privilege, anxious to maintain the status quo and feather his own nest, even as he aspired to social advancement. To men of Jex's odious type fear of revolution was greater than fear of the pox.

'I cannot say more, Mr Jex, but I have had some experience in these matters . . . you may verify the facts with the quartermaster Tregembo, if you cannot take the word of a gentleman,' he added.

Jex was silent, his mind hunting for any advantage he might have gained from the web of words that Drinkwater was spinning. He was not sure where the area of mystery lay; with the man in the Blue Fox, the landsman Waters or the murder with its strange, coincidental surname. The rum was confusing him and he could not quite grasp where the ascendancy he had felt a few minutes earlier had now gone. He had meant to press Drinkwater for a return of his money, or at least establish some hold over his captain that he might turn to his own advantage. He had been certain of his arguments as he had rehearsed them in the spirit room half an hour ago. Now he was dimly aware of a mystery he did not understand but which was vaguely dangerous to him, of Drinkwater's real authority and the awesome power of the Articles of War which even a pip-squeak lieutenant might invoke against him. Jex's intelligence had let him down. Only his cunning could extricate him.

'I am not . . .'

'Mr Jex,' said Drinkwater brusquely, suddenly sick of the whole charade, 'you are the worse for drink. I have already confided in you more than I should and I would caution you to be circumspect with what I have told you. I am unhappy about both your motive and your manner in drawing this whole matter to my attention.' He stood up, 'Good night Mr Jex.'

The purser turned away as *Virago* sat her stern heavily in a trough. Jex stumbled and grabbed for the edge of the table.

Drinkwater suddenly grinned. 'Take your time, Mr Jex, and be careful how you go. After all if Waters is a murderer you may find yourself eased overboard one dark night. I've known it happen.' Drinkwater, who knew nothing of the purser's cowardice, had touched the single raw nerve that Jex possessed. The possibility of being killed or maimed had never occurred to him when he had solicited the post of purser aboard the *Virago*. Indeed there seemed little likelihood of the ship ever putting to sea again. Now, since witnessing the horribly wounded Mason die in agony, he thought often of death as he lay in the lonely coffin-like box of his cot.

Drinkwater watched the purser lurch from the cabin. He felt like a fencer who had achieved a lucky parry, turned aside a blade that had seemed to have penetrated his guard, yet had allowed his opponent to recover.

He did not know if Jex had approached Edward, and could only hope that Tregembo's explanation, which he was sure Jex would seek in due course, would not betray him. But it was the only alibi he had. He found his hands were trembling again now that he was alone. From the forward bulkhead the portraits of Elizabeth and Charlotte Amelia watched impassively and brought the sweat to his brow at the enormity of what he had done. He wondered how successfully he had concealed the matter behind the smokescreen of duty. What was it Lettsom had said about concealing inadequacy that way? He shrugged off the recollection. Such philosophical niceties were irrelevant. There was no way to go but forwards and of one thing he was now sure. He had no alternative but to carry out his bluff. There was no time to wait for a reply to his letter to Lord Dungarth.

He would have to land Edward very soon.

The following morning dawned fine and clear. The wind had hauled north westerly and the fleet made sail to the eastward. The little gun-brigs were taken in tow by the battleships. Soon after dawn the whole vast mass of ships, making six or seven knots, observed to starboard the low line of the Danish coast. First blue-grey, it hardened to pale green with a fringe of white breakers. At nine o'clock on the morning of March 19th the fleet began to pass the lighthouse on The Skaw and turned south east, into the Kattegat. The Danes had extinguished the lighthouse by night, but in the pale morning sunshine it formed a conspicuous mark for the ships as each hauled her yards for the new course. At one o'clock Parker ordered the frigate *Blanche* to proceed ahead and gain news of the progress of Nicholas Vansittart. He had left Harwich a fortnight earlier in the Hamburg packet with a final offer to Count Bernstorff, the Danish Minister.

After the hardships of the last few days the sunshine felt warm and cheering. First lieutenants throughout the fleet ordered their men to wash clothes and hammocks. The nettings and lower rigging of the ships were soon bright with fluttering shirts and trousers. The sight of the enemy coast to starboard brought smiles and jokes to the raw faces of the men. Officers studied its monotonous line through their glasses as though they might discern their fates thereby.

The sense of corporate pride that could animate British seamen, hitherto absent from Parker's fleet, seemed not dead but merely dormant, called forth by the vernal quality of the day. This reanimation of spirit was best demonstrated by Nelson himself, ever a man attuned to the morale of his men. As the wind fell light in the late afternoon he called away his barge and an inquisitive fleet watched him pulled over to the mighty *London*. One of his seamen had caught a huge turbot and presented it as a gift to the little one-armed admiral.

In a characteristically impetuous gesture beneath which might be discerned an inflexible sense of purpose, Nelson personally conveyed the fish to his superior. It broke the ice between the two men. When the story got about the fleet by the mysterious telegraphy that transmitted such news, Lettsom composed his now expected verse:

'Nelson's prepared to grow thinner
And give Parker a turbot bright,
If Parker will only eat dinner,
And let Lord Nelson fight.'

But Mr Jex had not shared the general euphoria as they passed the Skaw. He had slept badly and woke with a rum-induced hangover that left his head throbbing painfully. He had lost track of the cogent arguments that had seemed to deliver Lieutenant Drinkwater into his hands the previous evening. His mind was aware only that he had been thwarted. To Jex it was like dishonour.

Soon after the change of watch at eight in the morning as the curious on deck were staring at the lighthouse on the Skaw, Jex waylaid Tregembo and offered him a quid of tobacco.

'Thank 'ee, zur,' he said, regarding the purser with suspicion.

'Tregembo isn't it?'

'Aye, zur.' Tregembo bit a lump off the quid and began to chew it.

'You have known Lieutenant Drinkwater a long time, eh, Tregembo?' The quartermaster nodded. 'How long?'

'I first met Mr Drinkwater when he were a midshipman, aboard the *Cyclops*, frigate, Cap'n Henry Hope . . . during the American War.'

'And you've known him since?'

'No zur, I next met him when I was drafted aboard the *Kestrel* cutter, zur, we was employed on special service.'

'Special service, eh?'

'Aye zur, very special . . . on the French coast afore the outbreak of the present war.' A sly look had entered the Cornishman's eyes. 'I'm in Mr Drinkwater's employ, zur . . .'

'Ah yes, of course, then perhaps you can tell me if Mr Drinkwater has a brother, eh?' Tregembo regarded the fat, peculating officer and remembered what Drinkwater had said about Waters and what he had learned at Petersfield. He rolled the quid over his tongue:

'Brother? No zur, the lieutenant has no brother, Mr Jex zur.'

'Are you sure?'

'I been with him constant these past nine years and I don't know that he ever had a brother.'

'And this special service . . .'

'Aye zur, we was employed on the *Hellebore*, brig, under Lord Nelson's orders.' Tregembo remembered what Drinkwater had said to him and now that he had seen what Jex was driving at he was less forthcoming.

'Under Lord Nelson, eh, well, well . . . so Mr Drinkwater's highly thought of in certain quarters then?'

'Aye zur, he's well acquainted with Lord Dungarth.' Tregembo was as proud of Drinkwater's connection with the peer as Jex was impressed.

'It is surprising then Tregembo, that he is no more than a lieutenant.'

'Beggin' your pardon but 'tis a fucking disgrace . . . It's a long story, zur, but Mr Drinkwater thrashed a bugger on the *Cyclops* and the bastard got even with him in the matter of a commission . . .' A smile crossed Tregembo's face. 'Leastaways he thought he'd bested him, but he ended in the hospital at the Cape, zur.' He leaned forward, his jaw rotating the quid as he spoke. 'Men don't cross the lieutenant too successfully, zur, leastaways not sensible men.'

'Bloody wind's still freshening, sir, and I don't like the look of it.' Rogers held his hat on, his tarpaulin flapping round him as he stared to windward. The white streaks of sleet blew across the deck, showing faintly in the binnacle lamplight. Both the officers staggered as *Virago* snubbed round to her anchor, sheering in the wind, jerking the hull and straining the cable.

'Rouse out another cable, Sam,' Drinkwater shouted in Rogers's ear, 'we'll veer away more scope.'

The good weather had not lasted the day. Hardly had the fleet come to an anchor in Vingå Bay than the treacherous wind had backed and strengthened. Now, at midnight, a full gale was blowing from the west south west, catching them on a lee shore and threatening to wreck them on the Swedish coast.

Drinkwater watched the grey and black shapes of the hands as they moved about the deck. He was glad he had been able to provide them with warm clothing. Tonight none of them would get much sleep and it was the least he could do for them. They were half-way through bringing up the second cable when they saw the first rocket. It reminded them that out in the howling blackness, beyond the circumscribed limit of their visible horizon, other men in other ships were toiling like themselves. The arc of sputtering sparks terminated in a baleful blue glare that hung in the sky and shone faintly, illuminating the lower masts and spars of the *Virago* before dying.

'Someone in distress,' shouted Easton.

'Mind it ain't us, Mr Easton, get a lead over the side to see if we are dragging!'

Suddenly from forward an anonymous voice screamed: 'Starb'd bow! 'Ware Starb'd bow!'

Drinkwater looked up to see a pyramid of masts and spars and the faint gleam of a half-set topsail above a black mass of darkness: the interposition of a huge hull between himself and the tumbling wavetops that had been visible there a moment earlier.

'Cut that cable!' he shouted with all the power in his lungs. Forward a quick-witted man took up an axe from under the fo'c's'le. Drinkwater waited only long enough to see the order understood before shouting again:

'Foretopmast stays'l halliards there! Cast loose and haul away! Sheet to starboard!' There was a second's suspense then the grinding crunch and trembling as the strange ship drove across their bow, carrying away the bowsprit. She was a huge ship and there was shouting and confusion upon her decks.

'Christ! It's the fucking *London*!' shouted Rogers who had caught a glimpse of a dark flag at her mainmasthead. All Drinkwater was aware of were the three pale stripes of her gun decks and the fact that in her passing she was pulling *Virago* round to larboard. There was more shouting including the unmistakably patrician accents of a flagship lieutenant demanding through his speaking trumpet what the devil they were doing there.

'Trying to remain at anchor, you stupid blockhead!' Rogers bawled back as a final rendering from forward told where *Virago* had torn her bowsprit free of *London*'s main chains. The unknown axeman succeeded in cutting the final strands of her cable.

'We're under way, Easton, keep that God damn lead going.'

Easton had a lantern in the chains in a flash and Quilhampton ran aft reporting the foretopmast staysail aloft.

'Sheet's still a-weather, sir . . .'

'Cast it loose and haul aft the lee sheet.'

'Aye, aye . . .'

Virago's head had been cast off the wind, thanks to *London*. Now Drinkwater had to drive her to windward, clear of the shallows under their lee.

'Spanker, Rogers, get the bloody spanker on her otherwise her head'll pay off too much . . .' Rogers shouted for men and Drinkwater jumped down into the waist. He wished to God he had a cutter like the old *Kestrel* that could claw to windward like a knife's edge. Suddenly *Virago*'s weatherly, sea-kindly bluff bows were a death trap.

'Mr Matchett! Will she take a jib or is the bowsprit too far gone?'

'Reckon I c'd set summat forrad . . .'

'See to it,' snapped Drinkwater. 'Hey! You men there, a hand with these staysails!' He attacked the rope stoppings on the mizen staysail and after two men had come to his aid he moved forward to the foot of the foremast where the main staysail was stowed. His hands felt effeminately soft but he grunted at the freezing knots until more men, seeing what he was about, came to his assistance.

'Halliards there lads! Hoist away . . . up she goes, lively there! Now we'll sail her out like a yacht!' He turned aft. 'Belay that main topsail, Graham, she'll point closer under this canvas . . .'

'Aye, aye, sir.'

'Cap'n, cap'n, zur.'

'Yes? Here Tregembo, I'm here!'

'Master says she's shoaling . . .'

'God's bones!' He hurried aft to where Easton was leaning outboard, gleaming wetly in the lamplight from where a wave had sluiced him and the leadsman. Drinkwater grabbed his shoulder and Easton looked up from the leadline. He shook his head. 'Shoaling, sir.'

'Shit!' he tried to think and peered over the side. The faint circle of light emitted by the lantern showed the sea at one second ten feet beneath them, next almost up to the chains. But the streaks of air bubbles streaming down-wind from the tumbling wave-caps were moving astern: *Virago* had headway. He recalled the chart, a shoaling of the bay towards its southward end. He patted Easton's shoulder. 'Keep it goin', Mr Easton.' Then he jumped inboard and made for the poop.

'Steer full and bye!'

Out to starboard another blue rocket soared into the air and he was aware that the sleet had stopped. He could see dark shapes of other ships, tossing and plunging with here and there the gleam of a sail as some fought their way to windward while others tried to hold onto their anchors. He remembered his advice to Quilhampton on the subject of anchors. He had lost one now, and although he had not lost the ship, neither had he yet saved her.

A moment later another sleet squall enveloped them. He looked up at the masthead pendant. *Virago* was heading at least a point higher without square sails and Matchett had succeeded in getting a jib up on what was left of the bowsprit. He wondered how much leeway they were making and tried looking astern at the wake but he could see nothing. He wondered what had become of the *London* and what old Parker was making of the night. Perhaps 'Batter Pudding' would be a widow before dawn. Parker would not be the first admiral to go down with his ship. He did not know whether Admiral Totty had survived the wreck of the *Invincible*, but Balchen had been lost with *Victory* on the Caskets fifty years earlier, and Shovell had died on the beach in the Scillies after the wreck of the *Association*. But poor Parker might end ignominiously, a prisoner of the Swedes.

'Quite a night, sir,' Rogers came up. He had lost his hat and his hair was plastered upon his head.

'Quite a night, Sam.'

'We've set all the fore and aft canvas we can, she seems to sail quite well.'

'She'll do,' said Drinkwater tersely, 'If she weathers the point, she'll do very well.'

'Old Willerton's been over the side on the end of the foretack.'

'What the devil for?'

'To see if his "leddy" is still there.'

'Well is it?' asked Drinkwater with sudden superstitious anxiety.

'Yes,' Rogers laughed and Drinkwater felt a sense of relief, then chid himself for a fool.

'Pipe "Up spirits", Sam, the poor devils deserve it.'

Virago did weather the point and dawn found her hands wet, cold and red-eyed, anxiously staring astern and out on either beam. Of the fifty-eight ships that had anchored in Vingå Bay only thirty-eight were now in company. They beat slowly to windward, occasionally running perilously close together as they tacked, grey shapes tossing in heavy grey seas on which was something new, something to add greater danger to their plight: ice floes.

Many of the absent ships were the smaller members of the fleet, particularly the gun-brigs, but most of the bombs were still in company and the *Anne Reed* made up under *Virago*'s larboard quarter. Once they had an offing they bore away to the southward.

The wind shifted a little next day then, at one bell in the first watch, it backed south westerly and freshened again. Two hours later *Virago* followed the more weatherly ships into the anchorage of Skalderviken in the shelter of the Koll. Drinkwater collapsed across his cot only to be woken at four next morning. The wind had increased to storm force. Even in the lee of the land *Virago* pitched her bluffbow into the steep seas and flung the spray over her bow to be whipped aft, catching the unwary on the face and inducing the agonising wind-ache as it evaporated. Rain and sleet compounded the discomfort and Drinkwater succeeded in veering a second cable onto his one remaining anchor. At daylight, instead of rigging out a new bowsprit, the tired men were aloft striking the topgallant masts, lowering the heavy lower yards in their jeers and lashing them across the rails.

Then, having exhausted themselves in self-preservation, the wind eased. It continued to drop during the afternoon and just after midnight the night-signal to weigh was made from *St George*. Nelson, anxious to prosecute the war in spite of, or perhaps because of, the disappearance of Parker, was thwarted before the fleet could move. The wind again freshened and the laboriously hove in cables were veered away again.

Nelson repeated the signal to weigh at seven in the morning and this time the weather obliged. An hour and a half later the remnants of the British squadrons in the Baltic beat out of Skalderviken and then bore away towards the Sound and Copenhagen.

By noon the gale had eased. *London* rejoined, together with some of the other ships. The flagship had been ashore on an uncharted shoal off Varberg castle and the *Russell* had had a similar experience attempting to tow off the gun-brig *Tickler*. Both had escaped.

Less fortunate was the gun-brig *Blazer* which also ran ashore at Varberg and was captured by the Swedes.

The fleet was hove to when Parker rejoined to await the results of Vansittart's embassy. Just before dark the *Blanche* was sighted making up from the south. The news that she brought was eagerly awaited by men who had had a bellyful of shilly-shallying.

Chapter Thirteen *24–28 March 1801*

Councils of Timidity

There are many levels at which a man can worry and Drinkwater was no exception. Over-riding every moment of his life, waking and sleeping, was concern for his ship and its performance within so large a fleet. Beneath this constant preoccupation lay a growing conviction that the expedition had been left too late. In the two days since *Blanche* rejoined the fleet a number of alarming rumours had circulated. It was learned that Vansittart's terms had been rejected by Count Bernstorff and the Danish government. Both Vansittart and Drummond, the accredited British envoy to the Danish court, had been given their passports and told to leave. Britons resident in Denmark had been advised to quit the country while the Swedish navy, already possessing its first British prize, the *Blazer,* was making belligerent preparations at Carlscrona. Worse still, the Russians were reported cutting through the ice at Revel.

But it was the inactivity of their own admiral that most worried the British. Every hour the Commander-in-Chief waited, robbed them of surprise, and every hour the fleet lay idle increased the gossip and rumour that spread from passing boat to gunroom to lower deck. Vansittart had given Parker formal instructions to commence hostilities in one breath and warned him of the formidable preparations made at Copenhagen in another. Drummond endorsed the determination of the Danes and promised the hesitant Parker a bloody nose. After the first conference aboard *London,* at which Nelson was present, Parker had excluded his second-in-command and Rear Admiral Graves from further consultation. Instead he interviewed the pilots from the Hull Trinity House who were as apprehensive as the admiral and informed Parker that they were familiar with the navigation of The Sound alone, and could undertake no responsibility for the navigation of the Great Belt. Nelson, who saw the Russians as the greatest threat, thought that defeat of the Tsar would automatically destroy the Baltic Alliance, wished to take a detachment of the fleet by the Great Belt and strike directly at Revel. He had made his recommendations in writing and Dommett, the captain of the fleet, had emerged from Parker's cabin, his face a mask of agony, to reveal to the assembled officers on the *London*'s quarterdeck that Parker had struck out every single suggestion made by Vice-Admiral Nelson.

It was a story that had gone round the fleet like wildfire and, together with the rumour circulated from *Blanche* about Danish preparations, added to the feeling that they were too late.

Lieutenant Drinkwater was a prey to all these and other worries as he stood upon *Virago's* poop on the freezing morning of March 26th. He was staring through his glass at a large boat flying the red flag of Denmark together with a white flag of truce, as it pulled through the fifty-two British ships anchored off Nakke Head at the entrance to The Sound.

Meanwhile in *London*'s great cabin, a confident young aide-decamp with a message from Governor Stricker at Elsinore told Parker that if his guns were no better than his pen he had better return to England. There were two hundred heavy cannon at Cronbourg Castle, together with a garrison of three thousand men and Parker, used to the clear waters of the West Indies, was apprehensive of dark nights and fields of ice. Parker's hesitation was obvious to the young Danish officer and the worried countenances of *London*'s officers, as they waited in the cold, led him to conclude they shared their admiral's apprehensions.

Drinkwater began to pace *Virago*'s poop as the watch idled round the deck, needlessly coiling ropes and unenthusiastically chipping the scale off a box of shot set on the after mortar hatch. A low mumble came from them and exactly reflected the mood of the entire fleet.

Two days earlier, after conferring with Parker, Vansittart and Drummond had been sent home in the lugger *Kite*. Drinkwater had taken advantage of the departure of the lugger to send a letter to Lord Dungarth and the subject of that letter was the fundamental worry that underlay every thought of every waking hour. Since the interview with Jex, Drinkwater had striven to work out a solution to the problem of Edward. Sweating at the thought of his guilt, of the reception of his first letter to Dungarth sent by Lady Parker, and of Jex's knowledge, he had spent hours formulating a plan, considering every turn of events and of how each circumstance would be regarded by others. Now the constant delays denied him the opportunity to land Edward. The last few days had had a nightmare quality enhanced by the bad weather, the freezing cold and the continual nagging worries over the fleet itself.

For the first time in months he had a nightmare, the terrifying spectre of a white clad woman who reared over his supine body to the clanking of chains. With the illogical certainty of dreams she seemed to rise higher and higher above him, yet never diminished in size, while her Medusa head became the smiling face of someone he knew. He woke shivering yet soaked in sweat, his heart beating violently. Compelled by some subconscious urge he had risen in his night-shirt and struck a light to the cabin lantern and spread out the roll of canvas from the bottom of his sea-chest. Already the paint was cracking but, in the light of the lantern, it did not detract from the face that looked back at him: the face in his dream. The portrait was larger than the two now hanging on the forward bulkhead. It showed a young woman with auburn hair piled upon her head. Pearls were entwined in the coiffure that was at once negligent and contrived. Her creamy shoulders were bare and her breasts were just visible behind a wisp of gauze. The grey eyes looked directly out of the canvas and Drinkwater shivered, not from cold, but with the sensation of someone walking upon his grave. The lovely Hortense Montholon had been brought off a French beach in the last days of peace. For months she had masqueraded as an émigrée, sending information from England to her lover Edouard Santhonax in Paris. She had been returned to France by Lord Dungarth and married Santhonax on his escape following the battle of Camperdown.

Drinkwater had acquired the portrait by his capture of the French frigate *Antigone* in the Red Sea. She had been commanded by the same Santhonax and, though he had escaped yet again, Drinkwater had kept the canvas. It had lain in the bottom of his sea-chest, cut from its wooden stretcher and hidden from his wife, for it was unlikely that Elizabeth would understand its fascination. But to Drinkwater it symbolised something more than the likeness of a beautiful woman. The face of Hortense Santhonax was the face of the enemy, not the face of the tow-haired Danes but a manifestation of the force now consuming the whole continent of Europe.

He could not see it objectively yet, but the liberal allure of the French Revolution had long faded. Even those staunch republicans, the Americans, had disassociated themselves from the lawless disregard for order with which the French pursued their foreign policies or instructed their ragged, irresistible and rapacious armies. He remembered something Dungarth had said the night they landed Hortense upon the beach at Criel: 'Nine parts of humanity is motivated by a combination of self-interest and apathy. Only the tenth part hungers for power, and it is this which a prudent people guards itself against. In France the tenth part has the upper hand.' As he stood shivering in the dawn Drinkwater glimpsed the future in a flash. This rupture with Denmark, whatever its sinister motivations from the steppes, was a single symptom of a greater cancer, a cancer that fed upon a doctrinaire philosophy with a spurious validity. He was engaged in a mighty struggle between moderation and excess, and his spartan life had filled him with a horror of excess.

A wild knocking at his door caused him to roll the portrait up. 'What is it?'

'The admiral's made the signal to prepare to weigh, sir.' It was Quilhampton's voice. 'Wind is fresh westerly, sir, and it's eight bells in the middle watch.'

'Very well, call all hands, I'll be up directly.'

The day that followed had been a disaster. In a rising wind which caused problems to the smaller vessels in weighing their anchors, the fleet had got under way at daylight. Led by the 74-gun *Edgar* with her yellow topsides, they beat to the westward, along the north coast of the flat, featureless, coast of Zeeland. *Edgar*'s captain, George Murray, had recently surveyed the Great Belt and it was by this passage that Sir Hyde Parker had finally decided to pass into the Baltic. The Commander-in-Chief did not hold his determination very long. In the wake of *Edgar*, slightly inshore of the main battle fleet, the smaller ships tacked wearily to windward. Ahead of *Virago* were the seven bombs, astern of her the other tenders. At eleven o'clock while Drinkwater consulted his chart, listened to the monotonous chant of the leadsman and occasionally referred to the old, worn notebook left him years earlier as part of Blackmore's bequest, the *Zebra* struck the Zeeland's Reef.

Alarmed by the lookout's shout, Drinkwater watched *Zebra*'s fore topgallant go by the board and ordered *Virago* tacked at once. Soon after, *Edgar* had flown *Virago*'s pennant with the order to assist *Zebra* and he had sent away his boats with two spare spars to lash across their gunwhales in order to carry out her anchor.

He had watched Rogers pull away over the choppy grey sea and been forced to kick his own heels in idleness until, just before dark, the combined efforts of the bomb ships' boats succeeded in getting *Zebra* off the reef.

While Drinkwater had spent the afternoon at anchor, Parker had been told an even more alarming piece of news. Someone in the flagship had informed the Commander-in-Chief that greater risks would have to be run by taking the fleet through the Great Belt. Alarmed by this and the accident to *Zebra*, Parker countermanded his orders and the fleet was ordered to return to its anchorage off Nakke Head. *Virago*, escorting the *Zebra*, had once again dropped her anchor at midnight, and now, in the chilly sunshine of the following morning, Drinkwater looked across to where Mr Quilhampton and a party from *Virago* were helping the *Zebra*'s people get up a new fore topgallant mast.

On his own fo'c's'le Mr Matchett was putting the finishing touches to the gammoning of their own refitted bowsprit. Over the rest of *Virago* the mood of listless despair hung like a cloud.

At last Drinkwater saw the Danish boat leave *London*'s side and though during the afternoon reports came down to him where he dozed in his cabin, that Murray, Nelson, Graves and other officers were all visiting the flagship, nothing else happened.

Drinkwater woke from his sleep at about four o'clock. He could not afterwards explain it, but his mind was resolved over the problem of Edward. He would brook no further delay. He passed word for Quilhampton and Rogers.

'Ah, Mr Rogers, I wish you to have the long boat made ready an hour before daylight with a barrel of biscuit in it, together with water barricoes, mast and sail. I want a crew told off tonight, say six men, with Tregembo as leading hand. Mr Quilhampton will command the boat and I shall accompany it. In the unlikely event of our being absent when the signal is made to weigh, you are to take charge. I will give you that order in writing when I leave.'

'Very good, sir, may I ask . . .?'

'No, you may not.'

Rogers looked offended and turned on his heel. Drinkwater called him back.

'I do not want any of your irreverent speculation on this matter, Sam. Be pleased to remember that.'

'Aye aye, sir.' Drinkwater raised his eyebrows and stared significantly at Quilhampton.

'The same goes for you, Mr Q.'

'Yes sir.'

'Very well. Now pass word for the volunteer Waters to come aft and do you, Mr Q, mount a guard on my cabin and see we are not disturbed.'

Rogers opened his mouth to protest, thought better of it, and strode from the cabin. Drinkwater waited for Edward to appear, occupying the time by rummaging in a canvas bag he had had brought into the cabin by an inquisitive Mr Jex.

A knock at the door was followed by Mr Quilhampton's head. 'Waters is here now, sir.'

'Very well, show him in.'

Edward entered the cabin and stood awkwardly, looking around with a curious sheepishness. It suddenly struck Drinkwater that a month or two more might have made Edward into a seaman. Already he was lean and fit and had not been long enough on salt beef for it to have made much difference to him. But it was his attitude that most struck Drinkwater. Four months ago they had met as equals, now Edward had all the inherent awkwardness of one who felt socially inferior. The realisation embarrassed Drinkwater.

'How are you?' he asked too brusquely for Edward to perceive any change in their bizarre relationship.

'Well enough . . . sir.'

'How have you been treated?'

'The same as all your seamen,' Edward replied with a trace of bitterness, 'I have no complaints.'

Drinkwater bit off a tart rebuke and poured two glasses of blackstrap. He handed one to Edward then went to the door. 'Mr Q, I want a bowl of hot water from the galley upon the instant.'

'A bowl of hot water, sir?' He caught the gleam in Drinkwater's eye. 'Er, yes sir.'

'Sit down Ned, sit, down.' Drinkwater closed the door. 'Your circumstances are about to change. Whether 'tis for the better I cannot say, but listen carefully to what I tell you.' He paused to collect his thoughts.

'Jex, the purser, has tumbled you. He saw a cursed newspaper report about the murder and also saw you in the Blue Fox, at Chatham. You knew of this?'

Edward nodded. 'I did not know how he had found out, but he approached me . . .'

'You did not . . .?'

'Confess? Good God no! I merely acted dumb, as any seaman does in the presence of an officer.' The ghost of a smile crossed Edward's face. 'What did you do about Mr Jex?' The anxiety was now plain.

Drinkwater sighed. 'Bluffed, Ned, bluffed. Denied you were my brother, said the name of the suspected murderer was a coincidence then gave him to understand that there might be something of a mystery surrounding the whole affair, but that it was not his concern . . . come in!'

A heavy silence hung in the cabin as Quilhampton ushered in the messman with the bowl of water. Both rating and mate could scarcely disguise their curiosity. It would be all over *Virago* in a matter of moments that Waters, the landsman volunteer, was taking wine with *Virago's* commander. But Nathaniel no longer cared. Perhaps some apparent unconcern would lend credibility to what he proposed. Edward did not seem to have noticed, but waited only for the intruders to leave before bursting out:

'What the hell d'you mean you told him there was something of a mystery . . .'

'God damn it, Ned, I've lied for you, risked my career, abused my position of command and maybe jeopardised my whole life for brotherly bloody affection! D'you not think a flat denial would only have increased Jex's inquisitiveness. Mr Jex is not to be counted among my most loyal officers, he is seeking to avenge a grudge. But he is not stupid enough to risk his suspicions against the Articles of War, nor bright enough not to be a little confused by what I have told him. Perhaps he will work it all through and conclude I have deceived him; if that is the case his malice will be thereby increased. But by that time you will be gone.'

Edward shook his head. 'I don't understand . . .'

'My shaving things are lying on the cabin chest there,' he indicated the cotton roll, 'do you shave while I talk . . . Now, I wrote from Yarmouth to Lord Dungarth. I was employed by him some years ago in secret operations on the French and Dutch coasts. He is a spy-master, a puppet-master he calls himself, and *may* be able to find you some employment . . .'

'What the devil did you say about me for God's sake?' asked Edward lathering himself.

'Only that a person known to me was anxious to be of service to his country, had asked for my protection and spoke fluent French. That this person might prove of some value for a patriotic service in a Baltic state. His lordship is intelligent enough to draw his own conclusions . . .'

'Especially if he reads the newspapers,' muttered Edward as the razor rasped down his tanned cheek. He swished the razor in water and turned to his brother.

'So I am to become a puppet, to dance to his lordship's string-pulling, eh?'

'You have scant reason for bitterness, Edward,' said Drinkwater sharply, 'I would have thought it preferable to dancing on the gallows.' Drinkwater mastered his anger at Edward's peculiar petulance and poured himself another glass of blackstrap.

'I am about to land you on the Danish coast. You should acquire a horse and make for Hamburg. The Harwich packet calls fortnightly and when the *Kite* left for England with the envoys she carried mails. Among them was a letter to Lord Dungarth stating that the person of whom I had written earlier would take his instructions from the packet master in the name of 'Waters'.'

'And d'you think the security of these letters will be breached?'

'I doubt it. The second is hardly incriminating, the first I sent by special delivery. To be precise the Commander-in-Chief's wife.'

'Good God!'

'It is the best I can do for you Ned, for I must land you.' He had thought to say 'disencumber myself of you', but refrained.

'Yes, of course. How long must I wait in Hamburg?'

'I should give it two months . . . meet the Harwich packet when she berths.'

'After which this Lord Dungarth will have abandoned me much as you now wish to.' The two brothers stared at each other.

'That is right, Ned,' Drinkwater said quietly, 'And damned sorry I am for it.'

Edward shrugged. 'I need money.'

Drinkwater nodded and reached into his chest. 'You can take the money I took from you at Yarmouth, plus twenty sovereigns of mine. I should like to think that one day you were in a position to redeem the debt . . . as for clothes these will have to suffice.' He upturned a canvas bag. Shirts, pantaloons, shoes and a creased blue broadcloth coat fell out.

'A dead man's?'

'Yes, named Mason.'

'It seems you have thought of everything . . .'

Drinkwater ignored the sarcastic tone. 'You had better take his sword and his pistol. I have renewed the flint and there is a cartouche box with a spare flint and powder and ball for half a dozen rounds.' He watched Edward put on one of the shirts and try the shoes. They were a tolerable fit. 'If you are careful you have sufficient funds to purchase a horse and lodgings for your journey. I suggest you speak only in French. Once in Hamburg you must trust to luck.'

'Luck,' repeated Edward ironically, pulling on Mason's coat, 'I shall need a deal of that . . . and if she fails me, as she has done before, then I may always blow my brains out, eh? Nathaniel?' He turned to find his brother gone and the cabin filling with the grey light of dawn.

Drinkwater looked astern once at the dark shape of *Virago* as the first of the daylight began to illuminate the anchorage. A freezing wind blew in their faces as the boat, her sheets trimmed hard in, butted her way to the south eastwards, through the anchored ships. The only advantage to be had from the multitude of delays they had been subjected to in the past weeks was that a boat working through the anchorage was unlikely to attract much attention. There had been too much coming and going between the ships for any suspicions to be aroused.

The boat's crew were muffled against the cold. Beside him in the stern sat Edward, staring at the approaching shore and ignoring the curious looks of his former messmates. He had one hand on the rail and the other round Mason's canvas bag, sword and cocked hat.

The two brothers sat in silence. There had been no formal leave taking, Drinkwater having re-entered the cabin merely to announce the readiness of the boat.

Edward's ingratitude hurt Nathaniel. He could not imagine the emotions that tore his brother, how the comparison of their situations had seemed heightened by the social gulf that had divided them during Edward's short sojourn before the mast. Nor could Edward, to whom precarious existence had become a way of life, fully realise the extent to which Drinkwater had risked his all. And a man used to gambling and living upon his wits with no-one to blame but himself for his misfortunes usually casts about for a scapegoat. But this was lost on Drinkwater who charitably assumed the bleak prospect looming before his brother accounted for Edward's attitude.

Quilhampton tacked the boat seaward again in the growing light. The low coast of Zeeland was now clearly visible to the south of them and after half an hour they went about again and stood inshore where the tree-lined horizon was broken by the harder edges of roofs and the spire of Gilleleje. Drinkwater nudged Quilhampton and pointed at the village. Quilhampton nodded.

Forty minutes later they lowered the sail and got out the oars, running the boat on the sand in a comparative lee.

Drinkwater walked up the beach alongside Edward. Neither man said a word. Behind them Quilhampton stilled a speculative murmur among the boat's crew.

The two brothers strode past fishing boats drawn up on the beach. From the village a cock crowed and rising smoke told of stirring life. They saw a man emerge from a wooden privy who looked up in astonishment.

'I think I will take my leave now,' Edward said, his voice devoid of any emotion.

'Very well,' replied Nathaniel, his voice flat and formally naval.

Edward paused then gripped the canvas bag flung over his shoulder with both fists, avoiding the necessity of shaking hands. He nodded to his brother then turned and strode away. Drinkwater stood and watched him go. The man from the privy had reappeared at the door of a neat wooden house. With him was a woman with yellow hair and a blue shawl wrapped about her shoulders. They stood staring at the approaching stranger. Edward made no attempt to conceal himself but walked up to them and raised his hat. The woman retreated behind her husband but after a few minutes, during which it was clear that Edward was making himself understood to the Dane, curiosity brought her forward again.

Though the two looked twice at Drinkwater, Edward did not turn and after a moment Nathaniel walked back to the boat.

The wind before which *Virago*'s longboat returned was foul for the fleet to attempt The Sound. But the day proved more eventful than could have been expected as that dismal realisation permeated every wardroom and gun-room in the fleet. About ten in the morning the Commander-in-Chief began signalling various ships for boats. There followed hours during which, in a grey and choppy sea, the boats of the fleet pulled or sailed about, commanded by blue midshipmen with notes and orders, while the weary seamen toiled at the oars to invigorate their circulation.

The cold was bitter, following an unseasonal early spring, winter had reasserted itself. In England daffodils, new budded in the warmth of early March, now froze on the stem, an omen from the North that did not go unnoticed among the ignorant and neglected womenfolk who waited eagerly for news of the vaunted Baltic expedition.

But a new air gradually transformed the weary ships. The battleships hauled alongside the cumbersome flat-bottomed boats they had so laboriously towed or carried from England and lowered 24-pounder guns into them. Colonel Stewart's detachment of the 49th Foot improvised musket drill over the hammock nettings, while his riflemen were said to be ready to shoot the Tsar's right eye out. Even the bombs were part of this rejuvenation, the artillery detachments being ordered out of their tenders and on board the vessels they were to attend in action.

Mr Tumilty's rubicund, smiling face came over the side and the red haired Irishman pumped Drinkwater's hand enthusiastically.

'Why Mr Drinkwater, but I'd sure never like to see you naval boys try to do anything secret, 'tis for sure the whole population of Denmark has seen us cruising up and down the coast, by Jesus!' Drinkwater grinned, thinking of his own private secret expedition that had only been accomplished an hour or two earlier.

'I'm damned glad to see you, Mr Tumilty, but what's the cause of all this sudden activity?'

'Don't you know? Why, Admiral Parker has at last decided to let Lord Nelson have his way. The bombs are to join a squadron under his lordship's command. And for certain 'tis Revel or Copenhagen for us, m' dear fellow.'

'Are we to go with the bombs, then?'

'Aye, Nat'aniel. They say Nelson has been nagging the poor old admiral 'til he was only too glad to get rid of him.' Tumilty shivered and rubbed his hands. 'God, but it's cold. To be sure a man that'd go to sea for fortune would go to hell for pleasure . . .'

'Well, Mr Tumilty, do you go to see Mr Jex and give him my compliments and ask him to issue a greygoe to you, and sheepskins to your men. We should have enough.'

'That's mighty kind of you Nat'aniel, mighty kind. Sure an'it'll be hotter than the hobs of hell itself when we kindle those big black kettles you've got skulking beneath those hatches,' he added, rubbing his hands again, this time with enthusiasm.

'Beg pardon, sir, message from the admiral . . .' Drinkwater took the packet from Quilhampton and noted the boat pulling away from the ship's side. In his delight at welcoming Tumilty he had not seen it arrive.

He scanned the order: *The ships noted in the margin are . . .* Drinkwater looked down the list. There, at the bottom he found *Virago . . . to form a squadron under my command ordered forward upon a special service . . . The ships and vessels placed under my directions are to get their sheet and spare anchors over the side, ready for letting go at the shortest notice . . . commanding officers are to take especial notice of the following signals . . . No 14 to anchor by the stern . . .* It was signed in the admiral's curious, left-handed script: *Nelson and Brontë.*

'Mr Rogers!'

'Sir?'

'The vice-admiral is to shift his flag to *Elephant* this morning.'

'What the devil for?'

'She draws less than the *St George,* Mr Rogers. Do you direct the watch officers to pay particular attention to all signals from the *Elephant.* We are to form part of a detachment under Nelson . . .'

The sudden activity of the fleet and the disencumbering of Edward had coincided to throw off Drinkwater's depression. He suddenly felt ridiculously buoyant, a feeling shared by the impish Tumilty whose smile threatened to disappear into his ears.

''Twill be a fine music we'll be playing to these damned knaves, Mr Rogers, so it will, a fine *basso profundo* with the occasional crescendo to make 'em jump about like eejits.'

'Let's hope we're not too late, Mr Tumilty,' said Rogers who had not yet forgiven Drinkwater for his mysterious behaviour over Waters.

'Beg pardon, zur, but Mr Trussel sent me down with more orders just come, zur.'

'Thank you Tregembo.' Drinkwater took the packet and broke the wafer.

'Beg pardon, zur, but may I speak, zur?'

'What is it?'

' 'Tis well-known about the ship that the man we landed yesterday was a spy, zur.'

Drinkwater looked at the Cornishman. They both understood.

'Mr Jex approached me some days ago, zur. It cost him two plugs of tobacco to learn you ain't got no brother, zur.'

'Thank you.'

'Now, with your permission, zur, I'll see to your sword and pistols, zur.'

'They are all right, thank you Tregembo, I have not used them since last you attended to them.'

'I'll look at them, just the same.'

Drinkwater bent over the new orders. It was a general instruction to the bomb vessels to place themselves under the orders of Captain Murray of the *Edgar*. It was anticipated that they would be used against the fortress at Cronbourg. A note was included from Martin. The commander's crabbed script drew Drinkwater's attention to the fact that it was suspected that *Zebra* had suffered some damage on the Zeeland's Reef and he might yet be able to render Drinkwater a service. Drinkwater fancied he could read the unwritten thought that lay behind that fatuous phrase, that he, Nathaniel Drinkwater, was an intimate of Lord Dungarth. Drinkwater wondered what Martin would do if he knew that the lieutenant, with whom he was currently currying favour, had just assisted a murderer to escape the noose.

Late in the afternoon the brig *Cruizer* was ordered forward to send in a boat to make a final demand of Governor Stricker at Cronbourg as to his intentions if the British fleet attempted to pass The Sound. It revealed to all, including the Danish commander, that Parker was still vacillating.

The following morning, Saturday March 28th, the wind hauled westerly and the temperature rose. The sun shone and the fleet weighed, setting all sail to the royals in an attempt to enter and pass The Sound. But the wind fell light and the contrary current held up the lumbering battleships so that Parker, learning from Brisbane of the *Cruizer* that Stricker had laughed in his face, could not risk his ships drifting under the heavy guns of the fortress. Once again the fleet anchored and in *Virago*'s cabin that night they debated how long it took to wear an anchor ring through the shank.

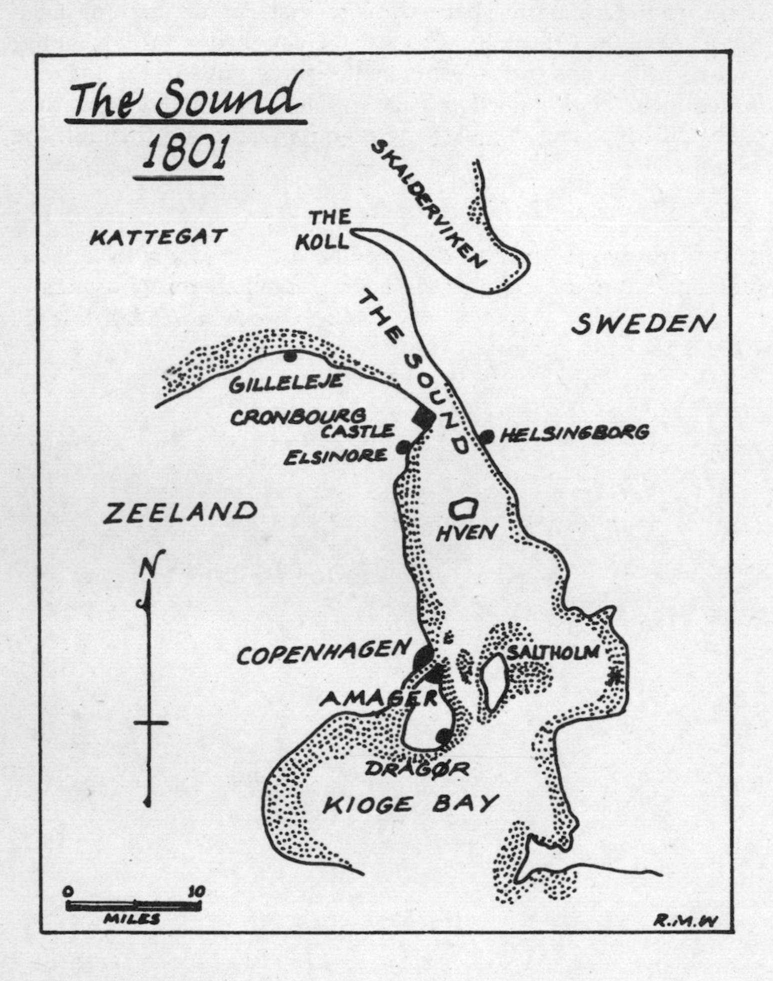
The Sound
1801
KATTEGAT
THE
KOLL
SKALDERVIKEN
THE SOUND
SWEDEN
GILLELEJE
CRONBOURG
CASTLE
ELSINORE
HELSINGBORG
ZEELAND
HVEN
N
COPENHAGEN
SALTHOLM
AMAGER
DRAGØR
KIOGE BAY
0
10
MILES
R.M.W

PART THREE

Lord Nelson

'It is warm work; and this day may be the last to any of us at a moment. But mark you! I would not be elsewhere for thousands.'

NELSON, COPENHAGEN, 2 April, 1801

Chapter Fourteen *29–30 March 1801*

The Sound

'Two guns from the flagship, sir.'

'Very well, what o'clock is it?'

'It wants a few minutes of midnight, sir; wind's freshened a little from the west.'

Drinkwater struggled into his greygoe and hurried on deck. He looked up at the masthead pendant and nodded his approval as Rogers reported the hands mustering to weigh.

'Sheet home the topsails, Mr Rogers, and have headsails ready for hoisting. Mr Easton!'

'Sir?'

'Have you a man for the chains?'

'All ready.'

'Very well.'

'One thing we *can* do is weigh the bloody anchor in the middle of the night,' offered Rogers in a stage whisper.

'*Virago* 'hoy!'

'Hullo?' Drinkwater strode to the rail to see the dim shape of a master's mate standing in the stern of a gig.

'Captain Murray desires that you move closer inshore towards Cronbourg Castle, sir. The bombs are to prepare to bombard at daylight!'

'Thank you.' Drinkwater turned inboard again. 'Can you make out *Edgar* in this mist?'

'Aye, sir, just, she's hoisted lanterns.'

Drinkwater saw the flare of red orpiment from the *Edgar*'s stern.

'Bengal light, sir, signal to weigh.'

'Very well. Mr Matchett!'

'Sir?'

'Heave away!'

Virago filled her topsails as the anchor came a-trip and the water began to chuckle under her round bow. Keeping a careful watch to avoid collision Drinkwater conned the old ship south-eastwards in the wake of the *Edgar*. On either beam dark shapes with the pale gleam of topsails above indicated the other bombs creeping forward ready to throw their fire at the intransigent Danes. Then, barely an hour after they had got under way, the wind shifted, backing remorselessly and beginning to head them.

'Topsail's a-shiver, zur,'

'Brace her hard up, Mr Easton, God damn it!'

'Hard up, sir, aye, aye . . . it's no good sir, wind's drawing ahead.'

The concussion of guns from the darkness ahead and the dark rose glow of twin Bengal lights together with a blue rocket signalled the inevitable.

'Main braces, Mr Easton, down helm and stand by to anchor!'

Once again the anchor splashed overboard, once again *Virago*'s cable rumbled through the hawse pipe and once again her crew clambered aloft to stow the topsails, certain in the knowledge that tomorrow they would have to heave the cable in again. They were nowhere near close enough to bombard as Murray intended.

All morning Drinkwater waited for the order to weigh as the light wind backed a little. During the afternoon the rest of the ships worked closer inshore and by the evening the whole fleet had brought to their anchors four miles to the north west of Cronbourg castle. Drinkwater surveyed the shore. The dark bulk of the fortress was indistinct but the coast of Zeeland was more heavily wooded than at Gilleleje. The villages of Hellebaek and Hornbaek were visible, the latter with a conspicuous church steeple looking toylike as the sun westered to produce a flaming sunset. It picked out not only the villages of Denmark but small points of metallic fire and the pink planes of sunlit stone where the guns of the Swedish fortress at Helsingborg on the opposite side of The Sound peered from their embrasures.

Men lingered on deck in silence watching the Danish shore where figures could be seen on foot and horseback. Here and there a carriage was observed as the population of Elsinore came out to look at this curiosity, the heavy hulls of the British ships, the tracery of their masts and yards silhouetted against the blood red sunset. It seemed another omen, and to the Danes a favourable one. The image of those ships reeking in their own blood-red element was not lost on Drinkwater who wrote of it in his journal before turning again to the stained notebook he had consulted when the fleet had made for the Great Belt.

The book was one of several left him after the death of Mr Blackmore, the old sailing master of the *Cyclops*. Drinkwater had been his brightest pupil on the frigate and the old man had left both his notebooks and his quadrant to the young midshipman. The notebooks had been meticulously kept and inspired Drinkwater to keep his own journal in considerable detail. Blackmore had carried out several surveys and copied foreign charts, particularly of the Baltic, an area with which he had been familiar, having commanded a ship in the Scandinavian trade.

Drinkwater looked at the chartlet of The Sound. The ramparts of Cronbourg were clearly marked together with the arcs of fire of the batteries and a note that their range was no more than one and a half miles. The Sound was two and a half miles wide and the fleet could not hope to pass unscathed if they received fire from both Helsingborg and Cronbourg.

Drinkwater was familiar with the current. It had frustrated them already, usually running to the north but influenced by the wind with little tidal effect. The Disken shoal formed a middle ground but should not present any problem to the fleet. It was the guns of Cronbourg that would do the damage, those and the Swedish cannon on the opposite shore.

Drinkwater went on deck before turning in. It was bitterly cold again with a thin layer of high cloud: Trussel was on deck.

'All quiet, Mr Trussel?'

'Aye sir, like the grave.'

'Moonrise is about two-fifteen and the almanac indicates an eclipse.'

'Ah, I'd better warn the people, there's plenty of them as still believes in witchcraft and the like.'

'As you like, Mr Trussel.' Drinkwater thought of his own obsession with Hortense Santhonax and wondered if there were not something in old wives' tales. There were times when a lonely man might consider himself under a spell. He thought, too, of Edward, and where he might be this night. Trussel recalled him.

'To speak the truth, Mr Drinkwater, I'd believe any omen if it meant making some progress. This is an interminable business, wouldn't you say?'

'Aye, Mr Trussel, and the Danes have been well able to observe every one of our manoeuvres.'

'And doubtless form a poor opinion of 'em, what with all the shilly shallying. I've never seen so much coming and going even when the Grand Fleet lay at St Helen's. Why your little boat-trip t'other morning went unremarked by anyone.'

The point of Trussel's chat emerged and Drinkwater smiled.

'Indeed, Mr Trussel, that was the point of it.'

'The point of it, sir . . .?' said Trussell vaguely.

'Come, what is the rumour in the ship, eh? Ain't it that the mysterious fellow we took aboard at Yarmouth is, in truth, a spy?'

'Aye, sir. That's what scuttlebutt says, but I don't always hold that scuttlebutt's accurate.'

'But in this case it is, Mr Trussel, in this case it most certainly is. Good night to you . . .'

In his coffin-like cot Mr Jex lay unsleeping. He felt a growing sense of unease at the quickening pace of events. The fruitless comings and goings of the last week, the weary handling of ground tackle and sails had scarcely affected him since he did no special duty at such times. True the bad weather had confined him sick and miserable in his cabin but he had at least a measure of satisfaction in abusing and belabouring his steward, a miserable, cowed man who was loved by no-one. But even Jex had overcome his sickness eventually and the prolonged periods at anchor had pacified his internal disquiet. Like his Commander-in-Chief, Jex did not wish to pass the fortress at Cronbourg, but whereas Parker was merely excessively cautious, Jex was a coward. He found it increasingly difficult to concentrate upon his columns of figures, even when they showed a rise in the fortunes of Hector Jex to the extent of yet wiping out the amount extorted by Lieutenant Drinkwater. Instead he found unbidden images of mutilated bodies entering his mind; of bloody decks strewn with limbless corpses, of the surgeon's tubs filled with arms and legs.

Lieutenant Rogers's bloodthirsty yarns lost nothing in the telling and Jex's disgrace in the action with the luggers had left him a prey to the cruel and merciless wit of his brother officers. Rogers's lack of either tact or compassion only fuelled the constant references to Jex's cowardice so that the purser conceived a hatred for the first lieutenant that began to exceed that he already felt for his commander.

As for the latter, Jex had felt a hopelessness at having been outmanoeuvred yet again by Mr Drinkwater. The ostentatious departure of Waters from the ship had seemed to him to prove the accuracy of Drinkwater's assertions about the mysterious landsman. All Jex could do was hope to determine whether or not a real murder had taken place at Newmarket, and whether or not the Marquis de la Roche-Jagu really existed. He could not himself conceive that it would have been reported without it being known in Newmarket whether or not the event had actually taken place. And it was this desire to live long enough to prove the arrogant Mr Drinkwater wrong that was constantly undermined by the growing horror of premature death.

Even as he lay there, a deck below the anchor watch who marvelled at the lunar eclipse, he saw himself dead; torn apart by cannon shot, his bowels spilling from his paunch.

Drinkwater stood in the sunshine and looked round the deck. He had done all he could to move *Virago* forward to a position where she might assist the seven bomb vessels if they required it, yet remain out of range of the guns of Cronbourg with her vulnerable cargo of explosives and combustibles.

He looked beyond the masts of the bomb vessels at their target. Anchored in a line, just outside the known arc of fire of the Danish guns they were preparing to bombard the castle.

Despite the fact that he had already trodden the soil of Denmark, his preoccupation with Edward's plight had so far blinded him to a full realisation of the enemy's country. To date he had seen it as a series of landmarks to take bearings of, a flat coast with hidden, offshore dangers and a population amply warned of their approach. This morning he realised the alien nature of it. Weighing at daylight the bombs with the battleship *Edgar* and the frigate *Blanche* had taken up the positions attempted the previous day. The castle of Cronbourg loomed before them, an edifice of unusual aspect to English eyes, used to the towers of the Norman French. The redbrick walls, towers and cupolas with their bright green copper roofs had a fantastic, even fairy-like quality that seemed at first to totally disarm Sir Hyde Parker's fears.

But even as they let their anchors go at six in the morning of March 30th the Danish flag was hoisted in the north westerly breeze that set fair for the passage of The Sound. The white cross on a red, swallow-tail ground had the lick of a dragon's tongue about it, as it floated above the fortress, over the roofs of the town of Elsinore.

The men had breakfasted at their stations and Lettsom had come on deck to see for himself the progress of the fleet. Easton was pointing out the landmarks.

'The town is Helsingør, Mr Lettsom, which we call Elsinore, the castle is called Cronbourg, or Cronenbourg on some charts.'

'Then that is Hamlet's castle, eh? Is that so Mr Drinkwater?'

'I suppose it is, Mr Lettsom.'

'And they tell me you had an eclipse last night.'

'I think 'twas the moon that had an eclipse. Happily it had no effect upon us.'

'Quite so, sir.' Lettsom paused for a moment. ' "The moist star, upon whose influence Neptune's empire stands, Was sick almost to doomsday with eclipse . . ." Hamlet, gentlemen, Act One . . .'

'Sick to doomsday with anchoring more like, Bones,' put in Rogers.

Lettsom ignored the first lieutenant and produced another quotation: ' "But look, the morn, in russet mantle clad, Walks o'er the dew of yon high eastern hill . . ." '

'But it ain't high, Mr Lettsom, thus proving Shakespeare did not know the lie of the land hereabouts.'

'True, sir, but there's such a thing as poetic licence. And here, if not the dawn, is Mr Jex.'

The assembled officers laughed as the purser came on deck, and the surgeon, in fine form now he had the attention of all, continued his thespian act.

'Good morning Mr Jex,' he said, then added darkly, ' "here is a beast that wants discourse of reason".'

Bewildered by the laughter, yet conscious that he was the cause of it, Jex looked sullenly round.

' "A dull and muddy-metalled rascal", eh, Mr Jex?' Even Lettsom himself was scarce able to refrain from laughter and Jex was roused to real anger.

'Do you mind your manners, Mr Lettsom,' he snarled, 'I've given you no cause to abuse me.'

' "Use every man after his desert and who would 'scape whipping?"'

'Why,' laughed Rogers unwilling to let Lettsom have all the fun, 'both you and your eighth man would qualify there, Mr Jex . . .' Laughter spread along the deck among the seamen who well understood the allusion to Jex's corruption.

'Aye, "be thou as chaste as ice, as pure as snow, thou shalt not escape calumny." '

'Hold your God damn tongue . . .' burst out Jex, the colour mounting to his face at this public humiliation.

'Gentlemen, gentlemen,' Drinkwater temporised, 'I beg you to desist . . . Mr Jex, I assure you the surgeon meant no offence but merely wished to air his knowledge of the Bard. I am by no means persuaded his powers of recall are accurate . . .'

'Sir!' protested Lettsom but Drinkwater called their attention to the fleet.

'Let us see whether aught is rotten in the state of Denmark shall we?'

'Mr Drinkwater, you o'erwhelm the powers of my muse,' grinned Lettsom, 'I shall betake myself to my cockpit and sulk like Achilles in his tent.'

The surgeon and purser were instantly forgotten as glasses were lifted to watch the fleet weigh from the anchorage and begin the approach to Copenhagen through the sound.

Led by *Monarch*, the foremost ship of Lord Nelson's division, the ships of the line stood south eastwards in brilliant sunshine. It presented a magnificent spectacle to the men watching from the huddle of bomb ships that waited eagerly to play their part in the drama of the day. The wind had settled to a fine breeze from the north north westward, as *Monarch* approached Cronbourg. They could see her topmen racing aloft to shake out the topgallants from their stoppings.

'*London*'s signalling, sir, "General bombs, commence the bombardment".'

'Thank you, Mr Easton. Mr Rogers, have the crews in the boats ready to render assistance, and Mr Tumilty, perhaps you will give us the benefit of your opinion in the action.'

'I shall be delighted, Nat'aniel. Mark *Zebra* well, I hear she took a pounding on the reef t'other day and, though I believe her to be well built, if Bobbie Lawson overloads his mortars I think she may be in trouble.'

'Is Captain Lawson likely to over-charge his mortars, Tom?'

'To win the five guineas I wagered that he couldn't sustain one round a minute for more than half an hour he may become a mite careless, Nat'aniel, so he may . . .'

Drinkwater laughed just as the first bomb fired. 'That's *Explosion*,' snapped Tumilty, suddenly concentrating. The concussion rolled over the water towards them as they saw *Explosion*'s waist billow clouds of smoke.

'She certainly lives up to her name.'

'They'll remark the fall of shot before anyone else fires,' said Tumilty informatively. They could see the arc of the shell reach its apogee and then they were distracted as the batteries at Cronbourg opened a rolling fire. For a moment *Monarch*'s hull disappeared behind a seething welter of splashes, then behind the smoke of her own discharge as first she, and then successive ships astern returned the fire of the castle. It was six forty-five in the morning.

For the next hour the air was rent by the explosions of the guns. The deep rolling of British broadsides was answered by the heavy fire from Cronbourg. Nearer, the powerful and thunderous bark of the ten- and thirteen-inch mortars enveloped the lower masts of the bomb vessels in heavy clouds of smoke. No signals came from the bombs and the Viragos were compelled to stand idle, but it afforded them a rare and memorable sight.

'No fire from the Swedes, sir,' said Rogers, '*Monarch's* inclining to their side of the channel.'

Parker's centre division was abeam of them now, all the ships setting their topgallants but keeping their main courses in the buntlines so as to hamper neither the gunnery nor the conning of the battlefleet through The Sound.

' 'Tis a fine sight, Nat'aniel,' said Tumilty, 'at moments like this one is almost persuaded that war is a glorious thing.'

'Sadly, Tom, that is indeed true. See the *Elephant*, the two-decker with the blue flag at her foremasthead, that's Nelson's flagship, see how he holds his fire. That's the contempt of Old England for you, by God!'

'If that's war on the English style, wait until you see that Irish version, by Jesus,' Tumilty grinned happily, ' 'Tis not your cold contempt, but your hot-tempered fury that puts the enemy to flight . . .'

They both laughed. 'There goes the old *Isis*. See Mr Q, that is quite possibly the last time you'll see a fifty in the line of battle . . . included here for her shallow draught I imagine.'

Beyond the battleships, on the Swedish side of The Sound the smaller vessels were under way. The gun-brigs and the frigates towing the flat-boats, the sloops and the fire-ships *Otter* and *Zephyr*, the tenders and cutters all stood southward, sheltered by the rear division of Admiral Graves. Only *Blanche* and *Edgar* remained to cover the bomb vessels and at fifteen minutes to eight the rear repeating frigate hoisted a string of bunting.

'*Jamaica* signalling, sir, "Repeated from flag, bombs to cease fire and approach the admiral".' Mr Quilhampton closed the signal book.

'That's a touch of the naval Irish, Mr Tumilty,' said Rogers nudging the artillery officer. 'It means Parker wants us to play chase.'

'Is that a fact, Mr Rogers,' said Tumilty calling his non-commissioned officer to the break of the poop while Drinkwater and Rogers bawled orders through their trumpets to get *Virago* under way.

The order was obeyed with alacrity. Topmen raced aloft to shake out the topsails while the fo'c's'le party set to with their spikes at the windlass. At the fiferails there was much heaving as sheets were belayed and halliards manned.

'Now Hite,' asked Tumilty, leaning over the rail and addressing the bombardier who had a watch and tablet in his hands, 'what did you make it?'

'Mr Lawson was engaged for thirty-seven minutes, sir, both mortars in use and by my reckoning he threw forty-one shells . . .'

Tumilty whistled. 'Phew, he must have been working them poor artillerymen like devils, eh Hite?'

'Yes sir.'

'An' I've lost five guineas, devil take it!'

'You've lost your wager then?' asked Drinkwater as he strode forward to get a better view of the fo'c's'le party.

'To be sure an' I have.'

'You look damned cheerful about it.'

'An' why shouldn't I look cheerful? An' why shouldn't you look cheerful seeing as how you stand to benefit from it.'

'Me? Hoist away there, Mr Q. Lively there with the cat-tackle, Mr Matchett. Steer south east, Mr Easton . . . how should I be delighted in your misfortune, Tom?'

'Well I'll put up another five that says *Zebra* will be unfit for the next bombardment and *Virago* will stand in the line.'

Drinkwater looked curiously at the little Irishman before turning his attention again to getting *Virago* under way and taking station in the rear of the line of bomb vessels.

Standing across to the Swedish side the squat little ships left the Danish shore as the frustrated guns of Cronbourg fell silent.

By nine o'clock they were clear of The Narrows and at noon anchored with the rest of the fleet off the island of Hven.

'I wonder what damage the mortars did, Tom.'

Tumilty shrugged. ''Tis not what execution they did to Elsinore or Cronbourg that should interest you, Nat'aniel, but what damage they did to *Zebra*.'

Chapter Fifteen *30 March–1 April 1801*

Copenhagen Road

'Christ, but it's bloody cold again.' Rogers stamped upon the deck and his breath was steaming in the chilling air. It was not yet dark but the brief warmth of the sun had long gone. Pancakes of ice floated slowly past the ship and Lettsom, invigorated by the air's freshness after a day spent below and well muffled in sheepskins, watched curiously from the rail.

'I don't think I can stand much more of this blasted idling in ignorance Lettsom, stap me if I can!'

'Happen you have little choice,' answered Lettsom straightening up.

'No,' growled Rogers with angry resentment.

'I suppose you want to know what those two ships learnt . . .'

'Yes, *Amazon* and *Cruizer* went forward with the lugger *Lark;* her master's familiar with the approaches to Copenhagen. Someone said they thought Nelson was in the lugger but . . .' he shrugged resignedly. 'Bollocks to them; I suppose they'll tell us in good time when they want us to get shot.'

'How is our commander taking the delay, he seems an active man?'

'Drinkwater? He's a strange cove. He was promoted in '99 but because of some damned administrative mix-up he lost the commission. He took it blasted well; if it'd been me I'd have made an unholy bloody row about it.'

'I don't doubt it,' said Lettsom drily, 'I think our Mr Drinkwater something of a stoic, though an oddity too. What d'you make of this spy business?'

Rogers shrugged. 'What is there to make of it? As I said Drinkwater's a strange cove. Been mixed up in the business since before the war; ask Tregembo if you want to know about our commander. Lying old buzzard will tell you tales as tall as the main truck; about the young midshipman who slit the gizzard of some Frog and took the m'sieur's sword for his pains, or retook an American prize after her crew over-powered the prize crew. All in all it's a bloody mystery why our Nathaniel ain't commanding this bloody expedition against the festering Tsar . . . Let's face it, Bones, he couldn't make a worse mess of it than that old fool Parker and *he's* got Lord Nelson to prod his reluctant arse for him.'

'True, Mr Rogers, but it does seem that Mr Drinkwater was specially selected for his discretion in landing this spy fellow. I'd say he'd achieved that with a fair degree of success, wouldn't you?'

'Yes, I suppose . . . hey, what's that going on alongside *Cruizer*?' Rogers whipped the night-glass from its rack and stared hard at the grey shape of the brig half a mile away and partially hidden from them behind *Blanche*. 'By God, she's getting under way!'

Lettsom stared into the gathering darkness and had to confess he could see nothing remarkable.

'There man, are you blind? Damned good surgeon you'll make if you can't see a bloody brig getting under way with her boats alongside.'

'No, I can't see a thing. D'you want me to tell the captain on my way below?'

'Yes, I'd be obliged to you.' Rogers turned away. 'Hey fo'c's'le there! Can't you see anything unusual on the starboard beam. Keep your blasted eyes peeled, God damn it, unless you want a Danish guard-boat coming alongside to piss in your ear while you're asleep up there . . .'

'Aye, aye, sir.' Lettsom heard the aggrieved tone in the response.

In the cabin he told Drinkwater of the news of *Cruizer*.

'Thank you Mr Lettsom, pray take a seat. Will you take a glass and a biscuit with me? I daresay we will know what's amiss tomorrow morning, in the meantime a glass to keep the cold out before turning in would be a good idea, eh?'

'Indeed it would, sir, thank you.'

'Mr Lettsom, I don't care much for doggerel, but I hear that you command a superior talent upon the flute. Would you oblige me with an air?'

'With the greatest of pleasure, Mr Drinkwater. Are you familiar with the work of Lully?'

'No. Pray enlighten me.'

*

The fleet had moved south from Hven at daybreak. They were now anchored within sight of the roofs and spires of Copenhagen, at the northern end of Copenhagen Road. Another council of war had been held aboard *London* to which the artillery officers were summoned. Quilhampton returned from delivering Tumilty to the flagship with news for Drinkwater.

'*Amazon* and *Cruizer*, sir, they've been forward with the *Lark*, lugger. Lord Nelson's reconnoitred the Danish position, so one of the mids aboard *London* told me.'

Drinkwater nodded. 'Doubtless we'll learn all the details when he returns. I'm obliged to you Mr Q.' Drinkwater reached for the old notebooks of Blackmore and pored over the chart, lost in thought.

The Danish capital of Copenhagen straddled a narrow strait between the easternmost part of Zeeland and the smaller island of Amager. The strait formed the inner harbour and ran through the heart of the city. To the east the sea formed a large open roadstead separated from the main part of The Sound by the low, sandy island of Saltholm which supported little but a few huts and a quantity of marram grass. But the roadstead was deceptive. In addition to the shoals that lined the shores of Amager and Saltholm, which converged at the southern end off Dragør in The Grounds, a large elliptical mud-bank split the roadstead in two. Called the Middle Ground it divided the area into two navigable channels. The westernmost one, which from the British fleet's present anchorage led first towards, and then southwards past Copenhagen, was called the King's Deep. The easternmost which ran due south close to the Saltholm shore, and out of range of the guns at Copenhagen, was known as the Holland Deep.

The problem in attacking Copenhagen would be whether to enter the King's Deep from the north, which might bottle the ships up at the southern end with an unfavourable wind preventing them returning through the Holland Deep, or assembling at the southern end and forcing a passage to the north through the King's Deep when the wind changed.

Drinkwater was suddenly disturbed by the opening of his door and the gleam of gold coins flung across the chart before him. He looked up in astonishment. Tumilty's usually florid face was blue with cold and a large dewdrop depended from his nose. But his expression was one of utter joy.

'There's my stake in the wager, Nat'aniel, and sure it is that I've just as cheerfully parted with another five to Captain Lawson for his superior pyroballogy from the *Zebra*, so I have.'

'And what of *Zebra*, Tom?' asked Drinkwater cautiously.

'Would you believe they've strained the thirteen-inch mortar bed mortal bad! And would you believe that they've sprung a garboard on the reef, and while it ain't what her commander would call serious, what with the hands pumping for an hour a watch, but further concussions of her mortars might let the whole o' the Baltic into her bilge?'

'And *Virago*?' asked Drinkwater rising to pour two glasses of blackstrap.

'Nothing firm yet, Nat'aniel. Flag officer's minds don't leap to decisions with the same facility as that of your humble servant's, but 'tis only a matter of time until expedience itself must recommend *Virago* to fill the breach, an' there's me money as an act of faith.' He lifted the glass to his lips giving one of his heavily conspiratorial winks.

Drinkwater digested the news. 'What did you learn of the plans for the rest of the fleet?'

'Oh, Parker's increased the size of Nelson's detachment by adding *Edgar* and *Ganges*.'

'That makes twelve line of battle ships. D'you think he means Nelson to make the attack?'

Tumilty nodded. 'Certain of it . . . Fremantle is put in charge of those damned flat boats and there are some additional signals. Here, 'tis all in these orders.'

Tumilty tossed the papers onto the table. He added conversationally, '*Isis* lost seven men passing Cronbourg when one of her old guns blew up.' He emptied his glass, helped himself to another and went on, 'Nelson, it seems, went ahead yesterday afternoon in a lugger . . .'

'The *Lark*.'

'Just so; then last night Brisbane took the *Cruizer* and laid a couple of buoys at the north end o' the Holland Deep. D'you know where that is?'

Drinkwater pointed at the charts before him. Tumilty peered over his shoulder. 'Ah, and yesterday Nelson saw the Danes hacking down beacons off Dragør . . .'

'Here, at the southern end of the Channel leading to Copenhagen from the south. If we'd gone by the Great Belt we'd have had to pass the cannon at Dragør and as you see there is less room than through The Sound.'

'Just so, just so . . . apparently the whole operation is now in jeopardy because the beacons and buoys have been removed from the approach channels. There's a line of forts and floating batteries along the waterfront at Copenhagen and they command the approaches from the north or south. In their front lies a shoal . . .'

'Here,' Drinkwater pointed. 'The Middle Ground, between the flats round Saltholm and Copenhagen itself.'

'Nelson wants to attack from the south, waiting for a southerly wind so that he may have a breeze to carry himself north if he's forced to disengage. The position looks formidable enough . . .'

'And if it ain't buoyed . . .' Drinkwater's voice tailed off and a remote look came into his eyes. Then he suddenly slapped his hand down upon the papers.

'God's bones, why the deuce did I not think of it before . . . where the devil's Lord Nelson now?'

'Nelson? Why he's still on the *London*, or perhaps the *Elephant* . . . hey, where are you going?'

Drinkwater flung open his cabin door and shouted 'Have a boat ready for me at once there!' then re-entering the cabin he reached for his cloak, hat and sword.

'I'm off to see Nelson.'

'What about your orders?' Tumilty pointed to the packet lying unopened on the desk.

'Oh damn them! We ain't going anywhere until those channels are buoyed out!'

Nelson's barge was returning alongside *Elephant* as *Virago*'s boat approached. The barge had not left the battleship's side, although the admiral had gone on board by the time the *Virago*'s boat bumped alongside and a tall lieutenant jumped across into the barge, teetered for a second upon a thwart, grabbed a tossed oar for support, and with a muttered 'By your leave,' flung himself at the manropes and scaled the side of the *Elephant*.

Touching his hat to the quarterdeck and announcing himself to the astonished marine sentry at the entry port Drinkwater collared a passing midshipman and looked round. The tail of a posse of officers was disappearing under the poop and Drinkwater guessed they followed Nelson into his cabin.

'His lordship, cully, upon the instant . . .' he growled at the boy.

Nelson was dismissing the entourage of officers, rubbing his forehead and pleading fatigue as Drinkwater pushed through them.

'What is your business, sir?' Drinkwater found himself confronted by a tall man in the uniform of a senior captain. The midshipman had melted away.

'By your leave sir, a word with his lordship . . .'

'What the devil is it, Foley?'

'An officer who requests a word with you.' Foley half turned and Nelson appeared in the doorway of the great cabin.

'My lord, I beg a moment of your time . . .'

Nelson was frowning. 'I know you!'

'I entreat your lordship to permit me to assist in the surveying and buoyage duties attending the fleet's approach to Copenhagen . . .' He felt Foley's hand upon his arm.

'Come sir, this is no time . . .'

'No, wait, Foley.' Nelson's one good eye glittered, though his face was grey with fatigue. 'Let us hear what the lieutenant has to say.'

'I was employed during the last peace in the buoy yachts of the Trinity House . . .'

'The Trinity House has provided us with pilots who do not share your enthusiasm, Mr, er . . .?'

'Drinkwater, my lord. You misunderstand me. These men are from the Trinity House at Hull, unfamiliar with the techniques of buoy-laying. The buoy yachts of the London House are constantly about the matter.'

There was a pause, then Nelson asked: 'Have I not seen you somewhere before, Mr Drinkwater?'

'Aye, my lord, at Syracuse in ninety-eight. I was first of the brig *Hellebore* . . .'

'The *Hellebore*?' Nelson frowned.

'You sent her to the Red Sea to warn Admiral Blankett of French intentions in Egypt.'

'Ah, I recollect. And all to no avail, eh, Mr Drinkwater?' Nelson smiled wearily.

'Not at all, my lord, we destroyed a French squadron and brought home a fine French thirty-eight.'

'Ah . . .' Nelson smiled again, the wide, mobile mouth that

betrayed the wild passion of his nature showed too that he was still a man of no great age.

'Mr Drinkwater,' he said after a moment's consideration in the rather high-pitched Norfolk accent that he never attempted to disguise, 'your zeal commends you. What ship are you in?'

'I command the bomb-tender *Virago*, my lord. She has two mortars mounted and an artillery lieutenant as keen to use 'em as myself . . .' he held the admiral's penetrating gaze.

'The ruddy Irishman that was at this morning's conference aboard *London*, eh?'

'The same, my lord.'

'I shall take note of your remarks and employ you and your ship as seems most desirable. I will acquaint Captain Brisbane of the *Cruizer* of your familiarity with the matter now urgently in hand. In the meantime, I must ask you to excuse me, I am most fearfully worn out . . . Foley be a good fellow and see Mr Drinkwater off . . .'

'Thank you, my lord.' Drinkwater withdrew, never having thought to have an admiral ask to be excused, nor such a senior post-captain to escort him to his boat.

'I hope you are able to make good your claims, Mr Drinkwater,' remarked Foley.

'I have no doubt of it, sir.'

'The admiral's condescension is past the tolerable limits of most of us,' the captain added with a touch of irony, handing over the importunate Drinkwater to the officer of the watch.

But Drinkwater ignored the gentle rebuke. He felt the misconstruction placed upon his presence with Lady Parker at Yarmouth was now effaced. He had glimpsed that Nelson touch at Syracuse and now he knew it for what it really was. In contrast with the tradition of self-seeking that had divided and bedevilled fleet operations for generations, Nelson was destined to command men united in purpose, whose loyalty to each other overrode petty considerations of self. They might not triumph before the well-prepared defences of Copenhagen but if they failed they would do so without disgrace. In the last words of Edmund Burke, if die they must, they would die with sword in hand.

'Now gentlemen,' Drinkwater looked round the circle of faces: Rogers, the assembled warrant officers, the red-faced coat of

Tumilty, the thin visage of Quilhampton. 'Well gentlemen, we are to split our forces. Mr Tumilty is to continue his preparations with his party under the direct command of Mr Rogers who will assume command of the ship in my absence. The three watches will be taken by Messrs Trussel, Matchett and Willerton who will also attend to those other duties as may from time to time be required of them. Messrs Easton and Quilhampton will provide themselves with the materials on this list and select a boat's crew which is to be adequately wrapped up against the cold. Mr Lettsom, you and Mr Jex will serve additionally to your established duties to second those other officers as they require it, or as Mr Rogers or myself deem it necessary. This is a time for great exertion, gentlemen, I do not expect to have to recall anyone of you to your duty but there will be little rest in the next few days until the matter presently resolved upon is brought to a conclusion. What that conclusion will be rests largely upon the extent of our endeavours. Is that understood?'

There was a chorus of assent. 'Very well, any questions?'

'Aye sir.' It was Matchett, the boatswain.

'Yes?'

'Are we to stand in the line of bombs, sir, as I've heard?' Drinkwater shot a glance at Tumilty whose innocent eyes were studying the deckhead.

'I cannot tell you at present, Mr Matchett.' A murmur of disappointment ran through the little assembly. 'All I can say is that I represented our case to Lord Nelson himself not an hour since . . .'

There was a perceptible brightening of faces. 'That is all, gentlemen.'

'Sir! Beg pardon, sir.'

'Yes, what is it?' Drinkwater turned from the boatswain to Mr Quilhampton.

'For this surveying, sir, the tablet and board . . .'

'Yes?'

'Well, sir, I can hold a pencil in - my right hand but . . .' Quilhampton held up the hook that terminated his left arm.

'Damn it, I had clean forgot, accept my apologies, Mr Q . . .' Drinkwater tore his mind off the instructions he was giving to Matchett and rubbed his forehead.

'Why don't 'e see Mr Willerton, sir. Carpenter'd knock him up a timber claw to hold anything, sir.'

'See to it, Mr Q, obliged to you Mr Matchett, now to the matter of these buoys. I want as many nets as you can knock up, about a fathom square, use any old rope junk but the mesh must be small enough to stop a twenty-four pound ball from escaping. Fit the boat up with coils of ten fathoms of three inch rope, enough for as many nets as you make. Then I want some of those deal planks left over from fitting the magazines, you know, the ones that Willerton has been hiding since Chatham, and small stuff sufficient to square lash 'em into a cross. No, damn it we'll nail 'em. Then I want a dozen light spars, boat-hook shafts, spare cannon ramrods, that sort of thing, all fitted with wefts of bunting. Get the duty watch cracking on that lot at once.'

'How many balls to each net, sir?'

'Four'll be too heavy to manhandle over the gunwhale, better make it three.'

'Then we can make the nets a little smaller, sir.'

Drinkwater nodded, 'See to it then.' He turned aft and caught sight of the purser. 'Oh, Mr Jex!'

'Sir?'

'Mr Jex, Mr Tumilty has asked me that it be specially impressed upon you that your party of firemen be adequately trained in the use of pump and hoses. When we go into action their efforts are required throughout the period the mortars are in use.'

'When we go into action sir?' Jex queried uncertainly. 'But I thought that the matter was not yet . . '

'I hope that we will soon know . . . ah, Mr Willerton are you able to help Mr Q? You have little time . . .'

Drinkwater did not see the pale face of Mr Jex staring with disbelief at his retreating figure.

Half an hour later Drinkwater reported to Brisbane aboard *Cruizer.*

'Now see here, Drinkwater, what we achieved last night in the way of buoying the channel was little enough.' Brisbane leant over the sheet of cartridge paper spread upon the table in *Cruizer*'s cabin. On it the brig's master, William Fothergill, had pencilled in the outline of the islands of Saltholm and Amager. Upon the latter stood the city of Copenhagen. Also drawn in were the approximate limits of the shallow water.

'We are attempting to find out the five fathom line which will give us ample water for Nelson's squadron. Happily for us the tidal range hereabouts is negligible, although a strong southerly wind will reduce the water on the Middle Ground . . .'

'So I understand, sir.'

'Last night we sounded for the eastern limit of the Holland Deep, here, along the Saltholm shore and laid four buoys . . .'

'What are you using for buoys, sir?'

'Water casks weighted with three double-headed shot, why?'

'With respect, sir, though adequate, the casks may be difficult to see, particularly if the sea is covered with sea-smoke as has been the case the last three mornings. May I suggest planks or short spars lashed or nailed in a cross with a hole drilled for a light pole. Ropes stoppered at the ends of the plants and drawn together to a becket at the base of the pole will afford a securing for the mooring and assist the pole to remain upright. If the pole carries a weft or flag I believe you will find this method satisfactory . . .'

'Damn good idea, sir,' put in Fothergill, 'and if necessary a lantern may be hung from the pole.'

'Quite so.' The three men straightened up from the chart smiling.

'Very well, Mr Drinkwater, so be it. Now Mr Fothergill is about to ink in what we have done so far and then this chart will go across to Captain Riou aboard *Amazon*. From now on all surveying reports are to be returned to *Amazon* where this chart is to be completed. I understand they have a squad of middies and clerks making copies for all the ships as the information comes in.'

The meeting closed and Drinkwater urged his oarsmen to hurry back to *Virago*. Already his active mind was preparing itself for the coming hours. Away to the southward of them *Amazon* was anchored off Saltholm, together with the *Lark* and the other brig, *Harpy*, and the cutter *Fox*. Boats were out with leadsmen, their cold crews struggling through the floes of ice that reminded them all that further to the eastward the pack was breaking up and every day brought the combination of a Russian fleet closer. Even before they reached *Virago*, *Cruizer* was underway again with Lord Nelson on board to reconnoitre the enemy position.

It was late afternoon on the 31st before Drinkwater and his two boats pulled away from *Virago*'s side. Astern of them each towed the materials for two buoys, dismantled and lashed together so as not to inhibit the efforts of the oarsmen. Each boat was heavily laden with nets of round shot in the bilges, small barricoes of water under the thwarts and each oarsman had his feet on a coil of rope and a cutlass. The oars were double-banked with two spare men huddled in the bow. All, officers and men alike, were muffled in sheepskins and woollen scarves, mittens and assorted headgear. All had had a double ration of spirits before leaving the ship and two kegs of neat rum were stowed under the stern sheets of each boat. Mr Jex had protested at the extravagance but had been quietly over-ruled by Drinkwater.

Quilhampton sat in the stern next to his commander. His new left hand had been hurriedly fashioned from a lump of oak and was able to hold both a tiller and a notebook.

'It's good enough for the present,' Quilhampton had said earlier, and added with a grin, 'and impervious to the cold.'

Drinkwater felt the pressure of the crude hand against his arm as Quilhampton swung the boat to avoid an ice floe. On his own hands he wore fur mitts over a pair of silk stockings. Experiment had shown he could manage a pencil by casting off the mittens on their lanyard, and using his fingers through the stockings.

They headed for *Amazon*, reaching the frigate an hour after sunset, and Drinkwater reported to Captain Edward Riou. Not many years older than Drinkwater himself, Riou had made his reputation ten years earlier when he had saved the *Guardian* after striking an iceberg in the Southern Ocean. His remarkable energy had not deserted him and he had given up command of a battleship to carry out his special duties in the frigate *Amazon*. He fixed his bright, intelligent eyes on Drinkwater as the latter explained his ideas for buoying the edges of the shoals.

'You will find Brisbane has anchored *Cruizer* at the north end of the Middle Ground with lights hoisted as a mark for all the boats out surveying. I have instructed the masters and officers now out sounding to anchor their boats on the five fathom line until relieved by the launches carrying the buoys, but I admit the superiority of your suggestion. In view of your experience then, you should take your boats to the southern end of the Holland Deep and establish the run of the Middle Ground to the southward. It is essential that both limits of the Deep are buoyed out by the morning and, if possible, that its southernmost extension is discovered. Lord Nelson desires to move his squadron south tomorrow and to make his attack upon the Danish line from a position at the southern end of the Middle Ground.'

Virago's two boats lay gunwhale to gunwhale in the darkness. While Quilhampton supervised the issue of rum, Drinkwater gave Easton his final instructions.

'We steer west by compass, Mr Easton, until you find five fathoms, when you are to drop your anchor and show a light. I will pull round you to establish the general trend of the bottom at a distance of sixty or seventy yards. If I am satisfied that we've discovered the edge of the bank I will pull away from you to the south south east until I am approximately a cable southward, then I will turn west and sound for the five fathom line and signal you with three lights when I am anchored. If your bearing has not altered greatly we may reasonably assume the line of the bank to be constant between the two boats. If there is a great change it will show the trend of the bank towards the east or west and we will buoy it. Do you understand?'

'Perfectly sir.'

'Very well, now we will lay a buoy at the first point to determine the starting position, so make ready and take a bearing from *Cruizer* when it is laid.'

'Aye, aye, sir.'

'Very well, let's make a start. Give way, Mr Q.'

The night was bitterly cold and the leadsmen were going to become very wet. The wind remained from the north and the sea, though slight, was vicious enough for the deep boats, sending little patters of freezing spray into their faces so that first they ached intolerably and then they numbed and the men at the oars became automata. Just within sight of each other the two boats pulled west, the boat-compasses on the bottom boards lit by lanterns at the officers' feet. Forward the leadsman chanted, his line specially shortened to five fathoms so as not to waste time with greater depths.

Drinkwater kneaded the muscle of his right upper arm which was growing increasingly painful the longer they remained in this cold climate. The knotted fibres of the flesh sent a dull ache through his whole chest as the hours passed and he cursed Edouard Santhonax, the man who had inflicted the wound.

The shout of 'Bottom!' was almost simultaneous from the two

boats and Drinkwater nodded for Quilhampton to circle Easton's boat, listening to his leadsman while the splash over the bow of the other boat indicated where Easton got his anchor overboard. Drinkwater picked up the hand-bearing compass. He would need the shaded lantern to read it but they were roughly west of Easton now.

'Five, five, no bottom, five, four, three, shoaling fast, sir!'

'Very well, bring her round to the northward,' he said to Quilhampton, staring at the dark shape of the other boat which had swung to the wind.

'Three, three, four, three, four, three . . .'

'Bring her to starboard again, Mr Q.' The oars knocked rhythmically against the thole pins and spray splashed aboard.

'. . . three, three, four, four, five . . . no bottom sir, no bottom . . .' He looked back at Easton and then at the boat compass. Easton was showing a light now; presumably he had made his notes and could afford to exhibit the guttering lantern on the gunwhale.

'Head south, now, Mr Q, pass across his stern so we can hail him.'

'Aye, aye, sir.'

'Everything all right, Mr Easton?'

'Aye, sir. We anchored to the buoy sinker and have almost readied the first buoy . . .' The sound of hammering came from the boat.

'Keep showing your light, Mr Easton. Head south south east, Mr Q, pull for three minutes then turn west.'

Beside him Quilhampton began to whisper, 'One, and two, and three, and four . . .'

Drinkwater kept his eyes on the light aboard Easton's boat. Presently he felt the pressure of the tiller as Quilhampton turned west. He listened to the headsman's chant.

'No bottom, no bottom, no bottom . . . no bottom, five!'

'Holdwater all! Anchor forrard there!'

A splash answered Quilhampton's order, followed by the thrum of hemp over a gunwhale. 'Oars . . . oars across the boat . . .'

The men pulled their looms inboard and bent their heads over their crossed arms. Backs heaved as the monotonous labour ceased for a while. Drinkwater took a bearing of Easton's feeble light and found it to be north by east a half east.

'Issue water and biscuit, Mr Q.' He raised his voice. 'Change places, lads, carefully now, we'll have grog issued when we lay the first buoy. Well done the leadsman. Are you very wet Tregembo?'

'Fucking soaked, zur.' There was a low rumble of laughter round the boat.

'Serves 'ee right for volunteerin',' said an anonymous voice in the darkness and they all laughed again.

'Right, we wait now, for Mr Easton. Give him the three lights Mr Q.'

Quilhampton raised the lantern from the bottom boards and held it up three times, receiving a dousing of Easton's in reply, but then the master's lantern reappeared on the gunwhale and nothing seemed to happen for a long time. A restive murmur went round the boat as the perspiration dried on the oarsmen and the cold set in, threatening to cramp ill-nourished and overexerted muscles.

'I daresay he's experiencing some delay in getting the buoy over,' said Drinkwater and, a few moments later, the light went out. Five minutes afterwards Easton was hailing them.

'We tangled with a boat from *Harpy*, sir. He demanded what we were doing in his sector.'

'What did you say?'

'Said we were from *Virago* executing Lord Nelson's orders, he used the password "Westmoreland" to which I replied "Northumberland".'

'Did that satisfy him?'

'Well he said he'd never heard of *Virago*, sir, but Lord Nelson sounded familiar and would we be kind enough to find out how far to the south this damned bank went.'

'Only too happy to oblige . . . sound round me then carry on to the south . . .'

'D'you think the Danes'll attack us, sir?' asked Quilhampton.

'To be frank I don't know; if 'twas the French doing this at Spithead I doubt we would leave 'em unmolested. On the other hand they seem to have made plenty of preparations to receive us and may wish to lull us a little. Still, it would be prudent to keep a sharp lookout, eh?'

'Aye, sir.'

They waited what seemed an age before the three lights were shown from Easton's boat then they continued south, the men stiff with cold and eager to work up some warmth. After sounding round the master's boat they left it astern, the lead plopping overboard as the oars thudded gently against the thole pins.

As the leadsman found the five fathom line the boat was anchored to the net of round shot on its ten fathom line and Drinkwater had the oars brought inboard and stowed while they prepared the buoy. Hauling alongside the four planks and two spars the men pulled them aboard, dripping over their knees, and cast off the lashings.

'Do you make sure the holes in the planks coincide before you nail 'em, Mr Q, or we're in trouble . . .'

They hauled the awkward and heavy planks across the boat in the form of a cross and, holding the lantern up, aligned the holes. Nailing the planks proved more difficult than anticipated since the point at which the hammer struck was unsupported. Eventually the nails were driven home and spunyarn lashings passed to reinforce them.

The four arm bridle was soon fitted and the awkward contraption manoeuvred to take the pole up through its centre. Eventually, as Easton completed pulling round them and set off for the south, they bent their anchor line to the bridle and prepared to cast off.

'Three lights, sir,' reported Quilhampton.

'Yes,' said Drinkwater, holding up his hand compass, 'and I fancy the bank is trending a little to the westward. Very well,' he snapped the compass shut, 'cast off from the buoy!'

He looked astern as they pulled away. The thin line of the spar soon disappeared in the darkness but the weft streamed out just above the horizon against the slightly lighter sky.

They laboured on throughout the small hours of the night, celebrating their success from time to time in two-finger grog. The trend to the east did not develop although Easton laid a second buoy before the bank swung southward again.

Drinkwater's boat was on its fifth run towards the west and already the sky was lightening in the east when Drinkwater realised something was wrong.

'Oars!' he commanded and the men ceased pulling, their oars coming up to the horizontal. He bent over the little compass and compared its findings with the steering compass in the bottom of the boat. Easton's boat was well on the starboard quarter. Ahead of them he thought he could see the low coast of Amager emerging from the darkness, but he could not be sure. The boat slewed as an ice floe nudged it.

'I believe we've overshot the bank, Mr Q. Turn north, and keep the lead going forrard there!'

'Aye, aye, zur!'

As the daylight grew it became clear that they had misjudged their distance from Easton and over-run the tail of the bank for some distance, but after an anxious fifteen minutes Tregembo found the bottom.

As they struggled to get their second buoy over, Easton came up to them.

'Don't bother to sound round me, Mr Easton, this is the tail of the bank all right.'

'Well done, sir.'

'And to you and your boat. You may transfer aboard here, Mr Easton, with your findings. Mr Q you will take Mr Easton's boat back to the ship.'

'Aye, aye, sir.'

'Buoy's ready, zur.'

'Very well, hold on to it there . . .' The boats bumped together and Easton and Quilhampton exchanged places. 'A rum issue before we part, eh?'

The men managed a thin cheer and in the growing light Drinkwater saw the raw faces and sunken eyes of his two boats' crews. The wind was still fresh from the north west and it would be a hard pull to windward for them. A heavy ice floe bumped the side of the boat. 'Bear it off Cottrell!'

There was no move from forward. 'Cottrell! D'you hear man?'

'Beg pardon, sir, but Cottrell's dead sir.'

'Dead?' Drinkwater stood and pushed his way forward, suddenly realising how chilled and cramped his muscles had become through squatting over his lantern, chart and compasses. He nearly fell overboard and only saved himself by catching hold of a man's shoulder. It was Cottrell's and he lolled sideways like a log. His face was covered by a thin sheen of ice crystals and his eyes stared accusingly out at Drinkwater.

'Get him in the bottom.' Drinkwater stumbled aft again and sat down.

'Can't sir, he's stiff as a board.'

Drinkwater swore beneath his breath. 'Shall I pitch 'im overboard sir?'

He had not liked to give such an order himself. 'Aye,' he replied, 'Poor old Jack . . . We have no alternative, lads.'

'He weren't a bad old sod, were 'e?'

There was a splash from forward. The body rolled over once and disappeared. A silence hung over the boat and Quilhampton asked 'Permission to proceed sir?'

'Carry on, Mr Q.'

'Zur!' Tregembo's whisper was harsh and urgent.

'What the devil is it?'

'Thought I saw a boat over there!'

Tregembo pointed north west, in the direction of Copenhagen. Drinkwater stood unsteadily. He could see a big launch pulling to the southward. It might be British but it might also be Danish. He thought of recalling Mr Quilhampton who was already pulling away from them but if the strange boat had not yet seen them he did not wish to risk discovery of the buoy that marked so important a point as the south end of the Middle Ground. Perhaps they could remove the weft, the bare pole would be much more difficult to see . . .

He rejected the idea, knowing the difficulty of relocating the bank and the buoy themselves, particularly in circumstances other than they had enjoyed tonight.

In the end he decided on a bold measure. 'Let go the buoy!'

He grabbed the tiller and leaned forward to peer in the compass. 'Give way together!' He swung the boat to the north west.

Heading directly for Copenhagen they could scarcely avoid being seen from the big launch. It was vital that observers in the approaching launch did not see the spar-buoy at the southern end of the Middle Ground.

The men were tired now and pulling into the wind after labouring at the oars all night was too much for them. Adding to their fatigue was a concentration of ice floes that made their progress more difficult still. After a few minutes it was obvious that they had been seen from the launch. Drinkwater swung the boat away to the north east, across the Middle Ground, drawing the pursuing launch away from the southernmost buoy. From time to time he looked grimly over his shoulder. He closed his mind to the ironic ignominy of capture and urged the oarsmen to greater efforts. But they could see the pursuing launch and knew they were beaten.

'Hang on, sir, that's one of them damned flat boats!'

'Eh?' Drinkwater turned again, numb with the cold and the efforts of the night. He could see the boat clearly now.

'Boat 'hoy! "Spencer"!' Drinkwater cudgelled his brain for the countersign given him by Riou.

' "Jervis"!' he called, then, turning to the boat's crew, 'Oars!' The men rested.

The big boat came up, pulled by forty seamen who had clearly not spent the night wrestling with leadlines and ice floes.

'What ship?' A tall lieutenant stood in her stern.

'*Virago*, Lieutenant Drinkwater in command.'

'Good morning, Lieutenant, my name's Davies, off to reconnoitre the guns at Dragør. There's a lot of you fellows out among the ice. Did you take us for a Dane?'

'Aye.'

'Ah, well, sir, 'tis All Fool's day today . . . Good morning to you.'

The big boat turned away. 'Well I'm damned!' said Drinkwater and, as if to further confound him the wind began to back to the westward. 'Well I'm damned,' he repeated. 'Give way, lads, it's time for breakfast.'

Chapter Sixteen *1 April 1801*

All Fool's Day

Drinkwater's tired oarsmen pulled alongside *Amazon* as the frigate got under way. Riou complied with Drinkwater's request that his boat be allowed to return to *Virago* under the master and that he remain on board to give his findings to Fothergill.

Before passing off the quarterdeck into the cabin where Fothergill and other weary officers were collating information, Riou asked, 'How far south did you get, Mr Drinkwater?'

'I found the southern end of the bank, sir, and marked it with a spar buoy.'

'Excellent. I have recalled *Cruizer* as you see. Lord Nelson joins us and we are taking *Harpy, Lark* and *Fox* through the Holland Deep . . .'

'Sir . . .' A midshipman interrupted them. 'Begging your pardon, sir, but Lord Nelson's barge is close, sir . . .'

'Excuse me . . .' Drinkwater went aft as Riou stepped to meet the vice-admiral at the entry. He was soon lost in a mass of plotting and checking, working alongside Fothergill as the findings of the night were carefully laid on the master chart. For an hour they worked in total concentration as *Amazon* made her way southwards. When they emerged on the quarterdeck to take a breath of air they both looked astern. A master's mate came up to Fothergill to brief him as to what had been going on.

'*Cruizer*'s reanchored off the north end of the Middle Ground with *Harpy* a mile south and *Lark* a further mile to the south of her.'

'The admiral don't trust our buoys, eh?' smiled Fothergill, exhausted beyond protest.

'Don't trust the fleet not to see 'em or run 'em down, more likely.'

'The mark vessels are to hoist signals to indicate they are to be passed to starboard,' offered the master's mate helpfully.

Drinkwater heard his name called by Captain Riou. 'Sir?'

The admiral smiled. 'Morning, Drinkwater. I understand you found the end of the Middle Ground.' Nelson crossed the deck just as it canted wildly. The vice-admiral fell against Drinkwater who caught him, surprised at the frail lightness of his body.

Amazon had approached too closely to the Saltholm shore to avoid the occasional ranging shot ricochetting from the Danish batteries two miles away, and while Riou resolutely set more canvas and pressed the frigate over the mud, Nelson turned to a group of unhappy looking men in plain coats who Drinkwater realised were the pilots from the Trinity House at Hull. He remembered Nelson's poor opinion of their enthusiasm.

'There gentlemen,' he quipped, 'a practical demonstration of the necessity of holding to the channel.' The admiral turned again to Drinkwater, calmly ignoring Riou's predicament of getting *Amazon* into deeper water.

'The southern end of the shoal Mr Drinkwater . . .?'

'Marked, my lord, with a spar buoy.'

'Good.' The admiral paused then turned to a group of officers all heavily bedecked with epaulettes. 'Admiral Graves, Captains Dommett and Otway, may I present Mr Drinkwater, gentlemen, Lieutenant commanding the bomb *Virago*.'

Drinkwater managed a stiff bow.

'Mr Drinkwater has laid a spar buoy on the south Middle Ground . . .' There was a murmur of appreciation that was without condescension.

'Will a spar buoy be sufficient, my lord? If the division is to use it as a mark for anchoring may I suggest a more substantial mark.' It was Rear Admiral Graves and Dommett nodded.

'I concur with Admiral Graves, my lord.'

Nelson turned to the remaining captain. 'Otway?'

'Yes, my lord, I agree.'

'By your leave, my lord . . .'

'Yes, Drinkwater, what is it?'

'There is great movement of ice coming down from the south east, I observed the spar buoys were merely spun by the floes whereas I fear a larger object like a boat . . .'

'Oh, I doubt that, Drinkwater,' put in Captain Otway, 'a boat is a more substantial body with a stem to deflect the floes, no a boat, my lord, with a mast and flag . . .'

'And a lantern,' added Graves.

Drinkwater flushed as Nelson confirmed the opinion. 'Very well then, a boat it shall be. Don't be discouraged Mr Drinkwater, your exertions have justified you in my opinion, and Captain Dommett will write you orders to have your bomb vessel in the line when we attack the Danes.'

'Thank you, my lord.'

'And now will you be so kind as to direct Fothergill that when he returns to *Cruizer* he is to have one of the brig's boats placed in accordance with our decision.'

Drinkwater slept in a chair in *Amazon*'s wardroom as the frigate reached the end of the Holland Deep, sighted his spar buoy and turned north to order *Fox* anchored south of *Lark*. Nelson had concluded there was ample room to anchor his division off the southern end of the Middle Ground out of range of the Danish guns. The wind had veered again and *Amazon* had to beat laboriously back through the Holland Deep to report to Sir Hyde Parker. This delay enabled Drinkwater to sleep off most of his exhaustion.

He was pulled back to *Virago* with Fothergill who handed him his copy of the chart before leaving for *Cruizer* and his own trip south to replace Drinkwater's buoy.

'The cartography isn't up to your own standard, Mr Drinkwater, but it'll serve.'

Drinkwater unrolled the corner of the chart. 'A midshipman's penmanship if I ain't mistaken,' he grinned at Fothergill. 'Your servant, Mr Fothergill . . .' Reaching up for the manropes he hauled himself up *Virago*'s side, the chart rolled in his breast.

'Welcome back, sir,' said Rogers.

'Thank you. Where's Mr Tumilty?'

'Here, sir, here I am Nat'aniel . . .'

'I owe you five guineas, Tom . . .'

'You do? By Jesus, what did I tell 'ee, Mr Rogers, that's five from you too . . .' Tumilty burst into a fit of gleeful laughter. 'An' it's All Fool's Day so it is.'

'All ready, Mr Drinkwater?' Drinkwater leaned over the rail to look down at Nelson in his barge. He was an unimpressive sight, his squared cocked hat at a slouch and an old checked overcoat round his thin shoulders.

'We await only your signal to weigh, my lord.'

'Very good. Instruct that Irish devil to make every shot tell.'

'Aye, aye, my lord.' Nelson nodded to his coxswain and the barge passed to the next ship in his division.

An hour later the greater part of the British force placed under Lord Nelson's orders stood to the southward, leaving the two three deckers, *St George* and *London*, four seventy-fours and two sixty-fours with Sir Hyde Parker at their anchorage at the north end of the Middle Ground. Passing slowly south under easy sail between the lines of improvised buoys and the anchored warning vessels Drinkwater was able to steady his glass on the horizon to the westward.

Preoccupation with other matters had not given him leisure to study the object of all their efforts, the city of Copenhagen. Above its low stretch of roofs the bulk of the Amalienbourg Palace was conspicuous. So were several fantastic and exotic spires. That of Our Saviour's church had a tall elongated spire with an exterior staircase mounting its side, while that of the Børsen was equally tall and entwined by four huge serpents.

But in the foreground the fortress of Trekroner, the Three Crowns, and the batteries of the Lynetten that lay before them, guarded the approaches to the city and combined with the line of blockships, cut down battleships, floating batteries, frigates and gun vessels to form a formidable defensive barrier. The enemy was only a little over two miles away, just out of range, though an occasional shot was fired at the British as they boldly crossed the Danish front.

Nelson made few signals to his ships. At half past five he ordered the *Ardent* and *Agamemnon* to take the guard duty for the night and shortly after eight in the evening, the wind falling light and finally calm, the last ship came to her anchor in the crowded road. This was *Cruizer*, withdrawn from her station as a mark vessel.

As *Virago* came to her own anchor at about six-fifteen, Nelson made the signal for the night's password.

'Spanish jack over a red pendant. What does that signify, Mr Q?'

'Er . . . "Winchester", sir.'

'Very well. Pass word I want all the officers to dine with me this evening within the hour. I anticipate further work later in the night.'

'Aye, aye, sir.' It would scarcely be a 'dinner' since the galley stove was now extinguished and Tumilty and Trussel had begun to make their preparations for action, but Jex could hustle up something and Drinkwater wished to speak to them all.

He looked down into the waist in the gathering dusk. A party of artillerymen under the bombardier, Hite, were scouring the chamber of the after mortar to remove any scale. He wondered how the soldiers had got on between decks for there was little enough room for them all. They had slung their hammocks in the cable tier and he did not think either Tumilty or Rogers had spared much effort on their welfare.

At eight, just as *Virago*'s officers sat down to dinner, shells were reported coming over from howitzer batteries ashore, but the activity soon died away. Mr Quilhampton, shivering on the poop and excluded from the meal, recorded in *Virago*'s log various signals passed from the *Elephant* by guard boat and rocket. Mostly the signals concerned the direction of boats from the brigs and gun vessels as the admiral made his final dispositions. The bomb vessels were left largely alone.

But it was not for long. While Mr Tumilty was expatiating on the forthcoming employment of his beloved mortars, Mr Quilhampton had his revenge for missing dinner.

'Beg pardon, sir, but a boat's alongside from the flagship. His lordship's compliments and would you be kind enough to attend him at once.'

Drinkwater stood. 'It seems you must excuse me gentlemen. Please do not disturb yourselves on my account, but I would recommend that you rested. There is likely to be warm work for us tomorrow.' A cheer went up at this and only Jex remained silent as Quilhampton added:

'It is exceeding cold, sir . . .'

'I think I can manage, Mr Q, thank you,' Drinkwater replied drily.

Drinkwater scrambled down into the waiting boat. In his pocket he had stuffed notebook, pencil and bearing compass. As he settled alongside the unknown midshipman he observed the truth of Mr Quilhampton's solicitude. It was bitterly cold and the ice floes were even more numerous than they had been previously. The current, too, was strong, sweeping them northwards towards The Sound. The wind had died away to a dead calm. Above the surface of the sea the low wisps of arctic 'sea-smoke' almost hid the boat itself, though it was clear at eye level.

They crossed *Elephant*'s stern. The windows were a blaze of light with the shadows of movement visible within.

'Admiral's dining with the captains of the fleet, sir,' explained the midshipman, swinging the boat under the two-decker's quarter and alongside her larboard entry.

Drinkwater reported to the officer of the watch who conducted him to the ante-room. A number of officers were gathered there, mostly wearing the plain blue coats of sailing masters. There was a group of pilots who looked more worried than when Drinkwater had last seen them. From beyond the doors leading into the *Elephant*'s great cabin came the noise of conviviality.

A man in lieutenant's uniform detached himself from a small knot of masters and came over to Drinkwater with his hand extended.

'Evening. John Quilliam, third of *Amazon*.'

'Evenin'. Nathaniel Drinkwater, in command of *Virago*.' They shook hands.

'Captain Riou spoke highly of you after your visit to *Amazon* the other day.'

Drinkwater blushed. 'That was exceedingly kind of him.' He changed the subject. 'I trust your frigate was not damaged by the grounding?'

'I imagine she may have lost a little copper, but she'll do for today's work . . .' Quilliam smiled as a burst of cheering came from the adjacent room.

'Take no notice of that, Drinkwater, his lordship'll not let it interfere with tonight's business.'

'Which is . . .?'

'There is a little dispute about the water in the King's Deep. The pilots incline to the view that it is deeper on the Middle Ground side. Briarly, master of the *Bellona*, opposes their view, while Captain Hardy and Captain Riou are undecided. The Admiral has two boats assembled, one for Briarly and myself, the other for Hardy and you . . .'

'Me?'

Quilliam smiled again but any explanation as to why Drinkwater had been specially selected was lost as the double doors of the cabin were opened by an immaculate, pig-tailed messman and a glittering assembly of gold-laced officers emerged. They were all smiling and shaking hands, having dined well and in expectation of lean commons on the morrow. Drinkwater recognised Admiral Graves and Captain Foley, familiar too was 'Bounty' Bligh of the *Glatton*, Edward Riou and George Murray of the *Edgar*, but the remainder were largely unknown to him. At the rear of the group the short, one-armed admiral, his breast ablaze with orders and crossed by the red ribbon of the Bath, had his left hand on the elbow of a tall post-captain who ducked instinctively beneath the deckhead beams.

'Ah, Quilliam,' said his lordship, catching sight of the two lieutenants, 'is all made ready?'

'Aye, my lord.'

'And you have briefed Lieutenant Drinkwater?' Quilliam nodded. 'Very good. Captain Hardy, I commend these two officers to you and I rely upon you to find out the truth of the matter.'

'Very well, my lord,' the tall captain growled and turned to the two lieutenants. 'Come gentlemen . . . Mr Briarly, let us make a start.'

They climbed down into the boats and were about to leave *Elephant*'s side when Nelson's high-pitched voice called down to them.

'Arc your oars muffled?'

'Yes my lord.'

'Very well. Should the Danish guard boat discover you, you must pull like devils, and get out of his way as fast as you can.'

There was a murmur of enthusiastic assent from the seamen at the oars.

'Good luck then.'

Hardy, captain of the *St George* anchored eight miles to the north, had brought his own boat. A bright young midshipman leant against the tiller. He was muffled in an expensive bearskin coat provided by an indulgent parent well acquainted with the fleet's destination weeks earlier.

'I've had a long pole prepared for sounding, Mr Drinkwater, it'll make less noise than a lead.'

'Aye, aye, sir.'

Drinkwater wondered how close to the enemy they were to go

that they needed to take such a precaution. They pulled in silence for a few minutes and Drinkwater noted their course by the light of the shaded lantern on the bottom boards.

'This north-going current is damned strong . . .'

'About two knots, sir.'

'Did you lay the mark on the south end of the Middle Ground?'

'Yes, sir. I laid a buoy on it and Lord Nelson ordered the buoy substituted by a boat.'

'Let us hope we can find it in the dark.'

They did find it. After half an hour of pulling east and then west after finding five fathoms, they discovered the set of the current was considerable and had misled them. But, having established the bearing of the moored boat from the admiral's lights hung in *Elephant*'s rigging, they began to move away.

'May I suggest we pull round the mark boat, sir, in order to establish that it has not substantially dragged and still marks the south end of the shoal.'

Hardy grunted approval and Drinkwater directed the midshipman while a man dipped the long pole overboard like a quant and peered at the black and white markings painted on it.

'It seems to be holding sir. I was worried because I only laid moorings for a spar buoy. I think Mr Fothergill must have laid a proper anchor.'

' 'Tis no matter, Mr Drinkwater. Time in reconnaissance is seldom wasted.'

They pulled west, losing the edge of the bank and swinging across the King's Channel that ran north, parallel to the Amager shore, the waterfront of Copenhagen and the defensive line of the Danish guns. The water deepened rapidly and the call came back that there was 'No bottom' until it gradually began to shoal on the Amager side.

Hardy swung the boat to the north while a man forward with a boat hook shoved the ice aside and the oarsmen struggled to pull rhythmically despite the floes that constantly impeded their efforts.

'There seems to be between six and eight fathoms in the main channel, sir,' Drinkwater said in a low voice after crouching in the boat's bottom and consulting his notebook. He was by no means certain of their exact position, but their line of bearing from *Elephant* was still reasonably accurate. 'The Middle Ground seems to be steep-to, with gentler shoaling on the Amager shore.'

Hardy leaned over his shoulder and nodded. 'Now I think you had better shutter that lantern and wrap canvas round it . . . not a word now, you men. Pull with short easy strokes and let the current do the work . . . Mr Fancourt . . .' Hardy pointed to larboard and the midshipman nodded. Drinkwater looked up and it took some minutes for his eyes to adjust again after the yellow lamplight.

Then he saw the enemy, dark, huge and menacing ahead of them. The southernmost ship of the Danish line was an old battleship. The spars that reared into the night sky showed that she had been cut down and was not rigged to sail, but two tiers of gun ports could just be made out and she was moored head and stern to chains.

Perfect silence reigned, broken only by the occasional plash and dribble as Hardy himself wielded the sounding pole. They could hear voices that spoke in a totally unfamiliar tongue, but they were not discovered. They were so close as they sounded round the enemy vessel that they thought there must have been times when the upper end of the pole appeared above the enemy's rail.

Greatly daring, Hardy pulled once more across the channel while Drinkwater scribbled the soundings down blind, hoping he could sort out his notes later. Satisfied at last, Hardy turned to the midshipman.

'Very well, Mr Fancourt, you may rejoin the admiral.'

Six bells rang out on *Elephant*'s fo'c's'le and the sentries were crying 'All's well!' as Hardy's boat returned alongside. Drinkwater followed Hardy under the poop and into the brilliantly lit great cabin. Briarly and Quilliam had returned ahead of them. Clustered round the master-chart that now carried much greater detail than when Drinkwater had last seen it were Nelson, Riou and Foley.

Nelson looked up. 'Ah, Hardy, you are back . . . Mr Briarly, oblige these two with a glass . . . right, what have you for us, Hardy?'

Drinkwater slopped the rum that Briarly handed him. He was shaking from the cold and though the cabin was not excessively warm, the candles seemed to make it very hot after the hours spent in the boat. He swallowed the rum gratefully and slowly mastered his shivering. There was clearly a dispute going on over the comparative depths.

'Call the pilots,' said Nelson at length. After a delay the elderly men entered the cabin. They too had dined and drunk well and spoke in thick Yorkshire accents. Drinkwater listened to the debate in progress round the chart-table. He helped himself to a second glass of rum and began to feel better, the alcohol numbing the ache in his arm. At last Nelson suppressed further argument.

'Gentlemen, gentlemen, it seems that the greater depth of water is to be found on the Middle Ground side of the King's Deep, yet, if what Captain Hardy says holds good for the length of the Channel, some danger will attend holding too strictly to that assertion, for the rapid shoaling on that side will give little warning of the proximity of the bank. Foley, we must include some such reference in the orders. Masters must pay attention to the matter and remark the leadsmen's calls with great diligence. I see little risk to the fleet if this injunction is remembered. Mr Drinkwater's buoy at the southern end of the Middle Ground is the keystone to the enterprise. Gentlemen I wish you good night . . .'

Drinkwater returned to *Virago* in a borrowed boat. His mind was woolly with fatigue and Nelson's rum. But the ache in his arm had almost gone, together with his worries over Nelson's opinion of him.

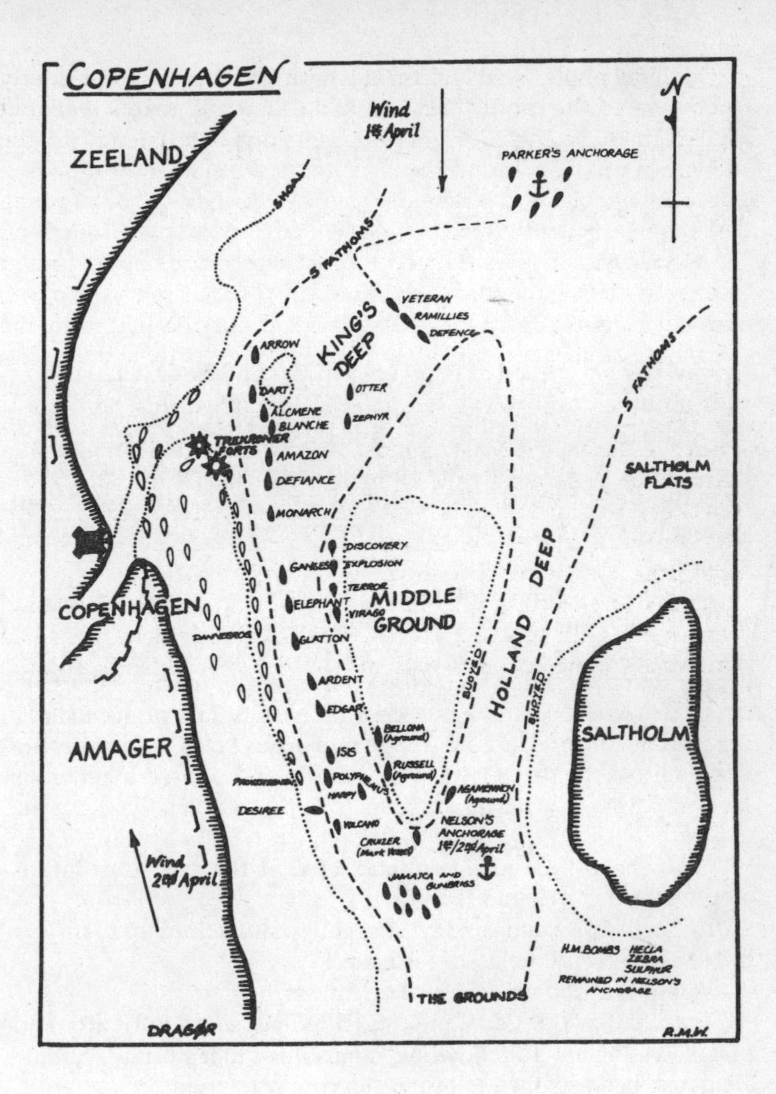
COPENHAGEN
Wind 1st April
N
ZEELAND
PARKER'S ANCHORAGE
SHOAL
5 FATHOMS
VETERAN
RAMILLIES
DEFENCE
KING'S DEEP
ARROW
DART
ALCMENE
BLANCHE
OTTER
ZEPHYR
TREKRONER FORTS
AMAZON
DEFIANCE
MONARCH
DISCOVERY
EXPLOSION
GANGES
TERROR
ELEPHANT
VIRAGO
MIDDLE GROUND
GLATTON
COPENHAGEN
ARDENT
EDGAR
BELLONA (Aground)
ISIS
RUSSELL (Aground)
POLYPHEMUS
HARPY
AGAMEMNON (Aground)
DESIREE
VULCANO
CRUIZER (Mark Vessel)
NELSON'S ANCHORAGE 1st/2nd April
JAMAICA AND GUNBRIGS
BUOYED
HOLLAND DEEP
5 FATHOMS
SALTHOLM FLATS
SALTHOLM
AMAGER
Wind 2nd April
H.M. BOMBS HECLA ZEBRA SULPHUR
REMAINED IN NELSON'S ANCHORAGE
THE GROUNDS
DRAGØR
R.M.W.

Chapter Seventeen *2 April 1801, Forenoon*

The Last Blunders

Drinkwater was called at eight bells in the middle watch. He was sour-mouthed and worse tempered. The chill in his cabin had brought back the ache in his arm and the insufficient sleep had left him feeling worse than ever. Rogers came in, having just taken over the deck from Trussel, with the news that the wind had sprung up from the south east. 'It seems our luck has changed at last, sir.'

'Huh! Get me hot water . . .'

'Tregembo's got the matter in hand . . .'

'Tregembo?'

'He spent yesterday sponging your best uniform and sharpening your sword. There was a deal of activity last night. *Blanche* dragged her anchor and there were numerous boats pulling about.' Rogers lifted the decanter from its fiddle and poured a generous measure. 'Here Nat, drink this, you'll feel better.' He held out the glass.

'God's bones!' Drinkwater shuddered as the raw spirit hit his empty stomach. 'Thanks Sam.'

'I've called all hands and got the galley stove fired up to fill 'em full of burgoo and molasses for ballast.'

'Very good. Did you enjoy your dinner?'

'Yes, thank you. Old Lettsom trilled us some jolly airs and Matchett sung us "Tom Bowling" and some other stuff by Dibdin.' He paused and seemed to be considering something.

'What is it?'

'Jex, sir . . .'

'Oh?'

'Acted rather oddly. Left us abruptly in the middle of dinner and we found him sitting on the bowsprit, tight as a tick and crying his bloody eyes out.'

'What time was this? Did any of the men see?'

'Well some did, sir. It happened about ten last night. Lettsom made us put him to bed, though I was inclined to put him under arrest . . .'

'No, no. You have been a trifle hard on him, Sam.'

'Bloody man's a coward, sir . . .'

'That's a stiff allegation to make. D'you have evidence to support it?'

'Aye, during the action with the luggers we found him cowering on the spare sails.'

'Why didn't you report him then?' asked Drinkwater sharply, getting up. Rogers was silent for a moment.

'Saw no point in bothering you . . .'

'Kept damned silent for your own purposes, more like it,' Drinkwater suddenly blazed. 'Jex is the worst kind of purser, Sam, but I had the measure of the man and now you have goaded him to this extreme . . .' Drinkwater fell silent as Tregembo knocked and entered the cabin. He brought a huge bowl of steaming hot water and put it down on the cabin chest, then he bustled about, laying out Drinkwater's best uniform and clean undergarments.

'You're worse than a bloody wife, Tregembo,' said Drinkwater partially recovering his good temper as the rum spread through him.

'Very well, Mr Rogers,' he said at last, 'let us forget the matter. As long as he stands to his station today we'll say no more about any aspect of it.'

'Aye, aye, sir,' replied Rogers woodenly, leaving the cabin.

After Tregembo had left Drinkwater stripped himself, decanted a little water with which to shave then lifted the bowl of water onto the deck. For a few shuddering moments he immersed as much of himself as he could, dabbing half-heartedly with a bar of soap and drying himself quickly. Bathing and putting on clean underwear was chiefly to reduce infection of any wounds he might suffer but, in fact, it raised his morale and when he stepped on deck in the dawn, his boat cloak over two shirts and his best coat, he had forgotten the labours of the night.

He paced the poop in the growing light, looking up occasionally at the masthead pendant to check the wind had not shifted. He could scarcely believe that after all the delays, disappointments and hardships, the wind that had played them so foul for so long should actually swing into the required quarter as if on cue.

Tregembo approached him with a crestfallen look. 'Mr Drinkwater, zur.'

'Eh? What is it Tregembo?'

'Your sword, zur, you forgot your sword.'

'Ah . . . er, yes, I'm sorry, and thank you for attending to it yesterday.'

Tregembo grunted and handed the weapon over. Drinkwater took it. The leather scabbard was badly worn, the brass ferrule at the end scratched. The stitching of the scabbard was missing at one point and the rings were almost worn through where they fastened to the sling. He half drew the blade. The wicked, thin steel glinted dully, the brass hilt was notched and scored where it had guarded off more than a few blows and the heavy pommel, that counterbalanced the blade and made the weapon such a joy to handle, reminded him of a slithering fight on the deck of a French lugger when he had consigned a man to oblivion with its weight. The thought of that unknown Frenchman's murder made him think of Edward and he looked at the horizon to the north west, where the spires of Copenhagen were emerging from the night. He could see the line of the Danish ships, even pick out the tiny points of colour where their red ensigns already fluttered above the batteries. He buckled on the sword.

A feeling that something was wrong entered his head and it was some time before he detected its cause. The boat marking the southern end of the Middle Ground was missing.

It was clear Nelson had not slept. Drinkwater learned afterwards that he had laid down in his cot and spent the night dictating. He reported the missing mark only to hear that Nelson had already been informed and had sent for Brisbane to move *Cruizer* onto the spot and anchor there as a mark.

'Thanks to you and Hardy we have the bearing from *Elephant* so Brisbane should have no very great trouble.'

'Yes, my lord.'

'Come, Drinkwater, help yourself to some coffee from the sideboard there . . .'

'Thank you, my lord.'

'There should be something to eat, I shall be sending for all captains shortly so you may as well wait. Ah Foley . . .' Drinkwater did as he was bid, breakfasted and tried not to eavesdrop on Nelson's complex conversations with a variety of officers, secretaries and messengers who seemed to come into the cabin in an endless procession.

At seven o'clock every commander in Nelson's division had assembled on board the *Elephant*. Among the blue coats the scarlet of Colonel Stewart and Lieutenant-Colonel Brock commanding the detachment of the 49th Foot made a bright splash of colour, while the dull rifle-green of Captain Beckwith's uniform reflected a grimmer aspect of war.

Apart from the council aboard the flagship the British fleet seethed with activity. Drinkwater had little choice but to trust to the energies of Rogers and Tumilty in preparing the *Virago* for action, but he was learning that as a commander in such a complex operation as that intended by Nelson, it was more important to comprehend his admiral's intentions. Boats swarmed about the ships. On the decks of the battleships red-coated infantrymen drilled under their sergeants and were inspected by the indolent subalterns. Mates and lieutenants manoeuvred the big flat-boats into station while on every ship the chain slings were passed round the yards, the bulkheads knocked down, the boats not already in the water got outboard and towed astern, the nettings rigged and the decks sanded. Officers frequently glanced up at the masthead to see if the wind still held favourable.

Nelson explained his intended tactics by first describing the Danish line of defence:

'The enemy has eighteen vessels along the western side of the King's Deep. They mount some seven hundred guns of which over half are estimated to be above twenty-four pounds calibre. At the northern end, the line is supported by the Trekroner Forts. It is also supported by shore batteries like the Lynetten . . .' Each officer bent over his copy of the chart and made notes. Nelson went on, '. . . the force of the batteries is thought to be considerable and may include furnaces for heating shot. The Trekroner also appears to be supported by two additional heavy blockships.

'The channel into the port, dockyard and arsenal lies behind the Trekroner Forts and joins with the King's Channel just north of the forts. It is thought to be closed by a chain boom and is covered by enfilading fire from batteries on the land. Other ships, a seventy-four, a heavy frigate and some brigs and smaller vessels are anchored on this line.

'Batteries are also mounted on Amager, supporting the southern end of the line. In all the Danish defences extend four miles.'

The admiral paused and sipped from a glass of water. Drinkwater thought his face looked grey with worry but a fierce light darted from his one good eye and he watched the expressions of his captains as if seeking a weakness. He cleared his throat and went on.

'Each of you will receive written orders as to your station in the action from my secretary as you leave. These are as concise as possible and written on card for ease of handling. However it is my intention to explain the general plan to avoid needless confusion.

'As you have already been made aware, all the line of battleships are to have their anchors ready for letting go by the stern. They will anchor immediately upon coming abreast of their allotted target. *Edgar* will lead with Mr Briarly temporarily serving in her. Fire may be opened at your discretion. Captain Riou in *Amazon* is to take *Blanche, Alcmène, Arrow* and *Dart* and co-operate with the van in silencing the guns commanding the harbour mouth, or as other circumstances might require. The bomb vessels will take station outside the line of battleships and throw their shells into the dockyard and arsenal. Captain Rose in the *Jamaica,* frigate, is to take the gun-brigs into position for raking the line at its southern end, thus discouraging reinforcement of the floating batteries from the shore. Captain Inman in *Désirée* will also take up this station. Captain Fremantle with five hundred seamen will concert his action with Colonel Stewart and the 49th Regiment to embark in the flat-boats and storm the Trekroner Forts as soon as their fire is silenced.' Nelson looked round the assembly. 'It looks formidable to those who are children at war,' he said smiling inspiringly, 'but to my judgement, with ten sail of the line I think I can annihilate them.' There was a murmur of agreement. 'That is all. Are there any questions? Very well then. To your posts, gentlemen, and success to His Majesty's Arms.'

The captains, commanders and lieutenants-in-command filed out, collecting their written instructions as directed and Drinkwater, looking for his boat among the throng of craft pressing alongside *Elephant*'s flanks, found himself button-holed by Mr Briarly of the *Bellona*.

'Hold hard, sir. I ask you for your support for a moment. Lord Nelson has sent for masters and these damned pilots. They are still arguing about the approach to the King's Deep. You know Fothergill's boat is missing this morning?'

'Aye, it must have been driven off station by an ice floe, I warned . . .'

Briarly nodded. 'I heard,' he broke in impatiently, 'Look, Mr Drinkwater, you seem to have the admiral's ear, can you not persuade him that although there may be greater water on the Middle Ground side it is so steep-to that a small miscalculation . . .'

'Mr Briarly, his lordship has appointed you to lead the fleet in *Edgar,* surely the rest will follow.' Drinkwater was getting anxious about preparations aboard *Virago.*

'I was out this morning at first light, if each ship steers with . . .' he pointed out some conspicuous marks to Drinkwater which ensured a lead through the King's Deep.

'Are you certain of that?'

'Positive.'

'And will tell the admiral so?' Briarly nodded. 'Then I am certain you will carry the day, Mr Briarly. I am sure you do not need my assistance and I beg you let me return to my ship . . .'

'Morning, Drinkwater.' Drinkwater turned to find Martin at his other elbow.

'Good morning sir,' Drinkwater said absently, fishing in his pocket and remembering he had left his pocket compass in his greygoe. He would have liked to check the bearing of *Cruizer* to ensure Brisbane had anchored her in the correct place. Briarly had already gone to try and brow-beat the pilots.

'You are to be in the battle, Drinkwater,' said Martin, 'thanks to my good offices.'

'Yours sir?' Drinkwater looked up in astonishment. Martin nodded.

'I put in a good word for you the other day when I attended Lord Nelson.'

Drinkwater choked back an insubordinate laugh. 'Ah . . . I see . . . er, I'm greatly obliged to you sir.' And then he added with irresistible impishness, 'I shall inform Lord Dungarth of my obligation to you.'

Martin further astonished him by failing to see the implied sarcasm. 'I'd be vastly pleased if you would my dear fellow, vastly pleased.'

It was only when he was being pulled back to *Virago* that he remembered he had failed to take a bearing of the *Cruizer* from the *Elephant*.

'The admiral's just hoisted Number 14, sir,' reported Rogers as Drinkwater returned once again to *Virago*. ' "Prepare for battle and for anchoring with springs on the anchors and the end of the sheet cable taken in at the stern port." '

'Very well.'

'The ship is cleared for action, sir.'

'Very well, I shall make my rounds now. Mr Easton! Mr Easton be so good as to attend the flagship's signals. Here,' he handed his instruction card to the master, 'Study that. I do not anticipate weighing until after the line of battle ships.'

Drinkwater led the way below with Rogers following. In the cabin space the bulkheads had been hinged up so that the after carronades and stern chasers could be fired if necessary. 'Only the gun captains and powder monkeys to remain with these guns, Mr Rogers. All other men to be mustered on deck as sailtrimmers, firemen or for Mr Tumilty's shell hoists . . .'

'Aye, aye, sir.'

Drinkwater looked at the place where his table had so long stood. Beneath it the previously locked hatch to the magazine had been removed. An artillery private armed with a short fusil stood guard over it.

'Mr Trussel and Bombardier Hite are below, sir. The felt curtains are well doused and Mr Tumilty is satisfied.'

Two men emerged carrying a box each. 'Mr Willerton's powder boxes, sir, checked for leaks and found correct.' Drinkwater remembered Tumilty's strictness on this point. A leaking powder box laid a gradual powder train directly from the deck to the magazine.

'Very well.' He nodded encouragingly at the men and reascended to the poop, striding the length of the waist alongside the carronades.

'Same arrangement for the waist batteries, Mr Rogers . . .'

'Aye, aye, sir.'

Drinkwater climbed onto the fo'c's'le where Matchett had his party of veteran seamen at the senior station. 'You will have the anchor ready?'

'Aye, sir. With a spring upon it sir, as soon as it's weighed and sighted clear.'

'Very good, Mr Matchett. Leave the spring slack when we anchor again. It is the line of battle ships his lordship wished to anchor by the stern to bring them swiftly into action and avoid the delays and risks in being raked as they swing. We shall most likely anchor by the head.'

'Aye, aye, sir.'

'Good luck, Mr Matchett . . . Mr Willerton what the devil are you up to?'

Willerton appeared suddenly from the heads with a pot of red paint in his hand and his eyes innocently blue in the sunshine that was now breaking through the cloud.

'Attending to my leddy, sir, giving her a nice red tongue and lips to smack at the Frogs, sir.'

Drinkwater smiled. 'They ain't Frogs, Mr Willerton, they're Danes.'

'All the same to 'er leddyship, sir.'

Drinkwater burst out laughing and turned aft, nodding to the men waiting by the windlass. 'You may heave her dead short, my lads.'

Dropping below by the forward hatch he ran into Lieutenant Tumilty who was no longer his usual flippant self but wore an expression of stern concentration. He was also uncharacteristically formal.

'Good morning sir. My preparations are all but complete. If you wish I will show you the arrangements I have made.' They walked aft through the hold where *Virago's* four score seamen had lived and messed, past the remaining cables and the space cleared for the artillerymen.

At the after end a hatch opened into the stern quarters giving access to the magazine under Drinkwater's cabin. Tumilty held out his arm.

'No further sir, without felt boots.'

'Of course,' said Drinkwater, almost colliding with Tumilty.

'Hite and Trussel are filling the carcases, the empty shells, with white powder. Hobbs here is sentry and will assist if the action goes on long . . .' Drinkwater nodded at another artillery-man who carried not a fusil, in such dangerous proximity to the magazine, but a truncheon. 'Once filled, the shells come through here to the after shell room.' Tumilty turned forward, indicating the huge baulks of timber below the after, thirteen-inch, mortar that formed a cavity in which the shells were lodged. Above his head a small hatch had been opened, admitting a patch of light below.

'We, or rather Rogers's men, whip up the charged shells through that hatch to the mortar above . . .'

'What about fuses?' asked Drinkwater.

'As you see the shells are all wooden plugged for storage. I cut the fuses on the fo'c's'le. It's clear of seamen once Matchett quits fooling with his anchors; he'll be busy aft here, whipping up the shells. I rig leather dodgers to protect the fuses from sparks. The sergeant or myself will cut the fuses. This controls the time of explosion. Time of flight, and hence range, is decided by the charge in the chamber of the mortar. As I was saying, the fuse is of special composition and burns four tenths of an inch per minute. A thousand yard flight takes 2.56 seconds, so you see, Nat'aniel, 'tis a matter for a man of science, eh?'

'Indeed, Tom, it is . . . what of the ten-inch shells forward?'

'They go up in shell hooks. Now, I've had all hands at mortar stations twice in your absence and they all know what to do. I think we'll take it easy to begin with but we should be firing more than one shell a minute from each gun when we get the range.'

'What about the dangers of fire? I understand they're considerable . . .'

'Mr Jex's party are well briefed. We've wet tarpaulins handy to go over the side, buckets and tubs o' water all over the deck and in the tops . . . sure an' 'twill be like nothing you've ever seen in your life, Nat'aniel,' Tumilty smiled, recovering some of his former flippancy.

'Sir! Sir!' Quilhampton scrambled over a pile of rope and caught hold of Drinkwater's arm. 'Beggin' your pardon, sir, but Mr Rogers says to tell you that the admiral's hoisted Number 66 and the preparative, sir, "General order to weight an' the leeward ships first." '

'Thank you, Mr Q, I'll be up directly.'

Drinkwater arrived on the poop, reached in his tail pocket and whipped out his Dollond glass. Already the fleet was in motion. On their larboard bow, just beyond the bomb vessel *Volcano*, the lovely *Agamemnon* was hoisting her topsails. *Edgar* was already under way, her yards being braced round and the canvas stiffening with wind. Water appeared white at her bow and somewhere a shout and three cheers were called for. Several of the ships cheered their consorts as the naval might of Great Britain got under way. Drinkwater's fatigue, aches, pains and worries vanished as his heart-beat quickened and the old familiar exciting tingle shot down his spine.

They might be dead in an hour but, by God, this was a moment worth living for! He tried to mask his idiotic enthusiasm and turned aft to begin pacing the poop in an effort to repress his emotions and appear calm.

Bunting rose and broke from *Elephant*'s yard arms as hard-pressed signalmen sweated to convey Nelson's last minute orders to the ships. Happily in the confusion none applied to the bomb vessels.

'*Agamemnon*'s in trouble, sir,' remarked Rogers, nodding in the direction of the sixty-four.

'Damned current's too much for her, she ain't got enough headway . . .'

'She'll fall athwart *Volcano*'s hawse if she ain't careful . . .'

'And ours by God! Veer cable Mr Matchett, veer cable!' They could see men on *Volcano*'s fo'c's'le hurriedly letting out cable as the battleship tried to clear the little bomb vessel while the current set her rapidly north.

They watched helplessly as the big ship crabbed awkwardly across their own bow, failed to weather the mark vessel, *Cruizer*, and brought up to her anchor on the wrong side of the Middle Ground. Within minutes a flat-boat was ordered to her assistance, to carry out another anchor and enable her to haul herself to windward.

Edgar, with Mr Briarly at the con, began to draw ahead unsupported and bunting broke out again from *Elephant*'s yards as Nelson ordered *Polyphemus* into the gap, followed by the old *Isis*. Drinkwater watched the next ship with some interest.

Bellona followed *Isis*, crossing close to *Cruizer*'s bowsprit as she turned into the King's Deep. Drinkwater wondered if her pilot could see his marks and transits through the smoke of *Edgar*'s fire as she engaged the *Provesteenen*, the most southerly Danish ship round which he and Hardy had sounded the night before. Beyond *Isis* Drinkwater could see *Désirée* which had got under way early and was already anchored and swinging to her spring to open a raking fire on the *Provesteenen*.

Russell, an old Camperdown ship and well-known to Drinkwater, was close behind *Bellona*, and *Elephant*'s topmen were aloft as the admiral's flagship moved forward to take station astern of *Russell*. *Ardent* and Bligh's *Glatton* were setting sail.

'God's bones,' muttered Drinkwater, 'I think they are ignoring Briarly's advice.' *Bellona* appeared to have inclined to a slightly more easterly course than the first ships. As they watched a sudden gap opened up between *Isis* and *Bellona*. 'What the devil . . .?'

'*Bellona*'s aground!' remarked Drinkwater grimly, 'hit the damned Middle Ground and look, by heaven, *Russell*'s followed him!'

'That'll set the cat among the bloody pigeons,' said Rogers.

Chapter Eighteen *2 April 1801, Afternoon*

The Meteor Flag

To the watchers on *Virago* nothing was known of the little drama on *Elephant*'s quarterdeck as Nelson took over the con of the battleship personally. Overhearing the pilots advising the master to leave the grounded *Bellona* and *Russell* to larboard the admiral ordered the helm put over the other way, leaving the stricken ships to starboard and averting complete catastrophe. All Drinkwater, Rogers and Easton could see were the leading British ships under their topsails, moving slowly north enveloped in a growing cloud of smoke as gun after gun in the Danish line bore on them. Tumilty and Lettsom had joined the knot of officers on the poop and the *Virago*'s rail was crowded with her people as they watched the cannonade.

Following *Elephant* were *Glatton*, *Monarch*, *Defiance* and *Ganges*, weathering the south end of the Middle Ground, while Riou's frigates, led by *Amazon*, were in line ahead for the entrance to the King's Deep.

Rose's little gun-brigs each with their waspish names: *Biter*, *Sparkler*, *Tickler*, were shaking out their topsails; seemingly as anxious to get among the enemy fire as their larger consorts. Fremantle's flatboats were also active, three or four of them clustered around *Agamemnon*'s bow assisting in carrying out her anchors, and converging on *Bellona* and *Russell* who were under fire from the *Provesteenen* and howitzer batteries on Amager.

'Hullo, old Parker's on the move.' The levelled telescopes swung to the north where the Commander-in- Chief's division was beating up to re-anchor at the north end of the Middle Ground.

'I wonder if he can see *Bellona* and *Russell* aground?' asked Easton.

'He'll have a damned fit if he can, two battleships out of the line is going to have quite an effect on the others,' offered Rogers.

'Your fire-eating brothers in Christ will have their whiskers singed, Mr Rogers,' said Lettsom philosophically. 'Here is a quatrain for you:

'See where the guns of England thunder
Giving blow for mighty blow,
Who was it that made the blunder,
Took 'em where they couldn't go?'

Rogers burst out laughing and even Drinkwater, keenly observing the progress of the action, could not repress a smile. He walked across to the deck log and looked at Easton's last entry: '10 o'clock, van ships engaged, cannonade became general as line of battle ships got into station.'

To the north of them most of Parker's squadron were reanchoring. But four of his battleships were beating up towards Copenhagen against wind and current to enter the action.

Astern of the bomb vessels, *Jamaica* and the gun brigs were having a similar problem. The crowded anchorage had not allowed all the ships to get sufficiently to the south to weather the Middle Ground in the wind now blowing, and though Drinkwater thought that the shallow draught gun-brigs could have chanced slipping inside *Cruizer*, it was clear that Parker's caution was now epidemic in the fleet.

'*Explosion*'s signalling, sir, "Bombs General, weigh and form line of battle." '

The noise of the cannonade reached Mr Jex as he bent down in the hold. He was outboard of the great coils of spare cable, in the carpenter's walk against the ship's side. He had left the deck on the pretext of checking the sea inlet cock. From here water was drawn on deck by the fire engine, to spout from the two hoses his party had laid out on the deck. The spigot had been opened hours earlier and Jex merely crouched over it. His fear had reduced him to a trembling jelly. He could hear above the still distant sound of cannon the distinct chuckle of water alongside a hull under way: *Virago* was going into action.

For five minutes Jex huddled terrified against the ship's side before recovering himself. Standing uncertainly he began to make his way towards the spirit room.

*

Drinkwater stared through the vanes of his hand compass at the main mast of *Cruizer.*

'Damn! She won't weather *Cruizer,* Mr Easton, can you stretch the braces a little?'

Easton looked aloft then shook his head. 'Hard against the catharpings, sir.'

Rogers came and stood anxiously next to Drinkwater as he continued to stare through the brass vanes. He was swearing under his breath.

'Keep her full and bye, Tregembo!' Drinkwater could feel the sweat prickling his armpits. He took his eye off *Cruizer* for a second and saw how the stern of the grounded Russell was perceptibly nearer.

'*Hecla's* having the same trouble, Nat,' Rogers muttered consolingly.

'That's bloody cold comfort!' snapped Drinkwater, suddenly venomous. Were they to go aground ignominiously after all their tribulations? He snapped the compass vanes shut and pocketted the little instrument.

'Set all sail, Mr Rogers, and lively about it!'

Rogers did not even bother to acknowledge the order. 'Tops there! Aloft and shake out the t'gallants! Fo'c's'le! Hoist both jibs . . .'

Easton had jumped down into the waist and was chivvying the waisters onto the topgallant halliards.

'Get those fucking lobsters to tail on, Easton. You there! Aloft and let fall the main course . . .'

The loose canvas flopped downwards, billowed and filled. *Virago* heeled a little more. Here and there a knife flashed to cut a kink jammed in a sheave but the constant days of battling with gales, of making and reducing sail now brought its own dividends and the Viragos caught something of the urgency of the hour.

The bomb vessel increased her speed, leaning to leeward with the water foaming along her side.

'Up helm and ease her a point.' Drinkwater had not taken his eyes off *Cruizer*'s stern. Suddenly the men looked up from coiling the ropes to see the brig's stern very close as they sped past, with a row of faces watching the old bomb vessel going into action.

Brisbane raised his hat, 'Tally ho, Drinkwater, by God! Tally ho and mind the mud!'

Drinkwater felt the thrill of exhilaration turn to that of fear as the deck heaved beneath his feet.

'God damn and blast it!' screamed Rogers, beside himself with angry frustration, but suddenly they were free and a ragged cheer broke from those who realised that for an instant their keel had struck the Middle Ground.

In a moment they could bear up for the battle . . .

'Larboard bow, sir!' Drinkwater looked up. Coming round *Cruizer*'s bow was *Explosion*, just swinging before the wind to make her own approach to her station. Drinkwater could not luff without colliding or losing control of *Virago*, neither dare he bear away for a little longer since *Russell* was indicating the bank dangerously close to his starboard side. He resolved to stand on, aware that Martin was screeching something at him through a trumpet.

'Damn Captain Martin,' he muttered to himself, but a chorus of 'Hear, hear!' from Rogers and Easton indicated the extent of his concentration. Martin was compelled to let fly his sheets to check *Explosion*'s headway.

'Up helm, Tregembo . . . reduce sail again!'

Astern Martin was still shouting as *Explosion*, closely followed by *Volcano*, *Terror* and *Discovery* weathered the *Cruizer* and the Middle Ground.

'For what we are about to receive, may we be truly . . . Jesus!' A storm of shot swept *Virago*'s deck. They had left astern *Désirée*, anchored athwart the Danish line with a spring straining on her cable, and *Polyphemus* was drawing onto the larboard quarter. She too was anchored, though by the stern. As *Virago* crossed the gap between *Polyphemus* and the next anchored ship, the *Isis*, a broadside from *Provesteenen* hit her, cutting up the rigging and sails and wounding the foremast. On their own starboard side they had already passed *Russell*, flying the signal for distress and with flat-boats heaving out cables from her bow and stern while cannon shot dropped all round them. As they passed *Bellona* a terrific bang occurred and screams rent the air.

Beside Drinkwater Lieutenant Tumilty wore a seraphic smile. 'Gun exploded,' he explained for the benefit of anyone interested. *Bellona*'s guns were returning the Danish fire and Drinkwater looked ahead. From this close range the enemy defences took on a different aspect. From a distance the exiguous collection of prames, radeaus, cut down battleships, floating batteries, transports and frigates had had a cheap, thread-bare look about them, compared with the formal naval might of Great Britain with its canvas, bunting and wooden walls. But from the southern end of the King's Deep it looked altogether different. Already *Bellona* and *Russell* were of little use, although both returned fire and strove throughout the day to get afloat again. Against the remaining ships the massed cannon of the Danish defences looked formidable. Spitting fire and smoke, the blazing tiers of guns were the most awesome sight Drinkwater had ever seen.

The gaps between the British ships were greater now, occasioned by the loss of *Bellona* and *Russell* from the line. Shot whined over the decks, ripping holes in the sails and occasionally striking splinters from *Virago*'s timber.

There was a scream as the bomb vessel received her first casualty, an over-curious artilleryman who spun round and fell across the ten-inch mortar hatch while his shattered head flew overboard.

The Danes were defending their very hearths, and kept up the gunfire by continually sending reinforcements from the shore to relieve their tired men, and sustain the hail of shot against the British.

Virago's fore topgallant was shot away as she passed *Edgar*, engaged against the *Jutland*, an old, cut down two-decker. Rogers leapt forward, temperamentally unable to remain inactive for long in such circumstances. He began to clear the mess while Drinkwater concentrated upon the calls of the leadsman in the starboard chains. Beyond *Jutland* the odd square shapes of two floating batteries and a frigate were firing at both *Edgar* and the next ship ahead, Bligh's *Glatton*. The former East Indiaman which had once compelled a whole squadron to surrender to her deadly, short range batteries of carronades was keeping up a terrific fire. Most of her effort was concentrated on her immediate opponent, another cut-down battleship, the *Dannebrog*, flagship of the Danish commander, Commodore Olfert Fischer. But *Virago* did not pass unmolested, three more men were wounded and another killed as the storm of shot swept them.

'Bring her to starboard a little, Mr Easton, and pass word to Mr Matchett, Mr Q, to watch for my signal to anchor; we are almost on our station abeam the admiral.'

The two officers acknowledged their orders.

Drinkwater studied *Elephant* for a moment. He could see the knot of glittering officers on her quarterdeck in the sunshine. Beyond the flagship lay the *Ganges* and then a gap, filled with boats pulling up and down the line. Just visible in the smoke were *Monarch* and Graves's flagship *Defiance*, and somewhere ahead of them, in the full fire of the heavy batteries of the Trekroner Forts, were Riou and his frigates.

'Bring the ship to the wind, Mr Easton.' *Virago* began to turn. 'You may begin your preparations, Mr Tumilty.' As they had closed *Elephant* the Irishman had been observing his targets and taking obscure measurements with what looked like a pelorus.

To his astonishment Tumilty winked. 'And now, my dear Nat'aniel, you'll see why we've brought all this here.' Leprechaun-like he hopped onto the foredeck and began to bawl instructions at his artillerymen.

Drinkwater felt the wind on his face and dropped his arm as the main topsail flogged back against the mast. 'Bunt lines and clew lines there! Ease the halliards! Up aloft and stow!' Rogers paused, looking along the deck to see his orders obeyed. 'You there, up aloft . . . Bosun's mate, start that man aloft, God damn it, and take his name!'

Virago's anchor dropped just as the leadsman called 'By the mark five!'

'Perfect, by God,' Drinkwater muttered to himself, pleased with his positioning, and suddenly thinking of Elizabeth in his moment of self-conceit.

'How much scope, sir?' Matchett was crying at him from forward.

'Half a cable, Mr Matchett,' he called through the speaking trumpet. He felt *Virago* tug round as her anchor bit and she brought up. She lay quietly sheering a few degrees in the current.

'Brought up, sir,' reported Easton, straightening up from taking a bearing.

'Very well, Mr Easton.' Drinkwater looked round. Astern of them *Terror* was turning into the wind to anchor while *Explosion* and *Discovery* continued past *Virago*. Of *Volcano* there was no sign, though Drinkwater afterwards learned she had been ordered to anchor and throw shells against the howitzer battery on Amager at the southern end of the line.

He raised his hat to Martin as the commander went past, partly out of bravado, partly to mollify the touchy man. To the south the confusion caused by the groundings had resulted in *Isis* anchoring prematurely to cover *Bellona* and *Russell*. The consequence of this was a dangerous extension of the line of battleships north of the *Elephant* with the lighter frigates absorbing enormous punishment from the Trekroner Forts, the Lynetten, Quintus and other batteries, plus the guns of the inner line commanded by Steen Bille. The whole area was a mass of smoke and fire while Parker's three relieving battleships, *Ramilles*, *Defence* and *Veteran* were making no apparent headway to come to Riou's assistance.

'Mr Drinkwater! I'm ready to open fire if you can steady the ship a little.'

Drinkwater turned his attention inboard. Rogers had a gang of men aft, their arms extended above their heads where they prepared to whip up the shells; groups of artillerymen, stripped to their braces in the biting wind, clustered round the mortars which, looking like huge, elongated cauldrons pointed their blunt, ineffective looking muzzles out to starboard, at the sky over Copenhagen.

'Mr Easton, let fall the mizzen topsail and keep it backed against the mast. Fire as you will, Mr Tumilty.'

'Thank 'ee, sir, and will you be kind enough to observe the fall o' shot?'

Drinkwater nodded. Tumilty hopped back to the fo'c's'le where he bent behind the leather dodger then walked aft beside the sergeant to the thirteen-inch mortar. Tapping the prepared fuse into the first shell Tumilty saw the monstrous ball, more than a foot in diameter and which contained ten pounds of white gun powder, safely into the chamber of the mortar. He had already loaded the powder he judged would throw the carcase over the opposing lines of ships into the heart of the Danish capital.

Handing the linstock to his sergeant he leaped up onto the poop and pulled his telescope from his pocket. '*Festina lente*, eh Nat'aniel . . . Fire!'

The roar was immense, drowning the sound of the guns of the fleets, and white smoke rolled reeking over them.

'Mark it! Mark it!' yelled Tumilty, his glass travelling up and then down as a faint white line arced against the blue sky to fall with increasing speed onto the roofs of the city.

At the mortar bed the artillerymen crowded round, swabbing

out the chamber of the gun. The elevation remained unchanged, being set at forty-five degrees.

Drinkwater stared at the arsenal of Copenhagen trying to see where the shell burst. He saw nothing.

'Over, by Jesus,' said Tumilty happily, 'and at least the fuse was not premature.' Drinkwater watched him fuss round the mortar again as the whipping up gang began to work. The ten inch had been readied but Tumilty held its fire until he was satisfied with the performance of the after mortar.

Although he felt the deck shudder under the concussion and gasped as the smoke and blast passed over him, Drinkwater was ready for the next shot. The carcase descended on the arsenal and Drinkwater saw it burst as it hit the ground.

'A little short Mr Tumilty, I believe.' The landing of the third shot was also short but at his next Tumilty justified his claim to be the finest pyroballogist in the Royal Artillery. The explosion was masked by the walls of the arsenal but Tumilty was delighted with the result and left the poop to supervise both mortars from the waist.

Dutifully Easton and Drinkwater reported the fall of the shells as well as they could. From time to time Tumilty would pause to traverse his mortar-beds but he maintained a steady fire. Beneath his feet Drinkwater was aware that *Virago* had suddenly become a hive of activity. All the oddities of her construction had been built for this moment: the curious hatches, the fire-screens, the glazed lantern niches; the huge futtocks and heavy scantlings; the octagonal hatches. Mr Trussel and Bombardier Hite received instructions from Tumilty and made up the flannel cartridges in the filling room. The artillery sergeant cut fuses on the now deserted fo'c's'le. In the waist seamen and soldiers scurried about as they carried shells, fuses, cartridges and buckets of water with which to douse the hot mortars. Orchestrating the whole was Lieutenant Tumilty, his face purple with exertion, his active figure justifying his regiment's motto as he seemed everywhere at once like some hellish fiend.

As they fired over the main action Drinkwater was able to see something of the progress of the battle. Already damage to the British ships was obvious. Several had lost masts and others flew signals of distress. Amongst the splashes of wide cannot shot the flat-boats and boats of the fleet pulled about, coolly carrying out anchors. Through this hail of shot Brisbane sailed the *Cruizer* from her now redundant duty of marking the south end of the Middle Ground, the length of the line to Riou's support. Of the Danish line Drinkwater could see little beyond those hulks and prames on his beam. One appeared to have got out of the line and several seemed to strike their flags, but as they had reappeared the next time he looked he could not be sure what was happening. *Terror, Explosion* and *Discovery* were throwing shells into Copenhagen. Neither *Hecla, Zebra* nor *Sulphur* appeared to have weathered the Middle Ground and got into the action.

'Fire! Fire!' Drinkwater swung round. A flicker of flames raced along the larboard rail but Rogers was equal to it. 'Fire party, hoses to the larboard waist!'

Drinkwater looked in vain for Jex, but his men were there, dragging an already pulsing hose towards the burning spars lying on the rail.

'Part-burnt wads, Nat'aniel,' shouted Tumilty unconcerned, identifying the cause of the fire.

'Where the devil's Mr Jex?' Drinkwater called out, frowning.

'Don't know, sir,' replied Rogers, as he had men cutting the lashing round the spars and levering them overboard. A shot whined over his head and he ducked.

'Mr Easton!'

'Sir!'

'Find Jex!'

'Aye, aye, sir.'

But Easton had not left the poop when Jex appeared through the smoke that billowed back from the ten-inch mortar forward. He was drunk and in his shirt-sleeves. 'I hear the cry of fire!' he shouted, holding up his hands above his head and staggering over a ring-bolt. 'Here I am you bastards, at my fucking action station, God rot you all . . .'

Men turned to look at the purser as he reached the after mortar and was again engulfed in the smoke of discharge. He emerged to the astonished onlookers like a theatrical wraith, his face flaccid, his cheeks wet with tears. Drinkwater was aware of a sniggering from the men at the shell-hatch.

'Bastards, you're all bastards . . .' Jex flung his arms wide in a gesture that embraced them all.

'Mr Jex . . .!' Drinkwater began, his jaw dropping as Jex's right arm flew off, spun round and slapped a topman across the face. The astonished man put up his hands and caught the severed limb.

'Cor! Pusser's give me back me bleeding eighth . . .'

The grotesque joke ended the brief hiatus on *Virago*'s deck. Jex looked stupidly at his distant arm then down at the gouts of his blood as it poured from the socket. He began to scream and run about the deck.

Rogers felled him with one end of a burning royal yard he was heaving overboard. Jex fell to the deck, his legs kicking and his back arching, the red stain growing on the planking.

'Jesus Christ,' muttered Easton watching, fascinated.

At last Jex grew still. Jumping down from the rail having tossed overboard all the burning spars Rogers pointed to the body and addressed two seamen standing stock still beside a starboard carronade.

'Throw that damned thing overboard.'

Then Tumilty's after mortar roared again.

'Mr Drinkwater, sir! The Commander-in-Chief is signalling, sir!'

'Well Mr Q, what is it?'

'Number 39, sir: "Discontinue the action," sir.'

' "Discontinue the action"? Are you certain? Drinkwater raised his Dollond glass and levelled it to the north. *Ramilles, Veteran* and *Defence* were still clawing to windward and he could see *London* still at anchor, with her blue admiral's flag at the main. And there too were the blue and white horizontal stripes of Number 3 flag over the horizontal red, white and blue of Number 9.

'Mr Easton, what o'clock d'you have?'

'Twenty minutes after one, sir.'

'You must log receipt of that signal, Mr Easton . . . Mr Matchett . . . where the devil's the bosun?'

'Here sir.'

'Prepare to weigh.'

'Aye, aye, sir.' Drinkwater looked again at the *London*. There was no mistaking that signal. It was definitely Number 39.

'Cease fire, Mr Tumilty . . . Mr Rogers, disperse the hands to their stations for getting under way . . .' Drinkwater looked anxiously about him. Disengagement was going to be difficult. The battleships had only to cut their cables, they were already headed north and would soon be carried out of the action but the bombs had to weigh and turn. *Virago* could not turn to larboard, away from the Danish guns, because of the Middle Ground upon whose edge she had been anchored. To turn to starboard would put the ship under a devastating raking fire. Drinkwater swallowed. If he weighed immediately he might obtain a little shelter behind the battleships but he ran two risks in doing so. The first was that with the prevailing current he might run foul of one of the bigger ships; the second was that too precipitate a departure from the line of battle could be construed as cowardice.

'What the devil d'you want me to cease fire for?' Tumilty's purple face peered belligerently through the smoke.

'The Commander-in-Chief instructs us to abandon the action, damn it!'

'What the bloody hell for?'

'Do as you're told, Tumilty!' snapped Drinkwater.

'Beg pardon, sir, Flag's only acknowledged the signal . . .'

'Eh?' Drinkwater looked where Quilhampton pointed. *Elephant* had not repeated Parker's order. He looked astern and saw *Explosion* had repeated Number 39.

'What the bloody hell . . .?'

'Can you see *Defiance*, Mr Q?' Quilhampton stared over the starboard quarter and levelled the big watch-glass.

'I can't be sure, sir, but I *think* Admiral Graves has a signal hoisted but if he has it ain't from a very conspicuous place . . .'

'Not very conspicuous . . .?' Drinkwater frowned again and returned his attention to the *Elephant*. Nelson had signalled only an acknowledgement of sighting Number 39 to Parker but not repeated it to his ships, and Number 16, the signal for Close Action, hoisted at the beginning of the battle, still flew.

Drinkwater tried to clear his head while the concussion of the guns went on. Nelson was clearly not eager to obey. From Parker's distant observation post it must be obvious that Nelson was in trouble. *Bellona* and *Russell* were aground, both flying conspicuous signals of distress; there was a congestion of ships at the southern end of the line which, combined with the presence of some bombs and the gun-brigs still in the southern anchorage, suggested that something had gone dreadfully wrong with Nelson's division. *Agamemnon*, after repeated efforts to kedge round *Cruizer*, had given up and sent her boats to the assistance of the fleet while *Cruizer*, the mark vessel, had abandoned her station to support Riou.

Parker could see the northern end of the line more clearly. Frigates engaged with prepared positions presaged disaster, while his three battleships were clearly going to be unable to relieve Riou as they were still too far off.

'Pusillanimous Parker's lost his bloody nerve, eh?' said Rogers levelling a glass alongside Drinkwater.

'I think,' said Drinkwater, 'he's giving Nelson the chance to get out while he may. But I think he little appreciates what bloody chaos there will be if Nelson tries to disengage at this juncture . . .'

'Well Nelson ain't moving!' Rogers nodded across at *Elephant*.

'No.' Drinkwater paused. 'Tell Matchett to veer that cable again, Sam . . . Mr Tumilty! Re-engage!' A cheer went along *Virago*'s deck and the next instant her waist filled with smoke and noise as the mortars roared.

'Flag to *Virago*, Number 214, for a "Lieutenant to report on board the Admiral," sir,' said Quilhampton diligently.

'Very well, pass word to Lieutenant Rogers, Mr Q.' Quilhampton went in search of the first lieutenant who had disappeared off the poop. Astern of them *Explosion* hauled down Number 39.

It was twenty minutes before Rogers returned. Rogers was elated.

'By God, sir, you should see it from over there, Nelson himself claims it's the hottest fire he's ever been under and the Danes are refusing to surrender. They're striking, then firing on the boats sent to take 'em . . .'

'What did the admiral want?' cut in Drinkwater.

'Oh, he remarked that *Virago*'s shells were well directed and could we drop some into the Trekroner Forts.'

'Mr Tumilty!' Drinkwater shrieked through the din. He beckoned the Irishman onto the poop. 'His lordship wants us to direct our fire at the Trekroner Forts.'

Tumilty's eyes lit up. 'Very good. I'll switch the ten-inch to firing one pound shot, that'll shake the eejits if they haven't got casemates over there.'

Tumilty took ten minutes and four careful shots to get the range. The Trekroner Forts were at extreme range and the increased charge of twice the amount of powder used to reach the arsenal made *Virago* shake to her keel.

The one-pound shot arrived in boxes, and stockingette bags of them were lifted into the forward mortar, one hundred to a shot. Drinkwater found the trajectory of these easier to follow than the carcases as they spread slightly in flight.

For half an hour *Virago* kept up this bombardment until Quilhampton reported a flag of truce flying at *Elephant's* masthead. All along both lines the fire began to slacken and an air of uncertainty spread over the fleet.

Looking northwards Drinkwater saw *Amazon* leading the frigate squadron towards Parker's anchored ships and rightly concluded that Riou, unable to see Nelson's signal for close action, had obeyed Parker's order to withdraw. It was only later that he learnt Riou had been cut in two by a round shot an instant after giving the order.

Desultory firing still rippled up and down the line as observers saw boats of both nations clustered round *Elephant* flying flags of truce. As the sun westered it appeared some armistice had been concluded, for Nelson made the signal to his ships to make sail. A lieutenant was pulled across to the line of bomb vessels to order them to move nearer the Trekroner Forts and remain until the admiral sent them further orders.

'That will bring the whole city in range,' grinned the smoke-grimed Tumilty.

'I think, gentlemen,' said Drinkwater shutting the Dollond glass with a snap, 'that we are to be the ace of trumps!'

Chapter Nineteen *2–9 April 1801*

Ace of Trumps

'Oh, my God!' Drinkwater peered down into the boat alongside *Virago*. By the lantern light he could see the body of Easton lying inert in the stern sheets.

'Where's the other boat? Mr Quilhampton's boat,' he demanded, suddenly, terribly anxious.

'Here sir,' the familiar voice called as the cutter rounded the stern. There were wounded men in her too.

'What the devil happened?'

'*Elephant* ordered us to carry out a cable, sir, and then, when we had done that, Captain Foley directed us to secure one of the Danish prizes . . .'

'Foley?'

'Yes, sir. Lord Nelson returned to *St George* when *Elephant* grounded trying to get away to the north . . .'

'Go on . . .'

'Well sir, we approached the prize about two o'clock and the bastards opened fire on us . . .'

Drinkwater turned away from the rail to find Rogers looming out of the darkness.

'Get those men out, Mr Rogers, and then take a fresh crew and get over the *Monarch*.'

'The *Monarch*, sir?'

'I sent Lettsom over there earlier tonight, she was in want of a surgeon.'

'Bloody hell.'

Drinkwater did what he could while he waited for the surgeon's arrival. It was little enough but it occupied the night and he emerged aching into the frozen dawn. It was calm and a light mist lay over the King's Deep.

The hours of darkness had been a shambles. After the exertions of the previous nights and the day of the battle, Drinkwater was grey with exhaustion. The British ships had not extricated themselves from the battle without difficulty. In addition to *Elephant*, *Defiance* had gone aground. *Monarch*, which had been badly damaged in the action and suffered fearful loss of life, had become unmanageable and run inshore only to collide with *Ganges*, run aground and come under the renewed fire of the Danes. Fortuitously the impact of *Ganges* drove *Monarch* off the mud and both ships got away in the growing night. One of the Danish ships had exploded with a fearful concussion and the air was still filled with the smell of burning.

Drinkwater had worked his own ship across the King's Deep during the evening, answering *Elephant*'s signal for a boat to attend her cables and *Monarch*'s for a surgeon. *Virago* was now anchored closer to the city, commanding the Trekroner Forts with her still-warm mortars and in company with *Explosion*, *Terror* and *Discovery*.

A rising sun began to consume the mist revealing that the majority of the British fleet had joined Sir Hyde Parker at the north end of the Middle Ground. Lettsom returned with Rogers, whose boat's crew had worked like demons. To the south *Bellona* and *Russell* had gone, the former by picking up *Isis*'s cable and hauling herself off. *Désirée*, too, seemed to have got off. Nearer them *Defiance* was still fast, but by the time Drinkwater sent the hands to breakfast she too was under way.

Shutting the magazines and exhorting his officers to use the utmost caution bearing in mind the weary condition of the men, Drinkwater had the galley range fired up and all enjoyed a steaming burgoo. Drinkwater was unable to rest and kept the deck. The excitement and exertions of the last hours had driven him beyond sleep and, though he knew reaction must come, for the moment he paced his poop.

The Danish line presented a spectacle that he would never forget. From his position during the battle Drinkwater's view had been obscured by smoke. He had been able to see only the unengaged sides of the British ships and had formed no very reliable opinion of the effects of the gunfire. But now he was able to see the effect of the cannonade on the Danish vessels.

The sides of many of the blockships and hulks were completely battered in, with huge gaps in their planking. Many were out of position, driven inshore onto the flats off Amager. Some still flew the Danish flag. Looking at the respective appearance of the two protagonists, the shattered Danish line to the west, the British battleships licking their wounds to the north east, Drinkwater concluded there seemed little to choose between them. Possession of the field seemed to be in the hands of the Danes, since no landing of the troops had taken place; no storming of the Trekroner from the flat-boats had occurred.

And then his tired mind remembered his own words of the previous night. Here they were, the line of little bomb vessels, the tubby Cinderellas of the fleet, holding the field for the honour of Great Britain and turning a drawn battle into victory.

'Sir, boat approaching, and I believe his lordship's in it!'

'What's that?' Drinkwater woke abruptly as Quilhampton's bandaged head appeared round the door. He stretched. His head, his legs and above all his mangled arm ached intolerably. He could not have slept above half an hour.

'What did you say? Lord Nelson?'

'Yes sir . . .'

Drinkwater dragged himself on deck to see the admiral's barge approaching *Explosion*. It passed down the line of bomb vessels. The little admiral wore his incongruous check overcoat and sat next to the taller Hardy. The Viragos lined the rail and gave the admiral a spontaneous cheer. Nelson raised his hat as he came abeam.

'Morning Drinkwater.'

'Good mornin', my lord.'

'I have been in over a hundred actions, Mr Drinkwater, but yesterday's was the hottest. I was well pleased with your conduct and will not forget you in my report to their Lordships.'

'Obliged to you, my lord.' Drinkwater watched the boat move on. Beside him Lettsom emerged reeking of blood.

'His lordship has paid a heavy price in blood for his honours,' the surgeon said sadly.

'How was *Monarch*?'

'A bloody shambles. Fifty-six killed, including Mosse, her captain, and one hundred and sixty-four wounded seriously. They say her first lieutenant, Yelland, worked miracles to bring her out. Doubtless he will be promoted . . .' Lettsom broke off, the implied bitterness clear. How many surgeons and their mates had laboured with equal skill would never be known.

'Flat-boats approaching, sir.'

'Mr Q, will you kindly desist with your interminable bloody reports . . .'

'Aye, aye, sir.'

Drinkwater was immediately ashamed of his temper. Quilhampton's crestfallen expression was eloquent of hurt.

'Mr Q! I beg your pardon.'

Quilhampton brightened immediately. 'That's all right, sir.'

Drinkwater looked at the flat-boats. 'Let me know what they are up to, Mr Q.' He went below and immediately fell asleep.

He woke to the smell of smoke rolling over the sea. Going on deck he found an indignant knot of officers on the poop. 'What the devil's this damned Dover court, eh?' He was thoroughly bad-tempered now, having slept enough to recover his spirits but not to overcome his exhaustion.

'Old Vinegar's ordered the prizes burned,' said Rogers indignantly. 'We won't have the benefit of any prize money, God rot him.' In a fleet that had subsisted for weeks upon rumour and gossip no item had so speedily offended the seamen. It was true that there was little of real value among the Danish ships but one or two were fine vessels wanting only masts and spars. Only the *Holstein* was to be spared and fitted as a hospital ship for the wounded. Nelson was reported to be furious with Parker and had remonstrated with his commander-in-chief on behalf of the common seamen in the fleet, arguing that their only reward was some expectation of prize and head money.

The vice-admiral seemed indefatigable. He was known to have arranged the truce and that evening went ashore to dine with his former enemies. Although peace had not been formally concluded the fleet had persuaded itself that the Danes were beaten.

Drinkwater shut the prayer book and put on his hat. The gospel of the resurrection had a hollow ring this Easter Sunday.

'On hats!' bellowed Rogers. Drinkwater stepped forward to address the men.

'My lads, I do not propose to read the Articles of War today, simply to thank you for acquitting yourselves so well on

Thursday.' A cheer went up from the men and Drinkwater mistily realised it was for him. The shouting died away. 'But . . . but we may not yet have finished work . . .' The hands fell silent again, staring apprehensively at him. 'I received orders this morning that the truce ends at noon. If no satisfactory explanation is heard as to why our terms have not been accepted we will bombard the city.'

He went below and Rogers dismissed the hands.

'Sir! Mr Rogers says to tell you there's boats coming and going between the shore and the Trekroner . . .'

Drinkwater went on deck and stared through his glass. There was no doubt about it – the Danes were reinforcing the defences.

'So much for his lordship's toasts of everlasting fraternity with the Danes,' remarked Rogers sourly.

'Man a boat, Mr Rogers, and take command of the ship in my absence.'

The boat could not go fast enough for Drinkwater and it wanted a few minutes before noon when he clambered up *London*'s side and reported to the commander-in-chief. Parker astonished him by remembering his name. 'Ah, Drinkwater, the officer of the watch informs me you have intelligence regarding the Trekroner Forts.' Drinkwater nodded. 'By the way, my wife writes and asks to be remembered to you, it seems I was not appreciative of your services to her last year when we met before.'

Drinkwater bowed. 'That is most kind of her ladyship, sir.' He was desperately anxious to communicate the news about the Danish reinforcements.

'The Danes are pouring men into the Trekroners, sir, reinforcements . . .'

'I think you may compose your mind on that score, Mr Drinkwater. The Danish envoys have just left me. The truce is extended.' It was only much later that Drinkwater wondered if Lady Parker implied anything in her kindness.

For two days the British fleet repaired the damage to itself, took out of the remaining prizes all the stores that were left and burnt the hulls. A south westerly wind swept a chill rain down over them and once again all was uncertainty. The seamen laboured at the sweeps of the flat-boats as they pulled between the plundered prizes and the British anchorage.

The cutter *Fox* left to survey the shallows over The Grounds to the south, past Dragør, in an attempt to find a channel suitable for the deep hulls of the first-rates and enable them to get through to the Baltic. Eager to assist, Drinkwater was ordered to remain on his bomb and keep his mortars trained on the city of Copenhagen.

Nelson and Colonel Stewart again dined ashore and the truce was further extended. News came that letters might be written and transported to England. Drinkwater sat at his reinstated table, snapped open the inkwell and paused before drawing a sheet of paper towards him. There was one duty he was conscious of having put off since the battle. Instead of the writing paper he pulled the muster book from its place and opened it.

He ran his finger down the list of names, halting at Easton. He paused for a second, recalling the man's face, then his mouth set in a firm line and he carefully wrote the legend *'D.D.'* for 'discharged dead'. He repeated the process against the name Jex, suppressing the unchristian relief that clamped his lips even more tightly, then hurried down the list, and inserted the cryptic initials against four other names.

At the bottom of the column he paused again. Then, dipping his pen in the inkwell with sudden resolution he wrote *'D.D.'* against the entry *'Ed 'd. Waters, Landsman Volunteer'*, sanded the page and pushed the book aside.

He found his hand shaking slightly as he began his letter to Elizabeth.

H.M Bomb Virago
Copenhagen Road
Wednesday 8th April 1801

My Darling Elizabeth,

Cruizer *is about to leave with despatches and I have time to tell you that on Thursday last the fleet was engaged before this city. The action was furious but I escaped unscathed, so your prayers were answered. Many brave fellows have fallen but you may tell Louise that James got only a scratch. He has done well and exceeded my expectations of him. Peace is still not confirmed, but I think it likely. You will read in the papers of great exertions by Lord Nelson and I flatter myself that his lordship took notice of me. Some good may yet come of it, although I must not be too sanguine, his lordship not having the chief command.*

Tell Susan that Tregembo is fit and in good health.

I hope you continue in health and your condition is not irksome. Kiss Charlotte Amelia for me and remember me as your devoted husband . . .

He signed the letter, disappointed that it was not more personal. Somehow Elizabeth's remoteness made her existence unreal. Reality was this penetrating chill and the endless ache in his right arm.

The cutter *Fox* returned to the fleet anchorage on the following evening. She had found a passage over the shoals into the Baltic. The next day came news of a fourteen week armistice. The Danes would supply the fleet with water and other necessaries and in return the bomb vessels would haul off. Other news came aboard too, news that had little impact on anyone except Lieutenant Nathaniel Drinkwater.

Danish and Prussian troops had entered Hamburg and the port had been closed to all communication with Britain.

Chapter Twenty *10 April–19 June 1801*

Kioge Bay

'General signal from Flag, sir: "All ships to send boat".'

'That ought to be for mails, see to it Mr Rogers.'

Every glass in the fleet had trained on *Lynx* when she arrived at Kioge Bay. Captain Otway was on board with news of the outside world. After the efforts and tribulations of the last few weeks almost any news that was not pure gossip about the fleet was welcome.

Strenuous efforts had been made to work the big ships, particularly *London* and *St George*, over the shallows. Their guns and stores had been hoisted out into merchant ships while the lightened battleships, riding high in the water, were hauled into the Baltic. Following the *London*, *St George* had grounded. Parker heard that the Swedish fleet was at sea and sent for Nelson to leave *St George* and rejoin *Elephant* anchored with the rest of the British warships at Kioge Bay. Nelson had his barge pull the twenty-four miles in the teeth of a rising and bitter wind to rejoin his former flagship.

While the big ships sailed to seek out the squadron from Carlscrona, the bombs and small fry waited in Kioge Bay and wondered if they were to sail against the Russians. Despite the recent carnage of the battle, relations with the Danes were good and the anchorage was usually enlivened by the sight of several Danish galliots among the anchored ship, selling cream for the officers' coffee and cheese and chickens to those who could afford them.

Then Parker had returned with the news that Tsar Paul had been assassinated and that his son Alexander had succeeded to the throne and declared his friendship with Britain. It was news already three weeks old.

So were the letters brought by *Lynx*, but nobody minded. The distribution of the mail had its usual effect. Men with letters ran off to sit in obscure corners or in the tops, painfully to spell out the ill-written scrawl of loved ones. Those without went off to sulk or affected indifference, according to their temperament. Saddest were the letters that arrived for the dead. There was one such for Easton, scented with lavender and superscribed in a delicate, feminine hand. It lay upon Drinkwater's table waiting to be returned unopened with his condolences.

There were three letters for Drinkwater. One was in Elizabeth's hand and one in Richard White's, but it was the third that he opened first.

Dear Drinkwater,

Your letters reached me safely and I desire that you wait upon me directly you return to London.

Dungarth.

It was frigidly brief and reawakened all Drinkwater's doubts about his conduct over Edward. Jex's death, though it had freed him from accusation from one quarter, had not released him entirely. It came as small consolation to learn that the Danish and Prussian troops had abandoned Hamburg.

He had gone on deck and paced the poop for over an hour before remembering the other letters. When he had sufficiently calmed himself he returned below and picked up the next. It was from his old friend Richard White, now a post-captain and blockading Brest in a frigate.

My Dear Nathaniel,

We are still here, up and down the Goulet and in sight of the batteries at St Matthew. I am sick of the duty and the incessant wearing of men and ships, but I suppose you would say there was no help for it. So thinks the First Lord, and no-one is disposed to argue with him. I heard you had command of a tender and if you can make nothing of it I would welcome a head I can rely on here. Write and let me know if you wish to serve as my first lieutenant . . .

Drinkwater laid the letter down. If he could contrive to get transferred to White's ship directly, without the need to call upon Dungarth, he could serve for years on the Brest blockade. The affair of Edward Drinkwater would blow over. He picked up the third letter and opened it. Elizabeth had been right all along; he was no dissembler, he knew that he would have to face the music. Sighing, he began to read.

My Dearest Nathaniel,

Charlotte and I are well, although we miss you. I grow exceedingly rotund. Louise is a great solace and constantly asks if I have heard of James.

We are starved of news from the Baltic and I wait daily to hear from you. Unrest in the country grows and there is uncertainty everywhere. We long for peace and I pray daily for your safe return, my dearest . . .

Drinkwater waited in *London*'s ante-room, nervous and tense, the subject of Edward uppermost in his mind. There had been ample time for the authorities to make arrangements for his arrest, perhaps Otway himself had brought a warrant . . . Sweat prickled between his shoulder blades. The dapper little midshipman who had brought Parker's summons had 'requested' he wore full uniform. Wondering if that insistence might not be sinister, he looked down at his coat and breeches.

The uniform was mildewed from languishing in his closet and the lace had become green. Tregembo's efforts prior to the battle had not been very successful and the smell of powder smoke was still detectable from the heavy cloth. Drinkwater felt exceedingly uncomfortable as he waited.

Parker's secretary appeared at last and called him into the great cabin. It was richly appointed; the furniture gleamed darkly, crystal decanters and silver candelabra glittered from the points of light that were reflected upwards from the sea through the stern windows and danced on the white-painted deckhead.

'Ah, Drinkwater . . .' the old man paused, apparently weighed down by responsibilities. 'I am to be superseded you know . . .' Drinkwater remained silent. 'Do you think I did wrong?'

'*I* sir??' That Parker should consult him was ludicrous. He felt out of his depth, aware only of the need to be tactful. 'Er, no, sir. Surely we have achieved the object of our enterprise.'

Parker looked at him intently, then seemed to brighten a little. 'It was not an easy task . . .' he muttered, more to himself than to Drinkwater. It was clear from his next remark that Drinkwater's acquaintance with his wife had allowed the friendless old man to speak freely.

'My wife reminds me constantly of my duty towards you in her letters . . .'

'Her ladyship is too kind, sir,' Drinkwater flushed; this solicitude on the part of Lady Parker was becoming a trifle embarrassing. Nelson had jumped to the wrong conclusion; was Parker about to do the same? Were not elderly husbands supposed to suspect young wives of all manner of infidelities?

'. . .And Lord Nelson is constantly complaining that I have failed to recognise your services both before and during the recent action. I believe you commanded *Virago* in the bombardment?'

'That is so, sir,' Drinkwater's heart was thumping painfully. Parker's nepotistic promotions after the battle of Copenhagen had aroused a storm of fury and it had taken all Nelson's persuasive powers to have a small number of highly deserving officers given a step in rank.

Parker picked up a paper and handed it to Drinkwater. 'Perhaps they will leave an old man in peace now.'

Drinkwater picked up the commission that made him Master and Commander.

The celebratory dinner in *Virago*'s cabin was a noisy affair. Out of courtesy Drinkwater had invited Lord Nelson, but the new Commander-in-Chief had taken his battleships off to demonstrate British seapower before the guns of Carlscrona and Revel.

The senior officer present was Captain Martin who did his best to hide his mortification at not being made post. He consoled himself by getting drunk. From some macabre source available in the aftermath of a bloody battle Rogers had acquired an old epaulette which they now presented to their commander.

''Tis a trifle tarnished, Drinkwater, but in keeping with the rest of your attire,' said Martin as he banged a spoon against a glass and called for silence. 'Gentlemen, I ask you to charge your glasses. To your swab, Drinkwater!'

'Drinkwater's swab!' The glasses banged down on the table and Tregembo and the messman moved rapidly to fill them again. Drinkwater looked round the grinning faces. Rogers flushed and half-drunk; Quilhampton, smiling seraphically, slipping slowly down in his chair banging on the table the fine, new wooden hand that Willerton had fashioned for him. Lettsom dry and birdlike; Tumilty red-faced and busy getting roaring drunk.

'An' I suppose I'll be having to call you "sir", Nat'aniel,' he shouted thickly, slapping Drinkwater's back in an insubordinate way.

'Sit down you damned Hibernian!' shouted Rogers.

'Take your damned fingers off me! An' I'm standing to make a pretty speech, so I am . . .' There were boos and shouts of 'Sit down!'

'I'll sit down upon a single condition . . . that Mr Lettsom makes a bit o' his versifying to mark the occasion.'

'Aye! Make us an ode, Lettsom!'

'Come, a verse!'

Lettsom held up his hand for silence. He was forced to wait before he could make himself heard.

At last he drew a paper from his pocket and struck a pose:

'The town of Copenhagen lies
Upon the Baltic shore
And here were deeds of daring done
'Twere never seen before.

'Bold Nelson led 'em, glass in hand
Upon the Danes to spy,
When Parker said "that's quite enough"
He quoth, "No, by my eye!"

'The dead and dying lay in heaps
The Danes they would not yield
Until the bold *Virago* came
Onto the bloody field.'

Lettsom paused, drank off his glass while holding his hand up to still the embryonic cheer. Then he resumed:

'Lord Nelson got the credit,
And Parker got the blame,
But 'twas the bold *Virago*
That clinched old England's fame.'

He sat down amid a storm of cheering and stamping. Mr Quilhampton's enthusiasm threatened to split his new hand until someone restrained him, at which point he gave up the struggle to retain consciousness and slid beneath the grubby tablecloth.

Drinkwater sat clapping Lettsom's dreadful muse.

'Your verse is like Polonius's advice, Mr Lettsom, the sweeter for its brevity,' Drinkwater grinned at the surgeon as Tregembo put another bottle before each officer. 'Mr Tumilty's contribution, sir,' he whispered in Drinkwater's ear.

'Ah, Tom, I salute you . . .'

Tumilty stood up. 'Captain Drinkwater . . .' he began, enunciating the words carefully, then he slowly bent over and buried his head in the remains of the figgy duff.

'What a very elegant bow,' said Martin rising unsteadily to take his leave. Drinkwater saw him to his boat.

'Good night Drinkwater.'

Returning to the cabin Drinkwater found Rogers dragging Tumilty to Easton's empty cot while Tregembo was carrying Quilhampton to bed. Martin had left and only Lettsom and Rogers sat down to finish a last bottle with Drinkwater.

Tregembo cleared the table. 'Take a couple of bottles, Tregembo, share 'em with the cook and the messman.'

'Thank 'ee, zur. I told 'ee you'd be made this commission, zur.' He grinned and left the cabin.

Lettsom blew through his flute. 'You, er, don't seem too pleased about it all, if I might say so,' said Lettsom.

'Is it that man Waters that's bothering you, sir?' asked Rogers.

Drinkwater looked from one to the other. There was a faint ringing in his ears and he was aware of a need to be careful of what he said.

'And why should Waters bother me, gentlemen?'

He saw Rogers shrug. 'It seemed an odd business to be mixed up in,' he said. Drinkwater fixed Rogers with a cold eye. Reluctantly he told the last lie.

'What d'you think I got my swab for, Samuel, eh?'

Lettsom drowned any reaction from Rogers in a shower of notes from his flute and launched into a lively air. He played for several minutes, until Rogers rose to go.

When the first lieutenant had left them Lettsom lowered his flute, blew the spittle out of it and dismantled it, slipping it into his pocket.

'I see you believe in providence, Mr Drinkwater . . .'

'What makes you say that?'

'Only a man with some kind of faith would have done what you did . . .'

'You speak in riddles, Mr Lettsom . . .'

'Mr Jex confided in me, I've known all along about your brother.'

'God's bones,' Drinkwater muttered as he felt a cold sensation sweep over him. He went deathly pale.

'I'm an atheist, Mr Drinkwater. But you are protected by my Hippocratic oath.' Lettsom smiled reassuringly.

A week later Admiral Pole took command of the fleet. The Baltic States were quiescent and, like Lord Nelson, the bomb vessels were ordered to England.

Chapter Twenty-One *July 1801*

A Child of Fortune

Commander Nathaniel Drinkwater knocked on the door of the elegant house in Lord North Street. Under his new full-dress coat with its single gleaming epaulette he was perspiring heavily. It was not the heat of the July evening that caused his discomfort but apprehension over the outcome of the forthcoming interview with Lord Dungarth.

The door opened and a footman showed him into an anteroom off the hall. Turning his new cocked hat nervously in his hands he felt awkward and a little frightened as he stood in the centre of the waiting room. After a few minutes he heard voices in the hall following which the same footman led him through to a book-lined study and he was again left alone. He looked around him, reminded poignantly of the portrait of Hortense Santhonax for, above the Adam fireplace, the arresting likeness of an elegant blonde beauty gazed down at him. He stared at the painting for some time. He had never met Dungarth's countess but the Romney portrait was said not to have done justice to her loveliness.

'You never met my wife, Nathaniel?' Drinkwater had not heard the door open and spun to face the earl. Dungarth was in court dress, his pumps noiseless upon the rich Indian carpet. Dungarth crossed the room and stood beside Drinkwater, looking up at the painting.

'Do you know why I detest the French, Nathaniel?'

'No my lord?' Drinkwater recollected Dungarth had conceived a passionate hatred for Jacobinism which was at variance with his former Whiggish sympathies with the American rebels.

'My wife died in Florence. I was bringing her body back through France in the summer of '92. At Lyons the mob learnt I was an aristocrat and broke open the coffin . . .' he turned to a side table. 'A glass of oporto?'

Drinkwater took the wine and sat down at Dungarth's invitation. 'We sometimes do uncharacteristic things for those close to us, and the consequences can last a lifetime.'

Drinkwater's mouth was very dry and he longed to swallow the wine at a gulp but he could not trust his hand to convey the glass to his lips without slopping it. He sat rigid, his coat stiff as a board and the silence that followed Dungarth's speech seemed interminable. Drinkwater was no longer on his own quarterdeck. After the heady excitement of battle and promotion the remorseless process of English law was about to engulf him. The colour was draining from his face and he was feeling light-headed. An image of Elizabeth swam before his eyes, together with that of Charlotte Amelia and the yet unseen baby, little Richard Madoc.

'Do you remember Etienne Montholon, Nathaniel?' Dungarth suddenly said in a conversational tone. 'The apparently wastrel brother of that bitch Hortense Santhonax?'

Drinkwater swallowed and recovered himself. 'Yes, my lord.' His voice was a croak and he managed to swallow some of the port, grateful for its uncoiling warmth in the pit of his stomach.

'Well, it seems that he became so short of funds that he threw in his lot with his sister and that fox of a husband of hers. The emergence of the consulate in France is attracting the notice of many of the younger émigrés who thirst for a share in *la gloire* of the new France.' Dungarth's expression was cynical. 'The rising star of Napoleon Bonaparte will recruit support from men like Montholon who seek a paymaster, and couples like the Santhonaxes who seek a vehicle for their ambition.'

'So Etienne Montholon returned to France, my lord?'

'Not at all. He remained in this country, leading his old life of gambling and squabbling, like all the émigré population. He served Bonaparte by acting as a clearing agent for information of fleet movements, mainly at Yarmouth in connection with the blockage of the Texel, but latterly watching Parker's squadron. The intransigence of the Danish Government was largely due to knowledge of Parker's dilatory prevarications and delays . . .' Dungarth rose and refilled their glasses. 'Etienne Montholon is dead now, he called himself *Le Marquis De La Roche-Jagu* and was killed by a jealous lover when in bed with his mistress at Newmarket . . .'

The point of his lordship's narrative struck Drinkwater like a blow. He felt his body a prey to the disorder of his mind which presented him with a bewildering succession of images: of Edward shivering on the bank of the River Yare, of Jex confronting him with the truth, of Edward walking ashore without looking back, of Jex's drunken death. Faintly he heard Dungarth say, 'By an odd coincidence the man suspected of the double murder had the same surname as yourself . . .'

Drinkwater turned to look the earl in the face. An ironic smile twisted Dungarth's mouth. ' 'Tis curious, is it not,' he said, 'how a man may flinch in perfect safety who would not deign to quail under a hail of shot?'

'I, er, I . . .'

'You need a little more wine, Nathaniel . . .' The glasses were again refilled and Dungarth resumed his tale.

'The suspect's cloak was found on the bank of the River Yare and it was supposed he drowned himself in a fit of remorse. Odd, though, that he should do his country such a service, eh?' Dungarth smiled. 'As for the girl, a certain Pascale Vrignaud, she suffered the fate of many whores. Odd little story, ain't it?'

'Yes.' Drinkwater swallowed the third glass of port at a gulp.

'I thought it would interest you,' added Dungarth smiling. 'You need give no further thought to the matter. Now, as to this fellow you feel may be of interest to me, whoever he is, I sent him from Hamburg with letters to Prince Vorontzoff in St Petersburg. The prince is a former ambassador to the Court of St James and has agreed to find him employment. Not unlike yourself, Nathaniel, this fellow Waters seems to be a child of fortune. Has a gambler's luck, wouldn't you say?'

Drinkwater returned Dungarth's grin. He felt no remorse for the death of Etienne Montholon, regretting that the man's rescue from the Jacobins had cost the lives of two British seamen. He wondered if Hortense would ever learn the name of her brother's executioner. It was a strange, small world. He saw the wheels of fate turning within each other and recalled Lettsom's observations on providence. As for Pascale, Edward would have her upon his own conscience. But Edward had a gambler's amorality as well as a gambler's luck. Drinkwater smiled at the aptness of Dungarth's last remark. The earl rose and refilled their glasses for the fourth time.

'I must thank you for your efforts . . . on my behalf, my lord,' said Drinkwater carefully, not wishing to break the delicate ice of ambiguity around the subject.

'It only remains,' replied Dungarth smiling, 'to see whether this man Waters is to be of any real use to us.'

Drinkwater nodded.

'And, of course, to drink to your swab . . .'

The Corvette

For my Mother

Contents

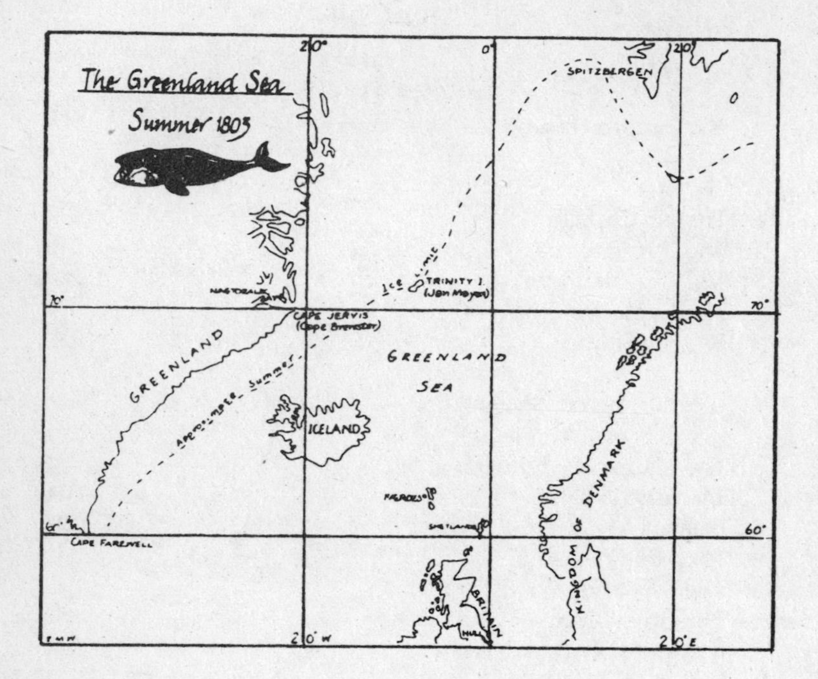
The Greenland Sea
Summer 1803
20°
0°
20°
SPITZBERGEN
TRINITY I.
(Jan Mayen)
70°
CAPE JERVIS
(Cape Brewster)
GREENLAND
GREENLAND
SEA
ICELAND
FAEROES
SHETLANDS
60°
CAPE FAREWELL
BRITAIN
HULL
KINGDOM OF DENMARK
20° W
20° E

PART ONE

The Convoy

'. . . and there came a report that the French were away to murder a' our whalers . . .'

The Man O' War's Man BILL TRUCK

May 1803

London

'He has *what?*'

The First Lord of the Admiralty swung round from the window, suddenly attentive. He fixed a baleful eye on the clerk holding the bundle of papers from which he was making his routine report.

'Resigned, my Lord.'

'Resigned? *Resigned*, God damn and blast him! What does he think the Service is that he may resign it at a whim? Eh?'

The clerk prudently remained silent as Earl St Vincent crossed the fathom of Indian carpet that lay between the window and his desk. He leaned forward, both hands upon the desk, his face approximating the colour of the Bath ribbon that crossed his breast in anticipation of a court levée later in the morning. He looked up at Mr Templeton.

Considerably taller than the first lord, Templeton nevertheless felt his lack of stature before St Vincent. Although used to his lordship's anger, his lordship's power never failed to impress him. The earl continued, his deep frustration obvious to the clerk.

'As if I have not enough with the war renewed and the dockyards but imperfectly overhauled, that I have to teach a damned kill-buck his duty. Good God, sir, the Service is not to be trifled with like a regiment. It has become altogether *too fashionable.*'

St Vincent spat the word with evident distaste. Since the Peace of Amiens he had laboured to clean the dockyards of corruption, to stock them with naval stores and to end the peculation and jobbery which beset the commissariat of his rival, Sir Andrew Snape Hammond, Comptroller of the Navy and head of the powerful Navy Board. He had found suppression of mutiny in the Cadiz squadron an easier task. He could not hang every grasping malefactor who stole His Majesty's stores, nor break every profiteer in the business of supplying His Majesty's Navy. Yet his affection for his ships and their well-being demanded it, and his honest opposition to the worldliness of the London politicians had made him many enemies.

Lord St Vincent hunched his shoulders and wiped his nose on a fine linen handkerchief. Templeton knew the gesture. The explosion of St Vincent's accumulated frustration would be through the touch-hole of his office, since his opponents stopped his muzzle.

'Be so kind, Templeton, as to add upon the skin of Sir James Palgrave's file that he is not to be employed again during the present war . . .'

'Yes my Lord.' St Vincent turned back to the window and his contemplation of the waving tree-tops in St James's Park. It was now his only eye upon the sky he had watched from a hundred quarterdecks. Templeton waited. St Vincent considered the folly of allowing a man a post-captaincy on account of his baronetcy. He recollected Palgrave; an indifferent lieutenant with an indolent fondness for fortified wines and a touchy sense of honour. It was perhaps a result of the inconsequence of his title. St Vincent, whose own honours had been earned by merit, disliked inherited rank when it eclipsed the abilities of better men. Properly the replacement of Palgrave should not concern the First Lord. But there was a matter of some importance attached to the appointment.

Templeton coughed. 'And the *Melusine*, my Lord?' St Vincent remained silent. 'Bearing in mind the urgency of her orders and the intelligence . . .'

'Why did he resign, Templeton?' asked St Vincent suddenly.

'I do not know, my Lord.' It was not the business of the Secretary's third clerk to trade in rumour, no matter how impeccable the source, nor how fascinating it sounded in the copy-room. But Sir James's hurried departure was said to stem from an inconvenient wound acquired in an illegal duel with the master of one of the ships he had been ordered to convoy. Templeton covered his dissimulation: 'And the *Melusine*, my Lord? It would seem she was in your gift.'

St Vincent looked up sharply. Only recent illness, a congestive outbreak of spring catarrh among the senior clerks, and including his Lordship's secretary Benjamin Tucker, had elevated Templeton to this daily tête-à-tête with the First Lord. Templeton flushed at his presumption.

'I beg pardon, my Lord, I meant only to allude to the intelligence . . .'

'Quite so, the intelligence had not escaped my recollection, Templeton,' St Vincent said sharply, and added ironically, 'whom had you in mind?'

'No one, my Lord,' blustered the clerk, now thoroughly alarmed that the omniscient old man might know of his connection with Francis Germaney, first lieutenant of the *Melusine*.

'Then who is applying, sir? Surely we are not in want of commanders for the King's ships?'

The barb drove home. 'Indeed not, my Lord.' The clerks' office was inundated daily with letters of application for employment by half-pay captains, commanders and lieutenants. All were neatly returned from the secretary's inner sanctum where the process of advancement or rejection ground its pitiless and partial way.

'Bring me the names of the most persistent applicants within the last month, sir, and jump to it.'

Templeton escaped with the alacrity of a chastened midshipman while St Vincent, all unseeing, stared at the rolling cumulus, white above the chimneys of Downing Street.

Since the renewal of the war two weeks earlier, officers on the half-pay of unemployment had been clamouring for appointments. The lieutenant's waiting-room below him was filled with hopeful officers, a bear-pit of demands and disappointments from which the admiralty messengers would be making a fortune in small coin, God rot them. St Vincent sighed, aware that his very overhaul of the navy had caused a dangerous hiatus in the nation's defences. Now the speed with which the fleet was recommissioning was being accomplished only by a reversion to the old vices of bribery, corruption and the blind eye of official condonement. St Vincent felt overwhelmed with chagrin while his worldly enemies, no longer concerned by the First Lord's zealous honesty, smiled with cynical condescension. Templeton's return broke the old man's bitter reverie.

'Well?'

'Three, my Lord,' said Templeton, short of breath from his haste. 'There are three whose persistence has been most marked.'

'Go on, sir, go on.'

'White, my Lord, Captain Richard White . . .'

'Too senior for a sloop, but he must have the next forty-four, pray do you note that . . .'

'Very well, my Lord. Then there is Yelland. He did prodigious well at Copenhagen . . .'

St Vincent sniffed. Whatever Yelland had done at Copenhagen was not enough to overcome the First Lord's prejudice. Templeton, aware that his own desire to please was bordering on the effusive, contrived to temporise: 'Though of course he is only a commander . . .'

'Just so, Templeton. *Melusine* is a twenty, a post-ship. Who is the third?'

'Er . . . Drinkwater, my Lord. Oh, I beg your pardon he is also only a commander.'

'No matter,' St Vincent mused on the name, trying to recall a face. 'Drinkwater?'

'I shall have to return . . .' began Templeton unhappily, but the First Lord cut him off.

'Read me his file. We may appoint him temporarily without the necessity of making him post.'

Templeton's nerve was near breaking point. In attempting to shuffle the files several papers came loose and floated down onto the rich carpet. He was beginning to regret his rapid promotion and thank his stars it was only temporary. He had forgotten all about his promises to his kinsman on the *Melusine*.

'Er, Nathaniel Drinkwater, my Lord, commissioned lieutenant October 1797 after Camperdown. First of the brig *Hellebore* sent on special service to the Red Sea by order of Lord Nelson. Lieutenant-in-command of the bomb tender *Virago* during the Baltic Campaign, promoted Master and Commander for his services prior to and during the battle of Copenhagen on the recommendation of both Parker and Nelson. Lately wounded in Lord Nelson's bombardment of Boulogne the same year and invalided of his wound until his present persistent application, my Lord.'

St Vincent nodded. 'I have him now. I recollect him boarding *Victory* in '98 off Cadiz before Nelson incurred their lordships' displeasure for sending that brig round Africa. Did he not bring back the *Antigone*?'

Templeton flicked the pages. 'Yes, my Lord. The *Antigone*, French National Frigate was purchased into the Service.'

'H'm.' St Vincent considered the matter. He remembered Mr Drinkwater was no youngster as a lieutenant in 1798. Yet St Vincent had remarked him then and had a vague recollection of a firm mouth and a pair of steady grey eyes that spoke of a quiet ability. And he had impressed both Parker *and* Nelson, no mean feat given the differences between the two men, whilst his record and his persistent applications marked him as an energetic officer. Maturity and energy were just the combination wanted for the *Melusine* if the intelligence reports were accurate. St Vincent began to cheer up. Palgrave had not been his choice, for he had commanded *Melusine* throughout the Peace, a fact that said more about Palgrave's influence than his ability.

'There's one other thing, my Lord,' offered Templeton, eager to re-establish his own reputation in his lordship's eyes.

'What is it?'

'Drinkwater, sir,' said the clerk, plucking the fact from the file like a low trump from a bad hand, 'has been employed on secret service before: the cutter *Kestrel*, my Lord, employed by Lord Dungarth's department.'

A gleam of triumph showed in St Vincent's eye. 'That clinches it, Templeton. Have a letter of appointment drawn up for my signature before eight bells . . . noon, Templeton, noon, and instructions for Captain Drinkwater to attend here with all despatch.' He paused reflecting. 'Desire him to wait upon me on Friday.'

'Yes, my Lord.' Templeton bent to retrieve the papers scattered about the floor. St Vincent returned to his window.

'Does one *smoke* a viper from his nest, Templeton?' The clerk looked up.

'Beg pardon, my Lord, but I do not know.'

'No matter, but let us see what Captain Drinkwater can manage, eh?'

'Yes, my Lord.' Templeton looked up from the carpet, aware that his lordship was no longer angry with him. He wondered if the unknown Captain Drinkwater knew that the First Lord's receiving hours were somewhat eccentric and doubted it. He reflected that there were conditions to the patronage of so punctilious a First Lord as John Jervis, Earl St Vincent.

'Be so kind as to have my carriage sent round, Templeton.'

The clerk rose, his bundle of papers clasped against his chest. 'At once, my Lord.' He was already formulating the letter to his kinsman aboard the *Melusine*:

My Dear Germaney,

In my diurnal consultations with his excellency The First Lord, I have arranged for your new commander to be Captain Nathaniel Drinkwater. He is not to be made post, but appointed as Job Captain so there is hope yet for your own advancement . . .

Chapter One *May 1803*

The Job Captain

'Non, m'sieur, non . . . Pardon,' Monsieur Bescond smote his forehead with the palm of his right hand and switched to heavily accented English. 'The shoulder, Capitaine, it must be 'igher. More . . . 'ow you say? Elevated.'

Drinkwater gritted his teeth. The pain in his shoulder was still maddening but it was an ache now, a manageable sensation after the agony of splintered bone and torn muscle. And he could not blame Bescond. He had voluntarily submitted himself to this rigorous daily exercise to stretch the butchered fibres of his shoulder whose scars now ran down into the right upper arm and joined the remains of an old wound given him by the French agent Santhonax. That had been in a dark alley in Sheerness the year of the Great Mutiny and he had endured the dull pain in wet or cold weather these past six years.

Monsieur Bescond, the emigré attorney turned fencing master, recalled him to his purpose. Drinkwater came on guard again and felt his sword arm trembling with the effort. The point of his foil seemed to waver violently and as Bescond stepped back he lunged suddenly lest his opponent notice the appalling quivering.

Mr Quilhampton's attention was elsewhere. The foible of Drinkwater's foil bent satisfyingly against the padding of Quilhampton's plastron.

'Bravo, M'sieur, tres bien . . . that was classical in its simplicity. And for you, M'sieur,' he said addressing Quilhampton and avoiding the necessity of using his name, 'you must never let your attention wander.'

Pleased with his unlooked for success Drinkwater terminated the lesson by removing his mask before Quilhampton could avenge himself.

'Were you distracted, James?' Whipping off his own mask

Quilhampton nodded in the direction of the door. Drinkwater turned.

'Yes, Tregembo, what is it?'

Drinkwater peeled off his plastron and gauntlet. His shirt stuck to his lean body, still emaciated after his wounding. A few loose locks of hair had escaped the queue and were plasted down the side of his head.

'I brought it as soon as I saw the seal, zur,' rumbled the old Cornishman as he handed the packet to Drinkwater. Quilhampton caught sight of the red wafer of the Admiralty with its fouled anchor device as Drinkwater tore it open.

Waiting with quickening pulse Quilhampton regarded his old commander with mounting impatience. He saw the colour drain from Drinkwater's face so that the thin scar on the left cheek and the blue powder burns above the eye seemed abruptly conspicuous.

'What is it, m'sieur? Not bad news?' Bescond too watched anxiously. He had come to admire the thin sea-officer with the drooping shoulder and his even skinnier companion with the wooden left hand. To Bescond they personified the dogged resistance of his adopted country to the monsters beyond the Channel who had massacred his parents and driven a pitchfork into the belly of his pregnant wife.

'Mr Q,' said Drinkwater with sudden formality, ignoring the Frenchman.

'Sir?' answered Quilhampton, aware that the contents of the packet had transformed the *salle d'armes* into a quarterdeck.

'It seems we have a ship at last! M. Bescond, my best attentions to you, I give you good day. Tregembo, my coat! God's bones, Mr Q, I have been made a "Job Captain", appointed to a sloop of war!'

An elated James Quilhampton accompanied Drinkwater to his house in Petersfield High Street. Since his widowed mother had obtained him a midshipman's berth on the brig *Hellebore*, thanks to the good offices of Lieutenant Drinkwater, Quilhampton had considered himself personally bound to his senior. Slight though Drinkwater's influence was, Quilhampton recognised the fact that he had no other patron. He therefore accorded Drinkwater an absolute loyalty that was the product of his generous nature. His own mother's close ties with Elizabeth Drinkwater had made him an intimate of the house in the High Street and it had been Quilhampton who, with Mr Lettsom, late surgeon of the bomb vessel *Virago*, had brought Drinkwater home after his terrible wounding off Boulogne.

To Quilhampton the Drinkwater household represented 'home' more than the mean lodgings his mother maintained. Louise Quilhampton, a pretty, talkative widow assisted Elizabeth Drinkwater in a school run for the poor children of the town and surrounding villages. Her superficial qualities were a foil to Mistress Drinkwater's and she was more often to be found in the house of her friend where her frivolous chatter amused five-year-old Charlotte Amelia and the tiny and newest arrival in the Drinkwater ménage, Richard Madoc.

James Quilhampton was as much part of the family as his mother had become. He had restrained Charlotte Amelia from interfering while her father sat for his portrait to the French prisoner of war, Gaston Bruilhac. And he had rescued her from a beating by Susan Tregembo, the cook, who had caught the child climbing over a fire to touch the cleverly applied worms of yellow and brown paint with which Bruilhac had painted the epaulette to mark Drinkwater's promotion to Master and Commander. That had been in the fall of the year one, when Drinkwater had returned from the Baltic and before he rejoined Lord Nelson for the fateful attack on Boulogne.

Quilhampton smiled at the recollection now as he looked at Bruilhac's creditable portrait and waited for Drinkwater to return from informing Elizabeth of their imminent departure.

That single epaulette which had so fascinated little Charlotte Amelia ought properly to have been transferred to Drinkwater's right shoulder, Quilhampton thought. Apart from concealing the drooping shoulder it was scandalous that Drinkwater had not been made post-captain for his part in extricating the boats after Nelson's daring night attack had failed. Their Lordships did not like failure and Quilhampton considered his patron had suffered because there were those in high places who were not sorry to see another of Nelson's enterprises fail.

Quilhampton shook his head, angry that even now their Lordships had stopped short of giving Drinkwater the post-rank he deserved. Allowed the title 'captain' only by courtesy, Commander Drinkwater had been made a 'Job Captain', given an acting appointment while the real commander of His Britannic Majesty's Sloop *Melusine* was absent. It was damned unfair, particularly after the wounding Drinkwater had suffered off Boulogne.

The young master's mate had spent hours reading to the feverish Drinkwater as he lay an invalid. And then, ironically, peace had replaced war by an uneasy truce that few thought would last but which made those who had suffered loss acutely conscious of their sacrifices. The inactivity eroded the difference in rank between the two men and replaced it with friendship. Strangers who encountered Drinkwater convalescing with energetic ascents of Butser Hill in Quilhampton's company, were apt to think them brothers. From the summit of the hill they watched the distant Channel for hours, Drinkwater constantly requesting reports on any sails sighted by Quilhampton through the telescope. And boylike they dodged the moralising rector on his lugubrious visits.

Gaston Bruilhac had been repatriated after executing delightful portraits of Drinkwater's two children and, Quilhampton recalled, he himself had been instrumental in persuading Elizabeth to sit for hers. He turned to look at the painting. The soft brown eyes and wide mouth stared back at him. It was a good likeness, he thought. The parlour door opened and Elizabeth entered the room. She wore a high-waisted grey dress and it was clear from her breathing and her colour that the news of their departure had caught her unawares.

'So, James,' she said, 'you are party of this conspiracy that ditches us the moment war breaks out again.' She caught her bottom lip between her teeth and Quilhampton mumbled ineffectual protests. He looked from Elizabeth to Drinkwater who came in behind her. His face was immobile.

'Oh, I know very well how your minds work . . . You are like children . . .' Her voice softened. 'You are worse than children.' She turned to her husband. 'You had better find something with which to drink to your new command.' She smiled sadly as Drinkwater stepped suddenly forward and raised her hand to his lips. She seated herself and he went in search of a bottle, waving Quilhampton to a chair.

'Look after him for me James,' she said quietly. 'His wound will trouble him for many months yet, you know how tetchy he becomes when the wind is in the south-west and the weather thickens up.'

Quilhampton nodded, moved by Elizabeth's appeal.

'This is the last of Dick White's malmsey.' Drinkwater re-entered the room blowing the dust off a bottle. He was followed by the dark-haired figure of his daughter who swept into the room in a state of high excitement.

'Mama, mama! Dickon has fallen into the Tilbrook!'

'What did you say?' Elizabeth rose and Drinkwater paused in the act of drawing the cork.

'Oh, it's all right,' Charlotte said, 'Susan has him quite safe. He's all wet, though . . .'

'Thank God for that. How did it happen?'

'Oh, he was a damned lubber, Mama . . .'

'Charlotte!' Elizabeth suppressed a smile that rose unchecked on the features of the two men. 'That is no way for a young lady to speak!'

Charlotte pouted until she caught the eye of her father.

'Perhaps,' said Elizabeth, seeing the way the wind blew, 'perhaps it would be better if you two went to sea again.' And then she began to explain to Charlotte Amelia that old King George had written a letter to Papa from Windsor and that Papa was to go away again and fight the King's enemies. And James Quilhampton sipped his celebratory malmsey guiltily, aware of the reproach in Elizabeth's gentle constancy.

Captain Drinkwater eased his shoulders slightly and settled the heavy broadcloth coat more comfortably. The enlarged shoulder pad which he had had the tailor insert to support the strained and wasted muscles of his neck did not entirely disguise the misalignment of his shoulders nor the cock of his head. The heavy epaulette only emphasised his disfigurement but he nodded his satisfaction at the reflection in the mirror and pulled his watch from his waistcoat pocket. It wanted fifteen minutes before six in the morning. Earl St Vincent, First Lord of the Admiralty, had already been at his desk for forty-five minutes. Drinkwater swallowed the last of his coffee hitched his sword and threw his cloak round his shoulders. Picking up his hat from its box, he blew out the candle and lifted the door latch.

Three minutes later he turned west into the Strand and walked quickly through the filth towards Whitehall. He dismissed any last minute additions he should have made to the shopping list he had left with Tregembo and composed his mind for his coming interview with the First Lord. He paused only to have his shoes blacked by a skinny youth who polished them with an old wig.

As the clock at the Horse Guards, the most accurate timepiece in London, struck the hour of six he turned in through the screen wall that separated the Admiralty from the periodical rioting seamen who besieged it for want of pay. He touched two fingers to his hat brim at the sentry's salute.

Beyond the glass doors he stopped and coughed. The Admiralty messenger woke abruptly from his doze and almost fell as he rose to his feet, extricating them with difficulty from the warming drawer set in the base of his chair. This he contrived to do without too much loss of dignity before leaving the hall to announce Commander Nathaniel Drinkwater.

Earl St Vincent rose as Drinkwater was ushered into the big office. He wore an old undress uniform with the stars of his orders embroidered upon his breast.

'Captain Drinkwater, pray take a seat.' He used the courtesy title and motioned Drinkwater to an upright chair and re-seated himself. Somewhat nervously Drinkwater sat, vaguely aware of two or three portraits that stared down at him and a magnificent sea-battle that he took for a representation of the action of St Valentine's Day off Cape St Vincent.

'May I congratulate you, Captain, upon your appointment.'

'Thank you, my Lord. It was unexpected.'

'But not undeserved.'

'Your Lordship is most kind.' Drinkwater bowed awkwardly from the waist and submitted himself to the First Lord's scrutiny. St Vincent congratulated his instinct. Commander Drinkwater would be about forty years of age, he judged. The grey eyes he remembered from their brief encounter in '98, together with the high forehead and the mop of hair that gave him a still youthful appearance despite the streaks of grey at his temples. The mouth was a little compressed, hiding the fullness of the lips and deep furrows ran down from his nose to bracket its corners. Drinkwater's complexion was a trifle pale beneath its weathering but it bore the mark of combat, a thin scar down the left cheek from a sword point, St Vincent thought, together with some tiny powder burns dotted over one eye like random inkspots.

'You have quite recovered from your wound, Captain?'

'Quite, my Lord.'

'What were the circumstances of your acquiring it?'

'I commanded the bomb tender *Virago*, my Lord, in Lord Nelson's attack on the Invasion Flotilla in December of year one. I had gone forward in a boat to reconnoitre the position when a shell burst above the boat. Several men were regrettably lost. I was more fortunate.' Drinkwater thought of Mr Matchett dying in his arms while the pain from his own wound seeped with a curiously attenuated shock throughout his system.

St Vincent looked up from the papers on his desk. The report of Commander Drinkwater's boat expedition into Boulogne was rather different, but no matter, St Vincent liked his modesty. A hundred officers would have boasted of the night's exploit and measured the risk according to the number of corpses in their boats. Palgrave would have done that, St Vincent was certain, and the thought pleased the old man in the rightness of his choice.

'Lord Dungarth speaks well of you, Captain.'

'Thank you, my Lord.' Drinkwater was beginning to feel uneasy, undermined by the compliments and aware that an officer with St Vincent's reputation was tardy of praise.

'You are perhaps thinking it unusual for a newly appointed sloop-captain to be interviewed by the First Lord, eh?'

Drinkwater nodded. 'Indeed, my Lord.'

'The *Melusine is* a fine sloop, taken from the French off the Penmarcks in ninety-nine and remarkably fast. What the French call a "corvette", though I don't approve of our using the word. Not an ideal ship for her present task . . .'

'No, my Lord?'

'No, Captain, your old command might have been better suited. Bomb vessels have proved remarkably useful in Arctic waters . . .'

Drinkwater opened his mouth and thought better of it. Before he could reflect further upon this revelation St Vincent had passed on.

'But it is not intended that you should linger long in northern latitudes. Since the King's speech in March it has been clear that the Peace would not last and we have been requested by the northern whale-fishery to afford some protection to their ships. During the last war it was customary to keep a cruiser off the North Cape and another off the Faeroes during the summer months while we still traded with Russia. Now that Tsar Alexander has reopened trade this will have to be reinstated. The whale-fishery, however, is sensitive. A small cruiser, the *Melusine* to be exact, was long designated to the task, principally because she was in commission throughout the peace.

'Now that war has broken out again her protection is the more necessary and the Hull ships are assembled in the Humber awaiting your convoy. That is where the *Melusine* presently lies. Her captain has recently become, er, indisposed, and you have been appointed in his stead . . .'

Drinkwater nodded, listening to the First Lord and eagerly wishing that he had known his destination was the Arctic before he despatched Tregembo and Quilhampton on their shopping expeditions. But there was also a feeling that this was not the only reason that he was waiting on the First Lord.

'During the peace,' St Vincent resumed, 'the French have despatched a vast number of privateers from their ports. These letters-of-marque have been reported from all quarters, most significantly on the routes of the Indiamen and already cruisers are ordered after them. That is of no matter to us this morning . . .' St Vincent rose and turned to the window. Drinkwater regarded the small, hunched back of the earl and tried to catch what he was saying as he addressed his remarks to the window and the distant tree-tops of the park.

'We believe some of these private ships have left for the Greenland Sea.' St Vincent spun round, a movement that lent his words a peculiar significance. 'Destruction of the northern fishery would mean destitution to thousands, not to mention the removal of prime seamen for His Majesty's ships . . .' He looked significantly at Drinkwater. 'You understand, Captain?'

'Aye, my Lord, I think so.'

St Vincent continued in a more conversational tone. 'The French are masters of the war upon trade, whether it be Indiamen or whalers, Captain. This is no sinecure and I charge you to remember that, in addition to protecting the northern whale-fleet you should destroy any attempt the French make to establish their own fishery. Do you understand?'

'Yes, my Lord.'

'Good. Now your written instructions are ready for you in the copyroom. You must join *Melusine* in the Humber without delay but Lord Dungarth asked that you would break your fast with him in his office before you left. Good day to you, Captain Drinkwater.'

Already St Vincent was bent over the papers on his desk. Drinkwater rose, made a half-bow and went in search of Lord Dungarth.

'Nathaniel! My very warmest congratulations upon being given *Melusine*. Properly she is a post-ship but St Vincent won't let that stop him.'

Lord Dungarth held out his hand, his hazel eyes twinkling cordially. He motioned Drinkwater to a chair and turned to a side table, pouring coffee and lifting the lid off a serving dish. 'Collops or kidneys, my dear fellow?'

They broke their respective fasts in the companionable silence of gunroom tradition. Age was beginning to tell on the earl, but there was still a fire about the eyes that reminded Drinkwater of the naval officer he had once been; ebullient, energetic and possessed of that cool confidence of his class that so frequently degenerated into ignorant indolence. Lord Dungarth wiped his mouth with a napkin and eased his chair back, sipping his coffee and regarding his visitor over the rim of the porcelain cup.

When Drinkwater had finished his kidneys and a servant had been called to remove the remains of the meal, Dungarth offered Drinkwater a cheroot which he declined.

'Finest Deli leaf, Nathaniel, not to be found in London until this war is over.'

'I thank you, my Lord, but I have not taken tobacco above a dozen times in my life.' He paused. Dungarth did not seem eager to speak as he puffed earnestly on the long cigar. 'May I enquire whether you have any news of, er, a certain party in whom we have . . .'

'A mutual interest, eh?' mumbled Dungarth through the smoke. 'Yes. He is well and has undertaken a number of tasks for Vorontzoff who is much impressed by his horsemanship and writes that he is invaluable in the matter of selecting English Arabs.' Drinkwater nodded, relieved. His brother Edward, in whose escape from the noose Drinkwater had taken an active part, had a habit of falling upon his feet. 'I do not think you need concern yourself about him further.'

'No.' In the service of a powerful Russian nobleman Edward would doubtless do very well. He could never return to his native country, but he might repay some of his debt by acting as a courier, as was implied by Dungarth. Vorontzoff, a former ambassador to the Court of St James, was an anglophile and source of information to the British government.

'I am sorry you were not made post, Nathaniel. It should have happened years ago but,' Dungarth shrugged, 'things do not always take the turn we would wish.' He lapsed into silence and Drinkwater was reminded of the macabre events that had turned this once liberal man into the implacable foe of the French Republic. Returning through France from Italy where his lovely young wife had died of a puerperal fever, the mob, learning that he was an aristocrat, had desecrated her coffin and spilled the corpse upon the roadway where it had been defiled. Dungarth sighed.

'This will be a long war, Nathaniel, for France is filled with a restless energy and now that she has worked herself free of the fervour of Republican zeal we are faced with a nationalism unlikely to remain within the frontiers of France, "natural" or imposed.

'Now we have the genius of Bonaparte rising like a star out of the turmoil, different from other French leaders in that he alone seems to possess the power to unite. To inspire devotion in an army of starving men and secure the compliance of those swine in Paris *is* genius, Nathaniel. Who but a fated man with the devil's luck could have escaped our blockade of Egypt and returned from the humiliation of defeat to retake Italy and seize power in France, eh?'

Dungarth shook his head and stood up. He began pacing up and down, stabbing a finger at Drinkwater from time to time to make a point.

'It is to the navy that we must look, Nathaniel, to wrest the advantage from France. We must blockade her ports again and nullify her fleets. God knows we can do little with the army, except perhaps a few conjoint operations, and they have been conspicuously unsuccessful in the past. But with the Navy we can prop up our wavering allies and persuade them to persist in their refusal to bow to Paris.'

'You think it likely that Austria will ever reach an accommodation with a republic?'

'There are reports, Nathaniel, that Bonaparte would make himself king and found a dynasty. God knows, but a man like that might stoop to divorce La Josephine and marry a Hohenzollern or a Romanov, even a Hapsburg if he can dictate a peace from a position of advantage. *You* know damned well he reached for India.' Dungarth looked unhappily at Drinkwater who nodded.

'Yes, my Lord, you are right.'

'On land France will exhaust herself and it is our duty to outlast her.'

'But she will need to be defeated on land in the end, my Lord, and if our own forces . . .'

Dungarth laughed. 'The British Army? God, did you see what a shambles came out of Holland? No, the Horse Guards will achieve nothing. We must look to Russia, Nathaniel, Russia with her endless manpower supported by our subsidies and the character of Tsar Alexander to spur her on.'

'You purport to re-establish liberty, my Lord, with the aid of Russia?' Drinkwater was astonished. Enough was known of Holy Russia to mark it as a strange mixture of refinement and barbarism. Russian ships had served with the Royal Navy in the North Sea, their officers a mixture of culture and incompetence. Russian troops had served in the Dutch campaign and relations between the two armies had been strained, while Suvorov's veterans had established a name in Northern Italy as synonymous with terror as anything conceived in Paris. Only two years earlier Alexander's father, the sadistic Tsar Paul, had turned on his British ally and leagued himself with France in a megalomaniac desire to carve up Europe with Bonaparte. Although Alexander professed himself the friend of England and a Christian Prince, he was suspected of conniving at his own father's assassination.

'I am informed,' Dungarth said with heavy emphasis and a nod that implied a personal connection, 'that Tsar Alexander wishes to atone for certain sins and considers himself a most liberal prince.' Dungarth's tone was cynical.

'So Vorontzoff's man is of some use . . .?'

Dungarth nodded. 'Together with a certain Countess Marie Narishkine . . . Still, this is not pertinent to your present purpose, Nathaniel. It is more in the line of, er, shall we say, family news, eh?'

Drinkwater grinned. Clearly Edward was more than a courier and Dungarth had made him an agent in his own right. He wondered how Edward liked his new life and, recalling the man aboard the *Virago*, decided he would manage.

'Doubtless St Vincent mentioned that the late and unlamented Peace afforded the French every opportunity to get ships away to cruise against our trade. This is the most dangerous weapon the French can bring against our sea-power. Look at the success enjoyed by privateers in the American War. Yankees, French and Irish snapped up prizes on our own doorstep, reduced our ports to poverty, raised insurance rates to the sky and induced the merchant classes to whine until the government rocked to their belly-aching. There won't be a captain in command of an escort like yours that don't bear a burden as heavy as that of a seventy-four on blockade duty. Mark me, Nathaniel, mark me. Loss of trade is loss of confidence in the Royal Navy and, bearing in mind the effort we must sustain for the foreseeable future, that augurs very ill.

'Now, to be specific, there are some whispers lately come from sources in Brittany that a number of ships, well armed and equipped, sailed north a year ago. They have not returned, neither has any news of them. Their most obvious destination is Canada where they may make mischief for us. But no news has come from the Loyalists in New Brunswick who keep a sharp eye on our interests. Neither have they been seen in American waters . . .'

'Ireland?'

'Perhaps, but again, nothing. The Norwegian coast provides ample shelter for privateers and was used by the Danes before Copenhagen but I am inclined to think they lie in wait for our whalers. Two disappeared last summer and although the loss of these ships is not remarkable, indeed they may simply have wintered in the ice, there is a story of some sighting of vessels thought not to be whalers by the Hull fleet last season.'

'You mean to imply that two whalers might have been taken by French privateers during the peace?'

'I do not know, Nathaniel. I only tell you this because these ships have not been heard of since they left France bound to the northward. It is a possibility that they have wintered in a remote spot like Spitzbergen and are waiting to strike against the whale-fishery on the resumption of hostilities. It is not improbable. French enterprise has sent letters-of-marque-and-reprisal to cruise in most of the areas frequented by British merchantmen. Opportunism may sometimes have the appearance of conspiracy and most of us knew the peace would not last.'

'Do you know the force of these vessels?'

'No, I regret I do not.'

Drinkwater digested the news as Dungarth sat down again. 'There is one other thing you should know.' Dungarth broke into his thoughts.

'My Lord?'

'Captain Palgrave did not leave his command willingly.'

'I heard he was indisposed.'

'He was shot in a duel. A very foolish affair which I heard of due to the loose tongue of one of the clerks here who is related to your first lieutenant. It seems that Palgrave had some sort of altercation with one of the captains of the whalers. Nothing will be done about it, of course; Palgrave cannot afford scandal so he has resigned his command and he has enough clout to ensure the facts do not reach the ears of the Court. But it is exceedingly unusual that a merchant master should incapacitate the captain of the man-of-war assigned to give him the convoy he has been bleating for.'

'Perhaps some affair locally, my Lord, an insult, a woman . . .'

'I grow damnably suspicious in my old age, Nathaniel,' Dungarth smiled, 'but since you speak of women, how is Elizabeth and that charming daughter of yours. And I hear you have an heir too . . .'

Chapter Two *May 1803*

The Corvette

Drinkwater leaned from the window of the mail-coach as the fresh horses were whipped up to draw them out of Barnet. Dusk was already settling on the countryside and he could make out little of the landmarks of his youth beyond the square tower of Monken Hadley church whose Rector had long ago recommended him to Captain Hope of the *Cyclops*.

From above his head a voice called, 'Why she flies like a frigate going large, sir.' Looking up he saw Mr Quilhampton's face excited by their speed, some eight or nine miles to the hour.

Drinkwater smiled at the young man's pleasure and drew back into the coach. Since his breakfast with Lord Dungarth it had been a busy day of letter writing and last minute purchases. There had been a brace of pistols to buy and he had invested in a chronometer and a sextant, one of Hadley's newest, which now nestled beneath his feet. They had seen the bulk of their luggage to the Black Swan at Holborn and left it in the charge of Tregembo to bring on by the slower York Stage.

He and Quilhampton had arrived at Lombard Street just in time to catch the Edinburgh Mail, tickets for which Quilhampton had purchased earlier in the day. He smiled again as he remembered the enthusiasm of Mr Quilhampton at the sight of the shining maroon and black Mails clattering in and out of the Post Office Yard, some dusty from travel, others new greased and washed, direct from Vidler's Millbank yard and ready to embark on their nocturnal journeys. The slam of the mail boxes, shouts of their coachmen and the clatter of hooves on the cobbles as their scarlet wheels spun into motion was one of affecting excitement, Drinkwater thought indulgently as he settled back into the cushions, and vastly superior to the old stage-coaches.

The lady opposite returned his smile, removing her poke bonnet to do so and Drinkwater suffered sudden embarrassment as he realised that not only had he been grinning like a fool but his knees had been in intimate contact with those of the woman for some minutes.

'You are going to join your ship, Captain?' Her Edinburgh accent was unmistakable as was the coquettish expression on her face.

'Indeed, ma'am, I am.' He coughed and readjusted his position. The woman was about sixty and surely could not suppose . . .

'Catriona, my niece here,' the lady's glove patted the knee of a girl in grey and white sitting in the centre of the coach, 'has been visiting with me in London, Captain, at a charming villa in Lambeth. Do you live in London, Captain?'

Drinkwater looked at the girl, but the shadow of her bonnet fell across her face and the lights would not be lit until the next stop. As she boarded the coach he remembered her as tall and slim. He inclined his head civilly in her direction.

'No, ma'am, I live elsewhere.'

'May one ask where, sir?' Drinkwater sighed. It was clear the widow was determined to extract every detail and he disliked such personal revelations. He answered evasively. 'Hampshire, ma'am.'

'Ah, Hampshire, such a *fashionable* county.'

As Mistress MacEwan rattled on he smiled and nodded, taking stock of the other passengers. To his left an uncomfortably large man in a snuff-coloured coat was dozing, or perhaps feigning to doze and thus avoid the widow's quizzing; while to his right a soberly dressed divine struggled to read a slim volume of sermons in the fast fading light. Drinkwater suspected he, like the corpulent squire, affected his occupation to avoid the necessity of conversation.

There was, however, no doubt about the condition of the sixth occupant of the swaying coach. He was sunk in a drunken stupor, snoring gracelessly and sliding further down in his seat.

'. . . And at the reception given by Lady Rochford, Catriona was fortunate enough to be presented to . . .'

The widow MacEwan's prattle was beginning to irritate him. The overwhelming power of her nonsense was apt to give the impression that all women were as ridiculously superficial. His thoughts turned to Elizabeth and their children and the brief note he had written to her explaining the swift necessity of his departure. Elizabeth would understand, but that did not help the welling sadness that filled his heart and he cursed the weakness acquired from a long convalescence at home.

'. . . And then the doctor advised the poor woman to apply poultices of green hemlock leaves to her breast and to consume as many millipedes as her stomach could take in a day and the tumour was much reduced and the lady restored to health. Is that not a remarkable story, Captain? You are a married man, sir?'

Drinkwater nodded wearily, aware that the clergyman next to him had let his book fall in his lap and his head droop forward.

'Of course, sir, I knew you were, you have the unmistakable stamp of a married man and a gallant officer. My husband always said . . .'

Drinkwater did not attend to the late Mr MacEwan's homespun wisdom. He had a sudden image of Richard standing naked after his fall in the Tilbrook while Susan Tregembo rubbed him dry.

'. . . But I assure you, Captain, it was not something to smile about. She died of smallpox within a month, leaving the child an orphan . . .' Catriona's knee was patted a second time.

'My apologies, ma'am, I was not smiling.'

Drinkwater felt the coach slow down and a few minutes later it stopped to change horses at Hatfield. 'Your indulgence ma'am, but forgive me.' He rose and flung open the coach door, going in search of the house of office and, having returned, shouted up to Quilhampton.

'Mr Q, we will exchange for a stage or two.'

'Aye, aye, sir.' Quilhampton descended. The new horses were already being put to and the guard was consulting his stage-watch. 'Half-a-minute, gentlemen.'

'Your boat cloak, Mr Q.' Drinkwater took the heavy cloak and whirled it round his shoulders. He reached inside the coach for his hat.

'I beg your forgiveness ma'am, but I am a most unsociable companion. May I present Mr Quilhampton, an officer of proven courage now serving with me. Mr Q, Mrs MacEwan.' He ignored Quilhampton's open jaw and shoved him forward. 'Have a care for the instruments.'

'Oh!' he heard Mrs MacEwan say, 'Honoured I'm sure, but Captain, the night air will affect you to no good purpose, sir and may bring on a distemper.' The speech ended in a little squeal of horror and Drinkwater grinned as he hoisted himself up. Mrs MacEwan had discovered Mr Quilhampton's wooden hand.

'All aboard!' called the guard mounting the box and raising his horn. He jammed his tricorne down on his head as the coach leapt forward. The blast of the horn covered his laughter. They had been less than the permitted five minutes in changing their horses.

Above the racing coach the sky was bright with stars. A slim, crescent moon was rising. The mail was passing through the market-garden country north of Biggleswade and the horses were stretching out. He did not encourage his fellow outsiders to converse, indeed their deference to his rank made it clear that Mr Quilhampton had been telling tall stories. He was left alone with his thoughts and dismissed those of Elizabeth and the children to concentrate upon the future. He was pleased to be appointed to the *Melusine* even as a 'Job Captain', a stand-in. It was a stroke of good fortune, for she would be manned by volunteers having been in service throughout the peace. All her men would be thorough-going seamen. The officers, however, were likely to be different, probably place-seekers and time-servers. Influence and patronage had triumphed once again, even in the short period of the Peace of Amiens. Worthy officers of humble origins had been denied appointments. *Melusine* was unlikely to have avoided this blight. He knew nothing about Palgrave beyond the fact that he was a baronet and had been compelled to resign his command after being seriously wounded in a duel. In the sober judgement of Nathaniel Drinkwater those two facts spoke volumes.

He shivered and then cursed the widow MacEwan for her sagacity. The night air and the cold had found the knotted muscles in his shoulder. Holding fast with one hand he searched for the flask of brandy in his tail-pocket with the other. The coach swayed as the guard rose to pierce the night with his post-horn. As he swigged the fiery liquid Drinkwater was aware of a toll-keeper wrapped in a blanket as he threw wide his toll-gate to allow the mail through.

The glorious speed of the coach seemed to speak to him of all things British and he smiled at himself, amused that such considerations still had the power to move him. His grim experience off Boulogne and the brush with death that followed had shaken his faith in providence. The ache in his shoulder further reminded him that he was going to venture into Arctic waters where he would need all the fortitude he could muster. Command of the *Melusine* and her charges would be his first experience of truly independent responsibility and, in that mid-night hour, he began to feel the isolation of it.

He took another swig of brandy and remembered the melancholia he had suffered after the fever of his recovery had subsided. The 'blue-devils' were an old malady, endemic among sea-officers and induced by loneliness, responsibility and, some men maintained, the enforced chastity of the life. Drinkwater was acutely conscious that he owed his full recovery from these 'megrims' to the love of his wife and friends. This thought combined with the stimulation of the brandy to raise his spirits.

Tonight he was racing to join a ship beneath a cloudless sky at what surely must be twelve miles to the hour! His thoughts ran on in a more philosophic vein, recalling Dungarth's long speech on the ambitions of France and the defence of liberty. He might talk of freedom being the goal of British policies, but at this very moment the press was out in every British sea-port, enslaving Britons for service in her Navy with as savage a hand as her landowners had appropriated and enclosed the countryside through which he was passing. The complexities of human society bewildered and exasperated Drinkwater and while his ordered mind was repelled by the nameless perfidies of politics, he was aware of the conflict it mirrored in himself.

There were many in Britain and Europe who welcomed the new order of things that had emerged from the bloody excesses of the French Revolution. Bonaparte was the foremost of these, an example of the exasperation of youth and talent at the blind intractability of vested interest. Surely Dungarth had overplayed the real danger posed by Bonaparte alone? Yet he would sail in command of his 'corvette' to drive the tricolour of France from the high seas with the same eagerness that the mail-guard consulted his watch and urged his charge through the night. He suppressed the feeling of radical zeal easily. The excitement of the night was making him foolish. He had a duty to do in protecting the Hull whale-fleet. The matter was simplicity itself.

Then a precarious sleep swallowed him, sleep that was interrupted by sudden jolts and the contraction of aching muscles, and accompanied by the memory of Elizabeth's sadness at his departure.

They broke a hurried fast at Grantham after the terrifying descent of Spitalgate Hill and by noon had crossed the Trent at Muskham. Drinkwater rode inside for a while but, assaulted again by Mrs MacEwan who seemed desirous of information regarding the 'gallant and charming Mr Quilhampton', he returned irritably to the box. He did not observe Mr Quilhampton's look of joy as he again exchanged seats and he was thoroughly worn out by the time the mail rolled into the yard of the Black Swan at York.

'And what, my dear, did you think of Mr Quilhampton?' asked Mrs MacEwan staring after the captain and the tall young officer beside him.

'I thought, Aunt,' said the young woman, removing her bonnet and shaking her red-gold hair about her shoulders, 'That he was a most personable gentleman.'

'Ahhh.' Mrs MacEwan sighed with satisfaction. 'See, my dear, he has turned . . .' She waved her gloved hand with frivolous affectation while Catriona simply smiled at James Quilhampton.

Drinkwater took to his bed before sunset, waiting only to instruct Quilhampton to mind the baggage and engage a conveyance to take them to Hull the following morning. Quilhampton was left to walk the streets of York alone, unable to throw off the image of Catriona MacEwan.

The good weather held. The following day being a Sunday they were obliged to hire a private chaise but the drive over the gentle hills was delightful. Drinkwater was much refreshed by his long sleep at York where, by a stroke of good fortune, he had enjoyed clean sheets. They ate at Beverly after hearing mattins in the beautiful Minster, reaching Kingston-upon-Hull at five in the afternoon.

First Lieutenant Francis Germaney stood in his cabin and passed water into the chamberpot. His eyes were screwed up tight against the pain and he cursed with quiet venom. He was certain now that 'the burns' had been contracted in a bawdy house in Kingston-upon-Hull and he wondered if Sir James Palgrave were similarly afflicted. It would serve the God-damned smell-smock right for he deserved it, that pistol ball in his guts notwithstanding.

'Oh Christ!' He saw the dark swirl of blood in the urine. And their blasted surgeon had not been sober since the morning of the duel. Not that he had been sober much before that, Germaney reflected bitterly, but there had been periods of near sobriety long enough to attend the occasional patient and maintain an appearance of duty. But now, God rot him, just when he was wanted . . .

Germaney resolved to swallow his pride and consult a physician without delay. Mr Surgeon Macpherson with his degree from Edinburgh could go to the devil. As he refastened his breeches his eyes fell on the letter from cousin Templeton. Commander Drinkwater's arrival was imminent and Templeton indicated that the First Lord himself was anxious to brook no further delay. Germaney reached for his coat and hat when a knock came at the door. 'What is it?'

The face of Midshipman the Lord Walmsley peered round the door.

'Mr Bourne's compliments, sir, but there's a shore-boat approaching answering the sentry's hail with "*Melusine*".'

'God damn!' Germaney knew well what that meant. The boat contained the new captain. 'Trying to catch us out,' he muttered.

'That's what Mr Bourne says.'

'Get out of my fucking way.'

Drinkwater folded his commission after reading it aloud and looked about him. Beneath a cloudless sky the corvette *Melusine* floated upon the broad, muddy Humber unruffled by any wind. Her paint and brass-work gleamed and her yards were perfectly squared. She lay among the tubby black and brown hulls of the whalers and the squat shapes of the other merchantmen and coasters at anchor off the port of Hull, a lady among drabs.

Not a rope was out of position beneath the lofty spars that rose to a ridiculous height. Named after a Breton sprite, *Melusine* showed all the lovely hallmarks of her French ancestry. Drinkwater's spirits soared and although he knew her for a showy thing, he could not deny her her beauty. He clamped the corners of his mouth tightly lest they betrayed his pleasure and frowned, nodding to the first lieutenant.

'Mr Germaney, I believe.'

'Your servant, sir. Welcome aboard.' Germaney removed his hat and bowed. 'May I present the officers, sir?'

Drinkwater nodded. 'Mr Bourne and Mr Rispin, sir; second and third lieutenants.' Two young officers in immaculate uniforms bowed somewhat apprehensively.

'Mr Hill, the Master . . .'

'Hill! Why, 'tis a pleasure to see you again. When was the last time?'

'Ninety-seven, sir, after Camperdown . . .' Hill was beaming, his face ruddy with broken veins and little of his fine black hair left beyond a fringe above his nape. Drinkwater remembered he had been wounded when a master's mate in the cutter *Kestrel*.

'How is the arm?'

'An infallible barometer signalling westerly gales, sir.' They both laughed. 'I heard you was wounded off Boulogne, sir . . .'

'I am a trifle sagged amidships, Mr Hill, but otherwise sound. I have an excellent second for you. May I present Mr James Quilhampton, Master's Mate, lately qualified at the Trinity House of London and a veteran of Copenhagen.' He stepped aside allowing the little knot of officers to receive Quilhampton's bow. Drinkwater turned to Germaney who resumed the introductions.

'Mr Gorton, sir, whose six years are nearly up.'

'How many have you served at sea, Mr Gorton?'

'All of them, sir,' replied the midshipman, looking Drinkwater in the eye. 'I was two years a volunteer before that, sir.' Drinkwater nodded with satisfaction. Mr Gorton seemed to possess more potential than either of the two commissioned lieutenants. He turned to the next youth, perhaps a year or two younger than Gorton.

'Lord Walmsley, sir.'

Drinkwater caught his jaw in time and merely nodded and turned to the next. Another seventeen-year-old, the Honourable Alexander Glencross essayed a bow and was received with similar frigidity. Drinkwater had the impression that neither of these two young gentlemen took their profession very seriously and was relieved to see two fairly commonplace specimens at the end of the line.

'Messrs Wickham and Dutfield, sir and Mr Frey.'

Mr Frey emerged from behind Dutfield where, Drinkwater suspected, the latter young gentleman had been holding him. Palgrave, it appeared, let his midshipmen fool about and skylark. That was all very well but it led too often to bullying and Mr Frey was a child of no more than twelve years of age.

Germaney produced a purser named Pater, a bosun and a carpenter before drawing Drinkwater's attention to a disreputable figure half hidden behind the mizenmast.

'Mr Macpherson, our surgeon.'

'Macpherson of Edinburgh, Captain,' slurred the surgeon, his face wet with perspiration, his eyes watery with rheum, '*À votre service*.' Drinkwater could smell the rum at a yard distant and noted the dirty coat and stained linen.

'Lieutenant Mount, sir,' Germaney ploughed on, distracting Drinkwater from the state of the surgeon. Macpherson's shortcomings would be the subject of some conversation between captain and first lieutenant, but later, and on Germaney's terms. 'Lieutenant Mount, sir, of His Majesty's Marines.'

'*Royal* Marines, Mr Germaney, you should not neglect the new title.' Drinkwater indicated the blue facings of a royal regiment. 'An improvement upon the old white, Mr Mount,' he said conversationally and paced along the line of scarlet and pipe-clayed soldiers drawn up for his inspection. Mr Mount glowed with pleasure. He had spotted the glitter of gold lace a good fifteen minutes before the midshipman of the watch and had turned his men out in time to create a good impression.

'Your men do you credit, Mr Mount. I would have them all proficient marksmen to a high degree and I should like you to take charge of all the small-arms training on the ship. I have a prejudice against the junior lieutenant being responsible for the matter. He is better employed with his division and at the great guns.'

Drinkwater looked round, pleased with the obvious stir this small innovation had caused. He strode forward to stand by the larboard hance. A solitary brass carronade marked the limit of the hallowed quarterdeck of Captain Sir James Palgrave and the non-regulation addition to *Melusine*'s long guns shone with an ostentatious polish.

'I hope, Mr Germaney,' said Drinkwater in a clear voice, 'that all this tiddley work ain't at the expense of the ship's true fighting qualities, eh?'

He was facing the men assembled in the waist and caught half a dozen swiftly suppressed grins.

'N . . . no, of course not, sir.'

'Very well.' He looked over the ship's company. They seemed to be made up of the usual mixture. Tow headed Scandinavians, swarthy Portuguese, three negroes, an Indian and an Arab amongst a herd of old and young from the two kingdoms and the emerald isle. 'Do your duty men and you have nothing to fear.' It was an old formula, hack words but good enough for the moment. And if it lacked inspiration it at least encapsulated all that was required of them.

'Pray take a seat, Mr Germaney.' Drinkwater hung his hat and turned to his first lieutenant. Captain Palgrave's hurried departure had made Drinkwater temporary heir to some handsome cabin furniture and a full decanter of rich malmsey.

He poured a glass for himself and the first lieutenant, aware that they had just inspected parts of the ship that he doubted Mr Germaney even knew existed.

'That cockpit, Mr Germaney, is an ill-ventilated spot at best. I want it white-washed as soon as possible. There are marks there, and in the demeanour of the young gentlemen, of a slackness that I do not like. Now, your good health.' They drank and Drinkwater looked shrewdly at the lieutenant. He was on edge, yet displayed a certain lassitude to the task of showing the captain round the ship. An officer intent on creating a good impression would have shown off some of *Melusine*'s good points rather than ignoring them. Well, it was no matter. For the present there were more urgent considerations.

'The ship is well enough, Mr Germaney, although I withhold my full approbation until I see how her people make sail and work the guns. What I am not happy about is the surgeon.'

A surprising and noticeable interest stirred Germaney.

'Tell me,' Drinkwater continued, 'how was such a slovenly officer able to hold his position under an officer as, er, punctilious as Captain Palgrave?'

'I am not certain, sir. It seemed Sir James owed him some service or other.'

'Is the man perpetually drunk?'

Germaney brightened. Things were turning a little in his favour. 'I regret to say that that is most usually the case, sir. There is no confidence in him among the people.'

'That does not surprise me. His instruments were filthy with rust and his loblolly boys looked perilous close to being gangrenous themselves. Come, another glass of this excellent malmsey . . .' Drinkwater watched the first lieutenant shrewdly. In the few hours he had been aboard much had already been made clear. He did not find the weakness of his three lieutenants comforting.

'What made your late captain leave such a taut ship, Mr Germaney?'

Germaney was beginning to relax. Captain Drinkwater seemed amiable enough: a trifle of a democrat, he suspected, and he had a few bees in his bonnet, to which his rank entitled him. But there was little to mark him as special, as Templeton had intimated. If anything he seemed inclined to tipple. Germaney drained his glass and Drinkwater refilled it.

'Oh, er, he resigned, sir. He was a man of some wealth as you see,' Germaney indicated the richness of the cabin furnishings and the french-polished panels of the forward bulkhead.

'An odd circumstance, wouldn't you say, to resign command of such a ship on the outbreak of war?'

Germaney shrugged, aware of the imputed slight. 'I was not a party to Sir James's affairs, sir.'

'Not even those most touching his honour, Mr Germaney?'

Germaney moved uneasily. 'I . . . I do not understand what you mean, sir.'

'I mean that I doubt if Captain Palgrave engaged in an affair of honour without the support of yourself as his second.'

'Oh, you know of that . . . some damned gossip hereabouts I . . .'

'I learned at the Admiralty, Mr Germaney, and I do not need to tell you that the news was not well received.' The implication went home. It was fairly logical to suppose that Germaney would have served as Palgrave's second in the duel. Often a first lieutenant was bound to his commander by greater ties than mere professional loyalty. It was inconceivable that a peacetime captain like Palgrave would not have had such a first lieutenant.

Germaney regretted his gossiping letter to Templeton and swore to have his cousin answer for this indiscretion. 'Was my name . . . am I, er . . . ?'

'I think,' said Drinkwater swiftly, avoiding a falsehood, 'I think that you had better tell me the precise origin of the quarrel. It seems scarcely to contribute to the service if the commander of the escort is to be called out by the masters he is sent to protect.'

'Well, sir, I er, it was difficult for me . . .'

'I would rather the truth from you, Mr Germaney,' said Drinkwater quietly, 'than rumour from someone else. You should remember that Hill and I are old messmates and I would not want to go behind your back because you concealed information from me.'

Germaney was pallid. The Royal proscription against duelling or participating in such affairs could be invoked against him. Palgrave had abandoned him and his thoughts would not leave the discomfort in his loins. Palgrave had his share of the responsibility for that too.

'There was an altercation in public, sir. An exchange of insults ashore between Captain Palgrave and the captain of one of the whale-ships.'

'How did this happen? Were you present?'

Germaney nodded. 'Sir James met Captain Ellerby, the master of the *Nimrod*, in the street. Ellerby was out walking with his daughter and there had previously been some words between him and Sir James about the delays in sailing. It is customary for the whale-ships to sail in early April to hunt seals before working into the ice in May . . .'

'Yes, yes, go on.'

Germaney shrugged. 'Sir James paid some exaggerated and, er, injudicious compliments to the daughter, sir, to which Ellerby took exception. He asked for a retraction at which Sir James, er . . .'

'Sir James what?'

'He was a little the worse for liquor, sir . . .'

'I should hope he was, sir, I cannot think an officer would behave in that manner sober. But come, what next? What did Sir James say?'

'He made the observation that a pretty face was fair game for a gentleman's muzzle.'

'Hardly an observation, Mr Germaney. More of a highly offensive *double-entendre*, wouldn't you say?'

'Yes, sir.'

'Then what happened?'

'Ellerby struck him with his stick and Sir James was restrained by myself and Mr Mount. Sir James said he would call for satisfaction if Ellerby had been a gentleman and Ellerby shouted that he would meet him if only to teach a gentleman manners . . . And so the unhappy affair progressed. Sir James was not entirely well the following morning and though he fired first his ball miscarried. Ellerby's ball took him in the spleen.'

'So the affair was public hereabouts?'

'As public as a Quaker wedding, sir,' concluded Germaney dejectedly.

'And hushed up, I don't doubt, with public sympathy supporting Ellerby and the town council firmly behind the move, eh?'

'Yes, sir. They provided a doctor and a chaise to convey Sir James away to his seat as fast as possible. It was not difficult to persuade him to resign, though damnably difficult to stop Macpherson leaving with him. But the city fathers would not hear of it. Macpherson had become too well-known in the taverns for a loud-mouthed fool. Until you told me I had supposed the matter hushed outside the town. I stopped all shore-leave, though I expect that by now the water-folk have spread the news among the men.'

'I don't doubt it. You and Mount stood seconds, did you?'

'Mount refused, sir.'

'Ahhh.' Mount's conduct pleased Drinkwater. It must have taken considerable moral courage. 'Well, Mr Germaney, your own part in it might yet be concealed if we delay no further.'

'Thank you, sir . . . About the surgeon, sir. It is not right that we should make a voyage to the Arctic with such a man.'

'No.' Drinkwater refilled the glasses. Germaney's explanation made him realise the extent of his task. The whale-ship captains, already delayed by government proscription pending the outcome of developments with France, had been further held up by Palgrave's dilatoriness, to say nothing of his arrogance and offensiveness. He knew from his own orders that the Customs officers would issue the whale-ships their clearances at a nod from *Melusine*'s captain, and he had no more desire than the whalers to wait longer. Delay increased the risk of getting fast in the ice. If that happened *Melusine* would crack like an egg-shell.

'But there is now no alternative. We will sail without delay. Now I desire that you send a midshipman to visit each of the whale-ships, Greenlanders they call 'emselves, don't they? He is to invite them to repair on board tomorrow forenoon and we can settle the order of sailing and our private signals. And tell the young gentleman that I would have the invitation made civilly with my cordial compliments.'

'Yes, sir,' said Germaney unhappily, 'and the surgeon?'

'Tell the surgeon,' said Drinkwater with sudden ferocity, 'that if I find him drunk I shall have him at the gratings like any common seaman.'

Two hours later Drinkwater received a round-robin signed by a dozen names stating that the whale-ship commanders 'Would rather their meeting took place ashore at the Trinity House of Kingston-upon-Hull . . .'

Drinkwater cursed Sir James Palgrave, annoyed that he must first set out to woo a set of cantankerous merchant masters who set the King's commission so lightly aside. Then he calmed himself and reflected they had little cause to love the Royal Navy. It plundered their ships of prime seamen, usually when they were entering the Humber and after the hardships of an Arctic voyage. There was already a Regulating Captain set up in the city with all the formal machinery of the Impress Service at his finger tips. Drinkwater remembered the story of a whaler abandoned by her entire crew off the Spurn Head as the cruising frigate hove in sight to press her crew.

No, they had no cause to love the Navy hereabouts and suddenly the vague, universal preoccupation of the justice of the present war came back to him. And as quickly was dismissed as irrelevant to the task in hand.

Chapter Three *May 1803*

The Greenlanders

The tie-wigged usher conducted Drinkwater through the splendid corridors of the Trinity House of Kingston-upon-Hull. His previous connections with the corporation had been with the Baltic pilots it had supplied for the Copenhagen campaign two years earlier. Their performance had been disappointing and had clouded his opinions, so that he had forgotten the Arctic connection of the brotherhood.

The usher paused for a second before a heavy door from beyond which came the noise of heated argument. Drinkwater caught the phrase 'two months late' and the angrier, 'what guarantee have we of a bounty . . .?' Then the usher opened the door and announced him.

Drinkwater advanced into the room. He was in full dress with cocked hat and sword. The room was lit by tall windows and rushes were strewn across the plain boarded floor. Sitting and standing round a long mahogany table about two dozen men in all shades of civilian clothing turned towards him. Their complexions varied from the effects of their diet, the privations of their calling and the present heat of their passions. He was acutely aware of a wall of prejudice and remained observantly circumspect. He inclined his head.

'I give you good day, gentlemen.'

'Huh!' A huge black bearded man who sat cross-armed and truculent upon the nearer edge of the table turned his face away. Drinkwater kept his temper.

'Thou woulds't do better to keep thyself civil, Friend Jemmett.' A man in the dark green and broad-brimmed hat of a Quaker rose from a seat behind the table. He came forward and indicated an upright chair.

'Pray seat thyself, sir. I am Abel Sawyers, master of the *Faithful*.' The Quaker's voice was low and vibrant.

Drinkwater sat. 'I am indebted to you, Captain Sawyers.' He looked round the circle of faces. They remained overwhelmingly hostile, clearly awaiting his first move.

'I am aware, gentlemen, that there has been disruption of your intentions . . .'

'Some disruption!' The big, black bearded man spoke after spitting into the straw for emphasis. 'Some disruption! We are nearly two months late, too late to qualify for the bounty, God damn it! I do not expect you to give a toss for our dependents, *Captain*, but by God do not *you* try to prevent us sailing by trading our clearances against men out of our ships.'

A chorus of agreement greeted this remark. Drinkwater knew the *Melusine* was short of a dozen hands but the idea of pressing men out of his charges had not occurred to him. Indeed he considered the deficiency too small to worry over. It seemed that Sir James Palgrave's iniquities extended to the venal.

'Aye, Cap'n, *my* guns are loaded and if you sends a boat to take a single man out of my ship I swear I'll not answer for the consequences,' another cried.

A further chorus of assent was accompanied by the shaking of fists and more shouts.

'First they reduce the bounty, then they take half our press exemptions and then they order us not to sail until there is a man o'war to convoy us . . .'

'Bloody London jacks-in-office . . .'

'The festering lot of 'em should be strung up!'

'Do they think that we're fools, Captain?' roared the bearded captain, 'that we cannot see they wish to delay us only to take the men out of our ships to man the fleet now that war has broken out again.'

'Gentlemen!' Drinkwater stood and faced them. 'Gentlemen! Will you be silent God damn you!' He was angry now. It was quite likely that all they said was true. There might yet be a frigate cruising off the Spurn to relieve the Hull whale-fleet of 'surplus men', pleading the excuse that they could recruit replacements in Shetland or Orkney as they were entitled to. Drinkwater would not have been at all surprised if the authorities had it in mind, but at least his presence made it more difficult if he refused to co-operate . . . 'Gentlemen . . .'

'Friends!' The mellow roar of Sawyers beside him seemed to

carry some authority over the angry Greenlanders and they eventually subsided. 'Let us hear what Captain Drinkwater has to say. He has come hither at our request. Please continue, Captain.'

'I have been to the Custom House this morning . . .'

'We do not want you or your damned government orders,' said the bearded Ellerby again.

'Except in the matter of bounty, friend,' put in the Quaker Sawyers quickly, which drew a hum of 'Ayes' and showed the first split in the assembly's unanimity.

'*You* would sail alone, Jemmett, but I could not risk an encounter with a cruiser off the Spurn. Men have been reluctant to sail this year for fear of the press. Let us see what Captain Drinkwater says about the matter of his own complement.'

Drinkwater looked at the new speaker. Dressed in brown drab he had a heavily pocked face with thin lips and snub nose which was, despite its inherent ugliness, possessed of a certain charm, enhanced by the kindness of the eyes. He caught Drinkwater's glance and bowed from his seat.

'Jaybez Harvey, Captain, master of the *Narwhal*.' He smiled. 'Your colleagues are too eager to press our men and pay scant regard to any exemptions . . .'

Drinkwater nodded and felt the need to exonerate his service. 'There is a war . . .'

'If there was no wars, Captain, thou knowest there woulds't be no navies to press innocent and God-fearing men from their unfortunate wives and children,' reproved the Quaker Sawyers.

'This endless debate shows no sign of ending, Captain Drinkwater. Will you tell us, when you propose to sail?' A tall man dressed in a sky-blue uniform elaborately trimmed with fur rose from his place. A similarly dressed colleague joined him and the two officers picked up lavishly trimmed hats and made for the door.

'Commander Malim and myself will await your instructions at the White Hart. Perhaps you will oblige us with your company at dinner, Captain.'

'And where are your ships, sir?' asked Drinkwater sharply, aware that the two officers, commanders of two vessels belonging to the Hudson's Bay Company, threatened to break the meeting up.

'Off Killingholme where they have been at a short scope this past sennight.'

Drinkwater restrained them from leaving as a babble of talk engulfed the whale-captains round the table.

'Be silent!' he bawled, 'may I suffer you to be silent for a moment!'

Eventually the noise diminished.

'This morning I visited the Custom House and authorised the release of your clearances.' He paused as this revelation found its mark. At last the Greenlanders fell silent. He turned to the pock-marked Harvey.

'Do I understand that it is customary to embark additional men at Shetland whether or not men are pressed out of your ships?'

Harvey nodded cautiously. 'If we are bound for the Greenland fishery. If we are bound for the Davis Strait we recruit in Orkney. We also fill up our water casks.'

'And to which fishery are you bound, gentlemen?' He looked round expecting a further outbreak of argument but apparently this matter, at least, had been brought to a conclusion.

'We have resolved that, due to the advance of the season, sir, we shall repair to the Greenland fishery. Shoulds't the fish not prove to be swimming there we may then catch some favourable effects from rounding Cape Farewell and entering the Davis Strait. But this matter we hold in abeyance, to be decided upon later by a majority and for those that wish to try the enterprise.'

'Thank you, Captain Sawyers. Then I must advise you that I cannot winter in the ice . . .'

'We do not need you, Captain,' said the black bearded Ellerby aggressively, 'and we shall in any case fish where the whim takes us, so do not expect us to hang upon your skirts like frightened children.'

'I have no intention of so doing. I shall require that you attend me upon the passage as I have word that there are French cruisers already at sea. I shall cruise in company with those captains who wish for my protection on grounds of their own choosing. I further propose we sail the instant we are ready. Shall we say the first of the ebb at daylight tomorrow morning?'

A murmur of surprise greeted this news and the Greenlanders debated briefly among themselves. After a while Sawyers rose.

'Thou hast our agreement.'

'Very well. You should each send a boat to the *Melusine* at six of the clock this evening for your written instructions. I shall include a table of signals to be used by us all for our mutual support and the direction of the convoy. The rendezvous will be Bressay Sound until the end of the first week in June. That is all, but for reminding you that I was informed in London that French private ships of war have sailed for the Polar regions, gentlemen. You may yet have need of *Melusine*.' Drinkwater watched for reaction to this slight exaggeration. It would do no harm to induce a little co-operation from these independent ship-masters. He was quite pleased with the result. Even the black bearded ruffian Ellerby exchanged glances of surprise with a captain near him.

Drinkwater rose and picked up his hat. The meeting broke up into groups. The Hudson Bay Company officers made for the door. The one who had spoken introduced himself as Commander Learmouth and congratulated Drinkwater on taming 'the polar bears'. He repeated his invitation to dinner which Drinkwater declined on the grounds of insufficient time. Learmouth and Malim departed and Drinkwater paused only to thank the curious Quaker Sawyers for his help.

'Thou hast an evil calling, friend, but thou dost not discredit it.' Sawyers smiled. 'And now I shall attend the Custom House and tomorrow pilot thy ship to sea.'

Drinkwater moved towards the door and found himself behind the big, bearded Greenlander. Suddenly the man turned, barring the way so that Drinkwater almost bumped into him and was forced to take a step backwards.

Drinkwater looked up at the face. Beneath the mass of dark hair and the beard he noticed a sharpness of feature and the eyes were a peculiar pale blue which caused the pupils to seem unnaturally piercing.

'Have you ever been to the polar regions, Captain?'

'No, I have not.' The big man turned to his companion, the same whaler captain who had sat next to him.

'They send a novice to protect us, God damn and blast them.' The Greenlander turned on his heel. Behind him Drinkwater was aware of other men gathered in a group. His reserve snapped.

'Captain!' There was no response and Drinkwater stepped quickly into the corridor where his voice echoed: 'Captain! '

With ponderous contempt the big man turned slowly.

'What is your name?'

The big man retraced his steps, intimidating Drinkwater with his height. 'Ellerby, Jemmett Ellerby of the *Nimrod*.' Drinkwater put out his hand to prevent a further dismissal.

'I understood, Captain Ellerby,' he said quickly but in a voice that carried to the curious group behind him, 'I understood you had a *reputation* for good manners. It seemed I was mistaken. Good day to you, gentlemen.'

'No, sir, you may not go ashore. I require the services of three midshipmen as clerks this afternoon to make copies of my orders to the convoy. You must make the final rounds of the ship to ensure that she is ready to weigh tomorrow morning. We will refill our water casks in Shetland so you may stum a few casks in readiness. Tell me, did Captain Palgrave lay in a store of practice powder?'

'Yes, sir,' replied Lieutenant Germaney unhappily.

'Good. Will you direct the purser to attend me and extend to the gunroom my invitation to dinner. Mr Quilhampton and Mr Gorton are also invited. I shall rate Mr Gorton as master's mate. As for the rest of the young gentlemen I may make their acquaintance in due course.' He turned and peered through the stern windows at the high, white mare's tails in the west.

'We shall have a westerly breeze in the morning,' he rose, 'that is all.'

'Aye, aye, sir. There is a gentleman come aboard, sir, with a trunk and God knows what besides. He has a letter of introduction and says he is to sail with us.'

Drinkwater frowned. 'Sail with us? What imposition is this?'

Germaney shrugged. 'He is in the gunroom.'

'Send him in.'

'Yes, sir . . . sir, may I not take an hour . . .?'

'God's bones, Mr Germaney, can you not take no for an answer! We are about to sail for the Arctic, you have a hundred and one things to attend to. I have no objection to your sending a midshipman ashore on an errand. Send Dutfield or Wickham, neither can write a decent hand, judging from their journals. Now where the devil is that pen . . .?'

Drinkwater cursed himself for a fool. In the luxury of Palgrave's cabin he had forgotten he was without half of his own necessaries. Tregembo had not yet arrived and here he was giving orders to sail!

He swore again, furious with Palgrave, Ellerby and that cabal of whale-ship masters that had distracted him. Sudden misgivings about Germaney's competence and the fitness of his ship for Polar service seized him. He had made no preparations himself, relying on those made by Palgrave. But now Palgrave's whole reputation threw doubts upon the matter. He remembered Ellerby's taunt about being a novice in Arctic navigation. His eyes fell on the decanter and he half-rose from the table when a knock came at the door.

'Yes?'

The man who entered was dressed from head to foot in black. He was about thirty years of age with hair short cropped and thinning. His features were strong and his shaved beard gave his lantern jaw a blue appearance. His brown eyes were full of confidence and his self-assurance had led him into the centre of the cabin where the skylight allowed him to draw himself up to his full height.

'I give you good day, sir. My credentials.' He handed Drinkwater a packet sealed with the fouled anchor wafer of the Admiralty. It contained a second letter and simply instructed Captain Drinkwater to afford every facility to the bearer consistent with the service he was presently engaged upon, as was set out in the bearer's letter of introduction.

Drinkwater opened the enclosed letter. It was dated from London three days earlier.

Honourable Sir,

Having been lately acquainted with Their Lordships' Intention of despatching a ship into Arctic Regions, the Governors of this body conceived it their Christian Duty to carry the word of Christ to the peoples Domiciled upon the Coasts of Greenland. It is with this purpose in mind that you are asked to convey thither the bearer of this letter, the Reverend Obadiah Singleton, D.D., M.D.

Your landing him at a Settlement of the Esquimaux, or causing him to be landed at some such Settlement, will assure you the Warmest Approbation from this Society for your furtherance in the Spread of the Christian Gospel.

The signature was illegible but was accredited to the Secretary of the Church Missionary Society.

Drinkwater put down the letter and looked up. He was beginning to feel the burden of command too great for him and the decanter beckoned seductively.

'Mr Singleton, pray take a seat. Will you take a glass of wine?' He rose.

'I do not drink intoxicating liquors, sir.' Drinkwater sat again, aware that the splendid isolation, the power and the purpose of command was, in reality, a myth. Only men like Palgrave sustained the illusion.

'Mr Singleton, are you aware of the extreme climate of the Arctic regions? Do you mean to winter there among the Eskimos?'

'I do, sir.'

'Entirely alone?'

'With God, sir,' Singleton answered with devastating simplicity. Drinkwater rose, a sense of helpless exasperation filling him. Almost defiantly he helped himself from the decanter, ignoring the disapproval in Singleton's eyes. Well damn Singleton! There would be much that Singleton did not approve of aboard a King's ship.

'But like me, Mr Singleton,' he said sipping the wine, 'you are flesh and blood.'

'Imbued with the Holy Spirit, sir, and the faith that can move mountains.'

'Let us hope,' remarked Drinkwater, 'that your faith sustains you.'

'Amen to that, sir.'

Drinkwater looked at the missionary, searching for some gleam of humour evident in the man. There was none. He was an alien amongst them, uncomprehending of their jack-ass humour, unable to understand the bawdy small talk, the rigid divisions that made a man-of-war. Singleton was an academic, a product of universities where the distilled wisdom of a thousand generations might be assimilated within the confines of a library. Drinkwater sighed and drained his glass. Singleton's insufferable self-righteousness would doubtless combine with an assumed right to criticise. That augured ill for the future and Drinkwater could see squalls ahead.

'Where have you been berthed, Mr Singleton? There is little room in the gunroom.'

'I do not think a *gun*room a fit place for a missionary, sir. No, Lieutenant Germaney has permitted me to use the cockpit.'

Drinkwater could well imagine it! The harassed lieutenant would not want the intrusion of a priggish irrelevance challenging his position in the gunroom.

'I doubt you will find it to your liking, but this is a small ship and there is no alternative.'

'It is true the air is mephitic, sir, but it will be a fit preparation for my ministry. The darkness alone will condition me to the Arctic winter.'

'It was not the darkness I had in mind, Mr Singleton, but no matter. You will see soon enough.' He ignored Singleton's puzzlement and went on: 'There is one thing you should know and that is that while you remain aboard this ship you are answerable for your conduct under the Articles of War as surely as if you were truly a midshipman. You will doubtless observe things that you do not approve of. Have you ever seen a flogging, sir? No? Well, it does not matter but you must accept that the usages of the naval service will come as a surprise to you and you would do well to remember that the wooden bulwarks behind which your church so comfortably nestles, are purchased at the price of blood, sweat and indignity.'

Singleton ignored this homily. 'When do you propose to land me, sir?'

'Land you? Good heavens, do not trouble me with such matters now. First I have to get these confounded ships out of this Goddamned river!'

Drinkwater saw the look of shock on Singleton's face and found that it gave him a pleasurable sensation. 'Saving your cloth, Mr Singleton,' he said ironically and added, 'I should like you to join the officers and dine with me this evening. And I should like you to make no hasty judgements about the sea service; parsons have a bad reputation at sea, far worse than that of seamen ashore.'

He rose and smiled, dismissing Singleton abruptly as another knock came at the cabin door. The purser entered.

'You sent for me, sir?'

'I did, Mr Pater . . . I shall see you at dinner, Mr Singleton.'

'Your man has arrived, sir,' put in the purser, 'they are swinging your baggage aboard now.'

'Excellent. Will you take a glass, Mr Pater?'

'With pleasure, sir.'

'Thou should'st address the ship's head a half-point more to starboard.'

Drinkwater nodded at Hill as the master sought his approval.

Melusine leaned slightly as the wind shifted forward a trifle as they altered course. The distant banks of the broad river were low and barely perceptible as the steeples and roofs of Hull dropped astern. Drinkwater raised his glass and studied the two vessels hoisting their topsails off Killingholme. The Hudson Bay Company's ships were superbly fitted, of a similar size to *Melusine* and with the appearance of sixth-rates of the smallest class. They were certainly a contrast to the squat whalers following *Melusine* down the river.

'Thou hast competition in the matter of elegance, Captain.'

'You object to elegance, Captain Sawyers?'

'It is irrelevant to the true meaning of life, Captain.'

'How will the *Faithful* fare with you piloting *Melusine* from the Humber?' asked Drinkwater, changing the subject and feeling preached at for the second time in as many days.

'My son is a chief mate, Captain Drinkwater, a man as skilled as myself.'

'Come, sir,' put in Drinkwater grinning, 'that is immodest!'

'Not at all. Ability is a gift from God as manifest as physical strength or the fact that I have brown hair. I do not glory in it, merely state it.'

Drinkwater felt out-manoeuvred on his own quarterdeck and turned to look astern. Alone among the whale-ships foaming in their wake, *Faithful* was without a garland slung between fore and mainmasts. The ancient symbol of a Greenlander's love-tokens was absent from her topgallant rigging, neither were there so many flags as were flying from the other ships. Drinkwater wondered how many of Sawyers's crew shared his gentle and sober creed. Perhaps his rumoured success at the fishery reconciled them to a lack of ostentation as was customary on sailing day.

The other ships were under no such constraint. The otherwise dull appearance of the whale-ships was enlivened by streamers, ensigns and pendants bearing their names, lovingly fashioned by their wives and sweethearts whose fluttering handkerchiefs had long since vanished. The embroidered pendant that flew from *Nimrod's* mainmasthead was fifty feet long, an oriflamme of scarlet, and Drinkwater could see the dominating figure of Jemmett Ellerby at the break of her poop.

Nimrod was crowding on sail and bid fair to pass *Melusine* as she slipped easily along at six knots, going large before the wind under her topsails and foretopmast staysail, leading the slower whalers towards the open waters of the North Sea.

'He hath the pride of Goliath before the Philistine Host,' Sawyers nodded in Ellerby's direction. 'He shall meet David at God's will.'

Drinkwater looked at the Quaker. He was not surprised that there were divisions of opinion and rifts between a group of individuals as unique as the whale-captains. Once on the fishing grounds there would be a rivalry between them that Drinkwater foresaw would make his task almost impossible. But the remark had either a touch of the venom of jealousy or of a confidence. Given what he had seen of Sawyers he doubted the man was a hypocrite and marked the remark as a proof of the Quaker's friendship. He responded.

'I am most grateful, Captain Sawyers, for your kind offer to pilot us clear of the Humber. It is an intricate navigation, given to much change, but I had not supposed that a gentleman of your persuasion would countenance boarding a King's ship.' He gestured towards the lines of cannon housed against the rail.

'Ah, but thou hast also doubtless heard how those of my persuasion, as thou has it, are not averse to profit, eh?' Sawyers smiled.

'Indeed I have,' replied Drinkwater smiling back.

'Well I shall confess to thee a love of the fishery, both for its profits and its nearness to God. It seems that thy presence is indispensable this season and so,' he shrugged, 'in order to practise my calling, sir, I have needs to assist thee to sea. Now, thou must bring her to larboard two points and square the yards before that scoundrel Ellerby forces you ashore on the Burcom.'

Nimrod was foaming up on their quarter, a huge bow wave hissing at her forefoot.

'May I give her the forecourse, sir?' asked Germaney eagerly.

'Aye, sir, he knows well enough to keep astern according to the order of sailing,' added Hill indignantly.

Drinkwater shook his head. 'This is not a race. Mr Q!'

'Sir?'

'Make to *Nimrod*, "Keep proper station".'

'Aye, aye, sir.'

Drinkwater turned his full attention to the *Nimrod*. She was almost level with the *Melusine*'s mizen now, no more than a hundred feet off as she too swung to larboard.

In the waist of the sloop men milled about watching the whaler and looking aft to see the reaction of their new commander. Officers too, advised of the trial of strength taking place above, had come up from their watch below. Drinkwater saw Singleton's sober black figure watching from the rail while Mr Gorton explained what was happening.

Drinkwater felt an icy determination fill him. After the days of being put upon, of being the victim of circumstance and not its master, he secretly thanked Ellerby for this public opportunity. By God, he was damned if he would crowd an inch of canvas on his ship.

Quilhampton and little Frey were sending up the signal. It was a simple numeral, one of two score of signals he had circulated to his charges the evening before. Mr Frey had even tinted the little squared flags drawn in the margins with the colours from his water-colour box. Drinkwater smiled at the boy's keenness.

Amidships the newly joined Tregembo nudged the man next to him.

'See that, mate. When he grins like that the sparks fly.' There was renewed interest in the conduct of their captain, particularly as the *Nimrod* continued to surge past.

Drinkwater turned to his first lieutenant. 'Give him the larboard bow chaser unshotted, if you please.'

'Larbowlines! Spitfire battery stand by!'

It was all very modish, thought Drinkwater ruefully, the divisions told off by name as if *Melusine* had been a crack seventy-four. Still, the men jumped eagerly enough to their pieces. He could see the disappointment as Germaney arrived forward and stood all the guncrews down except that at the long twelve pounder in the eyes.

Germaney looked aft and Drinkwater nodded.

The gun roared and Drinkwater saw the wadding drop right ahead of *Nimrod's* bowsprit. But still she came on.

'Mr Germaney! Come aft!'

Germaney walked aft. 'Sir?'

'Have your topmen aloft ready to let fall the forecourse, but not before I say. Mr Rispin!' The junior lieutenant touched his hat. 'Load that brass popgun with ball. Maximum elevation.'

'Aye, aye, sir.'

'Do you propose to fire on him, friend?' There was anxiety in Sawyers's voice.

'Merely putting a stone in David's sling,' said Drinkwater raising his glass.

'But I do not approve . . .'

Drinkwater ignored him. He was staring at Ellerby. The Greenlander was pointing to the men ascending *Melusine*'s foremast and spreading out along the foreyard, casting off alternate gaskets.

'Pass me the trumpet, Mr Hill.' He took the megaphone and clambered up into the mizen rigging.

'Take station, Ellerby! do you hear me! Or take the consequences!'

He watched the big man leap into *Nimrod*'s mizen chains and they confronted one another across eighty feet of water that sloshed and hissed between them, confused by the wash of the two ships.

'Consequences? What consequences, eh, Captain?' There was a quite audible roar of laughter from *Nimrod*'s deck. Without climbing down Drinkwater turned his head.

'When his mainmast bears, Mr Rispin, you may open fire.'

Drinkwater felt the wave of concussion from the brass carronade at the larboard hance. The hole that appeared in Nimrod's main topsail must have opened a seam, for the sail split from head to foot. A cheer filled *Melusine*'s waist and Drinkwater leapt inboard. 'Silence there!' he bawled. 'Give her the forecourse, Mr Germaney.'

The big sail fell in huge flogs of billowing canvas. In an instant the waisters had tailed on the sheets and hauled its clews hard down. *Melusine* seemed to lift in the water and start forward. *Nimrod* fell astern.

'Tell me, Captain Sawyers,' Drinkwater asked conversationally, 'do you throw a harpoon in person?'

'Aye, Captain, I do.'

'And cause more harm than that ball, I dare say.' Drinkwater was smiling but the Quaker's eyes were filled with a strange look.

'That was a massive pride that thou wounded, Captain Drinkwater, greater than the greatest fish in the sea.'

But Drinkwater did not hear. He was sweeping the horizon

ahead, beyond the low headland of Spurn and its slim lighthouse. There were no topsails to betray the presence of a frigate cruising for men.

'Mr Hill, please to back the main topsail and heave the *Faithful*'s boat alongside. Captain Sawyers, I am obliged to you, sir, for your assistance, but I think you may return to your ship.' He held out his hand and the Quaker shook it firmly.

'Recollect what happened to David, sir. I give you God's love.'

Chapter Four *June 1803*

The Captain's Cloak

Captain Drinkwater nodded to his first lieutenant. 'Very well, Mr Germaney, you may secure the guns and pipe the hammocks down.' He turned to the lieutenant of the watch. 'Mr Rispin, shorten sail now and put the ship under easy canvas.'

'Aye, aye, sir.'

Drinkwater paced aft, ignoring the stream of superfluous orders with which Mr Rispin conducted the affairs of the deck. He was tempted to conclude the young officer hid his lack of confidence beneath this apparent efficiency. It deceived no-one but himself. But in spite of misgivings about his lieutenants Drinkwater was well satisfied with the ship. *Melusine* handled like a yacht. He stared aft watching a fulmar quartering the wake, its sabre wings rigid as it moved with astonishing agility. He eased his shoulders beneath his coat aware that he could do with some exercise. There were other compensations besides the qualities of his former French corvette. Mr Hill, the master, had proved an able officer, explaining the measures taken in the matter of stores for the forthcoming voyage. Furthermore his two mates, Quilhampton and Gorton, seemed to be coming along well. Drinkwater was pleased with Hill's efficiency. He seemed to have assumed the duties of both sailing master and executive officer, and not for the first time Drinkwater regretted the system of patronage that promoted a man like Germaney and denied a commission to Stephen Hill.

Drinkwater turned forward and began pacing the windward side of the quarterdeck. Since they had returned Sawyers to his ship off the Spurn lighthouse the wind had held at west-north-west and they had made good progress to the north. Four more whalers had joined them from Whitby and this evening they were well to the eastward of the Firth of Forth, the convoy close hauled on the larboard tack and heading due north.

Drinkwater stopped to regard the whalers as the sun westered behind him. He could see a solitary figure on the rail of *Narwhal.* Taking off his hat he waved it above his head. Jaybez Harvey returned the salute and a few seconds later Drinkwater saw the feather of foam in the whaler's wake jerk closer to her stern as Harvey's men pulled in the cask at which *Melusine*'s gunners had been firing.

It had been a good idea to practise shooting in this manner. He had been able to manoeuvre up to, cross astern of and range alongside the cask, making and taking in sail for a full six hours while Harvey maintained his course. Finally to test both their accuracy and their mettle after so protracted an exercise, he had hauled off and let the hands fire three rounds from every gun, before each battery loosed off a final, concussive broadside.

The Melusines were clearly pleased with themselves and their afternoon's work. There was nothing like firing guns to satisfy a British seaman, Drinkwater reflected, watching the usual polyglot crowd coiling the train tackles and passing the breechings. He took a final look at the convoy. One or two of the whalers had loosed off their own cannon by way of competition and Drinkwater sensed a change of mood among the whale-ship masters. It was clear that preparations were under way for the arrival at the fishing grounds and he fervently hoped the differences between them were finally sunk under a sense of unanimous purpose.

He had stationed the Hudson Bay Ships at the van and rear of the convoy where, with their unusual ensigns, they gave the impression of being additional escorts, while *Melusine* occupied a windward station, ready to cover any part of the convoy and from where all her signals could be seen by each ship. He turned forward and looked aloft. The topmen were securing the topgallants and he could see the midshipmen in the fore and main tops watching over the furling of the courses. He considered himself a fortunate man in having such a proficient crew. Convoy escort could frustrate a sloop captain beyond endurance but the whalers, used to sailing in company and manoeuvring with only a handful of men upon the deck while the remainder were out in the boats after whales, behaved with commendable discipline. They were clearly all determined to reach the fishing grounds without delay. Even Ellerby seemed to have accepted his humiliation off the

Spurn in a good grace, although it was at *Nimrod* that Drinkwater first looked whenever he came on deck.

'Beg pardon, sir.'

'Mr Mount, what is it?'

'I should like to try my men at a mark, sir, when it is convenient.'

'By all means. May I suggest you retain the gunroom's empty bottles and we'll haul 'em out to the lee foreyard arm tomorrow forenoon, eh?'

'Very good, sir.'

'Have the live marines fire at the dead 'uns,* eh?' Mr Mount's laughter was unfeigned and, like Hill, he too inspired confidence.

'Are there any fencers in the gunroom? Mr Quilhampton and I have foils and masks and I am not averse to going a bout with a worthy challenger.'

The light of interest kindled in Mount's eye. 'Indeed, yes, sir. I should be pleased to go to the best of . . .'

A scream interrupted Mount and both men looked aloft as the flailing body of a seaman fell. He smacked into the water alongside. Drinkwater's reaction was instantaneous.

'Helm a-lee! Main braces there! Starboard quarterboat away! Move God damn you! Man overboard, Mr Rispin!' Mount and Drinkwater ran aft, straining to see where the hapless topman surfaced.

'Where's your damned sentry, Mount?'

'Here, sir.' The man appeared carrying a chicken coop. He hove it astern to the fluttering, squawking protest of its occupants.

'Good man.' The three men peered astern.

'I see him, sir.' The marine pointed.

'Don't take your eyes off him and point him out to the boat.'

Melusine was swinging up into the wind like a reined horse. Men were leaping into the quarter-boat and the knock of oars told where they prepared to pull like devils the instant the boat hit the water. Mr Quilhampton, holding his wooden hand out of the way as he vaulted nimbly over the rail, grabbed the tiller.

'Lower away there, lower away lively!'

The davits jerked the mizen rigging and the boat hit the water with a flat splash.

**A dead marine* – naval slang for an empty bottle.

'Come up!' The falls ran slack, the boat unhooked and swung away from the ship, turning under her stern.

'Hoist *Princess Charlotte*'s number and "Man overboard".' Drinkwater heard little Frey acknowledge the order and hoped that Captain Learmouth would see it in time to wear his ship round into *Melusine*'s wake. The marine was up on the taffrail, one hand gripping a spanker vang, the other pointing in the direction of the drowning man. He must remember to ask Mount the marine's name, his initiative had been commendable.

'Ship's hove to, sir,' Rispin reported unnecessarily.

'Very well. Send a midshipman to warn the surgeon that his services will be required to revive a drowning man.'

'You think there's a chance, sir . . . Aye, aye, sir.' Rispin blushed crimson at the look in Drinkwater's eye.

Everyone on the upper deck was watching the boat. Men were aloft, anxiety plain upon their faces. They could see the boat circling, disappearing in the wavetroughs.

'Can you still see him, soldier?'

'No sir, but the boat is near where I last saw 'im, sir.'

'God's bones.' Drinkwater swore softly to himself.

'Have faith, sir.' The even features of Obadiah Singleton glowed in the sunset as he stopped alongside the captain. The pious sentiment annoyed Drinkwater but he ignored it.

'Do you see the coop, soldier?'

'Aye, sir, 'tis about a pistol shot short of the boat . . . there, sir!'

Drinkwater caught sight of a hard edged object on a wave crest before it disappeared again.

'What's your name?'

'Polesworth, sir.'

'Oh! May God be praised!' Singleton clasped his hands on his breast as a cheer went up from the Melusines. A man, presumably the bowman, had dived from the boat and could be seen dragging the body of his shipmate back to the boat. The boat rocked dangerously as willing hands dragged rescued and rescuer inboard over the transom. Then there was a mad scramble for oars and the boat darted forward. Drinkwater could see Quilhampton urging the oarsmen and beating the time on the gunwhale with his wooden hand.

The boat surged under the falls and hooked on. Drinkwater looked at the inert body in the bottom of the boat.

'Now is the time for piety, Mr Singleton,' he snapped at the missionary as the latter stared downwards.

'Heave up!' The two lines of men ranged along the deck ran away with the falls and held the boat at the davit heads while the body was lifted inboard. The blue pallor of death was visible to all.

'Where's Macpherson?'

'Below, sir,' squeaked Mr Frey.

'God damn the man. Get him to the surgeon and lively there!' Men hurried to carry the dripping body below. Drinkwater felt the sudden anger of exasperation fill him yet again. He was damned if he wanted to lose a man like this!

'Mr Rispin! Don't stand there with your mouth open. Clap stoppers on those falls and secure that boat, then put the ship on the wind.' The boat's bowman slopped past, his ducks flapping wetly about his legs, his knuckle respectfully at his forehead as he crossed the hallowed planking of the quarterdeck.

'What's your name?'

'Mullack, sir.'

'That was well done, Mullack, I'll not forget it. Who was the victim?'

'Jim Leek, sir, foretopman.'

'A messmate of yours?' Mullack nodded. 'Did you see what happened?' The seaman met Drinkwater's eyes then studied the deck again. 'No, sir.' He was lying, Drinkwater knew, but that was nothing to hold against him in the circumstances.

'Very well, Mullack, cut along now.' Drinkwater watched for a second as *Melusine* paid off to steady on her course again.

'Begging your pardon, sir,' offered Lord Walmsley, stepping forward, 'but the man was only skylarking, sir. Leek was dancing on the yardarm when he missed his footing.'

'Thank you, Mr Walmsley. He is in your division ain't he?'

'Yes, sir.'

'Kindly inform the midshipmen that they will be put over a gunbreech every time they permit a man in their division to fool about aloft . . . and Mr Rispin! Set the main t'gallant again, we are three miles astern of our station.'

The smell of tobacco smoke filled the dimly lit cockpit which housed the midshipmen. For a second Drinkwater was a 'young gentleman' again, transported back to an afternoon in Gibraltar

Bay when he had caught a messmate in the throes of sodomy. As he paused to allow his eyes to adjust he took in the scene before him.

Leek's body was thrown over a chest, his buttocks bared while a loblolly boy held his abdomen face downwards. Behind him Surgeon Macpherson stood with a bellows inserted into Leek's anus. The clack-hole was connected to a small box in which tobacco was burning and, in addition to the aroma of the plug and the stink of bilge, the smell of rum was heavy in the foetid air.

'He's ejecting water,' said the loblolly boy. Drinkwater felt himself pushed aside in the darkness and looked round sharply as Singleton elbowed his way into the cockpit.

'What diabolical nonsense is this?' he snapped with uncommon force, opening a black bag. Macpherson looked up and his eyes narrowed, gleaming wetly in the flickering light of the two lanterns.

'The Cullenian cure,' he sneered, 'by the acrimony of the tobacco the intestines will be stimulated and the action of the moving fibres thus restored . . .'

'Get that thing out of his arse!' Macpherson and the loblolly boys stared at Singleton in astonishment as the missionary completed his preparations and pushed the drunken surgeon to one side.

Drinkwater had recovered from his shock. He was remembering something in Singleton's letter of introduction; the two letters 'M.D.'.

'Do as he says, Macpherson!' The voice of the captain cut through the gloom and Macpherson stepped back, his rum-sodden brain uncomprehending.

'By my oath . . . here, on his back and quickly now or we'll have lost him . . .'

Singleton waved two onlookers, Midshipmen Glencross and Gorton, to assist. Leek was laid face up on the deck and Singleton knelt at his head and shoved a short brass tube into his mouth. Pinching Leek's nose Singleton began to blow into the tube. After a while he looked at Gorton.

'Sit astride him and push down hard on his chest when I take my mouth away.'

They continued thus for some ten minutes, alternately blowing and punching down while the watchers waited in silence. About them *Melusine* creaked and groaned, her bilge slopping beneath them, but in the cockpit a diminishing hiatus of hope suspended them. Even Macpherson watched, befuddled and bewildered by what he was seeing.

Suddenly there was a contraction in Leek's throat. Singleton leapt up and pushed Gorton to one side, rolling Leek roughly over and slapping him hard between the shoulder blades. There was a massive eructation and Leek's chest heaved and continued to heave of its own accord. A quantity of viscid fluid ran from his mouth.

Singleton stood up and fixed Macpherson with a glare. 'I suggest you forget about Cullen, sir. The Royal Humane Society has advocated resuscitation since seventy-four.' He bumped into Drinkwater. 'Oh, I beg your pardon, sir.'

'That is quite all right, Mr Singleton. Thank you. Have that man conveyed to his hammock and excused watches until noon tomorrow, Mr Gorton.'

'Aye, aye, sir.'

Lieutenant Germaney leant on the rail and endeavoured to distract his preoccupied mind by concentrating upon the wine bottle at the yard arm. The pain was constant now and he thought his bowels were on fire and melting away.

The snap of a musket called his attention momentarily. The bottle swung intact, a green pinpoint at the extremity of the yard, catching the morning sun and twinkling defiantly.

A second musket spat and the bottle shattered. The marines were forbidden to cheer but there were congratulatory grins and one or two sullen faces. Mount was not under the same constraint.

'Ho! Good shooting, Polesworth. Next man, fire!' Mount's voice was bright with exhilaration and Germaney cursed him for his cheerfulness, seeing in the merriment of others a barometer of his own despair. Since the ship was witness to the remarkable medical talents of the Reverend Obadiah Singleton, Germaney had seen an opportunity to end his suffering. But fate had dealt him a mean trick, providing him with the means of a cure but entailing him in the awkward business of a confession before a gentleman of the cloth. Germaney writhed with indecision, an indecision made worse by the sudden popularity of Mr Singleton and the fact that he was seldom alone, was universally courted by all sections of the ship's company and encouraged in it by the captain, having seen the disgusting state of *Melusine*'s own surgeon.

The revival of Leek had also stimulated a sudden religious fervour, for the topman claimed he had died and seen God. While Singleton's attitude to his own medical abilities was purely professional, the theologian in him was intrigued. This circumstance seemed to make Germaney's distress the more acute.

A second bottle shattered and, a few minutes later, Mount dismissed his men. The Marine officer crossed the deck and removed his sword belt, sash, gorget and scarlet coat, laying them over the breech of the quarterdeck carronade next to Germaney. He doffed his hat and held it out.

'Be a good fellow, Germaney . . .' Germaney took the hat.

'What the deuce are you up to?'

Mount smiled and bent down to rummage in a canvas bag. He pulled a padded plastron over his shirt, produced a gauntlet, foil and mask and made mock obeisance.

'I go, fair one, to joust with the captain. Wilt thou not grant me a favour?'

'Good God.' Germaney was in no mood for Mount's humour but Mount was not to be so easily suppressed.

'See where he comes,' he whispered.

Commander Drinkwater had emerged on deck in his shirt sleeves and plastron. Germaney could see the extent of the rumoured wound. The right shoulder sagged appreciably and the reason for the cock of his head, that Germaney had dismissed as a peculiarity of the man, now became clear.

Drinkwater ignored the frank curiosity of the idlers amidships, whipped his foil experimentally, donned his mask and strode across the deck. He flicked a salute at his opponent.

'Best of seven, sir?' asked Mount, hooking the mask over his head.

'Very well, Mr Mount, best of seven.' Drinkwater lowered his mask and saluted.

Mount dropped his mask and came on guard. Both men called 'Ready' to Quilhampton, who was presiding, and the bout commenced.

The two men advanced and retreated cautiously, feeling their opponent by an occasional change of line, the click of the blades inaudible above the hiss of the sea and the thrum of the wind in the rigging.

There was a sudden movement. Mount's lunge was parried but the marine was too quick for Drinkwater, springing backwards then extending as the captain came forward to riposte.

Drinkwater conceded the hit. They came on guard again. Mount came forward, beat Drinkwater's blade and was about to extend and hit Drinkwater's plastron when the captain whirled his blade in a circular parry, stepped forward and his blade bowed against Mount's breast.

They came on guard again and circled each other. Mount dropped his left hand and threw himself to the deck, intending to extend under Drinkwater's guard but the captain pulled back his pelvis, then leaned forward, over Mount's sword and dropped his point onto the Marine officer's back.

'Oh very good, sir!' There was a brief round of applause from the knot of officers assembled about the contest.

Mount scored two more points in quick succession before a hiatus in which each contender circled warily, seeking an opening without exposing himself. The click of the blades could be heard now as they slammed together with greater fury. Mount's next attack scored and he became more confident, getting a fifth hit off the captain.

Mount came in to feint and lunge for the sixth point. Drinkwater realised the younger man was quicker than Quilhampton and he was himself running short of breath. But he was ready for it. He advanced boldly, bringing his forte down hard against Mount's blade and executing a croisé, twisting his wrist and pulling his elbow back so that his sword point scratched against Mount's belly. He leaned forward and the blade curved. Mount straightened and stepped back to concede the point. The second he came on guard again Drinkwater lunged. It would have gratified M. Bescond. Mount had not moved and Drinkwater had another point to his credit.

The muscles in Drinkwater's shoulder were hurting now, but the two quick hits had sharpened him. He caught Mount's next extension in a bind and landed an equalising hit. The atmosphere on the quarterdeck was now electric and the quartermaster called the helmsmen to their duty.

Drinkwater whirled a *molinello* but Mount parried quinte. There was a gasp as the onlookers watched Mount drop his blade to attack Drinkwater's unguarded gut, stepping forward as he did so.

But Drinkwater executed a brilliant low parry. The two blades met an instant before they collided *corps-à-corps*. They separated and came on guard again.

'A guinea on Mount,' muttered Rispin.

'Done!' said Hill, remembering the slithering deck of the *Draaken* one dull October afternoon off Camperdown.

Drinkwater scored again as Mount slipped on the deck then lost a point to the marine with an ineffectual parry. They came on guard for the last time. There was a *conversazione* of blades then Mount's suddenly licked out as he lunged low. Drinkwater stepped back to cutover but Mount seemed to coil up his rear leg and thrust himself bodily forward. His blade curved triumphantly against the captain's breast.

The fencers removed their masks, smiling and panting. They shook their left hands.

'By God you pressed me damned hard, sir.'

'You were too fast for me, Mr Mount.' Drinkwater wiped the sweat from his brow.

'You owe me a guinea, Mr Hill.'

'I shall win it back again, Mr Rispin, without a doubt.'

Drinkwater returned below, nodding acknowledgement to the marine sentry's salute as he entered the cabin. Tregembo had the tub of salt water ready in the centre of the cabin and Drinkwater immersed himself in it.

'I've settled all your things now, zur, but we have too many chairs.'

'Strike Palgrave's down into the hold. Get the sailmaker to wrap some old canvas round them.'

'I hope the pictures are to your liking, zur.'

He looked at the portraits by Bruilhac and nodded. Sluicing the icy water over his head he rose and took the towel from Tregembo.

'Don't cluck like an old hen, Tregembo. Don't forget I'm short of good topmen.'

'Aye, zur, I doubt you'll take to Cap'n Palgrave's lackey,' replied Tregembo familiarly, brushing Drinkwater's undress coat, 'but I'll exchange willingly, zur, I'm not too old yet.'

'D'you think I could stand Susan's reproaches if I sent you aloft again?' Drinkwater stepped out of the bath-tub. 'Where's Germaney put Palgrave's man?'

'He is mincing about the gunroom, sir,' replied Tregembo with a touch of ire and added under his breath, 'and 'tis the best bloody place for 'im.'

The Cornishman picked up the tub and sluiced its contents down the quarter gallery privy.

Dressing, Drinkwater sent for Mr Midshipman the Lord Walmsley. Donning his coat he sat behind his desk and awaited the appearance of his lordship. A glance out of the stern window showed the tail of the convoy. The sea was a dazzling blue and the wind still steady from the north of west, blowing fluffy cumulus clouds to leeward. It was more reminiscent of the Mediterranean than the North Sea: too good to last.

'Come in!' Lord Walmsley entered the cabin, his uniform immaculate, his hose silk. Drinkwater could imagine that he and his servant were popular in the confines of the cockpit.

'You sent for me, sir.'

'I did. The man Leek fell from the fore t'gallant yard yesterday, a consequence of skylarking didn't you say.'

Walmsley nodded. 'That is so, sir.'

'Skylarking upon the yards is irresponsible when it leads to losing men . . .'

'But sir, it was only high spirits, why Sir James . . .'

'Damn Sir James, Mr Walmsley,' Drinkwater said quietly. 'I command here and I intend to flog Leek this morning.' He paused. 'I see that disturbs you. Do you have a weak stomach, or a feeling of solicitude for Leek? Eh?' Drinkwater suppressed the smile that threatened to crack his face as he watched perplexity cross his lordship's face. '*Do* you have any feeling for Leek?'

'Why . . . I, er . . . yes, er . . .'

'Is he a good seaman?'

'Yes, sir.'

'Then I rely upon you to intercede for him. Do you understand? When I call for someone to speak for him. Now, kindly tell the first lieutenant to pipe all hands aft to witness punishment and to rig the gratings.'

Drinkwater gave way to suppressed mirth as Walmsley retreated, his face a picture of confusion. The lesson would be better learned this way.

Half a minute elapsed before the marine drummer began to beat the tattoo. Drinkwater heard the pipes at the hatchways and the thump of marines' boots and the muffled slap of bare feet. He rose, hitched his sword and tucked his hat under his arm. He picked up the slim brown book that gave him the right to do what he was about to.

Germaney's head came round the door. 'Ship's company mustered to witness punishment, sir. Lord Walmsley tells me it's Leek.'

'That's correct, Mr Germaney.'

'Begging your pardon, sir, but I conceive it my duty to inform you that Sir James encouraged . . .'

'. . . Such rash bravado. I know. Walmsley has already informed me. But, Mr Germaney, I would have you know that I command here now and I would advise you to recollect that Sir James's example is not to be followed too closely.' He was unaware that his remark pierced Germaney to his vitals.

Drinkwater stepped on deck into the sunshine. Half a mile to leeward the convoy foamed along. Mount's marines glittered across the after end of the quarterdeck and the officers were gathered in uniform with their swords. Forward a sea of faces was mustered. 'Off hats!'

Drinkwater cleared his throat and read the Thirty-Sixth Article of War.

'All other crimes not Capital, committed by any Person or Persons in the Fleet, which are not mentioned in this Act, or for which no Punishment is hereby directed to be inflicted, shall be punished according to Laws and Customs in such cases used at Sea.'

It was colloquially known as the Captain's Cloak, a grim pun which covered every eventuality likely to be encountered in a man-of-war not dealt with by the other thirty-five Articles.

'Able-Seaman Leek step forward.' The murmur from amidships as Leek stepped out in utter surprise was hostile. 'Silence there! You stand condemned by the provisions of this Article, in that you did skylark in the rigging, causing risk to yourself and to others in your rescue, and that you did delay the passage of His Majesty's sloop *Melusine* engaged in the urgent convoy of other ships. What have you to say?'

Leek hung his head and muttered inaudibly. He was bewildered at this unexpected ordeal. He had never been flogged, he was a volunteer, he began to tremble.

Drinkwater's eye was caught by a movement on his right.

Singleton was pushing through the midshipmen. Drinkwater turned his head and fixed Singleton with a glare. 'Stand fast there!' Singleton paused.

'I sentence you to one dozen lashes. Does anyone speak for this man?' He sought out Lord Walmsley. The young man came forward.

'Well, sir?'

'I, er . . . I wish to speak for the man, sir. He is a topman of the first rate and I have previously entertained no apprehensions as to his good behaviour, sir. I should be prepared to stand guarantor against his good conduct.'

Drinkwater bit his lip. Walmsley's speech was nobly touching and he had played his part to perfection.

'Very well. I shall overlook the matter on this occasion. But mark me, my lads, we are bound upon a service that will not tolerate the casual loss of good seamen. But for Mr Singleton, Seaman Mullack and Marine Polesworth, Leek, we would be gathered here this morning to send you over the standing part of the foresheet.* Do you reflect on that.' He turned to Germaney. 'Dismiss the men and pipe up spirits, Mr Germaney.'

Drinkwater chuckled to himself. Talk at dinner over the mess kids would be about this morning's theatricals. He hoped they would conclude that he would stand no nonsense, that although he might only be a 'job captain', temporarily commanding a post-captain's ship, he was not prepared to tolerate anything but the strictest adherence to duty.

*Naval slang for death or burial. Bodies were usually slid overside where the foresheet was belayed.

Chapter Five *June 1803*

Bressay Sound

The wind held fair and they raised Sumburgh Head at daylight after a passage of three days from the Spurn Head. By previous agreement the Hudson Bay ships, usually escorted to longitude twenty west, left them off the Fair Isle. Due to the mild weather the convoy had kept together and by the afternoon all the ships had worked into the anchorage in Bressay Sound and lay within sight of the grey town of Lerwick.

That evening Drinkwater received a deputation of whale-ship masters in his cabin. It consisted of Jaybez Harvey, Abel Sawyers and another captain whose name he did not know. Sawyers introduced him.

'Captain Waller, Captain Drinkwater. Captain Waller is master of the *Conqueror*.'

'Your servant.' Drinkwater remembered him as having sat next to Ellerby at the meeting in Hull. He was surprised that Ellerby was not among the announced deputation. Drinkwater hoped Ellerby realised he was no longer dealing with a man of Palgrave's stamp and had come to his senses. In any event Waller seemed a mild enough character, leaving most of the talking to Sawyers.

'Well, gentlemen,' Drinkwater said when he had settled them with a glass and placed Palgrave's decanter on the table before them, 'to what do I owe this honour?'

'As thou knowest, Captain Drinkwater, since we cast anchor we have been taking water and augmenting our crews. The islanders are as eager as ourselves to avoid delay, the season already being far advanced. It is therefore hoped that within these twenty-four hours thou also wilt be ready to weigh.'

'I see no reason for thinking otherwise.'

'Very well. We have therefore to decide upon the procedures to be adopted when we reach the fishing grounds. Know therefore that we have agreed to consider ourselves free to pursue whales once we cross the seventy-second parallel. Opinion is divided, as to the most advantageous grounds, the mysticetus . . .'

'Mysticetus?' broke in Drinkwater frowning.

'*Baleana Mysticetus*, the Greenland Right Whale . . .' Drinkwater nodded as Sawyers continued, 'has become wary of the approach of man in recent years. There are those who advocate his pursuit upon the coast of Spitzbergen, those who are more disposed to favour a more westerly longitude, along the extremity of the ice.'

'I gather you favour this latter option?' Sawyers nodded while a silent shake of the head indicated that Waller did not. 'I see, please go on.'

'I do not think this late arrival on the grounds will inconvenience us greatly. It was our practice to spend the first month in the Greenland Sea in sealing, waiting for the ice to open up and spending the first days of continuous daylight in the hunting of seal, walrus and bear. However, those of us that have, of late, pursued mysticetus into the drift ice, have been rewarded by a haul as high as ten or even a dozen fish in a season, which amply satisfies us.'

It was clear that Harvey and Sawyers were of one mind in the matter. But if the whale-fleet dispersed his own task became impossible.

'Would you be kind enough to indicate the degree to which these options are supported by the other masters?' The three men consulted together while Drinkwater rose and pulled out a chart of the Greenland Sea. Seven hundred miles to the north-north-west of Bressay Sound lay the island of Jan Mayen. His present company, he knew, still referred to it as Trinity Island, after their own corporation.

'I think, sir,' said Harvey in his broad accent, 'that a few favour the Spitzbergen grounds while the majority will try the ice-edge.'

'Very well.' Drinkwater paused to think. He could not cover both areas so which was the better post to take up with the *Melusine*? During the last war Danish privateers had operated out of the fiords of Norway. Would these hardy men attempt to entrap British whaleships on the coast of Spitzbergen? The battle of Copenhagen and Britain's new alliance with Russia must surely persuade Denmark that she had nothing to gain by provoking Britain from her Norwegian territories. Drinkwater cleared his mind of these diplomatic preoccupations. His own responsibilities were to the whalers and he conceived the greater threat, as indicated at the Admiralty, to come from French privateers. Long experience of French corsairs had led Drinkwater to admire their energy. He did not share the contempt of many of his contemporaries for French abilities. The Republican Navy had given the Royal Navy a bloody nose from time to time, he recalled, thinking that even the great Sir Edward Berry, one of Nelson's Band of Brothers, had nearly caught a tartar in the *Guillaume Tell* off Malta in 1800. And the corsairs were of greater resource than the Republican Navy. What of those Breton ships that had sailed north? Where were they now?

He looked at the chart. The huge area of the Greenland Sea was imperfectly surveyed. Hill had added every scrap of detail he could glean but it was little enough. Drinkwater concentrated on the problem from the French point of view. If the intention of the privateers was to harass British whalers then they would probably hide in the fiords of Iceland or around Cape Farewell. The former, ice free on its southern and eastern coasts would threaten the Greenland fishery whilst the less hospitable coast of Greenland would permit a descent upon the trade in the Davis Strait. Either station would give the ships a favourable cast well to the windward of British cruisers in the Western Approaches and a clear passage back to the French coast where they had only to run the British blockade to reach safety. And given the fact that they were unlikely to be making for the great French naval arsenals this would be relatively simple. It was clear that if the Hull ships were determined to fish in the Greenland Sea he must conceive the greater threat, if it existed at all, would come from Iceland and that he should support the whalers on the ice-edge.

'I shall make known to you that I shall cruise upon the ice-edge in company with the majority of ships. I would ask you therefore that you appoint one of your number to consult and advise me as to your intentions, that we may not be at cross-purposes.'

'That matter has already been settled, Captain. Abel Sawyers, here, has been elected to be our commodore.' Harvey's ugly face smiled.

'Then that is most satisfactory . . .'

'There is one thing, Captain.' Waller's apparent insignificance was enhanced by a thin voice with an insinuating quality.

'What is that, Captain Waller?'

'I do not think you understand the diversity of individual method employed by masters in the whalefishery. We do not expect to be constrained by you in *any* way. We wish to be free to chase fish wherever we think it to our advantage.'

Drinkwater shrugged, irritated by the man's pedantic manner. Alone among the whale-ship masters Waller seemed the least appropriate to his calling.

'Captain Waller, I have my orders and they are to *extend to you* the protection of a ship of war. I cannot prevent you from hunting the whale wherever you desire, but I can and have arranged a rendezvous and a distress signal to use if you are attacked.'

'And what do you propose?'

'My gunner is preparing Blue Lights for you. A Blue Light shot into the sky and accompanied by two guns may transmit your distress over a large distance and if this signal is used whenever strange sails are sighted I am sanguine that *Melusine* may be deployed to cover you.'

'And if we are attacked from two directions simultaneously?' asked Waller.

'I shall deal with hypothetical situations when they become real, sir, you ain't the only people used to active operations with boats, Captain.'

'And you are not the only people fitted with cannon. There have been instances where whale-ships have driven off an enemy . . .'

'Chiefly, I believe,' snapped Drinkwater, 'when the enemy was one of their own kind disputing the possession of a fish. Frankly, Captain Waller, since you have made it clear that you intend to fish off Spitzbergen I cannot see why you wish to enquire into the methods I intend to employ to protect the trade.'

Waller did not retort but lolled back into his chair. 'Aye, Captain, you will perfectly satisfy me if you do not interfere.'

Angrily Drinkwater looked at Harvey and Sawyers. They were clearly out of sympathy with Waller but said nothing as he equally obviously represented a body of opinion among this curious Arctic democracy. Drinkwater swallowed pride and anger. 'Another glass, gentlemen,' he conciliated. 'I suggest that we remain in company until the seventy-second parallel in eight degrees easterly longitude.' He laid a finger on the chart and the three men bent over the table. 'From here the Spitzbergen ships can detach.'

'I think that would be most agreeable,' said Sawyers.

'Agreed,' added Harvey.

Waller on the left, smoothed the chart out and nodded. 'Aye, 'twill do,' he said thoughtfully. Drinkwater saw his three visitors to their boats. The sun had disappeared behind a bank of cloud as they came on deck.

'I shall hoist the signal to weigh at noon tomorrow then, gentlemen.' They all agreed. Drinkwater looked across the Sound at the whalers. Odd shapes had appeared at their mastheads.

'Crow's nests,' explained Sawyers in answer to Drinkwater's question. 'It is necessary to provide an elevated lookout post both for sighting the fish and for navigating through the ice. I myself have spent many hours aloft there and have a nest of my own devising.'

'I see . . . Good night, Captain Waller.'

'They are also indispensable for shooting unicorns, Captain,' added Harvey.

'Unicorns? Come sir you haze me . . .'

'A name given to the Narwhal or Tusked Dolphin, Captain Drinkwater, after which my own ship is named. He may be hit from the masthead where a shot from the deck will be deceived by the refraction of the sea.'

'Ahhh . . . Your boat, Captain Harvey.'

Harvey's ugly face cracked into a grin and he held out his hand. 'If a King's Officer won't take offence from an old man, may I suggest that excessive concern will have a bad effect on you. Whatever heated air may have been blown about back in Hull, no-one expects the impossible. While we don't want to be attacked by plaguey Frenchmen we are more anxious to hunt fish.'

'I fear I cut a poor figure.'

'Not at all, man, not at all. You are unfamiliar with our ways and your zeal does you credit.'

'Thank you.'

'And I'll go further and say, speaking plainly as a Yorkshireman, you'm a damned sight better than that bloody Palgrave.' Harvey went over the side still smiling. Drinkwater turned to say farewell to Sawyers. The Quaker was staring aloft.

'Thou woulds't oblige thyself, Captain, by constructing a similar contrivance aloft.'

'Crow's nest? But it would incommode the striking of my t'gallant masts in a gale, Captain Sawyers.'

Sawyers nodded. 'Thou hast a dilemma, Friend; to keep thy lofty spars in order to have the advantage in a chase, or to snug thy rig down and render it practical.'

Drinkwater looked aloft and Sawyers added, 'Come, Friend, visit the *Faithful* tomorrow forenoon and familiarise yourself with the workings of a whale-ship.'

'I am obliged to you, Captain.' They shook hands and Sawyers clambered down into his boat. Drinkwater watched him pulled away, across the steel-grey waters of the Sound.

Immediately after Lieutenant Germaney had seen the captain over the side the following morning he returned to the gunroom and kicked out those of its occupants who lingered over their breakfasts. He took four glasses of blackstrap in quick succession and sent for the Reverend Obadiah Singleton.

'Take a seat, Mr Singleton. A glass of blackstrap?'

'I do not touch liquor, Mr Germaney. What is it you wish to see me about?'

'You are a physician are you not?'

Singleton nodded. 'Can you cure clap?'

Singleton's astonishment was exceeded by Germaney's sense of relief. The wine now induced a sense of euphoria but he deemed it prudent to restrain Singleton from any moralising. 'I don't want your offices as a damned parson, d'you hear? Well, what d'you say, God damn it?'

'Kindly refrain from blasphemy, Mr Germaney. I had thought of you as a gentleman.'

Germaney looked sharply at Singleton. 'A gentleman may be unfortunate in the matter of his bedfellows, Singleton.'

'I was referring to the intemperance of your language, but no matter. You contracted this in Hull, eh?'

Germaney nodded. 'A God da . . . a bawdy house.'

'Were you alone?'

'No. I was in company.'

'With whom, Mr Germaney? Please do not trifle with me, I beg you.'

'Captain Sir James Palgrave, the Lord Walmsley and the Honourable Alexander Glencross.'

'All gentlemen,' observed Singleton drily. 'May I ask you whether you have advertised your affliction to these other young men?'

'Good God no!'

'And why have you not consulted Mr Macpherson?'

'Because the man is a drunken gossip in whom I have not the slightest faith.'

'He will have greater experience of this sort of disease than myself, Mr Germaney, that I can assure you.'

Germaney shook his head, the euphoria wearing off and being again replaced by the dread that had been his constant companion since his first intimation of the disease. 'Can you cure me Singleton? I'll endow your mission . . .'

'Let us leave it to God and your constitution, Germaney. Now what are your symptoms?'

'I have a gleet that stings like the very devil . . .'

Germaney described his agony and Singleton nodded. 'You appear to be a good diagnostician, Mr Germaney. You are not a married man?'

'Affianced, Singleton, affianced, God damn and blast it!'

The deck of the *Faithful* presented a curious appearance to the uninitiated. Accompanied by Quilhampton, Gorton and Frey, Drinkwater was welcomed by Sawyers who introduced his son and chief mate. He directed his son to show the younger men the ship and tactfully took Drinkwater on a private tour.

The *Faithful* gave an immediate impression of strength and utility, carrying five boats in high davits with three more stowed in her hold. Her decks were a mass of lines and breakers as her crew attended the final preparations for fishing and the filling of her water casks. The men worked steadily, with little noise and no attention paid to their commander and his guest as they picked their way round the cluttered deck.

Sawyers pointed aloft. 'First, Captain, the rig; it must be weatherly but easily handled. Barque rig with courses, top and t'gallant sails. Thou doubtless noticed the curious narrow-footed cut to our courses, well this clears the davits and allows me to rig the foot to a 'thwartships boom. The boom is secured amidships to those eyebolts on the deck and thus tacks and sheets are done away with. As thou see'st with course and topsail braces led thus, through that system of euphroes I can handle this ship, of three hundred and fifty tons burthen, with five men.'

'Ingenious.'

'Aye, 'tis indeed, and indispensable when working after my boats in pursuit of fish running into the ice. Now come . . .' Sawyers clambered up onto the rail and leaned his elbows on the gunwhale of one of the carvel-built whale-boats. Drinkwater admired the lovely sheer and sharp ends of the boat and at his remark a man straightened up from the work of coiling a thin, white hemp line into a series of tubs beneath the thwarts.

'Whale line,' explained Sawyers, 'six tubs per boat, totalling seven hundred and twenty fathoms. The inner end accessible to the boat steerer, so that the lines of another boat may be secured and thus extend the line. This is done in the event of a fish sounding deep or running under ice. The outer end at the bow is secured to the foreganger, a short line attaching it to the harpoon which is kept to hand here, on this rest.' The instrument itself was not in place and Sawyers added, 'This is Elijah Pucill, Captain, speksioneer and chief harpooner; a mighty hunter of mysticetus.' The man grinned and Sawyers pointed to various items in the boat.

'Five oars and a sixth for steering. We prefer the oar for steering as it doth not retard the speed of a boat like a rudder. By it the boat may be turned even when stopped. By sculling, a stealthy approach may be made to a fish caught sleeping or resting upon the surface of the ocean. Of course a whale-boat may, by the same method, be propelled through a narrow ice-lead where, by the lateral extension of her oars, she would otherwise be unable to go.'

Drinkwater nodded. 'The oars,' Sawyer tapped an ash loom, 'are secured by rope grommets to a single thole pin and may thus be trailed without loss, clearing the boat of obstruction and allowing a man two hands to attend to any other task.'

'Who commands the boat?'

'In our fishery the harpooner, although in America they are sufficiently democratic to prohibit the officer from pulling an oar and he combines the duties of mate and steersman. My boats are commanded by the chief and second mates and the speksioneer, here. They pick their boat-steerers and line managers and all are men with whom they have sailed for many seasons.

'Remember, Captain, the harpooner is the man who places the harpoon, who must cut the fish adrift if danger threatens and who, having exhausted the fish, finally comes up with him and attacks with the lance.' Sawyers pointed to half a dozen slim bladed, long shafted weapons like boarding pikes. 'The lance is plied until the vitals of the fish are found and he is deprived of life.'

'It is not against your sensibilities to deprive the fish of life, Captain?'

Sawyers looked surprised. 'Genesis, Captain, Chapter One, verses twenty-six to twenty-eight, "God gave man dominion over the fish of the sea, and over the fowl of the air, and every living thing that moveth upon the earth." And in the Eighth Psalm "the Almighty madest him to have dominion over the works of Thy hands; thou hast put all things under his feet . . . the fowl of the air, and the fish of the sea, and whatsoever passeth through the paths of the seas. O, Lord, our Lord, how excellent is thy name in all the earth . . .".'

'Amen.' The speksioneer added fervently and then Sawyers resumed his discourse as though nothing had interrupted it.

'It is ordained thus.' He looked at Drinkwater, 'But I do not hold with the practice used by Jaybez Harvey and others, including thy friend Ellerby, of discharging the harpoon from a gun. It is a method lately introduced and not much in favour among the more *feeling* masters. Now there,' he said indicating a massive vertical post set near the bow of the whale-boat, 'is the bollard, round which a turn of whale-line may be taken to retard his progress and the more quickly tire him. This is very necessary in the case of a young whale or one which swims under the ice. It is, as you see, deeply scored by the friction of the line and may require water, supplied by this piggin, to prevent it setting fire to the timber.'

'Good heavens, and the line is able to take this strain?'

'Aye. The line is of the very best hemp and the finest manufacture. I have seen a boat pulled under when a fish dives and towed along underwater until the fish surfaced exhausted.'

'And you recovered the boat?'

'Yes. It does not always occur and here is an axe with which the harpooner can, at any time, cut free. But once a boat is fast, the harpooner is reluctant to let it go and he may, as we say, give the fish the boat, to induce fatigue or drown it.'

'Drown it? I do not understand.'

'The fish breathes air, respiring on the surface. He is able, however, to sustain energetic swimming for many minutes before nature compels him to return to the surface for more air. Should he dive too deep, as is often the case with young fish, he may gasp many fathoms down and thus drown.'

'I see,' said Drinkwater wondering. 'It must be of the first importance to ensure that the line is properly coiled and does not foul.' The man in the boat grinned and nodded.

'Aye, Cap'n, for if it fouls and the line-tender or harpooner don't cut it through quick enough, it may capsize the boat and take a man down in its 'tanglement.'

'Thou hast seen that, Elijah, hast thou not?'

'Aye, Cap'n. Once in the Davis Strait and once off Hackluyt's Head.'

Drinkwater shook his head in admiration. 'I do not see a harpoon, Captain Sawyers, and am curious to do so.'

'Ah.' Sawyers regained the deck and led Drinkwater forward. Three men sat upon a hatch, each carefully filing the head of a harpoon. A forge was set up on deck, with bellows and anvil at which a fourth man was fashioning another.

'The harpoon is made of malleable iron allowing it to twist but not to break. Here, Matthew, pray show Captain Drinkwater what I mean.'

A huge man rose from the hatch and grasped the harpoon he was sharpening, holding it at each end of the shank. Drinkwater noted the narrow shank which terminated at one end in the barbed head and at the other in a hollow socket intended to take the wooden stock used by the harpooner to throw the deadly weapon.

The man Matthew walked to the rail and hooked the shank round a belaying pin. With a grunt he bent and then twisted it several times.

'The devil!'

'Old horseshoe nails, Captain, that is what the finest harpoons are made from.'

'And the barbs on the harpoon's head are sufficient to secure it in the flesh of the fish enough to tow a boat?' Drinkwater asked uncertainly.

'Aye, Friend. The mouth, or head as thou calls't it, has withered barbs as you see. The barbs become entangled in the immensely strong ligamentous fibres of the blubber and the very action of the fish in swimming away increases this. The reverse barb, or stop-wither, collects a number of the reticulated sinews which are very numerous near the skin and once well fast, it is unusual to draw it.'

They passed on along the deck. Sawyers pointed out the various instruments used to flens a whale. They were razor sharp and gleaming with oil as each was inspected.

'They are cleaner than my surgeon's catling.'

The two men peered into the hold where, Sawyers explained, the 'whale-bone' and casks of blubber would be stowed, 'If God willed it that they had a good season.'

Drinkwater followed Sawyers into his quarters. It was a plain cabin, well lit by stern lights through which Drinkwater could see *Melusine*.

'I see you have struck your main topgallant mast, Friend.'

'I took your advice.' Drinkwater took the offered glass of fine port, 'To the mortification of several officers, I am amputating the upper twelve feet.'

'You will not regret it.'

'Thank you for your hospitality, Captain Sawyers. I have to admit to being impressed.'

Sawyers smiled with evident pleasure. 'The ship is but a piece of *man's* ingenuity, Captain Drinkwater. You have yet to see the wonders of the Almighty in the Arctic Seas.'

PART TWO

The Greenland Sea

'Oh Greenland is a cold country,
And seldom is seen the sun;
The keen frost and snow continually blow,
And the daylight never is done,
Brave boys! And the daylight never is done.'

Sea-song, *The Man O' War's Man*

Chapter Six *June 1803*

The Matter of a Surgeon

'You are entirely to blame, Mr Singleton,' shouted Drinkwater above the howl of the wind in the rigging. He stood at the windward rail, holding a backstay and staring down at the missionary who leaned into the gale on the canting deck.

'For what, sir?' Singleton clasped the borrowed tarpaulins tightly, aware that they were billowing dangerously. In an instant they were as wet with rain and spray as the captain's.

'For the gale!'

'The gale? *I* am to blame?' Singleton made a grab for a rope as *Melusine* gave a lee lurch. 'But that is preposterous . . .'

Drinkwater smiled, Singleton's colour was a singular, pallid green. 'Breathe deeply through the nose, you'll find it revivifying.'

Singleton did as he was bid and a little shudder passed through him. 'That is a ridiculous superstition, Captain Drinkwater. Surely you do not encourage superstition?'

'It don't matter what *I* think, Mr Singleton. The people believe a parson brings bad weather and you cannot deny it's blowing.'

'It is blowing exceedingly hard, sir.' Singleton looked to windward as a wave top reared above the horizon. *Melusine* dropped into the trough and it seemed to Singleton that the wave crest, rolling over in an avalanche of foam, would descend onto *Melusine*'s exposed side. Singleton's mouth opened as *Melusine* felt the sudden lift of the advancing sea imparted to her quarter. The horizon disappeared and Singleton's stomach seemed far beneath the soles of his feet. He gasped with surprise as the breaking crest crashed with a judder against *Melusine*'s spirketting and shot a column of spray into the air. As *Melusine* felt the full force of the wind on the wave-crest she leaned to leeward and dropped into the next trough. Singleton's stomach seemed to pass his eyes as the wind whipped the spray horizontally over the rail with a spiteful patter. Beside him an apparently heartless Captain Drinkwater raised his speaking trumpet.

'Mr Rispin, you must clear that raffle away properly before starting the fid or you will lose gear.' He turned to the missionary, 'It is an article of faith to a seaman, Mr Singleton,' he grinned, 'but it is, I agree, both superstitious and preposterous. As for the wind I must disagree, if only to prepare you for what may yet come. It blows hard, but not *exceedingly* hard. This is what we term a whole gale. It is quite distinct from a storm. The wind-note in the rigging will rise another octave in a storm.'

'Mr Bourne sent below to the cockpit to turn the young gentlemen out to strike the topgallant masts,' Singleton said, the colour creeping back into his cheeks and checking the corpse-like blue of his jaw. 'I had supposed the term to apply to some form of capitulation to the elements.'

Drinkwater smiled and shook his head. 'Not at all. The ship will ride easier from a reduction in her top hamper. It will lower her centre of gravity and reduce windage, thus rendering her both more comfortable and more manageable.' He pointed to leeward. 'Besides we do not want to outrun our charges.' Singleton stared into the murk to starboard and caught the pale glimpse of sails above the harder solidity of wallowing hulls that first showed a dull gleam of copper and then seemed to disappear altogether.

'And this,' Singleton said, feeling better and aware that any distraction, even that of watching the sailors, was better than the eternal preoccupation with his guts, 'is what Rispin is presently engaged upon?'

'Aye, Mr Singleton, that was my intention,' the speaking trumpet came up again. 'Have a care there, sir! Watch the roll of the ship, God damn it!' The trumpet was lowered. 'Saving your cloth, Mr Singleton.'

'I begin to see a certain necessity for strong expressions, sir.'

Drinkwater grinned again. 'A harsh environment engenders a vocabulary to match, Mr Singleton. This ain't a drawing-room at Tunbridge nor, for that matter, rooms at . . . at, er at whatever college you were at.'

'Jesus.'

'I beg your pardon?'

'Jesus College, Oxford University.' There was a second's pause and both men laughed.

'Ah. I'm afraid I graduated from the cockpit of a man o'war.'

'Not an *alma mater* to be recommended, sir, if my own experiences . . .'

'A cesspit, sir,' said Drinkwater with sudden asperity, 'but I do assure you that England has been saved by its products more than by all the professors in history . . .'

'I did not mean to . . .'

'No matter, no matter.' Drinkwater instantly regretted his intemperance. But the moment had passed and it was not what he had summoned Singleton for. Such levity ill became the captain of a man o'war. 'We were talking of the wind, Mr Singleton, and the noise made by a storm, beside which this present gale is nothing. I believe, Mr Singleton, that the wind in Greenland is commonly at storm force, that the particles of ice carried in it can wound the flesh like buckshot and that a man cannot exist for more than a few minutes in such conditions.'

'Sir, the eskimos manage . . .'

'Mr Singleton,' Drinkwater hurried on, 'what I am trying to say is that I need your services here. On this ship, God damn it. If the eskimos manage so well without you, Mr Singleton, cannot you leave them in their primitive state of savagery? What benefits can you confer . . .?'

'Captain Drinkwater! You amaze me! What are you saying? Surely you do not deny the unfortunate natives the benefits of Christianity?'

'There are those who consider your religion to be as superstitious in its tenets as the people's belief that you can raise a gale, Mr Singleton.'

'Only a Jacobin Frenchman, sir! Not a British naval captain!' Singleton's outrage was so fervent that Drinkwater could not resist laughing at him any more than he could resist baiting him.

'Sir, I, I protest . . .' Drinkwater mastered his amusement.

'Mr Singleton, you may rest easy. The solitude of command compels me to take the occasional advantage . . . But I am in desperate need of a surgeon. Macpherson has, as you know, been in a straitjacket for three days . . .'

'The balance of his mind is quite upset, sir, and the delirium tremens will take some time to subside. Peripheral neuritis, the symptom of chronic alcoholic poisoning . . .'

'I am aware that he is a rum-sodden wreck, devil-take it! That is why I need your knowledge as a physician.'

Melusine's motion eased as Rispin came across the deck and knuckled his hatbrim to report the topgallant masts struck. 'Very well, Mr Rispin. You may pipe the watch below.'

'Aye, aye, sir.'

'And send Mr Quilhampton to me.' He dismissed Rispin and turned to Singleton. 'Very well, Mr Singleton. I admire your sense of vocation. It would be an unwarranted abuse of my powers to compel you to do anything.' He paused and fixed Singleton with his grey eyes. 'But I shall expect you to volunteer to stand in for Macpherson until such time as we land you upon the coast of Greenland. Ah, Mr Q, will you attend the quarterdeck with your quadrant and bring up my sextant. Have Frey bring up the chronometer . . .'

Singleton turned to windward as the captain left him. The wind and sea struck him full in the face and he gasped with the shock.

Mr Midshipman the Lord Walmsley nodded at the messman. The grubby cloth was drawn from the makeshift table and the messman placed the rosewood box in front of his lordship. Drawing a key from his pocket Lord Walmsley unlocked and lifted the lid. He took out the two glasses from their baize-lined sockets and placed one in front of himself and one in front of Mr Midshipman the Honourable Alexander Glencross whose hands shot out to preserve both glasses from rolling off the table.

'Cognac, Glencross?'

'If you please, my Lord.'

Walmsley filled both glasses to capacity, replaced the decanter and locking the box placed it for safety between his feet. He then took hold of his glass and raised it.

'The fork, Mr Dutfield.'

'Aye, aye, my Lord.' Dutfield picked up the remaining fork that lay on the table for the purpose and stuck it vigorously into the deck beam. The dim lighting of the cockpit struck dully off it and Walmsley and Glencross swigged their brandy.

'Damn fine brandy, Walmsley.'

'Ah,' said his lordship from the ascendancy of his position and his seventeen years, 'the advantages of peace, don't you know.' He frowned and stared at the two midshipmen at the forward end of the table then, catching Dutfield's eye raised his own to the fork above their heads. 'The fork, Mr Dutfield.'

Mr Frey looked hurriedly up from his book and then snapped it shut, hurrying away while Dutfield's face wrinkled with an expression of resentment and pleading. 'But mayn't I . . .?'

'You know damn well you mayn't. You are a youngster and when the fork is in the deck beam your business is to make yourself scarce. Now turn in!'

Mumbling, Dutfield turned away.

'What did you say?'

'Nothing.'

Walmsley grinned imperiously. 'Dutfield you have forgot your manners. I could have sworn he said "good night", couldn't you, Glencross?'

'Oh, indeed, yes.'

Dutfield began to unlash his hammock. 'Well, Dutfield, where *are* your manners? You know, just because The Great Democrat has forbidden any thrashing in the cockpit does not prevent me from having your hammock cut down in the middle watch. Now where are your manners?'

'Good night,' muttered Dutfield.

'Speak up damn you!'

'Good night! There, does that satisfy you?'

Walmsley shook his head. 'No, Dutfield,' said his lordship refilling his glass, 'it does not. Now what have I told you, Dutfield, about manners, eh? The hallmark of a gentleman, eh?'

'Good night, *my Lord*.'

'Ah . . .' His lordship leaned back with an air of satisfaction. 'You see, Glencross, he isn't such a guttersnipe as his pimples proclaim . . .'

'Are you bullying again?' Quilhampton entered the cockpit. 'Since when did you take over the mess, Walmsley?'

'Ah, the *harmless* Mr Q, together with his usual ineffable *charm* . . .' Walmsley rocked with his own wit and Glencross sniggered with him.

'Go to the devil, Walmsley. If you take my advice you'd stop drinking that stuff at sea. Have you seen the state of the surgeon?'

'Macpherson couldn't hold his liquor like a gentleman . . .'

'God, Walmsley, what rubbish you do talk. Macpherson drinks from idleness or disappointment and has addled his brain. Rum has rotted him as surely as the lues, and the same will happen to you, you've the stamp of idleness about you.'

'How dare you . . . !'

'Pipe down, Walmsley. You would best address the evening to consulting Hamilton Moore. I am instructed by the captain that he wishes to see your journals together with an essay upon the "Solution of the longitude problem by the Chronometer".'

'Bloody hell!'

'Where's Mr Frey?'

'Crept away to his hammock like a good little child.'

'Good. Be so kind as to tell him to present his journal to the captain tomorrow. Good night.' Quilhampton swung round to return to the deck, bumping into Singleton who entered the cockpit with evident reluctance.

'Cheer up, sir!' he said looking back into the gloom, 'I believe the interior of an igloo to be similar but without some of the *inconveniences* . . .' Chuckling to himself Quilhampton ran up the ladder.

'Good evening, gentlemen.' Singleton's remark was made with great forbearance and he moved stealthily as *Melusine* continued to buck and swoop through the gale.

He managed to seat himself and open the book of sermons, ignoring the curious and hostile silence of Walmsley and Glencross who were already into their third glass of brandy. They began to tell each other exaggerated stories of sexual adventure which, Singleton knew, were intended to discomfit him.

'. . . and then, my dear Glencross, I took her like an animal. My, there was a bucking and a fucking the like of which would have made you envious. And to think that little witch had looked at me as coy as a virgin not an hour since. What a ride!'

'Ah, I had Susie like that. I told you of Susie, my mother's maid. She taught me all I know, including the French way . . .' Glencross rolled his eyes in recollection and was only prevented from resuming his reminiscence by Midshipman Wickham calling the first watch. The two half-drunk midshipmen staggered into their tarpaulins.

Singleton sighed with relief. He had long ago learned that to remonstrate with either Walmsley or Glencross only increased their insolence. He put his head in his hands and closed his eyes. But the vision of Susie's French loving would not go.

Eight bells rang and Walmsley and Glencross staggered out of the cockpit. As he passed Dutfield's hammock, his lordship nudged it with his shoulder.

'Stop that at once, Dutfield,' deplored Walmsley in a matriarchal voice, 'or you will go blind!'

Captain Drinkwater looked from one journal to another. Mr Frey's was a delight. The boy's hand was bold and it was illustrated by tiny sketches of the coastline of east Scotland and the Shetlands. There were some neat drawings of the instruments and weapons used in the whale-fishery and a fine watercolour of *Melusine* leading the whalers out of the Humber past the Spurn Head lighthouse. The others lacked any kind of redeeming feature. Wickham's did show a little promise from the literary point of view but that of Lord Walmsley was clearly a hurried crib of the master's log. Walmsley disappointed him. After the business of Leek, Drinkwater had thought some appeal had been made to the young man's better feelings. He was clearly intelligent and led Glencross about like a puppy. And now this disturbing story about the pair of them being drunk during the first watch. Drinkwater swore. If only Rispin had done something himself, or called for Drinkwater to witness the matter, but Drinkwater had not gone on deck until midnight, having some paperwork to attend to. One thing was certain and that was that unpunished and drunken midshipmen could quickly destroy discipline. Men under threat of the lash for the least sign of insobriety would not thank their captain for letting two boys get drunk on the pretext of high spirits. And, thought Drinkwater with increasing anger, it would be concluded that Walmsley and Glencross were allowed the liberty because of their social stations.

He was on the point of sending for the pair when he decided that, last night's episode having gone unpunished though not unpublicised, he must make an example as public as the offence. And it was damned chilly aloft in these latitudes, he reflected grimly.

'Mistah Singleton, sah!' The marine sentry announced.

'Come in! Ah, Mr Singleton, please take a seat. What can I do for you?'

'First a message from Mr Bourne, sir, he says to tell you, with his compliments, that he has sighted the *Earl Percy* about three leagues to leeward but there is still no sign of the *Provident*.'

'Thank you. I had thought we might have lost contact with more ships during the gale but these whaling fellows are superb seamen. Now, sir. What can I do for you? It was in my mind that you might like to address the men with a short sermon on Sunday. Nothing too prolix, you understand, but something appropriate to our present situation. Well, what d'you say?'

'With pleasure, sir. Er, the other matter which I came about, sir, was the matter of the surgeon.'

'Ahhh . . .'

'Sir, Macpherson is reduced to a state of anorexy. I do not pretend that there is very much that can be done to save him. Already his groans are disturbing the men and he is given to almost constant ramblings and the occasional ravings of a lunatic.'

'You have been to see him?'

Singleton sighed. 'It seems you have carried the day, sir.'

Drinkwater smiled. 'Don't be down-hearted, Mr Singleton. I am sure that you would not wish to spend all your days aboard *Melusine* in idleness. If my gratitude is any consolation you have it in full measure.'

'Thank you, sir. After you have landed me you will find that the whalers each have a surgeon, should you require one. I shall endeavour to instruct the aptest of my two mates.'

'That is excellent. I shall make the adjustments necessary in the ship's books and transfer the emoluments due to Macpherson . . .'

'No, sir. I believe he has a daughter living. I shall have no need of money in Greenland and the daughter may as well have the benefit . . .'

'That's very handsome of you.'

'There is one thing that I would ask, Captain Drinkwater.'

'What is that?'

'That we transfer Macpherson to the hold and that I be permitted to use his cabin.'

Drinkwater nodded. 'Of course, Mr Singleton, and I'm obliged to you.'

The gale increased again with nightfall and Drinkwater waited until two bells in the first watch. An advocate of Middleton's three watch system he liked to know who had the deck at any time during the twenty-four hours without the wearisome business of recollecting who had been the officer of the watch on his last visit to the quarterdeck. He wrapped his cloak about him and stepped out onto the berth deck. The marine sentry snapped to attention. Drinkwater ran up the ladder.

Melusine buried her lee rail and water rolled into the waist. The air was damp and cold, the clouds pressed down on the mastheads, obscuring the sky but not the persistent daylight of an Arctic summer. It was past nine in the evening, ship's time, and in these latitudes the sun would not set for some weeks.

Drinkwater made for the lee rail, took a look at the convoy, remarked the position of the *Nimrod* as sagging off to leeward.

'Mr Rispin, have the midshipmen of the watch make *Nimrod*'s number and order that he closes the commodore.'

'Aye, aye, sir.'

Drinkwater took himself across the deck to the weather rail where the vertical side of the ship deflected the approaching wind up and over his head, leaving its turbulence to irritate those less fortunate to leeward. He began to pace ruminatively up and down, feigning concentration upon some obtuse problem while he watched the two midshipmen carry out the simple order. After a little he called the lieutenant of the watch.

'Mr Rispin, I desired you that the midshipmen of the watch hoisted the signal. Send that yeoman forward. How else do you expect the young gentlemen to learn without the occasional advantage of practical experience?'

The wind was strong enough to require a practised hand at the flag halliards.

Expecting a fouled line or even the loss of one end of the halliard Drinkwater was secretly delighted when he observed Number Five flag rise upside down from the deck.

'Mr Rispin!'

'Sir?'

'Have that yeoman called aft and instruct the young gentlemen in the correct manner to hoist numerals.' The exchange was publicly aired for the benefit of the watch on deck. There were a number of grins visible.

When the signal had been hoisted and *Nimrod*'s attention been called to it by the firing of a gun, Drinkwater called the two midshipmen to him.

'Well, gentlemen. What is your explanation of this abysmal ignorance?'

'An error, sir,' said Walmsley. Drinkwater leaned forward.

'I detect, sir,' he said, 'that you have been drinking. What about you, Mr Glencross?'

'Beg pardon, sir.'

'We are not drunk, sir,' added Walmsley.

'Of course not, Mr Walmsley. A gentleman does not get *drunk*, does he now, eh?'

The midshipmen shook their contrite heads. Experience had taught them that submission would purchase them a quick release.

'The problem is that I am not greatly interested in your qualities as gentlemen. You will find gentlemen forward among the lord mayor's men, you will find gentlemen lolling at Bath or Tunbridge, you will find gentlemen aplenty in the messes of His Majesty's regiments of foot and horse. Those are places proper to gentlemen with no other abilities to support them beyond a capacity for brandy.

'You may, perhaps, also find gentlemen upon the quarterdeck of a British man-o'-war, but they have no *right* there unless they are first and foremost seamen and secondly officers, capable of setting a good example to their men.

'In a few years you will be bringing men to the gratings for a check-shirt for the offence your gentility has led you into. Now, Mr Glencross, the fore topmasthead for you; and Mr Walmsley the main. There you may reflect upon the wisdom of what I have just told you.'

He watched the two young men begin to ascend the rigging. 'Mr Rispin, bring them down at eight bells. And not a moment earlier.'

Chapter Seven *June 1803*

The First Whales

Drinkwater turned from the stern window and seated himself at the table. He drew the opened journal towards him. The brilliant sunlight that reflected from the sea onto the deckhead of the cabin was again reflected onto his desk and the page before him. He picked up his pen and began to write.

The ships favouring the Spitzbergen grounds left us in latitude 72° North and 8° East'ly longitude. Among those left under my convoy are Faithful, *Capt. Sawyers, and* Narwhal, *Capt. Harvey. Their appearance much changed as they disdain to shave north of the Arctic Circle. It fell calm the next morning and the air had a crystal purity. Towards evening I detected a curious luminosity to the northward, lying low across the horizon. This the whale-fishers denominate 'ice blink'. Towards midnight, if such it can be described with no need to light the binnacle lamps, a steady breeze got up, whereupon the ships crowded on sail and stood to the northwards. At morning the 'ice-blink' was more pronounced and accompanied by a strange viscid appearance of the sea. There was also an eerie and subtle change in the atmosphere that seemed most detectable by the olfactory senses and yet could not be called a smell. By noon the reason for these strange phenomenae was apparent. A line of ice visible to the north and west. I perceived immediately the advantages of a 'crow's nest'. All are well on board . . .*

He was interrupted by a loud and distant howl. It seemed to come from the hold and reminded Drinkwater of the unfortunate and now insane Macpherson.

. . . except for the surgeon, whose condition by its very nature, disturbs the peace of the ship.

But it was not Macpherson. The knock at the door was peremptory and Quilhampton's eager face filled with excitement. 'Whales, sir, they've lowered boats in chase!'

'Very well, Mr Q. I'll be up directly.'

At a more sedate pace Drinkwater followed him on deck. He saw the whales almost immediately, three dark humps, moving slowly through the water towards the *Melusine*. In the calm sea they left a gentle wake trailing astern of their bluff heads, only a few whirls visible from the effort of their mighty tails. One of them humped its back and seemed to accelerate. A fine jet of steamy spray spouted from its spiracle. They crossed *Melusine*'s stern not one hundred feet away, their backs marked by some form of wart-like growths. From the rail Drinkwater could clearly see the sphinctal contractions of the blow-hole as the mighty creature spouted.

The watch, scattered at the rails and in the lower rigging were silent. There was something profoundly awe-inspiring in the progress of the three great humps, as they moved with a ponderous innocence through the plankton-rich water. But then the boats passed in energetic pursuit and *Melusine*'s people began to cheer. Drinkwater marked Sawyers Junior, pulling the bow oar of *Faithful*'s number two boat. He wore a sleeveless jerkin and a small brimmed hat. In the stern stood the boat-steerer, leaning on the long steering oar, the coloured flag attached to a staff with which they signalled their ship fluttered like an ensign.

Drinkwater also noticed Elijah Pucill sweep past in *Faithful*'s number one boat. There were more than a dozen boats engaged in the pursuit now, their crews pulling at their oar looms until they bent, springing from the water to whip back ready for the next stroke. Already the whalers were swinging their yards, to catch what breeze there was and work up in support of their boats.

'Don't impede the whalers, Mr Hill, let them pass before you trim the yards to follow.'

'Aye, aye, sir.'

He looked again at the whales and saw they had disappeared. The boats slowed and Drinkwater watched a few kittiwakes wheel to the south and wondered if they could see the whales. Within a few minutes the boats were under way again, following the kittiwakes. But two boats had veered away at a right angle and Drinkwater noticed with sudden interest that they were from *Faithful*. He hauled himself up on the rail and, leaning against the mizen backstays, pulled out his Dollond glass.

There was a flurry of activity among the boats to the south. One had struck and its flag was up as the whale began to tow it. The other boats set off in pursuit. Drinkwater swung his glass back towards Sawyers and Pucill. They were no more than eight cables away and Drinkwater could see both men standing up in the bows of their boats while the crews did no more than paddle them steadily forward.

Then there was a faint shout and Drinkwater saw the whale. He saw a harpoon fly and Sawyers's boat steerer throw up the flag. Pucill had dropped his harpoon and jumped back to his oar as Sawyers's boat began to slide forward. A faint cloud of smoke enveloped the harpoon and Drinkwater remembered the bollard and a snaking line. He could see the splash of water from the piggin and then the rushing advance of the whale stopped abruptly and it sounded. Pucill's boat came up alongside Sawyers's and lay on its oars. Through the glass Drinkwater could see Pucill stand up again, both he and Sawyers hefting their lances. They stayed in this position for several minutes, like two sculptures and Drinkwater began to tire of trying to hold the glass steady. He lowered it and rubbed his eye. He was aware now of a cloud of seabirds, gathered as if from nowhere over this spot in the ocean. He could hear their cries and suddenly the whale breached. For a split second he saw its huge, ugly head with its wide, shiny portcullis of a mouth and the splashes of whitened skin beneath the lower lip that curled like a grotesque of a negro's. The lances darted as the boats advanced and there was a splashing of foam and lashing of fins as the head submerged again and the back seemed to roll over. Then the tail emerged, huge, horizontally-fluked and menacing the boats as they back-watered. The crack as it slapped the water sounded like artillery, clearly audible to the watching Melusines. They saw the pale shape of a belly and the brief outline of a fin as the boats closed for the kill. The lances flashed in the sun and the beast seemed to ripple in its death flurry. Then Drinkwater was aware that the sea around the boats was turning red. Mysticetus had given up the ghost.

We passed into open pack ice, Drinkwater wrote, *shortly before noon on 13th June 1803, in Latitude 74° 25' North 2° 50' East. We have sighted whales daily and taken many. The masters speak of a good year which pleases me after our previous melancholy expectations. In light winds the watch are much employed in working the ship through the ice. The officers have greatly benefitted from this experience and I have fewer qualms about their abilities than formerly. Mr Q. continues to justify my confidence in him while I find Mr Hill's services as master indispensable. I believe Mr Germaney to be unwell, suffering from some torpor of the spirits. Singleton will say little beyond the fact that he suspects Germaney of suffering from the blue devils, which I conceive to be a piece of nautical conceit upon his part to deceive me as to the real nature of G's complaint.*

The people have been exercised at cutlass and small arms drill by Mr Mount and recently, when we had occasion, in the manner of the whaleships, to moor to a large ice floe, they played a game of football.

There has been a plentiful supply of meat for the table, duck in particular being very fine. Seal and walrus have also been taken. While flensing, the carcases of the whales are frequently attacked by the Greenland Shark, a brown or grey fish some twenty odd feet in length. It is distinguished by a curious appendage from the iris of its eye. It makes good eating.

We have observed some fully developed icebergs. Their shapes are fantastical and almost magical and beggar description. In sunlight their colours range from brilliant white to a blue of . . .

Drinkwater paused. The strange and awesome sight of his first iceberg had both impressed and disquieted him for some reason that he could not fathom. Then it came to him. That pale ice-cold blue had been the colour of Ellerby's eyes. He shook his head, as though clearing his mind of an unpleasant dream. Ellerby was two hundred and fifty miles to the north-east and could be forgotten. He resumed his journal: *. . . impressive beauty. We have used them as a mark for exercising the guns which delights the people who love to see great lumps of ice flying from their frozen ramparts.*

Drinkwater laid down his pen and rubbed his shoulder. Frequent exercise with the foil had undoubtedly eased it, but the cold became penetrating in close promixity to the ice and his shoulder sometimes ached intolerably. Palgrave's decanter beckoned, but he resisted the temptation. Better to divert his mind by a brisk climb to his new-fangled crow's nest. He pulled the greygoe on and stepped out of the cabin. As he came on deck his nostrils quivered to the stimulating effect of the cold air. Swinging himself into the main shrouds he began to ascend the mainmast.

The crow's nest had been built by the carpenter and his mate. It was a deep box, bound with iron and having a trap in its base through which to enter. Inside was a hook for a speaking trumpet and a rest for a long-glass. Turning the seaman on duty out of it from the top gallant mast cross trees, Drinkwater ascended the final few feet and wriggled up inside.

'Nothink unusual, yer honour,' the lookout had reported as they passed in the rigging. Settling himself on the closed trap Drinkwater swept the horizon. He could see open water to the south and a whaler which he recognised as one of the Whitby ships. The drift ice closed to open pack within a mile of them and he counted the whalers still inside the ice within sight of the ship. Reckoning on visibility of some forty miles, he was pleased to identify all his charges and to note that most had boats out among the floes. One ship's boats were engaged in towing a whale, tail first, back to their ship while two vessels were engaged in flensing.

A number of tall, pinnacled bergs could be seen three or four miles away, while one huge castellated monster lay some ten miles off to the north-north-eastward.

Satisfied he lifted the trap with his toe by the rope grommet provided and eased himself down. Nodding to the waiting seaman at the cross trees. 'Very well, Appleyard, up you go again.'

'Aye, aye, sir.' The man scrambled up to the relative warmth of the nest and Drinkwater noted the scantiness of his clothing. He descended to the deck where Bourne, the officer of the watch, saluted him. Drinkwater was warmed by the climb and in a good humour. 'Mr Bourne, I'd be obliged if you and your midshipmen would join me for dinner.'

He went below and sent for the purser. When Mr Pater arrived Drinkwater ordered an issue of additional warm clothing at his own expense to be made to topmen. Then he sent for Mr Mount.

'Sir?' Mount stood rigidly to attention, promptly attentive to Drinkwater's summons.

'Ah, Mr Mount, I wish you to take advantage of every opportunity of taking seal and any bears to fabricate some additional warm clothing. Mr Pater informs me our stocks are barely adequate and I rely upon your talents with a musket to rectify the situation. See Mr Germaney and take a boat this afternoon. The signal for recall will be three guns.'

'Yes, sir, with pleasure.'

'I perceived a few seals basking about two miles to the east.'

'Thank you, sir. I'll take a party and see what we can accomplish.'

*

Drinkwater watched the hunting party leave. Fitting out the cutter for the expedition as if for a picnic Mount, Bourne, Quilhampton and Frey had been joined at the last minute by Lord Walmsley and Alexander Glencross. Mr Germaney had relieved Bourne of the deck and Mount had ensured the seamen at the oars each took a cutlass as a skillet for butchering the meat. Drinkwater toyed with the idea of watching their progress from the crow's nest but rejected it as a pointless waste of time and advised Germaney to keep a sharp watch for the onset of a fog and fire the recall the moment he thought it possible.

In the still air he heard an occasional pop through the open window of his stern lights as he recorded the air temperature and dipped a thermometer into the sea. Closing the sash frame he sat, blew on his hands and wrote:

Sawyers sends to me that he is confident this will be a good season. The sea is of a rich, greenish hue which he says indicates a plentitude of plankton and krill, tiny forms of life upon which Mysticetus feeds. He states that his men took a Razorback, an inferior species of fish which contains little oil and sinks on dying.

There is a strange remote beauty about these regions and they seem far from the realities of war. I begin to think my Lord St Vincent too sanguine in his expectations.

Drinkwater snapped the inkwell shut and leaned back in his chair. Five minutes later he was asleep. He was woken by a confused bedlam of shouts that persuaded him they were attacked. He had slept for several hours and was stiff and uncomfortable. The sudden awakening alarmed him to the extent of reaching the door before he heard the halloos and the laughter. Muttering about the confounded hunting party he slumped back into his chair, rubbing his shoulder.

'Pass word for my coxswain!' he bawled at the sentry, listening to the order reverberate forward. Tregembo knocked and entered with the familiarity of a favoured servant. 'Coffee, zur?'

'Aye, and a bath.'

'A bath, zur?'

'Yes, God damn it! A bath, a cold bath of sea-water! You've seen three boats of whale-fishers upset in it and it'll not kill me.'

'Aye, aye, zur.' Tregembo's tone was disapproving.

'And find out what happened to Mr Mount's huntin' party.'

Despite his desire for invigoration the bath was unbelievably cold. But in the flush of blood as he towelled himself and put on the clean under-drawers laid out by Tregembo, he felt a renewal of spirits. What he had not written in his journal but which had taken root in his mind and filled it upon waking in such discomfort, was the growing conviction that *Melusine*'s services in the Arctic were going to be purely formal. The strange beauty of the ice and sea did not blind him to the dangers that a fog or storm could summon up, but the necessity of endangering his ship for such a needless cause, for working his crew hard to maintain their martial valour to no purpose, set a problematical task for their captain.

He drew the clean shirt over his head as his steward brought in the coffee.

'Thank you, Cawkwell, on the table if you please, and pass word to Mr Mount to come and see me.'

'Sir,' whispered Cawkwell, a shadow of a man who seemed in constant awe of everybody. Drinkwater suspected Tregembo of specially selecting Cawkwell as his servant so that his own ascendant position was not undermined.

'I told Mr Mount to wait until you'd had your bath, zur,' he waited until Cawkwell had left the cabin, 'when you was less megrimish.'

Drinkwater looked up. 'Damn you for your insolence, Tregembo,' Tregembo grinned, 'you should try a bath, yourself.' Tregembo sniffed with disapproval and the knock of Mr Mount put an end to the familiarities.

'Enter!'

Mount, wrapped in his great-coat, stepped into the cabin. 'Ah, Mr Mount, what success did you have, eh?'

'A magnificent haul, sir, eleven seals and,' Mount's eyes were gleaming with triumph, 'a polar bear, sir!'

'A polar bear?'

'Yes, sir. Mr Frey discovered him asleep alongside a seal that he had partly eaten. He got the scent of us and made off into the water but, I suppose conceiving himself safe after putting a distance between us, clambered up onto another floe. Quilhampton and I both hit him and he made off, but we called up the boat and I got a second ball into his brain at about sixty paces.'

Drinkwater raised his eyebrows. 'A triumph indeed, Mr Mount, my congratulations.'

'Thank you, sir.'

'Now we will butcher the seals but have a party skin them and scrape the inside of the skins. I asked Mr Germaney to determine whether any of the people were conversant with tanning.'

'Yes, sir. Er, there's one thing, sir.'

'Yes? What is it?'

'We brought back an eskimo, sir.'

'You did *what*?'

'Brought back an eskimo.'

'God bless my soul!'

After this revelation Drinkwater could no longer resist inspecting the trophies. The eskimo proved to be a young male, who appeared to have broken his arm. He was dressed in skins and had a wind-tanned face. His dark almond eyes were clouded with fear and pain and he held his left arm with his right hand. Mr Singleton was examining him with professional interest.

'A fine specimen of an innuit, Captain, about twenty years of age but with a compound fracture of the left ulna and considerable bruising. I understand he resisted the help of Mount and his party.'

'I see. What do you propose to do with him Mr Singleton? We can hardly turn him loose with his arm in such a state, yet to detain him seems equally unjust. Perhaps his family or huntin' party are not far away.' Drinkwater turned to Mount. 'Did you see any evidence of other eskimos?'

'No, sir. Mr Frey ascended an eminence and searched the horizon but nothing could be seen. He is very lucky, sir, we were some way from the ship and returning when we happened to see him. If he had not moved we would have passed him by.'

'And left him to the polar bears, eh?'

'Exactly so, sir.'

Singleton had reached under the man's jerkin and was palpating the stomach. Curiously the eskimo did not seem to mind but began to point to his mouth.

'He's had little to eat, sir, for some time,' Singleton stood back, 'and I doubt whether soap has ever touched him.' Several noses wrinkled in disgust.

'Very well. Take him below and get that arm dressed. Give the poor devil some laudanum, Mr Singleton. As for the rest of you, you may give me a full account of your adventure at dinner.' He turned aft and nearly bumped into little Frey. 'Ah, Mr Frey . . .'

'Sir?'

'Do you think you could execute a small sketch of our friend?'

'Of course sir.'

'Very good, I thank you.'

The meal itself proved a great success. The trestle table borrowed from the wardroom groaned under the weight of fresh meat, an unusual circumstance of a man-of-war. In an ill-disguised attempt to placate his commander Lord Walmsley had offered Drinkwater two bottles of brandy which the latter did not refuse. The conversation was naturally about the afternoon's adventure and Drinkwater learnt of little Frey's sudden, frightening discovery of the sleeping polar bear which the boy re-told, his eyes alight with wine and the excitement of recollected fear. He heard again how Quilhampton, his musket resting in his wooden hand, had struck the animal in the shoulder and how Mount had established his military superiority by lodging a ball in the bear's skull.

'By comparison Bourne's triumph over the seals was of no account, sir, ain't that so, Bourne?' Mount said teasing his young colleague.

'That is an impertinence, Mount, if I had not had to secure the boat while you all raced in pursuit of quarry I should have downed the beast with a single shot.'

'Pah!' said Mount grinning, 'you should have left the boat to Walmsley or Glencross. I conceive it that you were hanging back from the ferocity of those somnolent seals.'

'Come, sir,' said Bourne with mock affront, 'd'you insinuate that I was frightened of an old bear who ran away at the approach of Mr Frey . . .'

Drinkwater looked at Frey. The boy coloured scarlet, uncertain how to take this banter from his seniors. Was Bourne implying the bear was scared by his own size or his own courage? Or that polar bears really were timid and his moment of triumph was thereby diminished?

Drinkwater felt for the boy, particularly as Walmsley and Glencross joined the raillery. 'Oh, Mr Bourne, the bear was absolutely *terrified* of Frey, why I saw him positively roll his eyes in terror at the way Frey hefted his musket. Did you not see that, Glencross?' asked Lord Walmsley mischievously.

'Indeed I did, why I thought he was loading with his mouth and firing with his knees . . .' There was a roar of laughter from the members of the hunting party who had witnessed the excited midshipman ascend an ice hummock with a Tower musket bigger than himself. He had stumbled over the butt, tripped and fallen headlong over the hummock, discharging the gun almost in the ear of the recumbent bear.

Poor Frey was in no doubt now, as to the purpose of his seniors' intentions. Drinkwater divined something of the boy's wretchedness.

'Come, gentlemen, there is no need to make Mr Frey the butt of your jest . . .'

There was further laughter, some strangled murmurs of 'Butt . . . butt . . . oh, very good, sir . . . very apt' and eventual restoration of some kind of order.

'Well, Mr Singleton,' said Drinkwater to change the subject and addressing the sober cleric, 'what d'you make of our eskimo friend?'

'He is named Meetuck, sir and is clearly frightened of white men, although he seems to have reconciled himself to us after he was offered meat . . .'

'Which he ate raw, sir,' put in Frey eagerly.

' 'Pon my soul, Mr Frey, raw, eh? Pray continue, Mr Singleton.'

'He claims to come from a place called Nagtoralik, meaning a place with eagles, though this may mean nothing as a location as we understand it, for these people are nomadic and follow their food sources. He says . . .'

'Pardon my interruption, Mr Singleton but do I understand that you converse with him?'

Singleton smiled his rare, dark smile. 'Well not converse, sir, but there are words that I comprehend which, mixed with gesture, mime and some of Mr Frey's quick drawings, enabled us to learn that he had found a *putulik*, a place with a hole in the ice through which he was presumably catching fish when he was attacked by a bear. He made his escape but in doing so fell and injured himself, breaking his arm. I think that *scuppers* the arguments of Mr Frey's persecutors, sir, that even an experienced hunter may fall in such terrain and also that the polar bear is capable of great ferocity.'

'Indeed, Mr Singleton, I believe it does,' replied Drinkwater drily. Cawkwell drew the cloth in his silent ghost-like way and the decanters began to circulate.

'Tell us, Mr Singleton how you came to learn eskimo,' asked Mount, suddenly serious in the silence following the loyal toast.

Singleton leaned forward with something of the proselytiser, and the midshipmen groaned inaudibly, but sat quiet, gulping their brandy avidly.

'The Scandinavians were the first Europeans to make contact with the coast of Greenland sometime in the tenth century. Their settlements lasted for many years before being destroyed by the eskimos in the middle of the fourteenth century. When the Englishman John Davis rediscovered the coast in 1585 he found only eskimos. Davis,' Singleton turned his gaze on the midshipmen with a pedagogic air, 'gave his name to the strait between Greenland and North America . . . The Danish Lutheran Hans Egedé was able to study the innuit tongue before embarking with his family and some forty other souls to establish a permanent colony on the West Coast of Greenland. When he returned to Copenhagen on the death of his wife he wrote a book about his work with the eskimos among whom he preached and taught for some fifteen years. His son Povel remained in Greenland and completed a translation of Our Lord's Testament, a catechism and a prayer book in eskimo. Povel Egedé died in Copenhagen in '89 and I studied there under one of his assistants.' Singleton paused again and this time it was Drinkwater upon whose face his gaze fixed.

'I refused to leave during the late hostilities and was in the city when Lord Nelson bombarded it.'

'That,' replied Drinkwater meeting Singleton's eyes, 'must have been an interesting experience.'

'Indeed, Captain Drinkwater, it persuaded me that no useful purpose can be served by armed force.'

A sense of affront stiffened the relaxing diners. To a man their eyes watched Drinkwater to see what reply their commander would make to this insult to their profession. From little Frey, ablaze with brandy and bravado; the arrogant insensitivity of Walmsley and Glencross and the puzzlement of Mr Quilhampton, to the testy irritation of a silent Mr Hill and the colouring anger of Mr Mount, the table seethed with a sudden unanimous indignation. Drinkwater smiled inwardly and looked at his first lieutenant. Mr Germaney had said not a word throughout the entire meal, declined the brandy and merely toyed with his food.

'That, Mr Singleton, is an interesting and contentious point. For my own part, and were the world as perfect as perhaps its maker intended, I should like nothing better than to agree with you. But since the French do not seem to be of your opinion the matter seems likely to remain one for academic debate, eh? Well, Mr Germaney, what do you think of Mr Singleton's proposition?'

The first lieutenant seemed at first not to have heard Drinkwater. Hill's nudge was far from surreptitious and Germaney surfaced unsure of what was required of him.

'I . . . er, I have no great opinion on the matter, sir,' he said hurriedly, hoping the reply sufficient. Remarking the enormity of Germaney's abstraction with some interest Drinkwater turned to the bristling marine officer.

'Mr Mount?'

'Singleton's proposition is preposterous, sir. The Bible is full of allusions to the use of violence, Christ's own eviction of the moneylenders from the Temple notwithstanding. Had he argued the wisdom of bombarding a civilian population I might have had some sympathy with his argument for it is precisely to preserve our homes that we serve here, but the application of force is far from useless . . .'

'But might it not become an end, rather than a means, Mr Mount?' asked Singleton, 'and therefore to be discouraged lest its use be undertaken for the wrong motives.'

'Well a man does not stop taking a little wine in case he becomes roaring drunk and commits some felonious act, does he?'

'Perhaps he should, Mr Mount,' said Singleton icily, raising a glass of water to his lips.

'I don't understand you, Mr Singleton,' said Hill at last. 'I can see you may argue that if Cain had never slain Abel the world might have been a better place but given that it is not paradise, do you advocate that we simply lie down and invite our enemies to trample over us?'

'To turn the other cheek and beat our swords into ploughshares?' added Mount incredulously.

'Why not?' asked Singleton with impressive simplicity. There was a stunned silence while they assimilated the preposterous nature of this suggestion. Then the table erupted as the officers leaned forward with their own reasons for the impossibility of such a course of action. The candle flames guttered under the discharge of air from several mouths. In the ensuing babel Drinkwater heard such expressions as 'march unchecked on London . . . dishonour our women . . . destroy our institutions . . . rape . . . loot . . . national honour . . .'

He allowed the reaction to continue for some seconds before banging sharply on the table.

'Gentlemen, please!' They subsided into silence. 'Gentlemen, you must have some regard for Mr Singleton's cloth. Preposterous as his ideas sound to you, your own conversations have disturbed him these past weeks. He doubtless finds equally odd your own assertions that you will "thrash Johnny Crapaud", "cut the throats of every damned frog" you encounter not to mention "flog any man that transgresses the Articles of War or the common usages of the service". Yet you appear devout enough when Divine Service is read, an act which Mr Singleton may regard as something close to hypocrisy . . . eh?' He looked round at them, his eyes twinkling as he encountered mystification or downright astonishment.

'Now, if you ignore abstract considerations and deal with the pragmatic you will see that we have all chosen professions which require zeal. In Mr Singleton's case religious zeal and in your case, gentlemen, the professional zeal of strict adherence to duty. Zeal is not something that admits of much prevarication or equivocation and since argument and debate might be said to be synonyms for quibbling, your two positions are quite irreconcilable. And if two opposing propositions are irreconcilable I would suggest the arguing of them a fatuous waste of time.'

Drinkwater finished his speech with his eyes on Singleton. The man appeared disappointed, as though expecting unreserved support from Drinkwater. He felt slightly guilty towards Singleton, as though owing him some explanation.

'I believe in providence, Mr Singleton, which you might interpret as God's will. To me it incorporates all the forces that you theologists claim as evoked by "God" whilst satisfactorily explaining those you do not. It is a creed much favoured by sea-officers.'

'Then you do not believe in God, Captain Drinkwater,' pronounced Singleton dolefully, 'and the power of your intellect prevents you from spiritual conversion.'

Drinkwater inclined his head. 'Perhaps.'

'Then I find that a matter of the profoundest sadness, sir,' Singleton replied quietly. The silence in the cabin was touching;

even Walmsley and Glencross had ceased to wriggle, though their condition was more attributable to the brandy they had consumed than interest in polemics.

'So do I, Mr Singleton, so do I. But the moment when a man has to say whether God, as you theologists conceive him, exists or not is a profound one, not to be taken lightly. We cannot conceive of any form of existence that does not entail physical entity, witness your own archangels. Indeed even a devout man may imagine eternal life as some sort of transmigration of our corporeal selves during which all disabilities, uglinesses, warts and ill-disposed temperaments disappear. This is surely understandable, though not much above the primitive, something which our eskimo friend would comprehend.

'Now I ask you, as rational beings living in an age of scientific discovery and more particularly being seamen observing the varied phenomena of atmosphereology can you convince me of the whereabouts of these masses of corporeal souls? Of course not . . .'

'You deny the Resurrection, sir!'

Drinkwater shrugged. 'I have seen too much of death and too little of resurrection to place much faith in it applying to common seamen like ourselves.'

'But you are without faith!' Singleton cried.

'Not at all, sir!' Drinkwater refilled his glass. 'Belief in atheism surrenders everything too much to hazard. I cannot believe that. I see only purpose in all things, a purpose that is made evident by science and manifests itself in the divine working of providence. As for the corporeal self why Quilhampton, Hill and I hold together like a trio of doubled frigates. If the enemy gets a further shot at our carcases there will likely be little left to refurbish for the life hereafter.'

The facetious jest raised a little laughter round the table and revealed that all three midshipmen were asleep.

'I agree with the Captain,' said Germaney suddenly. 'I recollect something Herrick wrote. Er,' he thought for a moment and then sat up and quoted: '"Putrefaction is the end, of all that nature doth intend." There is great truth in that remark, great truth . . .'

Drinkwater looked sharply at his first lieutenant. Germaney's silence had seemed as uncharacteristic as his sobriety and now this sudden quotation seemed to be significant. It appeared that

Singleton considered it so, for he seemed disinclined to pursue the discussion and Drinkwater himself fell silent. Mount rose and thanked him for his hospitality and the hint was taken up by the others. As the chairs scraped back the midshipmen awoke and guiltily made their apologies. Drinkwater waved them indulgently aside.

As he watched them leave the cabin he called Singleton back. 'A moment, Mr Singleton, if you please.'

Drinkwater blew out the candles that had illuminated the table. The cabin was thrown into penumbral gloom from the midnight daylight of the Arctic summer.

'You must not think that I wish to ridicule your calling. In my convalescence I met a priest of your persuasion possessed of the most enormous spiritual arrogance. I found it most distasteful. It is not that I disbelieve, it is simply that I *cannot* believe as you do. After the birth of my children I had the curious *natural* feeling that I had outlived my usefulness. My liberal ideals were in conflict with this, but I could not deny the emotion. It seemed that all thereafter was merely vanity.'

Singleton coughed awkwardly. 'Sir, I . . .'

'Do not trouble yourself on my account, Mr Singleton, I beg you. I hear that Leek is a faithful convert and protests not only the existence of God but can vouch for his very appearance.'

'Leek was very close to death by drowning, sir, perhaps a little of the great mystery was unfolded to him.' Singleton was deadly serious.

'But the intervention of science prevented it: *your* knowledge, Mr Singleton.'

'Now you do ridicule me.'

Drinkwater laughed. 'Not at all. Perhaps we are, as you said earlier, too well-informed for our own good, as it says in the Bible, "unless ye be as little children . . ."'

'That is perhaps the wisest thing you have said, sir,' Singleton at last smiled back.

'Touché. And good night to you.'

'Good night, sir.'

Drinkwater went on deck. Mr Rispin had the watch and pointed out the closer drift ice and identified the whalers in sight. There was scarcely a breath of wind and *Melusine* lay upon a sea that only moved slightly from the ground swell. Rispin's unconfident, fussy manner irritated Drinkwater until he reflected that he had been particularly lugubrious this evening and dominated the conversation. Well, damn it, it was a captain's privilege to talk nonsense.

Lieutenant Germaney sat in his hutch of a cabin contemplating the bundle of scented paper tied with a blue ribbon. After a while he opened the lantern and removed the candle tray. He began to burn the letters, a little pile of ash mounting up and spilling onto the deck.

When he had completed his task he turned to his cot and lifted the lid of the walnut case that lay upon it. Taking out one of the pair of pistols it contained, he checked its priming. Turning again to the candle he carefully replaced the tray inside the lantern and closed it, returning the thing to its hook in the deck-head.

Reseating himself he lifted the pistol, placed its muzzle in his mouth. For a moment he sat quite still then, with the cold steel barrel knocking his teeth he said, 'Putrefaction!'

And pulled the trigger.

Chapter Eight *June 1803*

Balaena Mysticetus

'Why in God's name was I not told of this?'

'The confidentiality which exists between a patient and his physician . . .'

'God's bones, Singleton, I will not bandy words with you. The man should have been on the sick book, along with the others that have lues and clap.' Drinkwater swore again in self reproach and added, 'I remarked some morbid humour in him.'

'I am not the ship's surgeon, Captain Drinkwater, a fact which you seem to have lost sight of . . .'

'Have a care, sir, have a care!' Both men glared angrily at each other across the cabin table. At last Singleton said, 'It seems we have adopted irreconcilable positions which, by your own account are a waste of time trying to harmonise.' The ghost of a smile crossed Singleton's dark features. Drinkwater sighed as the tension ebbed. He gestured to a chair and both men sat, thinking of the broken body of Lieutenant Francis Germaney lying on its cot. *Melusine* lay becalmed, rolling easily in a growing swell among the loose drift ice. On deck the watch fended off the larger flocs while the sun shone brilliantly, dancing in coruscating glory from several fantastically shaped bergs to the north. Within the cabin the gloom of death hung like a stink.

'How long will he live?'

'Not very long. The condylar process of the left mandible is shattered, the squamous part of the temporal bone is severely damaged and there is extensive haemorrhaging from the ascending pharyngeal artery. How the internal carotid and the associated veins were not ruptured I do not know but a portion of the left lower lobe of the cortex is penetrated by pieces of bone.'

Drinkwater sighed. 'I marked some preoccupation in him from

our first acquaintance, but I never guessed its origin,' he said at last. 'Might you have achieved a cure?'

Singleton shrugged. 'I believed that I might have achieved a clinical cure, he was receiving intra-urethral injections of caustic alkali and a solution of ammoniated mercury with opium. His progress was encouraging but I fear that his humour was morbid and the balance of his mind affected. He confided in me that he was affianced; I think it was this that drove him to such an extremity as to attempt his own life.'

Drinkwater shuddered, feeling a sudden guilt for his unsympathetic attitude to Germaney. 'Poor devil,' he said, adding 'you have him under sedation?'

Singleton nodded, 'Laudanum, sir.'

'Very well. And what of our other lost cause, Macpherson?'

'He will not last the week either.'

After Singleton had left the cabin Drinkwater sat for some minutes recollecting the numbers of men he had seen die. Of those to whom he had been close he remembered Madoc Griffiths, Master and Commander of the brig *Hellebore* who had died on the quarterdeck of a French frigate in the Red Sea; Blackmore, the elderly sailing master of the frigate *Cyclops* worn out by the cares and ill usage of the service. Major Brown of the Lifeguards had been executed as a spy and hung on a gibbet above the battery at Kijkduin as a warning to the British cutters blockading the Texel. More recently he thought of Mason, master's mate of the bomb vessel *Virago* who had died after the surgeon had failed to extract a splinter, of Easton, *Virago*'s sailing master, who had fallen at Copenhagen during a supposed 'truce'. And Matchett who had died in his arms. Now Germaney, a colleague who might, in time, have been a friend.

A sudden world-weariness overcame him and he was filled with a poignant longing to return home. To lie with Elizabeth would be bliss, to angle for minnows in the Tilbrook with his children charming beyond all reason.

But it was impossible. All about him *Melusine*, with her manifold responsibilities, creaked and groaned as the swell rolled her easily and the rudder bumped gently. He suddenly needed the refreshment of occupation and stood up. Flinging on his greygoe he went on deck.

A light breeze had sprung up from the westward and he

received Bourne's report with sudden interest. Most of the whalers were flensing their catches, rolling the great carcases over as the masthead tackles lifted strips of pale blubber from the dead whales whose corpses were further despoiled by scores of Greenland sharks. Flocks of screaming and hungry gulls filled the air alongside each of the whalers and only one had her boats out in search of further prey.

'Very well, Mr Bourne, be so kind as to rig out the gig immediately. I shall require a day's provisions and, tell Mr Pater, two kegs of rum, a breaker of water well wrapped in canvas. One of the young gentlemen may accompany me and Mr Quilhampton is to command the boat. They may bring muskets. You will command in my absence.'

'Aye, aye, sir.' Drinkwater watched Bourne react to this news by swallowing hard.

He turned away to pace the quarterdeck while the boat was being prepared. A day out of the ship would do him good. He had a notion to cruise towards the *Faithful* or the *Narwhal* and renew his acquaintance with Sawyers or Harvey. The expedition promised well and already he felt less oppressed.

It was so very easy to forget Germaney dying in his cot. The wind steadied at a light and invigorating breeze which set the green sea dancing in the sunlight. The ice shone with quite remarkable colours which little Frey identified as varying tints of violet, cerulean blue and viridian. The larger bergs towered over the gig in wonderful minarets, towers and spires, appearing like the fantastic palaces of fairy folk and even the edges of the ice floes were eroded in their melting by the warmer sea into picturesque overhangs and strange shapes that changed in their suggestion of something else as the boat swept past.

Somehow Drinkwater had imagined the Arctic as a vast area of icy desert and the proliferation and variety of the fauna astonished him. Quilhampton suggested taking potshots at every seal they saw but Drinkwater forbade it, preferring to encourage Mr Frey's talents with his pencil. It seemed there was scarcely a floe that did not possess at least one seal. They saw several walruses while the air was filled with gulls, ivory gulls, burgomaster gulls, the sabre winged fulmar petrels and the pretty little kittiwakes with their chevron-winged young. The rapid wing beats of the auks as they lifted hurriedly from the boat's bow seemed ludicrous until they spotted a pair swimming beneath the water. The razorbills raced after their invisible prey with the agility of tiny dolphins.

Under her lugsail the gig raced across the water, Quilhampton's ingenious wooden hand on the tiller impervious to the cold.

'She goes well, Mr Q.'

'Aye, sir, but not as fast as the Edinburgh Mail.' Mr Q gazed dreamily to windward his thoughts far from the natural wonders surrounding him and filled only with the remembered image of Catriona MacEwan.

Shooting between two ice floes they came upon the *Faithful* in the very act of lowering after a whale. Captain Sawyers hailed them and Drinkwater stood up in the boat to show himself.

'I give you God's love, Captain, follow us by all means but I beseech thee to lower thy sail or the fish will see it and sound,' the Quaker called from his quarterdeck through a trumpet. 'Thou seest now the wonders of God, Captain . . .' Drinkwater recollected their valedictory remarks in Bressay Sound and waved acknowledgement.

'Douse the sail, Mr Q, let us warm the hands at the oars and, Tregembo, do you show these whale-men how they are not the only seamen who can pull a boat.'

'Aye, zur.'

Melusine's gig took station astern of *Faithful*'s Number One boat with the redoubtable Elijah Pucill at her bow oar. The gig's crew did their best, but their boat was heavier and it was not long before they were overtaken by young Sawyers and then left astern as a third boat from the whaler, her crew grinning at the out-paced naval officers as they sat glumly regarding the sterns of the racing whale-boats.

There were two spare oars in the boat and Drinkwater touched Quilhampton's arm and nodded at them. Quilhampton took the hint.

'Mr Frey, do you ship an oar and lay your back into it eh? Better than looking so damned chilly,' he added with rasping kindness. The men lost stroke as Frey shipped an oar forward, but the boat was soon under way again and began to close upon the whalers.

'Come lads, pull there! We gain on them!' There were grins in the boat but Drinkwater, who had been studying events ahead cooled them.

'I fear, Mr Q, that you are not gaining. The others have stopped. I suspect the whale has sounded . . . there, see that flock of birds, the gulls that hover above the boats . . .'

'Oars!' ordered Quilhampton and the blades came up horizontally. The men panted over their looms, their breath cloudy and their faces flushed with effort. The boat lost way and they lay about half a cable from the whale-boats.

Carefully Drinkwater stood as Quilhampton ordered the oars across the boat.

'Issue a tot of grog, Mr Q,' said Drinkwater without taking his eyes from the patch of swirling water that lay between the whale-boats. In each of them the harpooners were up in their bows, weapons at the ready, while at the stern each boat-steerer seemed coiled over his steering oar. Drinkwater was aware of a fierce expectancy about the scene and while in his own boat a mood of mild levity accompanied the circulation of the beaker, the whale-boat crews were tense with the expectation of a sudden order.

Just ahead of them the *Faithful*'s third boat lay, with Pucill's slightly broader on the starboard bow and Sawyers's to larboard.

Suddenly it seemed to Drinkwater that the circling gulls ceased their aimless fluttering. He noted some arm movements in the boat ahead, then it began to backwater fast. The gulls were suddenly overhead, screaming and mewing.

'Give way, helm hard a-starboard!'

Even as he shouted the instruction it seemed the sea not ten yards away disappeared and was replaced by the surfacing leviathan. The great jaw with its livid lower lip covered by strange growths seemed to tower over them. Then the blue-black expanse of the creature's back rolled into view as it spouted, covering them with a warm, foetid-smelling mist. The oar looms bent as the men pulled the boat clear and Quilhampton held the tiller over to bring the gig round onto a course parallel with that of the whale.

As the sea subsided round the breaching monster they caught a glimpse of its huge tail just breaking the surface. From somewhere Pucill's boat appeared and they saw the other two beyond the cetacean. The whale did not seem to have taken alarm and, pulling steadily, they managed to keep pace as Pucill raced past them. Drinkwater saw the speksioneer raise his harpoon as his boat drew level with the whale's hump and it spouted again.

The weapon struck the whale and for a second the monster

seemed not to have felt it. Then it increased speed. Drinkwater could see the harpoon line snaking round the loggerhead and the faint wisp of smoke from the burning wood as Pucill paid it out. But the whale began to tow Pucill's boat. Already it was leaving *Melusine*'s gig behind and its flag was up to signal to the *Faithful* and the other boats on the far side of the whale that he was fast to a fish.

Then mysticetus lifted his mighty tail and sounded again. Pucill paid out line and Drinkwater judged the whale's dive to be almost vertical, as though the great animal sought safety in depth. Pucill's boat ceased its forward rush and the others, including the gig closed on him. Drinkwater saw frantic signals being made and Sawyers's boat ran alongside Pucill's to pass him more line. The speksioneer's boat began to move forward again, indicating the whale had levelled off and was swimming horizontally. Both the speksioneer's and the mate's boats were now in tandem, Sawyers's astern of Pucill's and Drinkwater bade Quilhampton follow as the third of *Faithful*'s boats was also doing.

Although they had no real part in the chase it seemed to every man in the gig that it was now a matter not only of honour but of intense interest to keep up with the frightened and wounded whale. But it was back-breaking work and soon clearly a vain effort, for the towed boats swung north and headed inexorably for the ice edge where a large floe blocked their passage.

They could hear faint shouts. 'Cut! Cut!' and 'Give her the boat, Elijah! Give her the boat!' There was a scrambling of bodies from the speksioneer's boat into that of the young mate then the latter was cut and free and swung aside. Pucill's boat was smashed against the edge of the floe under which the whale had passed yet the two remaining boats seemed to disregard this unhappy circumstance. Their courses diverging, they each headed for opposite extremities of the floe.

'I think, Mr Q, that it is time we set our sail again, I believe the wind to have strengthened.'

'Aye, aye, sir.'

Taking the nearer gap in the ice Quilhampton gave chase the instant the sail was sheeted home. Both the remaining whale-boats had hoisted flags and from occasional glimpses of these over the lower floes they were able to keep in touch. However it was soon apparent that the freshening of the wind was now to their advantage and they made gains on the nearer whale-boat as they wove between the ice. It was an exhilarating experience, for in the narrow leads the water was smooth yet the wind was strong as it blew over the flatter floes or funnelled violently between those with steeper sides. It seemed the whale was working to leeward. Unaware of the dangers of unseen underwater ledges of ice they were fortunate to escape with only a slight scraping of the boat as they rounded a small promontory of rotten ice from which half a dozen surprised seals plopped hurriedly into the sea, surfacing alongside to peer curiously at the passing gig.

Then, quite suddenly they came upon the death throes of the whale. Sawyers's boat was already alongside as the beast rolled and thrashed with its huge flukes. They let fly the sheets and watched as the unbarbed lances were driven into the fish again and again in an attempt to strike its heart. After a few minutes of agony it seemed to lie still and Quilhampton pointed to the approach of the second boat. Of the wrecked boat there was no sign, though the drag it had imposed upon the whale had clearly exhausted it. There was suddenly a boiling of the sea and a noise like gunfire. The whale's flukes struck the surface of the water with an explosive smack several times and then, as Sawyers continued to probe for its life, it twisted over and brought those huge flukes down upon the stern of its tormentor's boat. The Melusines watched in stupefied horror as the boat's bow flew into the air and her crew tumbled out and splashed into the sea.

But leviathan was dead. His heart had burst from the deadly incisions of Sawyers's lance and the muscle-rending effort of his dying act. The open water between the floes was red with its blood.

'Get that sail down, Tregembo! Give way and pick those men out of the water. Mr Frey, have the rum ready, the poor devils are going to need it.'

'Aye, aye, sir.'

'I thank thee for thy assistance, Friend.' Captain Sawyers raised his glass and Drinkwater savoured the richness of the Quaker's excellent port. A bogie stove in *Faithful*'s cabin burned cheerfully and Drinkwater felt warmed within and without. There remained only the ache in his neck and shoulder which he had come almost to disregard now. The sodden whale-boat's crew had been rolled in hot blankets and seemed little the worse for their experience, though Drinkwater had been chilled to the very marrow from a partial wetting in getting the hapless seamen out of the water. He remarked upon this to Sawyers.

'Aye, 'tis often to be wondered at. We have found men die of the cold long after being chafed with spirits and warmed with blankets. But the over-setting of a boat, whilst not common, is not unusual. Whalers are naturally hardy and wear many woollen undergarments, also the nature of their trade and the almost natural expectation of mishap, leads them to suffer less shock from the experience. These factors and a prompt rescue, Friend, I believe has preserved the life of many an immersed whale-man.'

'It was fortunate the fish turned down-wind or we could not have followed with such speed.'

'Aye, 'tis true that mysticetus will commonly run to windward but he sensed dense ice in that direction and from the exertions necessary to his escape had, perforce, to turn towards open water where he might breathe. Also friend, the wind freshened, which reminds me that if it backs another point or two thou shoulds't expect a gale of wind. For your assistance in rescuing my men I thank you as I do also for thy assistance in towing the fish alongside; there cannot be many who command King's ships who engage in such practices.' Sawyers smiled wryly.

Drinkwater tossed off his glass and picked up his hat. He grinned at the older man. 'The advantages of being a Tarpaulin officer, Captain, are better employed in the Arctic than in Whitehall.'

They shook hands and Drinkwater took his departure. Scrambling down the *Faithful*'s easy tumble-home he was aware that the cutting-in of the whale had already begun. Undeterred by his ducking, Elijah Pucill was already wielding his flensing iron as the try-tackles began to strip the blanket-piece from the carcase.

'By God, sir,' remarked Quilhampton as he settled himself in the stern sheets of the gig, 'they don't work Tom Cox's traverse aboard there.'*

'Indeed not, Mr Q.'

*To work Tom Cox's traverse meant to idle.

'The ship bore east-nor'-east from the whaler's mizen top, sir, about two leagues distant.'

'Very well, Mr Q, carry on.'

'Wind's freshening all the time, Mr Hill.'

'And backing Mr Gorton, wouldn't you say?'

'Aye, and inclined to be a trifle warmer I think, not that there's much comfort to be derived from that.'

'Ah, but what should you deduce from that observation, Mr Gorton?'

Gorton frowned and shook his head.

'Fog, Mr Gorton, fog and a whole gale before the day is out or you may rate me a Dutchman. You had better inform Mr Bourne and then hoist yourself aloft and see if you can spot the captain's boat.'

'Aye, aye, sir.'

Bourne came on deck, anxiety plain on his face. 'Have you news of the Captain, Mr Hill?'

'No, Mr Bourne, but Gorton's going aloft with a glass.'

Bourne looked aloft. *Melusine* lay under her spanker and fore-topmast staysail, her reefed maintopsail aback. Hove-to she drifted slowly to leeward, ready to fill her topsail and work to windward. Bourne looked to starboard. The nearest ice lay a league under the sloop's lee.

'D'you know the bearing of the nearest whaler, Mr Hill?'

'*Faithful*'s west-sou'-west with the *Narwhal* and *Truelove* further to the west among heavier ice.'

'Very well. Fill the main tops'l, we'll work the ship towards the ice to windward. That will be . . .' he looked at the compass.

'West-sou'-west,' offered Hill.

'Very well.' Bourne clasped his hands behind his back and walked to the windward rail. Standing at the larboard hance by Captain Palgrave's fussy brass carronade now covered in oiled canvas, Lieutenant Bourne felt terribly lonely. He began to worry over the rising wind while Hill had the watch brace the mainyards round. The last few days had demonstrated the dangers of the ice floes to a ship of *Melusine*'s light build. The speed with which the ice moved had amazed them and all their skill had been needed to manoeuvre the ship clear of the danger. Captain Drinkwater's written orders to his watch-keeping officers had been specific: *At all costs close proximity with the ice is to be avoided and offing is to be made even at the prospect of losing contact with the whalers.* To move *Melusine* to safety now meant that the captain might be unable to relocate them and with fog coming on there was no longer the refuge contained in Captain Drinkwater's order book: *If in any doubt whatsoever, do not hesitate to inform me.*

In a moment of angry uncertainty Bourne damned Germaney for his insanity. Then worry reasserted itself, worming in the pit of his stomach like some huge parasite. He looked again and looked in vain for the ice edge. Already a white fog was swirling towards them. He ran forward and lifted the speaking trumpet.

'Masthead there!'

'Sir?' Gorton leaned from the crow's nest.

'D'you see anything of the gig?'

'Nothing, sir.'

'God damn and blast it!' He thought for a moment longer and then made up his mind, hoping that Captain Drinkwater had remained safe aboard one of the whalers.

'Mr Hill! Put the ship about, course south, clear of this damned ice.'

Like the good sailing master he was, Hill obeyed the order of the young commissioned officer and brought *Melusine* onto the starboard tack. Then he crossed the deck and addressed Bourne.

'Mr Bourne, if the captain's adrift in this fog he'll lose the ship. My advice is to give him minute guns and heave to again after you've run a league to the southward.'

Bourne looked at the older man and Hill saw the relief plain in his eyes.

'Very well, Mr Hill, will you see to it.'

Already the white wraiths curled across the deck and the next instant every rope began to drip moisture and the damp chill of a dense fog isolated the ship.

Chapter Nine *June–July 1803*

The Mercy of God

It was intuition that told Drinkwater a change in the weather was imminent, intuition and a nervous awareness of altering circumstances. He was slowly awakened to a growing ache in his neck and a dimming of the brilliance of the ice which combined with a softening of its shadows. The day lost its colour and the atmosphere began to feel oddly hostile. The birds were landing on the sea and were airborne in fewer numbers.

He touched Quilhampton's arm as the boat ran between two ice floes some seven or eight feet tall. The lead through which they were running was some hundred yards across, with a patch of open sea visible ahead of them from which, when they reached it, they hoped to catch sight of *Melusine*. Quilhampton turned. 'Sir?'

'Fog, Mr Q, fog and wind,' he said in a low voice.

Their eyes met and Quilhampton replied, 'Pray God we make the ship, sir.'

'Amen to that, Mr Q.'

Quilhampton, who had been dreaming again of Catriona, pulled himself together and concentrated on working the gig even faster through the lead to reach the open water before the fog closed over them.

Drinkwater ordered Frey to pass another issue of rum to the men who sat shivering in the bottom of the boat. The warmth had gone out of the sun and the approaching fog made the air damp. He heard Quilhampton swear and looked up. The lead between the floes was narrowing as they spun slowly in the wind. He was conscious of a strong and unpleasant smell from the algae on the closing ice.

'Get the oars to work, Tregembo!' Drinkwater snapped and the men, looking round and grasping the situation at a glance, were quick to obey. Already the lead had diminished by half.

'Pull, damn you!'

The boat headed for the narrowing gap with perhaps a cable to run before reaching the open water. The men grunted with effort as they tugged the gig forwards while in the stern Drinkwater and Quilhampton watched anxiously. The gap ahead was down to twenty yards. The sail flapped uselessly as the wind died in the lee of the converging ice. Drinkwater looked anxiously on either side of them, seeking some ledge on the ice upon which they could scramble when the floes ground together and crushed the boat like an eggshell. But both floes were in an advanced state of melting, their waterlines eroded, their surfaces overhanging in an exaggerated fashion. In a minute or two the oars would be useless as there would be insufficient room to extend them either side of the boat. He wished he had a steering oar with which to give the boat a little more chance.

'Keep pulling, men, then trail oars as soon as you feel the blades touch the ice. Mr Frey, get that damned mast down.' He tried to keep his voice level but apprehension and a sudden bitter chill from the proximity of the ice made it shake. The floes had almost met overhead so that they pulled in a partial tunnel. Then there was a crash astern. Drinkwater looked round. The lead had closed behind them and a wave of water was rushing towards the gig's transom.

'Pull!' he shouted, turning forward to urge the men, but as he did so he saw them leaning backwards, the looms of their oars sweeping over their heads as they allowed them to trail. They tensed for the impact of the ice when the wave hit them. The boat was thrust abruptly forward as the ice met overhead. Lumps of it dropped into the boat and there were muttered curses as the midshipman, helped now by idle oarsmen got the mast into the boat not an instant too soon.

Suddenly they were in open water and, a moment later in a dense fog.

'Did anyone see the ship?' Drinkwater asked sharply.

There was a negative muttering.

'We have exchanged the frying pan for the fire, Mr Q.'

'Aye, sir.' Quilhampton sat glumly. The heart-thumping excitement of the race against the closure of the ice had had at least the advantage of swift resolution. Catriona might one day learn he had died crushed in Arctic ice and it seemed to him a preferable death to freezing and starving in an open boat. He was about to ask how long Captain Drinkwater thought they could survive when he saw the men exchange glances and Midshipman Frey looked aft, his face pale with anxiety. He pulled himself together. He was in command of the boat, damn it, despite the fact that *Melusine*'s captain sat beside him.

'Permission to re-ship the mast, sir.'

Drinkwater nodded. He looked astern. They were well clear of the ice and already feeling the effect of the wind. 'Aye, but do not hoist the sail.'

'Aye, aye, sir.' Quilhampton nodded at the junior midshipman. 'Step that mast forrard!'

There was a scrambling and a knocking as the stumpy spar with its iron traveller and single halliard was relocated in the hole in the thwart. The men assisted willingly, glad of something to do. When it was done they subsided onto the thwarts and again looked aft.

'Have all the oars secured inboard and two watches told off. You will take one and I the other. Tregembo pick the hands in Mr Quilhampton's watch and Mr Frey you will pick those in mine. I will take the tiller, Mr Q, whilst you make an issue of grog and biscuit. We will then set the watches and heave the gig to. At regular intervals the bowman will holloa and listen for the echo of his voice. If he hears it we may reasonably expect that ice is close but from what we saw there is little ice to leeward, though some may drift that way at a greater speed than ourselves. In this case we have only to put up the helm and run away from it while its protection to windward will reduce the violence of the sea. The watch below will huddle together to get what warmth it can. Captain Sawyers was only just relating many whaleboat crews have survived such circumstances so there is little to be alarmed about.'

The last sentence was a bare-faced lie, but it had its effect in cheering the men and they went about their tasks with a show of willingness.

With greater misgivings and the pain in his shoulder nagging at him appallingly, Drinkwater sat hunched in the stern-sheets.

Singleton looked at the blade of the catling as the loblolly boy held the lantern close. There was no trace of mist upon it. Francis Germaney had breathed his last.

'One for the sail-maker, eh sir?' The loblolly boy's grin was wolfish. It was always good to bury an officer, especially one who had the sense to blow his brains out. Or make a mess of it, the man thought, thereby casting doubts on whether he had them in the first place.

Singleton looked coldly at Skeete who stared back.

'I'll plug his arse and lay him out for the sail-maker, sir.'

'Be silent, Skeete, you blackguard!' snapped Singleton impatiently, rising and for the hundredth time cracking his head on the deckbeam above. He left the first lieutenant's cabin hurriedly to the accompaniment of Skeete's diabolical laughter. A loblolly 'boy' of some twenty years experience and some fifty years of age, Skeete was enjoying himself. To the added pleasure of witnessing the demise of an officer, a circumstance which in Skeete's opinion was all too rare an occurrence, he derived a degree of satisfaction from the office he was about to perform upon such an august corpse as that of Lieutenant Francis Germaney, Royal Navy. Further, since ridding themselves of the drunken oppression of Macpherson, Skeete and his mate had enjoyed an autonomy previously unknown to them. Mr Singleton's remarkable ability in reviving Leek had impressed the surgeon's assistants less than the rest of the crew. To Skeete and his mate, Singleton was not a proper ship's officer and, being a damned parson with pronounced views upon flogging and the Articles of War, could be insulted with a fair degree of impunity. Skeete could not remember enjoying himself so much since he last visited Diamond Lil's at Portsmouth Point.

In search of Drinkwater Singleton arrived on deck to be knocked to his knees by a seaman jumping clear as Number Nine gun fired and recoiled.

'Mind you f . . . Oh, beg pardon, sir,' the man grinned sheepishly and helped the surgeon to his feet. Somewhat shaken and uncertain as to the cause of the noise and apparent confusion as the gun crew reloaded and hauled up the piece, Singleton made his way aft.

'Is something the matter, Mr Hill?' he asked the master.

'Bosun's mate, take that man's name and tell him I'll give him a check shirt at the gangway the next time he forgets to swab his gun . . . matter, Mr Singleton? Merely that there is a fog and the captain has yet to return.'

'Fog?' Singleton turned and noticed the shroud that covered the ship for the first time. He looked sharply at Hill. 'You mean that the captain's lost in this fog? In that little boat?'

'So it would seem, Mr Singleton. And the little boat is his gig . . . now if you will excuse me . . . Mackman, you Godforsaken whoreson, coil that fall the other way, God damn you bloody landsmen!'

Singleton pressed aft aware that not only was the *Melusine* shrouded in dense fog but that the wind was piping in the rigging and that the ship was beginning to lift to an increasingly rough sea as she came clear of the ice.

Mr Bourne, now in command, stood miserably at the windward rail with a worried looking Rispin, promoted abruptly and unwilling to first lieutenant. It was clear, even to Singleton's untutored eye, that Stephen Hill was in real command. Although he realised with a pang that he felt very uneasy without Drinkwater's cock-headed presence on the quarterdeck, he felt a measure of reassurance in Hill's competence. Knowing something of the promotion-hungry desires of lieutenants and midshipmen Singleton wondered to what extent efforts were being made to recover the captain, then he recollected his duty and struggled across the deck towards Bourne.

A patter of spray flew aft and drove the breath from his body as he reached the anxious lieutenant. 'Mr Bourne!'

'Eh? Singleton, what is it?'

Bourne's cloak blew round him and his uncertainty seemed epitomised by the way he clutched the fore-cock of his hat to prevent it blowing away.

'Mr Germaney has expired.'

'Oh.' There seemed little else to say except, 'Thank you, Mr Singleton.'

Frozen to the marrow Singleton made his way to the companionway. As he swung himself down a second dollop of spray caught him and Number Nine gun roared again. Reaching the sanctuary of his cabin he flung himself on his knees.

Afterwards Drinkwater was uncertain how long they nursed the gig through that desperate night, for night it must have been. Certainly the fog obscured much of the sunlight and prevented even a glimpse of the sun itself so that it became almost dark. After the twists and turns of their passage through the ice, and his preoccupation in avoiding damage to the boat, Drinkwater had to admit to being lost. The pain in his neck and the growing numbness of his extremities seemed to dull his brain so that his mental efforts were reduced to the sole consideration of keeping the boat reasonably dry and as close to the wind as they were able. He dare not run off before it for, although its effect would be less chilling, he feared far more the prospect of being utterly lost, while every effort he made to retain his position increased his chances of being not too far distant from the whalers or the *Melusine* when the fog lifted.

The boat's crew spent a miserable night and at one point he recovered sufficient awareness to realise he had his arm round the shoulders of little Frey who was shuddering uncontrollably and trying desperately to muffle the chattering of his teeth and the sobbing of his breath. Tregembo and Quilhampton huddled together, their familiarity readily breaking down the barriers of rank, while further forward the other men groaned, swore and crouched equally frozen.

Occasionally Drinkwater rallied, awakened to full consciousness by a sudden, agonising spasm in his shoulder, only to curse the self-indulgence that had led to this folly and probable death. He realised with a shock that he was not much moved by the contemplation of death, and with it came the realisation that his hands and feet felt warmer. For a second sleep threatened to overwhelm him and he knew it was the kiss of approaching death. A picture of Charlotte Amelia and Richard Madoc swam before his eyes, he tried to conjure up Elizabeth but found it impossible. Then he became acutely aware that the boy beside him was his son, not the baby he had left behind, but Richard at ten or eleven years. The boy's face was glowing, his full lips sweet and his eyes the deep brown of his mother's.

'Farewell, father,' the boy was saying, 'farewell, for we shall never meet again . . .'

'No, stay . . .!' Drinkwater was fully conscious, his mind filled with the departing vision of his son. A seaman whose name he could not remember looked aft from the bow. Drinkwater came suddenly to himself, aware that the extremities of his limbs were lifeless. He tried to move the midshipman. Mr Frey was asleep.

'Mr Frey! Mr Frey! Wake up! Wake up, all of you! Wake up, God damn it . . . and you, forrard, why ain't you holloaing like you were ordered . . . Come on holloa! All of you holloa and sing! Sing

God damn and blast you, clap your hands! Stamp your feet! Mr Frey give 'em grog and make the bastards sing . . .'

'Sing, sir?' Frey awoke as though recalled from a distant place.

'Aye, Mr Frey, sing!'

Realisation awoke slowly in the boat and men groaned with the agony of moving. But Frey passed the keg of grog and they drained it greedily, the raw spirit quickening their hearts and circulation so that they at last broke into a cracked and imperfect chorus of 'Spanish Ladies'.

And just as suddenly as Drinkwater had roused them to sing, he commanded them to silence. They sat, even more dejected now that the howl of the wind reasserted itself and the boat bucked up and down and water slopped inboard over them.

The minute gun sounded again.

'A six-pounder, by God!'

'M'loosine, zur,' said Tregembo grinning.

'Listen for the next to determine whether the distance increases.' They sat silent for what seemed an age. The concussion came again.

' 'Tis nearer, zur.'

'Further away . . .'

They sat through a further period of tense silence. The gun sounded yet again.

Three voices answered at once. They were unanimous, 'Nearer!'

'Let us bear off a little, Mr Q. Remain silent there and listen for the guns, but each man is to chafe his legs . . . Mr Frey perhaps you would oblige me by checking the priming of those muskets. Then you had better rub Mr Q's calves. His hand may be impervious to the cold but his legs ain't.'

Half an hour later they were quite sure the *Melusine*'s guns were louder, but the sea was rising and water entering the boat in increasing amounts. The hands were employed baling and Drinkwater decided it was time they discharged the muskets. They waited for the sound of the guns. The boom seemed slightly fainter.

The muskets cracked and they waited for some response. Nothing came. The next time the minute gun fired it was quite definitely further away.

The fog lifted a little towards dawn. Those on *Melusine*'s quarter-deck could see a circle of tossing and streaked water some five cables in radius about them.

'With this increase in visibility, Mr Bourne, I think we can afford to take a chance. I suggest we put the ship about and stand back to the northward for a couple of hours.'

Bourne considered the proposition. 'Very well, Mr Hill, see to it.'

Melusine jibbed at coming into the wind under such reduced canvas as she was carrying and Hill wore her round. She steadied on the larboard tack, head once more to the north and Hill transferred the duty gun-crew to a larboard gun. It was pointless firing to windward. After a pause the cannon, Number Ten, roared out. *Melusine* groaned as she rose and fell, occasionally shuddering as a sea broke against her side and sent the spray across her rail.

'Sir! Sir!' Midshipman Gorton was coming aft from the foremast where he had been supervising the coiling of the braces.

'What is it?'

'I'm certain I heard something ahead, sir . . .'

'In this wind? . . .'

'A moment, Mr Rispin, what did you hear?'

'Well sir, it sounded like muskets, sir . . .'

The quarterdeck officers strained their eyes forward.

'Fo'c's'le there!' roared Hill. 'Keep your eyes open, there!'

'There sir! There!' Midshipman Gorton was crouching, his arm and index finger extended over the starboard bow.

'Mark it, Mr Gorton, mark it. Leggo lee mizen braces, there! Mizen yards aback!'

'Thank God,' breathed Mr Rispin.

'Thank Hill and Gorton, Mr Rispin,' said Lieutenant Bourne.

Mr Frey saw the ship a full minute before Mr Gorton heard the muskets.

'Drop the sail, Mr Q! Man the oars my lads, your lives depend upon it!'

They were clumsy getting the oars out, their tired and aching muscles refusing to obey, but Tregembo cursed them from the after thwart and set the stroke.

Drinkwater took them across *Melusine*'s bow to pull up from leeward. He could see the sloop was hove-to and making little headway but he felt easier when he saw the mizen topsail backed.

As they approached it was clear that even on her leeward side it was going to be impossible to recover the boat. He watched as several ropes' ends were flung over the side and men climbed into the chains to assist. The painter was caught at the third and increasingly feeble throw and the gig was dashed against *Melusine*'s spirketting and then her chains. The tie-rods extending below the heavy timbers of the channels smashed the gunwhale of the boat, but as the gig dropped into the hollow of the sea Drinkwater saw one pair of legs left dangling over the ledge of the chains where willing hands reached down. It was not a time for prerogative and Drinkwater refused to leave the boat until all the others were safe. He had little fear for the seamen, for all were fit, agile and used to scrambling about. But Frey was very cold and his limbs were cramped. Drinkwater called for a line and a rope snaked down into the boat. He passed a bowline round Frey's waist as the men scrambled out of the boat. As the gig rose and the rope was hauled tight, Drinkwater tried to support the boy. Suddenly the boat fell, half rolling over as the inboard gunwhale caught again and threatened to overset it. Frey dangled ten feet overhead, the line rigged from the cro'jack yardarm had plucked him from the boat. One of his shoes fell past Drinkwater as he grabbed a handhold. He looked down to find the gig half full of water. The mizen whip was already being pulled inboard and Drinkwater shouted.

'Mr Q! Up you go!' Quilhampton waited his moment. As the boat rose he leapt, holding his wooden left hand clear and extending his right. He missed his footing but someone grabbed his extended arm and his abdomen caught on the edge of the channel. Hands grabbed the seat of his trousers and he was dragged inboard winded and gagging.

Only Drinkwater was left. He felt impossibly weak. Above him the whole ship's company watched. He was aware of Tregembo, wet to the skin and frozen after his ordeal, leaning outboard from the main chains. One hand was extended.

'Come *on*, zur!' he shouted, a trace of his truculent, Cornish independence clear in his eyes.

Drinkwater felt the boat rise sluggishly beneath him. She would not swim for many more minutes. He leaped upwards, aware that his outstretched arm was only inches from Tregembo's hand, but the boat fell away and he with it, suddenly up to his waist in water as the gig sank under him.

'Here, zur, here!'

He felt the rope across his shoulders and with a mighty effort passed a bight about his waist, holding the rope with his left hand

and the loose end with his right. He felt himself jar against the barnacled spirketting and the weight on his left arm told where he hung suspended by its feeble grip, then that too began to slide while he tried to remember how to make a one-handed bowline with his right hand. Then *Melusine* gave a lee roll and a sea reached up under his shoulders. He was suddenly level with the rail, could see the faces lining the hammock nettings. In an instant the sea would drop away again as the sloop rolled to windward. He felt the support of the water begin to fall yet he was quite unable to remember how to make that first loop.

Then hands reached out for him. He was grabbed unceremoniously. The sea dropped away and he was pulled over the nettings and laid with gentle respect upon the deck. He looked up to see the face of Singleton.

'The mercy of God, Captain Drinkwater,' he said, 'has been extended to us all this day . . .'

And the fervent chorus of 'Amens' surprised even the semi-conscious Drinkwater.

Chapter Ten *July 1803*

The Seventy-second Parallel

'Sir! Sir!'

Drinkwater swam upwards from a great depth and was aware that Midshipman Wickham was shaking him. 'Eh? What is it?'

'Mr Rispin's compliments, sir, but would you come on deck.'

'What time is it?'

'Nearly eight bells in the morning watch, sir.'

'Very well.' He longed to fling himself back into his cot for he had been asleep no more than three or four hours and every muscle in his body ached. He idled for a moment and heard a sudden wail of pipes at the companionways and the cry for all hands as *Melusine*'s helm went down and she came up into the wind. Two minutes later, in a coat and greygoe that were still wet under his tarpaulin, he was on deck.

'The smell made me suspicious, sir,' cried Rispin, his voice high with anxiety, 'then the wind fell away and then we saw it . . .' He pointed.

Drinkwater's tired eyes focussed. Half a mile away, rearing into the sky and looming over their mastheads the iceberg seemed insubstantial in the grey light. But the smell, like the stink he had noticed in the ice lead, was strongly algaic and the loss of wind was evidence of its reality. *Melusine* seemed to wallow helplessly and, although Rispin had succeeded in driving her round onto the larboard tack, there seemed scarcely enough wind now to move her as the mass of ice loomed closer.

Drinkwater stood stupefied for a moment or two, trying to remember what he had learned from fragments of conversation with the whale-ship captains. It was little enough, and he felt the gaps in his knowledge like physical wounds at such a moment.

He had read of the submerged properties of icebergs, that far more of them existed below the level of the sea than above. Part of the monster that threatened them might already be beneath them.

'A cast of the lead, Mr Rispin, and look lively about it!'

Above his head *Melusine*'s canvas slatted idly. 'T'gallant halliards there, topman aloft and let fall the t'gallants! Fo'c's'le head there! Set both jibs!' The waist burst into life as every man sought occupation. Drinkwater was left to reflect on Newton's observations upon the attraction of masses. Ship and iceberg seemed to be drawn inexorably together.

'By the mark seven, sir!'

'That'll be ice, sir,' Hill remarked, echoing his own thoughts.

'Aye.'

'Let fall! Let fall!' Lieutenant Bourne had taken the deck from Rispin and the topgallants hung in folds from their lowered yards.

'Hoist away!' The yards rose slowly, their parrels creaking up the slushed t'gallant masts as the topmen slid down the backstays.

'Sheet home!'

'Belay!'

Amidships the braces were ready manned as the halliards stretched the sails. Watching anxiously Drinkwater thought he saw the upper canvas belly a little.

'By the mark five, sir!' The nearest visible part of the iceberg was half a musket shot away to starboard. Drinkwater sensed *Melusine*'s deck cant slightly beneath his feet. He was so tense that for a moment he thought they had touched a spur of ice but suddenly *Melusine* caught the wind eddying round the southern extremity of the berg. Her upper sails filled, then her topsails; she began to move with gathering swiftness through the water.

'By the deep nine, sir!'

Drinkwater began to breathe again. *Melusine* came clear of the iceberg and the wind laid her on her beam ends. Just as suddenly as it had come the fog lifted. The wind swung to the north-northwest and blew with greater violence, but the sudden shift reduced the lift of the sea, chopping up a confused tossing of wave crests in which *Melusine* pitched wildly while her shivering topmen lay aloft again to claw in the topgallants they had so recently set.

As the visibility cleared it became apparent that the gale had dispersed the ice floes and they were surrounded by pieces of ice of every conceivable shape and size. Realising that he could not keep the deck forever, Drinkwater despatched first Bourne and then

Rispin aloft to the crow's nest from where they shouted down directions to the doubled watches under Drinkwater and Hill, and for three days, while the gale blew itself out from the north they laboured through this vast and treacherous waste.

The huge bergs were easy to avoid, now that clear weather held, but the smaller bergs and broken floes of hummocked ice frequently required booming off from either bow with the spare topgallant yards. Worst of all were the 'growlers', low, almost melted lumps of ice the greater part of whose bulk lay treacherously below water. Several of these were struck and *Melusine*'s spirketting began to assume a hairy appearance, the timber being so persistently scuffed by ice.

Drinkwater perceived the wisdom of a rig that was easily handled by a handful of men as Sawyers had claimed at Shetland. He also wished he had the old bomb vessel *Virago* beneath his feet, a thought which made him recollect his interview with Earl St Vincent. It seemed so very far distant now and he had given little thought to his responsibilities during the last few days, let alone the possibility of French privateers being in these frozen seas. He wished St Vincent had had a better knowledge of the problems of navigation in high latitudes and given him a more substantial vessel than the corvette. Lovely she might be and fast she might be, but the Greenland Sea was no place for such a thoroughbred.

They buried Germaney the day following Drinkwater's return to *Melusine*. It was a bleak little ceremony that had broken up in confusion at a cry for all hands to wear ship and avoid a growler of rotten ice. Singleton's other major patient, the now insane Macpherson, lay inert under massive doses of laudanum to prevent his ravings from disturbing the watch below.

On the fifth day of the gale they sighted *Truelove* and made signals to her across eight miles of tossing ice and grey sea. She was snugged down under her lower sails and appeared as steady as a rock amid the turmoil about her. A day later they closed *Diana*, then *Narwhal*, *Provident* and *Earl Percy* hove in sight, both making the signal that all was well. On the morning that the wind died away there seemed less ice about and once again *Faithful* was sighted, about ten miles to the north-west and making the signal that whales were in sight.

Greatly refreshed from an uninterrupted sleep of almost twelve hours, wrote Drinkwater in his journal, *I woke to the strong impression that my life had been spared by providence* . . . He paused. The vision of Midshipman Frey as his son had been a vivid one and he was certain that had he not awakened to full consciousness at the time he would not have survived the ordeal in the open boat. The consequences of his folly in leaving the ship struck him very forcibly and he resolved never to act so rashly again. In his absence Germaney had died and he still felt pangs of conscience over his former first lieutenant. He shook off the 'blue devils' and his eye fell upon the portraits upon the cabin bulkhead, and particularly that of his little son. He dipped his pen in the ink-well.

The conviction that I was awoken in the boat by the spirit of my son is almost impossible to shake off, so fast has it battened upon my imagination. I am persuaded that we were past saving at that moment and would have perished had I not been revived by the apparition. He paused again and scratched out the word apparition substituting *visitation*. He continued writing and ended: *the sighting of* Faithful *reassured me that my charges had made lighter of the gale than ourselves, for though nothing carried away aloft* Melusine *is making more water than formerly.* Faithful *made the signal for whales almost immediately upon our coming up and the whale ships stood north where, inexplicably, there seems to be less ice. The cold seems more intense.*

He laid his pen down, closed his journal and slipped it into the table drawer.

'Pass word for Mr Hill!'

He heard the marine sentry's response passed along and rose, pulling out the decanter and two glasses from the locker where Cawkwell had secured them.

'Come in,' he called as Hill knocked and entered the cabin. 'Ah, take a seat, Mr Hill, I am sure you will not refuse a glass on such a raw morning.'

'Indeed not, sir . . . thank you.'

Drinkwater sipped the blackstrap and re-seated himself.

'Mr Hill, we have known each other a long time and now that Germaney is dead I have a vacancy for a lieutenant . . . no, hear me out. I can think of no more deserving officer on this ship. I will give you an acting commission and believe I possess sufficient influence to have it ratified on our return. Now, what d'you say, eh?'

'That's considerate of you, sir, but no, I . . .'

'Damn it, Bourne's told me that without you he'd have been

hard pushed to work the ship through the fog, he's a good fellow and does you the credit you deserve. With a master's warrant you'll never get command and the advancement you should have. Recollect old James Bowen, Earl Howe's Master of the Fleet, when asked what he would most desire for his services at the First of June, asked for a commission.'

'Aye, sir, that's true, but Bowen was made prize agent for the fleet, he'd no need to worry about the loss of pay. I've no private income and have a family to support. Besides, Bowen still had the earl's patronage whilst I, with all due respect to yourself, sir, would likely remain a junior lieutenant for the rest of my service. At least now I receive ninety-one pounds per annum, which even less five guineas for the income tax, is more than a junior lieutenant's pay. In addition, sir, with my warrant I'm a standing officer and even if the ship is laid up I still receive pay. Thank you all the same, sir.'

Drinkwater refilled Hill's glass. It was no less than he expected Hill to say and he reflected upon the stupidity of a system which denied men of Hill's ability proper recognition.

'Very well then. Whom do you think I should promote? Gorton has his six years almost in and is the senior, Quilhampton is but a few months his junior but holds a certificate from the Trinity House as master's mate. I am faced with a dilemma in that my natural inclination is to favour Quilhampton because he is known to me. I would welcome your advice.'

Hill sighed and crossed his legs. 'I have seen neither of them in action, sir, but I would rate both equally.'

'The decision is invidious, but you incline to neither . . .?'

'Sir, if I may be frank . . .?'

'Of course.'

'Then I should favour Mr Gorton, sir. Mr Quilhampton is both junior and a mite younger, I believe. Your favouring him would seem like patronage and I think that his hand might prove a handicap.'

Drinkwater nodded. 'Very well, Mr Hill. I do not approve of your pun but your reasoning is sound enough. Be so kind as to have a quiet word with Mr Q, that his disappointment is tempered by the reflection that he has not lost my confidence.'

'Aye, aye, sir.' Hill rose.

'One other thing . . .'

'Sir?'

'Do not mention the matter of the hand as deciding one way or another. I do not really think it a great disadvantage. It is quite impervious to cold, d'you know.'

Singleton looked with distaste at what had once been the person of Mr Macpherson the surgeon. He lay stupefied under ten grains of laudanum, his face grey, the cheeks cadaverous and pallid with a sheen of sweat that gleamed like condensation on a lead pipe under the lantern light.

He could almost *feel* Skeete grinning in the shadows next to him. Singleton thought a very un-Christian thought, and was mortified by the ferocity of it. Why, why did Macpherson not die? Rum had long since destroyed his brain and now deprivation of it had turned him into a thrashing maniac. Yet his punished organs refused to capitulate to the inevitable, and he came out of his stupor to roll and rave in his own stink until Skeete cleaned him up and Singleton sedated him once more.

Singleton forbore to hate what Drinkwater had trapped him into accepting. He saw it as a God-given challenge that he must overcome his revolted instincts. This was a testing for the future and the squalor of life among the eskimos. He tried to thank God for the opportunity to harden himself for his coming ordeal. Attending Macpherson was as logical a piece of divine intervention as was the discovery of Meetuck, and Singleton knew he had been right, that men's cleverness did indeed obscure the obvious. Was it not crystal clear that God himself had intervened in thus providing him with a means of preparing himself for the future?

There was also the matter of Drinkwater's survival in the gig. It appalled Singleton that the matter was taken so lightly on board. It struck Singleton as a kind of blasphemy. He was not used to the thousand tricks that fate may play a seaman in the course of a few days. He could not lie down and forget how close he had been to death a few hours ago, and worse, he could not forget how the ship had missed the steadying presence of her commander. There had been no doubt as to Hill's competence, indeed it was enhanced by the lower deck opinions he had heard about the other officers, but Hill had been alone and his isolation emphasised the loss of Drinkwater.

From the rough, untutored tarpaulin of first impression, Singleton had come to like the sea-officer with the cock-headed figure and the lined face. The mane of brown hair pulled impatiently behind his head in a black-ribboned queue told of a still youthful man, a man in his prime, a man of implicit reliability. Singleton began to lose his unfortunate prejudice against the profession of arms, though his own principles remained admirably steadfast. They might appear impractical to the world of sophistry, the world in which Drinkwater was enmeshed, but Singleton was bound upon a mission inspired by the Son of God. Among the primitive peoples of the earth he would prove a theory practical, a theory more shattering in its simplicity than the prolix vapourings of the Revolutionary pedagogues that had apostrophised the French Revolution. He would prove practical the Gospel of Christ.

But although he was motivated by the spirit, Singleton was unable to ignore reality, and he had become aware that without Drinkwater he would be unlikely to find the kind of co-operation he required to land upon the coast of Greenland. He began to be obsessed with the preservation of Drinkwater's health, particularly since the ordeal in the open boat, after which the captain had become thin and drawn. Looking down on the inert body of the *ci-devant* surgeon he decided there were more pressing things for him to attend to.

'Try and get some portable soup into him,' he said dismissively to Skeete, and turned in search of the companionway and the freezing freshness of the upper deck.

And there Singleton found further evidence of the beneficence of the Almighty in the person of Meetuck engaged, with two seamen as his assistants to supplement his broken arm, in completing the preparations of the bear and seal skins. Meetuck's conversation had enabled Singleton to turn the theoretical knowledge he had acquired at Copenhagen into a practical instrument and already Meetuck had submitted himself to baptism.

But in his eagerness to converse colloquially, to perfect his knowledge of the eskimo tongue and to test his ability to spread the gospel of Christ, Singleton had paid little attention to those things he might have learned from the eskimo. Beyond the knowledge that Meetuck had lost touch with his companions in a fog, fallen and injured himself, losing his kayak in the process, Singleton learned only that he came from a place called Nagtoralik, and called his people the Ikermiut, the people of the Strait. Some prompting from a more curious, though preoccupied Drinkwater, elicited the information that this 'strait' was far to the westward, and thus, by deduction, on the coast of Greenland. In his heart Singleton believed that it was where he would establish his mission on behalf of the Church Missionary Society. Eager to convert Meetuck it never occurred to Singleton that a male of Meetuck's maturity ought to have survived better on the ice, and the eskimo's lack of intelligence never prompted him to volunteer information he was not specifically asked for. All Meetuck knew was that Singleton was a *gavdlunaq*, a white man, and that he seemed to be a good one. In his simple mind Meetuck strove to please the men that had rescued him and fed him so well.

Seeing Singleton, Meetuck looked up and smiled, his thin lips puckering the wind-burned cheeks and his mongol eyes became dark slits. He said something and indicated the skins, particularly that of the polar bear, which he gently smoothed.

'It was a great bear,' Singleton translated for the puzzled seamen, 'and he who killed it was a mighty hunter . . .' The two men seemed to think this a quaint turn of phrase and giggled, having been much amused by Meetuck's antics and incomprehension at their inability to speak as did Singleton. Singleton was affronted by their attitude, his almost humourless disposition unable to see the amusement caused by the eskimo. 'Like Nimrod . . .' His voice trailed away and he turned aft to see the captain coming on deck, his boat cloak over the greygoe in the intense cold. It struck him that Drinkwater would benefit himself from warmer clothing and he turned below again in search of Mount.

The marine lieutenant was dicing with Rispin when he entered the gunroom.

'Ho, there, Singleton, d'you come to taste the delights of damnation then?' Mount grinned at the sober missionary whose disapproval extended to almost all the leisure activities of both officers and midshipmen, especially, as was now the case, it was accompanied by the drinking of alcohol. Singleton swallowed his disapproval and gave one of his rare, dry smiles.

'Ah, Mount, I wish you to prove that you deceive my eyes and are not yet sunk to a depravity that is beyond redemption.'

Mount rolled his eyes at Rispin, 'Lo, Rispin, I do believe I am being granted a little Christian forbearance. What is it you want?'

'Your polar bear's hide.'

'Egad,' Mount smote his breast in mock horror, 'you press me sore, good sir. Why?'

'I wish to have it for a good cause.'

'Ah-ha! Now it becomes clear, Mr Singleton, you wish to deprive me of the spoils of my skill so that I shall freeze and you will be warm as an ember, eh?'

'You misunderstand . . .'

Mount held up his hand, 'Are you aware what trouble I went to, to stop that whelp Quilhampton from claiming the damned animal was his. He had the nerve to claim that without his winging the brute I should not have struck him. There! What d'you think of that, eh?'

'I think it most likely, certainly he did very well to hit a target with his wooden hand.'

'Oh, I do not think you need worry about Mr Q's abilities. He does not seem in any way handicapped. No, Mr Singleton, you want the bear's pelt and so do I. Now what do you suggest we do with it, Rispin? How would you, old Solomon, decide between the two of us, eh?' Mount's eyes fell significantly upon the dice.

'But, Mount, it is not for myself that I wish to have the skin, I have already purchased several of the seal-skins.'

'What is it for then? Not that damned eskimo friend of ours?'

'No. For the Captain, I fear he may have taken a chill and you know that in this weather a chill may become bronchitic or worse, induce a pulmonary inflammation.'

'Why this *is* Christian charity . . . come, Singleton, let us ask Rispin to resolve the matter.'

'Very well,' said Singleton, refusing to rise to Mount's bait. 'Mr Rispin?'

'Let the dice decide,' Rispin said, incurring a furious glare from Singleton.

'That is dishonourable, Mr Rispin, you know I do not approve . . .'

'But it would be amusing, Singleton, come, let us see whether the Almighty will influence the dice . . .'

'That's blasphemy, Mr Mount! I do not mind you having your joke at my expense but I will not tolerate this.' Singleton turned on his heel indignantly and smashed his forehead against a deck-beam. 'God-damn!' he swore, leaving the gunroom to the peals of laughter from the two officers.

Drinkwater lowered his glass and addressed Bourne. 'Heave-to under his stern, Mr Bourne.'

'Aye, aye, sir.' Raising the telescope again Drinkwater stared at *Narwhal*. It was the third time that forenoon she had lowered her boats after whales and the third time she had recovered them as the beasts eluded the hunt and swam steadily north-west. For two days the *Narwhal, Faithful, Diana, Earl Percy* and *Provident* and *Truelove* had worked their way north-west with *Melusine* accompanying them. Only Captain Renaudson of the *Diana* had hit a whale using his brass harpoon gun, and that had turned out to be a razorback.

As *Melusine* came up under *Narwhal*'s lee, Drinkwater hoisted himself onto the rail, holding onto the mizen rigging.

'*Narwhal*, ahoy!' He saw Jaybez Harvey's pock-marked features similarly elevate themselves and he waved in a friendly fashion. 'No success, Captain?'

Harvey shook his head. 'No, there be sommat curious about the fish,' he shouted. ' 'Tis unusual for them to swim north-west in such schools. Happen they know sommat, right whales is slow, but these devils aren't wanting to fill the lamps of London Town, Captain, that I do know.'

Drinkwater jumped down on deck as *Narwhal*'s hands squared her yards and she moved forward again, bumping aside an ice floe upon which a seal looked up at her in sudden surprise.

'If I hit him, may we lower, sir?' asked Walmsley, eagerly lifting a musket. Drinkwater looked at the seal as it rolled over.

'It's hardly sport, Mr Walmsley, ah . . . too late . . .' Drinkwater was saved the trouble of a decision as the seal, worried by the shadow of the *Narwhal* that passed over it, sought the familiarity of the sea.

Drinkwater saw the grin of pleasure that it had escaped cross Mr Frey's face as he sorted the signalling flags with the yeoman. 'Bad luck, Mr Walmsley, perhaps another time.'

'Aye, aye, sir.' Walmsley grimaced at Frey who grinned back triumphantly. 'God knows what you'll do when you meet a Frenchman, Frey, ask him to sit for his bloody portrait I shouldn't wonder . . .'

Drinkwater heard the jibe, but affected to ignore it. Walmsley's concern was unnecessary, the likelihood of their meeting a Frenchman so remote a possibility that Drinkwater considered Mr Frey's talents with pencil and watercolour box the only profitable part of the voyage.

They braced the yards round and *Melusine* reached east, across the sterns of the *Narwhal*, the *Diana* and the *Faithful*, tacking at noon in a sea that was scattered with loose floes. Only a dozen ice bergs were visible from the deck and the light north-easterly breeze had re-established clear weather. It was still bitterly cold, but the wind was strong enough to keep the surface of the sea moving, otherwise Drinkwater suspected it might freeze over. Although this would be unseasonable it was a constant worry for him as he inspected the readings of the thermometer in the log book.

Another problem he had faced was that of employment in the ship. During the days since the abatement of the gale there had been less danger from the ice, and they had worked slowly north in the wake of the whalers under easy sail. The diversions they had used on the passage north from the Humber had been re-started, although the weather was too cold for fencing, making the foil blades brittle. But the cutter had been lowered to pursue seals, for Drinkwater wanted all hands to be better clad than Palgrave's slops would allow, and hunting had ceased to be the prerogative of the officers. Marines and topmen trained in the use of small arms under Lieutenant Mount's direction, made up the shooting parties and it was certain that *Melusine* was the best fed warship in the Royal Navy. This fresh meat was most welcome and thought to be an excellent anti-scorbutic.

Drinkwater devised what amusements he could, even to the extent of purchasing some of the baleen from the whalers, in order that the seamen might attempt to decorate it in the same manner as the men in the whale-ships. As he looked along the waist where Meetuck supervised the cleaning of a fresh batch of seal skins and the gunner checked the flints in the gun-locks, he felt that the ship's services were somewhat wasted. They still went to quarters twice a day and exercised the guns with powder every third day; the unaccustomed presence of a marine sentry at his door and the pendant of a 'private' ship of war at the mainmasthead were constant reminders that *Melusine* was a King's ship, a man-of-war.

But Drinkwater was aware of a feeling seeping through the ship that she had undergone some curious enchantment, that, for all the hazards they had and would encounter, these were natural phenomena. He could not throw off the growing feeling that they were on some elaborate, dangerous but nevertheless curious pleasurable yachting excursion. Preoccupied with this consideration he was surprised at the little party of officers that suddenly confronted him.

'Beg pardon, sir.'

'Yes, Mr Mount, what is the matter?' It seemed like some deputation and for a moment his heart missed a beat in alarm, for his thoughts had run from yachting to naval expeditions like Cook's and, inevitably, Bligh's. He looked at the officers. With Mount were Rispin and Hill, Gorton, Quilhampton.

Walmsley, Glencross, Dutfield and Wickham with an angry Obadiah Singleton apparently were bringing up the rear with some reluctance. They seemed to be carrying a bundle.

'We thought, sir, that you might consider accepting a gift from us all . . .'

'Gift, Mr Mount . . .?'

'Something to keep you warm, sir, as Mr Hill informs me we crossed the seventy-second parallel at noon.'

They offered him the magnificent pelt of the polar bear.

Greatly daring Mount said, 'The Thirty-sixth Article of War is of little use in a boat sir.' It was an impropriety, but an impropriety made in the spirit of the moment, in tune with the bitingly cold, clean air and the sunshine breaking through the clouds. It was all thoroughly unreal for the quarterdeck of a sloop of war.

'Thank you, gentlemen,' he said, 'thank you very much. I am indebted to you all.'

Bourne crossed the deck to join them. 'Perhaps, sir, at a suitable occasion you will honour the gunroom for dinner.'

Drinkwater nodded. 'I shall be delighted,' he said, removing cloak and greygoe and flinging the great skin around him. 'What happened to the animal's head?'

'We had him *Mount*ed, sir,' said Walmsley mischieviously and they drifted forward in high spirits, just as if they were on a yachting cruise.

Chapter Eleven *July 1803*

The Great Hunt

Mr Quilhampton swung the glass from larboard beam to starboard bow. At first he saw nothing unusual for they had been aware that the loose floes would give way to close pack ice and probably to an ice shelf, from the ice blink that had been in sight for some twelve hours. He was taking some comfort from the isolation of the crow's nest to nurse his wounded pride. He was disappointed at Mr Gorton's advancement, and although he acknowledged the kindness of Mr Hill in mollifying him, it did not prevent him from suffering. He would have liked to return home a lieutenant, to indulge in a little swagger with a new hanger at his hip and a cuff of buttons instead of the white collar patches of the novice, when he entered the Edinburgh drawingroom of Catriona MacEwan. He had already furnished and populated the room in his imagination, but he was still perfecting the manner of his entrance, torn between an amusing frightening of Catriona's perfectly awful aunt with his wooden hand, or the upstaging of a languid rival who would probably be wearing the theatrical uniform of a volunteer yeomanry regiment. Although amusing, he had already astonished the old lady with his hand, and, in any case, the jape smacked more of the cockpit he wished to leave, than the gunroom to which he aspired. No, the discomfiture of the rival it must be, then . . .

'Masthead there!' He looked down. The master was looking aloft.

'Sir?'

'*Narwhal*'s signalling, what d'you make of it?'

Recalled to his duty Quilhampton levelled the big watch glass. The six whalers were bowling along on the larboard tack. *Melusine* was slightly to leeward of them all, but astern of *Narwhal*. The whaler's signal flaps streamed out in a straight line towards the sloop and were impossible to read. He struggled with the glass but could not make head or tail of the flag hoist. He hailed the deck and told Hill. Looking round the horizon again he saw the reason almost at once. The fast moving school of whales that they had so patiently followed for three days now, beating to windward as the great fish swam with steady purpose to the north-west had slowed. They were circling and there were more of them. Quilhampton wondered if it was the entire school on the surface at the same time or whether they had made some sort of rendezvous for breeding purposes. And then he saw something else, something quite extraordinary.

Opening up upon their larboard beam was a great channel in the ice shelf. Quilhampton realised the extent of his preoccupation in not noticing it before. Apart from loose floes he estimated the opening was several miles wide, partly hidden by a low raft of hummocked ice. In the channel the water appeared greener, forming an eutrophid strait between great continents of ice. Here was the reason for the whales' mysterious migration, a krill and plankton-rich sea which they had sensed from a distance.

Already *Narwhal* had two boats in the water. *Provident*, *Earl Percy* and *Faithful* were heaving to. *Diana* had still to come up and *Truelove*, fallen off to the eastward, had seen *Narwhal*'s signal and altered to the west.

Quilhampton swung himself through the trapdoor and hurried down the mainmast rigging.

Drinkwater realised the significance of the great ice-free lead as soon as he reached the crow's nest. He was perceptive enough to know that the strange channel that seemed to exist as far as the eye could see to the westward was unusual. Entering the channel the right whales had slowed. He could see twenty or thirty at any one time on the surface, their spouts so numerous as to form a cloud above them as they vented through their spiracles. From time to time a great, blunt head would appear, the baleen gleaming in a rigid grin while seawater poured from the corners of the gaping mouth as the fibrous whale-bone strained the tiny organisms from the sea.

He sensed, too, a change of tempo from the pursuing whalers. As he swung his glass on the two nearer ships he counted the boats already in the water. *Narwhal* and the nearer ships had all their boats out, *Diana*, a little to the east was lowering, while *Truelove* had hoisted her topgallants in her haste to join the great hunt.

Surprisingly he saw a boat from *Narwhal* turn away from the whales towards the sloop and through the glass he could see Harvey himself standing in the bow. He swung his glass once more to the west. The open lead, with hardly a floe loose on its extraordinary surface, beckoned them to the westwards. It seemed to Drinkwater that the ice shelf had suddenly split, moved by some elemental force, and pulled apart. Momentarily he wondered whether that force might be reversed, that if they entered the channel they might be trapped and crushed. Shaking off his apprehension he made his way below, arriving on the quarterdeck as Harvey's boat came up under the quarter and Lieutenant Rispin, at a nod from Drinkwater, invited Harvey on board.

Harvey's eyes were shining with excitement, illuminating his snubnosed face and eradicating the disfigurements of the smallpox. Drinkwater immediately warmed to him. 'Good morning, Captain Harvey, I am surprised you are not in hot pursuit of the fish.'

Harvey grinned and dispensed briefly with the formalities. 'There will be enough pickings here, captain, if we can hold the whales, to fill all our empty casks and send us safe back to Hull, but we want your assistance.'

'How so?'

'Well, the whales will likely follow th'krill and all into yonder lead. Once we get amongst them they'll swim to west, like. If you'd put this ship ahead of the fish and drop cannon fire ahead of them it'll slow them like, stop them escaping . . . will you do it?'

A quick kill, a short voyage, the success of a task that had seemed once so very difficult and French privateers a figment of the First Lord's overworked imagination. He had only one reservation, and his inexperience in ice nagged him.

'How far into the lead will they go, Captain Harvey? That looks like dense shelf ice to me, if it closes you may survive but this ship will be crushed like an egg-shell.'

Harvey shook his head. 'I've heard of this happening once before, Captain Drinkwater, in my father's day, sixty-eight or nine, I think. Happen if the whales take themselves into the lead then it'll not close.'

Drinkwater could see Harvey's argument, but it was imperfect. The whales might turn and swim back faster than a ship could beat to windward, the wind might shift and blow the ice to the south-west of them to the north again. He said as much to Harvey and watched the disappointment in the Yorkshireman's eyes.

'The ice'll not close, not for a week at least, and we'll have our casks full by then . . .' The lust of the hunter was strong in him. Drinkwater could sense his sudden impatience to be gone, to be pointing the harpoon gun that gleamed dully in the bow of his whale-boat.

A short voyage. Home and an end to the ache in his shoulder. Elizabeth . . .

'Very well, three days, damn you.' He grinned and Harvey grinned and smacked him painfully upon his shoulder. The *lése-majesté* caused the waiting officers to hide their grins and the instant Harvey had regained his boat Drinkwater called for all hands. He would make them pay for their impertinence, damn it!

'Set the t'gallants, Mr Rispin!'

'Set t'gallants, sir.' He watched Rispin pick up the speaking trumpet as the watch below tumbled up the hatchways. The lieutenant launched into his customary stream of largely superfluous orders.

'After guard to hoist the main t'garns'ls. Bosun's mate, send the after guard to man the main t'garns'l halliards, there! Corporal of marines, send the marines aft to man the mizen t'garns'ls halliards. Master at arms! Send below and turn up the idlers, stewards and servants, messmen, cooks-mates, sweepers and loblolly boys!'

This volley of orders was answered by the petty officers who thumped the fife-rails for good effect with their starters, cursing and shouting at the men.

'Topmen aloft, aloft . . .' Rispin's strange, hysterical system seemed to galvanise the hands, as though they were all suddenly aware that the hunt for whales had taken on a new, more primitive flavour. And yet, watching from the larboard hance, one foot upon the slide of Palgrave's fancy brass carronade, Drinkwater once again received the strong impression that they were engaged upon a yachting excursion. Perhaps it was just the excitement, perhaps the extravagance of Rispin's fancy orders that had about it that ritual quality he had observed aboard such craft as the Trinity House Yacht back in eighty-eight, or perhaps it was the fantastic cake-icing seascape that surrounded him that induced the Arctic calenture.

'Let fall! Sheet home!' The yards rose as the canvas fell.

He shook off the ridiculous feeling. 'Mr Quilhampton!'

'Sir?'

'Aloft with you, we shall run into the ice lead and work ahead of the whales.'

'Aye, aye, sir.' Drinkwater looked at the compass.

'Steer west by north.'

'West by north, sir . . . west by north it is, sir.'

'Sheet home there! Belay!' Rispin at last pronounced topgallants hoisted.

'Square the yards, Mr Rispin, course west by north.'

Rispin acknowledged the order and his voice rose again as he bawled through the trumpet.

'After guard and marines to the weather mainbrace! Forebrace there! Bosun's mate start those men aft here! Haul in the main brace, pull together damn you and mind the weather roll! That's very well with the main yard! Belay there! Belay! Belay the fore-yard, don't come up any . . .!'

It went on for some minutes before Mr Rispin, fussing under his captain's eye, was satisfied with the trim of the yards and *Melusine* had already gathered way. From her leeward position she was up among the whalers and their boats now. Two boat-flags were already up, with *Narwhal*'s colours on them, Drinkwater noticed. He raised his hat to Harvey's mate who conned the whaler while his commander was out after the fish. He saluted Abel Sawyers as *Melusine* swept past the Quaker in his boat, his men pulling furiously to catch a great bull whale a musket shot on the sloop's starboard bow. Then they were in among the whales, the air misty with their breathing, a foetid taint to it. The humps of the shining backs, the flick of a great tail and once a reappearance of that great ugly-noble head as it sluiced the water through the baleen in an ecstasy of surfeit.

'Beat to quarters, Mr Rispin,' Drinkwater said it quietly, watching the young officer's reaction. He noted the surprise and the hesitation and then the acknowledgement.

Pipes squealed again and the marine drummer began to beat the *rafale*. Men ran to their stations and knelt by the guns, the officers and midshipmen drew their dirks and swords and the gun-captains raised their hands as their guns became ready.

'Sail trimmers, Mr Hill. We'll heave-to and fire a broadside ahead of the leading whales!' Hill was at his station and had relieved Rispin. There was now an economy of orders as Hill deployed the men chosen to trim the *Melusine*'s sails and spars in action. Bourne too was beside him, ready to pass orders to the batteries. 'Load ball, Mr Bourne, all guns at maximum depression, both broadsides to be ready.'

'Aye, aye, sir.'

Melusine had entered the lead now. On either side the backs of whales still emerged, their huge tails slowly thrusting the water as they drove majestically along. Beyond the whales, close to larboard and some miles distant to starboard, the ice edge glittered in the sunlight, full of diamond brilliants shading to blue shadows with green slime along the waterline.

He was aware of Mr Singleton on the quarterdeck. 'Should you not be at your station?' he asked mildly.

'I beg your pardon, sir, I took it to be another of these interminable manoeuvres that . . .'

'Never mind, never mind. You may watch now you are here.'

Singleton turned to see Meetuck pointing excitedly from the fo'c's'le as a female whale rolled luxuriously on her side, exposing her nipple for her calf. 'It seems scarcely right to kill these magnificent creatures,' he muttered to himself, remembering the *Benedicite*. The mother and calf fell astern.

'Down helm, Mr Hill, you may heave the ship to . . .' There were more orders and *Melusine* swung to starboard, easing her speed through the water to a standstill.

'Larboard battery! Make ready!' The arms went up and he nodded to Bourne.

'Fire!'

The broadside erupted in smoke and flame with a roar that made the ears tingle. The balls raised splashes, a cable to leeward where two big whales had been seen. Through the drifting smoke Drinkwater saw one huge fluke lift itself for a moment as the whale dived, but he had no idea whether he had reversed its course.

'Reload!' There was a furious and excited activity along the larboard waist. There was nothing to compare with firing their brute artillery that so delighted the men, officers and ratings alike.

'You may give them another broadside, Mr Bourne.'

Again the arms went up and again the shots dropped ahead of the whales. Drinkwater turned to starboard, to look back up the strait. The whalers were three miles away and between them and the *Melusine* was a most extraordinary sight. The sea seemed to boil with action. He could see more than a dozen boats. Three were under tow by harpooned whales, others were in the act of striking, their harpooners up in the bows as the tense steersmen brought their flimsy oars into the mass of whales that had now taken alarm and were swimming south-west, along the line of the lead. Beyond these two boats crews were lancing their catches, probing for the lives of the great beasts as their victims rolled and thrashed the water with their great tails. Through his glass Drinkwater could see the foam of their death agonies tinged with blood. A few flags were up on dead carcases and these were either under tow to the whalers or awaiting the few boats that could be spared for this task.

Drinkwater saw at once that he could not fire his starboard guns without endangering the boats but their crews were excitedly awaiting the order that would send their shot in amongst the whales.

'By God,' he heard Walmsley mutter to Glencross, 'this is better than partridge.'

'Secure the starboard guns, Mr Bourne, and draw the charges!' He heard the mutter of disappointment from the starbowlines. 'Silence there!'

A new danger suddenly occurred to him. The sloop lay in the path of the advancing animals. The death of some of their number had communicated an alarm to the others and their motion was full of turbulent urgency. He did not wish to think what effect one of those bluff heads would have upon *Melusine*'s hull. 'Haul the mainyard, Mr Hill and put the ship before the wind . . .' Hill grasped the sudden danger and *Melusine* turned slowly to larboard as she again gathered headway. She had hardly swung, presenting her stern to the onrushing whales when their attention was attracted by shouts to the south, to larboard. One of the boats that had been fast to a fish had been dashed to fragments on the ice edge two miles away as the tortured beast had dived under the ice. The alarm had been raised by another boat, towing past *Melusine*'s stern, who hailed the sloop to request her rendering assistance and allowing them to hold onto their whale. It was while clearing away the quarterboat that the whale struck them. A large gravid female in the last stages of her pregnancy had been terrified by the slaughter astern of her. The ship shook and the stunned animal rolled out from under the quarter, almost directly beneath the boat. Her astonished crew, half-way down to the water's surface looked down into the tiny eye of the monster. The whale spouted, then dived, her flukes hitting the keel of the suspended boat but not upsetting it.

A few minutes later, under the command of Acting Lieutenant Gorton the boat was pulling across a roil of water, avoiding the retreating whales with difficulty, on her way to rescue the crew of the smashed whale-boat. It did not appear that *Melusine* had suffered any damage from the collision.

The whalers hunted their quarry for fifty hours while the sun culminated and then began its slow unfinished setting, its azimuth altering round the horizon to rise again to each of two successive noons. *Melusine* was quite unable to stem the escape of the whales and in the end Drinkwater agreed to the boats securing their captured whales to her sides.

'As fenders!' Harvey had hailed, his eyes dark and sunken in his head with the fatigue of the chase, 'in case the ice closes on you!' The jest was made as he went in pursuit of his eighth whale, his cargo almost complete. Now the five ships lay secured along the ice edge on the northern side of the lead, tied up as though moored to a quay, their head and stern lines secured to ice anchors. Each had a pair of whales alongside, between hull and ice, while rafted outboard in tier after tier lay the remainder of the catch. While *Melusine*'s company stood watch, the exhausted whalers turned below to sleep before the flensing began. They had taken more than thirty whales between them and the labour of cutting up the blubber and packing it in casks took a further two days of strenuous effort.

Melusine's midshipmen went out on the ice with Mount and a party of marines and took some more seals, returning to the ship to pick off the brown sharks that clustered round the whale corpses as they sank after flensing. The fine weather held and the whale-captains expressed their good fortune, accepting an invitation to dine with Drinkwater the instant the flensing was completed. Even Sawyers seemed to be un-Quakerishly cheerful, and Drinkwater, anticipating an early departure from the Greenland Sea, ordered Tregembo to get Palgrave's carvers, silver and plate out of storage.

The high good humour that seemed to infect them all after the success of the last few days allayed his worries about the possible closure of the ice. Besides, he twice-daily ascended the mainmast to the crow's nest, spending as much as half an hour aloft with the big watch glass and making note of the bearings of familiar ice hummocks with a pocket compass. The variation in their positions was minimal, the movement of the ice, like the weather, seemed suspended in their favour. His own natural suspicions, those fine tunings of his seaman's senses, were blunted by the triumphant confidence of Harvey, Renaudson, Sawyers and Atkinson of the *Truelove*.

As they gathered in Drinkwater's cabin sipping from tankards of mimbo, a hot rum punch that Cawkwell concocted out of unlikely materials, their elation was clear. So great had been their success that the customary jealousy of one whaler who had done less well than his more fortunate colleague was absent. It was true that Harvey's harpoon gun had proved its value, netting him the largest number of whales, but he endured only mild rebukes from Sawyers who claimed the method un-Godly.

'Never a season like it, Captain,' Renaudson said, his face red from the heat in the cabin and the effects of the mimbo. 'Abel bleats about God like your black-coated parson,' he nodded in Singleton's direction, 'but 'tis luck, really. A man may fish the Greenland Seas for a lifetime, like, then, ee,' he shook his head slightly, a small grin of disbelief in his good fortune crossing his broad, sweating features, 'his luck changes like this.' He became suddenly serious. 'Mind you, Captain, it'll not happen again. No. Not in my lifetime, any road. I've seen the best and quickest catch I'm ever likely to make and I doubt my son'll see owt like it himself, not if he fishes for twenty year'n more. Abel's lucky there, both him and his son together in one great hunt.' He drained the tankard. 'I see tha's children of thee own, Captain.' He nodded at the portraits on the bulkhead, his accent thickening as he drank.

'Yes,' said Drinkwater, sipping the mimbo more cautiously. It was not a drink he greatly cared for, but his stocks of good wine were almost exhausted and Cawkwell had suggested that he served a rum punch to warm his guests. Harvey joined them.

'Ee, Captain, your guns weren't as much good as mine.' He grinned, clearly happy that his beloved harpoon gun had established its reputation for the swift murder of mysticetae. 'I shall patent the modifications I've made and make my fortune twice over from this voyage.' He nudged Renaudson. 'Get th'self a Harvey's patent harpoon gun for next season, Thomas, then th'can shoot whales instead of farting at them.' The dialect was thick between them and Drinkwater turned away, nodding to Atkinson, a small, active man with a lick of dark hair over his forehead, who was talking to Mr Gorton. Drinkwater had invited only Hill, Singleton and the lieutenants to the meal, there was insufficient room for midshipmen. Besides, he knew the whalemen would not want the intrusion of young gentlemen at their celebrations.

He found himself confronted by Singleton's blue jaw. His sobriety was disquieting amongst all the merriment. 'Good evening, Mr Singleton.'

'Good evening, sir. A word if you please?'

'Of course.'

'I deduce this gathering is to mark the successful conclusion of the fishery.'

'So it would appear. Is that not so, Captain Sawyers?' He turned to the Quaker who had, as a mark of the relaxation of the occasion, removed his hat.

'Indeed it is, although a few of us have an empty cask or two left. The Lord has provided of his bounty . . .'

'Amen,' broke in Singleton, who seemed to have some purpose in his abruptness. 'Then may I ask, sir, when you intend landing me?'

'Landing thee . . .?' Sawyers seemed astonished and Drinkwater again explained for Sawyers's benefit.

'It seems the Almighty smiles upon all our endeavours then, Friend,' he said addressing Singleton, 'and perhaps thine own more than ours.' He smiled. 'This lead towards the south-west will bring you close to the coast of East Greenland, somewhere about latitude seventy. I have heard the coast is ice-free thereabouts, although I have never seen it close-to myself. You may see the mountain peaks in clear weather for a good distance. *Nunataks*, the eskimos call them . . .'

'Then we had better land you,' Drinkwater said to Singleton, 'but I am still uncertain of the wisdom of following this lead into the ice shelf. Do you not think it might prove a cul-de-sac?'

Sawyers shook his head. 'No, the fish would not have entered it if some instinct had not told them that the krill upon which they feed were rich here, and that open water did not exist ahead of them . . .'

'But surely,' Singleton put in, his scientific mind engaged now, 'the whales may dive beneath the ice. My observations while you have been hunting them show they can go prodigious deep.'

'No, Friend,' Sawyers smiled, 'their need of air and their instinct will not persuade them to dive beneath such an ice shelf as we have about us now. Surely,' he said with a touch of irony, the dissenter gently teasing the man of established religion, 'surely thou sawest how, even in their terror, they made no attempt to swim under the ice?'

Singleton flushed at the mocking of his intelligence. Sawyers mollified him. 'But perhaps in the confusion of the gun smoke thine eyes were misled. No, mysticetus will dive only under floes in the open sea and beneath bay ice through which he breaks to inhale . . .'

'Bay ice?' queried Drinkwater.

'A first freezing of the sea, Captain, through which he may appear with a sudden and majestic entrance . . .'

They sat to dinner, cod, and whale meat steaks with dried peas and a little sauerkraut for those who wanted it, all washed down with the last bottles of half-decent claret that Tregembo had warmed slightly in the galley. As was usual in the gloom of the cabin despite the low sunshine outside, Drinkwater had had the candles lit and the spectacle of such a meal etched itself indelibly upon his mind. Alternating round the table the whale-ship masters and the naval officers made an incongruous group. In eccentric varieties of their official uniform the lieutenant and the master agreed only in their coats. Beneath these they wore mufflers, guernseys and an assortment of odd shirts. Gorton, presumably slightly over-awed to be included in the company, wore shirt and stock in the prescribed manner, but this was clearly over some woollen garment of indeterminate shape and he presented the appearance of a pouter pigeon. The whale-captains were more fantastic, their garb a mixture of formality, practicality and individual choice.

Sawyers, with the rigidity of his sect, appeared the most formal, clearly possessing a thick set of undergarments. His waistcoat and coat were of the heaviest broadcloth and he wore a woollen muffler. Renaudson, on the other hand, marked the perigee of Arctic elegance, in seal-skin breeches over yellow stockings, a stained mustard waistcoat and a greasy jacket, cut short at the waist and made of some nondescript fur that might once have been a seal or a walrus. Atkinson was similarly equipped, although his clothes seemed a little cleaner and he had put on fresh neck-linen for the occasion, while Harvey, his neckerchief filthy, sported a brass-buttoned pilot jacket. Drinkwater himself wore two shirts over woollen underwear, his undress uniform coat almost as salt-stained as Harvey's pilot jacket. But he was pleased with the evening. The conviviality was infectious, the wine warming and the steaks without equal to an appetite sharpened by cold.

The conversation was of whales, of whale-ships and captains, of harpooners and speksioneers and the profits of owners. There were brief, good-natured arguments as one challenged the claims of another. For the most part the whalers dominated the conversation, the young naval officers, under the eye of their commander and overwhelmed by the ebullience of their guests, playing a passive part. But Drinkwater did hear Singleton exchanging stories of the eskimos with Atkinson who seemed to have met them whilst sealing, and they were debating the reasons why they took their meat raw, when methods of cooking it had been shown to them on many occasions. Thus preoccupied he was suddenly recalled by Sawyers on his right. Above the din Sawyers had been shouting at him to catch his attention.

'I beg your pardon, Captain, I was distracted. What was it you were saying?'

'That thy guns were of little use, Friend.'

'In the matter of stopping the whales? Oh, no . . . very little, but it allowed my people to share the excitement a little, although,' he recollected with the boyish grin that countered the serious cast to his cock-headed features, 'I think that my order to secure the starboard guns without them being fired, near sparked a mutiny.'

'That was not quite what I meant, Friend. I had said that we had no *need* of thy guns, that thy presence here has proved unnecessary. Oh, I mean no offence, but whatever hobgoblins the enemy were supposed to have in the Arctic seas have proved imaginary.'

Drinkwater smiled over the rim of his glass as he drained it, leaning back so that Cawkwell could refill it. 'So it would seem . . .'

'Sir! Sir!' Midshipman Frey's face appeared at the opposite end of the table and the conversation died away.

'*Narwhal*, sir! *Narwhal*'s taken fire . . . !'

Chapter Twelve *July 1803*

Fortune's Sharp Adversity

From *Melusine*'s deck they saw *Narwhal* already blazing like a torch. Great gouts of flame bellied from her hold and tongues of fire leapt into the rigging. She was moored beyond *Truelove*, ahead of the sloop, and her crew could be seen rushing down upon the ice. For a second the diners stood as though stunned, then they made for the gangplank onto the ice, led by Harvey.

Pausing only to call for all hands and the preparation of the ship's fire-engine, Drinkwater followed, impelled by some irrational force that caused him to do anything but stand in idleness. Men were pouring down *Truelove*'s gangplank unrolling a canvas hose that was obviously too short to reach much beyond the barque's bowsprit. As he came abreast of *Narwhal*'s stern and among the milling of her crew, Drinkwater realised they were mostly drunk. Harvey was roaring abuse at them, his face demonic in his rage, lit by a blaze that spewed huge gobbets of flame into the sky as casks of whale kreng exploded. Harvey struck two men in his agony before he turned to his ship. He staggered forward into the orange circle of heat where the ice gleamed as it melted, holding his arms up before his face. He was still shouting, something more persistent than abuse, and Drinkwater was about to start after him when Bourne and Quilhampton arrived with a party of marines and seamen lugging the fire-engine.

'Just coming, sir!'

'Suction into the sea, Mr Q! And get two jets playing on the gangplank . . .'

To save the ship was clearly impossible, but there seemed some doubt among the men assembled on the ice as to the whereabouts of two or three of *Narwhal*'s company.

Harvey had already reached the gangplank and edged cautiously forward. Above his head the mainyard was ablaze, the furled canvas of the sail burning furiously. Ahead of him the main hatchway vented flame like a perpetually firing mortar and the deck planks could be seen lifting and curling back. The bulwarks had yet to catch and Harvey reached their shelter, hanging outboard of them and peering over the rail. Drinkwater stepped forward and the heat hit him, searing his eyes so that he stopped in his tracks. It was intense and the roaring of the fire deafening.

A man was crouching beside Drinkwater and he turned to see the marine Polesworth pointing the nozzle of the hose and shouting behind him to the men at the handles. The gurgle of the pump was inaudible and the jet, when it came in spurts to start with, quite inadequate. He felt Quilhampton pulling his left arm.

'Come back, sir, come back!'

'But Harvey, James, what the hell does he think he's doing?'

'They say there's a boy still board . . .'

'My God! But no-one could live in that inferno!'

Quilhampton shook his head, his face scarlet in the reflection of the flames. Their feet were sinking into the melting ice as they stared at Harvey. He was attempting to make his way aft outside the hull, by way of the main chains, but the hand by which he clutched the rail was continually seared and he was making painfully slow progress. And then Drinkwater saw the object of Harvey's foolhardy rescue attempt. The figure was lit from within the cabin where the bulkheads were already burning, silhouetted against the leaded glass of the larboard quarter-gallery. By contrast to the conflagration above, *Narwhal*'s hull was dark as lamp-black but as their eyes adjusted, the pale face with its gaping mouth pressed against the glass in a silent scream, riveted their attention.

'Polesworth! Direct your hose upon the quarter-gallery!' The marine obeyed and Drinkwater hoped he might thereby delay the fire spreading to the place. Harvey had scrambled the length of the main chains and was feeling for a footing to cross twenty feet of hull to the mizen chains. He found some plank land, a perilous footing, but he kept moving steadily aft.

'Rope, we need rope. From *Truelove*, Mr Q!' He saw Renaudson among the appalled crowd. 'Rope, Captain, rope from your ship!'

There was a hurried exchange of orders and men began to run towards *Truelove*.

Harvey gained the mizen chains and had leant outboard from

their after end to find a footing on the leaded top of the quarter-gallery. But he was too late.

With a roar an explosion shook *Narwhal*'s stern, the windows of the gallery shattered outwards and a small rag of humanity was ejected into the blackness. Harvey was blown off into the water.

As the explosion died away Drinkwater heard several voices shout that *Narwhal*'s small powder magazine was beneath the cabin aft, and then their attention was claimed by a great cracking and splitting of wood as the mainmast, closest to the origin of the fire, burnt through and toppled slowly over onto the ice, bringing the fore and mizen masts with it. The crowd of men moved backwards in fear and when the rope arrived, Renaudson, Quilhampton and Drinkwater made their way to the edge of the ice amid burning spars. Their footing was treacherous. The surface ice was reduced to slush, slush that had no longer the sharp edge of the ice shelf. It now formed a lethal declivity into the freezing black waters of the sea.

They looked down upon Harvey's pale face, curiously blotched and appearing like the head of John the Baptist upon Salome's salver. 'Quick! The rope!'

It snaked over Drinkwater and fell alongside Harvey, but his eyes closed and he did not seem to have seen it.

'God's bones!' Drinkwater began to struggle out of his coat but Quilhampton was quicker, splashing into the water as soon as he saw what the matter was. Drinkwater hesitated a second, concerned that Quilhampton's wooden hand might hamper him, remembering his own pathetic attempts to make a bowline.

But Quilhampton needed no help. He shouted to the men on the ice and Drinkwater stumbled back up the ice-slope to get men to tail onto the line and drag Harvey and Quilhampton to safety, while *Narwhal*'s hull finally erupted, splitting open along her topsides as the fire consumed her.

Despite the fierce heat both rescued and rescuer were shivering. Blankets miraculously appeared and Singleton arrived with an improvised stretcher and the surgeons of the *Truelove* and the *Narwhal* herself.

In seconds Harvey and Quilhampton were on their way back to *Melusine* and in their wake men followed, drifting away from the fire now that there was no longer anything that could be done.

'Captain Renaudson, ah, and you, Captain Sawyers. A word if

you please . . .' The two men approached, sober faces reflecting the glare of the fire, even though it was the midnight of an arctic summer and quite light.

'What do we do with these men, gentlemen?' Drinkwater asked.

'Hang the lubbers, God blast their bloody stupidity.' Renaudson turned on the shifty eyed and shamefaced Narwhals as they stood on the ice disconsolately, 'You should starve here, if I had my way . . . drunken bastards!' he said with venom.

'Steady, Friend . . .' put in Sawyers, putting out a restraining arm.

'A pox on your damned cant, Abel. These harlots' spawn deserve nothing . . .'

'You do not know that they all . . .'

'I do not need to know more than that Jaybez Harvey will not live to see his wife again, nay, them art shit,' and he spat for emphasis and turned away.

Drinkwater looked at the crowd of men. 'Which of you is the chief officer?'

The mate stepped forward. 'I'm the mate, Captain, John Akeroyd.'

'How did the ship catch fire?'

'I'm not certain, sir, I was below, turned in.'

'Who had the watch?' Drinkwater addressed the question to the huddle of men. There seemed to be some shoving and then a man came forward.

'Me.'

'What is your name?'

'Peter Norris, third mate . . . men got among the spirits, sir, there was some sort o'fight over a game o'cards . . . tried to stop it but it was too late . . .'

Drinkwater saw the raw bruising round Norris's left eye which indicated he spoke the truth. 'Hhmmm . . .'

'There is a custom, Friend, in the fishery,' offered Sawyers helpfully, 'that when a disaster such as this occurs the crew of the vessel lost is split up among the other vessels. Perhaps, Mr Akeroyd, thou would'st care to divide the men.' Sawyers caught Drinkwater's arm and turned him away. 'Come, Friend, this is not a naval matter.'

'But there is some degree of culpability . . . if Harvey should die . . .'

'The fishery has its own ways, Captain Drinkwater.' Sawyers

was tugging him as he tried to turn back, 'Come away, they have lost everything and will go home as beggars . . .'

'But, damn it, Sawyers, Harvey is like to die and that boy . . .'

'Aye, Friend, thou mayst be right, but thou cannot flog them and they will be penitent ere long. Come.' And Drinkwater returned reluctantly to *Melusine*.

Rispin met him formally at the side. 'I beg pardon sir, the sideboys are . . .'

'Oh, damn the sideboys, Mr Rispin, where is Mr Singleton?'

'He took the injured man below, sir, with the surgeons from two of the whaling vessels, sir.'

'Thank you.'

'And sir, the wind's freshening.'

'And damn the wind too!'

Drinkwater found Quilhampton in the cockpit, a mug of mimbo before him and blankets and midshipmen close about him. He was recovering in good company and although the midshipmen drew deferentially aside Drinkwater offered Quilhampton no more than a nod and the terse observation that he had 'Done very well.'

'Bit tight with the compliments, Q, old chap,' muttered Lord Walmsley as Drinkwater moved forward to where the midshipmen's chests had been dragged into a makeshift table.

'How is he?' The three surgeons turned, grunted and bent over Harvey. The pock-marked face was crusted with burnt flesh, the beard singed and smelling foully. Alongside lay the roll of Singleton's instruments, the demi-lunes, daviers and curettes gleaming in the light of the two battle lanterns suspended from the low beams. Drinkwater looked at the palms of the hands. They were black and swollen.

Singleton straightened. 'How is he?' Drinkwater repeated the question.

'We have administered laudanum as an anodyne, Captain Drinkwater, and *I* am of the opinion that the wounds *must* be debrided without delay.'

'If you cannot agree, gentlemen,' said Drinkwater with a sudden edge to his voice addressing the whale-ships' surgeons, 'then you may leave the patient to my doctor.' The surgeon of the *Narwhal* looked up angrily. He was a man of nearer seventy years than sixty, Drinkwater judged.

'I've been with Cap'n Harvey these last twenty-six years, Cap'n, an' I'll not leave him . . .'

'Then you will hold your tongue, sir; since you have nowhere else to go, you may remain. As for you,' he turned to the other man, 'I suggest you return and offer Captain Renaudson what assistance he requires in the matter of examining those of *Narwhal*'s crew that join *Truelove*.' He ignored the sullen glares in the two men's eyes. 'Now, Singleton, how is he?'

'We will debride the wounds, sir, while he is still in a state of shock, those about the face particularly, but . . .'

'Well . . .'

'Well what?'

'I have auscultated the pulmonary region and,' he paused, shaking his head, 'the trachea, the bronchia and larynx, indeed it appears the lungs themselves have been seared severely, by the intake of such hot air, sir.'

'Then there is little hope?'

'I fear not, sir.'

Drinkwater looked at the *Narwhal*'s surgeon. 'Who was the boy?'

'Cap'n Harvey's sister's son.'

Drinkwater sighed. His eye caught the edge of the circle of lamplight. A face, disembodied in the darkness of the cockpit, seemed to leer at him and for a second Drinkwater imagined himself in the presence of the personification of death. But it was only the loblolly 'boy', Skeete.

He turned in search of the fresh air of the deck, pausing at the foot of the ladder. 'You had better lie him in my cot. And you would best do your curettage in the cabin. There is more light.'

Lieutenant Rispin met him at the companion. 'Ah, sir, I was about to send for you. The wind continues to freshen, sir, and we are ranging a little.'

Drinkwater looked at the ice edge above the rail.

'Only a little, Mr Rispin, pray keep an eye upon it.'

'Aye, aye, sir.' Rispin touched the fore-cock of his hat and Drinkwater fell into a furious pacing of the deck. Forward the bell struck two and the sentries called their ritual 'All's well' at hatch, companionway and entry, on fo'c's'le and stern. It was two bells in the middle watch, one o'clock in the morning, bright as day and beneath his feet another man was dying.

It was the waste that appalled him most, that and the consideration that the loss of *Narwhal*, though it in no way affected the *Melusine* directly, seemed of some significance. He had liked Harvey, a tarpaulin commander of the finest sort, able, kindly and, in the end, heroic. Drinkwater began to see *Narwhal*'s loss as an epitome, a providential instruction, an illumination of a greater truth as he paced his few yards of scrubbed planking.

The folly of many had destroyed in a twinkling their own endeavours, a few had been victims of the consequence of this folly (for they had later learned that, in addition to the boy, two men were also missing). And one, upon whom all the responsibility had lain, was to be sacrificed; to die to no ultimate purpose, since *Narwhal* had been lost. Drinkwater could only feel a mounting anger at the irresponsibility of the men who had got among the spirits aboard the whaler. Renaudson had been furious with them, damning them roundly with all the obscene phrases at his disposal and yet Drinkwater began to feel a degree of anger towards himself. Perhaps he should not have had the masters to dinner; had Harvey been aboard *Narwhal*, his men might not have run wild. In that case Harvey would have been alive.

He clutched at his hat. 'God damn it!' he muttered to himself, suddenly mindful of his duty. Rispin had been right, the wind had an edge to it that promised more. He looked aloft, the pendant was like a bar, stretching towards the south-west as the gale began to rise from the north-east.

Drinkwater strode forward to the main rigging. Swinging himself onto the rail he began the ascent of the mainmast.

He felt the full violence of the gale by the time he reached the main top. It threatened to pluck him from the futtocks as he hung, back downwards. At the topgallant crossing, it tore at his clothes. He cursed as he struggled into the crow's nest, realising that his preoccupation had lasted too long. Commanders of ships should not indulge in morbid reflections. Even before he had levelled the long glass he knew something was wrong.

To the north-east the lead was not only filling with loose ice floes, blown into it by the gale, but it was narrower; quite noticeably narrower. The great ice raft to which they were moored which had cracked away from the shelf to the north and west of them and which was, perhaps, some fifty or sixty miles square, must have been revolving. Drinkwater tried to imagine the physical reasons for this. Had it just been the onset of the gale? Could a few hours of rising wind turn such a vast island of ice so quickly? The logic of the phenomena defeated him. What was certain was that the lead had closed to windward; he did not need take bearings to see that. He swung the glass the other way. If the ice island revolved, then surely the strait ought to open in that direction. It did not. Its unwillingness to obey the laws of nature as he conceived them disturbed Drinkwater. He was once again confronted by his ignorance. Kicking open the trapdoor, he dangled his legs for the topgallant ratlines.

Regaining the deck and without the ceremony required by the usages of the navy, he hastened precipitately down the makeshift gangplank onto the ice. Hurrying aboard *Faithful* he woke Sawyers with the news. The Quaker's eyes told him what he already felt in his bones.

'Thou dids't right, Friend. Happen the Lord was about to punish our pride. We must make sail without delay and take this fair wind to the south-west. We have no need to linger. I pray thee do not delay, thy ship is not fit to withstand a single fastening in the ice. Go, go!'

The watches were swiftly alerted on the other whalers and within a few minutes the hands were being tumbled up on all the ships. *Diana*, the leewardmost would have to leave first, for the wind pinned them slightly onto the ice, but her sturdy sides withstood a scrape or two before her rudder bit and her head came off. *Truelove*'s bow nudged the remnants of *Narwhal* that had rested, half sunk, upon a ledge of ice, and she too stood out into the lead, her hands dropping the forecourse as well as setting the topsails. *Melusine* followed, her spirketting grinding on *Narwhal* as her bow was thrust out into open water. As the hands dropped the forecourse in its buntlines it occurred to Drinkwater, as one of those savage ironies truth thrust before him, that had not *Narwhal*'s burnt timbers lain like a fender ahead of them, the onshore wind might have pinned *Melusine*'s hull against the ice forever.

He looked astern as *Diana*, *Earl Percy* and *Provident* bumped off the wreck and out into the safety of open sea. Then the six ships stood south-west, aware that the lead, once so wide and inviting, so apparently permanent and alive with whales, was already narrowing on either beam.

There was no longer any sign of a single whale.

PART THREE

The Fiord

'(Men) live like wild beasts in a deep solitude of spirit and will, scarcely any two being able to agree since each follows his own pleasure of caprice.'

Giambattista Vico (1668–1744)

Chapter Thirteen *July 1803*

The Fate of the 'Faithful'

Drinkwater kept the deck for three days. By the end of this time he was reduced to a stupor of fatigue, suffering from a quinsy and incipient toothache. But *Melusine* and the whalers had broken out of the lead to the south-west and, but for the presence of a thousand ice floes, were in what passed for 'open' water. Their escape from being set fast and crushed had been as remarkable, as much for the danger to the ship as to the frequency of its occurrence. Perhaps twenty or thirty times, Drinkwater had lost count, they tacked, wore, or threw all aback to make a stern-board clear of impending doom. Many more times than this the hands bore lighter floes off with the spare spars. There were several minor injuries, one rupture and a case of crushed ribs amongst the men. The days of hunting parties were long forgotten, the yachting atmosphere paid for ten times over. Despite their best endeavours *Melusine* was several times jarred by collision with floes and the increasing number of growlers that bore witness to the high summer of the region.

There was little conviviality in gunroom or cockpit. On the berth deck the men rolled in or out of their hammocks as the watches changed, dog-tired, cold and miserable. Amid this atmosphere Macpherson ceased his ravings and quietly gave up the ghost, while Harvey now awash with opiates, continued to breathe with increasing difficulty. The internal routines of the ship went on, hammocks were piped up, the decks scrubbed, spirits served and the hands piped to their dinners. The mess kids were scoured and the hammocks piped down The cook and his mates swore and blasphemed at the coppers, the bosun's mates cursed at the hatchways, the loblolly boys in the cockpit as they cleared night soil from the sick.

On the quarterdeck Hill and Bourne bore the brunt of the activity, for Drinkwater had doubled the watches, and Rispin and Gorton were stationed in the waist, or forward, supervising the staving off of the ice.

And through it all Drinkwater kept the deck, his mind numbed with weariness, yet continually aware of every influence upon the movement of his ship. At moments of greatest peril he was the first to be aware of a sudden set towards a berg, the swirl of undertow suggesting the submerged presence of a growler or the catspaw of a squall from the turbulent lee of a large ice hummock. And it was Drinkwater who first suspected there might be something wrong with the rudder. It was nothing serious, a suspicious creaking when he listened from the privacy of the quarter-gallery latrine, a certain sluggishness as *Melusine* came to starboard. In fact it was at first only a suspicion, a figment, he thought, of an over-anxious mind. In the face of more pressing problems he tended to dismiss it. When he came below at the end of his three-day vigil as they drifted into the 'open' water and the wind, perversely, fell to a dead calm, he flung himself across his cot in grateful oblivion.

But when he woke, with *Melusine* rolling gently on a long, low swell, he heard again the creak from the rudder stock below.

Wearily he came on deck to find Hill on watch.

'What time is it, Mr Hill?'

'Six bells in the afternoon watch, sir.'

'I have slept the clock round . . . tell me, do the quartermasters complain of the steering?'

'No, sir.' Drinkwater looked at the two men at the wheel.

'How does she steer?'

'She seems to drag a little, sir, a coming to 'midships.'

'When you've had helm which way?'

'Larboard, I think, sir.'

'Why didn't you report it?'

The man shrugged. 'Only noticed it today, sir, while we've bin tryin' to catch this fluky wind, sir.'

'Very well.' He turned to Hill. 'I'm mystified, Mr Hill, but we'll keep an eye on it. Damned if I don't think there's something amiss, but what, I'm at a loss to know.'

'Aye, aye, sir, I'll take a look in the steerage if you wish.' Drinkwater nodded and Hill slipped below to return a few minutes later shaking his head.

'Nothing wrong, sir. Not that I can see.'

'Very well.'

'That whale hit the rudder, sir, and we've had a fair number of these damned ice floes . . .'

'Deck there!' They both looked aloft. 'Deck there! Think I can see gun-fire three points to starboard!'

The two officers looked at each other, then Drinkwater shouted, 'silence there!' They stood listening. A faint boom came rolling over the limpid water. 'That's gun-fire, by God!' Drinkwater ran forward and swung himself up into the main rigging. As he climbed he stared about him, trying to locate the whalers, aware that they had become widely dispersed in their struggle through the ice. He could see *Diana*, about five miles away to the eastward and ahead of them eight, perhaps ten miles distant was *Truelove*. Yes, her barque rig could be plainly seen beneath the curved foot of the main topgallant. *Earl Percy* and *Provident* were also to the east. He struggled up into the crow's nest as Leek slid agilely down.

'Where away?' gasped Drinkwater with the effort of his climb.

'Four points now, sir. I think it's where I last saw *Faithful*, sir, lost her behind a berg.'

'Very well.' He picked up the glass and stared to the south-west. He could see nothing. 'Leek!'

'Sir?'

'Away to Mr Hill, ask him to rig out the booms and set stun's'ls aloft and alow.'

'Stun's'ls aloft 'n' alow, aye, sir.' He watched Leek reach out like a monkey, over one hundred feet above the deck, and casually grab a backstay. The man diminished in size as he descended and Drinkwater levelled his glass once more. He felt the mast tremble as the topmen mounted the shrouds, he heard the mates and midshipmen as they supervised the rigging of the booms and the leading of outhauls and downhauls, heel-ropes and sheets. And then, as his patience was running out, he felt *Melusine* heel as she increased her speed. Five minutes later he located the *Faithful*.

She was fifteen or twenty miles away, perhaps more, for it was hard to judge. Her shape was vertically attenuated by refraction. She seemed to float slightly above the surface of the sea amid a city of the most fantastic minarets, a fairy-tale picture reminiscent of the Arabian Nights displaced to a polar latitude. But Drinkwater's interest was diverted from the extraordinary appearance of refracted icebergs by the unusual shape alongside the *Faithful*. At first he took it for a mirror image of the whaler. But then he saw the little points of yellow light between the ships. Sawyers was a Quaker and carried no guns. The second image was a hostile ship; an enemy engaging *Faithful*. Drinkwater swore; he was seven leagues away in light airs at the very moment Earl St Vincent had foreseen his presence would be required to protect the whalers.

'An enemy sir?'

'Yes, Mr Bourne, at a guess twenty miles distant and already with a prize crew on board the *Faithful*, damn it . . . Mr Hill, bear up, bear up! D'you not see the growler on the starboard bow . . .' Drinkwater broke off to cough painfully. His throat was rasped raw by the persistent demands made on him to shout orders, but he felt an overwhelming desire to press after the ship that had taken one of his charges from under his very nose.

'I have a midshipman at the masthead and want a pair of young eyes kept on the enemy and prize until they're both under our lee. The midshipman that loses sight of them will marry the gunner's daughter!' He coughed again. 'Now double the watches, Mr Bourne, this may prove a long chase.'

'Aye, aye, sir.' Bourne hesitated, unwilling to provoke a captain whom he knew to be short-tempered if his orders were not attended to without delay. 'Beg pardon, sir, but what about the other ships?'

'I have made them a signal to the effect that I am chasing an enemy to the south-west. My orders to them oblige them to close together. Let us hope they do what they are told, Mr Bourne.'

Bourne took the hint, touched the fore-cock of his hat and hurried off. Drinkwater swallowed with difficulty, swore, and set himself to pace the quarterdeck, leaving the business of working the ship through the ice to Hill until he was relieved by Bourne himself at eight bells. He was beyond shouting orders, feeling a mild fever coming on and worrying over the loss of the *Faithful* and the ominous creaking that came from the rudder. But *Melusine* handled well enough and after another hour Tregembo appeared to announce Drinkwater's dinner, served late, as had become his custom in high latitudes to try and differentiate between day and night in the perpetual light.

It was while he was eating that Mr Frey came below to report they had lost the wind and the enemy.

'What . . .?' His voice whispered and he tried to clear his throat. 'Upon what point of sailing was the enemy and prize when last seen, Mr Frey?'

'Both ships were close hauled on the starboard tack, sir. They had a fair breeze before the fog closed in.'

'And their heading?'

'South-west, sir.'

'Very well. Tell Mr Bourne to strike the stun's'ls, and reduce to all plain sail. Double the forward lookouts and make a good course towards the south-west. A man to go to the mainmast head every hour to see if the enemy masts are above the fog. Kindly call me in two hours time.'

'Aye, aye, sir.' Frey hesitated in the doorway.

'Well, what is it?'

'If you please, sir, Mr Bourne said I was to ask you if you wanted Mr Singleton to attend you?'

'Damn Mr Bourne's impertinence, Mr Frey, you've your orders to attend to . . .' The boy fled and, rolling himself in his cloak, Drinkwater flung himself across his cot shivering.

Two hours later Mr Frey called him. Staggering to his feet, his head spinning, Drinkwater ascended to the quarterdeck. Although the thermometer registered some 36° Fahrenheit it seemed colder. Every rope and spar dripped with moisture and the decks were dark with it. Mr Bourne touched his hat and vacated his side of the quarterdeck. It could not by any stretch of the imagination be described as the 'windward side' for *Melusine* lay wallowing in a calm. Almost alongside her a ridge of ice, hummocked and cracked with apparent age gleamed wetly in the greyness. It was not daylight, neither was it night. The ship might have been the only living thing in an eternity of primordial mist, an atmosphere at once eerie and oppressive through which each creak of the ship's fabric, each slat of idle canvas or groan of parrel as she rolled in the low swell, seemed invested with a more than ordinary significance. The grinding creak from the rudder stock seemed deafening now. Drinkwater was too sick to attribute this heightened perception to his fever, and too unsteady on his legs to begin to pace the deck. Instead he jammed himself against the rail close to the mizen rigging and beckoned Bourne over.

'Sir?'

'Mr Bourne, my apologies. I was short with Frey when he offered the services of the doctor.'

' 'Tis no matter, sir, but I thought you looked unwell . . .'

'Yes, yes, Mr Bourne, thank you for your kindness. I will see Singleton in due course. But I am more concerned with the rudder. Had you noticed the noise?'

'Mr Hill drew it to my attention. The ship has long lost steerage way, sir. But I had no reason to doubt much was wrong, sir. She answered the helm well enough when last the wind blew.'

Drinkwater nodded, then spoke with great difficulty. 'Yes, yes, but I fear the matter is a progressive disintegration of some sort. No matter, there is nothing to be done at the moment. You have no sign of those ships?'

'None, sir.'

'Very well. That is all, Mr Bourne.'

Bourne turned away and Drinkwater hunched his shoulders into his cloak. His right shoulder ached with the onset of the damp weather, his throat was sore and his toothache seemed to batter his whole skull.

The fog lasted for four days and was followed by a south-westerly gale during which the visibility never lifted above a half a mile. The air was filled with particles of frozen rain so that Drinkwater was obliged to secure the *Melusine* to a large ice floe. At the height of the gale he submitted to the ministrations of Mr Singleton and suffered a brief agony which ended his toothache by the extraction of a rotten molar. But the removal of the tooth also signalled the end of his quinsy. On the advice of Singleton he kept to his cabin and his cot while the *Melusine* was alongside the ice. There was, in any case, little he could do on deck and, as Singleton pointed out, his recovery would be the quicker and he would be fitter to attend his duties, the instant the gale abated and the visibility lifted.

He did not protest. His general debility was, he realised himself, his own fault. In circumstances of such peril as *Melusine* had so often been, it was physically impossible to keep the deck permanently. His confidence in his lieutenants had not initially been high and he had found it very difficult to go below in circumstances of broad daylight. However, the days of working the ship through the ice had improved the proficiency of Bourne and Gorton. Even

Rispin showed more firmness and self-confidence, while Hill and the other warrant officers appeared to carry out their duties efficiently. In addition to the worry and sense of failure at the capture of *Faithful*, his shoulder plagued him, reducing his morale and subjecting him to fits of the 'blue devils' while the fever lasted. All the while the rudder ground remorselessly below him, like a long-fused petard waiting to explode. Despite its comparative idleness while they were secured to the floe, it continued to grind and groan as *Melusine* ranged and bumped the ice, rolling and sawing at her moorings as the gale moaned in the rigging. Meanwhile the watch stumbled about the deck, wound in furs, greygoes, even blankets, to combat the stinging particles in the air.

Ten days after the onset of the fog there came a change in the weather that was as abrupt as it was unexpected and delightful. A sense of renewed hope coincided with this change, sending Drinkwater on deck a fit man, all traces of quinsy and fever gone. He was burning to resume the pursuit of the unknown enemy ship that had taken the *Faithful* from under his nose. The situation of the *Melusine* had been transformed. The sun shone through a fine veil of cloud producing a prismatic halo upon the horizontal diameter of which appeared two parhelia, faint false suns, the results of atmospheric refraction. This phenomena was exciting some comment from the watch on deck and had so far absorbed Mr Rispin's interest that he had neglected to inform Drinkwater of the dramatic change in the weather. It was bitterly cold. On every rope and along the furled sails the moisture had frozen into tiny crystals which were glinting in the sunshine. Drinkwater sniffed the air and felt its chill tingle the membranes of his nasal passages. The resultant sneeze recalled Rispin belatedly to his duty.

'Oh, good morning, sir. As you see, sir, the wind has dropped and the visibility is lifting . . .'

'Yes, yes, Mr Rispin, I can see that for myself . . .' Drinkwater replied testily. The appearance of the twin sun dogs alarmed him, not on any superstitious account, but because he recollected something Harvey had said about their appearance indicating a change of weather. That much was obvious, but there had been something said about wind. He looked at the weft on the windward dog-vane. It hung down motionless. Casting his eyes aloft he saw that the masthead pendant was already lifting to a light air from the north. He also saw the crow's nest was empty.

'Mr Rispin!'

'Sir?'

'Direct a midshipman aloft upon the instant to look out for any sails, then have the topsails hard reefed and loosed in their buntlines, the foretopmast stays'l and spanker ready for setting and the longboat hoisted out and manned ready to pull the ship's head off.'

Rispin's mouth opened, then closed as his eyes filled with comprehension. He might be slow on the uptake, thought Drinkwater as he forced himself to a patience he was far from feeling, but Mr Rispin certainly made up for what he lacked in intelligence by a veritable out-pouring:

'Mr Glencross, aloft at once with a glass and cast about for sails. Bosun's mate! Pipe the watch aloft to loose topsails, topmen to remain at the yard arms and the bunts and await the order "let fall". Corporal of marines! Turn up the marines and send 'em aft to man the yard tackles. Master at Arms! Turn up the idlers below to man the stay tackles. Look lively there!' Rispin turned frantically, waving the speaking trumpet. 'Mr Walmsley! Have the afterguard cast loose the stops on the spanker. Fo'c's'le there! Cast loose the fore topmast stays'l!' Rispin's brow wrinkled in thought as he mentally ticked off the tasks Drinkwater had set him.

Already the dog-vanes pointed north and the wefts were lifting. Drinkwater watched a catspaw of wind ripple the surface of the clear water to starboard. A low raft of ice a cable to windward seemed to be perceptibly nearer.

'You may cut the moorings, Mr Rispin!'

'Cut the moorings, aye, aye, sir.' Rispin's relief was noticeable. He had clearly forgotten the necessity of putting a party onto the ice and the difficult business of recovering them by boat once the ship had got clear.

Hill and Bourne had come on deck, alarmed by the bellowing at the hatchways. Drinkwater nodded to them. 'We are about to get a blow from the north, gentlemen, I want the ship off this ice floe before we are trapped. The boat is about to be launched to pull her head off.'

Both Hill and Bourne acknowledged the immediacy of Drinkwater's alarm. There was already a perceptible breeze from the north, icy and dry after the southwesterly gale. 'Turn up the watch below, Mr Bourne!'

The longboat was already swaying up from the waist, the marines stamping aft as they leant their weight to the yard tackles that hoisted the boat out over the side. Mr Quilhampton was standing on the rail in charge of the launching party.

'Walk back all!' The boat descended below the rail as the last of her crew tumbled in. A second or two later she hit the water. 'Cone up all!' Marines and idlers relaxed as the tackles went slack and on the fo'c's'le Walmsley's party, having prepared the staysail, made a line ready for the boat. A carpenter's party was hacking through the moorings and in the tops Frey, Wickham and Dutfield held up their hands to indicate the topsails were ready.

A glance at the dog-vanes showed the wefts horizontal. It was not a moment too soon. There were pronounced white caps on the water to windward and *Melusine* was rubbing against the ice with some violence.

Drinkwater could feel the sensation of physical discomfort churning the pit of his stomach as his body adjusted to the state of acute worry. Ten minutes neglect by Rispin and they might remain pinned on the floe. He thought of setting sail in an attempt to spin the floe, but he had only the vaguest idea of its size. He was grasping at straws. Officers were reporting his preparations complete and he ordered the yards braced sharp up on the larboard catharpings. The boat was attempting to pull *Melusine*'s head round towards the wind and, although the bow came some six feet off the ice they seemed to be unable to increase that distance. Forward a resourceful Mr Gorton was getting out a spare topgallant yard and lashing it to prevent losing what the longboat had gained. Meanwhile Mr Quilhampton was urging his boat's crew to further efforts, but *Melusine* seemed unwilling to move. On the last occasion this had occurred they had bounced off the remains of *Narwhal*. This time they did not have such help.

'Mr Bourne!' The lieutenant's face turned anxiously towards him.

'Sir?'

'Man the larboard guns, two divisions to fire unshotted cartridges alternately. The breechings to be set up tight. We'll use the recoil to throw the ship off.'

'Aye, aye, sir! Larbowlines! Larboard battery make ready . . . !'

It took several minutes, much longer than if the men had been at their stations for action. But there was no-one on deck, except perhaps Meetuck, who was not seaman enough to appreciate the nature of their situation. Hill was dragging a pudding fender aft to heave over the larboard quarter.

'Well done, Mr Hill . . .'

Drinkwater watched the dog-vanes, his stomach churning. He felt his isolation from the comforting expertise of the whale-ship masters acutely. It prompted him to hail the mainmasthead.

'Masthead there!'

Glencross's head appeared. 'D'you have anything in sight?'

'No, sir! There seems to be clear water to leeward of this floe, but no sails, sir.'

'Very well.' Drinkwater directed his thoughts to the fate of the *Faithful*. In which direction should he chase once he got clear of their present situation? He tried not to think of the possibility of their failing to clear the floe. *Melusine* was not fit for such work in these latitudes. He began to see the weaknesses of St Vincent's reforms undertaken in a mere temporary truce, while the protagonists of this great war caught their breath. But he had no time for further considerations. Bourne reported the guns ready.

'Very well. Forward battery to fire first and to reload as fast as possible. Fastest guns' crew will receive a double tot of rum. But no rolling fire, Mr Bourne, half broadsides only, to make best use of the recoil.'

'Aye, aye sir. I took the liberty of double-loading . . .'

'Have a care then, one round only doubled, Mr Bourne. See to it yourself and open fire without delay.'

Drinkwater clasped his hands behind his back with anxiety as Bourne ran along the deck. It would certainly make the ship recoil, double charging the guns like that. But it might also blow the chambers of the guns . .

'Fire!' The forward division of guns jerked back against their lashed breechings and their crews leapt round them, swabs and rammers plied as *Melusine* trembled. Drinkwater leaned over the side to see the rope to the longboat curve slightly.

'Pull, Mr Q! Pull!'

He saw Quilhampton wave as a sea swept over the bow of the boat. The after division of the larboard battery roared, the guns leaping against the capsquares on the restrained carriages.

Drinkwater strode to the larboard side and looked overboard. There was a slight gap between the *Melusine*'s tumblehome and the ice edge. He raised his glance forward to see Gorton rigging out another foot of spare spar. They would not lose what they had gained. He must remember to congratulate Gorton on his initiative.

'Fire!' The forward division of six pounders roared again and this time Drinkwater saw the sloop move, her head falling off as Gorton rigged out his spar a little more. Aft, Hill let the fender down so that the larboard quarter could set in on the ice, increasing the angle with the floe. If they could achieve an angle of two points, twenty-two and a half degrees, they might theoretically sail off, but in practise a greater angle would be required, for they would fall back towards the ice as they got the ship underway. The after division fired a second time.

There was no doubt that they were gaining on the wind! But that too was increasing. The forward division fired a third time.

Gorton's spar jerked out again, but Drinkwater could see the strain it was bearing.

'Mr Bourne! Hold the after battery and reload the forrard. All guns to fire simultaneously!'

'Tops there! Let fall the instant the guns discharge!' The three midshipmen acknowledged. 'And, Mr Hill, direct the sheets to be hove to the yardarms the instant the buntlines are slackened!'

'Very well, sir!'

Drinkwater was sweating with excitement despite the numbness of his hands. Quilhampton's boat was a liability now, but he dare not cast if off just yet.

'Ready sir.'

'Very well, Mr Bourne. Fire!'

Melusine shuddered throughout her entire length. Somewhere amidships an ominous crack sounded. But it was not the spar. Gorton's party grunted and swore with effort as their yard, hove out with an extempore tackle at its heel, took up two feet of increased gap. Astern *Melusine*'s larboard quarter ground against the pudding-fender.

Above his head the sails creaked and cracked with ice as the men at the sheets hove down on the frozen canvas.

'Hoist away fore and aft!' The staysail rose from the fo'c's'le head and behind him the spanker was hauled out upon its gaff and boom.

'I can't hold her, sir!' Gorton cried from forward. Drinkwater's heart thumped with anxiety as *Melusine* gathered way.

'No matter, Mr Gorton . . .' The last words were drowned in the splitting crack that came from Gorton's breaking topgallant yard. *Melusine*'s head fell back towards the floe, but she was already gaining speed.

'Mr Gorton, cut the longboat free and hoist the jib!'

Drinkwater stared forward. 'Steady, keep her full and bye, quartermaster. Not an inch to loo'ard.'

'Nothing to loo'ard, sir, aye, aye.'

But she was falling back. The gap between the ice and *Melusine*'s hull was narrowing.

It was too late to order another broadside prepared. He gritted his teeth and watched the inevitable occur. The shock of collision was jarring, knocking some unsuspecting men to the deck, but *Melusine* bounced clear and began to stand off the ice. Half an hour later she hove-to in comparatively clear water and waited for the longboat to come up.

Drinkwater looked up from the chart and tapped it with the dividers. Bourne and Hill bent over the table at the broken and imperfect line that delineated the east coast of Greenland. There were a few identifiable names far to the south, Cape Farewell and Cape Discord, then innumerable gaps until Hudson's anchorage of Hold with Hope.

'I believe our present situation to be here, some sixty leagues west-nor'-west of Trinity Island.

'I believe that the enemy approached from, and retired to, the south-west. We should have seen him earlier had he attacked from any other quarter and it argues favourably to my theory that it was *Faithful* he took, the ship most advanced into that quarter. In addition the last sighting of him and his prize was to the south-west and sailing on the same point. I therefore propose that we chase in that direction. It is inconceivable that he did not experience the fog and south-westerly gale that we have just had and it may be that he is not far away.'

'What about the other whale ships, sir?' asked the cautious Bourne.

Drinkwater looked at the young man. 'There are times when it is necessary to take risks, Mr Bourne. They are armed and alerted to the presence of enemy cruisers while *Faithful was* unarmed and *is* a prize. It argues for our honour as well as our duty that we pursue *Faithful* with a view to retaking her.'

'D'you think there are more French cruisers in the area, sir?'

'It's a possibility that there are. I have reason to believe there may be.'

'You were aware of the possibility?' asked Hill.

'Yes,' Drinkwater nodded. 'That is why *Melusine* was appointed escort to the whale-fleet.'

Drinkwater understood what Hill was implying. It made the capture of *Faithful* highly discreditable to *Melusine* and her commander, despite the practical impossibilities of policing the whole Greenland Sea.

'What about the Spitzbergen ships, sir?'

Drinkwater shrugged. 'One can only be in one place at one time, Mr Hill. Besides I believe that the capture of *Faithful* at least argues to our being in the right area, if not in the right position to prevent the capture. At all events, now it is our duty to reverse that. Do you have any more questions?'

First lieutenant and master shook their heads.

'Very well, gentlemen. In the meantime there is no need to impress upon you the necessity of keeping a sharp lookout.'

Chapter Fourteen *July 1803*

The Corsair

Drinkwater awoke from a dream that had not disturbed him for many months since the nightmares of his delirium following the wounding he had received off Boulogne. But it terrified him as much as upon the first occasion he had experienced it, as a callow and frightened midshipman on the frigate *Cyclops*. Again the terrifying inability to move laid him supine beneath the advance of the ghastly white lady who over-rode his body to the accompanying clanking of chains. Over the years the white lady had assumed different guises. She had appeared to him with the face of Hortense Santhonax, sister to one of the French Republic's most daring frigate captains and secret agents, or as the sodomite tyrant of *Cyclops*'s cockpit, the unspeakably evil Augustus Morris. Now she had a visage as cold as the icebergs that had given him so many nightmares of a more tangible nature in recent weeks. Her eyes had been of that piercing and translucent blue he had noticed forming in the shadows of pinnacles and spires. Although she changed her appearance Drinkwater knew the white lady had not lost the power to awake in him a strong feeling of presentiment.

He lay perspiring, despite the fact that his exposed feet were registering air at a temperature well below the freezing of water. He began to relax as he heard the rudder grind. It had been grinding so long now with so little apparent ill-effect that he had almost ceased to worry about it. Was he being cautioned by fate to pay it more attention? He tossed aside the blankets and with them such a childish notion. He was about to call the sentry to pass word for Tregembo when he considered it was probably still night, despite the light that came through the cabin windows.

He had almost forgotten the dream as he ascended to the deck. But its superstitious hold was once more thrown over him as he stepped clear of the ladder.

Meetuck turned from the rail where he seemed to have been looking at something, and his almond eyes fell upon Drinkwater with an almost hostile glare. The eskimo, whom Drinkwater had not seen for several days, took a step towards him. Meetuck was muttering something: then he halted, looked at his arm, which was still splinted, shrugged and turned forward.

Mystified by this pantomime Drinkwater nodded to Mr Bourne, who had the deck, and swung himself into the main rigging, reaching the crow's nest and ousting Glencross who appeared to have made himself comfortable with a small flask of rum and a bag of biscuit.

'You may leave that there, Mr Glencross. I doubt you'll be requiring them on deck.' The midshipman cast a rueful glance at the rum and mumbled, 'Aye, aye, sir.'

'I shall return the flask, Mr Glencross, in due course.'

Drinkwater settled himself down with the telescope. In five minutes all thoughts of dreams or eskimos had been driven from his mind. The wind had held steady from the north and they sailed through an almost clear sea, the bergs within five miles being largely decayed and eroded into soft outlines. More distant bergs presented a fantastic picture which increased in its improbability as he watched. Munching his way through Glencross's biscuit and warmed by the rum, he had been aloft for over an hour, enjoying the spectacle of increasing refraction as the sun climbed. The distant icebergs, floes and hummocks seemed cast into every possible shape the imagination could devise. He sighted a number of polar bears and numerous seals lay basking upon low ice. Once the ship passed through a school of narwhals, the males with their curious twisted swords. He saw, too, a number of grampuses, their black and livid white skin a brilliant contrast to the sea as they gambolled like huge dolphins in *Melusine*'s wake as she pressed south-west. Drinkwater was reminded of Sawyers and the whale-captain's regard for the works of God in Arctic waters. He was also reminded of Sawyers's present plight.

It was four bells into the morning watch before Drinkwater saw what he had been looking for, amid the ice pinnacles on their starboard bow, almost indistinguishable from them except to one who had a hunter's keenness of purpose. The edges of sails, betrayed by the inverted image of two ships, their waterlines uppermost, jutted dark into the glare of the sky. They were perhaps thirty miles away and the easing of the wind and the comparative simplicity of navigation through such loose ice suited the slight and slender *Melusine*.

Descending to the deck, Drinkwater passed orders for the course to be amended three points closer to the wind and the corvette to hoist a press of sail. He doubted if *Melusine* presented such a conspicuous picture to the enemy, given her relative position to the sun, but if they were spotted he felt sure the ship's speed would close the gap between them and the distant *Faithful*, whose sea-keeping qualities were far superior to her speed.

At noon the distance between them had closed appreciably and at the end of the first dog-watch the enemy could be clearly seen from the head of the lower masts.

Drinkwater dined with Singleton and Bourne, remarking on the way the eskimo had startled him that morning.

'You mean you thought he had some hostile intent, sir?' asked Singleton.

'Oh, I conceived that impression for a second or two. His appearance was aggressive, but he seemed suddenly to recall some obligation relative to his arm.'

'So he damned well should,' said Bourne.

'Can you recall what he said to you, Captain?' asked Singleton, ignoring Bourne.

Drinkwater swallowed his wine and frowned. 'Not perfectly, but I recall something like "gavloonack" . . .'

'Gavdlunaq?'

'Yes, I think that was it. Why? Does it signify to you?'

'It means "white man". Was there anything else?'

Drinkwater thought again. 'Yes, nothing I could repeat though. Oh, he mentioned that place he said he came from . . .'

'Nagtoralik?'

'Aye, that was it, *Nagtoralik*.' Drinkwater experimented with the strange word. 'A place with eagles, didn't you say?'

'Yes, that's right, but I don't recall eagles being mentioned by Egedé . . .'

Drinkwater threw back his head and laughed. 'Oh, come, Mr Singleton, you academics! If a thing ain't in print in some dusty library it don't signify that it don't exist.' Bourne joined in the laughter and Singleton flushed.

'There is a Greenland Falcon, the *Falco Rusticolus Candicans* of

Gmelin which the innuits, in their unfamiliarity with the order Aves, may mistake for eagles. It is possible that an error in nomenclature took place in translation . . .' Bourne chuckled at Singleton's seriousness as Drinkwater said, somewhat archly, 'Indeed that may be the case, Mr Singleton.'

A silence filled the cabin. Singleton frowned 'To return to Meetuck, sir. You can recall nothing further, nothing specific, I mean?'

Drinkwater shook his head. 'No. He was looking over the side, saw me, turned and advanced, uttered this imprecation, looked at his arm and went off forward. I can scarcely expect anything better from a savage.' Then Drinkwater became aware of something preoccupied about Singleton. 'What is it, Mr Singleton? Why are you so interested in an incident of no importance?'

Singleton leaned back in his chair. 'Because I believe it may indeed be of some significance, sir. I understand you are chasing to the south-west, chasing an enemy ship, a French ship perhaps?'

Drinkwater looked at Bourne enquiringly. The first lieutenant shrugged. 'Yes,' said Drinkwater, 'that is correct.'

'Why do you think this ship is running south-west, sir?'

'Well, Mr Singleton, the wind is favourable, she is luring us away from our other charges and the sea is less encumbered by ice in this direction.'

'It is also in the direction of the coast, sir.'

'And . . .?'

'And I believe Meetuck, though he is not very intelligent, even for an eskimo, has seen white men before, white men who have been hostile to him. I believe that before setting out on the ice he may have come from the Greenland coast where white men were . . .'

'Frenchmen?' broke in Bourne.

'It is possible,' said Singleton, turning to the lieutenant.

'It is indeed,' said Drinkwater thoughtfully, remembering the cautionary words of Lord Dungarth in his room at the Admiralty.

'You have some information upon that point, Captain?' asked Singleton shrewdly, but before Drinkwater could reply the cabin door burst open. Midshipman Lord Walmsley stood in the doorway. His usual look of studied contempt was replaced by alarm.

'An enemy, sir, to windward a bare league . . .'

Drinkwater rose. 'Beat to quarters, damn it!'

*

Mr Rispin had been caught out again. The enemy ship had clearly sighted the pursuing sloop and whether she knew *Melusine* for a naval ship or took her for a whaler, she had left *Faithful* to head west-south-west alone and doubled back unobserved, to lurk behind a berg until *Melusine* came up. Drinkwater reached the quarterdeck as the marine drummer beat the *rafale*.

'Who was your masthead lookout, Mr Rispin?' he asked venomously, casting round for the enemy. He saw the Frenchman immediately, frigate-built and with the tricolour flying from her peak.

'As bold as bloody brass,' said Hill, taking up his station on the quarterdeck alongside the captain.

'Well sir?' Drinkwater stared unblinkingly at Rispin.

'Lord Walmsley, sir.'

'God damn and blast his lordship!'

'D'you wish me to take in sail, sir?'

'Aye, Mr Hill, turn down-wind and get the stuns'ls in. Mr Bourne, don't show our teeth yet, all guns load canister and ball but hold 'em inboard with closed ports.'

Hill altered course and Drinkwater watched the yards squared and the topmen work aloft, stiff monkeys in the frozen air as the studding sails fluttered on deck. He looked astern. A dozen burgomaster gulls flew in their wake and a few fulmars swept the sea to starboard but he no longer had time for such natural wonders. He was studying the strange ship coming up on their starboard quarter.

She was bigger than themselves, a frigate of twenty-eight guns, he reckoned, more than a match for the *Melusine* and wearing French colours.

A shot plunged into the water just astern of them. A second following a minute later struck the hull beneath his feet. Drinkwater hoped Cawkwell had lowered the window sashes. A third ball plunged under their stern. Her guns were well served and there was no doubt that, whether a national frigate or a well-appointed corsair, she was determined upon making a prize of the *Melusine*.

Drinkwater set his mouth in a grim line. He had fought the *Romaine* off the Cape of Good Hope from a position of disadvantage, but now there were no British cruisers in the offing to rescue him.

'Ship's cleared for action, sir.' Bourne touched his hat.

Drinkwater turned forward and looked along the deck. The gun crews were kneeling at their posts, the midshipmen with their parties in the fore and main tops, two men at each topgallant crossing and marines aloft in the mizen top. The sail trimmers were at the rails and pins; on the fo'c's'le the bosun stood, his silver whistle about his neck. The helm was in the hands of the two quartermasters with Mr Quilhampton standing casually alongside, his wooden hand holding the log slate. Gorton and Rispin commanded the two batteries, seconded by Glencross and Walmsley, while Mr Frey attended the quarterdeck, with Drinkwater, Hill, Bourne and Lieutenant Mount, whose marines lined the hammock nettings.

'Very well, Mr Bourne.' He raised his voice. 'Starboard battery make ready. I intend to haul our wind and rake from forward.' He paused as another enemy ball found their stern. 'You may fire as you bear, Mr Rispin, but take your time, my lads, and reload as if the devil was on your tail.' He nodded to Hill, 'Very well, Mr Hill, starboard tack, if you please.'

Melusine began to turn, heeling over as she brought the wind round on her beam. Gun captains pulled up their ports and drove home more quoins to counter-act the heel. Rispin, leaped from gun to gun, his hanger drawn.

'God damn! Mr Frey, pass word to Tregembo to get my sword . . . Where the devil have you been, Tregembo?'

'Sharpening your skewer, zur, 'twas as rusty as a church door knocker . . .' Tregembo buckled on the sword and handed Drinkwater a pair of pistols. 'An' I took down the portraits, zur.' He reproached Drinkwater, his old face wrinkling with a kind of rough affection.

Drinkwater managed a half smile and then turned his attention to the ship. Above their heads the braces were swinging the yards. From forward he heard the report of the first gun and watched the enemy for the fall of shot. He saw splinters fly from the vessel's knightheads. Each gun fired in turn as *Melusine* crossed the stranger's bow, and although one or two holes appeared in the Frenchman's fore course and several spouts of water showed on either bow, most seemed to strike home. But as *Melusine* stretched out on the starboard tack she too exposed her stern to the enemy. They fired a broadside and several balls furrowed the deck, one wounded the mizen topmast and holes opened in the spanker.

Somewhere below there rose the most horrible howl of agony and Drinkwater was aware of little Frey shaking beside him.

'Mr Frey,' said Drinkwater kindly, 'I don't believe anyone has loaded Captain Palgrave's fancy carronades. Would you and your two yeomen attend to it, canister might be useful later in the action, wouldn't you say?'

Frey focussed his eyes on the two brass carronades that Captain Palgrave's vanity had had installed at the hances. They still slumbered beneath oiled canvas covers. Frey nodded uncertainly and then with more vigour. 'Aye, aye, sir.' It would be good for the child to have something to do.

Astern of them the enemy hauled into their wake. The *Melusine*'s French build began to take effect. She started to open the distance between them.

'Mr Bourne, pass word for the gunner to report to me.'

The gunner was called for at the hatchways and made his appearance a moment or two later, his felt slippers sliding incongruously upon the planking.

'Ah, Mr Meggs, I want a caulked keg of powder with a three-minute fuse sealed up in canvas soon as you are able to arrange it.'

The gunner frowned, raised an eyebrow and compressed his toothless mouth. Then, without a word, knuckled his forehead and waddled below. Drinkwater turned to Bourne.

'Well, Mr Bourne, whatever our friend is, he'll not get a gun to bear at the moment.'

Hill came up. 'D'you intend to mine him, sir?'

Drinkwater grinned. 'We'll try. It's a long shot, but I'm not certain that he's a national frigate. I have an idea that he may be a letter-of-marque, in which case he'll be stuffed full of men and we cannot risk him boarding.'

'I am of the same opinion, sir. There's something about him that marks him as a corsair.'

'Yes. Now, we don't want him to see the keg dragging down on him so we will put it over forrard and lead the line out of a forrard port. That way he will not observe any activity around the stern here . . .'

'Use the log-line, sir? It's handy and long enough,' asked Hill.

'Very well. Do that if you please.' Drinkwater looked forward. 'But first, I think you had better luff, Mr Hill.'

'Jesus!' Hill's jaw dropped in alarm as the berg reared over them. Drinkwater held his breath lest *Melusine* struck some underwater projection from the icy mass that towered over the mastheads. 'Down helm!'

Melusine swooped into the wind, her sails shivering, then paid off again as the berg drew astern. Their pursuer, his attention focussed ahead, had laid a course to pass almost as clear as his quarry. That the *Melusine* could shave the berg indicated that it was safe for him to do so, and Drinkwater remarked to Hill on the skill of their enemy.

'Aye, sir, and that argues strongly that he's a letter-of-marque.'

Drinkwater nodded. 'And he'll be able to read our name across our stern and know all about our being a French prize.'

Hill nodded and Bourne rejoined them. 'Meggs says he'll be a further ten minutes, sir, before the keg is ready.'

'Very good, Mr Bourne. Will you direct Rispin to take watch on the fo'c'sle and warn us of any ice ahead. Take over the starboard battery yourself.'

Bourne looked crestfallen but acknowledged the order and moved forward to the waist.

Meggs brought the wrapped keg to the quarterdeck in person.

'Three-minute fuse, sir,' he said, handing over the keg to Hill who had mustered three sail-trimmers to carry the thing forward, together with the log-line tub. Five minutes later Drinkwater saw him straighten up and look expectantly aft. Drinkwater nodded and leaned over the side. The keg drifted astern as *Melusine* rushed past, the log-line paying out. Snatching up his glass Drinkwater knelt and focussed his telescope, levelling it on the taffrail and shouting for Quilhampton.

'Mr Q! The instant I say, you are to tell Hill to hold on.'

'Hold on, aye, aye, sir.'

Drinkwater could see the canvas sack lying in the water. It jerked a few times, sending up little spurts of water as the ship dragged it along when the line became tight, but in the main it drifted astern without appreciably disturbing the wake. He wondered if his opponent would have a vigilant lookout at the knightheads. He did not seem a man to underestimate.

Suddenly in the image glass he saw not only the keg, but the stem of the advancing ship. The bow wave washed the keg to one side.

'Hold on!'

'Hold on!' repeated Quilhampton and Drinkwater saw the line jerk tight and then the persistent feather of water as *Melusine* dragged the keg astern, right under the larboard bow of the pursuing Frenchman.

He wondered how long it had taken to veer the thing astern. Perhaps no more than a minute or a minute and a half. He wondered, too, how good a fuse Meggs had set. It was quite likely that the damned thing would be extinguished by now. It was, as he had admitted to Hill, a long shot.

'Stand by to tack ship, Mr Q!'

Quilhampton passed the order and Drinkwater stood up. He could do no more, and his shoulder hurt from the awkward position it was necessary to assume to stare with such concentration at the enemy's bow. The keg blew apart as he bent to rub his knees.

'Larboard tack!'

He felt the deck cant as the helm went down and Hill ran aft telling his men to haul in the log-line. Struggling down on his knees again he levelled his glass. At first he thought that they had achieved nothing and then he saw the Frenchman's bowsprit slowly rise. The bobstay at least had suffered and, deprived of its downward pull the jibs and staysails set on the forestays above combined with the leeward pull of the foremast to crack the big spar. He saw it splinter and the sails pull it in two. There was a mass of men upon the enemy fo'c's'le.

He spun his feet. 'We have him now, by God!' But *Melusine* had ceased to turn to starboard. She was paying off before the wind.

'She won't answer, sir! She won't answer!'

It was then that Drinkwater remembered the rudder.

Chapter Fifteen *28 July 1803*

The Action with the 'Requin'

Drinkwater did not know how much damage he had inflicted upon the enemy, only that his own ship was now effectively at the mercy of the other. It was true the loss of a bowsprit severely hampered the manoeuvrability of a ship, but by shortening down and balancing his loss of forward sail with a reduction aft, the enemy still had his vessel under command. And there was a good enough breeze to assist any manoeuvre carried out in such a condition.

As for themselves, he had no time to think of the loss of the rudder, beyond the fact that they were a sitting duck. But the enemy could not guess what damage had been inflicted by fortune upon the *Melusine.*

'Heave the ship to under topsails, Mr Hill!' Drinkwater hoped he might convey to his opponent the impression of being a cautious man. A man who would not throw away his honour entirely, but one who considered that, having inflicted a measure of damage upon his enemy, would then heave to and await the acceptance of his challenge without seeking out further punishment.

Despatching Hill to examine and report upon the damage to the rudder Drinkwater called Bourne aft.

'Now, Mr Bourne, if I read yon fellow aright, he ain't a man to refuse our provocation. It's my guess that he will work up to windward of us then close and board. I want every man issued with small arms, cutlasses, pikes and tomahawks. The larboard guns you are to abandon, the gun crews doubling to starboard so that the fastest possible fire may be directed at his hull. Canister and ball into his waist. Mr Mount! Your men to pick off the officers, you may station them where you like, but I want six marines and twenty seamen below as reinforcements. You will command 'em, Mr Bourne, and I want 'em out of the stern windows and up over the taffrail. So muster them in my cabin and open the skylight.

Either myself, Hill or Quilhampton will pass word to you. But you are not to appear unless I order it. Do you understand?'

'Aye, aye, sir.'

'Oh, and Mr Bourne, blacken your faces at the galley range on your way below.'

'Very good, sir.'

'And you had better warn Singleton what is about to take place. Tell him he'll have some work to do. By the way who was hit by that first ball?'

'Cawkwell, sir. He's lost a leg, I believe.'

'Poor devil.'

'He was closing the cabin sashes, sir.'

'Oh.'

Drinkwater turned away and watched the enemy. As he had guessed, the Frenchman was moving up to windward. They had perhaps a quarter of an hour to wait.

'Mr Frey!'

'Are your two carronades loaded?'

'Aye, sir.'

'I think you may have employment for them soon. Now you are to man the windward one first and you are not to fire until I pass you the express order to do so. When I order you to open fire you are to direct the discharge into the thickest mass of men which crowd the enemy waist. Do you understand?'

The boy nodded. 'I need a cool head for the job, Mr Frey.' He lowered his voice confidentially. 'It's a post of honour, Mr Frey, I beg you not to let me down.' The boy's eyes opened wide. He was likely to be dead or covered in glory in the next half-hour, Drinkwater thought.

'I will not disappoint you, sir.'

'Very good. Now, listen even more carefully. When you have discharged the windward carronade you are to cross to the other and train it inboard. If you see a number of black-faced savages come over the taffrail you are to sweep the waist ahead of them with shot, even, Mr Frey, even if you appear to be firing into our own men.'

The boy's eyes opened wider. 'Now that is a very difficult order to obey, Mr Frey. But that is your duty. D'you understand me now?'

The boy swallowed. 'Yes, sir.'

'Very good.' Drinkwater smiled again, as though he had just

asked Frey to fetch him an apple, or some other similarly inconsequential task. He went to the forward end of the quarterdeck and called for silence in the waist, where the men were sorting out the small arms, joking at the prospect of a fight.

'Silence there, my lads.' He waited until he had their attention. 'When I order you to fire I want you to pour in as much shot across his hammock nettings then hold him from boarding. If he presses us hard you will hear the bosun's whistle. That is the signal to fall back. Seamen forward under Lieutenants Rispin and Gorton. Marines aft under Mr Mount. When Mr Bourne's reserve party appears from aft you will resume the attack and reman your guns as we drive these impertinent Frenchmen into the sea. I shall then call for the fore course to be let fall in order that we may draw off.'

A cheer greeted the end of this highly optimistic speech. He did not say he had no intention of following the enemy and taking their ship. He did not know how many men knew the rudder was damaged, but some things had to be left to chance.

'Very well. Now you may lie down while he approaches.'

Like an irreverent church congregation they shuffled down and stretched out along the deck, excepting himself and Mount who kept watch from the quarterdeck nettings.

The enemy ship was almost directly to windward of them now and also heaving to. As Drinkwater watched, the side erupted in flame, and shot filled the air, whistling low overhead, like the ripping of a hundred silk shirts.

The second broadside was lower. There were screams from amidships and the ominous clang as one of the guns was hit on the muzzle and a section of bulwark was driven in. A marine grunted and fell dead. Drinkwater nudged Mount. It was Polesworth. Drinkwater felt his coat-tails being tugged. Mr Comley, the bosun, was reporting.

'I brought my pipe aft, sir.'

'Very good, Mr Comley. You had better remain with me and Mr Mount.'

'Aye, sir.'

'Have you served in many actions, Mr Comley?' asked Drinkwater conversationally.

'With Black Dick in the *Queen Charlotte* at the Glorious First, sir, with Cap'n Rose in the *Jamaicky* at Copenhagen, when you was in the *Virago*, sir, an' a score o'boat actions and cuttin' outs and what not . . .'

A third broadside thudded home. Aloft rigging parted and the main top gallant mast dangled downwards.

'You were with the gun brigs then, on the 2nd April?'

'Aye, sir. An' a precious waste of time they were, an' all. I says to Cap'n Rose that by the time we'd towed 'em damned things across to Denmark and then half the little barky's got washed ashore here an' there . . .'

But Drinkwater never knew what advice Mr Comley had given Captain Rose in the battle with the Danish fleet. He knew that the *Melusine* could stand little more of the pounding she was taking without fighting back.

'Open fire!' He yelled and immediately the starboard guns roared out. For perhaps ten whole minutes as the larger ship drove down upon the smaller, the world became a shambles of sights and sounds through which the senses peered dimly, assaulted from every direction by destructive forces. The shot that whistled and ricochetted; the canister that swept a storm of iron balls across the *Melusine*'s deck; the musket balls that pinged off iron-work and whined away into the air; the screams; the smoke; the splinters that crackled about, made it seem impossible that a man could live upon the upperdeck and breathe with anything like normality. Even more astonishing was the sudden silence that befell the two ships' companies as they prepared, the one to attack, the other to defend. It lasted perhaps no more than ten seconds, yet the peace seemed somehow endless. Until that is, it too dissolved into a bedlam of shouting and cursing, of whooping and grunting, of killing and dying. Blades and arms jarred together and the deck became slippery with blood. Drinkwater had lost his hat and his single epaulette had been shot from his left shoulder. It was he who had ended the silence, ordering Frey's brass carronade to sweep the enemy waist from its commanding position at the hance. He had pushed the boy roughly aside as he placed his foot on the slide to repel the first Frenchman, a young officer whose zeal placed himself neatly upon the point of Drinkwater's sword.

Simultaneously Drinkwater discharged his pistol into the face of another Frenchman then, disengaging his hanger, cut right, at the cheek of a man lowering a pike at Mount.

'Obliged, sir,' yelled Mount as he half-turned and shrugged a man off his shoulder who had tried leaping down from the enemy's mizen rigging. The smoke began to clear and Drinkwater was suddenly face to face with a man he knew instinctively was the enemy commander. Drinkwater fell back a step as the small dark bearded figure leapt through the smoke to *Melusine*'s deck. It was a stupid, quixotic thing to do. The man did not square up with a sword. He levelled a pistol and Drinkwater half-shielded his face as Tregembo hacked sideways with a tomahawk. The Frenchman was too quick. The pistol jerked round and was fired at Tregembo. Drinkwater saw blood on the old Cornishman's face and lunged savagely. The French captain jumped back, turned and leapt on the rail. Drinkwater's hanger caught him in the thigh. A marine's bayonet appeared and the French commander leapt back to his own deck. Drinkwater lost sight of him. He found himself suddenly assailed from the left and looked down into the waist. The defenders were bowed back as a press of Frenchmen poured across.

'Mr Comley, your whistle!' Drinkwater roared.

He had no idea where Comley was but the whistle's piercing blast cut through the air above the yelling mob and Drinkwater was pleased to see the Melusines give way; he skipped to the skylight.

'Now, Bourne, now, by God!'

A retreating marine knocked into him. The man's eyes were dulled with madness. Drinkwater looked at Frey. The boy had the larboard carronade lanyard in his hand.

'Fire, Mr Frey!' The boy obeyed.

Drinkwater saw at least one Melusine taken in the back, but there seemed a hiatus in the waist. Most of his men had disengaged and skipped back two or three paces. The marines were drawn up in a rough line through which Bourne's black-faced party suddenly appeared, passing through the intervals, each armed with pike or tomahawk. Bourne at their head held a boarding axe and a pistol. The hiatus was over. The bewildered Frenchmen were suddenly hardpressed. Drinkwater turned to Comley.

'Let fall the fore course, Mr Comley!'

The bosun staggered forward. 'Mr Frey!'

'Sir?'

'Reload that thing and get a shot into the enemy waist from there.'

'Aye, aye, sir.'

Slowly the Melusines were recovering their guns. There were dead and wounded men everywhere and the decks were red with their blood. Drinkwater followed Bourne down into the waist, joining Mount's marines as they bayoneted retreating Frenchmen. The quarterdeck was naked. If the French took advantage of that they might yet lose the ship. Drinkwater turned back. Two or three of the enemy were preparing to leap across. He shot one with his second pistol and the other two were suddenly confronting him. They looked like officers and both had drawn swords. They attacked at once.

Drinkwater parried crudely and felt a prick in his right leg. He felt that his hour had come but smote hard upon the blade that threatened his life. Both his and his assailant's blades snapped in the cold air and they stood, suddenly foolish. Drinkwater's second attacker had been beaten back by a whooping Quilhampton who had shipped his hook, caught the man's sword with it and twisted it from his grip. With his right he was hacking down at the man's raised arm as he endeavoured to protect his head. The tomahawk bit repeatedly into the officer's elbow.

'Quarter, give quarter, Mr Q!'

Drinkwater's own opponent was proffering his broken sword, hilt first as Tregembo, his cheek hanging down like a bloody spaniel's ear, the teeth in his lower jaw bared to the molars, pinned him against the rail.

Drinkwater was aware of the hull of the enemy drawing slowly astern as the foresail pulled *Melusine* clear. The French began to retreat to orders screamed from her deck and the two ships drifted apart. As they did so the enemy swung her stern towards the retiring *Melusine*. Drinkwater could see his opponent's name: *Requin*, he read.

Drinkwater bent over the table and pointed at the sketch he had drawn. The cabin was crowded. With the exception of Mr Rispin, who had been wounded, and Mr Gorton, who had the deck, every officer, commissioned and warrant, was in the room, listening to Drinkwater's intentions, offering advice on technical points and assisting in the planning of the rigging of a jury rudder.

For eight hours *Melusine* had run dead before the wind under a squared fore course which was occasionally clewed up to avoid too heavy a crash as she drove helplessly through the ice. There was no way they could avoid this treatment to the ship. His own cuts and scratches he had dressed himself, the wound in his thigh no more than an ugly gash. Since the action Drinkwater had had Singleton question Meetuck. It had been a long process which Singleton, exhausted after four hours of surgery, appalled by the carnage after the fighting and strongly disapproving of the whole profession of arms, had accomplished only with difficulty. But he had turned at last to Drinkwater with the information he wanted.

'Yes, he says there are places from which the ice has departed at this season and which our big *kayak* can come close to.'

But Drinkwater could not hope to close a strange coast without a rudder. In order to refit his ship with a rudder capable of standing the strain of a passage back to Britain he had to have one capable of allowing him to close the coast of Greenland. It was this paradox that he was engaged in resolving.

He straightened up from the table. 'Very well, gentlemen. If there are no further questions we will begin. Mr Hill, would you have the fore course taken in and we will unrig the mizen topmast without delay.'

There was a buzz of conversation as the officers filed out of the cabin. Drinkwater watched them go then leaned again over the plan. How long would it take them? Six hours? Ten? Twelve? And still the masthead lookout reported the *Requin* in sight to the east-north-east. He wondered what damage they had really inflicted on her. How seriously had her commander been wounded? Would his wound deter him, or goad him to resume the pursuit? The action had ceased by a kind of mutual consent. Each party had inflicted upon the other a measure of damage. He was certain the *Requin* was a letter-of-marque. It would be an enormous feather in the cap of a corsair captain to bring in a sloop of the Royal Navy, particularly one that was a former French corvette. First Consul Bonaparte might be expected to find high praise and honours for so successful a practitioner of *la guerre de course*. But his owners might not be pleased if it was at the expense of extensive damage to their ship, or too heavy a loss amongst their men. Privateering was essentially a profit-making enterprise. The *Requin* had clearly been built on frigate lines intended to deceive unwary merchantmen entering the Soundings. Certainly, ruminated Drinkwater, it argued that her owners had not spared expense in her fitting-out.

He sighed, hearing overhead the first thumps and shouts where the men began the task of rigging the jury rudder.

Sending down the mizen topmast was a matter of comparative simplicity, a standard task which the men might be relied upon to carry out in a routine manner. *Melusine* lay stationary, rolling easily upon a sea dotted with floes, but comparatively open. After an hour's labour the topmast lay fore and aft on the quarterdeck and was being stripped of its unwanted fittings. The topgallant mast was removed from it, but the cross-trees were left and the upper end of the topmast itself was rested on the taffrail. It was lashed there until the carpenter's mate had added a notch in the handsome carving. Meanwhile the carpenter had begun to build up a rudder blade by raising a vertical plane on the after side of the mast, coach-bolting each baulk of timber to its neighbour. In the waist the forge was

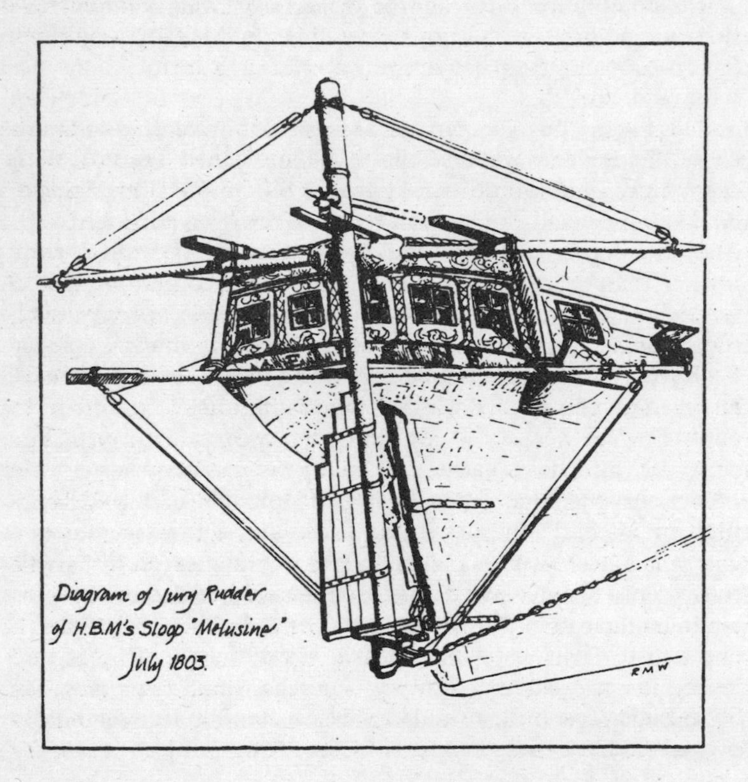

hoisted up and a number of boarding pikes heated up to be beaten into bars with which to bind the rudder blade.

Fabricating the jury rudder and stock was comparatively easy. What exercised Drinkwater's ingenuity was the manner of shipping it so that it could be used to steer the ship. After some consultation with the warrant officers, particularly regarding the materials available, it was decided that an iron ring to encircle the masthead could be fabricated from the head-iron at the top of the mizen lower mast. This was of a sufficient diameter to encompass the heel of the mizen topmast so, by fitting it to the lesser diameter of the topmast's other end, there was sufficient play to allow the mast to rotate. The head-iron also had the advantage of having a second ring, a squared section band, which capped the mizen lower masthead. To this could be secured two chains, made from the yard slings from the main yard and elongated by those from the foreyard. These could then be led as far forward as was practical and bowsed taught at the fore-chains. This iron would thus become the new heel-iron for the rudder stock, a kind of stirrup.

The first part of the work went well. Some considerable delay was experienced in driving the head-iron off the mizen lower mast, but while Bourne and the bosun were aloft struggling with wedges, two stout timbers were prepared to be lashed either side of the vertical mizen topmast when it was lowered upside down, over the stern. A large pudding-fender was also slung over the side and lashed against the taffrail. The jury rudder stock would then turn against this well-slushed fender, restrained from moving to left or right by the side timbers.

There remained two problems. The first was to keep tension on the heel arrangement which it would be impossible to attend to once the thing was hoisted over the side. And the other would be to fabricate a method of actually turning the rudder.

Drinkwater estimated that *Melusine*'s forward speed would contribute greatly to the first as long as her alterations of direction were small, such as would occur while steering a course. Terrific strain would be imposed if large rudder angles were necessary, as would be the case with tacking or wearing or, God help them, if they had to fight another action with the *Requin*. To this end Drinkwater had the mizen topgallant mast slung over the stem and lashed below the level of his quarter galleries. From here tackles were led to the mizen topmasthead which would, of course, be the heel of the rudder stock when rigged. The cross-jack yard was similarly readied across the upper taffrail from quarter to quarter and lashed to the stern davits. From here two tackles could be rigged to the upper end of the topmast which would extend some feet above the rail and give good leverage to steady the spar.

The problem of rigging some steering arrangement proved the most difficult. The idea of lashing a tiller was rejected owing to the great strain upon it which would almost certainly result in the lashing turning about the round mast. In the end it was found necessary to bore the mast, a long task with a hand auger that occupied some four hours work. Into the mortice thus made, the yard arm of the mizen royal yard was prepared to go to become a clumsy tiller.

While these works were in progress Drinkwater frequently called for reports from the masthead about the movement of the *Requin*. But she, too, seemed to be refitting, although her inactivity did not remit the anxiety Drinkwater felt on her account, and he fumed at every trivial delay.

His impatience was unjust for, as he admitted to himself, he could not have been better served, particularly by Hill, Bourne, Gorton and Quilhampton. Comley, the bosun and Mr Marsden, the carpenter were indefatigable, while the men, called upon to exert themselves periodically in heaving the heavy timbers into position, in fetching and carrying, in the rigging of tackles and the frequent adjustment of leads until all was to the demanding exactness Drinkwater knew was the secret of such an operation, carried out their multifarious orders willingly.

There were considerable delays and a few setbacks, but after eight hours labour the timbers assembled on the quarterdeck looked less like a lowered mast and more like a rudder and stock. In one of these delays Drinkwater took himself below to attend the wounded.

Melusine had suffered greatly in the action, not only in her fabric, but in her company. As Drinkwater made his way below to the cockpit he refused to allow his mind to dwell on the moral issues that crammed the mind in the aftermath and anti-climax of action. No doubt Singleton would hector him upon the point in due course and Drinkwater felt a stab of conscience at the way he had been instrumental in turning little Frey from a frightened boy to a murderous young man who had killed in the service of his King and Country. Still, Drinkwater reflected, that was better than fulfilling that mendacious platitude: *Dulce et decorum est, pro patria mori.*

But it was not Singleton's face that reproached him in the gloom of the cockpit. Skeete leered at him abruptly, holding up the horn lantern to see who it was.

'Are 'ee wounded, Cap'n, sir?' The foul breath of Skeete's carious teeth was only marginally worse than the foetid stink of the space, crammed as it was with wounded men. They lay everywhere, some twisted in agony, some slumped under the effects of laudanum or rum, some sobbed and cried for their wives or mothers. Singleton looked up as Drinkwater leaned over the body of Mr Rispin. Their eyes met and Singleton gave the merest perceptible shake to his head. Drinkwater knelt down beside the lieutenant.

'Well now, Mr Rispin. How goes it, eh?' he asked quietly.

Rispin looked at him as though he had no idea who it was. There was very little left of Rispin's chest and his eyes bore testimony to the shock his body had received. His pupils were huge: he was already a dead man, astonished to be still alive, if only for a little longer.

Drinkwater turned aside. He almost fell over one of the ship's nippers, a boy of some nine years of age named Maxted, Billy Cue Maxted, Drinkwater remembered from the ship's books, named for the battleship *Belliqueux*, from whence his father had come to ruin the reputation of poor Mollie Maxted. Now little Billy was a cripple. He had been carrying powder to his gun when a ball knocked off both his legs. They were no more than dry sticks and he was conscious of their loss. Drinkwater knelt down beside him.

The child's eyes alighted on the captain and widened with comprehension. He struggled to rise up, but Drinkwater pushed him back gently, feeling the thin shoulder beneath the flannel shirt.

'Oh, Cap'n Drinkwater, sir, I've lost both my legs, sir. Both on 'em, and this is my first action, sir. Oh, sir, what'm I going to do, sir? With no legs, who'll carry powder to my gun, sir, when next we fights the Frogs, sir?'

'There, Billy, you lie back and rest. It's for me to worry about the guns and for you to be a good boy and get well . . .'

'Will I get well, sir?' The boy was smiling through his tears.

'Of course you will, Billy . . .'

'And what'll happen to me, sir?' Drinkwater swallowed. How could you tell a nine-year-old he was a free-born Briton who would never be a slave? He was free to rot on whichever street corner took his fancy. He might get a pension. Perhaps ten pounds a year for the loss of two legs, if someone took up his case. Drinkwater sighed.

'I'll look after you, Billy. You come and see me when you're better, eh? We'll ship you a pair of stumps made of whale ivory . . . '

'Aye, sir, an' a pair o'crutches out o' the Frog's topgallant yards, eh, Cap'n?'

An older seaman lying next to Billy hoisted himself on one elbow and grinned in the darkness. Drinkwater nodded, rose and stepped over the inert bodies. Rispin had died. Somewhere in the stinking filth of the orlop his soul sought the exit to paradise, for there were no windows here to throw wide to the heavens, only a narrow hatchway to the decks above. At the ladder Drinkwater paused to look back.

'Three cheers for Cap'n Drinkwater!' It was little Billy's piping voice, and it was answered by a bass chorus. Drinkwater shuddered and reached for the ladder ropes.

Dulce et decorum est . . .

He had not seen Tregembo in the cockpit, he realised as he passed the marine sentry stationed outside his cabin. He opened the door only to find a party of men under Mr Quilhampton completing the lashings of the mizen topgallant mast across the stern.

'We had to break two of the glazings, sir,' said Quilhampton apologetically, pointing at the knocked-out corners of the stern windows.

'No matter, Mr Q. How does it go?'

'Just passing the final frappings now.'

'Very well.' Drinkwater paused and looked hard at one of the men. The fellow had his back to Drinkwater and was leaning outboard. 'Is that Tregembo?'

'Yes, sir. He refused to stay in the cockpit,' Quilhampton grinned, 'complained that he wasn't having a lot of clumsy jacks in *his* cabin.'

Drinkwater smiled. 'Tregembo!'

The Cornishman turned. 'Aye, zur?' His head was bandaged and he spoke with difficulty.

'How is your face?'

'Aw, 'tis well enough, zur. Mr Singleton put a dozen homeward bounders in it an' it'll serve. I reckon I'll be able to chaw on it.'

Drinkwater wondered what sort of an appearance Tregembo would make, his cheek crossed by the scars of Singleton's sutures. If they ever reached Petersfield again he could expect some hard words from Susan. He nodded his thanks to the man for saving his life. The Cornishman's eyes lit. There was no need for words.

'Very well.'

'You've broken your sword, zur.' Tregembo was reproachful. The French sword had hung on his hip since he had taken it from the dead lieutenant of *La Creole* twenty-odd years ago off the coast of Carolina. He had forgotten the matter.

'You'd better have Mr Germaney's, zur. For the time bein'.'

Drinkwater nodded again, then turned to Quilhampton.

'Carry on, Mr Q.'

'Aye, aye, sir.'

They were ready to heave the jury rudder over the taffrail when he returned to the deck. All the purchases were manned, each party under the direction of an officer or midshipman. The former mizen topmast, the ball from the *Requin* prised out of it and the improvised rudder blade bound to it, jutted out over the stern. The heel-iron at its extremity was fitted with the requisite chains and shackles and the head of the mast was, where it passed through the heel-iron, well slushed with tallow to allow free rotation.

'All ready, sir.' Bourne touched his hat.

'Very good, Mr Bourne. Let's have it over . . .'

'Aye, aye, sir. Set tight all. Ready, Mr Gorton?' Gorton was up on the taffrail, hanging overboard with two topmen.

'Ready, sir.'

Bourne lifted the speaking trumpet and turned forward. 'Mr Wickham! Mr Dutfield! Your parties to take up slack only!'

'Aye, aye, sir!' The tackles from the heel iron came inboard at the chess-trees and here the two midshipmen had half a dozen men each to set the heel of the rudder tight.

'Very well, Mr Comley, haul her aft.'

'Haul aft, aye, aye . . .'

The mast was pushed aft, the tackles overhauling or tightening as necessary. At the point of equilibrium the weight was slowly taken on the side tackles that led downwards from the mizen topgallant mast, Mr Gorton shouting directions to Quilhampton in the cabin below, where the hauling parts came inboard.

'Some weight on the retaining tackle, Mr Comley . . .'

'Holding now, sir.' They had rigged a purchase from the base of the mizen mast to the upper end of the rudder stock. This now took much of the weight until the stock approached a more vertical angle and the full weight was taken by Quilhampton's quarter tackles. The rudder blade dipped down and entered the sea. There was an ominous jerk as Comley eased his purchase and the weight came upon the quarter tackles. But they were heavy blocks, with sufficient mechanical advantage to handle the weight. The rudder stock approached the vertical, coming to rest on the pudding fender and, further down, the cross member formed by the mizen topgallant mast.

'I think some parcelling there, Mr Gorton, together with a loose frapping will make matters more secure,' said Drinkwater, leaning over the stern by the starboard stern davit.

'Aye, aye, sir.' He called down to Quilhampton and explained what Drinkwater wanted. Looking down, Drinkwater could see Quilhampton's quarter tackles disappear into the water. They were bar-tight. Above his head Comley was removing the purchase to the mizen mast and setting up two side purchases, stretched out to the arms of the cross-jack yard which was lashed up under the boat davits. This was to ease some of the effects of torsion the improvised rudder could be expected to undergo.

Forward Wickham and Dutfield were hauling their tackles tight under Bourne's direction. As Comley clambered down Drinkwater directed him to set up some additional bracing lines to support the extremities of the mizen topgallant mast and the cross-jack yard. He felt his anxiety subside and rubbed his hands with satisfaction.

'Well done, Mr Bourne, a splendid achievement.'

'Thank you, sir.'

Drinkwater hailed the masthead. Mr Frey looked over the rim of the crow's nest.

'Any sign of the *Requin*, Mr Frey?'

'No change, sir! East-nor'-east, distant three or four leagues, sir!'

'Very well!' Drinkwater turned to Bourne. 'Heave the ship to, Mr Bourne, then set an anchor watch. Pipe "Up spirits", all hands to have a double tot and then send 'em below. We'll lie-to, then get under way in four hours. The masthead is to be continually manned. Carry on.'

Drinkwater was cheered for the second time that day, only on this occasion he felt less guilty.

Chapter Sixteen *July-August 1803*

A Providential Refuge

'We therefore commit their bodies to the deep, to be turned into corruption, looking for the resurrection of the body (when the sea shall give up her dead) . . .'

Obadiah Singleton, the stole of ordained minister of the Church of England about his muffled neck, read the solemn words as *Melusine*'s entire company stood silently in the waist. Drinkwater nodded and the planks lifted. From beneath the bright bunting of the ensigns the hammocks slid over the standing part of the fore-sheet, to plunge into the grey-green sea.

There were fifteen to bury, with the likelihood of a further seven or eight joining them within a day or two. They did not go unmourned. Among *Melusine*'s company, friends grieved the loss of shipmates. For Drinkwater there was always the sense of failure he felt after sustaining heavy losses and among those rigid bundles lay Cawkwell, his servant. He wondered whether he had been wise to have held *Melusine*'s fire for so long, and yet he knew he had inflicted heavy casualties upon the *Requin*, that her reluctance to renew the action could only in part have been due to the physical damage they had done to her fabric. From what he had seen of her commander the purely commercial nature of privateering would not prevent him from seeking a chance of glory. Drinkwater knew that the ablest of French men were not in the Republic's battle-fleet, rotting in her harbours, penned in by the Royal Navy's weary but endless blockade. France's finest seamen were corsairs, aboard letters-of-marque like the *Requin*, as intrepid and daring as any young frigate captain in the Royal Navy. They were pursuing that mode of warfare at which they excelled: the war against trade, wounding the British merchants in their purses and thus bringing opposition to the war openly into Parliamentary debate. It was not without reason that First Consul Napoleon Bonaparte described the British as 'a nation of shopkeepers'. Singleton closed the prayerbook as the Melusines mumbled their final 'Amens'.

'On hats!'

Drinkwater turned away for the companionway and his cabin. Already Bourne was piping the hands to stations for getting under way.

Drinkwater looked up at the stump of the mizen mast. They would set no more than the spanker on that, but the wind, although it had swung round to the south, remained light. It had brought with it a slight lessening of the visibility and they had not seen the *Requin* for three hours.

However, although Drinkwater's anxiety was eased he was still worried about the rudder and had ordered Bourne to hoist only spanker, main topsail and foretopmast staysail to begin with. It was one thing to devise extempore measures and quite another to get them working. But while Bourne brought the ship onto a course for the Greenland coast there was something else Drinkwater had to attend to, an inevitable consequence of death.

'Pass word for Mr Quilhampton,' he said to the marine sentry who came to attention as Drinkwater opened the cabin door. Drinkwater took off his full-dress coat and changed it for the stained undress he wore over the blue guernsey that had become an inseparable, if irregular, part of his uniform clothing. The air had warmed slightly with the onset of the southerly breeze, but it had also become damp again and Drinkwater felt the damp more acutely in his bones and shoulder than the very cold, drier polar airstream of the northerly.

Drinkwater heard the knock at the door. 'Enter!'

'You sent for me, sir?'

'Ah, yes, sit down a moment. Pray do you pour out two glasses there.' He nodded at the decanter nestling between the fiddles on the locker top. Quilhampton did as he was bid while Drinkwater opened a drawer in his desk and removed a paper.

'Far be it from me to rejoice in the death of a colleague, James, but what may be poison to one man, oft proves meat to another.' He handed the sheet to Quilhampton who took it frowning. The young man's brow cleared with understanding.

'Oh . . . er, thank you, sir.'

'It is only an acting commission, Mr Q, and may not be ratified by their Lordships, and although you have passed your Master's

Mate's examination you have not yet sat before a Captains' board to pass for lieutenant . . . you understand?'

Quilhampton nodded. 'Yes sir, I understand.'

'Very well. You will take Mr Rispin's watch . . . and good luck to you.' Drinkwater raised his glass and they sipped for a moment in companionable silence. Quilhampton gazed abstractedly through the stern windows, the view was obscured by the spars and lashings of the jury rudder but he was unaware of them. He was thinking of how he could now swagger into Mrs MacEwan's withdrawing-room, to make a leg before the lovely Catriona, and send that damned lubber of a Scottish yeoman to the devil!

'I see,' said Drinkwater turning, 'that you are watching the effects of the ship getting under way upon the rudder.'

'Eh? Oh, oh, yes sir . . .' Quilhampton focussed his eyes as Drinkwater drained his glass, rose and picked up his hat.

'Well, Mr Q, let us go and see how it answers our purpose . . .'

It answered their purpose surprisingly well. Kept under easy sail after a little experimenting with balancing the rig, and running tiller lines to the mizen royal yard in a manner which best suited steering the ship, *Melusine* made west-north-west. There was a thinning of the floes and although the wind remained from the south, it began to get colder. Fog patches closed in and from these circumstances Drinkwater deduced that the coast of Greenland could not be very far distant. There were other indications that this was so; an increase in the number of birds, particularly eider ducks, and a curious attentive attitude on the part of Meetuck who, having hidden during the action with the *Requin* to the amusement of the Melusines, now hung about the knightheads sniffing the air like a dog.

Then, shortly before eight bells in the morning watch the next day he was observed pointing ahead with excitement. He repeated the same word over and over again.

'Nunataks! Nunataks!'

The hands, with their customary good-natured but contemptuous ignorance, laughed at him, tapping their foreheads and deriving a good deal of fun at the eskimo's expense. Quilhampton had the watch and was unable to see anything unusual. Nevertheless he went forward and had Singleton turned out of his cot to translate.

'What the devil does he mean, Obadiah? Noon attacks, eh?'

Singleton stared ahead, nodding as Meetuck pulled at his arm, his eyes shining with excitement.

'You need to elevate your glass, Mr Quilhampton. Meetuck refers to the light on the peaks of Greenland.' There was an uncharacteristic note of awe in Singleton's voice, but it went unnoticed by the practical Quilhampton.

'Well, I'm damned,' he said shortly, looking briefly at a jagged and gleaming outline in the lower clouds to the west. It was the sun shining on the permanent ice-cap of the mountains of Greenland.

'Mr Frey! Be so good as to call the captain . . .'

Drinkwater raised his glass for the hundredth time and regarded the distant mountains. They were distinguishable from icebergs by the precipitous slopes of dark rock on which the snow failed to lie. He judged their distance to be about twenty miles, yet he could close the coast no further because of the permanent coastal accretion of old ice, its hummocks smoothed, its ancient raftings eroded by the repeated wind-driven bombardment of millions upon millions of ice spicules. So far there was no break in that barrier of ice and mountains that indicated the existence of an anchorage. Drinkwater swore to himself. He was a fool to think a primitive savage of an eskimo could have any idea of the haven that he sought. And, he reflected bitterly, he was a bigger fool for actually looking. But he peered through his glass yet again in the fast-shrivelling hope that Meetuck might be right.

'It's a remarkable sight, isn't it?' Beside him Obadiah Singleton levelled the battered watch-glass he had borrowed from Hill.

Drinkwater could see little remarkable in the distant coast. It was as cold and forbidding as that of Arabia had been hot and hostile and his irritation was increased by the knowledge that Singleton had ceased to think like the *ad hoc* surgeon of *Melusine* and had reverted to being an Anglican divine sent on a mission to convert the heathen by a London Missionary society. When he had persuaded Singleton to assume the duties of surgeon Drinkwater had imagined it would prove regrettably impossible to find the time or opportunity to close the coast and land the missionary. Now it would be impossible to refuse, even if it meant landing Singleton on the ice.

'Don't you think it remarkable, sir?' asked Singleton again.

'I would think it so if I found an ice-free anchorage with a fine sandy bottom in five fathoms at low water, Mr Singleton. I should consider that highly remarkable.'

'But the colour, the colour, to what do you suppose it is due?'

'Eh?' Drinkwater took his glass from his eye and looked where Singleton was pointing. He had been scanning the coast ahead and failed to notice the strange coloration of the snow on the slopes of a mountain which plunged into the ice on the south side of what they took to be an ice-covered bay. This slope, just opening on their larboard beam was a dark, yet brilliant red.

'An outcrop of red-hued rock, perhaps . . .' he said with only a mild curiosity. 'The rocks and cliffs of Milford Haven are a not dissimilar colour . . .'

'No, that is too smooth and even for rock. It's snow . . . red snow. Egedé did not mention red snow . . .'*

'To the devil with red snow, Mr Singleton. Get that damned eskimo aft here and quiz him again. Is he sure, absolutely sure of this anchorage for big kayaks? Have you explained that we must anchor our ship, Singleton, not run it up the beach like a bloody dugout?'

Singleton sighed. 'I have asked him that several times, sir . . .'

'Well get him aft and ask him again.' Drinkwater raised his glass and trained it forward to where a cape jutted out. There was the faint shadow of further land. Could that be the expected opening in the coast that Meetuck assured them existed? And if it was, how the hell were they to break through this fast-ice with a leaky old hull and a jury rudder, a stump mizen and a truncated mainmast?

They had drawn maps for Meetuck, but he did not seem to comprehend the concept of a bird's eye view and Drinkwater was increasingly sceptical of Singleton's assurances of his use of other faculties.

The olfactory organs did not rate very highly as navigational aids, clouded by the eskimo's own inimitable musk. Drinkwater had scoffed at Singleton's adamant assertions, privately considering that whatever inner faith makes a man a priest, also betrays he lacks common sense.

*Caused by a single-celled plant: *Chlamydomonas nivalis*.

Drinkwater smelled Meetuck's presence and lowered the telescope. Since their dawn encounter Meetuck had appeared uneasy in Drinkwater's presence. He stuck close to Singleton and nodded as he fired the same questions yet again.

Meetuck answered, his flat speech with its monotonous modulation and clicking, minimal mouth movements seemed truly incomprehensible, but after some minutes Drinkwater thought he detected an unusual enthusiasm in Meetuck's answers.

Singleton turned to Drinkwater. 'He says, yes, he's sure that Nagtoralik is to the north, only a little way now.' Singleton gestured on the beam. 'This is *aquitseq*, a nameless place. It is also *anoritok*, very windy, and there are no fish, especially capelin. Soon, he says, we will see *vivak*, which is a cape to be skirted and beyond it we will see *ikersak*, the strait upon the northern shores of which his people live.' At each innuit word Singleton turned to Meetuck, as if for confirmation, and on each occasion the eskimo repeated the word and grunted agreement.

'He says it is *upernavsuak*, a good location to dwell in the spring, by which I assume he means that by this time of year it is ice free, but again he repeats that there are bad white men near Nagtoralik, white men like you, sir. He seems to have conceived some idea that you are connected with them after the action with the *Requin*. I cannot make it out, sir . . .'

'Perhaps your preaching has turned him into a proper Christian, Mr Singleton. Meetuck seems terrified by the use of force,' said Drinkwater drily. 'He certainly absented himself from the deck during the action. Ask him if that,' Drinkwater pointed to the distant cape, 'is the promontory to be skirted, eh?'

Meetuck screwed his eyes up and stared on the larboard bow. Then something odd happened. His weathered skin smoothed out as he realised this was indeed the cape they sought. He turned to speak to Singleton as if to confirm this and his face was so expressive that Drinkwater knew that, whatever the cape hid, and however it answered their purpose, Meetuck had brought them to the place he intended. But his eyes rested on Drinkwater and his expression changed, he muttered something which ended in a gesture towards the nearest gun and the noise 'bang!' was uttered before he ran off, disappearing below.

'Upon my soul, Mr Singleton, now what the devil's the meanin' of that?'

Singleton frowned. 'I don't know, sir, but he has an aversion to you and cannon-fire. And if I'm not mistaken it has something to do with the bad white men of Nagtoralik.'

'No bottom . . .' The leadsman's chant with its attenuated syllables had become a mere routine formality, a precaution for it was obvious that the water in the strait was extraordinarily deep.

'D'you have a name for the cape, sir?' asked Quilhampton who, with Hill and Gorton was busy striking hurried cross bearings off on a large sheet of cartridge paper pinned to a board.

'I think it should be named for the First Lord, Mr Q, except that he took his title off a Portuguese cape . . .' Drinkwater was abstracted, watching the dancing catspaws of increasing wind sweep down from the mountainous coast two miles to the southwards.

'How about Cape Jervis, sir,' suggested Quilhampton who, if the captain did not decide quickly would name the promontory Cape Catriona.

'A capital idea, Mr Q,' then to the quartermaster, 'Meet her, there, meet her.'

The katabatic squall hit the *Melusine* with sudden, screaming violence and the tiller party shuffled and tugged at the clumsy arrangement. It had succeeded in steering through an ice strewn lead that was now opening into what Meetuck called *Sermiligaq*: the fiord with many glaciers. *Melusine*, under greatly reduced canvas, leaned only slightly to the increased pressure of the wind and began to race westward with the cold wind coming down from the massive heights to larboard.

'No-o botto-o-m . . .'

Curiosity had filled the quarterdeck. Those officers not engaged in the sailing of the ship or the rough surveying of the coast, formed in a knot around Singleton. The missionary's eyes were alight with a proprietary fire as he pointed to the dark rock that rose in strata after horizontal strata, delineated by a rind of snow as erosion reduced successive layers, giving the appearance of a gigantic series of steps.

'It is more impressive, gentlemen,' Singleton was saying, 'than either Crantz or Egedé had led me to believe, more remarkable, perhaps, than those bizarre stratifications found in the Hebrides because of the enormous extent of this coastline . . . Is it not possible to imagine such a land as inflaming the imagination of the old Norse harpers when they composed their sagas? A land wherein giants dwelt, eh?'

Drinkwater strode up and down, catching snatches of Singleton's lyrical enthusiasm, watching the progress of the ship and casting an eye over the hurried mapping of the coastline. Hill had just completed a neat piece of triangulation from which he had established the elevation of the mountains closest to the extremity of Cape Jervis as 2,800 feet. From this he deduced a summit ten miles inland to the westward to be about 3,000 feet from its greater height. His proposal to name it after *Melusine*'s commander was gently rebuffed.

'I think not, Mr Hill, flattering though it might be. Shall we call it after the ship, eh?'

So Mount Melusine it became, a name of which nature seemed to approve because even as they made the decision there came a crack like gunfire. For an instant all the faces on the deck looked round apprehensively, until Singleton laughingly drew their attention to the calving glacier, one of many frozen rivers that ran down to the sea in the valleys between those mighty summits.

They watched with awe the massive lump of ice as it broke clear of the glacier and rolled with an apparent gentle slowness into the sea, finding its own floating equilibrium to become just one more iceberg in the Arctic Ocean.

'Nature salutes our eponymous ship, sir,' said Singleton turning to Drinkwater.

'Let us hope it is a salutation and not an omen, Mr Singleton. By the by, where is Meetuck?'

Singleton pointed forward. 'Upon what I believe you term "the knightheads", keeping a lookout for his kin, the *Ikermiut*.'

'Their village lies hereabouts, on this inhospitable shore?' Drinkwater indicated the mountains to the southward.

'No sir, to the north, where the land is lower. That is what I believe Meetuck means when he says we will find an anchorage at Nagtoralik.'

A lower coastline presented itself to them the following afternoon, but the lead failed to find the bottom and Meetuck was insistent that this was not the place. Nevertheless they stood close inshore and half a dozen glasses were trained upon the patches of surprising green undergrowth that sprouted between the dark outcrops of rock. There were flocks of eider ducks and geese paddling upon the black sandy beaches and Mr Frey spotted a whirring brace of willow grouse that rose into the air.

Melusine tacked offshore and Drinkwater luxuriated in the amazing warmth of the sun. It struck his shoulders, seeping into aching muscles and easing some of the tension he felt in his anxiety both for the ultimate safety of *Melusine* and also that of Sawyers and the *Faithful*. Forward, Meetuck still kept his self-appointed vigil, staring ahead and Drinkwater felt an odd reassurance in the sight, a growing confidence that the eskimo was right.

The sun was delicious and it was clear that its heat melted the snows, and the moraine deposits brought from higher ground by the action of the ice had deposited enough of a soil to root the chickweed and ground willow that covered the low shore. It argued an area that might support life, if only there was an anchorage . . .

They went about again and rounded a headland of frowning black rocks. It was a salient of the mountains that rose peak above peak to the distant, glistening *nunataks*. Standing close in, the dark, deeply fissured rocks showed a variety of colours in the sunshine where lodes of quartz and growths of multi-hued lichens relieved the drabness. They were also made uncomfortably aware of the existence of mosquitos, a surprising discovery and one that made even the philosophical Singleton short tempered.

Squatting on a carronade slide little Frey recorded the drab appearance of the rocks as a shrewdly observed mixture of greys, deep red and dark green. His brush and pencil had been busy since they had first sighted land and the active encouragement of the captain had silenced the jeers of Walmsley and Glencross, at least in public.

Above them the cliff reared, precipitous to man, but composed of a million ledges where the stains of bird-lime indicated the nesting sites of kittiwakes and auks. A number still perched on these remote spots, together with the sea-parrots whose brilliant coloured beaks glowed like tiny jewels in the blazing sunshine.

Alongside, an old bull seal rose, his nostrils pinching and opening, while two pale cubs, the year's progeny, dived as the shadow of the ship fell upon them. As they cleared the cape open water appeared to the westward, bounded to the northern shore by another distant headland. From forward came a howl of delight from Meetuck. He pointed west, down the channel where distant mountains rose blue against the sky.

Singleton crossed the deck, his ear cocked to catch Meetuck's words.

'It seems, sir, that the anchorage of Nagtoralik lies at the head of this fiord.'

Drinkwater nodded. 'Let us hope that it is the providential refuge that we so desperately need, Mr Singleton.'

'And where you can land me,' answered Singleton in a low voice, staring ahead.

Daylight diminished to a luminous twilight for the six hours that the sun now dipped beneath the horizon. The brief arctic summer was fast fading and with its warmth gone the wind dropped and a dripping fog settled over the ship. Lines hung slack and the sails slatted impotently. After the warmth of the day the chill, grey midnight struck cold throughout the ship, though in fact the mercury in the thermometer had fallen far lower among the ice-bergs of the Greenland Sea.

Shivering in his cabin Drinkwater wrote up his journal, expressing his anxiety over the state of *Melusine*'s steering gear and his inability to find and rescue Sawyers.

Assuming that we are able to effect repairs to the rudder by hauling down I am not optimistic of locating the Faithful. *The lack of belligerence in Captain Sawyers made of him and his ship a gift to the marauding French and it is unlikely that we shall be of further use to him.*

He paused, unwilling to admit to himself the extent of his sense of failure in carrying out Earl St Vincent's orders. At the moment the very real anxieties of a safe haven, the possibility of carrying out effective repairs and of returning to join the whalers for the homeward convoy were more immediately demanding. With a sigh he turned to a more domestic matter.

My desire to anchor will, of necessity, rob me of the services of Mr Singleton who is determined to pursue his mission among the eskimo tribes. I am torn between admiration and . . . He paused. He had been about to write 'contempt', but that would not be accurate, despite the fact that he considered Singleton a fool to think he could either convert the eskimos or survive himself. He did not doubt that men imbued with Singleton's religious zeal could endure incredible hardships, but his own years of seafaring had taught him never to gamble with fate, always to weigh the chances carefully before deciding upon a course of action. He had never seen himself as a dashing sea-officer of the damn-the-consequences type. Drinkwater sighed again. He admired Singleton for his fortitude and he was in awe of his faith. He scratched out his last sentence and wrote:

I admire Singleton's courage at undertaking his mission, but I do not understand the power of his faith. His presence on board as a surgeon will be sorely missed, but I fear my remonstrances fall upon deaf ears and he is determined to remain upon this coast.

Soon afterwards Drinkwater's head fell forward upon his chest and he dozed.

'Captain, sir! Captain, sir!'

'Eh? What is it?' Drinkwater woke with a start, cold and held in a rigor of stiff muscles.

'Mr Quilhampton's compliments, sir, and there's a light easterly breeze, sir.'

'Thank you, Mr Frey, I'll be up.'

The boy disappeared and Drinkwater dragged himself painfully to his feet. On deck he found the fog as dense as ever, but above his head the squared yards spread canvas before the light wind. Quilhampton touched his hat.

'Mornin' sir.'

'Mornin' Mr Q.'

'Wind's increasing sir. Course west by north. Beggin' your pardon sir, but d'you wish us to heave to, sir, or, if we stand on to sound minute guns?'

'D'you sound minute guns, Mr Q, and post a midshipman forrard to sing out the instant he hears an echo. We will put the ship on the wind and the moment that occurs on a course of east-nor'-east. '

'Aye, aye, sir.'

Drinkwater fell to pacing the quarterdeck. Before the fog closed down they had seen the fiord open to the westward. They could stand down it with a reasonable degree of safety, provided of course that they heard no echoes close ahead from the towering cliffs in answer to their minute guns. Eight bells rang, the end of the middle watch, four o'clock in the morning and already the sun had risen. He longed for its warmth to penetrate the nacreous vapour, consume the fog and ease the pain in his shoulder.

It was six hours later before the fog began to disperse. The wind had fallen light again and their progress had been slow, measured only by the anxious barking of the minute gun and the hushed silence that followed it. They saw distant mountain peaks at first and it became clear that they were reaching the head of the fiord for they lay ahead, on either bow and either beam. Snow gleamed as the sun seemed suddenly fierce and the fog changed from a pervasive cloud to dense wraiths and then drew back to reveal a little, misty circle of sea about them while the cliffs seemed to reach downwards from the sky.

It was a fantastic effect, but their vision was still obscured at sea level, and for a further hour they moved slowly westward, Drinkwater still anxiously pacing the quarterdeck while on the knightheads Meetuck waited with the expectancy of a dog.

And then, about five bells in the morning watch, the visibility suddenly cleared. *Melusine* was almost at the head of the fiord. To the south stretched the cliffs and mountains that culminated in the cape beneath whose fissured rocks they had tacked the previous afternoon. This wall of rock curved round to the west and north, bordering the fiord. The northern shore was comprised of mountains but these were less precipitous, the littoral formed of bays and inlets some of which were wooded with low conifers. At the head of the fiord, where once a mighty glacier had calved bergs into the sea, was a bay, backed by rising ground, an alpine meadow-land that turned to scree, then buttresses of dark rock rising to mountain peaks.

On the fo'c's'le Meetuck pointed triumphantly, capering about and clapping his hands, his lined face creased with happiness.

'My God!' exclaimed Drinkwater fishing for his glass. It was an anchorage without a doubt. Not a mile from them five ships lay tranquilly at anchor. One of them was the *Requin*, flying the tricolour of France.

An instant later she opened fire.

Chapter Seventeen *August 1803*

Nagtoralik Bay

'Beat to quarters, Mr Bourne!'

Drinkwater ignored the bedlam surrounding him while *Melusine* was put into a state to fight. He swept the anchorage, pausing only briefly on each ship to determine its force. But it occurred to him as he did so that there was something remarkable about three of the ships in the bay. Identification of the *Requin* was simple. She must have arrived off Cape Jervis well ahead of the *Melusine* and now she was swung, a spring on her cable, every gun pointing at the British ship which, by its minute guns, had warned her of its approach.

Drinkwater swore, for he realised that anchored to the south of the *Requin* was a large lugger, a *chassé marée*, and to the east of her, the unpierced topsides of the *Faithful*. To find Sawyers's ship in such circumstances was hardly reassuring, given that *Melusine* still laboured under her jury rudder.

To the west of *Requin* two more vessels lay at anchor and Drinkwater knew them instantly for whale ships. They were not immediately familiar and as Bourne reported the sloop cleared for action, Drinkwater ordered the course altered to starboard, risking raking fire, but anxious to close the distance a little before responding to *Requin*'s guns. Drinkwater began to calculate the odds. The big, French privateer made no obvious move to get under way. She would sit at anchor, in the centre of her captures, relying upon her superior weight of metal to keep *Melusine* at a distance. When she had driven off *Melusine* she would come in pursuit, to administer the *coup de grâce*.

Drinkwater swore again. Their jury rudder and obvious reduction of rig bespoke their weakness. He looked again at the *Requin* for signs of damage to her bow. She had a bowsprit, perhaps a trifle shorter than when they had first met, and therefore a jury rig, but it looked perfectly serviceable.

'That's the bloody *Nimrod*!' Hill called in astonishment, 'and the *Conqueror*!'

Drinkwater swung his glass left. The extent of his own ineptness struck him like a blow even as Bourne replied to the sailing master.

'They must have been taken off Spitzbergen, by God!'

Was Bourne right? Had the *Requin* taken *Nimrod* and *Conqueror* off Spitzbergen and cruised with complete impunity throughout the Greenland Sea? If so, *Melusine*'s presence had been a farce, a complete charade. Every exertion of her company a futile waste of time. He could see again the contempt for his own inexperience in Captain Ellerby's pale blue eyes. How mortifyingly justified that contempt was now proved. He had bungled his commission from Lord St Vincent and failure stared at him from every one of *Requin*'s gun muzzles.

Drinkwater swallowed hard. He felt as though he had received a physical blow.

'Make ready the larboard battery, Mr Bourne. Put the ship on the wind, Mr Hill, starboard tack. We will open fire on the *Requin*, Mr Bourne, all guns to try for the base of her mainmast.' His voice sounded steady and assured despite his inner turmoil.

He nodded as the two officers acknowledged their orders, then he raised his glass again, anxious to hide his face.

Melusine headed inshore, her bowsprit pointing at the stern of the *Faithful* as *Requin* fired her second broadside. It was better pointed than the first as the British sloop stood well into range. Drinkwater felt shots go home, holes appeared in several sails and he felt acutely vulnerable with his clumsy jury steering gear. But a plan was formulating in his mind. If he could lay *Melusine* alongside the *Faithful* he might be able to launch a boat attack on the *Requin* while partially protecting *Melusine*'s weak stern from the *Requin*'s heavier guns.

'Larboard battery ready, sir,' Bourne reported, and Drinkwater took his glass from his eye only long enough to acknowledge the readiness of the gunners.

'Fire when you bear, Mr Bourne.'

They were closing *Faithful* rapidly and more shots from *Requin* arrived, striking splinters from forward and sending Meetuck scampering aft and down the companionway like a scuttering rabbit. A roar of laughter ran along the deck and then *Melusine*'s guns replied, the captains jerking their lanyards in a rolling broadside.

'Mr Mount! Your men are to storm the whaler *Faithful* when I bring the ship under her lee. I doubt she has more than a prize crew aboard and . . .'

'Bloody hell!' A heavy shot thumped into the quarter rail and smashed the timbers inboard. It was perilously close to Mr Hill as he stood by the big tiller and he swore in surprise. Drinkwater looked up to determine the source of the ball and another hit *Melusine*, dismounting an after larboard gun. It was carronade fire.

'It's the fucking *Nimrod*, by God!' howled Hill, his face purple with rage as he capered to avoid the splinters. Whatever it was it was dangerous and Drinkwater decided to retire.

'Larboard tack, Mr Hill, upon the instant!'

Hill jumped to the order with alacrity and Drinkwater swung his glass onto the whaler *Nimrod*. Smoke drifted away from her side and he saw another stab of yellow fire and a second later was drenched in the spray from the water thrown up no more than five yards astern.

'By Christ . . .' Drinkwater saw a black-bearded figure standing on the rail. There was no doubt about it being Jemmett Ellerby and he was waving his hat as yet another shot was fired from his carronades.

Drinkwater's blood froze. He wanted to make sure of what he saw and studied the big figure intently. Yes, there could be no doubt about it. *Nimrod* flew no colours while above his own head the British ensign snapped out as *Melusine* lay over to the larboard tack, exposing her stern, but rapidly increasing her distance from the enemy.

'Ship full and bye on the larboard tack, sir,' Hill reported. Drinkwater nodded, his brain still whirling with the evidence his senses presented him with. It seemed impossible, but then, as the ship stood out of danger to the eastward and he could order the gun crews stood easy, he gave himself time to think.

'Beat to windward, Mr Hill. You may reduce sail and have the men served dinner at their guns . . .'

'Look at that, sir! Do you see it?' Lieutenant Bourne cried incredulously. He pointed astern to where, beyond the anchored ships what looked like stone huts, low and almost part of the beach, showed beyond the anchored ships. There was a flagpole and from it flew the unmistakable colours of Republican France.

Drinkwater attempted to make sense of the events of the forenoon. At first he was bewildered but after a while he set himself the task of assembling the evidence as he saw it. He retired to his cabin as *Melusine* stood eastward under easy sail, making short tacks. On a piece of paper he began to list the facts and as he wrote he felt a quickening of his pulse. Under the stimulus of a glass or two his memory threw up odd, remembered facts that began to slot neatly together. He was seized by the conviction that his reasoning was running true and he sent for Singleton, explaining that he would land the missionary as soon as it was safe to do so but what appeared to be Frenchmen held the post at Nagtoralik.

'I want you to question Meetuck exhaustively, Mr Singleton. His attitude to the guns has been odd, so has his attitude to myself. You recollect he talked of "bad" white men,' Drinkwater explained and Singleton nodded.

'I do not expect he is able to tell the difference between British, French, Dutch or Russians, all of whom have frequented these seas from time to time. He could not be expected to comprehend a state of war exists between us and the men occupying his village.'

'You saw a village then?'

Singleton nodded. 'I saw twenty or so *topeks* and a number of kayaks drawn up on the beach.'

Drinkwater sighed, biting off a sarcasm that Singleton would have been better employed in the cockpit. The divine was no longer bound to serve there, he was free to go ashore when circumstances permitted, and, thank God, *Melusine* had suffered no casualties thanks to Drinkwater's timely withdrawal.

'Very well. Be a good fellow and see what information you can extort from our eskimo friend. I am almost certain that Ellerby, the master of the *Nimrod*, is in league with whoever is ashore there. He opened fire on us.'

Singleton nodded. 'I wish to land in a place untainted by such doings, Captain Drinkwater. I shall see what I can do.'

After he had gone Drinkwater again gathered his thoughts. Of course St Vincent had not guessed that the French would attempt to make settlements in Greenland. Drinkwater could only imagine what privations the inhabitants endured during the Arctic winter. But since the loss of Canada forty years earlier France had held St

Pierre and Miquelon and it was not inconceivable that now she dominated Denmark, the country that claimed sovereignty over these remote coasts, France might attempt such a thing. St Vincent had mentioned Canada and had seemed certain that some moves were being made by Bonaparte's government or its agents, official or entrepreneurial, in these northern seas. 'This is no sinecure,' the Earl had said, 'and I charge you to remember that, in addition to protecting the northern whale-fleet you should destroy any attempt the French make to establish their own fishery . . .'

Was that what they were doing? It seemed possible. The Portuguese hunted the whale from island bases and, although the winter ice would close the bay, the collusion of a traitor like Ellerby to supply whales, blubber, oil and baleen to them began to make a kind of sense. He began to consider Ellerby and as he did so the figure of Waller insinuated itself into his mind. *Conqueror* was the other ship in the anchorage. Was Waller tied up with Ellerby? Had *Conqueror* also fired into *Melusine* unobserved?

Drinkwater thought back to Hull. Waller had seemed like Ellerby's familiar then. They had clearly acted together, Drinkwater concluded, as he recollected other things about the two men. Ellerby's hostility to Palgrave had resulted in a duel. It occurred to Drinkwater that whatever his prejudices against a man of Palgrave's stamp the quarrel might have been deliberately provoked. And there was Ellerby's affirmation at the Trinity House that he intended to fish for whales where the whim took him. 'Do not expect us to hang upon your skirts like frightened children,' he had said insolently. The recollection stimulated others. When Drinkwater had mentioned the menace of French privateers and the sailing of enemy ships for the Arctic seas he had intended a deliberate exaggeration, a hyperbole to claim attention. He remembered the look of surprise that the black-bearded Ellerby had exchanged with the master sitting next to him. That man had been Waller.

Later, in Bressay Sound, Waller had shown considerable interest in Drinkwater's intentions. It was with some bitterness that Drinkwater realised he had taken little note of these events at the time and had been hoist by his own petard to some extent. And there was something else, something much more significant and, to a seaman much less circumstantial. Waller's attitude to Drinkwater's offer of protection had been dismissive. How dismissive and how ineffectual that offer had been, now burned him with shame; but that was not the point. Waller had stated that the masters of whalers resented interference and when Drinkwater had nominated the rendezvous position Waller had smoothed the chart out. He had been on the left of Drinkwater, looking at the west Greenland coast, yet he and Ellerby intended to hunt whales off Spitzbergen!

The deception was simple. Ellerby, who had already attempted and failed to intimidate Drinkwater, took a back seat and sent Waller to the conference at Bressay Sound. Waller checked Drinkwater's methods and intentions, sounded him and gauged his zeal and ability before reporting back to Ellerby. Drinkwater cursed under his breath. It explained why, after his public humiliation leaving the Humber, Ellerby's *Nimrod* had behaved with exemplary regard for the convoy regulations. Yet Sawyers himself had remarked upon Ellerby's 'massive pride', spoken figuratively of David and Goliath and warned Drinkwater about Ellerby. For a fleeting second Drinkwater thought Sawyers too might be a part of the conspiracy, given his religious contempt for war and the rights and wrongs of the protagonists. Allied with the well-known Quaker liking for profit it made him an obvious suspect. But *Faithful* had been captured under Drinkwater's very nose and Sawyers's behaviour did not really give any grounds for such a suspicion.

Drinkwater sat back in his chair, certain that he had solved the riddle. For some reason the French had established a settlement on the Greenland coast in a position that was demonstrably ice-free, to use for shipping whale products back to France. The risks were high, given the closeness of the British blockade. How much easier to establish contact with British ship-masters who could facilitate the return of the cargoes to France via the good offices of a smuggler or two. From Hull the coast of the Batavian Republic was easily accessible and Drinkwater, like every other officer in the Navy, had heard that French soldiers preferred to march in Northampton boots, rather than the glued manufactures of their own country.

The provision of a powerful French privateer, more frigate than corsair, argued in favour of his theory. Encountered at sea she gave nothing away about official French involvement with the settlement, thus avoiding problems with the Danes, and her loss, if it occurred, would cause no embarrassment to First Consul Bonaparte.

Drinkwater nodded with satisfaction, convinced of Ellerby's treachery, almost certain of Waller's and then, with a start, recollected that Earl St Vincent would not so easily be satisfied.

A knock came at his door. Frey's head was poked round the door when Drinkwater called him in.

'Beg pardon, sir, but Mr Hill says to tell you that there's three ships crowding on sail astern.'

'Very well, Mr Frey. My compliments to the first lieutenant and he's to issue spirits to all hands and then we'll give these fellows a drubbin', eh?'

'Aye, aye, sir.'

Drinkwater sat a moment longer and considered the news. One of the ships would be *Requin* and the second almost certainly *Nimrod*. Was the third *Conqueror* or that damnable lugger? He sighed. He would have to go on deck to see. Whatever the third ship was, Drinkwater was uncomfortably aware that he was outnumbered, outgunned and might, in an hour, have followed Germaney and Rispin into the obscurity of death.

The third ship turned out to be the lugger, her big sails proving more efficient to windward than the other two. He had been right about them. They were indeed *Requin* and *Nimrod*. He studied them through his glass. *Nimrod* was astern of *Requin*, hiding behind the more numerous guns of the big privateer, but ready to bring the smashing power of those heavy carronades to bear upon a *Melusine* that, in her captain's mind's eye, was already a defenceless hulk under the *Requin*'s guns.

Drinkwater summoned Singleton and requested his help after the action which, he confided, he expected to be bloody. He also asked about Meetuck's interrogation.

'It is a complicated matter, but there is much about a big, bearded man with eyes the colour of, er "shadowed ice", if that makes sense to you.'

'I am indebted to you.' Drinkwater smiled and Singleton felt an immense compassion for the cock-headed captain and his terrible profession. 'And now, Mr Singleton, I'd be further obliged to you if you would read us the Naval Prayer.' Drinkwater called the ship's company into the waist. Seamen and officers bared their heads and Obadiah Singleton read the words laid down to be used before an action.

'Oh most powerful and Glorious Lord God, the Lord of Hosts, that rulest and commandest all things . . .'

When it was over Singleton exceeded his brief and led the ship's company into the Lord's Prayer with its slurred syllables and loud, demotic haste. He finished with the Naval Prayer and Bourne, casting an agonised look at the closing enemy, hastily ordered the men back to their stations.

Scarcely less impatient, Drinkwater ordered more sail and turned to Hill, explaining his intentions and those he thought that would be the enemy's.

'*Requin* will seek to disable us, Mr Hill, aiming high from a range that will favour her long guns. The instant we are immobilised he will board while the *Nimrod* ranges alongside and pummels us with those damned carronades. He hasn't many of them, but I'll wager they'll be nasty.'

'Beg pardon, sir, but is *Nimrod* manned by a prize crew?'

'I don't believe she is, Mr Hill. I'm not certain, but I am sure that she's commanded by her British master, one Jemmett Ellerby who deserves to swing for his treachery.'

'Jesus . . .'

'Very well. Now we will bear up and put the ship before the wind. Mr Bourne! A moment of your time. We will run down on the lugger. She is in advance of the other vessels and is doubtless ready to run alongside and pour in men when *Requin* boards. If we can hit her hard with round shot and canister I'll be happy. Then I intend to manoeuvre and avoid *Requin*, using *our* long guns to come up with *Nimrod* and disable her . . .' He outlined Ellerby's treachery for Bourne's benefit and saw the astonishment in his expression harden to resolution. Drinkwater did not say that he intended to destroy *Nimrod* in the belief that they stood little chance of ultimate survival after an action with *Requin*.

He knew now that word of Ellerby's treachery would spread like wildfire and his men fight better for the knowledge. He smiled at his first lieutenant and sailing master. 'Very well, gentlemen. Good luck. Now you may take post.'

They bore down on the lugger which attempted to sheer away. Drinkwater had decided that the jury rudder would take such strains that their manoeuvring might throw upon it. If the enemy did not shoot it away *Melusine* might be relied upon to handle reasonably well, despite the leaky condition a few months in the ice had caused. Her superior height and the fury of her fire cleared the lugger's deck and wounded her mainmast, but her doggedness worried Drinkwater. He was almost certain the officer commanding her had been trying to work round his stern, within range of his light carriage guns to attempt to hit the rudder. This intention to disable the British sloop argued that they knew all about her weak spot. Whatever their intent, the enemy's first move had been thwarted, now he had to deal with the real threat. The *Requin* was on their starboard bow, close hauled on the larboard tack. In a few minutes she would cross their bow, rake them and then bear up astern, holding the weather gauge and assailing their vulnerable rudder.

Drinkwater ordered the course altered to starboard, to bring *Melusine*'s guns to bear as the two ships passed.

'For what we are about to receive, may the Lord make us truly grateful.'

A murmur of blasphemous 'Amens' responded to Hill's facetious remark.

Chapter Eighteen *August 1803*

Ellerby

'Fire!'

The gun captains jumped back, jerking their lanyards and snapping the hammers on the gunlocks. *Melusine*'s larboard six-pounders recoiled inboard against their breechings and as their crews moved forward to sponge and reload them the storm of shot from *Requin*'s broadside hit them. Uncaring for himself Drinkwater watched its effect with anxiety, knowing his enemy possessed the greater weight of metal and the risk he had taken in turning back instead of running from his pursuers. But he knew any chase would ultimately lead to either damage to *Melusine*'s exposed jury rudder or capture due to her being overtaken under her cut-down rig. Besides, he had already determined that Ellerby should reap the just reward of his treachery and that duty compelled him to exercise justice.

He therefore watched the smoke clear from the waist and saw, with a pang of conscience, that Bourne was down and perhaps eight or nine other men were either killed or badly wounded.

'Mr Gorton! Take command of the batteries!' Gorton crossed the deck and saw Bourne carried below as Drinkwater swung round to study *Requin*, already half a cable astern on the larboard quarter. The big privateer had been closed hauled on the wind and her gunnery had suffered from the angle to *Melusine* and the heel of her deck. Nevertheless it was a heavy price to pay for a single broadside. Drinkwater hoped the effects of his own shot, fired from the more level deck of a ship before the wind, had had greater effect. He could see *Requin*'s sails begin to shiver as her captain brought her through the wind to bear down on *Melusine*'s undefended stern. If her gunners were anything like competent they could catch the British sloop with a raking broadside.

Drinkwater turned resolutely forward and raised his glass. They were already very close to *Nimrod*. Ellerby's big figure jumped into the image lens with a startling clarity. Drinkwater closed the glass with a vicious snap.

'Starboard battery, make ready!' Quilhampton looked along the line of guns, his sword drawn. He nodded at Gorton.

'All ready, canister and ball.'

Drinkwater raised his speaking trumpet. 'Sail trimmers to their posts,' he turned to Hill. 'Bear up under his stern, Mr Hill, I want that broad side into his starboard quarter.'

'Aye, aye, sir.'

They raced down upon the approaching whaler. Her bulk and ponderous motion gave her an appearance of greater force than she possessed. Her gunwhales were only pierced for three carronades on each side, but they were of a heavy calibre.

Drinkwater ran forward to the starboard cathead and raised the speaking trumpet again. The two ships were already level, bowsprit to bowsprit.

'Captain Ellerby! Captain Ellerby! Surrender in the King's name before you consign your men to the gallows!'

Ellerby's violent gesture was all that Drinkwater knew of a reply, although he saw Ellerby was yelling something. Whatever it was it was drowned in the roar of his guns, their wide muzzles venting red and orange flame at point-blank range.

Drinkwater nodded at Quilhampton and as Hill put the helm down and *Melusine* began to lean over as she turned, the starboard guns poured ball and canister into the whaler's quarter. Drinkwater fought his way aft, through the sweating gun crews and the badly maimed who had been hit by the langridge from Ellerby's cannon. A man bumped into him. He was holding his head and moaning surprisingly softly seeing that several assorted pieces of iron rubbish protruded from his skull. Drinkwater regained the quarterdeck and looked astern. *Nimrod* continued apparently unscathed on an easterly course.

'Put her on the wind, Mr Hill, and then lay her on the starboard tack!'

Hill began to give orders as the waist was cleared of the dead and wounded, the guns reloaded and run out again. The days of practice began to pay off. Each man attending to his allotted task, each midshipman and mate supervising his half-division or special party, each acting-lieutenant marking his subordinates, attending to the readiness of his battery while Hill, quietly professional on the quarterdeck, directed the trimming of the yards and the sheets to get the best out of the ship.

Melusine turned into the wind, then swung her bowsprit back towards the *Nimrod*, gathering speed as she paid off the starboard tack. Beyond the whaler, Drinkwater could see the *Requin* and was seized by a sudden feeling of intense excitement. He might, just *might*, be able to pull off a neat manoeuvre as *Requin* and *Nimrod* passed each other on opposite courses. He pointed the opening out to Hill.

'She'll do it, sir,' Hill said, after a moment's assessment.

'Let's hope so, Mr Hill.'

Never a doubt, sir.'

Drinkwater grinned, aware that *Melusine* with her jury rudder and ice-scuffed hull was no longer the yacht-like 'corvette' that had danced down the Humber in the early summer.

They crossed *Nimrod*'s stern at a distance of four cables. Not close enough for the six-pounder balls to have much effect on the whaler's massive scantlings. But there was no response from the *Nimrod*'s carronades and Drinkwater transferred his attention to the *Requin*, whose bearing was opening up on the sloop's starboard bow.

'He's not going to let us do it, Mr Hill . . .' They had hoped to cross the *Requin*'s stern too, and pour the starboard broadside into her but the privateer captain was no fool and was already turning his ship, to pass the British sloop on a reciprocal course. They would exchange broadsides as before . . .

'Up helm! Up helm!' Drinkwater shouted. 'Starbowlines, hold your fire!'

'Stand by the lee braces, there!' Hill bawled at his sail-trimmers, suddenly grasping Drinkwater's intention.

'Pick off the officers!' Drinkwater yelled at the midshipmen and marines in the tops. *Melusine* was already turning, an ominous creaking coming from the rudimentary steering gear as a terrific load came on it. *Requin*'s guns roared as the *Melusine*'s stern swung away from the arc of her fire, and although a shower of splinters flew from the taffrail the rudder stock and supporting timbers and spars were untouched.

'Steady her and then bring her round onto the larboard tack. So far so good.'

Drinkwater felt the exhilaration of having called the tune during the last half hour, despite the losses *Melusine* incurred. He was aware of a mood of high elation along the deck where the men joked and relived the last few moments with an outbreak of skylarking equally uncaring in the heady excitement for those below undergoing the agonies of Singleton's knife.

Melusine clawed back to windward while her two enemies came round in pursuit again. Already they were a mile away to the northwest and Drinkwater thought he could keep them tacking in his wake for an hour or two yet while he sought a new opening.

'That lugger's out of the running, sir,' offered Hill, pointing to the *chassé marée* half a mile away. Her crew had sweeps out and were pulling her desperately out of the path of the approaching British sloop which seemed to be bearing down upon them with the intention of administering the *coup de grâce*. In fact Drinkwater had long since forgotten about the lugger, although it had been no more than forty or fifty minutes since they had fired into her.

He nodded at Gorton with the good-natured condescension of a school-master allowing his pupils an indulgent catapult shot at sparrows. The larboard guns fired as they passed and several balls struck home, causing evident panic among the lugger's crew.

Drinkwater was seized by a sudden feeling that things had been too easy and recalled the dead and wounded. He turned and called sharply to the midshipman who was in attendance to the quarterdeck and whose obvious pleasure at still being alive had induced a certain foolish garrulousness with the adjacent gun crews.

'Mr Frey!'

'S . . . Sir?'

'Pray direct your attention to the surgeon, present him with my compliments and ascertain the extent of our losses. I am particularly concerned about Mr Bourne.'

'Aye, aye, sir.'

After Frey had departed Drinkwater called for reports of damage and the carpenter informed him that they had a shot between wind and water, but that otherwise most of the enemy's fire had been levelled at personnel on the upper deck.

Pacing up and down Drinkwater tried to assess the state of his enemies. He had not succeeded in forcing *Nimrod* to surrender and his chances of annihilating the *Requin* were slight. But the whaler had failed to take advantage of a clear shot at *Melusine*'s stern. Did that argue her untrained crew had simply missed an opportunity or that, having fired into a King's ship they might have taken heed of Drinkwater's earlier hail?

Discipline was not so tight on a merchantman and a crew might be seduced from its nominal allegiance to their master by the threat of the gallows. Drinkwater considered the point. Did it also signify that *Requin*'s fire had been at *Melusine*'s deck, not at her rigging? In the place of the privateer Captain Drinkwater thought he might have wanted the naval vessel disabled from a distance, without material damage to the *Requin* herself.

Unless, argued Drinkwater, *Requin's* superiority was over-estimated. Perhaps her crew were less numerous than he supposed and therefore to decimate the British had become a priority with *Requin's* commander.

'Wind's veering, sir.' Hill interrupted his train of thought.

'Eh?'

'Hauling southerly, sir.'

It was true. The wind had dropped abruptly and was chopping three, no, four points and freshening from the south-east. Drinkwater stared to the south, there was a further shift coming. In ten minutes or so the wind would be blowing directly off the mountain peaks to the southward. All the ships in the fiord would be able to reach with equal facility. It altered everything.

'That puts a different complexion on things, Mr Hill.'

Hill turned from directing a trimming of the yards and nodded his agreement. For a few moments Drinkwater continued pacing up and down. Then he came to a decision.

'Put the ship on an easterly course, Mr Hill. I want her laid alongside the *Nimrod* without further delay.'

It was a decision that spoke more of honour than commonsense, yet Drinkwater was put in an invidious position by his orders. It was doubtful if St Vincent could have foreseen the extent of the French presence in the Arctic, or of the treachery of Ellerby and, presumably, Waller. Yet Drinkwater's orders were explicit in terms of preventing any French ascendancy in the area. The red rag of honour was raised in encouragement; not to use his utmost endeavour was to court a firing squad as Byng had done fifty years before.

Requin's shot stove in the gunwhale amidships, dismounted a gun and wiped out two gun crews. The maintopmast was shot through and went by the board and the big privateer bore up under *Melusine*'s stern. The single report of a specially laid gun appeared to annihilate the four men steering by the clumsy tiller.

Then Drinkwater realised that the rudder stock had been shot to pieces and the tiller merely fallen to the deck, taking the men with it. They picked themselves up unhurt, but Drinkwater's eyes met those of Hill and both men knew *Melusine* was immobilised. Two minutes later she bore off before the wind and with a jarring crash that made her entire fabric judder she struck *Nimrod* amidships.

'Boarders awa-a-way!' Mad with frustration and anger Drinkwater lugged out his borrowed sword and grabbed a pistol from his waistband and ran forward. Men left the guns and grabbed pikes from the racks by the masts and cutlasses gleamed in the sunshine that beat hot upon their backs as they crowded over the fo'c's'le and scrambled down onto the whaler's deck.

Quilhampton was ahead of Drinkwater and had reached the *Nimrod*'s poop where Ellerby stood aiming his great brass harpoon gun into the *Nimrod*'s waist as Drinkwater led his boarders aft. A cluster of men had gathered round him but the majority of his crew, over twenty men, were dodging backwards into whatever shelter the deck of the whaler offered, making gestures of surrender and calling for quarter.

'Mr Q! Stand aside, damn it!' Drinkwater called, his voice icy with suppressed fury. He saw Ellerby raise the huge gun, saw its barrel foreshorten as the piece was aimed at his own breast and heard the big Yorkshireman yell:

'Stand fast, Cap'n Drinkwater! D'you hear me! Stand fast!'

But Drinkwater was moving aft and saw the smoke from the gun. He felt the rush of air past his cheek as the harpoon narrowly missed him and a second later he was shoving Quilhampton aside.

Somebody had passed Ellerby a whale-lance and its long shaft kept Drinkwater at a distance. 'You traitorous bastard, Ellerby. Put that thing down, or by God, I'll see you swing . . .'

Drinkwater was forced backwards, stumbled and fell over as Ellerby, his face a mask of hatred, stabbed forward with the razor-sharp lance. Suddenly Ellerby had descended the short ladder from *Nimrod*'s poop and stood over Drinkwater.

Aware of the quivering lance and the fanatical light in Ellerby's pale blue eyes Drinkwater could think only of the pistol he had half fallen on. Even as Ellerby stabbed downward Drinkwater rolled over, his thumb pulling the hammer back to full cock and his finger squeezing the trigger.

He felt the lance head cut him, felt the cleanness of the keen edge with a kind of detachment that told him that it was not fatal, that the lance had merely skidded round his abdomen, through the thin layer of muscles over his right ribs. He stood up, bleeding through the rent in his coat.

Ellerby was leaning drunkenly on the lance that, having wounded Drinkwater, had stuck in the deck. The beginnings of a roar of pain were welling up from him and streaming through his beard in a shower of spittle. Drinkwater could not see where the ball had entered Ellerby's body, but as he crashed forward onto the deck its point of egress was bloodily conspicuous. His spine was shattered in the small of his back and the roar of impotence and pain faded to a wheezing respiration.

Drinkwater pressed his hand to his own flank and looked down into his fallen foe. Ellerby's wound was mortal and, as the realisation spread men began to move again. The whale-ship crew threw down their weapons and James Quilhampton, casting a single look at Drinkwater, gave orders to take possession of the *Nimrod*.

Drinkwater turned, aware of blood warm on his hand. Before him little Mr Frey was trying to attract attention.

'Yes, Mr Frey? What is it?'

Frey pointed back across *Melusine*'s deck to where the *Requin* could be seen looming out of the smoke.

'B . . . beg pardon, sir, but Mr Hill's compliments and the *Requin* is bearing up to windward. '

As if to lend emphasis to the urgency of Frey's message the multiple concussion of *Requin*'s broadside filled the air, while at Drinkwater's feet Ellerby gave up the ghost.

Chapter Nineteen *August 1803*

The Plagues of Egypt

Drinkwater felt the relief of the broad bandage securing the thick pledget to his side. He stared through the smoke trying to ignore Skeete who was tugging his shirt down after completing the dressing.

'That'll do, damn it!' he shouted above the noise of the guns.

'Aye, aye, sir.' Skeete grinned maliciously through his rotten teeth and Drinkwater tucked his shirt tails impatiently into his waistband still trying to divine the intentions of *Requin*'s commander.

Leaving Lord Walmsley in command of *Nimrod* Drinkwater and the boarding party had returned to *Melusine* although the whaler and sloop still lay locked together. *Requin* lay just to windward, firing into the British ship with her heavier guns. At every discharge of her cannon they were swept by an iron storm. There were dead and dying men lying on the gratings where their mates had dragged them to be clear of the guns and from where the surgeon's party selected those worthy to be carried below to undergo the horrors of amputation, curettage or probing. The superficially wounded dressed themselves from the bandage boxes slotted into the bar-holes in the ship's capstans, and held against such an eventuality. Drinkwater saw that stained bandages had sprouted everywhere, that the larboard six-pounders were being served by men from both batteries and that Gorton was wounded.

The noise was deafening as the Melusines fired their cannon as fast as each gun could be sponged, charged and laid. Ropes and splinters rained down from aloft and below the mainmast three bodies lay where they had fallen from the top. Only the foremast stood intact, the foretopsail still filled with wind.

The stink of powder smoke, the noise and the confusion and above all the unbelievably hot sun combined with the sharp pain in his flank to exhaust Drinkwater. It crossed his mind to strike, if only to end the killing of his men and the intolerable noise.

Something of this must have been evident in his face, for Hill was looking at him.

'Are you all right, sir?' Hill shouted.

Drinkwater nodded grimly.

'Here sir . . .' Hill held out a flask and Drinkwater lifted it to his lips. The fiery rum stirred him as it hit the pit of his stomach.

'Obliged to you, Mr Hill . . .' He looked up at the spanker. It was too full of holes to be very effective, but an idea occurred to him.

'Chapel that spanker, Mr Hill, haul it up against the wind. Let us swing the stern round and try and put *Nimrod* between us and that bloody bastard to windward!'

A shower of splinters were struck from the adjacent rail and Drinkwater and Hill staggered from the wind of the passing ball, gasping for breath. But Hill recovered and bawled at the afterguard. Drinkwater turned. He must buy time to think. He saw Mount's scarlet coat approaching after posting his sentries over the prisoners aboard *Nimrod*.

'Mr Mount!'

'Sir?'

'Mr Mount, muster your men aft here . . .'

The katabatic squall hit them with sudden violence, screaming down from the heights to the south of them, streaking the water with spray and curling the seas into sharp, vicious waves in the time it takes to draw breath. The air at sea level in the fiord had been warmed for hours by the unclouded sun. Rising in an increasing mass, this air was replaced by cold air sliding down from its contact with the ice and snow of the mountain tops to spread out over the water as a squall, catching the ships unprepared.

Melusine's fore topgallant mast, already weighed down by the wreckage of the main topmast and its spars, carried away and crashed to leeward. But the chapelled spanker, hauled to windward by Hill's men, spun the sloop and her prize, while *Nimrod*'s sails filled and tended to drive both ships forward so that their range increased from their tormentor.

But it was a momentary advantage for, hove to, the *Requin* increased her leeway until the strain on her own tophamper proved too much. Already damaged by *Melusine*'s gunfire, her wounded foremast went by the board. Dragged head to wind and with her backed main yards now assisting her leeward drift, *Requin* presented her stern to Drinkwater and he was not slow to appreciate his change of fortune. A quick glance at *Nimrod*'s sails and he saw immediately that he might swiftly reverse their turning movement and bring *Melusine*'s battered larboard broadside to bear on that exposed stern.

'Belay that Hill!' He indicated the spanker. 'Brail up the spanker! Forrard there! Mr Comley! Foretopmast staysail sheets to windward . . .' His voice cracked with shouting but he hailed *Nimrod*.

'*Nimrod! Nimrod* 'hoy! Back your main and mizen tops'ls, Mr Walmsley, those whalemen that help you to be pardoned . . .' It was a crazy, desperate idea and relied for its success on a swifter reaction than the *Requin*'s captain could command. Drinkwater waited in anxious impatience, his temper becoming worse by the second. He raised his glass several times and studied the *Requin*, each time expecting to see something different but all he could distinguish with certainty was that the big privateer was drifting down on them. And then *Melusine* and her prize began to turn again, swinging slowly round, rolling and grinding together as the continuing wind built up the sea.

The katabatic squall had steadied to a near gale and swept the smoke away. The sun still shone from a cloudless sky although its setting could not be far distant. The altered attitude of the ships had silenced their gunfire and the air was filled now with the scream of wind in rigging and the groaning of the locked ships.

Drinkwater shook his head to clear it of the persistent ringing that the recent concussion of the guns had induced and raised his speaking trumpet again.

'Larboard guns! Gun captains to lay their pieces at the centre window of the enemy's stern. Load canister on ball. Fire on the command and then independently!'

He saw Quilhampton in the waist acknowledge and wondered what had become of Gorton. He raised his glass, aware that Mount was still beside him awaiting the instructions he was in the process of giving when the squall hit them.

'Any orders, sir?' Mount prompted.

Drinkwater did not hear him. He was watching *Melusine*'s swing and waiting for the raised arms that told him his cannon were ready. The last gun captain raised his hand. He waited a little longer. A quick glance along the gun breeches showed them at level elevation. They traversed with infinite slowness as *Nimrod* and *Melusine* cartwheeled . . . Now, by God!

'Fire!'

Noise, smoke and fire spewed from the ten six-pounders as sixty pounds of iron and ten pounds of small ball hit *Requin*'s stern. Drinkwater was engulfed in the huge cloud of smoke which was as quickly rent aside by the wind. Then the six-pounders began independent fire, each captain laying his gun with care. *Requin*'s stern began to cave in, beaten into a gaping wound, her carved gingerbread-work exploding in splinters.

'Sir! Sir!' Mr Frey was dancing up and down beside him.

'What the devil is it, Mr Frey?' Drinkwater suddenly felt anxious for the boy whose presence on the quarterdeck he had quite forgotten.

'She strikes, sir! She strikes!'

Drinkwater elevated his glance. The tricolour was descending from the gaff in hasty jerks.

'Upon my soul, Mr Frey, you're right!'

'Any orders, sir,' repeated the hopeful Mount.

'Indeed, Mr Mount. You and Frey take possession!'

Drinkwater jerked himself awake with a start. The short Arctic night was already over. His wound, pronounced superficial by an exhausted Singleton, throbbed painfully and his whole body ached in the chill of dawn. He rose and stared through the stern windows. *Melusine* and her assorted prizes lay at anchor in Nagtoralik Bay, the battered British sloop to seaward, a spring on her cable, covering any signs of trouble in the other ships. He had prize crews aboard the lugger *Aurore*, the *Requin* and the *Nimrod*, although the *Nimrod* had assumed the character of consort, having towed the helpless *Melusine* into the anchorage.

They had been met by boats from the whalers *Conqueror* and *Faithful* as the last of the daylight faded from the sky and the wounded ships had come to their anchors. It was clear from the expression of Captain Waller of the *Conqueror* that he had put an entirely different interpretation on the sight of *Melusine* towing in astern of *Nimrod* than was the case. His false effusions of congratulation had been cut short by Drinkwater arresting him and having him placed in the bilboes.

'Thou hast done right, Friend,' said Sawyers, holding out his hand. But Drinkwater gently dismissed the Quaker, pleading tiredness and military expediency for his bad manners. There would be time enough for explanations later, for the while it was enough that *Faithful* was recaptured and *Requin* a prize.

Drinkwater turned from the stern windows and slumped back in his chair. The low candle-flame in the lantern fell upon the muster book. In the two actions with the *Requin* he had lost a third of his ship's company. They were terrible losses and he mourned Lieutenant Bourne who had died of head wounds shortly after the *Requin* surrendered.

Hardly a man had not collected a scratch or a splinter wound. Little Frey had received a sword cut on his forearm which he had bravely bandaged until Singleton spotted the filthy linen and ordered the boy below. Tregembo had been knocked senseless and of the quarterdeck officers only Mount and Hill were unscathed.

He blew the sand off the muster book and closed it. Amid all the tasks that awaited him this morning he must bury the dead. His eyelids dropped. On deck Mr Quilhampton paced up and down, the watch ready at the guns. Mount was aboard *Requin* with a strong detachment of marines; Lord Walmsley commanded *Nimrod* and the Honourable Alexander Glencross the *Conqueror*.

He could allow himself an hour's sleep. He was aware that providence had chastened him but that luck had saved him. His head fell forward onto his breast and his ears ceased to ring from the concussion of guns.

'Will you receive the deputation now, sir?' Drinkwater nodded at Mr Frey's figure standing in the cabin doorway. It was frightening how fast the maturing process could work. Frey stood aside and half a dozen whale-men came awkwardly into the cabin under the escort of Mount's sergeant and two private marines.

'Well,' said Drinkwater coldly, 'who is to speak for you?'

A man was pushed forward and turned a greasy sealskin hat nervously in his hands. Addressing the deck he began to speak, prompted by shamefaced shipmates.

'B . . . beg pardon, yer honour . . .'

'What is your name?'

The man looked about him, as if afraid to confess to an identity that separated him from the anonymous group of whale-men.

'Give an answer to the captain!' Frey snapped with a sudden, surprising venom.

'J . . . Jack Love, sir, beggin' yer pardon. Carpenter of the *Nimrod*, sir . . .'

'Go on, Love. Tell me what you have to say.'

'Well sir, we went along of Cap'n Ellerby, sir . . .'

'An' of Cap'n Waller, sir . . .' another piped up to a shuffling chorus of agreement.

'Pray go on.'

'Well sir, there was a fair profit to be made, sir, during the peace like . . .' He trailed off, implying that trade with the French under those circumstances was not illegal.

'In what did you trade, Love? Be so good as to tell me.'

'We brought out necessaries, sir . . . comestibles and took home furs . . .'

'Furs?'

'Aye, sir,' an impatient voice said and a small man shoved forward. 'Furs, sir, furs for the Frog army what Ellerby could sell at a profit . . .'

Drinkwater digested the news and a thought occurred to him.

'Do you know anything about two Hull whale ships that went missing last winter?' He looked round the half-circle of faces. Love's hand rubbed anxiously across his mouth and he shook his head, avoiding Drinkwater's eyes.

'We don't want no traitorous doin's, sir. We was coerced, like . . .' He fell silent. The word had been rehearsed, fed him by some sea-lawyer and he was lying, although Drinkwater knew there was not a shred of evidence to prove it. They would have profited under Ellerby, war or peace, so long as no supercilious naval officer stuck his interfering nose into their business.

Love seemed to have mustered his defences, prodded on by some murmuring behind him.

'When we realised what Ellerby was doing, sir, we wasn't 'aving none of it. We didn't obey 'im sir . . .' Drinkwater remembered *Nimrod*'s failure to take full advantage of her position during the action.

'And *Conqueror*'s people. How are they circumstanced?'

'We were coerced too, sir. Cap'n Waller threatened to withhold our proper pay unless we co-operated . . .'

Drinkwater stared at them. He felt a mixture of contempt and pity. He could imagine them under the malign influence of Ellerby and he remembered the ice-cold fanaticism in his eyes. The men began to shuffle awkwardly under his silent scrutiny. They were victims of their own weakness and yet they had caused the death of his men by their treachery.

'Would you wish to prove your loyalty to King and Country, then?' he asked, rising to his feet, the picture of a patriotic naval officer. Their eagerness to please, to fall in with his suggestion, verged on the disgusting.

'Very well. You will find work enough refitting the ships under the direction of my officers. You may go now. Return to your ships; but I warn you, the first man that fails to show absolute loyalty will swing.'

Their delight was manifest. It was the kind of thing they had hardly dared hope for. They nodded their thanks and shambled out.

'You may discharge the guard, sergeant,' Drinkwater addressed Mr Frey. 'Do you go to the two whale ships, Mr Frey, and ransack the cabins of Captain Ellerby and Captain Waller. I want the press-exemptions of every man-jack of those whale-men.'

Drinkwater regarded Waller with distaste. Without Ellerby he was pathetic and Drinkwater was conscious that, as a King's officer, he represented the noose to Waller. Somehow hanging was too just an end for the man. He had tried a brief, unconvincing and abject attempt at blustered justification which Drinkwater had speedily ended.

'It is useless to prevaricate, Captain Waller. Ellerby fired into a British man-o'-war wearing British colours and I am well aware, from information laid before me by men from *Nimrod* and *Conqueror*, that you and he were in traitorous intercourse with the enemy for the purposes of profit. That fact alone put you in breach of your oath not to engage in any other practice other than the pursuance of whale-fishing. What I wish to know, is to what precise purpose did you trade here and with whom?'

Waller's face had drained. Drinkwater slammed his fist on the cabin table. 'And I want to know *now*!'

Waller's jaw hung slackly. He seemed incapable of speech. Drinkwater sighed and rose. 'You may,' he said casually, 'consider the wisdom of turning King's Evidence. I *do* have enough testimony against you to see you swing, Waller . . .'

Drinkwater's certainty was overwhelmingly persuasive. Waller swallowed.

'If I turn King's Evidence . . .'

'Tell me the bloody truth, Waller, or by God I'll see you at the main yardarm before another hour is out!'

'It was Ellerby . . . he said it couldn't fail. We did well out of it during the peace. There seemed no reason not to go on. When the war started again, I tried to stop it. Aye, I said it weren't worth the risk like. But Ellerby said it were worth it. Happen I should have known'd better. Anyroad I went along wi'it . . .'

The dialect was thick now. Waller in the confessional was a man turned in upon himself, contemplating his weaknesses. Again Drinkwater felt that surge of pity for a fool caught up in the ambitions of a strong personality.

'Went along with what?' he asked quietly

'Furs. French have this settlement. Just before Peace of Amiens Ellerby had run into a French privateersman, Jean Vrolicq. This Vrolicq offered us a handsome profit if we carried furs to England, like, and smuggled them across t'Channel. Easier, nay, safer than Vrolicq trying to run blockade. Furs for the French army taken to France in English smuggling boats . . .'

'Furs?' It was the second time Drinkwater queried the word, only this time he was more curious about the precise nature of the traffic and less preoccupied by the fate of the man before him.

'Aye, Cap'n. Furs for French army. They have bearskins on every cavalry horse, fur on them hussars . . .'

Drinkwater recollected the cartoons of the French army, the barefoot scarecrows motivated by Republican zeal . . . and yet he did not doubt Waller now.

'We ran cargoes of fox, ermine, bear and hares . . . four hundred pounds clear profit on top o' what the fish brought in . . .'

'Very well, Captain Waller. You may put this in writing. I shall supply you with the necessaries.'

Drinkwater called the sentry and Waller was taken out.

It was a strange tale, yet, thinking back to his interviews with Earl St Vincent and Lord Dungarth he perceived the first strands of the mystery had been evident even then. That he had stumbled on the core of it was a mixture of good and bad luck that was compounded, for those who liked to think of such matters in a philosophical light, as the fortune of war.

He poured a glass of wine and listened to the noise around him. *Melusine*'s jury rudder was being lifted and the blacksmith from *Faithful* was fashioning a yoke iron so that tiller lines might be fitted to its damaged head and so rigged for the passage home. Spars were being plundered from the *Requin* to refit the sloop and the *Aurore* was being put in condition to sail to Britain.

Mindful of the political strictures St Vincent had mentioned in respect of the whale fishery, Drinkwater was anxious that both *Nimrod* and *Conqueror* returned to the Humber. But his own desperate shortage of men prevented him from taking *Requin* home as a prize. He intended burning her before they left Nagtoralik Bay.

A knock at the cabin door preceded the entry of Obadiah Singleton. His blue jaw seemed more prominent as his face was haggard with exhaustion.

'Ah, Mr Singleton. What may I do to serve you?'

'I consider that I have completed my obligations to the sick, Captain Drinkwater. I shall leave them in the hands of Skeete . . .'

'God help them . . .'

'Amen to that. But there is work enough for me ashore . . .'

'You cannot be landed here, Mr Singleton, there is a French settlement . . .'

'Your orders were to land me, Captain Drinkwater. There are eskimos here. As for the French, I cannot think that you would invite them on board your ship . . .'

'My orders, Mr Singleton,' Drinkwater replied sharply, 'are to extirpate any French presence I find in Arctic waters. To that end I must root out and take prisoner any military presence ashore.'

'I think your concern for your own ship will not permit that,' Singleton said with a final certainty.

'What the devil d'you mean by that?'

'I mean that Mr Frey, whom you sent ashore for water, has returned with information that leads me to suppose the poor devils ashore here are afflicted with all the plagues of Egypt, Captain Drinkwater.'

Chapter Twenty *August–September 1803*

Greater Love Hath no Man

They had assembled all the French prisoners ashore prior to burning the *Requin*. Flanked by Mount and Singleton and escorted by a file of marines, Drinkwater inspected the hovels that made up the French settlement. Drawn apart from the privateersmen and regarded with a curious hostility by a crowd of eskimos, an untidy, starveling huddle of men watched their approach cautiously. They wore the remnants of military greatcoats, their feet bound in rags and their shoulders covered in skins. Most hid their faces. They were Bonaparte's Arctic 'colonists'.

Explanation came slowly, as though the revelation of horror should not be sudden. They were military ghosts, two companies of *Invalides*, a euphemism for the broken remnants of Bonaparte's vaunted Egyptian and Syrian campaigns. A handful of men who had regained France after the desertion of Bonaparte and the assassination of his successor Kleber; men who had returned home from annexed Egypt where their accounts of what had happened and the decay of their bodies were a double embarrassment to the authorities.

Drinkwater remembered the purulent eyes of the men he had fought hand to hand off Kosseir on the Egyptian coast of the Red Sea. Perhaps some of these poor devils had been in the garrison that had so gallantly resisted the British squadron under Captain Lidgbird Ball. He surveyed the diseased remnants of French ambition who had been trepanned to Greenland in an attempt to form a trading post to acquire furs for the French army. Here they could supply the voracious wants of the First Consul's armies at the expense of degrading the eskimos, exchanging liquor for furs, liquor that came through the agency of British whalers.

Under Drinkwater's scrutiny several of the Frenchmen drew

themselves up, still soldiers, such was the power of military influence. The rags fell away from their faces. The ravages of bilharzia, trachoma-induced blindness, skin diseases, frostbite and God alone knew what other contagions burned in them.

Drinkwater turned aside, sickened. He met the eyes of Singleton. *'Dulce et decorum est pro patria mori,'* said the missionary softly.

'Where is this man Vrolicq?' Drinkwater muttered through clenched teeth.

Mount had the privateer's commander and officers quartered in a wretched stone and willow-roofed hovel. They stood blinking in the pale sunshine that filtered through a thin overcast and stared at the British officers.

Jean Vrolicq, corsair, republican opportunist and war-profiteer regarded Drinkwater through dark, suspicious eyes. He was a small man whose hardiness and energy seemed somehow refined, as though reduced to its essence in these latitudes, and disdaining a larger body. His face was bearded, seamed and tanned, his eyes chips of coal. Drinkwater recognised the man who had wounded him during their first action with the *Requin*.

'So, Captain, today you remember you have prisoners, eh?' Vrolicq's English was good, his accent suggesting a familiarity with Cornwall that was doubtless allied to the practice of 'free trade'.

'Tell me, M'sieur, was this trade you had with Captain Ellerby profitable to yourself?'

Perhaps Vrolicq thought Drinkwater was corruptible instead of merely curious, angling for a speculative cargo aside from his duty.

'But yes, Captain, and also for the carrier.' The man grinned rapaciously. 'You British are expert at making laws from which profits can be made with ease. You are equally good at breaking your own laws, which is perhaps why you make them, yes? Ellerby, he traded furs for cognac, his friends traded gold for cognac. We French now have gold in France and cognac in Greenland. Ellerby has furs which he also trades. To us French. So we have gold, cognac and furs. Ellerby has a little profit. It is clever, yes? And because your King George has a wise Parliament who all like a little French cognac.' The disdain was clear in Vrolicq's voice. But it was equally clear why Ellerby had not wanted Drinkwater's presence in the Greenland Sea, yet needed his protection in soundings off the British coast where an unscrupulous naval officer might board him in search of men and discover he had tiers of furs over his barrels of whale blubber. If Ellerby's plan had not been disrupted he and Waller would have been at the rendezvous off Shetland at the end of September and allowed Drinkwater to escort them safely into the Humber. And how assiduously Drinkwater had striven to afford Ellerby the very protection he needed for his nefarious trade!

'It is quite possible,' said Vrolicq, breaking into Drinkwater's thoughts, 'that you might yourself profit a little . . .'

'Go to the devil!' snapped Drinkwater, turning away and striding down the beach towards the waiting boat.

Drinkwater stood on the quarterdeck wrapped in the bear-skin given him by the officers. It was piercingly cold, the damp tendrils of a fog reaching down into the bay from the heights surrounding them. The daylight was dreary with mist; the Arctic summer was coming to its end.

'Boat approaching, sir.' Drinkwater acknowledged Frey's report and watched one of the *Nimrod*'s boats, commandeered to replace *Melusine*'s losses, as it was pulled out from the curve of dark sand and shingle that marked the beach at Nagtoralik. He waited patiently while Obadiah Singleton clambered over the rail, nodded him a greeting, then ushered him below to the sanctuary of the cabin.

'Well Obadiah, you received my note. I am about to sail. All the ships are ready and the wind, what there is of it, will take us clear of the bay as soon as this fog lifts. This is the last chance to change your mind.'

'That is out of the question, Nathaniel.' Singleton smiled his rare smile. All pretence at rank had long since vanished between the two men. Singleton's determination to stay and minister to the human flotsam on the shores of the bay ran contrary to all of Drinkwater's instincts. He could not quite believe that Singleton would remain. 'Oh, I know what you intend to say. "Remember whom you are to cope withal; a sort of vagabonds, rascals and runaways, a scum of Bretagnes, and base lackey peasants whom their o'er cloyéd country vomits forth to desperate ventures, and assured destruction . . ." King Richard the Third, Nathaniel. That last clause is most appropriate. Scarcely any will survive the coming winter. There is evidence of typhus . . .'

'Typhus!'

'Yes, what you call the ship or gaol fever . . .'

'I know damned well what typhus is . . .'

'Well then you know that as a divine I should urge you to take mercy upon them, to have compassion even at the risk of infecting your ship's company. As a physician I warn you against further contact with them. There is not only typhus, there is . . .'

'I know, I know. I do not wish to reflect upon the whole catalogue of ills that infests this morbid place. So you advise me to take no action. To leave them here to rot.'

'This is the first time, Nathaniel, that I have seen you indecisive.' Singleton smiled again.

'There is no need to enjoy the experience, damn it!'

'Forgive me. Perhaps one thing I have learned during our acquaintance is that true decisions are seldom made upon philosophical lines. Sometimes the burdens of your position are too great for one man to bear. It is God's will that I surrogate for your conscience.'

'And what will happen to you, Obadiah? Eh?'

'I do not know. Let us leave that to God. You were bidden to land me upon the coast of Greenland. You have done your duty.'

'And Vrolicq?'

'Vrolicq is an agent of the devil. Leave him to me and to God. '

'I have already offered you whatever you wish for out of the ships. Surely you till take my pistols . . .'

'Thank you, no. I have taken such necessaries as I thought desirable out of the *Requin* before you fired her yesterday. I have everything I need.' He paused. 'I am at peace, Nathaniel. Do not worry on my account. It is you who work for implacable masters. It was Christ's essential gospel that we should love our enemies.'

'I do not understand you, damned if I do.'

'John, fifteen, verse thirteen,' he held out his hand. 'Farewell, Nathaniel.'

'Have you any questions, gentlemen?'

The assembled officers shook their heads. Sawyers of *Faithful* had loaned his speksioneer, Elijah Pucill, to assist Mr Quilhampton in bringing home *Nimrod*. Gorton was sufficiently recovered to command *Conqueror*, seconded by Lord Walmsley. Sawyers's son was assisting Glencross in the *Aurore*. The crews of the two whalers had been tempered by prize crews from *Melusine* while those elements whose loyalty might still be in doubt were quartered aboard the sloop herself. Drinkwater dismissed them, each with a copy of his orders. They filed out of the cabin. Captain Sawyers hung back.

'You wished to speak to me, Captain Sawyers?'

'Aye, Friend. We have both been busy men during the past five days. I wished for a proper opportunity to express to thee my gratitude. I have thanked God, for the force of thine arm was like unto David's when he slew Goliath, yet I know that to be an instrument of God's will can torture a man severely.'

Drinkwater managed a wry smile at Sawyers's odd reasoning. 'I am considering it less hazardous to be surrounded by ice than by theologians. But thank you.'

'I have left thy servant, the Cornishman, a quantity of furs. Perhaps thou might find some use for them better than draped over the horses of the un-Godly.'

Drinkwater grinned. Some explanation of Sawyers's activities in the last few days suggested itself to Drinkwater. It occurred to him that Sawyers knew all along of Ellerby's treachery but his religious abhorrence of war enabled him to overlook it. Besides, now the shrewd Quaker had most of *Nimrod*'s cargo of furs safely stowed aboard the *Faithful*.

'What have you entered in your log book concerning your capture?'

'That I was taken by a French privateer, conducted to an anchorage and liberated by thyself. I have no part in thy war beyond suffering its aggravations.'

'Good. It was not my intention to advertise this treachery. Much distress will be caused thereby to the families of weak and defenceless men.'

Sawyers raised an eyebrow. 'Canst thou afford such magnanimity? Seamen gossip, Friend.'

'Captain Sawyers, if you were to come upon two unmanned whalers anchored inside the Spurn Head, would you ensure they came safely home to their owners?'

A gleam of comprehension kindled in Sawyers's eyes. 'You mean to press the crews when you have anchored the ships?'

'There are a few of your men already on board to claim salvage. I am not asking you to falsify your log, merely amend it.'

Sawyers chuckled. 'A man who cannot write a log book to his

own advantage is not fit to command a ship, Captain Drinkwater.' He paused. 'But what advantage is there to thee?'

Drinkwater shrugged. 'I have a crew again.'

'Patriotism is an unprofitable business and thy acumen recommends thee for other ventures. But have you considered the matter of their press exemptions?'

'I had them collected from the two ships. They burned with *Requin*.'

'And Waller?' asked Sawyers, raising an eyebrow in admiration.

Drinkwater smiled grimly. 'Ellerby may take the burden of treachery dead. Waller can expiate his greed if not his treason by serving the King along with the rest of the whale-men. It is better for them to dance at the end of the bosun's starter rather than a noose. Besides, as Lord St Vincent was at pains to point out to me, loss of whale-men means loss of prime seamen. It seems a pity to deprive His Majesty of seamen to provide employment for the hangman.'

Sawyers laughed. 'I do not think that it is expiation, Friend. It seems to be *immolation*.'

Drinkwater lingered a while after the Quaker had departed, giving him time to return to *Faithful*, then he reached for his hat and went on deck to give the order to weigh anchor.

Drinkwater stared astern. Gulls dipped in *Melusine*'s wake and beside him the jury rudder creaked. As if veiling itself the coast of Greenland was disappearing in a low fog. Already Cape Jervis had vanished.

Far to the west, above the fog bank, disembodied by distance and elevation, the *nunataks* of the permanent ice-cap gleamed faintly, remote and undefiled by man.

Drinkwater turned from his contemplation and began to pace the deck. He thought of Meetuck who had disappeared for several days, terrified of the guns that rumbled and thundered over his head. He had reappeared at last, driven into the open by hunger and finally landed a hero among his own people. He remembered the thirty odd Melusines that would not return, Bourne among them. And the survivors; Mr Midshipman Frey, Gorton, Hill, Mount and James Quilhampton. And little Billie Cue about whose future he must write to Elizabeth.

He looked astern once more and thought of Singleton, ministering to the sick veterans of an atheist government who were corrupting the eskimos. Singleton would die attempting to alleviate their agonies and save their souls whilst proclaiming the existence of a God of universal love.

There was no sense in it. And yet what was it Singleton had said?

'Mr Frey!'

'Sir?'

'Be so kind as to fetch me a Bible.'

'A Bible, sir?'

'Yes, Mr Frey. A Bible.'

Frey returned and handed Drinkwater a small, leatherbound Bible. Drinkwater opened it at St John's Gospel, Chapter Fifteen, verse thirteen. He read:

Greater love hath no man than this, that a man lay down his life for his friends.

Then he remembered Singleton's muttered quotation as they had stared at the French veterans: *'Dulce et decorum est pro patria mori.'*

'It's all a question of philosophy, Mr Frey,' he said suddenly, looking up from the Bible and handing it back to the midshipman.

'Is it, sir?' said the astonished Frey.

'And the way you look at life.'

Chapter Twenty-One *November 1803*

The Nore

'Square the yards, Mr Hill, and set t'gallants.'

Drinkwater watched the departing whalers beat up into the Humber, carried west by the inrush of the flood tide. He had at least the satisfaction of having obeyed his orders, collecting the other ships, the *Earl Percy*, *Provident*, *Truelove* and the rest, at the Shetland rendezvous. He had now completed their escort to the estuary of the River Humber and most of them were taking advantage of the favourable tide to carry them up the river against the prevailing wind. Only *Nimrod*, *Conqueror* and *Faithful* remained at anchor in Hawke Road while Sawyers shipped his prize crews on board to sail the remaining few miles to the mouth of the River Hull.

Amidships Drinkwater watched Mr Comley's rattan flick the backsides of reluctant whalemen into *Melusine*'s rigging. Their rueful glances astern at their former ships tugged at Drinkwater's conscience. It had been a savage and cruel decision to press the crews of the *Nimrod* and *Conqueror*, but at least his action would appear to have the sanction of common practice and no-one would now hang for the treachery of Jemmett Ellerby. The irony of his situation did not escape him. A few months earlier he had given his word that no-one would be pressed from his convoy by a marauding cruiser captain intent on recruiting for the Royal Navy here off the Spurn. Now he had done the very thing he deplored. He did not think that waterfront gossip in Hull would examine his motives deeply enough to appreciate the rough justification of his action. But it was not local opinion that he was worried about.

He had collected all his scattered parties now, after the weary voyage home from Greenland. Aboard *Melusine* the watches had been reduced to the drudgery of regular pumping and Drinkwater himself had slept little, his senses tuned to the creaks and groans of the jury steering gear, every moment expecting it to fly to pieces under the strain. But it had held as far as Shetland where they had again overhauled it as the rest of the whalers prepared to sail south, and it would hold, God-willing, until they reached the Nore.

They passed *Faithful* as they stood out of the anchorage. She was already getting under way and Drinkwater raised his hat in farewell to Sawyers on his poop. The Quaker stood to make a small fortune from the voyage now that the 'salvage' of *Nimrod* and *Conqueror* could be added to his tally of profits on baleen, whale oil and furs. Drinkwater wished him well. He had given an undertaking to drop a few judicious words to any of the Hull ship-owners who sought to press the Government for reparation for the excessive zeal of a certain Captain Drinkwater in pressing their crews. Drinkwater was aware of the benefit of a precedent in the matter.

But there were other matters to worry Drinkwater. Sawyers's reassurances now seemed less certain as *Melusine* stood out to sea again. It was true Drinkwater had spent nearly two days in composing his confidential despatch to the Secretary of the Admiralty. In addition he had sent Mr Quilhampton to Hull on board the *Earl Percy* to catch the first London mail, a Mr Quilhampton who had been carefully briefed in case he was required to answer any question by any of their Lordships. Drinkwater doubted there would be trouble about the pressing of the whalemen. The Admiralty were not fussy about where they acquired their seamen. But what of Waller? Supposing Drinkwater's decision was misinterpreted? What of his leaving to their fate those pitiful French '*invalides*'? The Admiralty had not seen their condition. To the authorities they might appear more dangerous than Drinkwater knew them to be. As for Singleton, what had appeared on his part of an act of tragic courage, might now seem oddly fatuous. Drinkwater had carried a letter from Singleton to the secretary of his missionary society and had himself also written, but God alone knew what would become of the man.

'She's clear of the Spit, sir.'

'Very well, Mr Hill, a course for The Would, if you please.'

Drinkwater turned from contemplating the play of light upon the shipping anchored at the Nore. He had been thinking of the strange events of the voyage and the clanking of *Melusine*'s pumps had reminded him of his old dream and the strange experience when he had been lost in the fog. He came out of his reverie when Mr Frey reported the approach of a boat from Sheerness. Instinctively Drinkwater knew it carried Quilhampton, returning from conveying Drinkwater's report to Whitehall. He sat down and settled a stern self-control over the fluttering apprehension in his belly.

The expected knock came at the door. 'Enter!'

Mr Quilhampton came in, producing a sealed packet from beneath his boat cloak.

'Orders, sir,' he said with indecent cheerfulness. Drinkwater took the packet. To his horror his hand shook.

'What sort of reception did you receive, Mr Q?' he asked, affecting indifference as he struggled with the wax seals.

'They kept me kicking my heels all morning, sir. Then the First Lord sent for me, sir. Rum old devil, begging your pardon. He sat me down, as polite as ninepence, and asked a lot of questions about the action in Nagtoralik Bay, the force of the *Requin*, sir . . . I formed the impression he was judging the force opposed to us . . . then he got up, paced up and down and looked at the trees in the park and turned and dismissed me. Told me to wait in the hall. Kept me there two hours then a fellow called Templeton, one of the clerks, took me into the copy-room and handed me these,' he nodded at the papers which had suddenly fallen onto the table as Drinkwater succeeded in detaching the last seal.

'It was rather odd, sir . . .'

'What was?' Drinkwater looked up sharply.

'This cove Templeton, sir. He said, well to the best of my recollection he said: "You've smoked the viper out, we knew about him in May when we intercepted papers en route to France, but you caught him red-handed".' Quilhampton shrugged and went on. 'Then he asked after Lieutenant Germaney and seemed rather upset that he'd gone over the standing part of the foresheet . . .'

But Drinkwater was no longer listening. He began to read, his eyes glancing superficially at first, seeking out the salient phrases that would spell ruin and disgrace.

The words danced before his eyes and he shuffled the papers, looking from one to another. Quilhampton watched, uncertain if he was dismissed or whether further intelligence would be required from him.

With the silent familiarity of the trusted servant Tregembo entered the cabin from the pantry. He held a filled decanter.

'Cap'n's got some decent wine, at last, zur,' he said to Quilhampton conversationally. 'Happen you've a thirst since coming from Lunnon, sur . . .'

Quilhampton looked from the Cornishman's badly scarred face to the preoccupied Drinkwater and made a negative gesture.

'Give him a glass, Tregembo, and pour me one too . . .'

It was not unqualified approval. St Vincent considered Waller should have been handed over:

Bearing in mind the political repercussions upon the sea-faring community of Kingston-upon-Hull I reluctantly endorse your actions, acknowledging the extreme measures you were forced to adopt and certain that service in any of His Majesty's ships under your command will bring the man Waller to an acknowledgement of his true allegiance . . .

Drinkwater was aware of a veiled compliment. Perhaps Dungarth's hand was visible in that. But he was not sure, for the remainder of the letter was pure St Vincent:

It is not, and never has been, nor shall be, the business of the Royal Navy to make war upon sick men, and your anxieties upon that score should be allayed. The monstrous isolation which the Corsican tyrant has condemned loyal men to endure, only emphasises the nature of the wickedness against which we are opposed . . .

Drinkwater relaxed. He had been believed. He picked up the other papers somewhat absently, sipping the full glass Tregembo had set before him.

. . . I am commanded by Their Lordships to acquaint you of the fact that the condition of the sloop under your command being, for the present unfit for further service, you are directed to turn her over to the hands of the Dockyard Commissioner at Chatham and to transfer your ship's company entire into the frigate Antigone *now fitting at that place . . .*

'Good Heavens, James. I am directed to turn the ship's company over to the *Antigone*! Our old prize from the Red Sea!'

''Tis a small world, sir. Does that mean *Melusine* is for a refit?'

Quilhampton's anxiety for his own future was implicit in the question. Drinkwater nodded. 'I fear so, James.'

'And yourself, sir . . .?'

'Mmm?' Drinkwater picked up the final sheet and the colour left his face. 'God bless my soul!'

'What is it, sir?'

'I am posted to command her. Directly into a thirty-six gun frigate, James!'

'Posted, sir? Why my heartiest congratulations!'

Drinkwater looked at his commission as a Post-Captain. It was signed by St Vincent himself, a singular mark of the old man's favour.

'About bloody time too, zur,' muttered Tregembo, refilling the glasses.

Author's Note

It is a fact that damage was inflicted upon the northern whale-fishery by French cruisers during the Napoleonic War. For details of the fishery itself, Scoresby Jnr has been my chief authority. There are significant differences between the hunting of the Greenland Right whale and the better known Sperm Whale fishery of the South Pacific. Chief among these was the practice of not reducing the blubber to oil as the comparative brevity of the voyage did not warrant it. Similarly I have used the noun 'harpooner' in preference to the Americanism 'harpooneer'. Although it was well-known that the whale breathed air, it was still extensively referred to as a 'fish'. At this period the Right Whale was thought to have poor hearing but acute eye-sight. Although known to overset boats, Mysticetus was a comparatively docile animal, far less aggressive than the Sperm Whale.

The delay in the sailing of the Hull ships is my own fiction but it is based on the fact that in 1802, during the Peace of Amiens, the government removed some of the press-exemptions extended to the officers of whalers in anticipation of further hostilities. It is therefore not difficult to excuse the whale-ship masters their suspicions. There were indeed plans of Hull and the Humber discovered en route to France in early 1803 and this forms the basis for Ellerby's treachery. In addition he was not only acting traitorously but illegally, since he had breached an oath required of whaler captains that they would not profit from any activity in the Arctic Seas than that of whaling.

The extraordinary opening in the ice corresponds roughly to that found by Scoresby in 1806. It was however 1822 before the eponymous Scoresby discovered the great fiord, an inlet of which forms Nagtoralik Bay. Of Scoresby Sound the Admiralty Sailing Directions say 'This ice-free land consists mainly of rugged mountains but . . . near the open sea the vegetation is luxuriant and game is plentiful.' It is also 'considered to be the most easily accessible part of the coast of East Greenland.'

Drinkwater's reasons for suppressing his discovery are clear. When Beaufort was appointed Hydrographer to the Navy his habit of personally scrutinising all surveys combined with the remoteness of the locality to delay the publication of a spurious and anonymous survey of 'Nagtoralik Bay and its surroundings.' By this time, of course, Scoresby's name had become firmly connected with the area.

1805

For Liz and Brian Bell

Contents

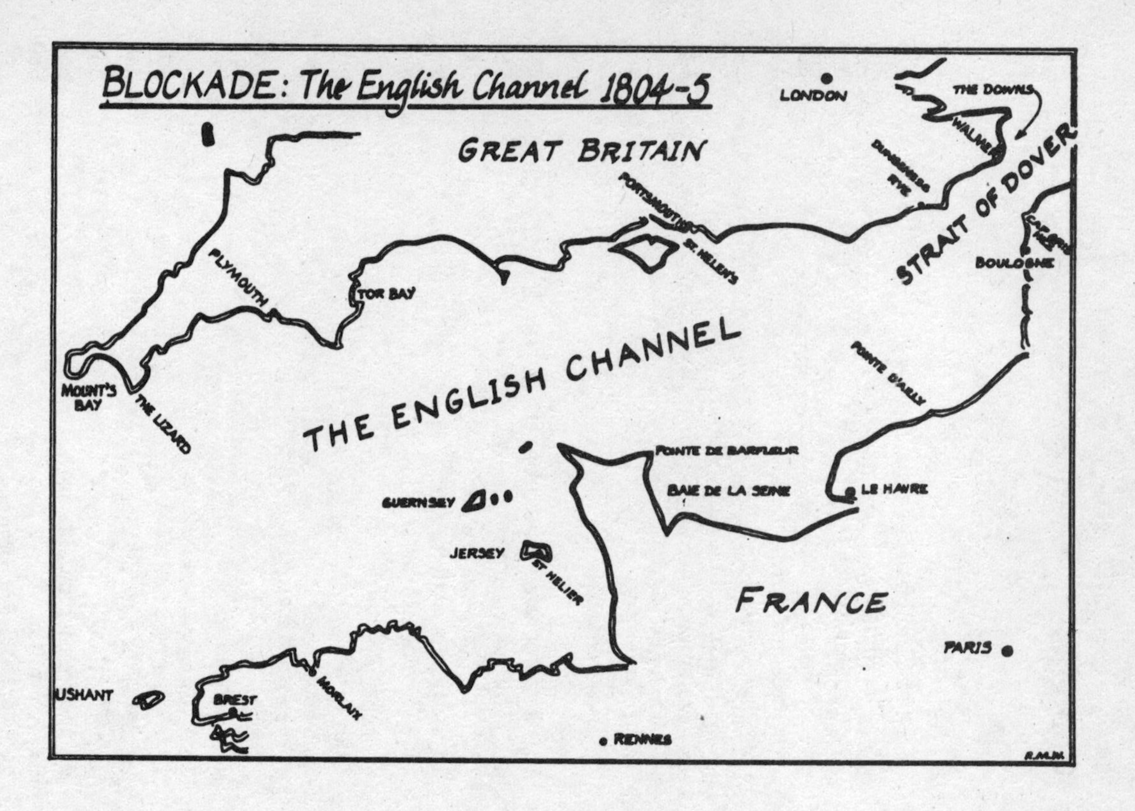
BLOCKADE: The English Channel 1804-5
LONDON
THE DOWNS
WALMER
DUNGENESS
RYE
GREAT BRITAIN
STRAIT OF DOVER
BOULOGNE
PORTSMOUTH
ST. HELEN'S
PLYMOUTH
TOR BAY
MOUNT'S BAY
THE LIZARD
THE ENGLISH CHANNEL
POINTE D'AILLY
POINTE DE BARFLEUR
BAIE DE LA SEINE
LE HAVRE
GUERNSEY
JERSEY
ST HELIER
FRANCE
PARIS
USHANT
BREST
MORLAIX
RENNES

PART ONE

Blockade

'Let us be master of the Channel for six hours and we are masters of the world.'

NAPOLEON TO ADMIRAL LATOUCHE-TRÉVILLE July 1804

'I do not say, my Lords, that the French will not come. I only say they will not come by sea.'

EARL ST VINCENT TO THE HOUSE OF LORDS 1804

Chapter One *March 1804*

The Club-Haul

'Sir! Sir!'

Midshipman Frey threw open the door of the captain's cabin with a precipitate lack of formality. The only reply to his urgent summons from the darkness within was the continuous creaking of the frigate as she laboured in the heavy sea.

'Sir! For God's sake wake up, sir!'

The ship staggered as a huge wave broke against her weather bow and sluiced over the rail into her waist. It found its way below by a hundred different routes. Outside the swinging door the marine sentry swore, fighting the impossibility of remaining upright. Frey stumbled against the leg of a chair overset by the violence of the ship's movement. He found the cabin suddenly illuminated as a surge of white water hissed up under the counter and reflected the pale moonlight through the stern windows. Mullender, the captain's steward, would catch it for not dropping the sashes if one of the windows was stove in, the boy thought irrelevantly as he shoved the chair aside and groped to starboard where, over the aftermost 18-pounder gun, the captain's cot swung.

'Sir! *Please* wake up!'

Frey hesitated. Pale in the gloom, Captain Nathaniel Drinkwater's legs stuck incongruously out of the cot. Still in breeches and stockings they seemed appendages not consonant with the dignity of a post-captain in the Royal Navy. Frey reached out nervously then drew back hurriedly as the legs began to flail of their own accord, responding to the squealing of the pipes at the hatchways and the sudden cry for all hands taken up by the sentries at their unstable posts about the ship.

'Eh? What the devil is it? Is that you, Mr Frey?'

The cot ceased its jumping and Captain Drinkwater's face,

haggard with fatigue, peered at the midshipman. 'Why was I not called before?'

'I had been calling you for some time . . .'

'What's amiss?' The captain's tone was sharp.

'Mr Quilhampton's respects . . .'

'What is it?'

'We've to tack, sir. Immediately, sir. Mr Quilhampton apprehends we are embayed!'

'God's bones!' The sleep drained from Drinkwater's face with the dawning of comprehension. Beyond the bulkhead the ship had come to urgent life with the dull thunder of a hundred pairs of feet being driven on deck by the bosun's mates.

'My hat and cloak, Mr Frey. On deck at once, d'you hear me!' Drinkwater forced his feet into his buckled shoes and tugged on his coat, stumbling to leeward as the frigate lurched again. He shoved past the midshipman and swore as his shin connected with the overset chair-leg. He swore a second time as he bumped into the marine sentry sliding across the deck in an attempt to avoid part of the larboard watch tumbling up from the berth-deck below via the after-ladder.

By the time Frey had collected the captain's hat and cloak he emerged onto an almost deserted gun-deck. The purser's dips glimmered, casting dull gleams on the fat, black breeches of the double-lashed 18-pounder cannon and the bright-work on the stanchions. A few round shot remained in the garlands, but most had been dislodged and rolled down to leeward where they rumbled up and down amid a dark swirl of water. Mr Frey paused in the creaking emptiness of the berth-deck.

'All hands means you too, younker. Get your arse on deck instanter, God damn you!'

Frey doubled up the ladder with a blaspheming Lieutenant Rogers at his heels. The first lieutenant had only roused himself from a drunken slumber with the greatest difficulty. He did not like being shown up in front of the whole ship's company and Frey's belated appearance served to cover his tardiness.

The first thing Drinkwater noticed when he reached the upper deck was the strength of the wind. He had gone below less than two hours earlier with the ship riding out a south-westerly gale under easy sail on the larboard tack. Hill, the sailing master, had observed their latitude earlier as being ten leagues south of the

Lizard and the ship was holding a course of west-north-west. Even allowing for considerable leeway Drinkwater could not see that Mr Quilhampton's fears were justified. He had left orders to be called at eight bells when, with both watches, they could tack to the southward and hope to come up with the main body of the Channel Fleet under Admiral Cornwallis somewhere west of Ushant.

Quilhampton's face was suddenly in front of him. The strain of anxiety was plain even in the moonlight; clear too was the relief at Drinkwater's appearance.

'Well, Mr Q?' Drinkwater shouted at the dripping figure.

'Sir, a few minutes ago the scud cleared completely. I'm damned certain I saw land to leeward . . . or something confounded like it.'

'Have you seen the twin lights of the Lizard?' Drinkwater shouted, a worm of uncertainty uncoiling itself in his belly.

'Half an hour ago we couldn't see much, sir. Heavy, driving rain . . .'

'Then it cleared like this?'

'Aye, sir, and the wind veered a point or two . . .'

It was on Drinkwater's tongue to ask why Quilhampton had not called him, but it was not the moment to remonstrate. He crossed quickly to the binnacle, aware by the grunts of the helmsmen that they were having the devil of a time holding the frigate on course. A glance confirmed his fears. The veering wind had cast the ship's head to the north-west and if that latitude was in error he did not dare contemplate further.

'Thank you, Mr Frey.' He flung the boat-cloak over his shoulder and very nearly lost it in the violence of the wind. The scream of air rushing through the rigging had a diabolical quality that Drinkwater did not ever remember hearing before in a quarter-century of sea-service. He looked aloft. Both the fore and main topsails were hard-reefed and a small triangle of a spitfire staysail strained above the fo'c's'le. Even so the ship was over-canvased, almost on her beam ends as spume tore over her deck stinging the eyes and causing the cheeks to ache painfully.

'Look, sir! Look!'

Quilhampton's arm pointed urgently as he fought to retain his footing on the canting deck. Drinkwater slithered to the lee rail as the look-out took up the cry.

'Land! Land! Land on the lee bow!'

Rogers cannoned into him. 'She'll never stay in this sea, sir!'

Drinkwater smelt the rum on his stale breath, but agreed with him. 'Aye, Sam, and there's no room to wear.' He paused, gathered his breath and shouted his next order so there could be no mistake. 'We must club-haul!'

'Club-haul? Jesus!'

'Amen to that, Mr Rogers,' Drinkwater said sarcastically. 'Now, Mr Q. D'you get the mizen topmen and the gunners below to rouse out the top cable in the starboard tier. Open the port by number nine gun and haul it forward outside all. Clap it on the starboard sheet-anchor. Ah, Mr Gorton,' Drinkwater addressed the second lieutenant who had come up with the master. 'Mr Gorton, you on the fo'c's'le with the bosun. Get Q's cable made fast and the anchor cleared away. I shall rely upon you to let the anchor go when I give the word.' Gorton turned away with Quilhampton and both officers hurried off.

'I hope your confidence ain't misplaced, sir.' Rogers stared after the figures of the two young men.

'Both demonstrated their resource in the Greenland Sea, Sam. Besides, I want you amidships to pass my orders in case they ain't heard.' Drinkwater refused to be drawn by Roger's touchiness respecting his two juniors. For all his obvious disabilities Drinkwater had dragged Lieutenant Rogers off the poop of an ancient bomb-vessel and placed him on the quarterdeck of one of the finest frigates in the service, so he had little cause to complain of partiality. 'See that the men are at their stations and all ropes will run clear.' That at least was something Rogers would do superbly and with a deal of invective to spur the men's endeavours.

'Well, Mr Hill?'

'I've told two of my mates off into the hold to sound the well and Meggs is mustering a party at the pumps. If you open number nine port she'll be taking water all the while.'

'That,' replied Drinkwater shouting, 'is a risk we'll have to take.'

There was little either captain or master could do until the preparations were completed. The ship was rushing through the water at a speed that, under other circumstances, they would have been proud of.

'Is it Mount's Bay, d'you think?' Hill's concern was clear. He, too, was worried about that latitude. 'We haven't sighted the Lizard lights, sir.'

'No.' Drinkwater hauled himself gingerly into the leeward mizen rigging and felt the wind catch his body as a thing of no substance. He clung on grimly and stared out to starboard. The thin veil of cloud which showed the gibbous moon nearly at the full was sufficient to extend a pale light upon the waves as the wind tore their breaking crests to shreds and sent the spume downwind like buckshot. With the greatest difficulty he made out what might have been the grey line of a cliff out on the starboard beam. He could only estimate its distance with difficulty. Perhaps a mile, perhaps not so much.

Then the moon sailed into a clear patch of sky. It was suddenly very bright and what Drinkwater saw caused his mouth to go dry.

A point or two on their starboard bow, right in their track as they sagged to leeward, rose a huge grey pinnacle of rock. In the moonlight its crags and fissures stood out starkly, and at its feet the breakers pounded white. But in the brief interval in the cloud Drinkwater became aware of something else. Atop the rock, perched upon its highest crag, a buttress and wall reared sheer from the cliff. Immediately he knew their position and that the danger to the ship and her company was increased a hundredfold. For beneath the ancient abbey on St Michael's Mount, stretching round onto their windward bow, the breakers pounded white upon the Mountamopus shoal.

There are few periods of anxiety greater in their intensity than that of a commander whose ship is running into peril, waiting for his people to complete their preparations. On the one hand experience and judgement caution him not to attempt a manoeuvre until everything is ready; upon the other instinct cries out to be released into immediate action. Yet, as the sweat prickled between his shoulder blades, Drinkwater knew that to act hastily was to court disaster. If the ship failed in stays there would be no second chance. It was useless to speculate upon the erroneous navigation that had brought them to this point, or why Rogers stank of rum, or, indeed, whether the two were connected. All these thoughts briefly crossed his mind in the enforced hiatus that is every captain's lot once orders have been given.

He looked again at the mount. The moon had disappeared now under a thick mantle of cloud, but they were close enough for its mass to loom over them, an insubstantial-looking lightening of the darkness to leeward, skirted about its base by the breakers that dashed spray half-way up its granite cliffs. This sudden proximity made his heart skip and he looked along the waist where men had been clustered in a dark group, hauling on the messenger that pulled the heavy cable along the ship's side. He could imagine their efforts being thwarted by the protruberances of the channels, the dead-eyes, the bead-blocks and all the other rigging details that at this precise moment seemed so much infernal nuisance. God, would they never finish?

The wind shrieked mercilessly and the frigate lay over so that he felt a terrible concern for that open gun-port into which, without a shadow of doubt, the sea would be sluicing continuously. He was unable to hear any noise above the storm and hoped that the pumping party were hard at it.

'Ready, sir!'

After the worry the word came aft and took him by surprise. It was Rogers, his face a pale blur of urgency abruptly illuminated as, again, the cloud was torn aside and the moon shone brightly. The light fell on the frigate, the sea and St Michael's Mount, sublime in its terrifying majesty.

'Stations for stays!' He left Rogers to bawl the order through the speaking trumpet, took Hill by the elbow and forced him across the deck. 'We'll take the wheel, Mr Hill. It'll need the coolest heads tonight.' He sensed Hill's bewilderment as to what had gone wrong with the navigation.

Captain and sailing master took over the head-wheel, the displaced quartermasters moving across the deck to assist the gunners to haul the main-yard.

'Ease down the helm, Mr Hill!' Drinkwater could feel the vibration of the hull as it rushed through the water, transmitted up from the rudder through the stock and tiller via the tiller ropes which creaked with the strain upon them. The ship lay over as she began to turn into the wind. A sea hit her larboard bow and threw her back a point. Drinkwater watched the angled compass card serenely illuminated by the yellow oil lamp, quietly obeying the timeless laws of natural science amid the elemental turmoil of the wind and sea.

Drinkwater raised his voice: 'Fo'c's'le there! Cut free the anchor! Let the cable run!'

Rogers took up the cry, bawling the first part forward and the latter part below to the party at the gun-port and by the cable-compressors. Drinkwater was dimly aware of a flurry of activity on the fo'c's'le and the hail that the anchor was gone. Behind him one of the two remaining helmsmen muttered, 'Shit or bust, mateys!'

'I hope it holds,' said Hill.

'It'll hold, Mr Hill. 'Tis sand and rock. The rock may part the cable in a moment or two but she'll hold long enough.' He wished he possessed the confidence he expressed. He could feel the cable rumbling through the port, there was no doubt about that strange sensation coming up through the thin soles of his shoes. Rogers was crouched at the companionway and suddenly straightened.

'Half cable veered, sir!'

Sixty fathoms of thirteen-inch hemp. Not enough, not yet. Drinkwater counted to three, then: 'Nip her!'

'I believe,' said Drinkwater to cover the extremity of his fear that in the next few seconds the anchor might break out or the cable part, 'I believe at this point when staying, both the French and the Spanish invoke God as a matter of routine.'

'Not such a bad idea, sir, beggin' yer pardon,' answered one of the helmsmen behind him.

And then the ship began to turn. For a moment he thought she might go the wrong way, for he had let go the lee anchor and that from a port well abaft the bow.

'Hard over now, my lads . . .' He began to spin the wheel, aware that the anchor and cable were snubbing the ship round into the wind and thus assisting them. With the courses furled there were no tacks and sheets to raise and she was suddenly in the eye of the wind. There was a thunderous clap which sent a tremble through the hull as the fore-topsail came aback and juddered the whole foremast to its step in the kelson.

'Main-topsail haul!' Thank God for his crew, Drinkwater thought. They were only a few days out of Chatham and might have had a crew that were raw and unco-ordinated, but he had drafted the entire company from the sloop *Melusine*, volunteers to a man. The main and mizen yards came round. So too did the ship, she was spinning like a top, her bow rising and her bowsprit stabbing at the very moon as she passed through the wind. The main-topsail filled with a crack that sent a second mighty tremor through the ship.

'We've done it, by God!' yelled Rogers.

'Cut, man! Cut the bloody cable!'

With the ship cast upon the other tack they had only a few seconds before the action of the anchor would pull the ship's head back again, but the backed fore-topsail was paying her off.

'Haul all!'

The foreyards came round and Rogers came aft and reported the cable cut. Drinkwater caught a glimpse of rock close astern, of the hollow troughs of a sea that was breaking in shallow water.

He handed the wheel back to the quartermasters. 'Keep her free for a little while. We are not yet clear of the shoals.'

'Aye, aye, sir.'

'Ease the weather braces, Mr Rogers.'

They made the final adjustments and set her on a course clear of the Mountamopus as a dripping party came up from the gun-deck and reported the port closed. Relief was clear on every face. As if cheated in its intention, the storm swept another curtain of cloud across the face of the moon.

'You may splice the main-brace, Mr Rogers, then pipe the watch below. My warmest thanks to the ship's company.'

Drinkwater turned away and headed for the companionway, his cabin and cot.

'Three cheers for the cap'n!'

'Silence there!' shouted Rogers, well knowing Drinkwater's distaste for any kind of show. But Drinkwater paused at the top of the companionway and made to raise his hat, only to find he had no hat to raise.

Squatting awkwardly to catch the light from the binnacle, Mr Frey made the routine entry on the log slate for the middle watch: *Westerly gales to storm. Ship club-hauled off St Michael's Mount, Course S.E. Lost sheet anchor and one cable.* He paused, then added on his own accord and without instruction: *Ship saved.*

The weather had abated somewhat by dawn, though the sea still ran high and there was a heavy swell. However, it was possible to relight the galley range and it was a more cheerful ship's company that set additional sail as the wind continued to moderate during the forenoon.

Drinkwater was on deck having slept undisturbed for four blessed hours. His mind felt refreshed although his limbs and, more acutely, his right shoulder which had been mangled by wounds, ached with fatigue. It was almost the hour of noon and he had sent down for his Hadley sextant with a view to assisting Hill and his party establish the ship's latitude. The master was still frustrated over his failure of the day before, for he could find no retrospective error in his working.

On waking Drinkwater had reflected upon the problem. He himself did not always observe the sun's altitude at noon. Hill was a more than usually competent master and had served with Drinkwater on the cutter *Kestrel* and the sloop *Melusine*, proving his ability both in the confined waters of the Channel and North Sea, and also in the intricacies of Arctic navigation.

As Mullender gingerly lifted the teak box lid for Drinkwater to remove the instrument he caught the reproach in Hill's eyes.

'It wants about four minutes to apparent noon, sir,' said Hill, adding with bitter emphasis, 'by my reckoning.'

Drinkwater suppressed a smile. Poor Hill. His humiliation was public; there could be few on the ship that by now had not learned that their plight last night had been due to a total want of accuracy in the ship's navigation.

Hill assembled his party. Alongside him stood three of the ship's six midshipmen and one of the master's mates. Lieutenant Quilhampton was also in attendance, using Drinkwater's old quadrant given him by the captain. Drinkwater remembered that Quilhampton and he had been discussing some detail the previous day and that the lieutenant had not taken a meridian altitude. Nor had Lieutenant Gorton. Drinkwater frowned and lifted his sextant, swinging the index and bringing the sun down to the horizon. The pale disc shone through a thin veil of high cloud and he adjusted the vernier screw so that it arced on the horizon. He peered briefly at the scale, replaced the sextant to his eye and noted that the sun continued to rise slowly as it moved towards its culmination.

'Nearly on, sir,' remarked Hill who had been watching the rate of rise slow down. The line of officers swayed with the motion of the ship, a picture of concentration. The sun ceased to rise and 'hung'. Its brief motionless suspension preceded its descent into the period of postmeridian and Hill called, 'On, sir, right on!'

'Very well, Mr Hill, eight bells it is.'

By the binnacle the quartermaster turned the glass, the other master's mate hove the log and eight bells was called forward where the fo'c's'le bell was struck sharply. The marine sentinels were relieved, dinner was piped and a new day started on board

His Britannic Majesty's 36-gun, 18-pounder, frigate *Antigone* as she stood across the chops of the Channel in search of Admiral Cornwallis and the Channel Fleet.

'Well, Mr Hill,' Drinkwater straightened from his sextant, 'what do we make it?' Drinkwater saw Hill bending over his quadrant, his lips muttering. A frown puckered his forehead, something seemed to be wrong with the master's instrument.

To avoid causing Hill embarrassment Drinkwater turned to the senior of the midshipmen: 'Mr Walmsley?'

Midshipman Lord Walmsley cast a sideways look at the master, swallowed and answered. 'Er, thirty-nine degrees, twenty-six minutes, sir.'

'Poppy cock, Mr Walmsley. Mr Frey?'

'Thirty-nine degrees six minutes, sir.' Drinkwater grunted. That was within a minute of his own observation.

'Mr Q?'

'And a half, sir.'

The two master's mates and Midshipman the Honourable Alexander Glencross agreed within a couple of minutes. Drinkwater turned to Mr Hill: 'Well, Mr Hill?'

Hill was frowning. 'I have the same as Lord Walmsley, sir.' His voice was puzzled and Drinkwater looked quickly at his lordship who had already moved his index arm and was lowering his instrument back into the box between his feet. It suddenly occurred to Drinkwater what had happened. Hill habitually muttered his altitude as he read it off the scale and Walmsley had persistently overheard and copied him. Yesterday, without Quilhampton and Drinkwater, Hill would have believed his own observation, apparently corroborated by Walmsley, and dismissed those of his juniors as inaccurate.

Drinkwater made a quick calculation. By adding the sum of the corrections for parallax, the sun's semi-diameter and refraction, then taking the result from a right angle to produce the true zenith distance, he was very close to their latitude. They were almost upon the equinox so the effect of the sun's declination was not very large and there would be a discrepancy in their latitudes of some twenty miles. Hill's altitude would put them twenty miles *south*, where they had thought they were yesterday.

'Very well, gentlemen. We will call it thirty-nine degrees, six and a half minutes.'

They bent over their tablets and a few minutes later Drinkwater called for their computed latitudes. Again only Walmsley disagreed.

'Very well. We shall make it forty-nine degrees, eleven minutes north . . . Mr Hill, you appear to have an error in your instrument.'

Hill had already come to the same conclusion and was fiddling with his quadrant, blushing with shame and annoyance. Drinkwater stepped towards him.

'There's no harm done, Mr Hill,' he said privately, reassuring the master.

'Thank you, sir. But imagine the consequences . . . last night, sir . . . we might have been cast ashore because I failed to check . . .'

'A great deal might happen *if*, Mr Hill,' broke in Drinkwater. 'There is too much hazard in the sea-life to worry about what did not happen. Now bend your best endeavours to checking the compass. We have an error there too, or I suspect you would have tumbled yesterday's inaccuracy yourself.'

The thought seemed to brighten Hill, to shift some of the blame and lighten the burden of his culpability. Drinkwater smiled and turned away, fastening his grey eyes on the senior midshipman.

'Mr Walmsley,' he snapped, 'I wish to address a few words to you, sir!'

Chapter Two *March 1804*

The *Antigone*

Captain Nathaniel Drinkwater turned his chair and stared astern to where patches of sunlight danced upon the sea, alternating with the shadows of clouds. The surface of the sea heaved with the regularity of the Atlantic swells that rolled eastwards in the train of the storm. In the wake of the *Antigone* herself half a dozen gulls and fulmars quartered the disturbed water in search of prey. Further off a gannet turned its gliding flight into an abrupt and predatory dive; but Drinkwater barely noticed these things, his mind was still full of the interview with Lord Walmsley.

Drinkwater had inherited Lord Walmsley together with most of the other midshipmen from his previous command. They had already been on board when he had hurriedly joined the *Melusine* for her voyage escorting the Hull whaling fleet into the Arctic Ocean the previous summer. The officer responsible for selecting and patronising this coterie of 'young gentlemen', Captain Sir James Palgrave, had been severely wounded in a duel and prevented from sailing in command of the *Melusine*. Now Drinkwater rather wished Walmsley to the devil along with Sir James whose wound had mortified and who had paid with his life for the consequences of a foolish quarrel. Walmsley was an indolent youngster, spoiled, vastly over-confident and of a character strong enough to dominate the cockpit. Occasionally charming, there was no actual evil in him, though Drinkwater would have instinctively written *bad* against his character had he been asked, if only because Lord Walmsley did not measure up to Drinkwater's exacting standards as an embryonic sea-officer. The fact was that his lordship did not give a twopenny damn about the naval service or, Drinkwater suspected, Captain Nathaniel Drinkwater himself. The captain was, after all, only in command of one of the many cruisers attached to the hastily raked-up collection of ships that made up the Downs Squadron. Lord Walmsley knew as well as Captain Drinkwater that, whatever hysteria was raised in the House of Commons about the menace of invasion across the Strait of Dover, it would not be Admiral Lord Keith's motley collection of vessels that stopped it but the might of the Channel Fleet under Admiral Cornwallis. Since Cornwallis's squadrons were bottling up the French in Brest it seemed unlikely that Keith's ships would be achieving anything more glorious than commerce harrying and a general intimidation of the north coast of France. It was well known that Keith himself did not want his job and that he considered his own post to be that usurped by the upstart Nelson: holding the key to the Mediterranean outside Toulon.

Drinkwater sighed; when the Commander-in-Chief of the station made common knowledge of his dissatisfaction, was it any wonder that a young kill-buck like Walmsley should adopt an attitude of indifference? What was more, Walmsley had influence in high places. This depressing reflection irritated Drinkwater. He turned, rose from his chair and, taking a key from his waistcoat pocket, unlocked his wine case. He took out one of the two cut-glass goblets and lifted the decanter. The port glowed richly as he held the glass against the light from the stern windows. Resuming his seat he hitched both feet up on the settee that ran from quarter to quarter across the stern and narrowed his eyes. Damn Lord Walmsley! The young man was a souring influence among a group of reefers who, if they were not exactly brilliant, were not without merit. Midshipman Frey, for instance, just twelve years old, had already seen action off the coast of Greenland, was proving a great asset as a seaman and had also demonstrated his talents as an artist. Drinkwater was not averse to advancing the able, and had already seen both Mr Quilhampton and Mr Gorton get their commissions and placed them on his own quarterdeck as a mark of confidence in them, young though they were. Messrs Wickham and Dutfield were run-of-the-mill youngsters, willing and of a similar age. The Honourable Alexander Glencross was led by Lord Walmsley. The sixth midshipman was even younger than Frey, a freckled Scot named Gillespy forced upon him as a favour to James Quilhampton. In his pursuit of Mistress Catriona MacEwan, poor Quilhampton had sought to press his suit by promising the girl's aunt to find a place for the child of another sister. Little Gillespy was therefore being turned into a King's sea-officer to enhance

Quilhampton's prospects as a suitable husband for the lovely Catriona. Drinkwater had had a berth for a midshipman and James had pleaded his own case so well that Drinkwater found himself unable to refuse his request.

'I believe Miss MacEwan is kindly disposed towards me, sir,' Quilhampton had said, 'but her festering aunt regards me as a poor catch . . .' Drinkwater had seen poor Quilhampton's eyes fall to his iron hook which he wore in place of a left hand. So, from friendship and pity, Drinkwater had agreed to the boy joining the ship. As for Gillespy, he had so far borne his part well despite being constantly sea-sick since *Antigone* left the Thames, and had spent the first half-dozen of his watches on deck lashed to a carronade slide. Drinkwater wondered what effect Walmsley and Glencross might have on such malleable clay.

'Damn 'em both!' he muttered; he had more important things to think about and could ill-afford his midshipmen such solicitude. They must take their chance like he had had to. Whatever his misgivings over the reefers, he was well served by his officers, Hill's error notwithstanding. That had been an unfortunate mistake and principally due to the badly fitted compass that was, in turn, a result of the chaotic state of the dockyards. They had found the error in the lubber's line small in itself, but enough to confuse their dead-reckoning as they steered down the Channel with a favourable easterly wind. That was an irony in itself after two months of the foulest weather for over a year; gales that had driven the Channel Fleet off station at Brest and into the lee of Torbay.

'Disaster,' he muttered as he sipped the port, 'is always a combination of small things going wrong simultaneously . . .' And, by God, how close they had come to it in Mount's Bay! He consoled himself with the thought that no great harm had been done. Although he had lost an anchor and cable, the club-haul had not only welded his ship's company together but shown them what they were themselves capable of. 'It's an ill wind,' he murmured, then stopped, aware that he was talking to himself a great deal too much these days.

'Now I want a good, steady stroke.' Tregembo, captain's coxswain regarded his barge crew with a critical eye. He had hand-picked them himself but since Drinkwater had read himself in at *Antigone*'s entry the captain had not been out of the ship and this was to be the first time they took the big barge away. He knew most of them, the majority had formed the crew of *Melusine*'s gig, but they had never performed before under the eyes of an admiral or the entire Channel Fleet.

He grunted his satisfaction. 'Don't 'ee let me down. No. Nor the cap'n, neither. Don't forget we owe him a lot, my lads,' he glowered round them as if to quell contradiction. There was a wry sucking of teeth and winking of eyes that signified recognition of Tregembo's partiality for the captain. 'No one but Cap'n Drinkwater'd've got us out o' Mount's Bay an' all three masts still standing . . . just you buggers think on that. Now up on deck with 'ee all.' Tregembo followed the boat's crew up out of the gloom of the gun-deck.

Above, all was bustle and activity. Tregembo looked aft and grinned to himself. Captain Drinkwater stood where, in Tregembo's imagination, he always stood, at the windward hance, one foot on the slide of the little brass carronade that was one of a pair brought from the *Melusine*. Ten minutes earlier the whole ship had been stirred by the hail of the masthead look-out who had sighted the topgallants of the main body of the Channel Fleet cruising on Cornwallis's rendezvous fifty miles west of Ushant. In the cabin below, Mullender was fussing over Drinkwater's brand new uniform coat with its single gleaming epaulette, transferred now to the right shoulder and denoting a post-captain of less than five years seniority. Mullender at last satisfied himself that no fluff adhered to the blue cloth with a final wipe of the piece of wool flag-bunting, and lifted the stained boat-cloak out of the sea-chest. He shook his head over it, considering its owner would benefit from a new one and cut a better dash before the admiral to boot, but, with a single glance out of the stern windows, considered the weather too fresh to risk a boat journey without it. Gold lace tarnished quickly and the protection of the cloak was essential. Drawing a sleeve over the knap on the cocked hat, Mullender left the cabin. He had been saving the dregs of four bottles to celebrate such a moment and retired to his pantry to indulge in the rare privilege of the captain's servant.

Drinkwater lowered his glass for the third time, then impatiently lifted it again. This time he was rewarded by the sight of a small white triangle just above the horizon. In the succeeding minutes others rose over the rim of the earth until it seemed that, for half of the visible circle where sea met sky, the white triangles of sails surrounded them. Beneath each white triangle the dark hulls emerged with their lighter strakes and chequered sides. The gay colours of flag signals and ensigns enlivened the scene and *Antigone* buzzed as officers and men pointed out ships they recognised, old friends or scandalous hulks that were only kept afloat by the prayers of their crews and the diabolical links their commanders enjoyed with the devil himself.

''Ere, ain't that the bloody *Himmortalitee*?' cried an excited seaman, and an equally effusive Hill agreed.

'Aye, Marston, that is indeed the *Immortalité*, and a damned fine ship she was when I was in her as a master's mate.'

'Gorn to the devil, Mister 'Ill, now we oldsters ain't there to watch. She used to gripe like a stuck porker in anything of a blow . . .'

'God damn it the *Belleisle*, by all that's holy . . .'

'And the *Goliath* . . .'

Drinkwater tolerated the excitement as long as it did not mar the efficiency of the *Antigone*. One of the look-out cruisers broke away and hauled her yards to intercept them.

'Permission to hoist the private signal, sir?' James Quilhampton crossed the deck, touching his hat.

'Very well, Mr Q.' Drinkwater nodded and lifted his glass, watching the frigate close hauled on the wind as she moved to intercept the new arrival. She was a thing of loveliness on such a morning and was sending up her royals to cut a dash and impress the *Antigone*'s company with her handiness and discipline. The two frigates exchanged recognition and private signals.

'Number Three-One-Three, sir. *Sirius*, thirty-six, Captain William Prowse.'

'Very well.' Drinkwater stood upon the carronade slide and waved his hat as the two cruisers passed on opposite tacks.

'The flagship's two points to starboard, sir,' the ever-attentive Quilhampton informed him.

'Very well, Mr Q, ease her off a little.' He wondered how *Antigone* appeared from *Sirius* as the look-out frigate tacked in her wake and hauled her own yards, swinging round to regain station. Drinkwater cast a critical eye aloft and then along the deck. Tregembo was mustering the barge's crew in the waist before ordering them into the boat. Although he was far from being a wealthy officer, he had managed a degree of uniformity for his boat's crew due to the large number of slops he had acquired in two previous ships. Over their flannel shirts and duck trousers the men wore cut-down greygoes that gave the appearance of pilot jackets, while upon their heads Tregembo had placed warm seal-skin caps, part of the profit of the *Melusine*'s voyage among the ice-floes of the Arctic seas. It was a piece of conceit in which Drinkwater took a secret delight.

He was proud of the frigate too. Notwithstanding the deplorable state of the dockyards and the desperate shortage of every necessity for fitting out ships of war caused by Lord St Vincent's reforms, she was cause for self-congratulation. The First Lord's zeal in rooting out corruption might have long-term benefits, but for the present the disruptions and shortages had made the commissioning of men-of-war a nightmare for their commanders. Drinkwater recognised his good fortune. The dreadful condition of *Melusine* on her return from the Arctic had removed her from active service and they had managed to take out of her a quantity of stores which, with what the dockyard at Chatham allowed, had enabled them to get *Antigone* down to Blackstakes for her powder in good time. Best of all he had employed seamen in her fitting out and not the convict labour St Vincent advocated. Besides, the ship herself had been in good condition. Built by the French in Cherbourg only nine years earlier, she had been captured in the Red Sea in September 1798 by a party of British seamen that included Drinkwater himself. His appointment to this particular ship was, he knew, a mark of favour from the First Lord. Originally armed with twenty-six long 24-pounder cannon, she had been taken with most of her guns on shore and the Navy Board had seen fit to reduce her force to conform with other frigates of the Royal Navy. Now she mounted twenty-six black 18-pounder long guns upon her gun-deck, two long 9-pounder bow-chasers upon her fo'c's'le together with eight stubby 36-pounder carronades. On her quarterdeck were eight further long nines and the two brass carronades that had formerly gleamed at the hances of *Melusine*.

Drinkwater grunted his satisfaction as Hill reported the flagship a league distant and gave his permission for sail to be shortened. There were occasions when he regretted not being able to handle the ship in the day-to-day routines but on an occasion such as the present one it gave him equal pleasure to watch the officers and men go about their duty, to remark on the performance of individuals and to note the weaker officers and petty officers in the ship. There was also the necessity to observe the whale-men he had pressed from the Hull whalers *Nimrod* and *Conqueror*; in particular a man named Waller, formerly the commander of the *Conqueror*, who had only escaped hanging by Drinkwater's clemency.* Waller was expiating treason before the mast as a common seaman and Drinkwater kept an eye on him. He had had Rogers, the first lieutenant, split all the whale-men into different messes so that they could not confer or form any kind of a combination. For a minute he was tempted to send Waller with the two score of pressed men taken aboard from the Nore guardship as replacements for the Channel Fleet. But he could not abandon his responsibilities that easily. It was better to keep Waller under his own vigilant eye than risk him causing trouble elsewhere in the fleet. The rest behaved well enough. Good seamen, most had come from the *Melusine* where they had originally been volunteers during the short-lived Peace of Amiens.

'Hoist the signal for dispatches, sir?'

Drinkwater turned to find the diminutive Mr Frey looking up at him. He nodded. 'Indeed yes, Mr Frey, if you will be so kind.' He smiled at the boy who grinned back. All in all, reflected Drinkwater, he was one of the most fortunate of all the post-captains hereabouts, and he cast his eyes round the horizon where ship after ship of the British fleet cruised under easy sail in three great columns with the frigates cast out ahead, astern and on either flank.

Drinkwater sniffed the fresh north-westerly breeze and felt invigorated by the delightful freshness of the morning. The storm of two nights previously had cleared the air. Even here, a hundred miles off the Isles of Scilly where already the first crocuses would be breaking through the soil, spring was in the air. He nodded at Rogers who walked over to him.

'Mornin', Sam.'

'Good morning, sir. Sail's shortened and the barge is ready for lowering.'

Drinkwater regarded his first lieutenant, remembering their previous enmity aboard the *Hellebore* when they had been wrecked

* See *The Corvette*

after an error of judgement made by Samuel Rogers, and of their successes together in the Baltic in the old bomb-vessel *Virago*. Rogers was a coarse and vulgar man, no scientific officer and only a passable navigator, but he was a competent seaman and his valour in action was too valuable an asset to be lightly set aside merely because he lacked social accomplishments. Besides, in his present situation he would have precious little opportunity to worry over such a deficiency. He was, Drinkwater knew, perfect as a first luff; the very man the hands loved to hate, who was indifferent to that hatred and who could take the blame for all the hardships, mishaps and injustices the naval service would press upon their unfortunate souls and bodies.

'She's looking very tiddly, Sam. Fit for an admiral's inspection already. I congratulate you.'

Rogers gave him a grin. 'I heard about your appetite for tiddly ships after the *Melusine*, sir.'

Drinkwater grinned back. 'She was a damned *yacht*, Sam. You should have heard the gunroom squeal when I cut off her royal masts and fitted a crow's nest to con her through the ice.'

'She was different from the old *Virago* then?'

'As chalk is from cheese . . .'

They were interrupted by Lieutenant Quilhampton. 'Flag's signalling, sir: "Captain to come aboard".'

'Very well. Bring the ship to under the admiral's lee quarter, Mr Q . . . Sam be so good as to salute the flag while I shift my coat.'

'Aye, aye, sir.' The two officers began to carry out their orders as Drinkwater hurried below to where an anxious Mullender had coat, hat, cloak and sword all ready for him.

Chapter Three *March 1804*

The Spy Master

Admiral Sir William Cornwallis rose from behind his desk and motioned Drinkwater to a chair. His flag-lieutenant took the offered packet of Admiralty dispatches and handed them to the admiral's secretary for opening.

'A glass of wine, Captain?' The flag-lieutenant beckoned a servant forward and Drinkwater hitched his sword between his legs, laid his cocked hat across his lap and took the tall Venetian goblet from the salver. 'Thank you. I have two bags of mail for the fleet in my barge and a draft of forty-three men for the squadron . . .'

'I shall inform the Captain of the Fleet, sir. Sir William, your permission?'

'By all means.' The admiral bent over the opened dispatches as the flag-lieutenant left the cabin. The servant withdrew and Drinkwater was left with Cornwallis, his immobile secretary and another man, a dark stranger in civilian clothes, who seemed to be regarding Drinkwater with some interest and whose evident curiosity Drinkwater found rather irksome and embarrassing. He avoided this scrutiny by studying his surroundings. The great cabin of His Britannic Majesty's 112-gun ship *Ville de Paris* was a luxurious compartment compared with his own. As a first-rate line of battleship the *Ville de Paris* was almost a new ship, built as a replacement for Rodney's prize, the flagship of Admiral De Grasse, taken at the Battle of Saintes in the American War and so badly knocked about that she had foundered on her way home across the stormy Atlantic. It was an irony that a ship so named should bear the flag of the officer responsible for keeping the French fleet bottled up in Brest. Drinkwater did not envy the admiral his luxury: the monotony of blockade duty would have oppressed him. Even in a frigate attached to the inshore squadron cruising off Ushant, the perils of tides and rocks would far outweigh the risk of danger from the enemy coupled as they were with the prevailing strong westerly winds. As his old friend Richard White constantly wrote and told him, he was lucky to have avoided such an arduous and thankless task. There were a few who had carved out a glorious niche for themselves with brilliant actions. Pellew, for instance, in the *Indefatigable* and with *Amazon* in company had caught the French battleship *Droits de l'Homme*, harried her all night and forced her to become embayed in Audierne Bay where she was wrecked. The thought of embayment still caused him a shudder and he recollected that Pellew's triumph had also caused the loss of *Amazon* from the same cause. No, for the most part the maintenance of this huge fleet with its frigates and its supply problems was simply to keep Admiral Truguet and the principal French fleet capable of operating in the Atlantic, securely at its moorings in Brest Road. By this means Napoleon would not be able to secure the naval supremacy in the Channel that he needed to launch his invasion. Whatever the monotony of the duty there was no arguing its effectiveness. All the same Drinkwater was not keen to be kept under the severe restraint of commanding a frigate on blockade.

There was a rustle as Cornwallis lowered the papers and leaned back in his seat. He was a portly gentleman of some sixty years of age with small features and bright, keen blue eyes. He smiled cordially.

'Well, Captain Drinkwater, you are not to join us I see.'

'No, Sir William. I am under Lord Keith's command, attached to the Downs Squadron but with discretionary orders following the delivery of those dispatches.' He nodded at the contents of the waterproof packet which now lay scattered across Cornwallis's table.

'Which are . . .?'

'To return to the Strait of Dover along the French coast, harrying trade and destroying enemy preparations for the invasion.'

'And not, I hope, wantonly setting fire to any French villages en route, Captain?' It was the stranger in civilian dress who put this question. Drinkwater opened his mouth to reply but the stranger continued, 'Such piracy is giving us a bad name, Captain Drinkwater, giving the idea of invasion a certain respectability among the French populace that might otherwise be not overenthusiastic about M'sieur Bonaparte. Hitherto, whatever the enmities between our two governments, the people of the coast have maintained a, er, certain friendliness towards us, eh?' He smiled, a sardonic grin, and held up his glass of the admiral's claret. 'The matter of a butt or two of wine and a trifle or two of information; you understand?'

Drinkwater felt a recurrence of the irritation caused earlier by this man, but Cornwallis intervened. 'I am sure Captain Drinkwater understands perfectly, Philip. But Captain, tell us the news from London. What are the fears of invasion at the present time?'

'Somewhat abated, sir. Most of the news is of the problems surrounding Addington's ministry. The First Lord is under constant attack from the opposition led by Pitt . . .'

'And we all know the justice of Billy Pitt's allegations, by God,' put in the stranger with some heat.

Drinkwater ignored the outburst. 'As to the invasion, I think there is little fear while you are here, sir, and the French fleet is in port. I believe St Vincent to be somewhat maligned, although the difficulties experienced in fitting out do support some of Mr Pitt's accusations.' Drinkwater judged it would not do him any good to expatiate on St Vincent's well-meaning but near-disastrous attempts to root out corruption, and he did owe his own promotion to the old man's influence.

Cornwallis smiled. 'What does St Vincent say to Mr Pitt, Captain?'

'That although the French may invade, sir, he is confident that they will not invade by sea.'

Cornwallis laughed. 'There, at least, St Vincent and I would find common ground. Philip here is alarmed that any relaxation on our part would be ill-timed.' Then the humour went out of his expression and he fell silent. Cornwallis occupied the most important station in the British navy. As Commander-in-Chief of the Channel Fleet he was not merely concerned with blockading Brest, but also with maintaining British vigilance off L'Orient, Rochefort and even Ferrol where neutral Spain had been coerced into allowing France to use the naval arsenals for her own. In addition there was the immense problem of the defence of the Channel itself, still thought vulnerable if a French squadron could be assembled elsewhere in the world, say the West Indies, and descend upon it in sufficient force to avoid or brush aside the Channel Fleet. On Cornwallis's shoulder fell the awesome burden of ensuring St Vincent's words were true, and Cornwallis had transformed the slack methods of his predecessor into a strictly enforced blockade, earning himself the soubriquet of 'Billy Blue' from his habit of hoisting the Blue Peter to the foremasthead the instant his flagship cast anchor when driven off station by the heavy gales that had bedevilled his fleet since the New Year. It was clear that the responsibility and the monotony of such a task were wearing the elderly man out. Drinkwater sensed he would have liked to agree with the current opinion in London that the threat of invasion had diminished.

'Did you see much of the French forces or the encampments, Captain?' asked the stranger.

'A little above Boulogne, sir, but I was fortunate in having a favourable easterly and was ordered out by way of Portsmouth and so favoured the English coast. I took aboard the Admiralty papers at Portsmouth.'

'It is a weary business, Captain Drinkwater,' Cornwallis said sadly, 'and I am always in want of frigates . . . by heaven 'tis a plaguey dismal way of spending a life in the public service!'

'Console yourself, Sir William,' the stranger put in at this show of bile, and with a warmth of feeling that indicated he was on exceptionally intimate terms with the Commander-in-Chief. 'Consider the wisdom of Pericles: "If they are kept off the sea by our superior strength, their want of practice will make them unskilful and their want of skill, timid." Now that is an incontestable piece of good sense, you must admit.'

'You make your point most damnably, Philip. As for Captain Drinkwater, I am sure he is not interested in our hagglings . . .'

The allusion to Drinkwater's junior rank, though intended to suppress the stranger, cut Drinkwater to the quick. He rose, having no more business with the admiral and having securely lodged his empty glass against the flagship's roll. 'I would not have you think, Sir William, that I am anxious to avoid any station or duty to which their Lordships wished to assign me.'

Cornwallis dismissed Drinkwater's concern. 'Of course not, Captain. We are all the victims of circumstance. It is just that I feel the want of frigates acutely. The Inshore Squadron is worked mercilessly and some relief would be most welcome there, but if Lord Keith has given you your orders we had better not detain you. What force does his Lordship command now?'

'Four of the line, Sir William, five old fifties, nine frigates, a dozen sloops, a dozen bombs and ten gun-brigs, plus the usual hired cutters and luggers.'

'Very well. And he is as anxious as myself over cruisers I doubt not.'

'Indeed, sir.'

Drinkwater moved towards the door as Cornwallis's eyes fell again to the papers. These actions seemed to precipitate an outburst of forced coughing from the stranger. Cornwallis looked up at once.

'Ah, Philip, forgive me . . . most remiss and I beg your pardon. Captain Drinkwater, forgive me, I am apt to think we are all acquainted here. May I introduce Captain Philip D'Auvergne, Duc de Bouillon.'

Drinkwater was curious at this grandiose title. D'Auvergne was grinning at his discomfiture.

'Sir William does me more honour than I deserve, Captain Drinkwater. I am no more than a post-captain like yourself, but unlike yourself I do not have even a gun-brig to command.'

'You are a supernumerary, sir?' enquired Drinkwater.

Both Cornwallis and D'Auvergne laughed, implying a knowledge that Drinkwater was not a party to.

'I should like you to convey Captain D'Auvergne back to his post at St Helier, Captain, as a small favour to the Channel Fleet and in the sure knowledge that it cannot greatly detain you.'

'It will be an honour, Sir William.'

'Very well, Captain,' said D'Auvergne, 'I am ready. Keep in good spirits, Sir William. It will be soon now if it is ever to occur.'

Unaware to what they alluded, Drinkwater asked: 'You have no baggage, Captain D'Auvergne?'

D'Auvergne grinned again. 'Good Lord no. Baggage slows a man, eh?' And the two men laughed again at a shared joke.

The meal had been a tense affair. Captain D'Auvergne had become almost silent and Drinkwater had remained curious as to his background and his function, aware only that he enjoyed a position of privilege as Cornwallis's confidant. The only clue to his origin was in his destination, St Helier. Drinkwater knew there were a hundred naval officers with incongruous French-sounding surnames who hailed from the Channel Islands. But Cornwallis had called St Helier D'Auvergne's 'post', whatever that meant, and it was clear from his appetite that he had not lived aboard ship for some time or he would have been a little more sparing with Drinkwater's dwindling cabin stores. The decanter had circulated twice before D'Auvergne, with a parting look at the retreating Mullender, leaned forward and addressed his host.

'I apologise for teasing you, Drinkwater. The fact is Cornwallis, like most of the poor fellows, is worn with the service and bored out of his skull by the tedium of blockade. Any newcomer is apt to suffer the admiral's blue devils. 'Tis truly a terrible task and to have been a butt of his irritability is to have rendered your country a service.'

'I fear,' said Drinkwater with some asperity, 'that I am still being used as a butt, and to be candid, sir, I am not certain that I enjoy it over much.'

The snub was deliberate. Drinkwater had no idea of D'Auvergne's seniority though he guessed it to be greater than his own. But he was damned if he was going to sit at his own table and listen to such stuff from a man drinking his own port! Drinkwater had expected D'Auvergne to bristle, rise and take his leave; instead he leaned back in his chair and pointed at Drinkwater's right shoulder.

'I perceive you have been wounded, Captain, and I know you for a brave officer. I apologise doubly for continuing to be obscure . . . Mine is a curious story, but I am, as I said, a post-captain like yourself. I served under Lord Howe during the American War and was captured by the French. Whilst in captivity I came to the notice of the old Duc de Bouillon with whom I shared a surname, although I am a native of the Channel Islands. His sons were both dead and I was named his heir after a common ancestry was discovered . . .' D'Auvergne smiled wryly. 'I might have been one of the richest men in France but for a trifling matter of my estates having been taken over by their tenants.' He made a deprecatory gesture.

'You might also have lost your head,' added Drinkwater, mellowing a little.

'Exactly so. Now, Drinkwater, that wound of yours. How did you come by that?'

Since his promotion to post-captain and the transfer of his epaulette from his left to his right shoulder, Drinkwater had thought his wound pretty well disguised. Although he still inclined his head to one side in periods of damp weather when the twisted muscles ached damnably, he contrived to forget about it as much as possible. He was certainly not used to being quizzed about it.

'My shoulder? Oh, I received the fragment of a mortar shell during an attack on Boulogne in the year one. It was an inglorious affair.'

'I recollect it. But that was your second wound in the right arm, was it not?'

'How the deuce d'you know that?'

'Ah. I will tell you in a moment. Was it a certain Edouard Santhonax that struck you first?'

'The devil!' Drinkwater was astonished that this enigmatic character could know so much about him. He frowned and the colour mounted to his cheeks. The relaxation he had begun to feel was dispelled by a sudden anger. 'Come, sir. Level with me, damn it. What is your impertinent interest in my person, eh?'

'Easy, Drinkwater, easy. I have no impertinent interest in you. On the contrary, I have always heard you spoken of in the highest terms by Lord Dungarth.'

'Lord Dungarth?'

'Indeed. My station in St Helier is connected with Lord Dungarth's department.'

'Ahhh,' Drinkwater refilled his glass, passing the decanter across the table, 'I begin to see . . .'

Lord Dungarth, with whom Drinkwater had first become acquainted as a midshipman, was the head of the British Admiralty's intelligence network. Drinkwater's personal relationship with the earl extended to a private obligation contracted when Dungarth had helped to spirit Drinkwater's brother Edward away into Russia when the latter was wanted for murder. The evasion of justice had been accomplished because he had killed a French agent known to Dungarth. Edward had in fact slaughtered Etienne de Montholon because he had found him in bed with his own mistress, but Dungarth's interest in Montholon had served to cover Edward's crime and protect Drinkwater's own career. It was an episode in his life that Drinkwater preferred to forget.

'What do *you* know of Santhonax?' he asked at last.

D'Auvergne looked round him. 'That he commanded this ship in the Red Sea; that you captured him and he subsequently escaped; that he was appointed a colonel in the French Army after transferring from the naval service; and that he is now an aide-de-camp to First Consul Bonaparte himself.'

'And your opinion of him?'

'That he is daring, brave and the epitome of all that makes the encampments of the French along the heights of Boulogne a most dangerous threat to the safety of Great Britain.'

Drinkwater's hostility towards D'Auvergne evaporated. The two had discovered a common ground and Drinkwater rose, crossing the cabin and lifting the lid of the big sea-chest in the corner. 'So I have always thought myself,' he said, reaching into the chest. 'Furthermore, I have this to show you . . .'

Drinkwater returned to the table with a roll of canvas, frayed at the edges. He spread it out on the table. The paint was badly cracked and the canvas damaged where the tines of a fork had pierced it. It was D'Auvergne's turn to show astonishment.

'Good God alive!'

'You know who she is?'

'Hortense Santhonax . . . with Junot's wife one of the most celebrated beauties of Paris . . . This . . .' He stared at the lower right hand corner, 'this is by David. How the devil did you come by it?'

Drinkwater looked down at the portrait. The red hair and the slender neck wound with pearls rose from a bosom more exposed than concealed by the wisp of gauze around the shoulders.

'It hung there, on that bulkhead, when we took this ship in the Red Sea. I knew her briefly.'

'Were you in that business at Beaubigny back in ninety-two?'

Drinkwater nodded. 'Aye. I was mate of the cutter *Kestrel* when we took Hortense, her brother and others off the beach there, *émigrés* we thought then, escaping from the mob . . .'

'Who turned their coats when their money ran out, eh?'

'That is true of her brother certainly. She, I now believe, never intended other than to dupe us.' He did not add that she had been Hortense de Montholon then, sister to the man his own brother Edward had murdered at Newmarket nine years later.

D'Auvergne nodded. 'You are very probably right in what you say. She and her husband are fervent and enthusiastic Bonapartists. I have no doubt that if Bonaparte continues to ascend in the world, so will Santhonax.'

'This knowledge is learned from your station at St Helier, I gather?'

D'Auvergne smiled, the sardonic grin friendly now. 'Another correct assumption, Drinkwater.' He regarded his host with curiosity. 'I had heard your name from Dungarth in the matter of some enterprise or other. He is not given to idle gossip about all his acquaintances, as a gentleman in our profession cannot afford to be. But I perceive you have seen a deal of service . . .' he trailed off.

Drinkwater smiled back. 'My midshipmen consider me an ancient and tarpaulin officer, Captain D'Auvergne. Very little of my time has been spent in grand vessels like the one I have the honour to command at this time. I take your point about the need to guard the tongue, but I also take it that you have a clearing house on Jersey where information is collected?'

'Captain,' D'Auvergne said lightly, 'you continue to amaze with the accuracy of your deductions.'

The decanter passed between them and Drinkwater began to relax for the first time since the morning. The silence that fell between them was companionable now. After a pause D'Auvergne said, 'Knowing the confidence reposed in you by Lord Dungarth, I will venture to tell you that it is part of my responsibility to gather information through a network of agents in northern France. My operations are of particular interest to Sir William, for I am able to pass on a surprising amount of news concerning Truguet's squadron at Brest. Hence my unease at the prospect of you harrying the actual sea-borders of France. Harry their trade and destroy the invasion barges wherever you find them, but have a thought for the sympathies of sea-faring folk who have never had much loyalty for the government in Paris . . .'

'Or London, come to that,' Drinkwater added wryly. The two men laughed again.

'Seriously, Drinkwater, I believe we are at the crisis of the war and I am sad that the government is not united behind a determination to face facts. This inter-party wrangling will be our undoing. The French army is formidable, everywhere victorious, a whole population turned to war. All we have to hope for is that Bonaparte might fall. There are indications of political upheavals in France. You have heard of the recent discovery of a plot to kill the First Consul; there are other reactions to him still fermenting. If they succeed I believe we will have a lasting peace before the year is out. But if Bonaparte survives, then not only will his position be unassailable but the invasion inevitable. The plans are already well advanced. Do not underestimate the power, valour or energy of the French. If Bonaparte triumphs he will have hundreds of Santhonaxes running at his horse's tail. Their fleet *must* be kept mewed up in Brest until this desperate business is concluded. This is the purpose of my visits to Cornwallis but I can see no harm in the captain of every cruiser being aware of the extreme danger we are in.' D'Auvergne leaned forward and banged the table for emphasis. 'Invasion and Bonaparte are the most lethal combination we have ever faced!'

Chapter Four *April 1804*

Foolish Virgins

'Where away?'

Drinkwater shivered in the chill of dawn, peering to the eastward where Hill pointed.

'Three points to starboard, sir. Ten or a dozen small craft with a brig as escort.'

He saw them at last, faint interruptions on the steel-blue horizon, growing more substantial as every minute passed and the gathering daylight grew. Squatting, he steadied his glass and studied the shapes, trying to deduce what they might be. Behind him he heard the shuffle of feet as other officers joined Hill, together with a brief muttering as they discussed the possibility of an attack.

Drinkwater rose stiffly. His neck and shoulder arched in the chilly air. He shut the telescope with a snap and turned on the officers.

'Well, gentlemen. What d'you make of 'em, eh?'

'Invasion barges,' said Hill without hesitation. Drinkwater agreed.

'"*Chaloupes*" and "*péniches*", I believe they call the infernal things, moving eastwards to the rendezvous at Havre and all ready to embark what Napoleon Bonaparte is pleased to call the Army of the Coasts of the Ocean.'

'Clear for action, sir?' asked Rogers, his pale features showing the dark shadow of an unshaven jaw and reminding Drinkwater that daylight was growing quickly.

'No. I think not. Pipe up hammocks, send the hands to breakfast. Mr Hill, have your watch clew up the fore-course. Hoist French colours and edge down towards them. No show of force. Mr Frey, a string of bunting at the fore t'gallant yardarms. We are Frenchbuilt, gentlemen. We might as well take advantage of the fact. Mr Rogers, join me for breakfast.'

As he descended the companionway Drinkwater heard the watch called to stand by the clew-garnets and raise the fore tack and sheet. Below, the berth-deck erupted in sudden activity as the off-duty men were turned out of their hammocks. He nodded to the marine sentry at attention by his door and entered the cabin. Rogers followed and both men sat at the table which was being hurriedly laid by an irritated Mullender.

'You're early this morning, sir,' grumbled the steward, with the familiar licence allowed to intimate servants.

'No, Mullender, you are late . . . Sit down, Sam, and let us eat. The morning's chill has made me damned hungry.'

'Thank you. You do intend to attack those craft, don't you?'

'Of course. When I've had some breakfast.' He smiled at Rogers who once again looked at though he had been drinking heavily the night before. 'D'you remember when we were in the *Virago* together we were attacked off the Sunk by a pair of luggers?'

'Aye . . .'

'And we beat 'em off. Sank one of them if I remember right. The other . . .'

'Got away,' interrupted Rogers.

'For which you have never forgiven me . . . ah, thank you, Mullender. Well I hope this morning to rectify the matter. Let's creep up and take that little brig. She'd make a decent prize, mmm?'

'By God, I'll drink to that!' Comprehension dawned in Rogers's eyes.

'I thought you might, Sam, I thought you might. But I want those bateaux as well.'

They attacked the skillygolee enthusiastically, encouraged by the smell of bacon coming from the pantry where Mullender was still muttering, each occupied with their private thoughts. Rogers considered a naval officer a fool if he did not risk everything to make prize-money. Since he had never had the chief command of a ship, he thought himself very hard done by over the matter. The event to which Drinkwater had alluded was a case in point. Both knew that they had been fortunate to escape capture when they were engaged by a pair of lugger privateers off Orfordness when on their way to Copenhagen. But whereas Drinkwater appreciated his escape, Rogers regretted they had not made a capture, even though the odds against success had been high. The *Virago* had been a lumbering old bomb-vessel whose longest-range guns were in her stern, an acknowledgement that an enemy attack would almost certainly be from astern! But a pretty little brig-corvette brought under the guns of the *Antigone* would be an entirely different story. With such an overwhelming superiority Drinkwater would not hesitate to attack and the outcome was a foregone conclusion. Nevertheless Rogers found himself hoping the brig would have a large crew, so that he might distinguish himself and perhaps gain a mention in *The Gazette*.

Drinkwater's thoughts, on the other hand, were only partially concerned with the brig. It was the other vessels he was thinking of. They were five leagues south-east of Pointe de Barfleur, on the easternmost point of the Contentin Pensinsula. The convoy of invasion craft were on passage across the Baie de la Seine bound for their rendezvous at Le Havre. It was here that the French were assembling vessels built further west, prior to dispersing them along the Pas de Calais, at Étaples, Boulogne, Wimereux and Ambleteuse, in readiness for the embarkation of the army destined to conquer Great Britain and make the French people masters of the world.

Perhaps Drinkwater's experiences of the French differed from those of his colleagues who were apt to ridicule the possibility of ultimate French victory; perhaps Captain D'Auvergne had alerted him to the reality of a French invasion; but from whatever cause he did not share his first lieutenant's unconditional enthusiasm. What Rogers saw as a possible brawl which should end to their advantage, Drinkwater saw as a matter of simple necessity. It was up to him to destroy in detail before the French were able to overwhelm in force. There had been much foolish talk, and even more foolish assertions in the newspapers, of the impracticality of the invasion barges. There had been mention of preposterous notions of attack by balloon, of great barges driven by windmills, even some crackpot ideas of under-water boats which had had knowledgeable officers roaring with laughter on a score of quarterdecks, despite the fact that such an attack had been launched against Admiral Howe in New York during the American War. Drinkwater was apt to regard such arrogant dismissal of French abilities as extremely unwise. From what he had observed of those *chaloupes* and *péniches* there was very little wrong with them as sea-going craft. That alone was enough to make them worthy targets for His Majesty's frigate *Antigone*.

'Beg pardon, sir.'

'Yes, Mr Wickham, what is it?' Drinkwater dabbed his mouth with his napkin and pushed back his chair.

'Mr Hill's compliments, sir, and the wind's falling light. If we don't make more sail the enemy will get away.'

'We cannot permit that, Mr Wickham. Make all sail, I'll be up directly.'

Rogers followed him on deck and swore as soon as he saw the distance that still remained. Hill crossed the deck and touched his hat.

'Stuns'ls, sir?'

'If you please, Mr Hill, though I doubt we'll catch 'em now.'

Drinkwater looked round the horizon. Daylight had revealed a low mist which obscured the sharp line of the horizon. Above it the sun rose redly, promising a warm day with mist and little wind. Already the sea was growing smooth, its surface merely undulating, no longer rippling with the sharp though tiny crests of a steady breeze. Hardly a ripple ran down *Antigone's* side: the wind had suddenly died away and Drinkwater now detected a sharp chill. Beside him Rogers swore again. He turned quickly forward.

'Mr Hill!'

'Sir?'

'Belay those stuns'ls. All hands to man yard and stay tackles, hoist out the launch!' He turned to Rogers. 'Get the quarter-boats away, Sam, there's fog coming. You're to take charge.'

Rogers needed no second bidding. Already alert, the ship's company tumbled up to sway out the heavy launch with its snubnosed carronade mounted on a forward slide. It began to rise jerkily from the booms amidships as, near at hand, the slap of bare feet on the deck accompanied a hustling of men over the rail and into the light quarter-boats hanging in the davits. Among the jostling check shirts and pigtails, the red coats and white cross-belts of the marines mustered with an almost irritating formality.

'Orders, sir?' Mr Mount the lieutenant of marines saluted him.

'Mornin', Mr Mount. Divide your men up 'twixt quarter-boats and launch. Mr Rogers is in command. I want those invasion craft destroyed!'

'Very well, sir.' Mount saluted and spun round: 'Sergeant, your platoon in the starboard quarter-boat. Corporal Williams, your men the larboard. Corporal Allen, with me in the launch!'

The neat files broke up and the white-breeched, black-gaitered marines scrambled over the rails and descended into the now waiting boats. Drinkwater looked at the enemy. The invasion craft had already vanished but the brig still showed, ghostly against the insubstantial mass of the closing fog.

'Mr Hill! A bearing of the brig, upon the instant!'

'Sou'-east-a-half-south, sir!'

'Mr Rogers!' Drinkwater leaned over the rail and bawled down at the first lieutenant in the launch. 'Steer sou'-east-a-half-south. We'll fire guns for you but give you fifteen minutes to make your approach.'

He saw Rogers shove a seaman to one side so that he could see the boat compass and then the tossed oars were being lowered, levelled and swung back.

'Give way together!'

The looms bent with sudden strain and the heavy launch began to move, followed by the two quarter-boats. In the stern of each boat sat the officers in their blue coats with a splash of red from the marines over which the dull gleam of steel hung until engulfed by the fog.

'Now we shall have to wait, Mr Hill, since all the lieutenants have left us behind.'

'Indeed, sir, we will.'

Drinkwater turned inboard. There was little he could do. Already the decks were darkening from condensing water vapour. Soon it would be dripping from every rope on the ship.

'I had hoped the sun would rise and burn up this mist,' he said.

'Aye, sir. But 'tis always an unpredictable business. The wind dropped very suddenly.'

'Yes.'

The two men stood in silence for a few minutes, frustrated by being unable to see the progress of the boats. After a little Hill pulled out his watch.

'Start firing in five minutes, sir?'

'Mmmm? Oh, yes. If you please, Mr Hill.' They must give Rogers every chance of surprise but not allow him to get lost. Drinkwater would not put it past a clever commander to launch a counter-attack by boat, anticipating the very action he had just taken in sending a large number of his crew off.

'Send the men to quarters, Mr Hill, all guns to load canister on ball, midshipmen to report the batteries they are commanding when ready.' He raised his voice. 'Fo'c's'le there! Keep a sharp look-out!'

'Aye, aye, sir!'

'Report anything you see!'

'Aye, aye, sir!'

He turned aft to where the two marine sentries stood, one on either quarter, the traditional protection for the officer of the watch. It was also their duty to throw overboard the lifebuoy for any man unfortunate enough to fall over the side. 'You men, too. Do you keep a sharp look-out for any approaching boats!'

He fell to restless pacing, aware that the fog had caught him napping, a fact which led him into a furious self-castigation so that the report of the bow chaser took him by complete surprise.

The boom of the bow chaser every five minutes was the only sound to be heard apart from the creaks and groans from *Antigone*'s fabric that constituted silence on board ship. Even that part of the ship's company left on board seemed to share some of their captain's anxiety. They too had friends out there in the damp grey fog. The haste with which the boats had been hoisted out had allowed certain madcap elements among the frigate's young gentlemen to take advantage of circumstances. In manning the guns, Drinkwater had learned, most of the midshipmen had clambered into boats, and those who had not done so were now regretting their constraint.

Lord Walmsley had gone, followed by the Honourable Alexander Glencross, both under Rogers in the launch. Being well acquainted with his temperament, Drinkwater knew that Rogers would have – what was the new expression? – turned a blind eye, that was it, to such a lack of discipline. Wickham had also gone in the boats, carting off little Gillespy. Dutfield had not been on deck and Frey had too keen a sense of obligation to his post as signal midshipman to desert it without the captain's permission, even though the lack of visibility rendered it totally superfluous. As a consequence Drinkwater had posted Hill's two mates, Caldecott and Tyrrell, in the waist and in charge of the batteries.

'Gunfire to starboard, sir!'

The hail came from the fo'c's'le where someone had his arm stretched out. Drinkwater went to the ship's side and cocked his head outboard, attempting to pick up the sound over the water and clear of the muffled ship-noises on the deck. There was the bang of cannon and the crackle of small-arms fire followed by the sound of men shouting and cursing. It did nothing to lessen Drinkwater's anxiety but it provoked a burst of chatter amidships.

'Silence there, God damn you!' The noise subsided. Side by side with Hill, Drinkwater strained to hear the distant fight and to interpret the sounds. The cannon fire had been brief. Had Rogers attacked the brig successfully? Or had the brig driven *Antigone*'s boats off? If so was Rogers pressing his attack against the invasion craft? And what had happened to little Gillespy and Mr Q? Anxiety overflowed into anger.

'God damn this bloody fog!'

As though moved by this invective there was a sudden lightening in the atmosphere. The sun ceased to be a pale disc, began to glow, to burn off the fog, and abruptly the wraiths of vapour were torn aside revealing *Antigone* becalmed upon a blue sea as smooth as a millpond. Half a mile away the brig lay similarly inert and without the aid of a glass Drinkwater could see her tricolour lay over her taffrail.

A cheer broke out amidships and beside him Hill exclaimed, 'She's ours, by God!' But uncertainty turned to anger as Drinkwater realised what Rogers had allowed to happen. He swept the clearing horizon with his Dolland glass.

'God's bones! What the hell does Rogers think he's about . . . Mr Hill!'

'Sir?'

'Hoist out my barge . . . and hurry man, hurry!'

Drinkwater swept the glass right round the horizon. There were no other ships in sight. But beyond the brig the convoy of *chaloupes* and *péniches* was escaping, quite unscathed as far as he could tell. In a lather of impatience Drinkwater sent Frey below for his sword and pistols.

'You will remain here, Mr Frey, to assist Mr Hill . . . Hill, you are to take command until Mr Rogers returns. I will take Tyrrell with me.' Frey opened his mouth to protest, then shut it again as he caught sight of the baleful look in his captain's eyes.

As he hurried into the waist, Drinkwater heard Hill acknowledge his instructions and then he was down in the barge and Tregembo was ordering the oars out and they were away, the oar looms bending under Tregembo's urging. He looked back once.

Antigone sat upon the water, her sails slack and only adding to the impression of confusion that the morning seemed composed of. He forced himself to be calm. Perhaps Rogers had had no alternative but to attack the brig. Drinkwater knew enough of Rogers's character to guess that the fog would have given him a fair excuse to ignore the invasion craft.

They were approaching the brig now. They pulled past three or four floating corpses. Someone saw their approach and then Rogers was leaning over the rail waving triumphantly.

'Pass under the stern,' Drinkwater said curtly to Tregembo, and the coxswain moved the tiller. Drinkwater stood up in the stern of the boat.

'Mr Rogers,' he hailed, 'I directed you to attack the invasion craft!'

Rogers waved airily behind him. 'Mr Q's gone in pursuit, sir.' The first lieutenant's unconcern was infuriating.

'You may take possession, Mr Rogers, and retain the quarter-boat. Direct Gorton and Mount to follow me in the launch!'

Rogers's crestfallen look brought a measure of satisfaction to Drinkwater, then they were past the brig and Drinkwater realised he had not even read her name as they had swept under her stern windows. Tregembo swung the boat to larboard as the invasion craft came into view.

Smaller than the brig and clearly following some standing order of the brig's commander, they had made off under oars as soon as Rogers's attack materialised. They were about a mile and a half distant and were no longer headed away from the brig. Seeing they were pursued by only a single boat they had turned, their oars working them round to confront their solitary pursuer. Mr Quilhampton's quarter-boat still pressed on, about half a mile from the French and a mile ahead of Drinkwater.

'Pull you men,' he croaked, his mouth suddenly dry; then, remembering an old obscenity heard years ago, he added, 'pull like you'd pull a Frenchman off your mother.'

There was an outbreak of grins and the men leaned back against their oars so that the looms fairly bent under the strain and the blades flashed in the sunshine and sparkled off the drops of water that ran along them, linking the rippled circles of successive oar-drips in a long chain across the oily surface of the sea. Drinkwater looked astern. The white painted carvel hull of the big launch was following them, but it was much slower. Drinkwater could see the black maw of the carronade muzzle and wished the launch was ahead of them to clear the way. The thought led him to turn his attention to the enemy. Did they have cannon? They would surely be designed to carry them in the event of invasion but were they fitted at the building stage or at the rendezvous? He was not long in doubt. A puff of smoke followed by a slow, rolling report and a white fountain close ahead of Quilhampton's boat gave him his answer. And while he watched Quilhampton adjust his course, a second fountain rose close to his own boat. For a second the men wavered in their stroke, then Tregembo steadied them. An instant later half a dozen white columns rose from the water ahead.

Beside him Tyrrell muttered, 'My God!' and Drinkwater realised the hopelessness of the task. What could three boats do against ten, no twelve, well-armed and, Drinkwater could now see, well-manned boats armed with cannon. One carronade was going to be damn-all use.

'Stand up and wave, Mr Tyrrell.'

'I beg pardon, sir?'

'I said stand up and wave, God damn you! Recall Quilhampton's boat before we are shot to bits!'

'Aye, aye, sir.' Tyrrell stood and waved half-heartedly.

'I said wave, sir, like this! ' Drinkwater jumped up and waved his hat above his head furiously. Someone at the oars in Quilhampton's boat saw him.

'Swing the boat round, Tregembo, I'm breaking off the attack.'

'Aye, aye, zur,' Tregembo acknowledged impassively and the barge swung round.

He waved again, an exaggerated beckoning, until Quilhampton's boat foreshortened in its turn. 'Pull back towards the launch.' He sat down, relieved. Ten minutes later the three boats bobbed together in a conferring huddle while, nearly a mile away, the French invasion craft had formed two columns and were pulling steadily eastwards.

'Well they've lost a brig, sir,' said Mount cheerfully. A ripple of acknowledgement went round the boat crews, a palliative to their being driven off by the French.

'Very true, Mr Mount, and doubtless we'll all be enriched thereby, but the smallest of those *péniches* can carry fifty infantry onto an English beach and you have just seen how well they can hold off the boats of a man-of-war. If the French have a few days of calm in the Channel it will not matter how many of their damned brigs are waiting to be condemned by the Prize Court, if the Prize Court ain't able to sit because a French army's hammering on the doors.' He paused to let the laboured sarcasm sink in. 'In carrying out an attack with a single boat you acted foolishly, Mr Q.' Quilhampton's face fell. Drinkwater rightly assumed Rogers had ordered him forward, but that did not alter the fact that Drinkwater had nearly lost a boat-load of men, not to mention a friend. It was clear that Quilhampton felt his public admonition acutely and Drinkwater relented. After all, there was no actual harm done and they *had* taken a brig, as Mount had pointed out.

'We have *all* been foolish, Mr Q, unprepared like the foolish virgins.'

This mitigation of his earlier rebuke brought smiles to the men in the boats as they leaned, panting on their oar looms.

'But I still have not given up those invasion craft. By the way, where's Mr Gorton?'

'Er . . . he was wounded when we boarded the brig, sir.' Quilhampton's eyes did not meet Drinkwater's.

'God's bones!' Drinkwater felt renewed rage rising in him and suppressed it with difficulty. 'Pull back to the ship and look lively about it.'

He slumped back in the stern of the barge, working his hand across his jaw as he mastered anger and anxiety. He was angry that the attack had failed to carry out its objective, angry that Gorton was wounded, and angry with himself for his failure as he wondered how the devil he was going to pursue the escaped invasion craft. And the parable he had cited to Quilhampton struck him as having been most applicable to himself.

Chapter Five *April 1804*

Ruse de Guerre

Captain Drinkwater's mood was one of deep anger, melancholy and self-condemnation. He stood on the quarterdeck of the 16-gun brig *Bonaparte,* a French national corvette whose capture should have delighted him. Alas, it had been dearly bought. Although surprised by the speed of Rogers's attack, the French had been alerted to its possibility. Two marines and one seaman had been killed, and three seamen and one officer severely wounded. In the officer's case the stab wound was feared mortal and Drinkwater was greatly distressed by the probability of Lieutenant Gorton's untimely death. Unlike many of his colleagues, Drinkwater mourned the loss of any of his men, feeling acutely the responsibility of ordering an attack in the certain knowledge that some casualties were bound to occur. He was aware that the morning's boat expedition had been hurriedly launched and that insufficient preparation had gone into it. The loss of three men was bad enough, the lingering agony of young Gorton particularly affected him, for he had entertained high hopes for the man since he had demonstrated such excellent qualities in the Arctic the previous summer. It was not in Drinkwater's nature to blame the sudden onset of fog, but his own inadequate planning which had resulted not only in deaths and woundings but in the escape of the invasion craft whose capture or destruction might have justified his losses in his own exacting mind.

But he had been no less hard on Rogers and Mount. He had addressed the former in the cabin, swept aside all protestations and excuses in his anger, and reduced Rogers to a sullen resentment. It simply did not seem to occur to Rogers that the destruction of the invasion craft was of more significance than the seizure of a French naval brig.

'God damn it, man,' he had said angrily to Rogers, 'don't you *see* that you could have directed the quarter-boats to attack the brig, even as a diversion! Even if they were driven off! You and Mount in the launch could have wrought havoc among those *bateaux* in the fog, coming up on them piecemeal. The others would not have opened fire lest they hit their own people!' He had paused in his fury and then exploded. 'Christ, Sam, 'twas not the brig that was important!'

Well it was too late now, he concluded as he glared round the tiny quarterdeck. Rogers was left behind aboard *Antigone* with a sheet of written orders while Drinkwater took over the prize and went in pursuit of the invasion craft.

'Tregembo!'

'Zur?'

'I want those prisoners to work, Tregembo, work. You understand my meaning, eh? Get those damned sweeps going and keep them going.'

'Aye, aye, zur.' Tregembo set half a dozen men with ropes' ends over the prisoners at the huge oars.

It was already noon and still there was not a breath of wind. The fog had held off, but left a haze that blurred the horizon and kept the circle of their visibility under four miles. Somewhere in the haze ahead lay the *chaloupes* and the *péniches* that Drinkwater was more than ever determined to destroy. He had taken the precaution of removing the brig's officers as prisoners on board *Antigone* and issuing small arms to most of his own volunteers. In addition he had a party of marines under a contrite Lieutenant Mount (who was eager to make amends for his former lack of obedience). Drinkwater had little fear that the brig's men would rise, particularly if he worked them to exhaustion at the heavy sweeps.

He crossed the deck to where Tyrrell stood at the wheel.

'Course south-east by east, sir,' offered the master's mate.

Drinkwater nodded. 'Very well. Let me know the instant the wind begins to get up.'

'Aye, aye, sir.'

He turned below, wondering if he would find anything of interest among the brig's papers and certain that Rogers had not thought of looking.

The wind came an hour after sunset. It was light for about half an hour and finally settled in the north and blew steadily. Drinkwater ordered the sweeps in and the prisoners below.

'Mr Frey.'

'Sir?' The midshipman came forward eagerly, pleased to have been specially detailed for this mission and aware that something of disgrace hung over the events of the morning.

'I want you to station yourself in the foretop and keep a close watch ahead for those invasion craft. From that elevation you may see the light from a binnacle, d'you understand?'

'Perfectly sir.'

'Very well. And pass word for Mr Q.'

Quilhampton approached and touched his hat. 'Sir?'

'I intend snatching an hour or two's sleep, Mr Q. You have the deck. I want absolute silence and no lights to be shown. Moonrise ain't until two in the mornin'. You may tell Mount's sentries that one squeak out of those prisoners and I'll hold 'em personally responsible. We may be lucky and catch those invasion *bateaux* before they get into Havre.'

'Let's hope so, sir.'

'Yes.' Drinkwater turned away and made for the cabin of the brig where, rolling himself in his cloak and laying his cocked pistols beside him, he lay down to rest.

He was woken from an uneasy sleep by Mr Frey and rose, stiff and uncertain of the time.

'Eight bells in the first watch, sir,' said Frey.

Drinkwater emerged on deck to find the brig racing along, leaning to a steady breeze from the north, the sky clear and the stars glinting like crystals. Quilhampton loomed out of the darkness.

'I believe we have 'em, sir,' he pointed ahead, 'there, two points to starboard.'

At first Drinkwater could see nothing; then he made out a luster of darker rectangles, rectangles with high peaks: lugsails.

'Straight in amongst 'em, Mr Q. Get the men to their quarters in silence. Orders to each gun-captain to choose a target carefully and, once the order is given, fire at will.' Fatigue, worry and the fuzziness of unquiet sleep left him in an instant.

' 'Ere's some coffee, sir.'

'Thank you, Franklin.' He took the pot gratefully. Night vision showed him the dark shadow of Franklin's naevus, visible even in the dark.

''S all right, sir.'

Drinkwater swallowed the coffee as the men went silently to their places. The brig's armament was of French 8-pounders; light guns but heavy enough to sink the *chaloupes* and *péniches*.

'Haul up the fore-course, Mr Q. T'gallants to the caps, if you please.'

'Rise fore-tacks and sheets there! Clew-garnets haul!' The orders passed quietly and the fore-course rose in festoons below its yard.

'T'gallants halliards . . .'

The topgallant sails fluttered, flogged and kicked impotently as their yards were lowered. The brig's speed eased so as to avoid over-running the enemy.

Drinkwater hauled himself up on the rail and held onto the forward main shroud on the starboard side. *Bonaparte* had eased her heel and he could clearly see the enemy under her lee bow.

'Make ready there! Mr Frey, stand by to haul the fore-yards aback.'

The sudden flash of a musket ahead was followed by a crackle of fire from small arms. The enemy had seen them but were unable to fire cannon astern.

'Steady as you go . . .'

'Steady as she goes, sir.'

He saw the dark blob of a *chaloupe* lengthen as it swung round to fire a broadside, saw its lugsails enlarge with the changing aspect, saw them flutter as she luffed.

'Starboard two points! Gun-captains, fire when you bear.'

There was a long silence, broken only by shouts and the popping of musketry. A dull thud near Drinkwater's feet indicated where at least one musket ball struck the *Bonaparte*. The *chaloupe* fired its broadside, the row of muzzles spitting orange, and a series of thuds, cracks and splintering sounded from forward. Then they were running the *chaloupe* down. He could see men diving overboard to avoid the looming stem of the brig as it rode over the heavy boat, split her asunder and sank her in passing over the broken hull. Along the deck the brig's guns fired, short barking coughs accompanied by the tremble of recoil and the reek of powder. Another boat passed close alongside and Drinkwater felt the hat torn from his head as musket balls buzzed round him.

'Mind zur.' Like some dark Greek Olympic hero Tregembo hefted a shot through the air and it dropped vertically into the boat. Next to him Quilhampton's face was lit by the flash of the priming in a scatter gun and the bell-muzzle delivered its deadly charge amongst the boat's crew as they drew astern, screaming in the brig's wake.

'Down helm!'

'Fore-yards, Mr Frey!'

The *Bonaparte* came up into the wind and then began to make a stern board as Drinkwater had the helm put smartly over the other way. Amidships the men were frantically spiking their guns round to find new targets. Individual guns fired, reloaded and fired again with hardly a shot coming in return from the invasion craft that lay in a shattered circle around them. Mount's marines were up on the rails and leaning against the stays, levelling their muskets on any dark spot that moved above the rails of the low hulls, so that only the cry of the wounded and dying answered the British attack.

'Cease fire! Cease fire!'

The reports of muskets and cannon died away. Drinkwater counted the remains of the now silent boats around them. He could see nine, with one, possibly two, sunk.

'I fear one has escaped us,' he said to no one in particular.

'There she is, sir!' Frey was pointing to the southwards where the dark shape of a sail was just visible.

'Haul the fore-yards there, put the ship before the wind, Mr Q.'

Bonaparte came round slowly, then gathered speed as they laid a course to catch the departing *bateau.* From her size Drinkwater judged her to be one of the larger *chaloupes canonnières,* rigged as a three-masted lugger. For a little while she stood south and Drinkwater ordered the fore-course reset in order to overhaul her. But it was soon obvious that the French would not run, and a shot was put across her bow. She came into the wind at once and the *Bonaparte* was hove to again, a short distance to windward.

'What the devil is French for "alongside"?' snapped Drinkwater.

'Try *accoster,* sir.'

'Hey, *accoster, m'sieur, accoster!'* They saw oar blades appear and slowly the two vessels crabbed together. 'Mr Mount, your men to cover them.'

'Very well, sir . . .' The marines presented their muskets, starlight glinting dully off the fixed bayonets. There was a grinding bump as the *chaloupe* came alongside. The curious, Drinkwater among them, stared down and instantly regretted it. Drinkwater felt a stinging blow to his head and jerked backwards as it seemed the deck of the vessel erupted in points of fire.

He staggered, his head spinning, suddenly aware of forty or fifty Frenchmen clambering over the rail from which the complacent defenders had fallen back in their surprise.

'God's bones!' roared Drinkwater suddenly uncontrollably angry. He lugged out his new hanger and charged forward. 'Follow me who can!' He slashed right and left as fast as his arm would react, his head still dizzy from the glancing ball that had scored his forehead. Blood ran thickly down into one eye but his anger kept him hacking madly. With his left hand he wiped his eye and saw two marines lunging forward with their bayonets. He felt a sudden anxiety for Frey and saw the boy dart beneath a boarding pike and drive his dirk into a man already parrying the thrust of a bayonet.

''Old on, sir, we're coming!' That was Franklin's voice and there was Tregembo's bellow and then he was slithering in what remained of someone, though he did not know whether it was friend or foe. His sword bit deep into something and he found he had struck the rail. He felt a violent blow in his left side and he gasped with the pain and swung round. A man's face, centred on a dark void of an open mouth, appeared before him and he smashed his fist forward, dashing the pommel of his hanger into the teeth of the lower jaw. The discharge of his enemy's pistol burnt his leg, but did no further damage and Drinkwater again wiped blood from his eyes. He caught his breath and looked round. Something seemed to have stopped his hearing and the strange absence of noise baffled him. Around him amid the dark shapes of dead or dying men, the fighting was furious. Quilhampton felled a man with his iron hook. Two marines, their scarlet tunics a dull brown in the gloom, their white cross-belts and breeches grey, were bayonetting a French officer who stood like some blasphemous crucifix, a broken sword dangling from his wrist by its martingale. A seaman was wrestling for his life under a huge brute of a Frenchman with a great black beard while all along the deck similar struggles were in progress. Drinkwater recognised the struggling seaman as Franklin from the dark, distinctive strawberry birthmark. Catching up his sword he took three paces across the deck and drove the point into the flank of the giant.

The man turned in surprise and rose slowly. Drinkwater recovered his blade as the giant staggered towards him, ignoring

Franklin who lay gasping on the deck. The giant was unarmed and grappled forward, a forbidding and terrifying sight. There was something so utterly overpowering about the appearance of the man that Drinkwater felt fear for the first time since they had gone into action. It was the same fear a small boy feels when menaced by a physical superior. Drinkwater's sword seemed inadequate to the task and he had no pistols. He felt ignominious defeat and death were inevitable. His legs were sagging under him and then his hearing came back to him. The man's mouth was open but it was himself that was shouting, a loud, courage-provoking bellow that stiffened his own resolve and sent him lunging forward, slashing at the man's face with his sword blade. The giant fell on his knees and Drinkwater hacked again, unaware that the man was bleeding to death through the first wound he had inflicted. The giant crashed forward and Drinkwater heard a cheer. What was left of his crew of volunteers encircled the fallen man, like the Israelites round Goliath.

The deck of the *Bonaparte* remained in British hands.

Antigone leaned over to the wind and creaked as her lee scuppers drove under water. Along her gun-deck tiny squirts of water found their way inboard through the cracks round the gun-ports. In his cabin Drinkwater swallowed his third glass of wine and finally addressed himself to his journal.

It is not, he wrote at last, *the business of a sea-officer to enjoy his duty, but I have often derived a satisfaction from achievement, quite lacking in the events of today. We have this day taken a French National brig-corvette of sixteen 8-pounder long guns named the* Bonaparte. *We have also destroyed twelve invasion bateaux, two of the large class mounting a broadside of light guns, taken upwards of sixty prisoners and thereby satisfied those objectives set in launching the attack at dawn. Yet the cost has been fearful. Lieutenant Gorton's wound is mortal and nineteen other men have died, or are likely to die, as a result of the various actions that are, in the eyes of the public, virtually un-noteworthy. Had we let the enemy slip away, the newspapers would not have understood why a frigate of* Antigone's *force could not have destroyed a handful of boats and a little brig. It was clear the enemy had prepared for the possibility of attack, that the brig was to bear its brunt while the bateaux escaped, and, that, at the end, we were nearly overwhelmed by a ruse de guerre that might have made prisoners of the best elements aboard this ship, to say nothing of extinguishing forever the career of myself. Even now I shudder at the possible consequences of their counter-attack succeeding.*

He laid his pen down and stared at the page where the wet gleam of the ink slowly faded. But all he could see was the apparition of the French giant and remember again how hollow his legs had felt.

Chapter Six *April–May 1804*

The Secret Agent

As April turned into a glorious May, Lieutenant Rogers continued to smart from Drinkwater's rebuke. It galled him that even the news that the *Bonaparte* had been condemned as a prize and purchased into the Royal Navy – thus making him several hundred pounds richer failed to raise his spirits. There were few areas in which Rogers evinced any sensitivity, but one was in his good opinion of himself, and it struck him that he had come to rely upon his commander's reinforcement of this. Such hitherto uncharacteristic reliance upon another further annoyed him, and to it he began to add other causes for grievance. Drinkwater's report had said little, certainly nothing that would elevate his first lieutenant and place him on the quarterdeck of the prize as a commander. In fact Drinkwater had sent the prize into Portsmouth with the wounded under the master's mate Tyrrell, so, apart from his prize money, Rogers had dismissed the notion that he could expect anything further from the capture. In addition to this it seemed that the impetus to *Antigone*'s cruise had gone, that no further chance of glory, advancement, or simply resuming his normal relationship with Drinkwater would offer itself to him. He took refuge in the only action left to him as first lieutenant; he harried the crew. *Antigone*'s people were employed constantly in a relentless series of drills. They shifted sails, exercised at small-arms and cutlasses, and sent down the topgallant and topmasts. To kill any residual boredom they even got the heavy lower yards across the rails aportlast. When Drinkwater drily expressed satisfaction, Rogers demurred respectfully and repeated the evolution until it was accomplished to his own satisfaction.

For his part, Drinkwater accepted this propitiation as evidence of Rogers's contrition, and his own better nature responded so that the difference between them gradually diminished. Besides, news of Gorton's slow death at Haslar Hospital seemed to conclude the incident.

Towards the end of April they had spoken to the 18-gun brigsloop *Vincejo* on her way to the westward, with orders to destroy the coastal trade off south Brittany. Her commander had come aboard and closeted himself with Drinkwater for half an hour. Their discussion was routine and friendly. After Wright's departure Drinkwater was able to confirm the speculations of the officers and explain that their late visitor was indeed the John Wesley Wright who, as a lieutenant, had escaped from French custody in Paris with Captain Sir Sydney Smith. He also mentioned that Wright was far from pleased with the condition of his ship, its armament, or its manning, and this seemed to divert the officers into a discussion about the *'Vincey Joe'*, an old Spanish prize, held to be cranky and highly unsuitable for its present task.

Drinkwater kept to himself the orders Wright had passed him and the knowledge that Wright, like himself twelve years earlier, had been employed by Lord Dungarth's department in the landing and recovery of British agents on the coast of France. The orders Wright had brought emanated from Lord Dungarth via Admiral Keith, and prompted Drinkwater to increase his officers' vigilance in the interception and seizure of French fishing boats. Hitherto fishermen had been largely left alone. They were, as D'Auvergne had pointed out, the chief source of claret and cognac in England, and were not averse to parting with information of interest to the captains of British cruisers. But their knowledge of the English coast and its more obscure landing places, the suitability of their boats to carry troops and their general usefulness in forwarding the grand design of invasion had prompted an Admiralty order to detain them and destroy their craft. In this way *Antigone* passed the first weeks of a beautiful summer.

It was from their captures, and from the dispatch luggers and cutters with which Lord Keith kept in touch with his scattered cruisers, that Drinkwater and his officers learned of the consequences of the attempt made by discontented elements in France to assassinate Napoleon Bonaparte. The Pichegru-Cadoudal conspiracy had implicated both wings of French politics and been exposed in the closing weeks of the previous year. It had taken some time to round up the conspirators and had culminated in the astounding news that Bonaparte's gendarmes had illegally entered the neighbouring state of Baden and abducted the young Duc D'Enghien. The duke had been given a drum-head court-martial which implicated the Bourbons in the plot against Bonaparte, and summarily shot in a ditch at Vincennes. Drinkwater's reaction to the execution of D'Enghien combined with the orders he had received from Wright to extend *Antigone*'s cruising ground further east towards Pointe d'Ailly.

'Standing close inshore like this,' Drinkwater overheard Rogers grumbling to Hill as he sat reading with his skylight open, 'we're not going to capture a damn thing. We're more like a bloody whore trailing her skirt up and down the street than a damned frigate. I wish we were in the West Indies. Even a fool of a Frenchman isn't going to put to sea with us sitting here for all to see.'

'No,' said Hill reflectively, and Drinkwater put down his book to hear what he had to say in reply. 'But it could be that that is just what the Old Man wants.'

'What? To be seen?'

'Yes. When I was in the *Kestrel*, cutter, back in ninety-two we used to do just this waiting to pick up a spy.'

'Wasn't our Nathaniel aboard *Kestrel* then?'

'Yes,' said Hill, 'and that cove Wright has been doing something similar more recently.'

'Good God! Why didn't you mention it before?'

Drinkwater heard Hill laugh. 'I never thought of it.'

In the end it was the fishing boat that found them as Drinkwater intended. She came swooping over the waves, a brown lugsail reefed down and hauled taut against the fresh westerly that set white wave-caps sparkling in the low sunshine of early morning. Drinkwater answered the summons to the quarterdeck to find Quilhampton backing the main-topsail and heaving the ship to. He levelled his glass on the approaching boat but could make nothing of her beyond the curve of her dark sail, apart from an occasional face that peered ahead and shouted at the helmsman. A minute or two later the boat was alongside and a man in riding clothes was bawling in imperious English for a chair at a yardarm whip. The men at the rail looked aft at Drinkwater.

He nodded: 'Do as he asks, Mr Q.'

As soon as the stranger's feet touched the deck he dextrously extricated himself from the bosun's chair, moved swiftly to the rail and whipped a pistol from his belt.

'What the devil are you about, sir?' shouted Drinkwater seeing the barrel levelled at the men in the boat.

'Shootin' the damned Frogs, Captain, and saving you your duty!' The hammer clicked impotently on a misfire and the stranger turned angrily. 'Has anyone a pistol handy?'

Drinkwater strode across the deck. 'Put up that gun, sir, d'you hear me!' He was outraged. That the stranger should escape from an enemy country and then shoot the men who had risked everything to bring him off to *Antigone* seemed a piece of quite unnecessary brutality.

'Here, take this.' Drinkwater turned to see Walmsley offering the stranger a loaded pistol.

'Good God! What, *you* here, Walmsley! Thank you . . .'

'Put up that gun, sir!' Drinkwater closed the gap between him and the spy and knocked up the weapon. The man spun round. His face was suffused with rage.

'A pox on you! Who the deuce d'you think you are to meddle in my affairs?'

'Have a care! I command here and you'll not fire into that boat!'

'D'you know who I am, damn you?'

'Indeed, Lord Camelford, I do; and I received orders to expect you some days ago.' He dropped his voice as Camelford looked round as though to obtain some support from Walmsley. 'Your reputation with pistols precedes you, my Lord. I must insist on your surrendering even those waterlogged weapons you still have in your belt.' He indicated a further two butts protruding from Camelford's waistband.

Camelford's face twisted into a snarl and he leaned forward, thrusting himself close to Drinkwater. 'You'll pay for your insolence, Captain. I do not think you know what influence I command, nor how necessary it was that I despatched those fishermen . . .'

'After promising them immunity to capture if they brought you offshore I don't doubt,' Drinkwater said, matching Camelford's anger. 'No fisherman would have risked bringing you off and under my guns without such assurance. It's common knowledge that we have been taking every fishing boat we can lay our hands on . . .'

'And now look, you damned fool, those two got clean away . . .' Camelford pointed to where the brown lugsail leaned away from the rail, full of wind and hauling off from *Antigone*'s side as her seamen stood and witnessed the little drama amidships.

'And you have kept your word, my Lord,' Drinkwater said soothingly, 'and now shall we go to my cabin? Put the ship on a course of north north-east, Mr Q. I want to fetch The Downs without delay.'

'Who the hell is he?' Rogers asked Hill as first lieutenant and master stood on the quarterdeck supervising their preparations for coming to an anchor in The Downs. 'D'you know?'

'Yes. Don't you recall him as Lieutenant Pitt? Vancouver left him ashore at Hawaii back in ninety-four for insubordination . . .'

'Is he the fellow that shot Peterson, first luff of the *Perdrix*, in, what, ninety-eight?'

'The same fellow. And the court-martial upheld his defence that Peterson, though senior, had refused to obey a lawful order . . .'

'Having the name Pitt helped a great deal, I don't doubt,' said Rogers. 'He resigned after it though, a regular kill-buck by the look of it. I thought Drinkwater was going to have a fit when he came aboard.'

'Oh he'll get away with almost anything. He's related to Lord Grenville by marriage, Billy Pitt by blood, and, I believe, to Sir Sydney Smith. I daresay it's due to the latter pair that he's been employed as an agent. I wonder what he was doing in France?'

'Mmmm. It must take some stomach to act as a spy over there,' Rogers's tone was one of admiration as he nodded in the direction of the cliffs of Gris Nez.

'Oh yes. Undoubtedly,' mused Hill, 'but I wonder what exactly . . .' The conversation broke off as a thunderous-looking Drinkwater came on deck.

'Are we ready to anchor, Mr Rogers?'

'Aye, sir, as near as . . . all ready, sir.' Rogers saw the look in Drinkwater's eye and went forward.

'Very well, bring-to close to the flagship, Mr Hill, then clear away my barge!'

Drinkwater had had a wretched time with the obnoxious Camelford. In the end he had virtually imprisoned the spy in his own cabin with a few bottles and spent most of the time on deck. Actually avoiding a ridiculous challenge from the man's deliberate provocation tested his powers of self-restraint to the utmost. He found it hard to imagine what on earth a person of Camelford's stamp was doing on behalf of the British government in France. After they had anchored, Drinkwater went below and found Camelford slumped in his own chair, the portrait of Hortense Santhonax spread on the table before him. He opened his mouth to protest at the ransacking of his effects but Camelford slurred:

'D'you know this woman, Captain Drinkwater?'

'The portrait was captured with the ship,' Drinkwater answered non-committally.

'I asked if you know her.'

'I know who she is.'

'If you ever meet her or her husband, Captain, do what I wanted to do to those fishermen. Shoot 'em both!'

Drinkwater sensed Camelford was in earnest. Whatever the man's defects, he was, at that moment, making an effort to be both conciliatory and informative. Besides, experience had taught Drinkwater that agents recently liberated from a false existence surrounded by enemies were apt to behave irrationally, and news of Santhonax or his wife held an especial fascination for him. He grinned at Camelford.

'In *his* case I doubt if I'd hesitate.'

'You know Edouard Santhonax too, then?'

Drinkwater nodded. 'He was briefly my prisoner on two occasions.'

'Did you know Wright was captured in the Morbihan?'

'Wright? Of the *Vincejo*?'

'Yes. He was overwhelmed in a calm by a number of gunboats and forced to surrender. They put him in the Temple and cut his throat with a rusty knife.' Camelford tapped the cracked canvas before him. 'Her husband visited the Temple the night before, with a commission from the Emperor Napoleon . . .'

'The *Emperor* Napoleon?' queried Drinkwater, bemused by this strange and improbable story.

'Hadn't you heard, Captain?' Camelford leaned back. 'Oh my goodness no, how could you? Bonaparte the First Consul is transfigured, Captain Drinkwater. He is become Napoleon, Emperor of the French. A plebiscite of the French people has raised him to the purple.'

Following Camelford's welcome departure, Drinkwater was summoned to attend Lord Keith. As he kicked his heels aboard Keith's flagship, the *Monarch*, Drinkwater learned that not only had Napoleon secured his position as Emperor of the French but his own patron, Earl St Vincent, had been dismissed from the Admiralty. The old man refused to serve under William Pitt who had just been returned as Prime Minister in place of Addington. Pitt had said some harsh things about St Vincent when in opposition and had replaced him as First Lord of the Admiralty with Lord Melville. But Drinkwater's thoughts were not occupied with such considerations for long. His mind returned to the image of Wright lying in the Temple prison with his throat cut and the shadowy figure of Edouard Santhonax somewhere in the background. He wondered how accurate Camelford's information was and what Camelford was doing in France. Was it possible that a man of Camelford's erratic character had been employed to do what Cadoudal and Pichegru had failed to do: to assassinate Napoleon Bonaparte? The only credible explanation for that hypothesis was that Camelford had been sent into France in a private capacity. Drinkwater vaguely remembered Camelford had avoided the serious consequences of his duel with Peterson. If that had been due to family connections, was it possible that someone had put him up to an attempt on the life of Bonaparte? Pitt himself, for instance, to whom Camelford was related and who had every motive for wishing the Corsican Tyrant dead.

There was some certainty nagging at the back of Drinkwater's mind, something that lent credibility to this extraordinary possibility. And then he remembered D'Auvergne's obscure remark to Cornwallis. Something about 'it would be soon if it was ever to be'. At the time he had connected it with D'Auvergne's passionate conviction that invasion was imminent; now perhaps the evidence pointed to Camelford having been sent into France to murder Napoleon. D'Auvergne's involvement in such operations could have made him a party to it. He was prevented from further speculation by the appearance of Keith's flag-lieutenant.

'The admiral will see you now, sir.'

He looked up, recalled abruptly to the present. Tucking his hat under his arm, Drinkwater went into the great cabin of the *Monarch*, mustering in his mind the mundane details of his need of firewood, fresh water and provisions. His reception was polite but unenthusiastic; his requisitions passed to Keith's staff. The acidulous Scots admiral asked him to take a protégé of his as lieutenant in place of Gorton and then instructed Drinkwater that his presence had been requested by the new Prime Minister, then in residence at Walmer Castle.

Drinkwater answered the summons to Walmer Castle with some misgivings. It chimed in uncomfortably with his train of thought while he had been waiting to see Keith and he could only conclude Pitt wished to see him in connection with the recent embarkation of his cousin, Camelford. It was unlikely that the interview would be pleasant and he recalled Camelford's threats when he had prevented the shooting of the fishermen.

The castle was only a short walk from Deal beach. Many years ago he had gone there to receive orders for the rendezvous that had brought Hortense and then Edouard Santhonax into his life. On that occasion he had been received by Lord Dungarth, head of the Admiralty's intelligence service. To his astonishment it was Dungarth who met him again.

'My dear Nathaniel, how very good to see you. How are you?'

'Well enough, my Lord.' Drinkwater grinned with pleasure and accepted the offered glass of wine. 'I hope I find you in health?'

Dungarth sighed. 'As well as can be expected in these troubled times, though in truth things could not be much worse. Our hopes have been dashed and Bonaparte has reversed the Republic's principles without so much as a murmur from more than a handful of die-hards. Old Admiral Truguet has resigned at Brest and Ganteaume's taken over, but I believe this imperial nonsense will combine the French better than anything, and that shrewd devil Bonaparte knows it . . . But I did not get you here to gossip. Billy Pitt asks for you personally. You did well to get Camelford back in one piece.'

'It was nothing, my Lord . . .'

'Oh, I don't mean embarking him. He's a cantankerous devil; I'm surprised he hasn't challenged half your officers. His honour, what there is of it, is a damned touchy subject.'

'So I had gathered,' Drinkwater observed drily.

Dungarth laughed. 'I'm sure you had. Anyway his capture would have been an embarrassment, particularly with the change of government.'

'You said "our hopes have been dashed", my Lord; might I assume that Bonaparte was not intended to live long enough to assume the purple?'

Dungarth's hazel eyes fixed Drinkwater with a shrewd glance. 'Wouldn't you say that Mr Pitt serves the most excellent port, Nathaniel?'

Drinkwater took the hint. 'Most excellent, my Lord.'

'And most necessary, gentlemen, most necessary . . .' A thin, youngish man entered the room and strode to the decanter. Drinkwater noticed that his clothes were carelessly worn, his stockings, for instance, appeared too large for him. He faced them, a full glass to his lips, and Drinkwater recognised the turned-up nose habitually caricatured by the cartoonists. 'So this is Captain Drinkwater, is it?'

'Indeed,' said Dungarth, making the introductions, 'Captain Drinkwater; the Prime Minister, Mr Pitt.'

Drinkwater bowed. 'Yours to command, sir.'

'Obliged, Captain,' said Pitt, inclining his head slightly and studying the naval officer. 'I wish to thank you for your forbearance. I think you know to what I allude.'

'It is most considerate of you, sir, to take the trouble. The service was a small one.' Drinkwater felt relief that the incident was to be made no more of.

Pitt smiled over the rim of his glass and Drinkwater saw how tired and sick his boyish face really was, prematurely aged by the enormous responsibilities of high office.

'He was the only midshipman that remained loyal to Riou when the *Guardian* struck an iceberg in the Southern Ocean,' said Pitt obliquely, as though this extenuated Camelford's behaviour. Drinkwater recalled Riou's epic struggle to keep the damaged *Guardian* afloat for nine weeks until she fetched Table Bay. The thought seemed to speak more of Riou's character than of Camelford's. 'Lord Dungarth assures me', Pitt went on, 'that I can rely upon your absolute discretion.'

So, Drinkwater mused as he bowed again and muttered, 'Of course, sir', it seemed that he *had* guessed correctly and that Pitt himself had sent his cousin into France to end Bonaparte's career.

But he was suddenly forced to consider more important matters.

'Good,' said Pitt, refilling his glass. 'And now, Captain, I wish to ask you something more. How seriously do you rate the prospects of invasion?'

The enormity of the question took Drinkwater aback. Even allowing for Pitt's recent resumption of office it seemed an extraordinary one. He shot a glance at Dungarth who nodded encouragingly.

'Well, sir, I do not know that I am a competent person to answer, but I believe their invasion craft capable of transporting a large body of troops. That they are encamped in sufficient force is well known. Their principal difficulty is in getting a great enough number of ships in the Strait here to overwhelm our own squadrons. If they could achieve that . . . but I am sure, sir, that their Lordships are better placed to advise you than I . . .'

'No, Captain. I ask *you* because you have just come in from a Channel cruise and your opinions are not entirely theoretical. I am told that the French cannot build barges capable of carrying troops. I do not believe that, so it is *your* observations that I wished for.'

'Very well, sir. I think the French might be capable of combining their fleet effectively. Their ships are not entirely despicable. If fortune gave them a lucky start and Nelson . . .' he broke off, flushing.

'Go on, Captain. "If Nelson . . ."'

'It is nothing, sir.'

'You were about to say: "if Nelson maintains his blockade loosely enough to entice Latouche-Tréville out of Toulon for a battle, only to lose contact with him, matters might result in that combination of their fleets that you are apprehensive of." Is that it?'

'It is a possibility talked of in the fleet, sir.'

'It is a possibility talked of elsewhere, sir,' observed Pitt with some asperity and looking at Dungarth. 'Nelson will be the death or the glory of us all. He let a French fleet escape him before Abukir. If he wasn't so damned keen on a battle, but kept close up on Toulon like Cornwallis at Brest . . .' Pitt broke off to refill his glass. 'So you think there is a chance of a French fleet entering the Channel?'

Drinkwater nodded. 'It is a remote one, sir. But the Combined Fleets of France and Spain did so in seventy-nine. They would have more chance of success if they went north about.'

'Round Scotland, d'you mean?'

'Yes, sir. There'd be less chance of detection,' said Drinkwater, warming to his subject and egged on by the appreciative expression on Dungarth's face. 'A descent upon the Strait of Dover from the North Sea would be quite possible and they could release the Dutch fleet en route. You could circumvent Cornwallis by . . .'

'A rendezvous in the West Indies, by God!' interrupted Pitt. 'Combine all your squadrons then lose yourself in the Atlantic for a month and reappear at our back door . . . Dungarth, d'you think it's possible?'

'Very possible, William, very possible, and also highly likely. The Emperor Napoleon has one hundred and seventy thousand men encamped just across the water there. I'd say that was just what he *was* intending.'

Pitt crossed the rich carpet to stare out of the window at the pale line of France on the distant horizon. The waters of the Strait lay between, blue and lovely in the sunshine beyond the bastions of the castle, dotted with the white sails of Keith's cruisers. Without turning round, Pitt dismissed Drinkwater.

'Thank you, Captain Drinkwater. I shall take note of your opinion.'

Dungarth saw him to the door. 'Thank you, Nathaniel,' the earl muttered confidentially, 'I believe your deductions to be absolutely correct.'

Drinkwater returned to his boat flattered by the veiled compliment from Dungarth and vaguely disturbed that his lordship, as head of the navy's intelligence service, needed a junior captain to make his case before the new Prime Minister.

Chapter Seven *June-July 1804*

The Army of the Coasts of the Ocean

'Six minutes, Mr Rogers,' said Drinkwater pocketing his watch, 'very creditable. Now you may pipe the hands to dinner.'

The shifting of the three topsails had been accomplished in good time and the tide was just turning against them. They could bring to their anchor and dine in comfort, for there was insufficient wind to hold them against a spring ebb. It was a great consolation, he had remarked to Rogers earlier, that they could eat like civilised men ashore at a steady table, while secure in the knowledge that their very presence at anchor in the Dover Strait was sufficient to keep the French army from invading.

For almost seven weeks now, *Antigone* had formed part of Lord Keith's advance division, cruising ceaselessly between the Varne Bank and Cap Gris Nez, one of several frigates and sixty-fours that Keith kept in support of the small fry in the shallower water to the east. Cutters, luggers, sloops and gun-brigs, with a few bomb-vessels, kept up a constant pressure on the attempts by the French army to practise embarkation. Drinkwater knew the little clashes between the advance forces of the two protagonists were short, sharp and murderous. His disfigured shoulder was proof of that.

Having frequently stood close inshore at high water, Drinkwater had seen that the invasion flotilla consisted of craft other than the *chaloupes* and *péniches* with which he was already familiar. There were some large *prames*, great barges, one hundred feet long and capable of carrying over a hundred and fifty men. A simple elevation of the telescope to the green hills surrounding Boulogne was enough to convince Drinkwater that he had been right in expressing his fears to Pitt. Line after line of tents spread across the rolling countryside. Everywhere the bright colours of soldiers in formation, little squares, lozenges, lines and rectangles, all tipped with the brilliant reflections of sunlight from bayonets, moved under the direction of their drill-masters. Occasionally squadrons of cavalry were to be seen moving; wheeling and changing from line to column and back to line again. Drinkwater was touched by the fascination of it all. Beside him Frey would sit with his box of water-colours, annoyed and impatient with himself that he could not do justice to the magnificence of the scene.

At night they could see the lines of camp-fires, the glow of lanterns, and occasionally hear the bark of cannon from the batteries covering the beaches which opened fire on an insolent British cutter working too close inshore.

Now Drinkwater waited for the cable to cease rumbling through the hawse and for Hill to straighten up from the vanes of the pelorus as *Antigone* settled to her anchor.

'Brought up, sir.'

'Very well. Mr Hill, Mr Rogers, would you care to dine with me? Perhaps you'd bring one of your mates, Mr Hill, and a couple of midshipmen.'

Mullender had fattened a small pig in the manger on scraps and that morning pronounced it ready for sacrifice. Already the scent of roasting pork had been hanging over the quarterdeck for some time and Drinkwater had been shamed into sending a leg into the gunroom and another into the cockpit. Mullender had been outraged by this largesse, particularly when Drinkwater ordered what was left after his own leg had been removed to be sent forward. But it seemed too harsh an application of privilege to subject his men to the aroma of sizzling crackling and deny them a few titbits. Besides, their present cruising ground was so near home that reprovisioning was no problem.

A companionable silence descended upon the table as the hungry officers took knife and fork to the dismembered pig.

'You are enjoying your meal, Mr Gillespy, I believe?' remarked Drinkwater, amused at the ecstatic expression on the midshipman's face.

'Yes, sir,' the boy squeaked, 'thanking you sir, for your invitation . . .' He flushed as the other diners laughed at him indulgently.

'Well, Mr Gillespy,' added Rogers, his mouth still full and a half-glass of stingo aiding mastication and simultaneous speech, 'it's an improvement on the usual short commons, eh?'

'Indeed, sir, it is.'

'You had some mail today, Mr Q, news of home I trust?'

Drinkwater asked, knowing three letters had come off in the despatch lugger *Sparrow* that forenoon.

'Yes, sir. Catriona sends you her kindest wishes.' James Quilhampton grinned happily.

'D'you intend to marry this filly then, Mr Q?' asked Rogers.

'If she'll have me,' growled Quilhampton, flushing at the indelicacy of the question.

'Can't see the point of marriage, myself,' Rogers said morosely.

'Oh, I don't know,' put in Hill. 'Its chief advantage is that you can walk down the street with a woman on your arm without exciting damn-fool comments from y'r friends.'

'Fiddlesticks!' Rogers looked round at the half-concealed smirks of Quilhampton and Frey. Even little Gillespy seemed to perceive a well-known joke. 'What the devil d'you mean, Hill?' demanded Rogers, colouring.

'That you cut out a pretty little corvette, trimmed fore and aft with ribbons and lace, with an entry port used by half the fleet in Chatham . . .'

'God damn it...'

'Now had you been *married* we would have thought it your wife, don't you see?'

'Why . . . I . . .'

'No, Hill, we'd never have fallen for that,' said James Quilhampton, getting his revenge. 'A married man would not have been so imprudent as to have carried so much sail upon his *bowsprit*!'

Upon this phallic reference the company burst into unrestrained laughter at the first lieutenant's discomfiture. Rogers coloured and Drinkwater came to his rescue.

'Take it in good part, Sam. I heard she was devilish pretty and those fellows are only jealous. Besides I've news for you. You need no longer stand a watch. I received notice this morning that Keith wants us to find a place for an élève of his, a Lieutenant Fraser . . .'

'Oh God, a Scotchman,' complained Rogers, irritated by Quilhampton and knowing his partiality in that direction. Mullender drew the cloth and placed the decanter in front of Drinkwater. He filled his glass and sent it round the table.

'And now, gentlemen . . . The King!'

Drinkwater looked round the table and reflected that they were not such a bad set of fellows and it was a very pleasant day to be dining, with the reflections of sunlight on the water bouncing off the painted deckhead and the polished glasses.

Two day's later the weather wore a different aspect. Since dawn *Antigone* had worked closer inshore under easy sail, having been informed by signal that some unusual activity was taking place in the harbour and anchorage of Boulogne Road. By noon the wind, which had been steadily freshening from the north during the forenoon, began to blow hard, sending a sharp sea running round Cap Gris Nez and among the considerable numbers of invasion craft anchored under the guns of Boulogne's defences.

The promise of activity, either action with the enemy or the need to reef down, had aroused the curiosity of the officers and the watch on deck. A dozen glasses were trained to the eastward.

'Mr Frey, make to *Constitution* to come within hail.'

'Aye, aye, sir.' The bunting rose jerkily to the lee mizen topsail yard and broke out. Drinkwater watched the hired cutter that two days earlier had brought their new lieutenant. She tacked and lay her gunwhale over until she luffed under the frigate's stern. Drinkwater could see her commander, Lieutenant Dennis, standing expectantly on a gun-carriage. He raised a speaking-trumpet.

'Alert Captain Owen of the movement in the Road!' He saw Dennis wave and the jib of *Constitution* was held aback as she spun on her heel and lay over again on a broad reach to the west where Owen in the *Immortalité* was at anchor with the frigate *Leda*. Owen was locally the senior officer of Keith's 'Boulogne division' and it was incumbent upon Drinkwater to let him know of any unusual movements of the French that might be taken advantage of.

'Well, gentlemen, let's slip the hounds off the leash. Mr Frey, make to *Harpy*, *Bloodhound* and *Archer* Number Sixteen: "Engage the enemy more closely".' The 18-gun sloop and the two little gun-brigs were a mile or so to the eastward and eager for such a signal. Within minutes they were freeing off and running towards the dark cluster of French *bateaux* above which the shapes of sails were being hoisted.

'Mr Hill, a man in the chains with a lead. Beat to quarters and clear for action, Mr Rogers.' He stood beside the helmsmen. 'Up helm. Lee forebrace there . . .'

Antigone eased round to starboard under her topsails and began to bear down on the French coast. The sun was already westering in a bloody riot of purple cloud and great orange streaks of mare's tails presaging more wind on the morrow. *Antigone* stood on, coming within clear visual range of the activity in the anchorage.

'Forty-four, forty-five brigs and – what've you got on that slate, Frey? – forty-three luggers, sir,' reported Quilhampton, who had been diligently counting the enemy vessels as the sun broke briefly through the cloud and shot rays of almost horizontal light over the sea, foreshortening distances and rendering everything suddenly clear. Then it sank from view and left the silhouettes of the *Immortalité* and *Leda* on the horizon, coming in from the west.

The small ships were close inshore, the flashes from their guns growing brighter as daylight diminished and the tide turned. Owen made the signal for withdrawal and the *Antigone*, in company with the *Harpy*, *Bloodhound* and *Archer*, drew off for the night and rode out the rising gale at anchor three leagues offshore.

At daylight on the following day, 20th July, Drinkwater was awoken by Midshipman Dutfield. 'Beg pardon, sir, but Mr Fraser's compliments, sir, and would you come on deck.'

Drinkwater emerged into the thin light of early morning. The north-north-westerly wind was blowing with gale force. The Channel waves were steep, sharp and vicious and *Antigone* rode uncomfortably to her anchor. The flood tide was just away and the frigate lay across wind and tide, rolling awkwardly. But it was not this circumstance that the new lieutenant wished to draw to Drinkwater's attention.

'There, sir,' he pointed, 'just beyond the low-water mark, lines of fascines to form a rough wall with artillery . . . see!' Fraser broke off his description as the French gave evidence of their purpose. The flash of cannon from the low-water mark was aimed at the gun-brigs anchored inshore. Out of range of the batteries along the cliffs, they were extremely vulnerable to shot from a half-mile nearer. The French, as if demonstrating their ingenious energy, had made temporary batteries on the dry sands and could withdraw their guns as the tide made. What was more, shot fired on a flat trajectory so near the surface of the sea could skip like stones upon a pond. They'd smash a gun-brig with ease and might, with luck, range out much further.

'It's bluidy clever, sir.'

'Aye, Mr Fraser . . . but why today?' Drinkwater adjusted his glass and immediately had his answer. At the hour at which it was normal to see lines of infantry answering the morning roll-call he was aware of something very different about the appearance of the French camps. Dark snakes wound their way down towards the dip in the hills where the roofs and belfries of Boulogne indicated the port.

'By heaven, Mr Fraser, they're embarking!'

'In this weather, sir?'

'Wind or not, they're damned well on the move . . .' The two officers watched for some minutes in astonishment. 'There are a lot less *bateaux* in the anchorage this morning,' Drinkwater observed.

'Happen they've hauled them inshore to embark troops.'

'That must have been a ticklish business in this wind with a sea running.'

'Aye.'

As the tide made, Owen ordered his tiny squadron under weigh and once again *Antigone* closed the coast. By now the batteries along the tideline had been withdrawn and there was sufficient water over the shoals for the bigger frigates to move in after the sloops and gun-brigs.

At noon *Antigone* came within range of the batteries and Drinkwater opened fire. After the weeks of aimless cruising, the stench of powder and the trembling of the decks beneath the recoiling carriages was music in the ears of *Antigone's* crew.

Their insolence was met by a storm of fire from the shore; it seemed that everywhere the ground was level the French had cannon. The practical necessity of having to tack offshore in the northerly wind allowed them to draw breath and inspect the ship for damage. There was little enough. A few holes in the sails and a bruised topgallant mast. Astern of them the gun-brigs and sloops were snapping around the two or three luggers that were trying to work offshore. The flood tide swept them northwards and, off Ambleteuse, Drinkwater gave orders to wear ship.

'Brace in the spanker there! Brace in the after-yards! Up helm!' The after-canvas lost its power to drive the frigate as Drinkwater turned her south.

'Square the headyards! Steady . . . steady as she goes!'

'Steady as she goes, sir.'

'Square the after-yards!'

Antigone steadied on her new course, standing south under her three topsails, running before the wind inside the shoals and parallel with the coast. It wanted an hour before high water but here the tide ran north for several hours yet and they could balance wind and tide, checking the ship's southward progress against the tide, and thus wreak as much havoc as they possibly could while the smoke from their own guns hung over their deck masking them from the enemy. The motion of the deck eased considerably.

'Mr Rogers! Shift over the starbowlines to assist at the larboard batteries. Every gun-captain to choose his target and fire as at a mark, make due allowance for elevation and roll. You may open fire!'

Drinkwater stared out to larboard. They were a mile from the cliffs at Raventhun and suddenly spouts of water rose on their beam. Drinkwater levelled his glass.

'Mr Gillespy!'

'Sir?'

'D'you see that square shape over there, where the ground falls away?'

The boy nodded. 'Yes, sir.'

'That's Ambleteuse fort. Be so kind as to point it out to Mr Rogers so that he may direct the guns.'

The little estuary that formed the harbour opened up on their beam as *Antigone* exchanged shot with the fort. Within the harbour they could see quite clearly a mass of rafted barges crammed with soldiers, rocking dangerously as the sharp waves drove in amongst them.

A shower of splinters sprouted abruptly from the rail where a ball struck home and more holes appeared in the topsails. Amidships the launch was hit by three shot within as many minutes and then they were passing out of range of the fort's embrasures. Rogers was leaping up and down from gun to gun, exhorting his men and swearing viciously at them when their aim failed. As the land rose again a battery of horse artillery could be seen dashing at the gallop along the cliff. Suddenly Drinkwater saw the officer leading the troop fling up his hand and the gunners rein in their horses.

'Mr Rogers! See there!' Rogers narrowed his eyes and stared through the smoke that cleared slowly in the following wind. Then comprehension struck him and he leant over the nearest gun and aimed it personally. The Frenchmen had got their cannon unlimbered and were slewing them round. They were shining brass cannon, field pieces of 8- or 9-pound calibre, Drinkwater estimated, and they were ready loaded. He saw white smoke flash from an almost simultaneous volley from the five guns and a second later the shot whistled overhead, carrying off the starboard quarter-boat davits and dumping the boat in the sea alongside, where it trailed in its falls amongst the broken baulks of timber.

Amidships Rogers was howling with rage as his broadside struck flints and chunks of chalk from the cliff a few feet below the edge. But his next shots landed among the artillerymen and they had the satisfaction of seeing the battery limbered up amid frantic cheers from the gunners amidships.

'We're too close inshore, sir. Bottom's shoaling.' Drinkwater turned to the ever-dutiful Hill who, while this fairground game was in progress, attended to the navigation of the ship.

'Bring her a point to starboard then.'

They were abeam of Wimereux now. Here too, there was a fort on the rocks at the water's edge, and below the fort two of the French invasion craft were stranded and going to pieces under the white of breakers. Drinkwater was suddenly aware that the cloud of powder smoke that rolled slowly ahead of the ship was obscuring his view. 'Cease fire! Cease fire!'

The smoke cleared with maddening slowness, but gradually it seemed to lift aside like a theatrical gauze, revealing a sight of confusion such as their own cannon could not achieve. They were less than two miles from Boulogne now, and under the cliffs and along the breakwaters of the harbour more than a dozen of the invasion barges lay wrecked with the sea breaking over them. Their shattered masts had fallen over their sides and men could be seen in the water around them.

They had a brief glimpse into the harbour as they crossed the entrance, a brief glimpse of chaos. It seemed as though soldiers were everywhere, moving like ants across the landscape. Yet, as *Antigone* crossed the narrow opening the guns of Boulogne were briefly silent, their servers witnesses of the drowning of over a thousand of their comrades. In this hiatus *Antigone* passed by, her own men standing at their guns, staring at the waves breaking viciously over rocking and overloaded craft, at men catching their balance, falling and drowning.

'I think there's the reason for the activity, sir,' said Fraser pointing above the town. 'I'll wager that's the Emperor himself.'

Drinkwater swung his glass and levelled it where Fraser pointed. Into the circle of the lens came an unforgettable image of a man in a grey coat, sitting on a white horse and wearing a large black tricorne hat. The man had a glass to his eye and was staring directly at the British frigate as it swept past him. As he lowered his own glass, Drinkwater could just make out the blur of Napoleon's face turning to one of his suite behind him.

'Napoleon Bonaparte, Emperor o' the French,' muttered Fraser beside him. 'He looks a wee bit like Don Quixote . . . Don Quixote *de la Manche . . .*'

Fraser's pun was lost in the roar of the batteries of Boulogne as they reopened their fire upon the insolent British frigate. Shot screamed all round them. Hill was demanding they haul further offshore and Rogers was asking for permission to re-engage. He nodded at both officers.

'Very well, gentlemen, if you would be so kind.' He turned for a final look at the man on the white horse, but he had vanished, obscured by the glittering train of his staff as they galloped away. 'The gale has done our work for us,' he muttered to himself, 'for the time being.'

Chapter Eight *July–August 1804*

Stalemate

'Will you damned lubbers put your backs into it and *pull*!'

Midshipman Lord Walmsley surveyed the launch's crew with amiable contempt and waved a scented handkerchief under his nose. He stood in the stern sheets of the big boat in breeches and shirt, trying to combat the airless heat of the day and urge his oarsmen to more strenuous efforts. Out on either beam Midshipmen Dutfield and Wickham each had one of the quarterboats and all three were tethered to the *Antigone*. At the ends of their towropes the boats slewed and splashed, each oarsman dipping his oar into the ripples of his last stroke, so that their efforts seemed utterly pointless. The enemy lugger after which they were struggling lay on the distant horizon.

Walmsley regarded his companion with a superior amusement. Sitting with his little hand on the big tiller was Gillespy, supposedly under Walmsley's tutoring and utterly unable to exhort the men.

'It is essential, Gillespy, to encourage greater effort from these fellows,' his lordship lectured, indicating the sun-burnt faces that puffed and grunted, two to a thwart along the length of the launch. 'You can't do it by squeaking at 'em and you can't do it by asking them. You have to bellow at the damned knaves. Call 'em poxy laggards, lazy land-lubbing scum; then they get so God-damned angry that they pull those bloody oar looms harder. Don't you see? Eh?'

'Yes . . . my Lord,' replied the unfortunate Gillespy who was quite under Walmsley's thumb, isolated as he was in the launch.

The lesson in leadership was greeted with a few weary grins from the men at the oars, but few liked Mr Walmsley and those that were not utterly uncaring from the monotony of their task and being constantly abused by the senior midshipman of their division, resented his arrogance. Of all the men in the boat there was one upon whom Walmsley's arrogant sarcasm acted like a spark upon powder.

At stroke oar William Waller laboured as an able seaman. A year earlier he had been master of the Greenland whale-ship *Conqueror*, a member of the Trinity House of Kingston-upon-Hull and engaged in a profitable trade in whale-oil, whale-bone and the smuggling of furs from Greenland to France where they were used to embellish the gaudy uniforms of the soldiers they had so recently been cannonading upon the cliffs of Boulogne. It had been this illicit trade that had reduced him to his present circumstances. He had been caught red-handed engaged in a treasonable trade with a French outpost on the coast of Greenland by Captain Nathaniel Drinkwater.

Although well aware that he could have been hanged for what he had done, Waller was a weak and cunning character. That he had escaped with his life due to Drinkwater's clemency had at first seemed fortunate, but as time passed his present humiliations contrasted unfavourably with his former status. His guilt began to diminish in his own eyes as he transferred responsibility for it to his partner who had been architect of the scheme and had died for it. The greater blame lay with the dead man and Waller was, in his own mind, increasingly a victim of regrettable circumstances. When he had been turned among them, many of *Melusine*'s hands had been aware of his activities. They had shunned him and despised him, but Waller had held his peace and survived, being a first-rate seaman. But he had kept his own counsel, a loner among the gregarious seamen of his mess, and long silences had made him morose, driven him to despair at times. He had been saved by the transfer to the *Antigone* and a bigger ship's company. Among the pressed and drafted men who had increased the size of the ship's company to form the complement of a frigate, there had been those who knew nothing of his past. He had taught a few ignorant landsmen the rudiments of seamanship and there were those among the frigate's company that called him friend. He had drawn renewed confidence from this change in his circumstances. He let it be known among his new companions that he was well-acquainted with the business of navigation and that many of *Antigone*'s junior officers were wholly without knowledge of their trade. In particular Lord Walmsley's studied contempt for the men combined with his rank and ignorance to make him an object of the most acute detestation to Waller.

On this particular morning, as Waller hauled wearily at the heavy loom of the stroke oar, his hatred of Walmsley reached its crisis. He muttered under his breath loudly enough for Walmsley and Gillespy to hear.

'Did you say something, Waller?'

Waller watched the blade of his oar swing forward, ignoring his lordship's question.

'I asked you what you said, Waller, damn you!'

Waller continued to pull steadily, gazing vaguely at the horizon.

'He didn't say nothing, sir,' the man occupying the same thwart said.

'I didn't ask you,' snapped Walmsley, fixing his eyes on Waller. 'This lubber, Mr Gillespy, needs watching. He was formerly the *skipper* of a damned whale-*boat* . . .' Walmsley laid a disparaging emphasis on the two words, 'a bloody merchant master who thought he could defy the King. And now God damn him he thinks he can defy you and I . . .'

Waller stopped rowing. The man behind him bumped into his stationary back and there was confusion in the boat.

'Give way, damn you!' Walmsley ordered, his voice low. Beside him little Gillespy was trembling. The oarsmen stopped rowing and the launch lost way.

'Go to the devil, you poxed young whoreson!' Waller snarled through clenched teeth. A murmur of approval at Waller's defiance ran through the boat's crew.

'Why you God-damn bastard!' Walmsley shoved Gillespy aside and pulled the heavy tiller from the rudder stock. In a single swipe he brought the piece of ash crashing into the side of Waller's skull, knocking him senseless, his grip on the oar-loom weakened and it swept up and struck him under the chin as he slumped into the bottom of the boat.

The expression on the faces of the launch's crew were of disbelief. Astern of them the towline drooped slackly in the water.

Drinkwater sat in the cool of his cabin re-reading a letter he had recently received from his wife Elizabeth, to see if he had covered all the points raised in it in his reply. The isolation of command had made the writing of his private journal and the committing of his thoughts to his letters an important and pleasurable part of his daily routine. Cruising so close to the English coast meant that Keith's ships were in regular contact with home via the admiral's dispatch-vessels. In addition to fresh vegetables and mail, these fast craft kept the frigates well supplied with newspapers and gossip. The hired cutter *Admiral Mitchell* had made such a delivery the day before.

He laid the letter down and picked up the new steel pen Elizabeth had sent him, dipping it experimentally in the ink-pot and regarding its rigid nib with suspicion. He pulled the half-filled sheet of paper towards him and resumed writing, not liking the awkward scratch and splatter of the nib compared with his goose-quill, but aware that he would be expected to reply using the new-fangled gift.

Our presence in the Channel keeps Boney and his troops in their camps. Last week he held a review, lining his men up so that they presented an appearance several miles long . . .

He paused, not wishing to alarm Elizabeth, though from her letters he knew of the arrangements each parish was making to raise an invasion alarm and call out the militia and yeomanry.

It is said that Boney himself went afloat in a gilded barge and that he dismissed Admiral Bruix for attempting to draw a sword on him when he protested the folly of trying an embarkation in the teeth of a gale. What the truth of these rumours is I do not know, but it is certain that many men were drowned and some score or so of barges wrecked.

He picked up his pen and finished the letter, then he sanded, folded and sealed it. Mullender came into the cabin and, at a nod from Drinkwater, poured him a glass of wine. He leaned back contented. Beyond the cabin windows the Channel stretched blue, calm and glorious under sunshine. Through the stern windows the reflected light poured, dancing off the deckhead and bulkheads of the cabin and falling on the portraits of his family that hung opposite. He became utterly lost in the contemplation of his family.

His reverie was interrupted by a shouting on deck and a hammering at his cabin door.

Drinkwater sat in his best uniform, flanked by Lieutenant Rogers and Lieutenant Fraser. The black shapes of their three hats sat on the baize tablecloth, inanimate indications of formality. Before them, uncovered, stood Midshipman Lord Walmsley. Drinkwater looked at the notes he had written after examining Midshipman Gillespy. The boy had been terrified but Drinkwater and his two lieutenants had obtained the truth out of him, unwilling to make matters worse by having to consult individual members of the boat's crew. Gillespy had withdrawn now, let out before Walmsley was summoned to hear the surgeon's report.

Drinkwater had once entertained some hopes of the midshipman but this episode disgusted him. He himself had no personal feelings towards Waller beyond a desire to see him behave as any other pressed seaman on board and to see him treated as such. Walmsley knew of Waller's previous circumstances and Drinkwater assumed that this had led to his contemptuous behaviour.

He looked up at the young man. Walmsley did not appear unduly concerned about the formality of the present proceedings. Drinkwater recollected his acquaintance with Camelford and wondered if Camelford's presence had set a portfire to this latent insolence and arrogance of Walmsley.

The silence of waiting hung heavily in the cabin. Following the incident in the launch, Drinkwater had had the boats hoisted inboard. Their progress to the west was no longer necessary since their chase, a lugger holding a breeze inshore, had long ago disappeared to the south-west. There was a knock at the door.

'Enter!'

'Come in, Mr Lallo. Pray take a seat and tell us what is the condition of Waller.'

The surgeon, a quiet, middle-aged man whose only vice seemed to be a messy reliance upon Sharrow's snuff, seated himself, sniffed and looked at Drinkwater. His didactic manner prompted Drinkwater to add: 'In words we all comprehend, if you please, Mr Lallo.'

Mr Lallo sniffed again. 'Well, sir,' he began, casting a meaningful look at the back of Lord Walmsley, 'the man Waller has taken a severe and violent blow with a heavy object . . .'

'A tiller,' put in Rogers impatiently.

'Just so, Mr Rogers. With a tiller, which has caused an aneurism . . . a distortion of the arteries and interrupted the flow of blood to the cere . . . to the brain . . .'

'You mean Waller's had a stroke?'

Lallo looked resentfully at Rogers and nodded. 'In effect, yes. He is reduced to the condition of an idiot.'

Drinkwater felt the particular meaning of the word in its real form. That Waller and his treason were no longer of any consequence struck him as an irony, but that a midshipman should have reduced him to that state by an over-indulgence of his authority was a reflection of his own powers of command. Drinkwater did not share Earl St Vincent's conviction that the men should respect a midshipman's coat if the object within was not worthy of their duty. He had always considered the training of his midshipmen a prime responsibility. With Walmsley he had failed. It did not matter that he had inherited his lordship from another captain. Nor, he reflected, could he hope that the processes of naval justice might redress something of the balance. The arrogance of well-connected midshipmen was nothing new in the navy, nor was the whitewashing of their guilt by courts-martial.

'Thank you, Mr Lallo. You do not entertain any hopes for Waller's eventual recovery then?'

'I doubt it, Captain Drinkwater. I believe him to have been a not unintelligent man, sir. He might be fit to attend the heads for the remainder of his days, though he is like to be afflicted with ataxia.' Lallo glared at the first lieutenant, defying him to require a further explanation.

'Thank you, Mr Lallo. That will be all.'

After the surgeon had left, Drinkwater turned his full attention upon Walmsley.

'Well, Mr Walmsley. Do you have anything to say?'

'I did my duty, sir. The man was insolent. I regret . . .'

'You *regret*! You regret hitting him so *hard*, I suppose. Eh?'

Walmsley swallowed. 'Yes, sir.'

'Lord Walmsley,' Drinkwater said, using the title for the first time, 'you are a young man with considerable ability, aware of your position in society and clearly contemptuous of your present surroundings. It is my intention to punish you as you are a midshipman. What you do after that as a gentleman is a matter for your own sense of honour. You may go now.'

'May I not know my punishment?'

'No. You will be informed. Whatever you appear at the gaming tables, you are, sir, only a midshipman on board this ship!'

Walmsley stood uncertainly and Drinkwater saw, for the first time, signs that the young man's confidence was weakening. There was a trembling about the mouth and a brightening of the eyes.

Walmsley turned away and the three officers watched him leave the cabin.

Next to him Drinkwater heard Lieutenant Fraser expel his breath with relief. Drinkwater turned to him. 'Well, Mr Fraser, it is customary upon these occasions to ask the junior officer present to give his opinion first.'

'Court-martial, sir . . .'

'But upon what charge, Fraser, for God's sake?' put in Rogers intemperately and Drinkwater smelt the drink on him. 'No, sir, he's too much influence for that. I doubt that'd do any of us any good.' Rogers spoke with heavy emphasis and Drinkwater raised an eyebrow. 'Besides he's done no more than many, and Waller was an insolent bastard at times. My advice, sir, is keep it in the ship.'

'Not a bluidy mastheading, for God's sake, sir,' expostulated Fraser who was showing signs of ability and perception far exceeding the first lieutenant's.

'No, gentlemen,' Drinkwater cut in. 'Thank you both for your opinions, so succinctly put,' he added drily. 'You are both right. The matter should not go outside the ship, but I do not hold with officers abusing their powers. Whatever Walmsley's expectations he is but a midshipman, and a midshipman going to the bad. It is not my intention to encourage him further. As for his punishment, we shall marry him to the gunner's daughter.'

Drinkwater rose from the table and took up his hat. The two lieutenants scrambled to their feet.

'Pipe all hands to witness punishment, Mr Rogers!'

Drinkwater emerged on deck some few minutes later, the punishment book in his hand. It contained few entries since Drinkwater was reluctant to administer corporal punishment for any but serious offences and had adopted such measures as stoppage of grog and the wearing of a collar as a public humiliation, finding them much more appropriate and effective for the trivial offences usually committed. This morning, however, would be different.

He took his place at the head of the officers who stood in a half-circle, their swords by their sides. Behind them in three ranks, Mount's marines were paraded, a glittering assembly of scarlet, white and steel. The men were crowded in the waist, over the boats and the hammock nettings in the gangways. Word had got about that Walmsley was to be punished and the hands were in a state of barely suppressed glee. In the circumstances and in view of the offender's station, Drinkwater called him forward and read the usually curtailed preamble with formal gravity.

'Silence there!' barked Rogers as the hands murmured their delight when Walmsley stepped uncertainly forward. He had lost his cocksure attitude and was clearly very apprehensive. It occurred to Drinkwater that Walmsley might have imagined such a thing as this could never happen to him, that it was something that affected others not of his standing.

'Mr Walmsley, the enquiry held by myself and the officers of His Britannic Majesty's frigate under my command have examined and condemned your conduct this forenoon and found you guilty of behaviour both scandalous and oppressive. This crime, not being capital, shall be punished according to the Custom of the Navy under the Thirty-Sixth Article of War, as enacted by the King's most excellent Majesty, by and with the advice and consent of', Drinkwater paused and fixed his eyes on the abject Walmsley, 'the Lords Spiritual and Temporal and Commons in Parliament assembled.

'You are, Mr Walmsley, to be flogged over the breech of a gun.' He snapped the book closed. 'Mr Comley!' The boatswain stepped forward. 'Two dozen strokes, sir. And lay 'em on!'

Comley put his hand on Walmsley's shoulder and pushed him forward until he stood by the breech of one of the quarterdeck guns. A shove sent the young man over the cannon and Comley drew back his rattan. In the next few minutes the boatswain did not spare his victim.

Captain Drinkwater continued walking the windward side of the quarterdeck long after sunset. The blazing riot of scarlet had faded by degrees to a pale lemon yellow and finally to a duck-egg blue that remained slightly luminous as the stars in their constellations blazed overhead. The air remained warm although there was enough of a breeze to enable *Antigone* to be steered under her topsails, and she cruised slowly southwards.

Drinkwater thought over the events of the day, distressed by the incident in the boats and aware that he had dealt with it in the only just way. Walmsley had begged an interview with him which he had refused, and the sight of Waller lying inert in the care of Mr

Lallo convinced him that he was right, that the longer the young man felt his punishment the better. Drinkwater sighed, worrying about the effect on the rest of the ship's company. The internal business of the ship was oppressing him, already the tedium of blockade, even in this relatively independent form of cruising, was making him irritable and the ship's company fractious. The fine summer weather and apparent inactivity of the French seemed to lend a quality of futility to their movements, although logic proclaimed the necessity of their presence, along with the other independent frigates and all the vessels of the various blockading squadrons. There was a quality of stalemate in the war and it was difficult to determine what would happen next. It seemed to Drinkwater that the equation was balanced, that even the weather, usually so impartial a player in the game, had assimilated some of this inertia and put no demands on his own skill or the energies of his people. It seemed an odd contrast to the previous summer when the changeable moods of the Greenland Sea kept them constantly about the business of survival.

He found himself longing for action. *Antigone* had missed the bombardment of Havre in late July and seen no more than some pedestrian chases after small fry which had achieved little. At the beginning of August had come the news that Admiral Ganteaume had attempted a break-out from Brest, but had turned back; so that the equation, showing for a moment signs of imbalance, had had its equilibrium re-established.

Drinkwater heard seven bells struck. Eleven o'clock. It was time he took himself below. Mr Quilhampton, who had been confined to the lee quarterdeck in the down-draught from the main-topsail for his entire watch, looked after the retreating figure and clucked his tongue sympathetically.

'Poor fellow,' he muttered to himself, taking up the weather side and ordering Gillespy to heave the log, 'fretting over a pair of ne'er-do-wells!'

Chapter Nine *August–December 1804*

Orders

'All hands, ahoy! All hands, reef topsails!'

Drinkwater staggered as *Antigone* slammed into a sea. A burst of spray exploded over her weather bow and whipped aft, catching the officers on the quarterdeck in the face to induce the painful wind-ache in their cheeks. The equinox had found them at last and Drinkwater experienced a pang of sudden savage joy. He had been warned of the onset of the gale by the increasing ache in his neck and shoulder that pressaged damp weather. During the long, warm, dry days of that exceptional summer he had hardly been reminded of his wound, but now the illusions were gone, stripped aside in that first wet streak of winter that incommoded his officers and afforded him his amusement.

He clapped his hand to his hat as a gust more violent than hitherto laid the ship over. 'Mr Rogers!'

'Sir?'

'We'll reef in stays, Mr Rogers. See what the hands can do!' He saw Rogers's look of incredulity and grinned as the first lieutenant turned away.

'Hands, tack ship and reef topsails in one!' bawled Rogers through his speaking trumpet. It amused Drinkwater to see the variety of reactions his order provoked. Hill caught his eye with a twinkle, Quilhampton grinned in anticipation, while Lieutenant Fraser, still considering Drinkwater something of an enigma, looked suitably quizzical. The hands milled at their mustering points.

'Man the rigging! 'Way aloft, topmen!'

Drinkwater crossed the deck and stood by the helm. 'Keep her off the wind a half point, quartermaster.'

'Aye, aye, sir.'

Drinkwater felt the thrill of anticipation. There was no real need to put the ship upon the other tack at this precise moment, but the evolution of going about and reefing the topsails at the same moment was an opportunity for a smart frigate to demonstrate the proficiency of her ship's company. By the eagerness with which the topmen lay aloft, some of this had communicated itself to them. One could always count on an appeal to a professional seaman's skill.

'Deck there!' The masthead look-out was hailing. 'Sail four points on the weather bow, sir. Looks like a cutter!'

Drinkwater acknowledged the hail, his sense of satisfaction growing. They now had a reason for tacking and an audience, and Fraser was looking at Drinkwater as if wondering how he had known of the presence of the other vessel.

'Down helm!'

Next to Drinkwater the four men at the double wheel spun the spokes through their fingers. *Antigone* came upright as she turned into the wind, the rush of her forward advance slowed rapidly and the scream of the wind across her deck diminished.

'Clew down topsails! Mainsail haul! Trice up and lay out!'

This was the nub of the manoeuvre, for the main and mizen yards were hauled with the topmen upon them at the same moment as the topsail yards were lowered on their halliards, the braces tended, the bowlines slacked off and the reef-pendants hauled up. Apart from Drinkwater's orders to the helmsmen and the general commands to the deck conveying the progress of the manoeuvre, there was a host of subsidiary instructions given by the subordinate officers and petty officers at their stations at the pin rails, the braces, the halliards and in the bunts of the topsails aloft.

As the yards were lowered, the studding sail booms lifted and the main and mizen topsails flogged, folding upwards as the reef-pendants did their work. *Antigone* continued her turn, heeling over to her new course as the fore topsail came aback, spinning her head with increasing speed.

'Midships and meet her.' Drinkwater peered forward and upwards where he could see the foretopmen having the worst time of it, trying to reef their big topsail while it was still full of wind.

'Man the head-braces! Halliards there!'

Rogers watched for the hand signals of the mates and midshipmen aloft to tell him the earings were secured and the reefpoints passed round the reduced portions of each topsail. Meanwhile *Antigone* crabbed awkwardly to leeward.

'Hoist away topsails! Haul all!'

Aloft the topsails rose again, stretched and reset, assuming the flat curve of sails close hauled against the wind as the forebraces hauled round their yards parallel with those on the main and mizen masts. On deck the halliards were sweated tight and the bowlines secured against the shivering of the weather leeches, belayed ropes were being coiled down and the topmen were sliding down the backstays, chaffing each other competitively. *Antigone* stopped crabbing and began to drive forward again on the new tack. She butted into a sea and the spray came flying aft over the other bow.

'Steady,' Drinkwater ordered the helmsmen, peering into the binnacle at the compass bowl. 'Course Nor'west by west.'

'Steady, sir. Course Nor'west by west it is, sir.'

Rogers came aft and touched his hat. He was grinning back at Drinkwater. 'Ship put about on the larboard tack, sir, and all three topsails reefed in one.'

'Very creditable, Mr Rogers. Now you may pipe "Up spirits" and let us see what this cutter wants.'

Drinkwater glanced through the stern windows where the *Admiral Mitchell* danced in their wake. The lieutenant in command of her had luffed neatly under their lee quarter half an hour ago and skilfully tossed a packet of dispatches on board from her chains. She now lay waiting for him to digest the news they contained. He studied the written orders for some moments, put aside the private letters and newspapers, and summoned Lord Walmsley. To Drinkwater's regret Walmsley had not offered to resign, though Drinkwater knew he could afford to and had therefore taken steps to settle the midshipman elsewhere. The young man knocked and entered the cabin.

'Sir?' Walmsley had been rigidly formal since his punishment. The experience had been deeply engraved upon his consciousness, yet Drinkwater sensed beneath this formality a deep and abiding resentment. Walmsley was still not convinced that he had erred.

'Mr Walmsley, I have for some time been considering your future. I have been successful in obtaining for you another berth. Rear-Admiral Louis who has, as you know, hoisted his flag aboard the *Leopard* to assist Lord Keith in the Strait of Dover, has agreed to take you on board.'

Walmsley had clearly not expected such a transfer and Drinkwater hoped that he would be appreciative of it. 'I hope,' he added, 'that you are sensible of the honour done you by Admiral Louis. No word of your conduct has been communicated to the *Leopard*. You will join with a clean slate. Do you understand?'

'Sir.'

'Very good. We will transfer you to the cutter as soon as the sea allows a boat to be launched. You may pack your traps.'

Drinkwater stared after the midshipman. He felt he had failed to make an impression on the youth and he feared that Walmsley would see that his sending him to a flagship only indicated his own lack of interest or influence.

It was two days before Walmsley departed, two days in which *Antigone* worked slowly south and west in obedience to her new orders. The formation of Rear-Admiral Louis's squadron had released her from her duties in the Channel and she was sent out to join Cornwallis and the Channel Fleet. Drinkwater greeted this news with mixed feelings. The close contact with the shore would be broken now, the arrival of mail less frequent and he would feel his isolation more. Nor was he very sure of the opinion Cornwallis had formed of him when they had last met. But his puritan soul derived that strange satisfaction from the anticipation of an arduous duty, and in his innermost heart he welcomed the change and the challenge.

It was two days, too, before he found the time to read the newspapers and mail. The most electrifying news for the officers and men of the *Antigone* was that war with Spain seemed imminent. Since the end of the Peace of Amiens 'neutral' Spanish ports had been shamelessly used by French warships. Their crews had enjoyed rights of passage through the country to join and leave their ships, and Spain had done everything to aid and abet her powerful and intimidating neighbour short of an actual declaration of war against Great Britain. Now the new British government had precipitated a crisis by sending out a flying squadron of four frigates to intercept a similar number of Spanish men-o'-war returning from Montevideo with over a million and a quarter in specie. Opposed by equal and not overwhelming force, the Spanish admiral, Don Joseph Bustamente, had defended the honour of his flag and in the ensuing action the Spanish frigate *Mercedes* had blown up with her crew and passengers. Although no immediate declaration of war had come from Madrid, it was hourly anticipated, and Drinkwater immediately calculated that the addition of the Spanish fleet to the French would augment it by over thirty ships of the line. They were superb ships too; one, the *Santissima Trinidad* had four gun-decks and was the greatest ship in the world.

It was while reflecting on the possible consequences of Mr Pitt's aggressive new policy, and on whether it would enable the French Emperor to attempt invasion, that his eye fell upon another piece of news; a mere snippet of no apparent importance. Thomas Pitt, second Baron Camelford, had been killed in a duel near Holland House. The circumstances of the affair were confused, but what was of interest to Drinkwater was that there was some veiled and unsubstantiated claims in the less respectable papers that Camelford's death had been engineered by French agents.

PART TWO

Break-Out

"I beg to inform your Lordship that the Port of Toulon has never been blockaded by me: quite the reverse – every opportunity has been offered to the Enemy to put to sea . . .'

NELSON TO THE LORD MAYOR OF LONDON August 1804

'Sail, do not lose a moment, and with my squadrons reunited enter the Channel. England is ours. We are ready and embarked. Appear for twenty-four hours, and all will be ended.'

NAPOLEON TO ADMIRAL VILLENEUVE August 1805

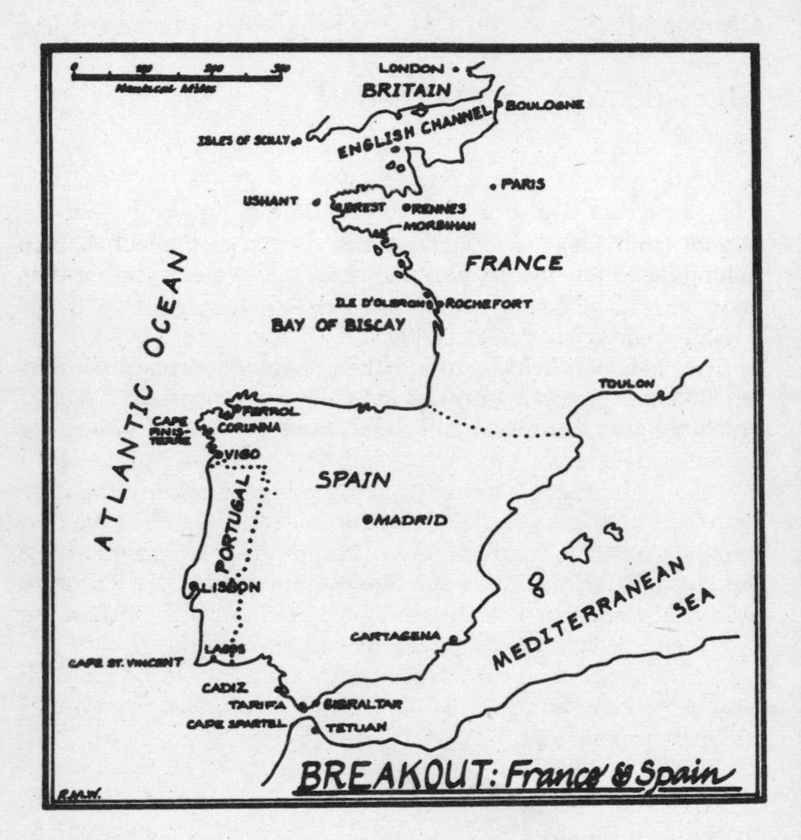
LONDON
BRITAIN
BOULOGNE
ENGLISH CHANNEL
ISLES OF SCILLY
PARIS
USHANT
BREST
RENNES
MORBIHAN
FRANCE
ATLANTIC OCEAN
ILE D'OLERON
ROCHEFORT
BAY OF BISCAY
TOULON
CAPE FINIS-TERRE
FERROL
CORUNNA
VIGO
SPAIN
PORTUGAL
MADRID
LISBON
MEDITERRANEAN SEA
CARTAGENA
LAGOS
CAPE ST. VINCENT
CADIZ
TARIFA
GIBRALTAR
CAPE SPARTEL
TETUAN
BREAKOUT: France & Spain
R.M.W.

Chapter Ten *January 1805*

The Rochefort Squadron

'Signal from Flag, sir.' Midshipman Wickham's cheerful face poking round the door was an affront to Drinkwater's seediness as he woke from a doze.

'Eh? Well? What o'clock is it?'

'Four bells, sir,' Wickham said, then, seeing the captain's apparent look of incomprehension added, 'in the afternoon, sir'.

'Thank you, Mr Wickham,' said Drinkwater drily, now fully awake. 'I shall be up directly.'

They had received and acknowledged the signal by the time Drinkwater reached the quarterdeck. Lieutenant Fraser handed him the slate as he touched his hat. Drinkwater had grown to like the ruddy Scotsman with his silent manner and dry humour. Drinkwater read the message scribbled on the slate. Midshipman Wickham was already copying it out into the Signal Log.

'Very well, Mr Fraser, we will close on *Doris* and see if Campbell has any specific orders for us. In the meantime watch the admiral for further signals.'

'Aye, sir.'

Drinkwater eased his right shoulder. Of all the stations to be consigned to during the winter months, the west coast of France with its damp procession of gales was possibly the worst for his wound. He drew the cloak closer around him and began to pace the deck, from the hance to the taffrail, casting an eye across the grey, white-streaked waves that separated him from the rest of the squadron. He watched the half-dozen ships of Rear-Admiral Sir Thomas Graves jockeying into line ahead, their yards braced up on the larboard tack as they began to move away to the north-north-westwards and the shelter of Quiberon Bay where they were to take in stores and water.

The two frigates *Doris* and *Antigone*, being late arrivals at this outpost of the Channel Fleet, were left to watch Rear-Admiral

Missiessy's ships anchored off Rochefort, in the shelter of the Basque Roads. Drinkwater turned his attention to the eastwards. On the horizon he could make out the blue blur of the Ile d'Oléron behind which the French squadron was anchored, comfortably secure under the lee of the island, the approach of its mooring blocked by batteries. He had reconnoitred them several times, sailing *Antigone* under the guns of the French batteries and carrying out manoeuvres between Oléron and the surrounding islands. It was, he admitted to himself a piece of *braggadocio;* but it was good for the men, enabling them to demonstrate before the eyes of the French their abilities. Best of all, it broke the monotony of blockade duty. They had received fire from the land batteries and from the floating battery the enemy had anchored off Oléron which mounted huge heavy mortars and long cannon of the heaviest calibres, together with furnaces for heating shot. Beyond the batteries they had countered the ships of Missiessy's squadron anchored in two neat lines. They appeared so securely moored that their situation seemed permanent, but Drinkwater knew that this was an illusion. There were French squadrons like Missiessy's in all the major French and Spanish ports, joined now, since the declaration of war against Great Britain, by the splendid ships of the Spanish navy. Nor were they entirely supine. Missiessy had sortied in the previous August, only being turned back by the appearance of Vice-Admiral Sir Robert Calder with a stronger force. From the Texel to Toulon the naval forces of the enemy were now united under the imperial eagle of France. Against this mass of shipping the British blockade was maintained unrelentingly. The ships of Keith, Cornwallis, Calder, Collingwood and Nelson watched each of the enemy ports, detaching squadrons like that of Graves's to close up the gaps.

Now that Graves had been driven off his station for want of the very necessaries of life itself, the Rochefort squadron of Missiessy was checked by the rather feeble presence of a pair of 36-gun frigates, *Antigone* and *Doris*.

'*Doris* signalling, sir.'

'Ah, I rather thought she might.' Drinkwater waited patiently while his people did their work and deciphered the numerical signal streaming from *Doris*'s lee yardarms. As senior officer it was up to Campbell of the *Doris* to decide how best to carry out their duties. Drinkwater listened to the dialogue between Wickham and Frey as the import of Campbell's intentions became clear.

'One-two-two.'

'Permission to part company . . .'

'Eight-seven-three.'

'To . . .'

'Seven-six-six.'

'See . . .'

'Two-four-nine.'

'Enemy . . . er, "Permission to part company to see enemy", sir.'

'Very well, Mr Frey. Thank you. You may lay me a course, Mr Fraser. Shake out the fore-course, if you please, let us at least give the impression of attending to our duty with alacrity.'

'Verra well, sir.' Fraser grinned back at the captain. He was beginning to like this rather stern Englishman.

Drinkwater woke in the darkness of pre-dawn with the conviction that something was wrong. He listened intently, fully awake, for some sound in the fabric of the ship that would declare its irregularity. There was nothing. They had reduced sail at the onset of the early January darkness and hove-to. Their leeway during the night should have put them between Oléron and the Ile de Ré at dawn, in a perfect position to reconnoitre Missiessy's anchorage with all the daylight of the short January day to beat offshore again. The westerly wind had dropped after sunset and it was inconceivable that their leeway had been excessive, even allowing for the tide.

Then it occurred to him that the reason for his awakening was something entirely different; his shoulder had stopped aching. He smiled to himself in the darkness, stretched luxuriously and rolled over, composing himself for another hour's sleep before duty compelled him to rise. And then suddenly he was wide awake, sitting bolt upright in his cot. An instant later he was feeling for his breeches, stockings and shoes. He stumbled across the cabin in his haste, fumbling for the clean shirt that Mullender should have left. If his shoulder was not aching it meant the air was drier. And if the air was drier it meant only one thing, the wind was hauling to the eastward. He pulled on his coat, wound a muffler around his neck to suppress the quinsy he had felt coming on for several days and, pulling on his cloak, went on deck.

The dozing sentry jerked to attention at this untimely appearance of the captain. As he emerged, Drinkwater knew immediately his instinct was right. Above the tracery of the mastheads the stars were coldly brilliant, the cloudy overcast of yesterday had vanished. A figure detached itself from the group around the binnacle. It was Quilhampton.

'Morning, sir. A change in the weather. Dead calm for the last half-hour and colder.'

'Why did you not call me, Mr Q?' asked Drinkwater with sudden asperity.

'Sir? But sir, your written orders said to call you if the wind freshened . . . I supposed that you were concerned with an increase in our leeway, sir, not . . . not a calm, sir. The ship is quite safe, sir.'

'Damn it, sir, don't patronise me!'

'I beg pardon, sir.' Even in the darkness Quilhampton was obviously crestfallen.

Drinkwater took a turn or two up and down the deck. He realised that the wind had not yet got up, that his apprehensions were not yet fully justified. 'Mr Q!'

'Sir?'

'Forgive my haste, Mr Q.'

'With pleasure, sir. But I assure you, sir, that I would have called you the instant I thought that the ship was in any danger.'

'It is not the ship that concerns me, James. It is the enemy!'

'The enemy, sir?'

'Yes, the enemy. In an hour from now the wind will be easterly and in two hours from now Missiessy, if he's half the man I think him to be, will be ordering his ships to sea. Now d'you understand?'

'Yes . . . yes I do. I'll have the watch cast loose the t'gallants ready to set all sail the moment it's light, sir.'

'That's the spirit. And I'll go below and break my fast. I've a feeling that this will be a long day.'

Over his spartan breakfast of skillygolee, coffee and toast, Drinkwater thought over the idea that had germinated from the seeds sown during his extraordinary conversation with Mr Pitt. He knew that he would not consciously have reasoned a grand strategy for the French by himself, but that game of shuttlecock with ideas at Walmer had produced the only convincing answer to the conundrum of Napoleon's intentions. It was clear that the French would not move their vast armies across the Channel until they had a fleet in the vicinity. Now, with Admiral Ver Huel's Dutch ships joining a Combined Franco–Spanish fleet, the preposterous element of such a grand design was diminishing. Drinkwater did not attempt to unravel the reasoning behind Pitt's deliberate provocation of Spain. It seemed only to undermine the solid foundation of Britain's defence based upon the Channel Fleet off Brest and the understanding that, if the enemy they blockaded escaped, then every British squadron fell back upon the chops of the Channel. In this grand strategy there still remained the factor of the unexpected. Navigationally the mouth of the Channel was difficult to make, particularly when obstructed by an enemy fleet. For the French Commander-in-Chief a passage round Scotland offered nothing but advantages: prevailing fair winds, a less impeded navigation, the element of surprise and the greater difficulty for the British of watching his movements. In addition the fleets of other nations could be more readily added. Russia, for instance, still not wholly committed to defying the new Emperor of France, perhaps the Danes, and certainly the Dutch. Worst of all was the consideration that the enemy might be in the Strait of Dover while the British waited for them off the Isles of Scilly. And the only place from which to launch such an attack was the West Indies, where the French might rendezvous, blown there by favourable winds to recuperate and revictual from friendly islands.

Nathaniel Drinkwater was not given to flights of wild imagination. He was too aware of the difficulties and dangers that beset every seaman. But during his long years of service intuition and cogent reasoning had served him well. He was reminded of the weary weeks of stalking the Dutch before Camperdown and how conviction of the accuracy of his forebodings had sustained him then. He called Mullender to clear the table and while he waited for the wind to rise he opened his journal, eager to get down this train of logic which had stemmed from some dim perception that lingered from his strange awakening.

8th January, he wrote, and added carefully, aware that he had still not become accustomed to the new year, *1805. Off the Ile d'Oléron in a calm. Woke with great apprehension that the day . . .* He paused, scratched out the last word and added: *year is pregnant with great events . . .*

'If you are going to record your prophecies,' he muttered to himself, pleased with his improving technique with Elizabeth's pen, 'you might as well make 'em big ones.'

It seems to me that a descent upon the British Isles might best be achieved by the French in first making a rendezvous . . .

But he got no further. There was a knock at the cabin door and Midshipman Wickham reappeared.

'Lieutenant Quilhampton's compliments, sir, and the wind's freshening from the east.'

The wind did not keep its early promise. By noon *Antigone* lay becalmed off the Ile d'Oléron, in full view of the French anchorage and with the tide setting her down towards the Basque Road; at one in the afternoon she had been brought to her anchor and Drinkwater was studying the enemy through his glass from the elevation of the mizen top. Beside him little Mr Gillespy was making notes at the captain's dictation.

'The usual force, Mr Gillespy: *Majestueux,* four seventy-fours, the three heavy frigates and two brig-corvettes. Nothing unusual in that, eh?' he said kindly.

'No, sir,' the boy squeaked, somewhat nonplussed at finding himself aloft with the captain. Gillespy had not supposed captains ascended rigging. It did not seem part of their function.

'But what makes today of more than passing interest,' Drinkwater continued, mouthing his words sideways as he continued to stare through the glass, 'is that they are taking aboard stores . . . d'you have that, Mr Gillespy?'

'Stores,' the boy wrote carefully, 'yes, sir.'

'Troops . . .'

'Troops . . . yes, sir.'

'And, Mr Gillespy,' Drinkwater paused. The cloudless sky let sunlight pour down upon the stretch of blue water between the green hills of the island and the main. The brilliantly clear air made his task easy and the sunlight glanced off the dull breeches of cannon. There was no doubt in Drinkwater's mind that Missiessy was going to break out to the West Indies and take back those sugar islands over which Britain and France had been squabbling for two generations. 'Artillery, Mr Gillespy, artillery . . . one "t" and two "ll"s.'

He closed his glass with a snap and turned his full attention to the boy. He was not so very many years older than his own son, Richard.

'What d'you suppose we'd better do now, eh?'

'Tell the admiral, sir?'

'First class, my boy.' Drinkwater swung himself over the edge of the top and reached for the futtocks with his feet. He began to descend, pausing as his head came level with the deck of the top. Gillespy regarded the captain's apparently detached head with surprise.

'I think, Mr Gillespy, that in the coming months you may see things to tell your grandchildren about.'

Midshipman Gillespy stared at the empty air where the captain's head had just been. He was quite bewildered. The idea of ever having grandchildren had never occurred to him.

The wind freshened again at dusk, settling to a steady breeze and bringing even colder air off the continent. *Antigone* stood offshore in search of *Doris* and, at dawn on the 9th, Drinkwater spoke to Campbell, informing him of the preparations being made by the French. Two hours later *Antigone* was alone apart from the distant topgallants of *Doris* in the north, as Campbell made off to warn Graves.

'Full and bye, Mr Hill, let us stop up that gap. I mislike those cloud banks building up over the land. We may not be able to stop the Frogs getting out but, by God, we must not lose touch with 'em.'

'Indeed not, sir.'

The wind continued light and steady throughout the day and at dawn on the 10th they were joined by the schooner *Felix* commanded by Lieutenant Richard Bourne, brother of Drinkwater's late lieutenant of the *Melusine*. Bourne announced that he had met Campbell and told him of Graves's whereabouts. Campbell had ordered *Felix* to stand by *Antigone* and act under Drinkwater's directions as a dispatch-boat in the event of Graves not turning up in time to catch Missiessy. Having an independent means of communicating such intelligence as he might glean took a great deal of weight off Drinkwater's mind. He had only to hang onto Missiessy's skirts now, and with such a smart ship and a crew tuned to the perfection expected of every British cruiser, he entertained few worries upon that score.

As the day wore on, the wind began to increase from the east and by nightfall was a fresh breeze. Drinkwater stretched out on his cot, wrapped in his cloak, and slept fitfully. An hour before dawn he was awakened and struggled on deck in a rising gale. As daylight grew it revealed a sky grey with lowering cloud. It was bitterly cold. The islands were no longer green, they were grey and dusted with snow. In the east the sky was even more threatening, leaden and greenish. Aloft the watch were shortening down, ready for a whole gale by mid-morning. Drinkwater was pleased to see Rogers already on deck.

'Don't like the smell of it, sir.'

'Happen you're right, Sam. What worries me more is what our friends are doing.'

'Sitting in Quiberon (he pronounced it 'Key-ber-ron') hoisting in fresh vittals.'

'I ken the Captain means the French,' put in Lieutenant Fraser joining them and reporting the first reef taken in the topsails. Fraser ignored Rogers's jaundiced look.

Drinkwater levelled his glass at the north point of Oléron. 'I do indeed, gentlemen, and here they are!'

The two officers looked round. Beyond the point of the island the white rectangles of topsails were moving as Missiessy's frigates led his squadron to sea.

'Mr Frey!'

'Sir?'

'Make to *Felix*, three-seven-zero.'

Drinkwater ignored Rogers's puzzled frown but heard Fraser mutter in his ear, 'Enemy coming out of port.'

A few minutes later the little schooner was scudding to the north-west with the news for Graves, or Campbell, or whoever else would take alarm from the intelligence.

'Heave the ship to, Mr Rogers. Let us see what these fellows are going to do.' He again raised the glass to his eye and intently studied the approaching enemy. The heavy frigates led out first. Bigger than *Antigone*, though not dissimilar in build, he tried to identify them, calling for Mr Gillespy, his tablet and pencil.

'And clear the ship for action, Mr Rogers. Beat to quarters if you please!'

He ignored the burst of activity, concentrating solely on the enemy. He recognised the *Infatigable*, so similar in name to Pellew's famous frigate. All three frigates seemed to be holding back, not running down upon the solitary *Antigone* as Drinkwater had expected. He could afford to hold his station for a little longer. Ah, there were the little brig-corvettes, exact replicas of the *Bonaparte*.

He counted the gun-ports; yes, eight a side, 16-gun corvettes all right. But then came the battleships, with Missiessy's huge three-decked 120-gun flagship, the *Majestueux* in the van. He heard the whistles of surprise from the hands now at their action stations and grinned to himself. This was what they had all been waiting for.

Astern of the *Majestueux* came four 74-gun battleships. All were now making sail as they altered course round the point, and foreshortened towards *Antigone*. One of the seventy-fours was detaching, moving out of line. He watched intently, sensing that this movement had something to do with himself. As the battleship drew ahead of the others the frigates made sail and within a few minutes all four leading ships were racing towards him, the gale astern of them and great white bones in their teeth. He shut his telescope with a snap and dismissed Gillespy to his action station. Hill and Rogers were staring at him expectantly.

'Hoping to make a prize of us, I believe,' Drinkwater said. 'Put the ship before the wind, Mr Hill.'

The helm came up and *Antigone* turned away. The braces clicked through the blocks as the yards swung on their parrels about the slushed topmasts and the apparent wind over the deck diminished. As the frigate steadied on her course, Drinkwater raised his glass once more.

Led by the seventy-four, the French ships were overhauling them rapidly. Drinkwater looked carefully at the relative angles between them. He longed to know the names and exact force of each of his antagonists and felt a sudden thrill after all the long months of waiting and worrying. For Drinkwater such circumstances were the mainspring of his being. The high excitement of handling an instrument as complex, as deadly, yet as vulnerable as a ship of war, in a gale of wind and with a superior enemy to windward, placed demands upon him that acted like a drug. For his father and brother the love of horse-flesh and speed had provided the anodyne to the frustrations and disappointments of life; but for him only this spartan and perilous existence would do. This was the austere drudgery of his duty transformed into a dangerous art.

He looked astern once more. Beyond the advancing French division the remaining French ships had disappeared. A great curtain of snow was bearing down upon them, threatening to obscure everything.

Chapter Eleven *January–March 1805*

The Snowstorm

Drinkwater stepped forward and held out his hand for Rogers's speaking trumpet. As *Antigone* scudded before the wind he could make himself understood with little difficulty.

'D'you hear, there! Pay attention to all my orders and execute them promptly. No one shall fire until I order it. All guns are to double shot and load canister on ball. All gun-captains to see their pieces aimed before they fire. I want perfect silence at all times. Any man in breach of this will have a check shirt.' He paused to let his words sink in. An excited cheer or shout might transform his intended audacity into foolhardiness. 'Very well, let us show these shore-squatting Frogs what happens to 'em when they come to sea. Lieutenant Quilhampton!'

'Sir?'

'Abandon your guns for the moment, Mr Q. I want you on the fo'c's'le head listening. If you hear anything, indicate with your arm the direction of the noise as you do when signalling the anchor cable coming home.'

'Aye, aye, sir.'

Drinkwater turned to the sailing master. 'Well, Mr Hill, take a bearing of that French seventy-four and the instant the snow shuts him from view, heave the ship to. In the meantime try and lay us in his track.'

Hill turned away and peered over the taffrail, returning to the binnacle to order an alteration of course to the north. Drinkwater also turned to watch the approaching French. He was only just in time to catch a glimpse of them before they vanished. They were well clear of the land now, catching the full fury of the gale and feeling the effects of carrying too much canvas in their eagerness to overtake *Antigone*. Then they were gone, hidden behind a white streaked curtain of snow that second by second seemed to cut off the edge of their world in its silent approach.

'Now, Hill! Now!'

'Down helm! Main-braces there! Leggo and haul!' *Antigone* began to turn back into the wind. As men hauled in on the fore and mizen braces to keep the frigate sailing on a bowline, the main-yards were backed against the wind, opposing the action of the other masts and checking her, so she lay in wait for the oncoming French. Drinkwater turned his attention to Quilhampton who had clambered up into the knightheads and had one ear cocked into the wind. *Antigone* bucked in the rising sea, her way checked and every man standing silent at his post.

''Tis a wonderful thing, discipline,' he heard Hill mutter to Rogers, and the first lieutenant replied with characteristic enthusiasm, 'Aye, for diabolical purposes!' And then the snow began to fall upon the deck.

'Keep the decks wet with sea-water, Mr Rogers. Get the firemen to attend to it.' He had not thought of the dangers of slush. Men losing their footing would imperil the success of his enterprise and wreak havoc when they opened fire. The snow seemed to deaden all noise so that the ship rose and fell like a ghost as minute succeeded minute. Drinkwater walked forward to the starboard hance. He wondered what the odds were upon them being run down. Even if they were, he consoled himself, mastering the feeling of rising panic that always preceded action, they would seriously jeopardise Missiessy's escape and the Admiralty would approve of that.

'Sir!' Quilhampton's voice hissed with urgent sibilance and he looked up to see the lieutenant's iron hook pointing off to starboard. For an instant Drinkwater hesitated, his mind uncertain. Then he heard shouting, the creak of rigging and the hiss of a bow wave. The shouting was not urgent, they themselves were undetected, but on board the Frenchman petty officers were lambasting an unpractised crew. And then he saw the ship, looking huge and black, the white patches of her sails invisible in the snow.

'Main-braces!' he hissed with violent urgency. 'Up helm!'

Drinkwater had no alternative but to risk being raked by the Frenchman's broadside. If the crew of the enemy battleship were at their guns, a single discharge would cripple the British frigate. But he hoped fervently that they would not see *Antigone* in so unexpected a place; that the novelty of being at sea would distract their attention inboard where, he knew, a certain amount of confusion was inevitable after so long a period at anchor. Besides, he could not risk losing control of his ship by attempting to tack from a standing start. Hove-to with no forward motion, *Antigone* would jib at passing through the wind and probably be caught 'in irons'.

A group of marines were at the spanker brails, hauling in the big after-sail as *Antigone* turned, gathering way and answering her helm. At the knightheads Quilhampton's raised arm indicated he still had contact with the enemy. They steadied the ship dead before the wind. Drinkwater went forward to stand beside Quilhampton and listen. The frigate was scending in the following sea and Drinkwater knew the wind, already at gale force, had not finished rising. If he was to achieve anything it would have to be soon. He strained his ears to hear. Above the creak of *Antigone*'s fabric and the hiss and surge of her bow-wave he caught the muffled sound of orders, orders passed loudly and with some urgency as though the giver of those instructions was anxious, and the recipients slow to comprehend. There were a few words he recognised: *'Vite! Vite!'* and *'Allez!'* and the obscenity *'Jean-Foutre!'* of some egalitarian officer in the throes of frustration. And then suddenly he saw the flat surface of the huge stern with its twin rows of stern windows looming through the snow. Drinkwater raced aft.

'Stand by larbowlines! Give her the main course!'

Then they could all see the enemy as a sudden rent in the snow opened up a tiny circle of sea. The gun-captains were frantically spiking their guns round to aim on the bow and Drinkwater looked up to see an officer on the battleship's quarter. He was waving his hat at them and shouting something.

'By God, he thinks we're one of his own frigates come too close!'

Drinkwater watched the relative angles between the two ships. There was a great flogging and rattle of blocks as the main clew-garnets were let run and the waisters hauled down the tacks and sheets of the main-course. The relative angle began to open and someone on the French battleship realised his mistake.

He heard someone scream *'Merde!'* and ordered *Antigone*'s course altered to starboard. Standing by the larboard hance he screwed up one eye.

'Fire!'

The blast and roar of the guns rolled over them, the thunderous climax of Drinkwater's mad enterprise. The yellow flashes from the cannon muzzles were unnaturally bright in the gloom as the snow closed round them once again. He caught a glimpse of the enemy's name in large gilt roman script across her stern: *Magnanime*.

The smoke from the guns hung in the air, drifting forward slowly then suddenly gone, whipped away. The gunners were swabbing, reloading and hauling out, holding up their hands when they were ready. The sound of enemy guns barked out of the obscurity and they were alone again, shut into their own tiny world, and the snow was falling thicker than ever.

'Fire!' yelled Rogers and the second broadside was discharged into the swirling wraiths of white. *Antigone*'s deck took a sudden cant as her stern lifted and she drove violently forward. Down went her bow, burying itself to the knightheads, a great cushion of white water foaming up around her.

'Too much canvas, sir!' yelled Hill. Drinkwater nodded.

'Secure the guns and shorten down!'

It took the combined efforts of fifty men to furl the mainsail. The huge, unreefed sail, set to carry them alongside the *Magnanime*, threatened to throw them off the yard as they struggled. In the end Lieutenant Fraser went aloft and the great sail was tamed and the process repeated with the fore-course. At the end of an hour's labour *Antigone* had hauled her yards round and lay on the starboard tack, her topsails hard reefed and her topgallant masts sent down as the gale became a storm and Drinkwater edged her north to report the break-out of Missiessy and the fact that he had lost contact with the enemy in the snow and violent weather.

Antigone was able to hold her new course for less than an hour. Laughing and chaffing each other, the watch below had been piped down when they were called again. Drinkwater regained the deck to find the wind chopping rapidly round, throwing up a high, breaking and confused sea that threw the ship over and broke on board in solid green water. For perhaps fifteen minutes the wind dropped, almost to a calm while the snow continued to fall. The ship failed to answer her helm as she lost way. The men milled about in the waist and the officers stood apprehensive as they tried to gauge the new direction from which the wind would blow. A few drops of rain fell, mingled with wet snow flakes.

'Sou'wester!' Hill and Drinkwater shouted together. 'Stand by! Man the braces!'

It came with the unimaginable violence that only seamen

experience. The squall hit *Antigone* like a gigantic fist, laying her sails aback, tearing the fore-topsail clean from its bolt ropes and away to leeward like a lost handkerchief. The frigate lay over under the air pressure in her top-hamper and water bubbled in through her closed gun-ports. From below came the crash and clatter of the mess kids and coppers on the galley stove, together with a ripe torrent of abuse hurled at the elements by the cook and his suddenly eloquent mates.

'Lee braces, there! Look lively my lads! Aloft and secure that raffle!'

With a thunderous crack and a tremble that could be felt throughout the ship the main-topmast sprang at the instant the main-topsail also blew out of its bolt ropes, and then the first violent spasm of the squall was past and the wind steadied, blowing at a screaming pitch as they struggled to bring the bucking ship under control again.

The gale blew for several days. The rain gave way to mist and the mist, on the morning of the 15th, eventually cleared. On the horizon to the north Drinkwater and Hill recognised the outline of the Ile d'Yeu and debated their next move. *Felix* must by now have communicated the news of Missiessy's break-out to Graves, in which case Graves would have withdrawn towards Cornwallis off Ushant. But supposing something had happened to Bourne and the *Felix*? After such an easterly wind Graves would be worried that Missiessy had gone, and gone at a moment when, through sheer necessity, his own back had been turned. Graves would have returned to Rochefort and might be waiting there now, unable to get close inshore to see into the Basque Road, for fear of the continuing gale catching him on a lee shore.

'He'd be locking the stable door after the horse had gone,' said Hill reflectively.

'Quite so,' replied Drinkwater. 'And we could fetch the Ile de Ré on one tack under close-reefed topsails to clarify the situation. If Graves is not there we will have lost but a day in getting to Cornwallis. Very well,' Drinkwater made up his mind, clapped his hand over his hat and fought to keep his footing on the tilting deck. 'Course south-east, let us look into the Basque Road and see if Graves has regained station.'

On the morning of the 16th they found Graves off the Ile d'Oléron having just been informed by the *Felix* of Missiessy's departure. In his search for the admiral, Bourne had also run across the French squadron heading north. During a long morning of interminable flag hoists it was established that this encounter had occurred after Drinkwater's brush with the enemy and therefore established that Missiessy's task was probably to cause trouble in Ireland. This theory was lent particular force by Drinkwater's report that troops were embarked. It was a tried strategy of the French government and the signalling system was not capable of conveying Drinkwater's theory about the West Indies. In truth, on that particular morning, with the practical difficulties in handling the ship and attending to the admiral, Drinkwater himself was not overconfident that he was right. Besides, there was other news that permeated the squadron during that blustery morning, news more closely touching themselves. In getting into Quiberon Bay to warn Graves, the *Doris* had found the admiral already gone. Struggling seawards again, *Doris* had struck a rock and, after great exertions by Campbell and his people, had foundered. *Felix* had taken off her crew and all were safe, but the loss of so fine a frigate and the escape of Missiessy cast a shadow over the morale of the squadron. Afterwards Drinkwater was to remember that morning as the first of weeks of professional frustration; when it seemed that providence had awarded its laurels to the Imperial eagle of France, that despite the best endeavours of the Royal Navy, the weeks of weary and remorseless blockade, the personal hardships of every man-jack and boy in the British fleet, their efforts were to come to naught.

But for the time being Graves's squadron had problems of its own. The morning of signalling had thrown them to leeward and in the afternoon they were unable to beat out of the bay and compelled to anchor. When at last the weather moderated, Graves reported to Cornwallis, only to find Sir William in ailing health, having himself been driven from his station to shelter in Torbay. For a while the ships exchanged news and gossip. Cornwallis was said to have requested replacement, while it was known that Admiral Latouche-Tréville had died at Toulon and been replaced by Admiral Villeneuve, the only French flag-officer to have escaped from Nelson's devastating attack in Aboukir Bay. Of what had happened to Missiessy no one was quite sure, but it was certain that he had not gone to Ireland. A few weeks later it was common knowledge that he had arrived at Martinique in the West Indies.

Chapter Twelve *April–May 1805*

The Look-Out Frigate

'Well, Mr Gillespy, you seem to be making some progress.' Drinkwater closed the boy's journal. 'Your aunt would be pleased, I'm sure,' he added wryly, thinking of the garrulous Mistress MacEwan. 'I have some hopes of you making a sea-officer.'

'Thank you, sir.' The boy looked pleased. He had come out of his shell since the departure of Walmsley, and Drinkwater knew that Frey had done much to protect him from the unimaginative and over-bearing Glencross. He also knew that James Quilhampton kept a close eye on the boy, ever mindful of Gillespy's relationship with Catriona MacEwan; while Lieutenant Fraser lost no opportunity to encourage a fellow Scot among the bear-pit of Sassenachs that made up the bulk of the midshipmen's berth. He was aware that he had been staring at the boy for too long and smiled.

'I trust you are quite happy?' he asked, remembering again how this boy reminded him of his own son. He should not care for Richard Madoc to go to sea with a man who did not take some interest in him.

'Oh yes, sir.'

'Mmmm.' The removal of Walmsley's influence charged that short affirmative with great significance. Drinkwater remembered his own life in the cockpit. It had not been happy.

'Very well, Mr Gillespy. Cut along now, cully.'

The boy turned away, his hat tucked under his arm, the small dirk in its gleaming brass scabbard bouncing on his hip. The pity of his youth and circumstance hit Drinkwater like a blow. The boy's account of the action with the *Magnanime* read with all the fervent patriotism of youth. There was much employment of unworthy epithets. The *Frogs* had *run from the devastating* (spelt wrongly) *thunder of our glorious cannon*. It was the language of London pamphleteers, a style that argued a superiority of ability Drinkwater did not like to see in one so young. It was not Gillespy's fault, of course; he was subject to the influence of his time. But Drinkwater had suffered enough reverses in his career to know the folly of under-estimation.

The *Magnanime* had been commanded by Captain Allemand, he had discovered, one of the foremost French naval officers. It was too easy to assume that because the major part of their fleets was blockaded in harbour they were not competent seamen. With Missiessy's squadron at sea, several hundred Frenchmen would be learning fast, to augment the considerable number of French cruisers already out. Drinkwater sighed, rose and poured himself a glass of blackstrap. He was at a loss to know why he was so worried. There were captains and admirals senior to him whose responsibilities far exceeded his own. All he had to do was to patrol his cruising area, one of a cloud of frigates on the look-out for any enemy movements, who linked the major units of the British fleet, ready to pass news, to pursue or strike at enemy cruisers, and hold the Atlantic seaboard of France and Spain under a constant vigilance.

It was all very well, Drinkwater ruminated, in theory. But the practicalities were different as the events of January had shown. To the east the French Empire was under the direction of a single man. Every major military and naval station was in contact with Napoleon, whose policy could be quickly disseminated by interior lines of communication. No such factors operated in Great Britain's favour. Britain was standing on the defensive. She had no army to speak of and what she had of one was either policing the raw new industrial towns of the Midlands or preparing to go overseas on some madcap expedition to the east under Sir James Craig. Her government was shaky and the First Lord of the Admiralty, Lord Melville, was to be impeached for corruption. Her dispersed fleets were without quick communication, every admiral striving to do his best but displaying that fatal weakness of disagreement and dislike that often ruined the ambitions of the mighty. Orde, off Cadiz, hated Nelson, off Toulon, and the sentiment was returned with interest. Missiessy at sea was bad enough (and Drinkwater still smarted from a sense of failure to keep contact with the French, despite the weather at the time), but the spectre of more French battleships at sea worried every cruiser commander. With that thought he poured a second glass of wine. He doubted

Ganteaume would get out of Brest, but Gourdon might give Calder the slip at Ferrol, and Villeneuve might easily get past Nelson with his slack and provocative methods. And that still left the Spanish out of the equation. They had ships at Cartagena and Cadiz, fine ships too . . .

His train of thought was interrupted by a knock at the cabin door. 'Enter!'

Rogers came in followed by Mr Lallo. There was enough in the expressions on their faces to know that they brought bad news. 'What is it, gentlemen?'

'It's Waller, sir . . .'

'He had a bad fit this morning, sir,' put in Lallo, 'I had confined him to a straitjacket, sir, but he got loose, persuaded some accomplice to let him go.' Lallo paused.

'And?'

'He went straight to the galley, sir, picked up a knife and slashed both his wrists. He was dead by the time I'd got to him.'

'Good God.' A silence hung in the cabin. Drinkwater thought of Waller defying him at Nagtoralik Bay and of how far he had fallen. 'Who let him go?'

'One of his damned whale-men, I shouldn't wonder,' said Rogers.

'Yes. That is likely. I suppose he may still have commanded some influence over them. There is little likelihood that we will discover who did it, Mr Lallo.'

The surgeon shrugged. 'No, sir. Well he's dead now and fit only for the sail-maker to attend.'

'You had better see to it, Mr Rogers.'

It was one of the ironies of the naval service, Drinkwater thought as he stood by the pinrail where the fore-sheet was belayed, that a man killed honourably in battle might be hurriedly shoved through a gun-port to avoid incommoding his mates as they plied their murderous trade, while a man whose death was as ignominious as Waller's, was attended by all the formal pomp of the Anglican liturgy. Casting his eyes over *Antigone*'s assembled crew, the double irony hit him that only a few would be even vaguely familiar with his words. The half-dozen negroes, three Arabs and sixty Irishmen might even resent their being forced to witness a rite that, in Waller's case, might be considered blasphemous. He doubted any of the others, the Swede, Norwegians, three renegade Dutchmen and Russians, understood the words. Nevertheless he ploughed on, raising his voice as he read from Elizabeth's father's Prayer Book.

'We therefore commit . . .' he nodded at the burial party who raised the board upon which Waller's corpse lay stiffly sewn into his hammock under the ensign, 'his body to the deep . . .'

The prayer finished he closed the book and put his hat on. The officers followed suit. 'Square away, Mr Rogers, let us continue with our duties.'

He turned away and walked along the gangway as the main-yards were hauled, and was in the act of descending the companionway when he was halted by the masthead look-out.

'Deck there! Sail-ho! Broad on the lee quarter!'

Drinkwater shoved the Prayer Book in his tail-pocket and pulled out his Dolland pocket glass. It was a frigate coming up hand over fist from the southward, carrying every stitch of canvas the steady breeze allowed. Even at a distance they could see bunting streaming to leeward.

'She's British, anyway.' Of that there could be little doubt and within half an hour a boat danced across the water towards them.

'Boat ahoy!'

'*Fisgard*!' came the reply, and Drinkwater nodded to his first lieutenant.

'Side-party, Mr Rogers.' He turned to Frey who was consulting his lists.

'Captain Lord Mark Kerr, sir.'

'Bloody hell,' muttered Rogers as he called out the marine guard and the white-gloved side-boys to rig their fancy baize-covered man-ropes. Captain Lord Kerr hauled himself energetically over the rail and seized Drinkwater's hand.

'Drinkwater ain't it?'

'Indeed sir,' said Drinkwater, meeting his lordship as an equal upon his own quarterdeck.

'The damnedest thing, Drinkwater. Villeneuve's out!'

'*What*?'

Kerr nodded. 'I was refitting in Gib when he passed the Strait. I got out as soon as I could; sent my second luff up the Med to tell Nelson . . .'

'You mean Nelson wasn't in pursuit?' Drinkwater interrupted.

Kerr shook his head. 'No sign of him. I reckon he's off to the east again, just like the year one . . .'

'East. Good God he should be going west. Doesn't he know Missiessy's at Martinique waiting for him?'

'The devil he is!' exclaimed Kerr, digesting this news. 'I doubt Nelson knows of it. By God, that makes my haste the more necessary!'

'What about Orde, for God's sake?'

'He was victualling off Cadiz. Fell back when Villeneuve approached.'

'God's bones!'

Kerr came to a decision. In the circumstances it did not seem to matter which was the senior officer, they were both of one mind. 'I'm bound to let Calder know off Ferrol, and then to Cornwallis off Ushant. I daresay Billy-go-tight will send me on to the Admiralty.'

'Billy's ashore, now. Been relieved by Lord Gardner,' interrupted Drinkwater. 'And what d'you want me to do? Cruise down towards the Strait and hope that Nelson comes west?'

Kerr nodded, already turning towards the rail. 'First rate, Drinkwater. He must realise his mistake soon, even if my lieutenant ain't caught up with him. The sooner Nelson knows that Missiessy's out as well, the sooner we might stop this rot from spreading.' He held out his hand and relaxed for an instant. 'When I think how we've striven to maintain this damned blockade, only to have it blown wide open by a minute's ill-fortune!'

'My sentiments exactly. Good luck!' Drinkwater waved his hastening visitor over the side. Something of the urgency of Kerr's news had communicated itself to the ship, for *Antigone* was under way to the southward even before Kerr had reached *Fisgard*.

As soon as Drinkwater had satisfied himself that *Antigone* set every inch of canvas she was capable of carrying, he called Rogers and Hill below, spreading his charts on the table before him. He outlined the situation and the import of his news struck home.

'By God,' said Rogers, 'the Frogs could outflank us!' Drinkwater suppressed a smile. The very idea that they could be bested by a handful of impudent, frog-eating 'mounseers' seemed to strike Rogers with some force. His lack of imagination was, Drinkwater reflected, typical of his type. Hill, on the other hand, was more ruminative.

'You say Nelson's gone east, sir, chasing the idea of a French threat to India again?'

'Something of that order, Mr Hill.'

'While in reality the West India interests will already be howling for Pitt's blood. Who's in the West Indies at the moment? Cochrane?'

'And Dacres, with no more than a dozen of the line between them,' added Rogers.

'If Missiessy and Villeneuve combine with whatever cruisers the French have already got out there, I believe that we may be in for a thin time. Meanwhile we have to edge down to the Strait. What strikes me as paramount is our need to tell Nelson what is happening. I dare not enter the Med for fear of missing him, so we must keep station off Cape Spartel until Nelson appears. He may then close on the Channel in good time if the French have to recross the Atlantic. If Gardner holds the Channel and Nelson cruises off the Orkneys, we may yet stop 'em.'

'If not,' said Hill staring down at the chart, 'then God help us all.'

'Amen to that,' said Drinkwater.

They did not meet Orde but five days later they found his sloop *Beagle* cruising off Cape Spartel, having observed the passage of Villeneuve's fleet and now lying in wait for Nelson. From *Beagle* Drinkwater learned that Villeneuve had been reinforced by Spanish ships from Cadiz under Admiral Gravina and that *Beagle* had lost contact when the Combined Fleet headed west.

'I knew it!' Drinkwater had muttered to himself when he learned this. He promptly ordered *Beagle* to rejoin Orde who was, he thought, falling back on the Channel to reinforce Lord Gardner. As *Beagle*'s sails disappeared over the horizon to the north and the Atlas Mountains rose blue in the haze to the east, Drinkwater remarked to Quilhampton and Fraser:

'There is nothing more we can do, gentlemen, until his lordship arrives.'

During the first week of May the wind blew westerly through the Strait of Gibraltar, foul for Nelson slipping out into the Atlantic. Drinkwater decided to take advantage of it and enter the Strait. He was extremely anxious about the passage of time as day succeeded day and Nelson failed to appear. If there was no news of Nelson at Gibraltar, he reasoned, he could wait there and still catch his lordship. In addition Gibraltar might have news carried overland, despite the hostility of the Spanish.

Off Tarifa they spoke to a Swedish merchant ship which had just left Gibraltar. There was no news of Nelson but much of a diplomatic nature. Russia was again the ally of Great Britain and Austria was dallying with Britain's overtures. However, there was an even more disturbing rumour that Admiral Ganteaume had sailed from Brest. That evening the wind fell light, then swung slowly into the east. At dawn the following day the topgallants of a fleet were to be seen, and at last Drinkwater breakfasted in the great cabin of *Victory*, in company with Lord Nelson.

It was a hurried meal. Drinkwater told Nelson all he knew, invited to share the admiral's confidence as much for the news he brought as for the high regard Nelson held him in after his assistance at the battle of Copenhagen.

'My dear Drinkwater, I have been in almost perpetual darkness as Hardy here will tell you. I had for some time considered the West Indies a likely rendezvous for the fleets of France and Spain. Would to God I had had some news. I have been *four months,* Drinkwater, without a word, *four months* with nothing from the Admiralty. They tell me Melville is out of office . . . My God, I hoped for news before now.' The admiral turned to his flag-captain. 'How far d'you think he's gone, Hardy?'

'Villeneuve, my Lord?'

'Who else, for God's sake!'

Hardy seemed unmoved by his lordship's bile and raised his eyebrows reflectively, demonstrating a stolidity that contrasted oddly with the little admiral's feverish anxiety. 'He has a month's start. Even the French can cross the Atlantic in a month.'

'A month. The capture of Jamaica would be a blow which Bonaparte would be happy to give us!'

'Do you follow him there, my Lord?' Drinkwater asked.

'I had marked the Toulon Fleet for my own game, Captain; you say Orde has fallen back from Cadiz?'

'It seems so, my Lord.'

'Then Gardner will not greatly benefit from my ships.' He paused in thought, then appeared to make up his mind. He suddenly smiled, his expression flooded with resolution. He whipped the napkin from his lap and flung it down on the table, like a gauntlet.

'They're *our* game, Hardy, damn it. Perhaps none of us would wish exactly for a West India trip; but the call of our country is far superior to any consideration of self. Let us try and bag Villeneuve before he does too much damage, eh gentlemen?'

'And the Mediterranean, my Lord?' asked Hardy.

'Sir Richard Bickerton, Tom, we'll leave him behind to guard the empty stable and watch Salcedo's Dons in Cartagena.' Nelson raised his coffee cup and they toasted the enterprise.

'You may keep us company to Cadiz, Captain, I shall look in there and see what Orde is about before I sail west.'

Orde was not off Cadiz, but his storeships were, and Nelson plundered them freely in Lagos Bay. Then intelligence reached the British fleet from Admiral Donald Campbell in the Portuguese Navy that confirmed Drinkwater's information. Campbell also brought the news that a British military expedition with a very weak escort under Admiral Knight was leaving Lisbon, bound into the Mediterranean. Nelson therefore ordered his foulest-bottomed battleship, the *Royal Sovereign*, together with the frigate *Antigone*, to see the fleet of transports clear of the Strait of Gibraltar.

Thus it was with something of a sense of anti-climax and of belonging to a mere side-show that *Antigone*'s log for the evening of 11th May 1805 read: *Bore away in company R-Ad Knight's convoy. Cape St Vincent NW by N distant 7 leagues. Parted company Lord Nelson. Lord Nelson's fleet chasing to the westward.*

Chapter Thirteen *May–July 1805*

Calder's Action

'Fog, sir.'

'So I see.' Captain Drinkwater nodded to Lieutenant Quilhampton as he came on deck and stared round the horizon. The calm weather of the last few days had now turned cooler; what had first been a haze had thickened to mist and now to fog. 'Take the topsails off her, Mr Q. No point in chafing the gear to pieces.' So, her sails furled and her rigging dripping, *Antigone* lay like a log upon the vast expanse of the Atlantic which heaved gently to a low ground swell that told of a distant wind but only seemed to emphasise their own immobility.

Captain and third lieutenant fell to a companionable pacing of the deck, discussing the internal details of the ship.

'Purser reported another rotten cask of pork, sir.'

'From the batch shipped aboard off Ushant?'

'Yes, sir.'

'That makes seven.' Drinkwater cursed inwardly. He had been delighted to have been victualled and watered off Ushant after returning from the Strait of Gibraltar and Admiral Knight's convoy. Lord Gardner had been particular to ensure that all the cruising frigates were kept well stocked, but if they found many more bad casks of meat then his lordship's concern might be misplaced.

'I was just wondering, sir,' said Quilhampton conversationally, 'whether I'd rather be here than off Cadiz with Collingwood. Which station offers the best chance of action?'

'Difficult to say, James,' said Drinkwater, dropping their usual professional formality. 'When Gardner detached Collingwood to blockade Cadiz it was because he thought that Villeneuve and Gravina might have already returned there. When the report proved false, Collingwood sent two battleships west to reinforce

Nelson and returned us to Calder. Opinion seems to incline towards keeping as many ships to the westward of the Bay of Biscay as possible. Prowse of *Sirius* told me the other day that both Calder and the Ushant squadron have virtually raised their separate blockades and are edging westwards in the hope of catching Villeneuve.'

'D'you think it will affect us, sir?'

Drinkwater shrugged. 'Not if my theory is right. Villeneuve will head more to the north and pass round Scotland. Besides, we don't know if Nelson caught up with him. Perhaps there has already been a battle in the West Indies.' He paused. 'What is it, James?'

Quilhampton frowned. 'I thought I heard . . . no, it's nothing. Wait! There it is again!'

Both men paused. As they listened the creaking of *Antigone*'s gear seemed preternaturally loud. 'Gunfire!'

'Wait!' Drinkwater laid his hand on Quilhampton's arm. 'Wait and listen.' Both men leaned over the rail, to catch the sound nearer the water, unobstructed by the noises of the ship. The single concussion came again, followed at intervals by others. 'Those are minute guns, James! And since we know the whereabouts of Calder . . .'

'Villeneuve?'

'Or Nelson, perhaps. But we must assume the worst. My theory is wrong if you are right. And they have a wind. Perhaps we will too in an hour.'

He looked aloft at the pendant flying from the mainmast head. It was already beginning to lift a trifle. Drinkwater crossed the deck and stared into the binnacle. The compass card oscillated gently but showed clearly that the breeze was coming from the west.

'You know, James, that report we had that Ganteaume got out of Brest proved false.'

'Yes, sir.'

'Well, perhaps Villeneuve is coming back to spring Ganteaume from the Goulet and *then* make his descent upon the Strait of Dover.'

'Possibly, sir,' replied Quilhampton, unwilling to argue, and aware that Drinkwater must be allowed his prerogative. In Quilhampton's youthful opinion the Frogs were not capable of that kind of thing.

Drinkwater knew of the young officer's scepticism and said, 'Lord Barham has the same opinion of the French as myself, Mr Q, otherwise he would not have gone to all the trouble of ensuring they were intercepted.'

Thus mildly rebuked, Quilhampton realised his minutes of intimacy with the captain were over. While Drinkwater considered what to do until the breeze gave them steerage way, Quilhampton considered that, as far as second lieutenants were concerned, it did not seem to matter if Lord Melville or Lord Barham were in charge of the Admiralty; the lot of serving officers was still a wretched one.

The breeze came from the west at mid-morning. Setting all sail, Drinkwater pressed *Antigone* to the east-north-east. Then, at six bells in the forenoon watch there was a brief lifting of the visibility. To the north-west they made out the pale square of sails over the shapes of hulls, while to the north-east they saw Calder's look-out ship, *Defiance*. Both *Antigone* and *Defiance* threw out the signal for an enemy fleet in sight and fired guns. Drinkwater knew that Calder could not be far away. Immediately upon making his signal, Captain Durham of the *Defiance* turned his ship away, squaring her yards before the wind and retiring on the main body of the fleet. Taking his cue, Drinkwater ordered studding sails set and attempted to cross the enemy's van and rejoin his own admiral. Shortly after this the fog closed in again, although the breeze held and Drinkwater cleared the frigate for action.

'We seem destined to go into battle blind, Sam,' he said to the first lieutenant as Rogers took his post on the quarterdeck. 'Snow in January and bloody fog in July and this could be the decisive battle of the war, for God's sake!'

Rogers grunted his agreement. 'Only the poxy French could conjure up a bloody fog at a moment like this.'

Drinkwater grinned at Rogers's prejudice. 'It could be providence, Sam. What does the Bible say about God chastising those he loves best?'

'Damned if I know, sir, but a fleet action seems imminent and we're going to miss it because of fog!'

Drinkwater felt a spark of sympathy for Rogers. Distinguishing himself in such an action was Rogers's only hope of further advancement.

'Look, sir!' Another momentary lifting of the fog showed the French much nearer to them now, crossing their bows and holding a steadier breeze than reached *Antigone*.

'We shall be cut off, damn it,' muttered Drinkwater, suddenly realising that he might very well be fighting for his life within an hour. He turned on Rogers. 'Sam, serve the men something at their stations. Get food and grog into them. You have twenty minutes.'

It proved to be a very long twenty minutes to Drinkwater. In fact it stretched to an hour, then two. Drinkwater had seen no signals from Calder and had only a vague idea of the admiral's position. All he did know was that the French fleet lay between *Antigone* and the British line-of-battle ships. At about one in the afternoon the fog rolled back to become a mist, thickening from time to time in denser patches, so that they might see three-quarters of a mile one minute and a ship's length ahead the next. Into this enlarged visible circle the dim and sinister shapes of a battle-line emerged, led by the 80-gun *Argonauta*, flying the red and gold of Castile.

'It *is* the Combined Fleet, by God,' Drinkwater muttered as he saw the colours of Spain alternating with the tricolour of France. He spun *Antigone* to starboard, holding her just out of gunshot as she picked up the stronger breeze that had carried the enemy thus far.

A vague shape to the north westward looked for a little like the topsails of a frigate and Drinkwater hoped it was *Sirius*. At six bells in the afternoon watch he decided to shorten sail, hauled his yards and swung north, crossing the Spanish line a mile ahead of the leading ship which was flying an admiral's flag. Rogers was looking at him expectantly. At extreme range it seemed a ridiculous thing to do but he nodded his permission. Rogers walked the line of the larboard battery, checking and sighting each gun, doing what he was best at.

As he reached the aftermost gun he straightened up. 'Fire!'

Antigone shook as the guns recoiled amid the smoke of their discharge and their crews swabbed, loaded and rammed home. She trembled as the heavy carriages were hauled out through the open ports again and their muzzles belched fire and iron at the long-awaited enemy. As the smoke from the second broadside cleared they were rewarded by an astonishing sight. Little damage seemed to have been inflicted upon the enemy at the extremity of their range, but the Combined Fleet was heaving to.

'Probably thinks that Calder's just behind us out of sight,' Rogers put in, rubbing his hands with glee.

Drinkwater wore *Antigone* round and immediately the yards were squared they made out the shapes of two frigates on their larboard bow, dim, ghostly vessels close-hauled as they approached from the east.

'The private signal, Mr Frey, and look lively!' He did not want to be shot at as he retreated ahead of the French, and already he recognised *Sirius* with her emerald-green rail.

The colours of flags clarified as the ships closed and Drinkwater turned *Antigone* to larboard to come up on *Sirius*'s quarter. The second British frigate, *Égyptienne*, loomed astern. Drinkwater saw Prowse step up on the rail with a speaking trumpet.

'Heard gunfire, Drinkwater. Was that you?'

'Yes! The Combined Fleet is just to windward of us!'

'Form line astern of the *Égyptienne*. Calder wants us to reconnoitre!'

'Aye, aye!' Drinkwater jumped down from the mizen chains. 'Back the mizen tops'l, Mr Hill. Fall in line astern of the *Égyptienne*.'

Drinkwater watched *Sirius* disappear into a fog patch and the second frigate ghosted past. For one glorious moment at about seven bells in the afternoon the fog lifted and the mist rolled back, giving both fleets a glimpse of each other. Astern of the three westward-heading British frigates, the British fleet of fifteen ships-of-the-line was standing south-south-west on the starboard tack, their topgallants set above topsails, but with their courses clewed up. From Sir Robert Calder's 98-gun flagship, the *Prince of Wales*, flew the signal to engage the enemy. This was repeated from the masthead of his second in command, Rear-Admiral Stirling, on board the *Glory*.

To the southward of the three frigates the Combined Fleet straggled in a long line of twenty ships and a few distant frigates. Since they had hove to, they had adjusted their course, edging away from the British frigates which, in order to hold the wind, were also diverging to the north-west. Prowse made the signal to tack and *Sirius* began to ease round on the enemy rear. She was holding the fluky wind better than either *Antigone* or *Égyptienne*. A few minutes later the mist closed down again. Drinkwater set his courses in an attempt to catch up with *Sirius* and lost contact with the *Égyptienne.* He heard gunfire to the south and then the sound of a heavier cannonade to the south-east. Next to him Rogers was beside himself with impatience and frustration.

'God damn it, God damn it,' he muttered, grinding the fist of one hand into the palm of the other.

'For God's sake relax, Sam. You'll have apoplexy else.'

'This is agony, sir . . .'

'Steer for the guns, Mr Hill.' It was agonising for Drinkwater too. But whereas all Rogers had to do was wait for a target to present itself, Drinkwater worried about the presence of other ships, dreading a collision. Ahead of them the noise of cannon-fire was growing louder and more persistent. Then, once again, the fog rolled back, revealing broad on their larboard bow the shape of a battleship. This time the enemy were ready for them.

The roar of forty cannon fire in a ragged broadside split the air. The black hull of the 80-gun vessel towered over them as Rogers roared, 'Fire!'

Antigone's puny broadside rattled and thudded against the stranger's hull as they saw the red and yellow of Spain and an admiral's flag at her mainmasthead. The wind of the battleship's broadside passed them like a tornado but most of the shot whistled overhead, parting ropes and holing sails. One casualty occurred in the main-top and the main-mast was wounded by two balls, but the *Antigone* escaped the worst effects of such a storm of iron. As the great ship vanished in the mist Drinkwater read her name across the stern: *Argonauta*.

Then there were other ships passing them, the *Terrible* and *America,* both disdaining to fire on a frigate, and Drinkwater realised that the Combined Fleet had tacked and were standing north. In the confusion he wondered what on earth Calder was doing, and whether the British admiral had observed this movement. Then the outbreak of a general cannonade told him that the two fleets were still in contact, and the sudden appearance of spouts of water near them convinced him that the British fleet were just beyond the line of the enemy and that *Antigone* was in the line of fire of the British guns.

A little after five in the afternoon they made contact again with the *Sirius*. Both frigates then hauled round and stood towards the gunfire. Once they caught a glimpse of the action and, from what could be discerned, the two fleets were engaged in a confusing mêlée.

'I don't know what the devil to make of it, damned if I do,' remarked Hill tensely, his tone expressing the frustration they all felt. *Antigone* continued to edge down in the mist until darkness came, although the gunfire continued for some time afterwards.

'What in God Almighty's name are we doing?' asked Rogers, looking helplessly round the quarterdeck.

'Why nothing, Mr Rogers,' said Hill, who was finding the first lieutenant's constant moaning a trifle tedious. To windward of the group of officers Captain Drinkwater studied the situation, privately as mystified as his officers. On the day following the action the weather had remained hazy and the two fleets had manoeuvred in sight of each other. Both had been inactive, as though licking their wounds. After the utter confusion of the 22nd, the British were pleased to find themselves masters of two Spanish prizes. It was also clear that they had badly damaged several more. However, the British ships *Windsor Castle* and *Malta* were themselves in poor condition and preparing to detach for England and a dockyard.

The wind had held, the Combined Fleet remained with the advantage of the weather gauge, and Calder waited for Villeneuve to attack. But the allied commander hesitated.

'All I've had to do today,' remarked Rogers in one of his peevish outbursts, 'is report another three casks of pork as being rotten! I ask you, is that the kind of work fit for a King's sea-officer?'

Although the question had been rhetorical it had brought forth a *sotto voce* comment from Midshipman Glencross for which the young man had been sent to the foremasthead to cool his heels and guard his tongue. As Drinkwater had written in his journal, the last days had been *inconclusive if our task is to annihilate the enemy.* And today, it seemed, was to be worse. The wind had shifted at dawn and every ship in the British fleet hourly expected Calder to form his line, station his frigates to windward for the repeating of his signals, and to bear down upon the enemy. As hour after hour passed and the wind increased slowly to a fresh breeze and then to a near gale, nothing happened. Villeneuve's fleet edged away to the north. By six o'clock in the evening the Combined Fleet was out of sight.

'Well,' remarked Lieutenant Fraser as he took over the deck and the hands were at last stood down from their quarters, 'at least we stopped them getting into Ferrol, but it's no' cricket we're playing. I wonder what they'll think o'this in London?'

Chapter Fourteen *July–August 1805*

The Fog of War

'Dear God, how many more?'

'Best part of the ground tier, sir, plus a dozen other casks among the batch shipped aboard off Ushant. I'd guess some of that pork was pickled back in the American War.'

Drinkwater sighed. Rogers might be exaggerating, but then again it was equally possible that he was not. 'If we ain't careful, Sam, we'll be obliged to request stores; just at the moment that would be intolerable. Apart from anything else we must wait on this rendezvous a day or two more.'

'D'you think there's going to be a battle then? After that farting match last week? There's a rumour that Calder is going to be called home to face a court-martial,' Rogers said, a note of irreverent glee in his voice.

'I'm damned if I know where these infernal rumours start,' Drinkwater said sharply. 'You should know better than believe 'em.'

Rogers shrugged. 'Well, it's not my problem, sir, whereas these casks of rotten pork are.'

'Damn it!' Drinkwater rose, his chair squeaking backwards with the violence of his movement. 'Damn it! D'you know Sam,' he said, unlocking the spirit case and pouring two glasses of rum, 'I've never felt so uncomfortable before. That business the other day was shameful. We should never have let the French get away unmolested. God knows what'll come of it . . . we don't know where the devil they are now. The only ray of hope is that Calder has joined forces with Gardner or Cornwallis if he's back on station, and that Nelson's rejoined 'em from the West Indies. With that concentration off Ushant, at least the Channel will be secure, but it is the uncertainty of matters that unsettles me.'

Rogers nodded his agreement. 'Worse than a damned fog.'

'But you want to know about the pork,' Drinkwater sighed. 'How many weeks can we last out at the present rate?'

Rogers shrugged, considered for a moment and said, 'Ten, possibly eleven.'

'Very well. I'll see what I can do about securing some from another ship in due course.'

'Beg pardon, sir, but what are *our* orders?'

'Well, we are to sit tight here on Calder's rendezvous for a week. *Aeolus* and *Phoenix* are within a hundred miles of us, with the seventy-four *Dragon* not so far. We are intended to observe Ferrol.' Drinkwater opened one of the charts that lay, almost permanently now, upon his table top. He laid his finger on a spot a hundred miles north-north-west of Cape Finisterre, 'The four of us are holding Calder's old post between us while he retires on the Channel Fleet in case Villeneuve makes his expected push for the Channel.'

'And if Villeneuve obliges and the Channel Fleet does no better than Calder did t'other day, then I'd say Boney had a better than even chance of getting his own way in the Dover Strait.'

'I doubt if Cornwallis would let him . . .'

'But you said yourself, sir, that Cornwallis might not yet be back at sea. What's Gardner's fighting temper?'

'We'll have little enough to worry about if Nelson's back . . .'

'But maybe he isn't. And even Nelson could be fooled by a fog. 'Tis high summer, just what the bloody French want. I reckon they'd be across in a week.'

Drinkwater fell silent. He was not of sufficiently different an opinion to contradict Rogers. He poured them each another glass.

'To be candid, Sam, things look pretty black.'

'Like the Earl of Hell's riding boots.'

No such strategic considerations preoccupied James Quilhampton as, for the duration of his watch and in the absence of the captain, he paced the weather side of the quarterdeck. His mind was far from the cares of the ship, daydreaming away his four hours on deck as *Antigone* rode the blue waters of the Atlantic under easy sail. He was wholly given to considering his circumstances in so far as they were affected by Miss Catriona MacEwan. From time to time, as he walked up and down, his right hand would clasp the stump of his left arm and he would curse the iron hook that he wore in place of a left hand. Although he possessed several alternatives, including one made for him on the bomb-vessel *Virago* that had been painted and was a tolerable likeness to the real thing, he felt that such a disfigurement was unlikely to enable him to secure the young woman as his wife. He cursed his luck. The wound that had seemed such an honourable mark in his boyhood now struck him for what it really was, a part of him that was gone for ever, its absence making him abnormal, abominable. How foolish it now seemed to consider it in any other way. The pride with which he had borne home his iron hook now appeared ridiculous. He had seen the pity in Catriona's eyes together with the disgust. As he recollected the circumstances it seemed that her revulsion had over-ridden her pity. He was maimed; there was no other way to look at the matter. Certainly that harridan of an aunt would point out James Quilhampton had no prospects, no expectations, no fortune and no left hand!

But she had been undeniably pleasant to him, surely. He pondered the matter, turning over the events of their brief acquaintanceship, recollecting the substance of her half-dozen letters that led him to suppose she, at least, viewed his friendship if not his suit with some favour. Reasoning thus he raised himself out of his despondency only to slump back into it when he considered the uncertainty of his fate. He was in such a brown study that the quartermaster of the watch had to call his attention to the masthead's hail.

'Deck! Deck there!'

'Eh? What? What is it?'

'Eight sail to the norrard, sir!'

'What d'you make of 'em?'

'Clean torps'ls, sir, Frenchmen!'

'Pass word for the captain!' Quilhampton shouted, scrambling up on the rail with the watch glass and jamming himself against the mizen shrouds. Within minutes Drinkwater was beside him.

'Where away, Mr Q?'

'I can't see them from the deck, sir . . . wait! One, two . . . six . . . eight, sir. Eight sail and they are French!'

Drinkwater levelled his own glass and studied the newcomers as they sailed south, tier after tier of sails lifting over the horizon until he could see the bulk of their hulls and the white water foaming under their bows as they manoeuvred into line abreast.

'Casting a net to catch us,' he said, adding, 'six of the line and two frigates to match or better us.' In the prevailing westerly breeze escape to the north was impossible. But the enemy squadron was sailing south, for the Spanish coast, the Straits of Gibraltar or the Mediterranean itself. Which? And why south if the main strength of the Combined Fleet had gone north? Perhaps it had not; perhaps Villeneuve had got past the cordon of British frigates and into Ferrol or Corunna, or back into the Mediterranean. Perhaps this detachment of ships was part of Villeneuve's fleet, an advance division sent out to capture the British frigates that were Barham's eyes and ears. Perhaps, perhaps, perhaps. God only knew what the truth was.

Drinkwater suddenly knew one thing for certain: he had seen at least one of the approaching ships before. The scarlet strake that swept aft from her figurehead was uncommon. She was Allemand's *Magnanime,* and there too was the big *Majestueux.* It was the Rochefort Squadron, back from the West Indies and now heading south!

'Mr Rogers!'

'Sir?'

'Make sail!' Drinkwater closed his glass with a snap. 'Starboard tack, stuns'ls aloft and alow, course sou' by east!'

'Aye, aye, sir!'

'Mr Quilhampton!'

'Sir?'

'A good man aloft with a glass. I want to know the exact progress of this chase and I don't want to lose M'sieur Allemand a second time.'

He fell to pacing the deck, occasionally turning and looking astern at the enemy whose approach had been slowed by *Antigone*'s increase in sail. The British frigate would run south ahead of the French squadron. It was not Drinkwater's business to engage a superior enemy, nor to risk capture. It was his task to determine whither M. Allemand was bound and for what reason. It was also necessary to let Collingwood, off Cadiz, know that a powerful enemy division was at sea and cruising on his lines of communication.

Drinkwater could not be expected to have more than the sketchiest notion of the true state of affairs during the last week of July and the first fortnight in August. But his professional observations and deductions were vital in guiding his mind to its decisions and, like half a dozen fellow cruiser captains, he played his part in those eventful weeks. Unknown to Drinkwater and after the action with Calder's fleet, Villeneuve had gone to Vigo Bay to land his wounded and refit his damaged ships. From Vigo he had coasted to Ferrol where the fast British seventy-four *Dragon* had spotted his ships at anchor. More French and Spanish ships had joined his fleet and he sailed from Ferrol on 13 August, being sighted by the *Iris* whose captain concluded from the Combined Fleet's westerly course that it was attempting a junction with the Rochefort Squadron before turning north. However, events turned out otherwise, for the wind was foul for the Channel. Villeneuve missed Allemand, encountered what he thought was part of a strong British force but was in fact *Dragon* and some frigates, swung south and arrived off Cape St Vincent on the 18th. Breaking up a small British convoy and forcing aside Vice-Admiral Collingwood's few ships, Villeneuve's Combined Fleet of thirty-six men-of-war passed into the safety of the anchorage behind the Mole of Cadiz. That evening Collingwood's token force resumed its blockade.

Drinkwater had tenaciously hung on to Allemand's flying squadron, running ahead of his frigates as the French commodore edged eastwards and then, apparently abandoning the half-hearted chasing off of the British cruiser, turning away for Vigo Bay. As soon as Drinkwater ascertained the French commander's intentions he made all sail to the south, arriving off Cadiz twenty-four hours after Villeneuve. He called away his barge and put off to HMS *Dreadnought*, Collingwood's flagship, to report the presence of the Rochefort ships at Vigo, expecting Collingwood's despatches for the Channel immediately.

Instead the dour Northumbrian looked up from his desk, his serious face apparently unmoved by Drinkwater's news.

'Have you looked into Cadiz, Captain Drinkwater? No? I thought not.' Collingwood sighed, as though weary beyond endurance. 'Villeneuve's whole fleet passed into the Grand Road yesterday . . .'

'I am too late then, sir.'

'With the chief news, yes.' Collingwood did not smile, but the tone of his tired voice was kindly.

'And my orders?'

'I have four ships of the line here, Captain, to blockade thirty to forty enemy men of war. You will remain with us.'

'Very well, sir.' Drinkwater turned to go.

'Oh, Captain . . .'

'Sir?'

'From your actions you appear an officer of energy. I should be pleased to see your frigate close inshore.'

Drinkwater acknowledged the vice-admiral's veiled compliment gravely. In the weeks to come he was to learn that this had been praise indeed.

Chapter Fifteen *August–October 1805*

Nelson

'The tower of San Sebastian bearing south-a-half-west, sir.' Hill straightened up from the pelorus vanes.

'Very well!' Drinkwater closed his Dolland glass with a snap, pocketed it and jumped down from the carronade slide. He took a look over Gillespy's shoulder as the boy's pencil dotted his final full stop.

'You make a most proficient secretary, Mr Gillespy,' he said, patting the boy's shoulder in a paternal gesture that spoke of his high spirits. He turned to the first lieutenant. 'Wear ship, Sam!'

'Aye, aye, sir. Sail trimmers, stand by!'

Antigone's company were at their quarters, the frigate cleared for action as she took her daily look into Cadiz harbour. The hills of Spain almost surrounded them, green and brown, spreading from the town of Rota to the north, to the extremity of the Mole of Cadiz, that long barrier which separated the anchorage of the Combined Fleets of France and Spain from the watching and waiting British. From *Antigone*'s quarterdeck the long mole had fore-shortened and disappeared behind the white buildings of the town of Cadiz which terminated in the tower of San Sebastian. The tower had fallen abaft their beam and ahead of them the islets of Los Cochinos, Las Puercas, El Diamante and La Galera barred their passage. Beyond the islets, beneath the distant blue-green summit of the Chiclana hill, the black mass of the Combined Fleet lay, safely at anchor.

Drinkwater turned to Midshipman Frey, busy with paint-box and paper at the rail. 'You will have to finish now, Mr Frey.' He looked from the masts of the enemy to the hurried watercolour executed by the midshipman. 'You do justice to the effects of the sunshine on the water.'

'Thank you, sir.' Frey and Gillespy exchanged glances. The captain was very complimentary this morning.

'Ready to wear, sir,' reported Rogers.

Drinkwater, his hands behind his back, drew a lungful of air. 'Very well, Sam. See to it.' He felt unusually expansive this bright morning, deriving an enormous sense of satisfaction from his advanced post almost under the very guns of Cadiz itself. He knew that *Antigone* had joined the fleet at a fortuitous moment and that Collingwood was desperately short of frigates. As soon as the admiral had seen Villeneuve into Cadiz he had sent off his fastest frigate, the *Euryalus*, commanded by one of the best cruiser captains in the navy, the Honourable Henry Blackwood. Blackwood was to inform Cornwallis off Ushant, and then Barham at the Admiralty in London. The departure of *Euryalus* left Collingwood with only one other frigate and the bomb-vessel *Hydra* until Drinkwater's arrival with *Antigone*. Their present task, although not so very different from their duties of the last eighteen months, seemed more crucial. There was an inescapable sense of expectancy in the fleet off southern Spain. Among the captains of the line-of-battleships cruising offshore this manifested itself in frustration. Collingwood was not an expansive man. His orders to his fleet were curt. The ship's commanders were forbidden to visit each other, there was to be no dining together, no gossip; just the remorseless business of forming line, wearing, tacking and, from time to time, running for Gibraltar or Tetuan for water, meat and other necessaries.

But close up to the entrance of Cadiz, Drinkwater was blissfully unconcerned. He had no desire to exchange stations, for it was here, opinion held, that an action would soon occur. He was not sure whence came these rumours. There was some extraordinary communication between the ships of a fleet that made even the Admiralty telegraph seem slow. Collingwood had been reinforced by the ships of Admiral Bickerton which Nelson had left in the Mediterranean when he chased the Toulon Fleet to the West Indies. Bickerton, his health in ruins, had gone home, but his ships had brought rumour from east of Gibraltar, while the regular logistical communication with Gibraltar ensured that news from Spain gradually permeated the fleet. It was a curious thing, reflected Drinkwater, as *Antigone* completed her turn and the after-sail was reset, that what began in a fleet as rumour was often borne out as fact a few days or weeks later.

'Ship's on the starboard tack, sir,' reported Rogers.

'Very well.' Drinkwater crossed the deck and watched the white walls of Cadiz slowly open out on the larboard beam, exposing the long mole to the south as the frigate beat out of Cadiz bay.

'Mr Frey, make ready the signal for "The enemy has topgallant masts hoisted and yards crossed".'

'Aye, aye, sir.'

Drinkwater idly watched Lieutenant Mount parading his marines for their daily inspection. He was reluctant to go below and break his mood by a change of scenery. Instead he continued his walk. They knew here, off Cadiz, that Pitt's alienation of Spain had been countered by the acquisition of Austria as an ally, and that there was word of a Russian and Austrian army taking the field. He learned also that the commander of the Rochefort Squadron that had so lately pursued him had been Commodore Allemand, promoted after the departure of Missiessy for Paris. What had become of Allemand now, no one seemed certain.

Drinkwater crossed the deck and began pacing the windward side, deep in thought. There was only one cloud on the horizon and that was their dwindling provisions. They had found more pork rotten, a quantity of flour and dried peas spoiled, and the purser and Rogers were reminding him daily of their increasingly desperate need to revictual. Despite Bickerton's ships, Collingwood was still outnumbered. He had hoped that events would have come to some sort of crux before now, but it seemed that Villeneuve delayed as long as possible in Cadiz. All coastal trade had ceased since Collingwood had detached a couple of small cruisers to halt it in an effort to starve Villeneuve out, and much of the business of supplying Cadiz with food was being carried out in Danish ships. It was known that things inside the town were becoming desperate: there seemed little love lost between the French and Spaniards and it was even rumoured that a few Frenchmen had been found murdered in the streets.

'Main fleet's in sight, sir,' reported Quilhampton, breaking his train of thought and forcing him to concentrate upon the matter in hand. He nodded at Frey.

'Very well. Mr Frey, you may make the signal.'

The rolled-up flags rose off the deck and were hoisted swiftly on the lee flag-halliards. The signal yeoman jerked the ropes and the flags broke out, streaming gaily to leeward and informing Collingwood of the latest moves of Villeneuve.

'Deck there! Vessels to the north . . .'

They watched the approach of the strangers with interest as they stood away from the *Dreadnought*. Collingwood threw out no signals for their interception and they were identified as more reinforcements for the British squadron securing Villeneuve in Cadiz, reinforcements from Ushant under Vice-Admiral Calder.

'Well, Sam,' remarked Drinkwater, 'that's one rumour that is untrue.'

'What's that, sir?'

'You said that Calder was going to be court-martialled and here he is as large as life.'

'Oh well, I suppose that shuts the door on Villeneuve then.'

'I wonder,' mused Drinkwater.

My dearest husband, Drinkwater read, Elizabeth's two-month-old letter having found its way to him via one of Calder's ships: *I have much to tell and you will want to know the news of the war first. We are in a fever here and have been for months. The French Invasion is expected hourly and the town is regularly filled with the militia and yeomanry which, from the noise they make, intend to behave most valiantly, but of which I hold no very great expectations. We hear horrid tales of the French. Billie has taught us all how to load and fire a blunderbuss and I can assure you that should they come they will find the house as stoutly defended as a handful of women and a legless boy can make it. The children thrive on the excitement, Richard particularly, he is much affected by the sight of any uniform . . .*

You will have heard of the Coalition with Austria. Much is expected of it, though I know not what to think at the moment. We are constantly disturbed by the passage of post-chaises and couriers on the Portsmouth Road that the turmoil makes it impossible to judge the true state of affairs and indeed to know whether anyone is capable of doing so . . .

There was much more, and with it newspapers and other gossip that had percolated through the officers' correspondence to the gunroom. There had been a movement by the Brest fleet under Ganteaume which had engaged British ships off Point St Matthew and seemed to have followed some direct instruction of the Emperor Napoleon's. It was conjectured that a similar order had gone out to Villeneuve, but the accuracy of this was uncertain.

The news was already old. He felt his own fears for his family abating. The uncertainty of the last months was gone. Whatever

French intentions were, it was clear that the two main fleets of the enemy were secured, the one in Brest, the other in Cadiz. This time the doors of the stables were double-bolted with the horses inside.

'Beg pardon, sir, but Mr Fraser says to tell you that *Euryalus* is approaching.'

'*Euryalus*?' Drinkwater looked up from the log-book in astonishment at Midshipman Wickham. 'Are you certain?'

'I believe so, sir.'

'Oh.' He exchanged glances with Hill. 'We are superceded, Mr Hill.'

'Yes,' Hill replied flatly.

'Very well, Mr Wickham, I'll be up directly.' He signed the log and handed it back to the sailing master.

Half an hour later Drinkwater received a letter borne by a courteous lieutenant from the *Euryalus*. He read it on deck:

Euryalus
Off Cadiz
27th September 1805

Dear Drinkwater,

I am indebted to you for so ably holding the forward post off San Sebastian. However I am ordered by Vice-Ad. Collingwood to direct you to relinquish the station to myself and to proceed to Gibraltar where you will be able to make good the deficiency in your stores. You are particularly to acquaint General Fox of the fact that Lord Nelson is arriving shortly to take command of His Majesty's ships and vessels before Cadiz, and it is his Lordship's particular desire that his arrival is attended with no ceremony and the news is kept from Admiral Decrès as long as possible.

May good fortune attend your endeavours. Lose not a moment.

Henry Blackwood.

Drinkwater looked at the lieutenant. 'Tell Captain Blackwood that I understand his instructions . . . Does he think that Decrès commands at Cadiz?'

The lieutenant nodded. 'Yes, sir. Captain Blackwood has come directly from London. Lord Nelson is no more than a day behind us in *Victory* . . .'

'But Decrès, Lieutenant, why him and not Villeneuve?'

'I believe, sir, there were reports in London that Napoleon is replacing Villeneuve, sir. Admiral Decrès was named as his successor.'

Drinkwater frowned. 'But Decrès is Minister of Marine. Does this mean the game is not yet played out?'

'Reports from Paris indicate His Imperial Majesty still has plans for his fleets, although I believe the French have decamped from Boulogne.'

'Good Lord. Very well, Lieutenant, we must be about our business. My duty to Captain Blackwood.'

'So,' muttered Drinkwater to himself as he watched the *Euryalus*'s boat clear the ship's side, 'the horse may yet kick the stable door down.'

'Port, Captain Drinkwater?'

'Thank you, sir,' Drinkwater unstoppered the decanter and poured the dark wine into his gleaming crystal glass. Despite the war the Governor of Gibraltar, General Fox, kept an impressive table. He had dined to excess. He passed the decanter to the infantry colonel next to him.

'So,' said the Governor, 'Nelson does not want us to advertise his arrival to the Dons, eh?'

'That would seem to be his intention, sir.'

'It would frighten Villeneuve. I suppose Nelson wants to entice them out for a fight, eh?'

'I think that would be Lord Nelson's intention, General, yes.' He remembered his conversation with Pitt all those months ago.

'Let's hope he doesn't damn well lose 'em this time then.' There was an embarrassed silence round the table.

'Is Villeneuve still in command at Cadiz, sir?' Drinkwater asked, breaking the silence. 'There was, I believe, a report that Napoleon had replaced him.'

Fox exchanged glances with the port admiral, Rear-Admiral Knight. 'We have not heard anything of the kind, though if Boney wants anything done he'd be well advised to do so.'

'The fleet is pleased to have Nelson out, I daresay,' put in Knight.

'Yes, Sir John. I believe his arrival will electrify the whole squadron.'

'Collingwood's a fine fellow,' said Fox, 'but a better bishop than an admiral. Pass the damn thing, John.'

Sir John Knight had his fist clamped round the neck of the decanter, withholding it from the Governor to signal his displeasure at having a fellow admiral discussed before a junior captain.

'Vice-Admiral Collingwood is highly regarded, sir,' Drinkwater remarked loyally, disliking such silly gossip about a man who was wearing himself out in his country's service. Fox grunted and Drinkwater considered that his contradiction of a General Officer might have been injudicious. Knight rescued him.

'I believe you will be able to sail and rejoin the fleet by noon tomorrow, Drinkwater.'

'I hope so, Sir John.'

'Well you may reassure Lord Nelson that he has only to intimate his desire to us and we shall regard it as a command. At this important juncture in the war it is essential that we all cooperate . . .'

'A magnificent sight is it not? May I congratulate you on being made post, sir.'

'Thank you . . . I er, forgive me, your face is familiar . . .'

'Quilliam, sir, John Quilliam. We met before Copenhagen . . .'

'On board *Amazon* . . . I recollect it now. You are still awaiting your step?'

'Yes. But resigned to my fate. To be first lieutenant of *Victory* is a better berth than many. Come, sir, his Lordship will see you at once and does not like to be kept waiting.'

Drinkwater followed Quilliam across *Victory*'s immaculate quarterdeck, beneath the row of fire-buckets with their royal cipher and into the lobby outside Lord Nelson's cabin. A minute later he was making his report to the Commander-in-Chief and delivering Sir John Knight's documents to him. The little admiral greeted him cordially. The wide, mobile mouth smiled enthusiastically, though the skin of his face seemed transparent with fatigue. But the single eye glittered with that intensity that Drinkwater had noted before Copenhagen.

'And you say it is still Villeneuve that commands at Cadiz, Captain?'

'I have learned nothing positive to the contrary, my Lord, but you well know the state of news.'

'Indeed I do.' Nelson paused and reflected a moment. 'Captain Drinkwater, I am obliged to you. I am reorganising my fleet. Rear-Admiral Louis is here, in the *Canopus* and I am attaching you to his squadron which is to leave to victual in Gibraltar. I know that you have come from there and I wish that you should station your frigate to the eastward of The Rock. I apprehend that Salcedo may break out from Cartegena and I am in my usual desperation for want of frigates.'

The order came like a blow to Drinkwater and his face must have shown something of his disappointment. 'My dear Drinkwater, I have no other means of keeping the fleet complete in provisions and water, but by this means. You may return with Louis but I cannot afford to have him cut off from my main body.'

Drinkwater subdued his disappointment. 'I understand perfectly, my Lord,' he said.

Nelson came round the table to escort Drinkwater to the door with his customary civility and in a gesture that made intimates of all his subordinates.

'We *shall* have a battle, Drinkwater. I *know* it. I *feel* it. And we shall all do our duty to the greater glory of our King and Country!'

And Drinkwater was unaccountably moved by the sincere conviction of this vehement little speech.

Drinkwater looked astern. The sails of Rear-Admiral Louis's squadron were purple against the sunset. Drinkwater wondered if Lord Walmsley had transferred from the *Leopard* with the rear-admiral. He did not greatly care. What he felt most strongly was a sense of anti-climax, and he felt it was common throughout all of Louis's squadron. He crossed the deck and looked at the log.

Thursday 3rd October 1805. 6 p.m. Bore up from the Straits of Gibraltar in company Canopus, *Rear-Ad. Louis,* Queen, Spencer, Zealous *and* Tigre. *Wind westerly strong breeze. At sunset handed t'gallants.*

'Very well, Mr Fraser, call me if you are in any doubt whatsoever.'

'Aye, aye, sir.' From his tone Fraser sounded depressed too.

Chapter Sixteen *3–14 October 1805*

Tarifa

'It's a ship's launch, sir.'

'I believe you to be right, Mr Hill. Very well, back the mizen topsail until she comes up.'

The knot of curious officers waited impatiently. For over a week *Antigone* had cruised east of Gibraltar, half hoping and half fearing that Salcedo would try and effect a juncture with Villeneuve. The only thing that could satisfy them would be orders to return to Cadiz. Was that what the launch brought them?

'There's a lieutenant aboard, sir,' observed Fraser. 'Aye, and a wee midshipman.'

The launch lowered its mainsail and rounded under *Antigone*'s stern. A moment later a young lieutenant scrambled over the rail and touched his hat to Drinkwater.

'Captain Drinkwater?'

'Yes. You have brought us orders?'

The officer held out a sealed packet which Drinkwater took and retired with to his cabin. In a fever of impatience he opened the packet. A covering letter from Louis instructed him to comply with the enclosed orders and wished him every success in his 'new appointment'. Mystified, he tore open Nelson's letter.

Victory
Off Cadiz
10th October 1805

My Dear Drinkwater

I am sensible of the very great services rendered by you before Copenhagen and the knowledge that you were exposed to, and suffered from, the subsequent attack on Boulogne. It is your name that I call to mind at this time. Poor Sir Robert Calder has been called home to stand trial for his actions in July last. I cannot find it in me to send him in a

frigate and am depriving the fleet of the Prince of Wales *to do honour to him. Brown of the* Ajax *and Letchmere of the* Thunderer *are also to go home as witnesses and it is imperative I have experienced captains in these ships. Leave your first lieutenant in command. Louis has instructions to transfer a lieutenant from one of his ships. You may bring one of your own, together with two midshipmen, but no more. These orders will come by the* Entreprenante *cutter, but she has orders to return immediately. Therefore hire a barca longa and join* Thunderer *without delay.*
Nelson and Brontë

'God bless my soul!' He was to transfer immediately into a seventy-four! 'How damnably providential!' he muttered, then recalled himself. He would be compelled to leave most of his effects . . .

'Mullender!' He began bawling orders. 'Rogers! Pass word for the first lieutenant!' He sat down and wrote out a temporary commission for Rogers, interrupting his writing to shout additional wants to his steward. Then he shouted for Tregembo and sent him off with a bewildering series of orders without an explanation.

Rogers knocked and entered.

'Come in, Sam. I am writing out your orders. You are to take command. This lieutenant is staying with you. I am transferring to *Thunderer.* You may send over my traps when you rejoin the fleet . . . Hey! Tregembo! Pass word for my coxswain, damn it! Ah, Tregembo, there you are. Tell Mr Q and Midshipmen Frey and Gillespy to pack their dunnage . . . oh, yes, and you too . . . Sam, set course immediately for Gibraltar. Take that damned launch in tow . . . Come, Sam, bustle! Bustle!' He shooed the first lieutenant out of the cabin. Rogers's mouth gaped, but Drinkwater took little notice. He was trying to think of all the essential things he would need, amazed at what he seemed to have accumulated in eighteen months' residence.

'Mullender! God damn it, where is the fellow?'

He would take Frey because he was useful, and Gillespy out of pity. He could not leave the child to endure Rogers's rough tongue. James Quilhampton he would have to take. If he did not he doubted if Quilhampton, like Tregembo, would ever forgive him the omission.

Antigone hove to off Europa Point and Drinkwater and his party transferred to the launch. The midshipman in command of the boat hoisted the lugsails and set his course for Gibraltar. Drinkwater looked back to see the hands swarming aloft.

'God bless my soul!' he said again. The cheer carried to him over the water and he stood up and doffed his hat. An hour later, still much moved by the sudden change in his circumstances, he stood before Louis.

'Sorry to lose you, Drinkwater, but I wish you well. I am fearful that my ships will miss the battle and I told Lord Nelson so, but . . .' the admiral shrugged his shoulders. 'No matter. I have hired a local lugger to take you down the coast. It is all that is available but the passage will not be long and you will not wish to delay for something more comfortable, eh?'

'Indeed not, sir. I am obliged to you for your consideration.'

By that evening, in a fresh westerly breeze, the *barca longa* was beating out of Gibraltar Bay. Below, in what passed for a cabin, Drinkwater prepared to sleep in company with Quilhampton and his two midshipmen.

'We must make the best of it, gentlemen,' he said, but he need not have worried. The events of the day had tired him and, shorn for a time of the responsibilities of command, he fell into a deep sleep.

He was awakened by a sharp noise and a sudden shouting. Against the side of the lugger something heavy bumped.

'By God!' he shouted, throwing his legs clear of the bunk, 'there's something alongside!' In the darkness he heard Quilhampton wake. 'For God's sake, James, there's something wrong!' The unmistakable sound of a scuffle was going on overhead and suddenly it fell quiet. Drinkwater had tightened the belt of his breeches and had picked up a pistol when the hatch from the deck above was thrown back and the grey light of dawn flooded the mean space.

A moustachioed face peered down at them from behind the barrel of a gun. '*Arriba!*'

Drinkwater lowered his pistol; there was no point in courting death. He scrambled on deck where a swarthy Spaniard twisted the flintlock from his grasp. They were becalmed off the town of Tarifa and the *Guarda Costa* lugger that had put off from the mole lay alongside, her commander and crew in possession of the deck of the *barca longa*. A glance forward revealed Tregembo still struggling beneath three Spaniards. 'Belay that, Tregembo!'

'Buenos Dias, Capitán.' A smirking officer greeted his emergence on deck, while behind him Quilhampton and Frey struggled over the hatch-coaming swearing. The master of the *barca longa* was secured by two Spanish seamen and had obviously revealed the nature of his passengers. For a second Drinkwater suspected treachery, but the Gibraltarian shrugged.

'Eet is not my fault, Captain . . . the wind . . . eet go,' he said.

'That's a damned fine excuse.' Drinkwater expelled his breath in a long sigh of resignation. Any form of resistance was clearly too late.

'Wh . . . what is the matter?' Little Gillespy's voice piped as he came on deck behind Frey, rubbing the sleep from his eyes. The Spanish officer pointed at him, looked at Drinkwater and burst out laughing, exchanging a remark with his men that was obviously obscene.

'We are prisoners, Mr Gillespy,' said Drinkwater bitterly. 'That is what is the matter.'

'Preesoners,' said the Coast Guard officer, testing the word for its aptness, '*si, Capitán*, preesoners,' and he burst out laughing again.

Had he not had Quilhampton and Tregembo with him and felt the necessity of bearing their ill-luck with some degree of fortitude in front of the two midshipmen, Drinkwater afterwards thought he might have gone mad that day. As it was he scarcely recollected anything about the ignominious march through the town beyond a memory of curious dark eyes and high walls with overhanging foliage. Even the strange smells were forgotten in the stench of the prison in which the five men were unceremoniously thrown. It was a large stone-flagged room, lined with decomposed straw. A bucket stood, half-full, in a corner and the straw moved from the progress through it of numerous rats. Drinkwater assumed it must be the Bridewell of the local *Alcaid*, emptied for its new inmates.

Conversation between the men was constrained by their respective ranks as much as their circumstances. Tregembo, with customary resource, commenced the murder of the rats while James Quilhampton, knowing the agony through which Drinkwater was going, proved his worth by reassuring the two midshipmen, especially Gillespy, that things would undoubtedly turn out all right.

'There will be a battle soon and Nelson will have hundreds of Spaniards to exchange us for,' he kept saying. 'Now, Mr Gillespy, do you know how many Spanish seamen you are worth, eh? At the present exchange rate you are worth three. What d'you think of that, eh? Three seamen for each of you reefers, four for me as a junior lieutenant, one for Tregembo and fifteen for the captain. So all Nelson has to do is take twenty-six Dagoes and we're free men!'

It went on all day, utterly exhausting Quilhampton, while Drinkwater paced up and down, for they drew back for him, clearing a space as though the cell was a quarterdeck and the free winds of the Atlantic blew over its stinking flagstones. Once or twice he stopped, abstracted, his fists clenched behind his back, his head cocked like one listening, though in reality from his mangled shoulder. They would fall silent then, until he cursed under his breath and went on pacing furiously up and down.

Towards evening, as darkness closed in, the heavy bolts of the door were drawn back and a skin of bitter wine and a few hunks of dark bread were passed in on a wooden platter. But that was all. Darkness fell and the place seemed to stink more than ever. Drinkwater remained standing, wedged into a corner, unable to compose his mind in sleep. But he must have slept, for he woke cramped, as another platter of bread and more raw wine appeared. They broke their fast in silence and an hour later the bolts were drawn back again. The Coast Guard officer beckoned Drinkwater to follow and led him along a passage, up a flight of stone steps and through a heavy wooden door. A strip of carpet along another passage suggested they had left the prison. The officer threw open a further door and Drinkwater entered a large, white-walled room. A window opened onto a courtyard in which he could hear a fountain playing. Leaves of some shrub lifted in the wind. On the opposite wall, over a fireplace, a fan of arms spread out. A table occupied the centre of the room, round which were set several chairs. Two were occupied. In one sat a tall dragoon officer, his dark face slashed by drooping moustaches, his legs encased in high boots. His heavy blue coat was faced with sky-blue and he wore yellow leather gloves. A heavy, curved sabre hung on its long slings beside his chair. He watched Drinkwater through a blue haze of tobacco smoke from the cigar he was smoking.

The other man was older, about sixty, Drinkwater judged, and presumably the *Alcaid* or the *Alcalde.* The Coast Guard officer made some form of introduction and the older man rose, his brown eyes not unkind. He spoke crude English with a heavy accent.

'Good day, Capitán. I am Don Joaquín Alejo Méliton Pérez, *Alcalde* of Tarifa. Here', he indicated the still-seated cavalry officer, 'is Don Juan Gonzalez De Urias of His Most Catholic Majesty's Almansa Dragoons. Please to take a seat.'

'Thank you, señor.'

'I too have been prisoner. Of you English. When you are defending Gibraltar under General Elliott.'

'Don Perez, I protest, my effects . . . my clothes . . .' he grasped his soiled shirt for emphasis, but the old man raised his hand.

'All your clothes and equipments are safe. I ask you here this morning to tell me your name. Don Juan is here coming from Cadiz. He is to take back your name and the ship that you are *capitán* from . . . This you must tell me, please.'

The *Alcalde* picked up a quill and dipped it expectantly in an ink-pot.

'I am Captain Nathaniel Drinkwater, Don Pérez, of His Britannic Majesty's frigate *Antigone* . . .'

At this the hitherto silent De Urias leaned forward. Drinkwater heard the name *Antigone* several times. The two men looked at him with apparently renewed interest.

'Please, you say your name, one time more.'

'Drink-water . . .'

'Eh?' The *Alcalde* looked up, frowned and mimed the act of lifting a glass and sipping from it, '*Agua?*'

Drinkwater nodded. 'Drink-water.'

'*Absurdo!*' laughed the cavalry officer, pulling the piece of paper from the *Alcalde,* then taking his quill and offering them to Drinkwater who wrote the information in capital letters and passed it back.

Don Juan De Urias stared at the letters and pronounced them, looked up at Drinkwater, then thrust himself to his feet. The two men exchanged a few words and the officer turned to go. As he left the room the Coast Guard officer returned and motioned Drinkwater to follow him once again.

He was returned to the cell and it was clear that much speculation had been in progress during his absence.

'Beg pardon, sir,' said Quilhampton, 'but could you tell us if . . .'

'Nothing has happened, gentlemen, beyond an assurance that our clothes are safe and that Cadiz is being informed of our presence here.'

Drinkwater saw Quilhampton's eyes light up. 'Perhaps, sir, that means our release is the nearer . . .'

It was an artificially induced hope that Quilhampton himself knew to be foolish, but the morale of the others should not be allowed to drop.

'Perhaps, Mr Q, perhaps . . .'

They languished in the cell for a further two days and then they were suddenly taken out into a stable yard and offered water and the contents of their chests with which to prepare themselves for a journey, the *Alcalde* explained. When they had finished they were more presentable. Drinkwater felt much better and had retrieved his journal from the chest. The *Alcalde* returned, accompanied by Don Juan De Urias.

'Don Juan has come', the *Alcalde* explained, 'to take you to Cadiz. You are known to our ally, *Capitán*.'

Drinkwater frowned. Had the French summoned him to Cadiz?

'Who knows me, señor?'

Perez addressed a question to De Urias who pulled from the breast of his coat a paper. He unfolded it and held it out to Drinkwater. It was in Spanish but at the bottom the signature was in a different hand.

'Santhonax!'

PART THREE

Battle

'Now, gentlemen, let us do something today which the world may talk of hereafter.'

VICE-ADMIRAL COLLINGWOOD TO HIS OFFICERS,
HMS *Royal Sovereign*, forenoon, 21st October 1805

'The enemy . . . will endeavour to envelop our rear, to break through our line and to direct his ships in groups upon such of ours as he shall have cut off, so as to surround them and defeat them.'

VICE-ADMIRAL VILLENEUVE TO HIS CAPTAINS
Standing Orders given on board the *Bucentaure*,
Toulon Road, 21st December 1804

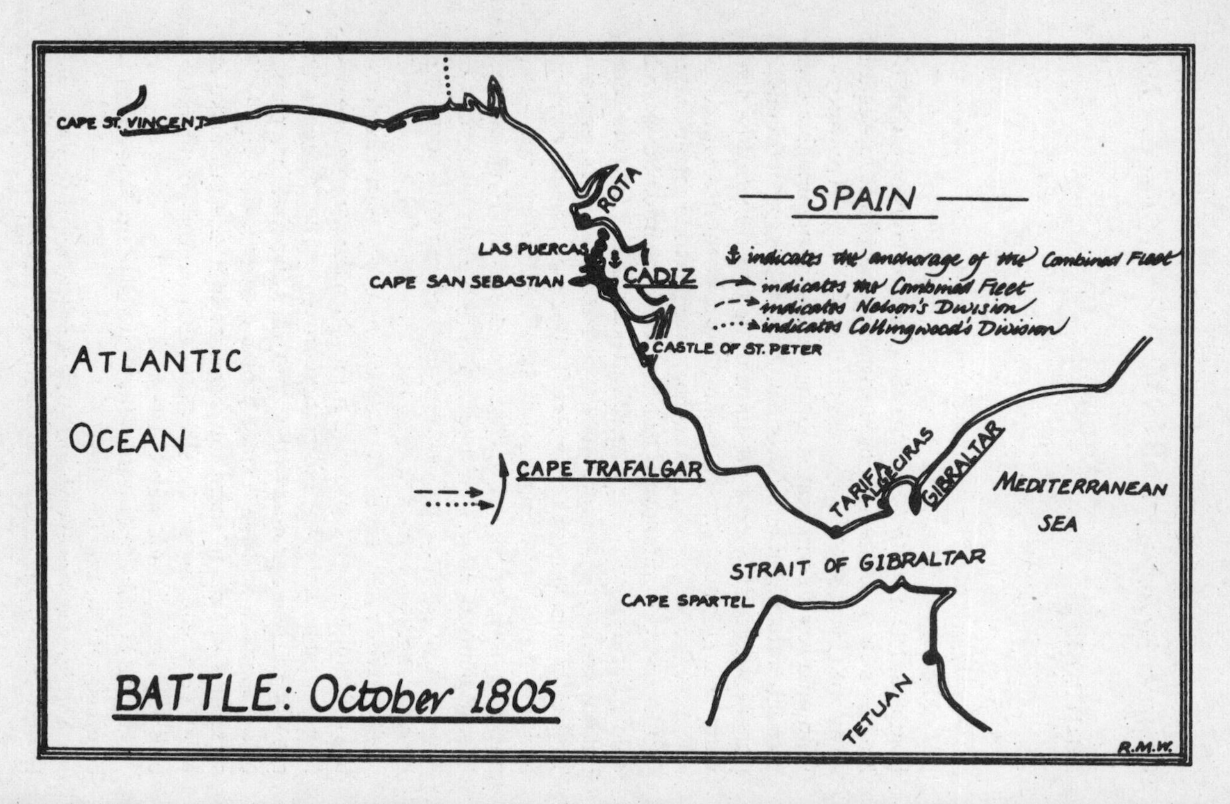
SPAIN
⚓ indicates the anchorage of the Combined Fleet
→ indicates the Combined Fleet
- - → indicates Nelson's Division
· · · → indicates Collingwood's Division
CAPE ST. VINCENT
ROTA
LAS PUERCAS
CAPE SAN SEBASTIAN
CADIZ
CASTLE OF ST. PETER
ATLANTIC
OCEAN
CAPE TRAFALGAR
TARIFA
ALGECIRAS
GIBRALTAR
MEDITERRANEAN
SEA
STRAIT OF GIBRALTAR
CAPE SPARTEL
TETUAN
BATTLE: October 1805
R.M.W.

Chapter Seventeen *14 October 1805*

Santhonax

Lieutenant Don Juan Gonzalez de Urias of His Most Catholic Majesty's Dragoons of Almansa flicked the stub of a cigar elegantly away with his yellow kid gloves and beckoned two of his troopers. Without a word he indicated the sea-chests of the British and the men lifted them and took them under an archway. Motioning his prisoners to follow, he led them through the arch to the street where a large black carriage awaited them. Dragoons with cocked carbines flanked the door of the carriage and behind them Drinkwater caught sight of the curious faces of children and a wildly barking dog. The five Britons clambered into the coach, Drinkwater last, in conformance with traditional naval etiquette. Tregembo was muttering continual apologies, feeling awkward and out of place at being in such intimate contact with 'gentlemen'. Drinkwater was compelled to tell him to hold his tongue. Behind them the door slammed shut and the carriage jerked forward. On either side, their gleaming sabres drawn, a score of De Urias's dragoons formed their escort.

For a while they sat in silence and then they were clear of the town, rolling along a coast-road from which the sea could be seen. None of them looked at the orange groves or the cork oaks that grew on the rising ground to the north; they all strove for a glimpse of the blue sea and the distant brown mountains of Africa. The sight of a sail made them miserable as they tried to make out whether it was one of the sloops Collingwood had directed to blockade coastal trade with Cadiz.

'Sir,' said Quilhampton suddenly, 'if we leapt from the coach, we could signal that brig for a boat . . .'

'And have your other hand cut off in the act of waving,' said Drinkwater dismissively. 'No, James. We are prisoners being escorted to Cadiz. For the time being we shall have to submit to our fate.'

This judgement having been pronounced by the captain produced a long and gloomy silence. Drinkwater, however, was pondering their chances. Freedom from the awful cell at Tarifa had revived his spirits. For whatever reason the French wanted them at Cadiz, it was nearer to the British battle-fleet than Tarifa and an opportunity might present itself for them to escape.

'Beg pardon, sir,' put in Quilhampton.

'Yes, James?'

'Did you say "Santhonax", sir, when we were in the stable yard? Is that the same cove that we took prisoner at Al Mukhra?'

'I believe so, yes.'

'I remember him. He escaped off the Cape . . . D'you remember him, Tregembo?'

'Aye, zur, I do. The Cap'n and I know him from away back.' Tregembo's eyes met those of Drinkwater and the old Cornishman subsided into silence.

Piqued by this air of mystery, Frey asked, 'Who is he sir?'

Drinkwater considered; it would do no harm to tell them. Besides, they had time to kill, the jolting of the coach was wearisome, and it is always the balm of slaves and prisoners to tell stories.

'He is a French officer of considerable merit, Mr Frey. A man of the stamp of, say, Captain Blackwood. He was, a long time ago, a spy, sent into England to foment mutiny among the fleet at the Nore. He used a lugger to cross the Channel and we chased him, I recollect, Tregembo. He shot part of our mast down . . .'

'That's right, zur,' added Tregembo turning on the junior officers, 'but we was only in a little cutter, the *Kestrel*, twelve popguns. We had 'im in the end though, zur.' Tregembo grinned.

'Aye. At Camperdown,' mused Drinkwater, calling into his mind's eye that other bloody October day eight years earlier.

'At Camperdown, sir? There were French ships at Camperdown?' asked Frey puzzled.

'No, Mr Frey. Santhonax was sent from Paris to stir the Dutch fleet to activity. I believe him to have been instrumental in forcing Admiral De Winter to sail from the Texel. Tregembo and I were still in the *Kestrel*, cruising off the place, one of Duncan's lookouts. When the Dutch came out Santhonax had an armed yacht at his disposal. We fought and took her, and Santhonax was locked up in Maidstone Gaol.' Drinkwater sighed. It all seemed so long ago and there was the disturbing image of the beautiful Hortense swimming into his mind. He recollected himself; that was no part of what he wanted to tell his juniors about Santhonax.

'Unfortunately,' he went on, 'whilst transferring Santhonax to the hulks at Portsmouth, much as we are travelling now . . .'

'He escaped,' broke in Quilhampton, 'just as we might . . .'

'He spoke unaccented and near perfect English, James,' countered Drinkwater tolerantly, ignoring Quilhampton's exasperation. 'How good is your Spanish, eh?'

'I take your point, sir, and beg your pardon.'

Drinkwater smiled. 'No matter. But that is not the end of the story, for Mr Quilhampton and I next encountered Edouard Santhonax when he commanded our own frigate *Antigone* in the Red Sea. He was in the act of re-storing her after careening and we took her one night, in a cutting-out expedition, and brought both him and his frigate out together from the Sharm Al Mukhra. Most of the guns were still ashore and we were caught in the Indian Ocean by a French cruiser from Mauritius. We managed to fight her off but in the engagement Santhonax contrived to escape by diving overboard and swimming to his fellow countryman's ship. We were saved by the timely arrival of the *Telemachus,* twenty-eight, commanded by an old messmate of mine.'

'And that was the last time you saw him, sir?'

'Yes. But not the last time I heard of him. After Napoleon extricated himself from Egypt and returned from Paris a number of officers that had done him singular services were rewarded. Santhonax was one of them. He transferred, I believe, to the army, not unknown in the French and Spanish services,' he said in a didactic aside for the information of the two young midshipmen who sat wide-eyed at the Captain's tale, 'who often refer to their fleets as "armies" and their admirals as "captains-general". Now, I suppose, he has recognised my name and summoned me to Cadiz.'

'I think he may want information from you, sir,' said Quilhampton seriously.

'Very probably, Mr Q. We shall have to decide what to tell him, eh?'

'Sir,' said Gillespy frowning.

'Yes, Mr Gillespy?'

'It is a very strange story, sir. I mean the coincidences . . . almost as if you are fated to meet . . . if you see what I mean, sir.'

Drinkwater smiled at the boy who had flushed scarlet at expressing this fantasy.

'So I have often felt, Mr Gillespy; but in truth it is not so very remarkable. Consider, at the time Tregembo, Mr Q and I were fighting this fellow in the Red Sea, Sir Sydney Smith was stiffening the defences of Acre and thwarting Boney's plans in the east. A little later Sir Sydney fell into Bonaparte's hands during a boat operation off Havre, along with poor Captain Wright, and the pair of them spent two years in The Temple prison in Paris,' he paused, remembering Camelford's revelations about the connection of Santhonax with the supposed suicide. 'The two of them escaped and Wright was put in command of the sloop-of-war *Vincejo*, only to be captured in a calm by gunboats in the Morbihan after a gallant defence. He was returned to the Temple . . .'

'Where Bonaparte had him murdered,' put in Quilhampton.

Drinkwater ignored the interruption. Poor Quilhampton was more edgy than he had been a few days earlier. Presumably the strain of playing Dutch uncle to this pair of boys had told on his nerves. 'Very probably,' he said, 'but I think the events not dissimilar to my own encounters with Santhonax; a sort of personal antagonism within the war. It may be fate, or destiny, or simply coincidence.' Or witchcraft, he wanted to add, remembering again the auburn hair of Hortense Santhonax.

Silence fell again as the coach rocked and swayed over the unmade road and the dragoons jingled alongside. From time to time De Urias would ride up abreast of the window and peer in. After several hours they stopped at a roadside *taverna* where a change of horses awaited them. The troopers had a meal from their saddlebags, watered their horses and remounted. For some English gold Drinkwater found in his breeches pocket he was able to buy some cold meat and a little rot-gut wine at an inflated price. The inn-keeper took the money, bit it and, having pocketed the coin, made an obscene gesture at the British.

'We are not popular,' observed Quilhampton drily, with a lordly indifference that persuaded Drinkwater he was recovering his spirits after the morning's peevishness. They dozed intermittently, aware that as the coast-road swung north the distant sea had become wave-necked under a fresh westerly breeze. Drinkwater was awakened by Quilhampton from one of these states of semi-consciousness that was neither sleep nor wakefulness but a kind of limbo into which his mind and spirit seemed to take refuge after the long, unremitting months of duty and the hopelessness of captivity.

'Sir, wake up and look, sir.'

From the window he realised they were headed almost north, running across the mouth of a bay. To the west he could see distant grey squares, the topsails of Nelson's look-out ships, keeping contact with the main fleet out of sight over the horizon to the westward. The thought made him turn to his companions.

'Gentlemen, I must caution you against divulging any information to our enemy. They are likely to question us all, individually. You have nothing to fear,' he said to young Gillespy. 'You simply state that you were a midshipman on your first voyage and know nothing.' He regretted the paternal impulse that had made the child his note-taker. 'You may say I was an old curmudgeon, Mr Gillespy, and that I told you nothing. Midshipmen are apt to hold that opinion of their seniors.' He smiled and the boy smiled uncertainly back. At least he could rely upon Frey and Quilhampton.

They crossed the back of a hill that fell to a headland whereon stood a tall stone observation tower. A picket of *Guarda Costa* horses and men were nearby and they turned and holloaed at the coach and its escort as it swept past.

'I recognise where we are,' said Drinkwater suddenly. 'That is Cape Trafalgar. Have we changed horses again?'

'Twice while you were dozing, sir.'

'Good God!' It was already late afternoon and the sun was westering behind great banks of cloud. On their right, above the orange and olive groves, Drinkwater caught sight of the Chiclana hill. They crossed a river and passed through a small town.

'Look sir, soldiers!' said Frey a little later as the coach slowed. They could hear De Urias shouting commands and swearing. Drinkwater looked out of the window but the nearest trooper gestured for him to pull his head in; he was not permitted to stare. The coach increased speed again and they were jolting through a bivouac of soldiers. Drinkwater recognised the bell-topped shakoes of French infantry and noted the numerals '67' and '16'. Someone saw his face and raised a shout: *'Hey, Voilà Anglais . . .!'*

The cooking fires of the two battalions drew astern as they began to go downhill and then they pulled up. Drinkwater saw water on either side of them before a dragoon opened each door and the window blinds were drawn. The trooper said something to them in Spanish from which they gathered that any attempt to see any more would be met by a stern measure. The doors were slammed and, in darkness, they resumed the last miles of their journey from Tarifa, aware that the coach was traversing the long mole of Cadiz.

They were hurried into their new place of incarceration. The building seemed to be some kind of a barracks and they were taken into a bare corridor and marched swiftly along it. Two negligent French sentries made a small concession to De Urias's rank as they halted by a door. A turnkey appeared, the door was unlocked and the two midshipmen, Tregembo and Quilhampton were motioned to enter. De Urias restrained Drinkwater whose quick glance inside the cell revealed it as marginally cleaner than the hole at Tarifa, but still unsuitable for the accommodation of officers.

'Lieutenant, I protest; the usages of war do not condemn officers doing their duty to kennels fit for malefactors!'

It was clear that the protest, which could not have failed to be understood by the Spanish officer, fell on deaf ears. As the turnkey locked the door De Urias motioned Drinkwater to follow him again. They emerged into a courtyard covered by a scrap of grey sky. The wind was still in the west, Drinkwater noted. As they crossed the square he saw a pair of horses with rich shabraques being held by an orderly outside a double door beneath a colonnade. The door was flanked by two sentries. Drinkwater's eye spotted the grenadier badges and the regimental number '67' again. They passed through the door. A group of officers were lounging about a table. One, in full dress, stood up from where he half sat on the end of the heavy table.

'Ah,' he said, smiling almost cordially, *'le capitaine anglais. Bienvenu à Cadiz!'* The officer bowed from the waist, his gaudy shako tucked under his arm. *'Je suis Lieutenant Leroux, Le Soixante-septième Régiment de Ligne.'*

'Bravo, Leroux!' There was an ironic laugh from his fellow officers which Leroux ignored. He twirled a moustache. *'Allez, Capitaine . . .'*

Ignoring De Urias, Drinkwater followed the insouciant Leroux up a flight of stairs and to a door at the end of another corridor. At the door Leroux paused and Drinkwater was reminded of a midshipman preparing to enter the cabin of an irascible captain. Leroux coughed, knocked and turned his ear to the door. Then he opened it, crashed to attention and announced Drinkwater. He stood aside and Drinkwater entered the room.

A tall, curly-haired officer rose from the table at which he had been writing. His dark and handsome features were disfigured by a broad, puckered scar which dragged down the corner of his left eye and split his cheek. His eyes met those of Drinkwater.

'So, Captain,' he said in flawless English, 'we meet again . . .' He indicated a chair, dismissed Leroux and sat down, his hand rubbing his jaw, his eyes fastened on his prisoner. For a moment or two Drinkwater thought the intelligence reports might have been wrong – Santhonax wore an elaborate, gold-embroidered uniform that was more naval than military – but he was soon made aware of Santhonax's status and the reason for Leroux's deference.

'I recollect you reminded me that it was the fortune of war that I was your prisoner when we last had the pleasure of meeting.' Santhonax's tone was heavily ironic. Drinkwater said nothing. 'I believe the more apt English expression to be "a turning of tables", eh?'

Santhonax rose and went to a cabinet on which a decanter and glasses stood in a campaign case. He filled two glasses and handed one to Drinkwater.

Drinkwater hesitated.

'It is good cognac, Captain Drinkwater.'

'Thank you.'

'Good. We have known each other too long to be hostile. I see you too have been wounded . . .'

Santhonax inclined his head in an imitative gesture, indicating Drinkwater's mangled shoulder.

'A shell wound, *m'sieur*, received off Boulogne and added to the scars you gave me yourself.'

'Touché.' Santhonax paused and sipped his cognac, never taking his eyes off Drinkwater, as though weighing him up. 'Not *"m'sieur"*, Captain, but *Colonel, Colonel* and *Aide-de-Camp* to His Imperial Majesty.'

'My congratulations,' Drinkwater said drily.

'And you are to be congratulated too, I believe. You have been commanding the frigate *Antigone*.' He paused, he had commanded her himself once. 'That is something else we have in common. She was a fine ship.'

'She *is* a fine ship, Colonel.'

'Yes. I watched her wear off San Sebastian a week or two ago. You and Blackwood of the *Euryalus* are well known to us.'

'You are no longer in the naval service, Colonel,' said Drinkwater attempting to steer the conversation. 'Could that be because it has no future?'

The barb went home and Drinkwater saw the ice in Santhonax's eyes. But the former agent was a master of self-control. 'Not at all, Captain. As you see from my present appointment, I have not severed my connections with the navy.'

'It occurs to me, however, that you may still be a spy . . .' He was watching Santhonax closely. That fine movement, no more than a flicker of the muscles that controlled the pupils of his eyes, was perceptible to the vigilant Drinkwater. There was no doubt that Santhonax was in Cadiz at the behest of his Imperial master. As an aide-de-camp Santhonax would be allowed the privileges of reporting direct to Napoleon. Even the Commander-in-Chief of the Combined Fleet, Vice-Admiral Villeneuve, would have to report to Paris through the Minister of Marine, Decrès.

Santhonax attempted to divert the conversation. 'You are still suspiciously minded, Captain Drinkwater, I see. There is little work for a spy here. The Combined Fleets of France and Spain are not as useless as you English would sometimes like to assume. They have twice crossed the Atlantic, ravaging the sugar islands off the West Indies, recovered British possessions in the islands, and fought an engagement with the British fleet . . .'

'In which with overwhelming force you managed to lose two ships . . .'

'In which the *Spanish* managed to lose two ships, Captain, and following which the British admiral is being tried for failure to do his utmost. I recall the last time this occurred it was found necessary to shoot him . . .'

Drinkwater mastered the anger mounting in him. Losing his temper would do no good. Besides, an idea was forming in his head. At that moment it was no more than a flash of inspiration, an intuition of opportunity, and it was laid aside in the need to mollify. He remained silent.

Santhonax seemed to relax. He sat back in his chair, although he still regarded Drinkwater with those unwavering eyes.

'Tell me, Captain, when you took *Antigone,* did you discover a portrait of my wife?'

'I did.'

'And . . . what became of it?'

'I kept it. You might have had it back had you not so unceremoniously left us off the Cape. It was removed from its stretcher, rolled up, and is still on board the *Antigone.* If I was to be liberated I should send it back to you as a mark of my gratitude.'

Santhonax barked a short laugh. 'Ha! But you were not on board *Antigone* when the Spanish *Guarda Costa* took you, were you, Captain? Where *were* you going?'

'It would be no trouble to send for the canvas, Colonel, most of my effects remain on board . . .'

'I asked', broke in Santhonax, his eyes hardening again, 'where you were going?'

'I was transferring to another ship, Colonel, the *Thunderer,* seventy-four.'

Santhonax raised one ironic eyebrow. 'Another promotion, eh? What a pity you were asleep the other morning. Our ally's vigilance has deprived Nelson of a captain.'

Drinkwater kept his temper and again remained silent.

'Tell me, Captain, is it correct that Admiral Louis's squadron is in Gibraltar?'

The idea sparked within Drinkwater again. Santhonax's intention was almost certainly similar to that when he had exerted pressure on de Winter in the autumn of '97. He was an aggressive French imperialist, known to be Bonapartist and a familiar of Napoleon's. Surely it was the French Emperor's intention that the Combined Fleet should sail? Even with those reports that Napoleon had broken up the camp at Boulogne, every indication was that he wanted the fleet of Villeneuve at sea. It was clear that Santhonax's question was loaded. The French were not certain about Louis, not absolutely certain, although the movements of British ships were reported to them regularly from Algeçiras.

Santhonax wanted extra confirmation, perhaps as added information with which to cajole Villeneuve as he had so successfully worked on de Winter.

And if Napoleon wanted Villeneuve at sea, so too did Nelson!

Anything, therefore, that smoothed Villeneuve's passage to sea was assisting that aim and, if he consciously aided the schemes of Napoleon, at least he had the satisfaction of knowing that the fleet that lay over the horizon to the west was equally anxious for the same result.

'Come, Captain,' urged Santhonax, 'we know that there are British line-of-battle ships in Gibraltar. Are they Louis's?'

'Yes.' Drinkwater answered monosyllabically, as though reluctant to reply.

'Which ships?'

Drinkwater said nothing. 'It is not a difficult matter to ascertain, Captain, and the information may make the stay of you and your friends,' Santhonax paused to lend the threat weight, 'a little pleasanter by your co-operation.'

Drinkwater sighed, as though resigning himself to his fate. He endeavoured to appear crestfallen. '*Canopus, Queen, Spencer, Tigre* and *Zealous*.'

'Ah, a ninety-eight, an eighty and three seventy-fours . . .'

'You are well informed, Colonel Santhonax.' Santhonax ignored the ironic compliment.

'And Calder, he has gone back to England in a frigate?'

'No, he has gone back to England in a battleship, the *Prince of Wales;* and the *Donegal* was to go to Gibraltar to join Louis.'

'You have been most informative, Captain.'

Drinkwater shrugged with the disdain he felt Santhonax would expect, and added, 'It is still a British fleet, Colonel . . .' He deliberately left the sentence unfinished.

'There is nothing to alarm us in the sight of a British fleet, Captain. Your seventy-fours have barely five hundred men on board, they are worn out by a two years' cruise; you are no braver than us, indeed you have infinitely less motive to fight well, less love of country. You can manoeuvre well, but we have also had sea-experience. I am confident, Captain Drinkwater, that we are about to see the end of an era for you and a glorious new era for the Imperial Navy.'

Drinkwater thought at first Santhonax was rehearsing some

argument that he would later put to Villeneuve, but there was something sincere in the speech. The guard was down, this was the soul of the man, a revealed intimacy born out of the long years of antagonism.

'Time will tell, Colonel.'

Santhonax rose. 'Oh yes indeed, Captain, time will tell, time and the abilities of your Admiral Nelson.'

Chapter Eighteen *15–16 October 1805*

The Spectre of Nelson

Drinkwater woke refreshed after a good night's sleep. He had been led from his interview with Santhonax to an upper room, presumably an officer's quarters within the barracks, which was sparsely, though adequately furnished, and served a plain meal of cold meat, fruit and wine. He had later been asked for and given his parole. When this formality had been completed his sea-chest was brought in by an orderly and he was returned his sword. He was refused leave to see the others but assured that they were quite comfortable.

For a long while he had lain awake, staring at a few stars that showed through the window and listening to the sounds of Cadiz; the barking of dogs, the calls of sentries, the periodic ringing of a convent bell and the sad playing of a distant guitar. He went over and over the interview with Santhonax, trying to see more in it than a mere exchange of words, and certain that his instinct was right and that Santhonax was there, in Cadiz, to force Villeneuve to sea. Eventually he had slept.

With the new day came this strange feeling of cheerfulness and he drew himself up in bed, a sudden thought occurring to him. He had been groping towards a conclusion the previous night, but he had been tired, his mind clogged by all the events of the day. Now, be began to perceive something very clearly. He had grasped Santhonax's purpose all right, but only half of its import. Santhonax's last remark, his sneering contempt for Nelson, was the key. He knew that few of the French admirals were contemptuous of Nelson, least of all Villeneuve who had escaped the terrible *débâcle* of Abukir Bay. But Santhonax would not sneer contemptuously without good cause; he had impugned Nelson's abilities, not his character. In what way was Nelson's ability defective?

And then he recalled his own complaint to Pitt. It was not a defect so much as a calculated risk, but it had twice cost Nelson dearly. Nelson's blockade out of sight of land had allowed Brueys to slip out of Toulon to Egypt, and Villeneuve to slip out of Toulon to the West Indies. Now, although he had Blackwood up at the very gates of Cadiz, it might happen again. If the wind went easterly the Combined Fleet could get out of Cadiz and would not run into Nelson unless it continued west. But at this time of the year the wind would soon swing to the west, giving the Combined Fleet a clear run through the Straits of Gibraltar. Nelson was fifty miles west of Cadiz. He might catch up, but then again he might not! And Napoleon was supposed to have decamped his army from Boulogne. They had not gone west, so they too must be marching east! Of course! Drinkwater leapt from the bed and began pacing the little room: Austria had joined the coalition and a small British expeditionary force under General Craig had gone east, he himself had escorted it through the Gut! The ideas came to him thick and fast now, facts, rumours, all evidence of a complete reversal of Napoleon's intentions but no less lethal. Craig would be cut off, British supremacy in the Mediterranean destroyed. *That* was why Ganteaume had not broken out of Brest. He could tie half the Royal Navy down there. And *that* was why Allemand had come no further south. He could not break through Nelson's fleet to reinforce Villeneuve but, by God, he could still keep 'em all guessing! And last, the very man whom Nelson had sent *Antigone* to guard against cutting Louis off in Gibraltar, Admiral Salcedo at Cartagena, had no need to sail west. He could simply wait until Villeneuve came past! It was a brilliant deception and ensured that British eyes were concentrated on the Channel.

Drinkwater ceased pacing, his mind seeing everything with a wonderful clarity. He felt a cold tingle run the length of his spine. 'God's bones,' he muttered, 'now what the devil do I do?'

His plan of the previous evening seemed knocked awry. If he added reasons persuading Santhonax that urging Villeneuve to sail was advantageous to Nelson, would Nelson miss the Combined Fleet? If, on the other hand, Villeneuve was left alone, would Nelson simply blockade him or would he attempt an attack? The long Mole of Cadiz could be cut off by the marines of the fleet and a thousand seamen, the anchorage shelled by bomb-vessels.

'This is the very horns of a dilemma,' he muttered, running his fingers through his hair. His thoughts were abruptly interrupted when the door of his room opened and Tregembo entered with hot shaving water. The sight cheered Drinkwater.

'Good morning, zur,' the old Cornishman rasped.

'God bless my soul, Tregembo, you're a welcome sight!'

'Aye, zur. I was passed word to attend 'ee, zur, and here I am.' Tregembo jerked his head and Drinkwater caught sight of the orderly just outside.

'Are you and the others all right?'

Tregembo nodded and fussed around the room, unrolling Drinkwater's housewife and stropping the razor.

'Aye, zur. All's as well as can be expected, considering . . .'

'No talk!' The orderly appeared in the doorway.

Drinkwater drew himself up. 'Be silent!' he commanded, 'I shall address my servant if I so wish, and desire him to convey my compliments to my officers.' Drinkwater fixed the orderly with his most baleful quarterdeck glare and went on, as though still addressing the French soldier, 'and to let 'em know I believe that things will not remain static for long. D'you hear me, sir?' Drinkwater turned away and caught Tregembo's eye.

'Not remain static long,' the Cornishman muttered, 'aye, aye, zur.' He handed Drinkwater the lathered shaving brush. They exchanged glances of comprehension and Tregembo left the room. Behind him the orderly slammed the door and turned the key noisily in the lock.

The silly incident left Drinkwater in a good enough humour to shave without cutting himself and the normality of the little routine caused him to reflect upon his own stupidity. It was quite ridiculous of him to suppose that he, a prisoner, could have the slightest influence on events. The best he could hope for was that those events might possibly provide him with an opportunity to effect an escape. At least he had Tregembo as a go-between; that was certainly better than nothing.

All day Drinkwater sat or paced in the tiny room. Towards evening he was taken down to walk in the courtyard, seeing little of his surroundings but enjoying half an hour in the company of Quilhampton and the two midshipmen.

'How are you faring, James?'

'Oh, well enough, sir, well enough. A little down-hearted I fear, but we'll manage. And you, sir? Did you see Santhonax?'

'Yes. Did you?'

'No, sir. By the way, I trust you have no objections, but our gaolers have allowed Tregembo to look after us. I hope you don't mind us poaching your coxswain, sir.'

'No,' said Drinkwater, brightening, 'matter of fact it might be a help. He can keep up communications between us. Have you learned anything useful?'

'Not much. From the way those French soldiers behave when a Spanish officer's about there's not much love lost between 'em.'

Drinkwater remembered the negligence of the two sentries in acknowledging De Urias. 'Good point, James.' He ought to have noticed that himself.

'And I believe there has been an epidemic in Andalucia recently, some sort of fever, and as a consequence there's a shortage of food. Cadiz is like a place under seige.'

'Good God! How d'you know that?'

Quilhampton shrugged. 'This and that, sir. Listening to the guards chatter. You can pick up some of the sense. I thought something of the kind must have happened as we came through the countryside yesterday. Not too many people in the fields, lot of young women and children . . . oh, I don't know, sir . . . just a feeling.'

'By heaven, James, that's well argued. I had not even noticed a single field.'

Quilhampton smiled thinly. 'We ain't too well liked, sir, I'm afraid. "Perfidious Albion" and all that.' He was suddenly serious and stopped strolling. He turned and said, 'D'you think we're going to get out, sir? I mean before the war's over or we're taken to France.'

Drinkwater managed a confident smile. 'D'you know, James, that an admiral is worth four post-captains on exchange. How many lieutenants d'you think that is, eh? By God, we'll be worth our weight in gold! After the battle they'll be queueing up to exchange us for admiral this and commodore that.' He patted Quilhampton's arm. 'Brace up, James, and keep up the spirits of those two reefers.'

'Oh, Frey's all right; he's as tough as a fore-tack despite appearances to the contrary. It's Gillespy I'm worried about. Poor boy cried last night. I think he thought I was asleep . . .'

'Poor little devil. Would it help if I had a word with him?'

'Yes, I think so. Tell him how many admirals there will be to exchange after the battle.'

Drinkwater turned but Quilhampton said, 'Sir . . . sir, do you think there's going to *be* a battle?'

'Damn sure, James,' Drinkwater replied. And for that instant, remembering Nelson's conviction, he was irrationally certain of the fact.

It is very curious Drinkwater wrote in his journal, *to sit and write these words as a prisoner. I am far from being resigned to my fate but while I can still hear the call of gulls and can hear the distant noise of the sea which cannot be very far from my little window I have not yet sunk into that despond that men who have been imprisoned say comes upon one. God grant that such a torpor is long in coming or fate releases me from this mischance . . .*

He stopped writing and looked at his pen. Elizabeth's pen. He closed his journal quickly and got up, falling to a violent pacing of the floor in an effort to drive from his mind all thoughts of Elizabeth or his children. He must not give way to that; that was the way to despair.

He was saved from further agony by the opening of his door. A strange officer in the uniform of the Imperial Navy stood behind the orderly. He spoke English.

'*Capitaine* Drinkwater? Good evening. I am Lieutenant René Guillet of the *Bucentaure*. Will you 'ave the kindness to follow me. It would be advisable that you bring your 'at.'

'This is a formal occasion?'

'*Oui*.'

Drinkwater was led into the same room in which he had been interviewed by Santhonax. Santhonax was there again, but standing. Sitting at the table signing documents was another man. After a short interval he looked up and studied the prisoner. Then he stood up and walked round the table, addressing a few words to Guillet who came smartly forward, collected the papers and placed them in a leather satchel. The strange man was tall and thin with an intelligent face. He wore a white-powdered wig over his high forehead. His nose was straight and his mouth well made and small. He had a firm chin, although his jowls were heavy. Drinkwater judged him to be much the same age as himself. He wore a long-skirted blue uniform coat with a high collar and corduroy pantaloons of a greenish colour, with wide stripes of gold. His feet were thrust into elegant black half-boots of the type favoured by hussars and light cavalry. Across his waist there looped a gold watch-chain from which depended a heavy gold seal.

'Introduce us, Colonel.' His voice sounded tired, but his English, although heavily accented, was good.

Santhonax stepped forward. 'Captain Nathaniel Drinkwater of the Royal Navy, formerly commander of His Britannic Majesty's frigate *Antigone* . . .'

'Ahhh . . . *Antigone* . . .' said the stranger knowingly.

'On his way to take command of the *Thunderer*,' Santhonax's voice was ironic, 'but taken prisoner *en route*.' He turned to Drinkwater, 'May I present Vice-Admiral Villeneuve, Commander-in-Chief of the Combined Squadrons of His Imperial and Royal Majesty Napoleon, Emperor of the French and of his Most Catholic Majesty King Ferdinand of Spain.'

The two men exchanged bows. 'Please sit down, Captain.' Villeneuve indicated a chair and returned behind the table where he sat, leaned forward with his elbows on the table and passed his hands over his face before resting his chin upon the tips of his fingers.

'Colonel Santhonax has told me much about you. Your frigate has made as much of a name for itself as *Euryalus*.'

'You do me too much honour, sir.'

'They are both good ships. The one was copied from the French, the other captured.'

'That is so, sir.'

'Colonel Santhonax also tells me you informed him that Nelson commands the British squadron off Cadiz. Is this true?'

Drinkwater frowned. He had said no such thing. He looked at Santhonax who was still standing and smiling, the candle-light and his scar giving the smile the quality of a grimace.

'You did not deny it when I said he was with the British fleet,' Santhonax explained. Drinkwater felt annoyed with himself for being so easily trapped, but he reflected that perhaps Santhonax had given away more. In any case, it was pointless to deny it. It seemed that Villeneuve would assume the worst, and if the worst was Nelson, then no harm was done. He nodded.

'Nelson *is* in command, sir,' he said.

He heard Villeneuve sigh and felt he had reasoned correctly.

The French admiral seemed abstracted for a second and Santhonax coughed.

'And several ships have gone to Gibraltar?' the admiral asked.

'Yes, sir.'

'Where is the *Superb*?' asked Villeneuve. 'She had gone to England for repair, no?'

'She had not rejoined the fleet when I left it, sir.' Drinkwater felt a quickening of his pulse. All Villeneuve's questions emphasised his desire to hear that Nelson's fleet was weakened by dispersal.

The admiral nodded. 'Very well, Captain, thank you.' He rang a little bell and Guillet reappeared. Drinkwater rose and bowed to the admiral who was turning towards Santhonax, but Santhonax ignored Villeneuve.

'Captain Drinkwater!'

Drinkwater turned. 'Yes?'

'I am leaving . . . to rejoin the Emperor tonight. You will send the picture to the Rue Victoire will you not . . . when you return to your ship?' Santhonax was sneering at him. Drinkwater remembered Camelford's words: 'Shoot 'em both!'

'When I rejoin my ship . . .'

The two men stared at each other for a second. 'Until the next time, *au revoir*.'

Walking from the room Drinkwater heard a suppressed confrontation between the two men. As the door closed behind him he heard Santhonax quite clearly mention *'Le spectre de Nelson . . .'*

Tregembo's brief visit the next morning disclosed little. 'They've got their t'gallants up, zur. Frogs and Dagoes all awaiting the order, zur . . . and pleased the Frogs'll be to go.'

'There's nothing new about that, Tregembo, they're always getting ready to go. It's the goin' they ain't so good at,' Drinkwater replied, lathering his face. 'But how the hell d'you know all this, eh?'

'There are Bretons in the guardroom, zur. I unnerstand 'em. Their talk, like the Kurnowic it is, zur . . .'

'Ahhh, of course.' Drinkwater smiled as he took the stropped razor from Tregembo, recalling Tregembo's smuggling past and the trips made to Brittany to evade the excise duty of His Majesty

King George III. 'Keep your spirits up, Tregembo, and tell Mr Q the same.'

'Aye, zur. Mr Gillespy ain't too good, zur, by the bye . . .'

'No talk!' The orderly, red-faced with fury, shoved Tregembo towards the door.

'Very well,' acknowledged Drinkwater. 'But there's very little I can do about it,' he muttered as, once again, the door slammed and he was left alone with his thoughts.

Meat and wine arrived at midday. He walked with the others after the hour of *siesta*, finding Quilhampton downcast and Gillespy in poor spirits. Today it seemed as if Frey was bearing the burden of cheering his fellow prisoners. At sunset a silent Tregembo brought him bread, cheese and wine. As the shadows darkened in the tiny room, Drinkwater found his own morale dropping. In the end it became irresistible not to think of his family and the 'blue-devils' settled on his weary mind. He did not bother to light his candle but climbed into the bed and tried to sleep. A convent bell tolled away the hours but he had fallen asleep when his door was opened. He woke with a start and lay staring into the pitch-darkness. He felt suddenly fearful, remembering Wright's death in the Temple. He reached for his sword.

'Get dressed please, *Capitaine*.'

'Guillet?'

'Please to 'urry, *m'sieur*.'

'What the devil d'you want?'

'Please, *Capitaine*. I 'ave my orders. Dress and come quickly with no noise.' Guillet was anxious about something. Fumbling in the dark Drinkwater found his clothes and his sword. Guillet must have seen the slight gleam of the scabbard mountings. 'Not your sword, *Capitaine* . . .'

Drinkwater left it on his bed and followed Guillet into the corridor. At the door of the guardroom Guillet collected a cloak and handed it to Drinkwater. Drinkwater threw the heavy garment over his shoulders.

'Allez . . .'

They crossed the courtyard and, with Guillet taking his arm, passed the sentry into the street. 'Please, *Capitaine*, do not make to escape. I have a loaded pistol and orders to shoot you.'

'Whose orders? Colonel Santhonax's? Do not forget, Lieutenant Guillet, that I have given my parole.' Drinkwater's anger was unfeigned and Guillet fell silent. Was it Santhonax's purpose to have him murdered in an alleyway?

They were walking down a gentle hill, the cobbled roadway descending in low steps, the blank walls of houses broken from time to time by dimly perceived wrought-iron gates opening onto courtyards. He could see the black gleam of water ahead and they emerged onto a quay. Drinkwater smelt decaying fish and a row of gulls, disturbed by the two officers, flapped away over the harbour. Guillet hurried him to a flight of stone steps. Drinkwater looked down at the waiting boat and the oars held upright by its crew. The lieutenant ordered him down the steps. He scrambled down, pushed by Guillet and sat in the stern-sheets. The bow was shoved off, the oars were lowered and bit into the water. The chilly night air was unbelievably reviving.

A mad scheme occurred to him of over-powering Guillet, seizing his pistol and forcing the boat's crew to pull him out to *Euryalus*. But what would become of Quilhampton and the others? The French, who had treated them reasonably so far, might not continue to do so if he escaped. In any case the plan was preposterous. The lift of the boat, as the water chuckled under the bow and the oars knocked gently against the thole pins, evoked a whole string of emotional responses. The thought that Santhonax was ruthless enough to have him murdered was cold comfort. Yet Guillet seemed to be pursuing orders of a less extreme nature. Nevertheless Drinkwater acknowledged the fact that, removed from his frigate, he was as impotent as an ant underfoot.

The boat was pulled out into the *Grande Rade*, among the huge hulls and towering masts of the Combined Fleet. Periodically a sentry or a guard-boat challenged them and Guillet answered with the night's countersign. A huge hull reared over them. Even in the gloom Drinkwater could see it was painted entirely black. He guessed her to be Spanish. Then, beyond her, he saw the even bigger bulk of a mighty ship. He could make out the greyer shade of lighter paint along her gun-decks. He counted four of these and was aware that he was looking at the greatest fighting ship in the world, the Spanish *navio Santissima Trinidad*.

He was still staring at her as the oarsmen eased their stroke. He looked round as they ran under the stern of a smaller ship. From the double line of lighted stern windows she revealed herself as a two-decker. The light from the windows made reading her name difficult, but he saw enough to guess the rest.

Bucentaure.

Guillet had brought him, in comparative secrecy, to Villeneuve's flagship.

Chapter Nineteen *16–17 October 1805*

Villeneuve

Vice-Admiral Pierre Charles Jean Baptiste Silvestre de Villeneuve sat alone in the great cabin of the *Bucentaure*. He stared at the miniature of his wife. He had painted it himself and it was not so much her likeness that he was looking at, as the remembrance of her as she had been on the day he had done it. He sighed resignedly and slipped the enamel disc in the pocket of his waist-coat. His eye fell on the letter lying on the table before him. It was dated a few days earlier and written by an old friend from Bayonne.

My dear friend,

I write to tell you news that will not please you but which you may otherwise not learn until it is brought to you by one who will not be welcome. I learned today that our Imperial master has despatched Admiral Rosily to Cadiz to take over the command from you. My old friend, I know you as undoubtedly the most accomplished officer and the most able tactician, whatever people may say, that the navy possesses. I recall to you the honour of the flag of our country . . .

Vice-Admiral Villeneuve picked up the letter and, holding it by a corner, burnt it in the candelabra that stood upon the table. The ash floated down upon the polished wood and lay upon Admiral Gravina's latest daily report of the readiness of the Spanish Fleet. Of all his flag-officers Gravina was the only one upon whom he could wholly rely. They were both of the nobility; they understood one another. Villeneuve clenched his fist and brought it down on the table top. It was on Gravina that would fall the responsibility of his own answer to defeating the tactics of Nelson. But he might yet avoid a battle with Nelson . . .

The knock at the cabin door recalled him to the present. *'Entrez!'*

Lieutenant Guillet, accompanied by the officer of the watch, Lieutenant Fournier, announced the English prisoner. The two stood aside as Drinkwater entered the brilliantly lit cabin from the gloom of the gun-deck with its rows of occupied hammocks.

The two officers exchanged glances and Fournier addressed a question to the admiral. Villeneuve seemed irritated and Drinkwater heard his own name and the word 'parole'. The two withdrew with a scarcely concealed show of reluctance.

'Please sit, Captain Drinkwater,' said Villeneuve indicating a chair. 'Do you also find young men always know best?' he smiled engagingly and, despite their strange meeting, Drinkwater warmed to the man. He was aware once again that the two of them were of an age. He smiled back.

'It is a universal condition, Your Excellency.'

'Tell me, Captain. What would British officers be doing in our circumstances?' Villeneuve poured two glasses of wine and handed one to Drinkwater.

Drinkwater took the glass. 'Thank you, sir. Much as we are doing. Taking a glass of wine and a biscuit or two in the evening at anchor, then taking their watch or turning in.'

The two men sat for a while in silence, Drinkwater patiently awaiting disclosure of the reason for this strange rendezvous. Villeneuve seemed to be considering something, but at last he said, 'Colonel Santhonax tells me you are an officer of great experience, Captain Drinkwater. He would not have been pleased that we are talking like this.'

Villeneuve's remark was an opening, Drinkwater saw, a testing of the ground between them. On what he said now would depend how much the enemy admiral confided in him. 'I know Colonel Santhonax to be a spy, Your Excellency. As an aide to your Emperor I assume he enjoys certain privileges of communication with His Majesty.' He paused to lend his words weight, 'I would imagine that could be a grave embarrassment to you, sir, particularly as Colonel Santhonax is not without considerable experience as a seaman. I would say, sir, that he shared something of the prejudices of your young officers.'

'You are very – what is the English word? Shrewd, eh? – Yes, that is it.' Villeneuve smiled again, rather sadly, Drinkwater thought. 'Do you believe in destiny, Captain?'

Drinkwater shrugged. 'Not destiny, sir. Providence, perhaps, but not destiny.'

'Ah, that is because you are not from an ancient family. A Villeneuve died with Roland at the Pass of Roncesvalles; a Villeneuve died in the Holy Land and went to battle with your Coeur-de-Lion, and a Villeneuve led the lances of Aragon with Bayard. I was the ninety-first Villeneuve to be a Knight of Malta and yet I saw the justice of the Revolution, Captain. I think as an Englishman you must find that difficult to understand, eh?'

'Perhaps less than you think, sir. My own fortunes have been the other way. My father was a tenant farmer and I am uncertain of my origins before my grandfather. I would not wholly disapprove of your Revolution . . .'

'But not our Empire, eh, Captain?'

Drinkwater shrugged. 'I do not wish to insult you, sir, but I do not approve of the Emperor's intentions to invade my country.'

Villeneuve was obviously also thinking of Napoleon for he said. 'Do you know what Santhonax is doing, Captain?'

'I imagine he has gone to Paris to report to His Imperial Majesty on the state of the fleet you command. And possibly . . .' he broke off, then, thinking it was worth a gamble, added, 'to tell the Emperor that he has succeeded in persuading you to sail.'

'Bon Dieu!' The blood drained from Villeneuve's face. 'H . . . how did you . . .?'

Villeneuve hesitated and Drinkwater pressed his advantage. 'As I said, Your Excellency, I know Santhonax for what he is. Did he kill Captain Wright in the Temple?'

The colour had not yet returned to the admiral's face. 'Is that what they say in England? That Santhonax murdered Wright?'

'No, they say he was murdered, but by whom only a few suspect.'

'And you are one of them, I think.'

Drinkwater shrugged again. 'On blockade duty, sir, there is ample time to ponder . . .' he paused seeing the admiral's puzzled look, 'er, to think about things.'

'Ah, yes, I understand. Your navy has a talent for this blockading. It is very tedious, is it not?'

'Very, sir . . .'

'And your ships? They wear out also?'

Drinkwater nodded, 'Yes.'

'And the men?'

Drinkwater held the admiral's gaze. It was no simple matter to convey to a Frenchman, even of Villeneuve's intelligence, the balance of the stubborn tenacity of a national character against a discipline that did not admit weakness. Besides, it was not his intention to appear over-confident. 'They wear out too, sir,' he said smiling.

Looking at the Englishman, Villeneuve noticed his hand go up under his coat to massage his shoulder. 'You have been wounded, Captain?'

'Several times . . .'

'Are you married?'

'Yes. I have two children.'

'I also am married . . . This war; it is a terrible thing.'

'I should not be here, sir, were it not for your Combined Fleet,' Drinkwater said drily.

'Ah, yes . . . the Combined Fleet. What is your opinion of the Combined Fleet, Captain?'

'It is difficult to judge, sir. But I think the ships good, particularly, with respect, the Spanish line-of-battle ships. The French are good seamen, but lack practice; the Spanish . . .' he shrugged again.

'Are beggars and herdsmen, the most part landsmen and soldiers,' Villeneuve said with sudden and unexpected vehemence. He stood up and began to pace with a slow dignity back and forwards between the table and the stern windows with an abstraction that Drinkwater knew to reveal he often did thus. 'And the officers are willing, but inexperienced. One cruise to the West Indies and they think they are masters of the oceans. They are all fire or venom because they think Villeneuve a fool! Do you know why I brought you here tonight, Captain, eh? No? Because it is not possible that I talk freely to my own officers! Only Gravina comprehends my position and he has troubles too many to speak of with his own court and that parvenu Godoy, the "Prince of Peace"!' Villeneuve's contempt filled him with a blazing indignation. 'Oh, yes, Captain, there is destiny,' he paused and looked down at Drinkwater, then thrust his pointing arm towards the windows. 'Out on the sea is Nelson and here, here is Villeneuve!' He stabbed his own chest with the same finger. Drinkwater sat quietly as Villeneuve took two more turns across the cabin then calmed himself, refilled the glasses and sat down again.

'How will Nelson attack, Captain?' He paused as Drinkwater protested, then held up his hand. 'It is all right, Captain, I know you to be a man of honour. I will tell you as I told my captains before we left Toulon. He will attack from windward if he can, not in line, but so as to concentrate his ships in groups upon a division of our fleet which he will annihilate with overwhelming force.' He slammed his right hand down flat upon the table making the candles gutter and raising a little whirl of grey ash. 'It was done at Camperdown and he did it to us at Abukir . . .' Again Villeneuve paused and Drinkwater watched him silently. The admiral had escaped from that terrible battle, Napoleon accounting him a lucky man, a man of destiny to be taken up to run at the wheels of the Imperial chariot.

'But it has never been done in the open sea with Nelson in command of a whole fleet,' Villeneuve went on, staring abstractedly into the middle distance. Drinkwater realised he was a sensitive and imaginative man and pitied him his burden. Villeneuve suddenly looked at him. 'That is how it will happen, yes?'

'I think so, sir.'

'If you were me, how would you counter it?'

'I . . . er, I don't know . . . It has never been my business to command a fleet, sir . . .'

Villeneuve's eyes narrowed and Drinkwater suddenly saw that the man did not lack courage, whatever might be said of him. 'When it is time for you to command a fleet, Captain, remember there is always an answer; but what you will lack is the means to do it . . .' He stood up again. 'Had I *your* men in *my* ships, Captain, I would astonish Napoleon!'

The admiral tossed off his second glass and poured a third, offering the wine to Drinkwater.

'Thank you, Your Excellency. But how would you answer this attack?' Drinkwater was professionally curious. It was a bold question, but Villeneuve did not seem to regard it as such and Drinkwater realised the extremity of the French admiral's loneliness and isolation. In any case Drinkwater was a prisoner, his escape from the heart of the Combined Fleet so unlikely that Villeneuve felt safe in using the opportunity to see the reaction to his plan of at least one British officer.

'A squadron of reserve, Captain, a division of my fleet kept detached to weather of my line and composed of my best ships, to reinforce that portion of my fleet which receives – how do you say? – the weight, no . . .'

'The brunt?'

'Yes, the brunt of your attack.'

Drinkwater considered Villeneuve's scheme. It was innovative enough to demonstrate his originality of thought, yet it had its defects.

'What if your enemy attacks the squadron of reserve?'

'Then the fleet tacks to *its* assistance, but I do not think this will happen. Your Nelson will attack the main line.' He smiled wryly and added, 'He may ignore the special division as being a badly manoeuvred part of the general line.'

'And if you are attacked from leeward . . .'

'Then the advantage is even more in our favour, yes.'

'But, Excellency, who have you among your admirals to lead this important division?'

'Only Gravina, Captain, on whom I can absolutely depend.' Villeneuve's face clouded over again. For a moment he had been visualising his counter-stroke to Nelson's attack, seeing the moving ships, hearing the guns and realising his dream: to save the navy of France from humiliation and raise it to the heights to which Suffren had shown it could be elevated. He sighed, obviously very tired.

'So you intend to sail, sir?' Drinkwater asked quietly. 'To offer battle to Nelson?'

'If necessary.' Villeneuve's reply was guarded, cautious, even uncertain, Drinkwater concluded, observing the admiral closely.

'But battle *will* be necessary if you wish to enter the Channel.'

'Perhaps . . .' There was an indifference now; Drinkwater felt the certainty of his earlier deliberations.

'Perhaps you are hoping to return to the Mediterranean?' he ventured. 'I hear his Imperial Majesty has withdrawn his camp from Boulogne?'

'*Diable!*' Villeneuve had paled again. 'How is this known? Do you know everything that comes to me?'

He rose, very angry and Drinkwater hurriedly added, 'Pardon, Excellency. It was only a guess . . . I, I made a guess . . .'

'A guess!' For a second Villeneuve's face wore a look of astonishment. Then his eyes narrowed a little. 'Santhonax was right, Captain Drinkwater, you are no fool. If I have to fight I will, but I have twice eluded Nelson and . . .' He shrugged, 'perhaps I might do it again.'

Drinkwater relaxed. He had been correct all along in his assumptions. The two men's eyes met. They seemed bound in an intensity of feeling, like the eyes of fencers of equal skill where pure antagonism had given way to respect, and only a superficial enmity prevented friendship. Then one of the fencers moved his blade, a tiny feinting movement designed to suggest a weakness, a concern.

'I think you might,' said Drinkwater in a voice so low that it was not much above a whisper. It was a terrible gamble, Drinkwater knew, yet he conceived it his duty to chance Nelson not missing the Combined Fleet.

For what seemed an age a silence hung in the cabin, then Villeneuve coughed and signalled their intimacy was at an end. 'After this conversation, Captain, I regret that you cannot leave the ship. You have given your parole and I will endeavour to make your stay comfortable.'

Drinkwater opened his mouth to protest. A sudden chilling vision of being on the receiving end of British broadsides overwhelmed him and he felt real terror cause his heart to thump and his face to blanch.

It was Villeneuve's turn to smile: 'You did not believe in destiny, Captain; remember?' Then he added, 'Santhonax wished that I left you to rot in a Spanish gaol.'

Drinkwater woke confused. After leaving Villeneuve he had been conducted to a small cabin intended for a warrant officer below the water-line on the orlop deck of the *Bucentaure*. A sentry was posted outside and for a long time he lay wide awake thinking over the conversation with Villeneuve, his surroundings both familiar and horribly alien. Eventually he had slept and he woke late, disgruntled, hungry and unable for some seconds to remember where he was. His lack of clothing made him feel irritable and the mephitic air of the unventilated orlop gave him a headache made worse by the strange smells of the French battleship. When he opened his door and asked for food he found the moustached sentry singularly unhelpful.

'I don't want your damned bayonet for my breakfast,' muttered Drinkwater pushing the dully gleaming weapon aside. He pointed to his mouth. '*Manger*,' he said hopefully. The sentry shook his head and Drinkwater retreated into the miserable cabin.

A few minutes later, however, the debonair Guillet appeared, immaculately attired as befitted the junior officer of a flagship, and conducted Drinkwater courteously to the gunroom where a number of the officers were breakfasting. They looked at him curiously and Drinkwater felt ill at ease in clothes in which he had slept. However he took coffee and some biscuit, observing that for a fleet in port the officers' table was sparsely provided. His presence clearly had something of a dampening effect, for within minutes only he and Guillet remained at the table.

'I should be obliged if I could send ashore for my effects, Lieutenant . . . I would like to shave . . .' He mimed the action, at which Guillet held up his hand.

'No, Captain, please it is already that I 'ave sent for your . . .' he motioned over his own clothes, stuck for the right word.

'Thank you, Lieutenant.'

They were not long in coming and they arrived together with Mr Gillespy.

'Good Lord, Mr Gillespy, what the devil do you do here, eh?' The boy remained silent and in the bad light it took Drinkwater a moment to see that he was controlling himself with difficulty. 'Come, sir, I asked you a question . . .'

'P . . . please, sir . . .' He pulled a note from his pocket and held it out. Drinkwater took it and read.

Sir,

The boy is much troubled by your absence. Permission has been obtained from our captors that he may join you wherever you have been taken and I have presumed to send him to you, believing this to be the best thing for him. We are well and in good spirits.

It was signed by James Quilhampton. He could hardly have imagined Drinkwater was on board the enemy flagship. 'Lieutenant Guillet . . . please have the kindness to return this midshipman to my lieutenant . . .'

'Oh, no, sir . . . please, please . . .' Drinkwater looked at the boy. His lower lip was trembling, his eyes filled with tears. '*Please*, sir . . .'

'Brace up, Mr Gillespy, pray remember who and where you are.'

He paused, allowing the boy to pull himself together, and turned towards Guillet. 'What are your orders regarding this young officer?'

Guillet shrugged. His new duty was becoming irksome and he was regretting his boasted ability to speak English. 'The admiral 'e is a busy man, *Capitaine*. 'E says if the, er, midshipman is necessary to you, then he 'as no objection.'

Drinkwater turned to the boy again. 'Very well, Mr Gillespy, you had better find yourself a corner of the orlop.'

'And now, *Capitaine*, perhaps you will come with me onto the deck, yes?'

Drinkwater was ushered on deck, Guillet brushing aside the boy in his ardour to show the English prisoner the puissant might of the Combined Fleet. Drinkwater emerged on deck, his curiosity aroused, his professional interest fully engaged. He was conducted to the starboard waist and allowed to walk up and down on the gangway in company with Guillet. The lieutenant was unusually expansive and Drinkwater considered he was acting on orders from a higher authority. It was difficult to analyse why Villeneuve should want an enemy officer shown his command. He must know Drinkwater was experienced enough to see its weaknesses as well as its strengths; no seaman could fail to do that.

The deck of the *Bucentaure* was crowded with milling seamen and soldiers as the last of the stores were brought aboard. The last water casks were being filled and there were obvious preparations for sailing being made on deck and in the rigging. Boats were out under the bows of the nearest ships, singling up the cables fastened to the buoys laid in the *Grande Rade*.

'Over there,' said Guillet pointing to a 74-gun two-decker, *'le Berwick* a prize from the Royal Navy, and there, the *Swiftsure,* also once a ship of your navy,' Guillet smiled, 'and, of course, we also 'ave one other ship of yours to our credit, but we could not bring it with us,' he laughed, 'His Majesty's sloop *Diamond Rock*!'

Guillet seemed to think this a great joke and Drinkwater remembered hearing of Commodore Hood's bold fortifying of the Diamond Rock off Martinique which had been held for some time before the overwhelming force of Villeneuve's fleet was brought to bear on it.

'I heard the garrison fought successive attacks off for nineteen hours without water in a tropical climate, Lieutenant, and that they capitulated upon honourable terms. Is that not so?' Guillet appeared somewhat abashed and Drinkwater changed the subject. 'Who is that extraordinary officer who has just come aboard?'

'Ah, that is *Capitaine* Infernet of the *Intrépide.*' Drinkwater watched a tall, flamboyant officer with a boisterous air climb on deck. ' 'E went to sea a powder monkey,' Guillet went on, 'and 'as escaped death a 'undred times, even when 'is ship it blows apart. 'E speaks badly but 'e fights well . . .'

'And who is that meeting him?'

'That is my *capitaine,* Jean Jacques Magendie, commandant of the *Bucentaure.*'

'Ah, and that man?' Drinkwater indicated a small, energetic officer with the epaulettes of a *Capitaine de Vaisseu.*

'Ah, that,' said Guillet in obvious admiration, 'is *Capitaine* Lucas of the *Redoutable.*'

'You obviously admire him, Lieutenant. Why is that?'

Guillet shrugged. 'He is a man most clever, and 'is crew and ship most, er, 'ow do you say it . . . er, very good?'

'Efficient?'

'*Oui*. That is right: efficient.'

Drinkwater turned away, Infernet was looking at him and he did not wish to draw attention to himself. He stared out over the crowded waters of Cadiz, the great battleships surrounded by small boats. He saw the massive hull of the four-decked Spanish ship *Santissima Trinidad,* 'That is the *Santissima Trinidad*, is it not?' Guillet nodded. 'She is Admiral Gravina's flagship?'

'No,' said Guillet, 'the Captain-General 'as 'is flag aboard the *Principe de Asturias* of one 'undred and twelve guns. The *Santissima Trinidad* flies the flag of Rear-Admiral Don Baltazar Cisneros. The ship moored next to 'er, she is the *Rayo* of one 'undred guns. She may interest you, *Capitaine;* she is commanded by Don Enrique Macdonnell. 'E is an Irish man who became a Spanish soldier to kill Englishmen. 'E fought in the *Regimento de Hibernia* against you when your American colonies bring their revolution. Later 'e is a sailor and when Gravina called for volunteers, Don Enrique comes to command the *Rayo.*'

'Most interesting. The *Rayo* is newly commissioned then?'

'Yes. And the ship next astern is the *Neptuno*. She is Spanish. We also 'ave the *Neptune.* She is', he looked round, 'there, alongside the *Pluton* . . .'

'We also have our *Neptune,* Lieutenant. She is commanded by Thomas Fremantle. He is rather partial to killing Frenchmen.' Drinkwater smiled. 'We also have our *Swiftsure* . . . but all this is most interesting . . .'

They spent the morning in this manner, talking always about ships and seamen, Drinkwater making mental notes and storing impressions of the final preparations of the Combined Fleet. He had a vague notion that they might be of value, yet was aware that he would find it impossible to pass them to his friends whose topsails, he knew, were visible from only a few feet up *Bucentaure's* rigging. But what was more curious was the strong conviction he had formed that it was Villeneuve himself who wished him to see all this.

A midday meal was served to Drinkwater in his dark and malodourous cabin. Eating alone he was reminded of his time as a midshipman in the equally stinking orlop of the British frigate *Cyclops.* The thought made him call for Gillespy. The only response was from the sentry, who put a finger to his lips and indicated the boy asleep in a corner of the orlop, curled where one of *Bucentaure*'s massive futtocks met the deck.

Guillet did not reappear in the afternoon and, after lying down for an hour, Drinkwater rose. The ship had become strangely quiet, the disorder of the forenoon was gone. The sentry let him pass and he went on deck, passing a body of men milling in the lower and upper gun-decks. As he emerged into a watery sunshine he was aware of the admiral's flag at the masthead lifting to seawards; an easterly wind had come at last!

On the quarterdeck a reception party which included Captain Magendie, his officers and a military guard was welcoming a short, olive-skinned grandee with a long nose. He courteously swept his hat from his head in acknowledgement of the compliments done him, revealing neatly clubbed hair.

Lieutenant Guillet hurried across the deck and took Drinkwater's arm. 'Please, *Capitaine,* is it not for you to be 'ere now.'

'Who was that man, Lieutenant?' asked Drinkwater suffering himself to be hastened below.

'Don Frederico Gravina. Now, *Capitaine,* please you must go to your cabin and to stay.'

'Why?'

'Why, *Mon Dieu, Capitaine,* the order to sail, it is being made.'

But the Combined Fleet did not sail. At four o'clock in the afternoon of 17th October the easterly wind fell away to a dead calm, and Drinkwater sat in his tiny cabin listening to the details of Mr Gillespy's family.

Chapter Twenty *18–21 October 1805*

Nelson's Watch-Dogs

Drinkwater woke with the calling of *Bucentaure*'s ship's company. He was denied the privilege of breakfasting with the officers and it was clear that he was not permitted to leave the hutch of a cabin he had been allocated. Nevertheless he was not required to be locked in, and by sitting in the cabin with a page of his journal before him he amused himself by getting Gillespy to attempt to deduce what was going on above them from the noises they could hear.

To a man who had spent most of his life on board ship this was not difficult, although for Gillespy the task, carried out in such difficult circumstances under the eye of his captain, proved an ordeal. There was a great deal of activity in the dark and stinking orlop deck. Further forward were the damp woollen curtains of the magazine and much of the forenoon was occupied by the barefoot padding past of the *Bucentaure*'s powder monkeys as they scrambled below for the ready-made cartridges. These were supplied by the gunner and his mates whose disembodied hands appeared with their lethal packages through slits in the curtains. Parties of seamen were carrying up cannon balls from the shot lockers and from time to time a gun-captain came down to argue some technicality with the gunner. The junior officers, or *aspirants*, were also busy, running hither and thither on errands for the lieutenants and other officers.

'What do you remark as the most significant difference, Mr Gillespy, between these fellows and our own, eh?' Drinkwater asked.

'Why . . . I don't know, sir. They make a deal of noise . . .'

Drinkwater looked pleased. 'Exactly so. They are a great deal noisier and many officers would judge 'em as inferior because of that; but remark something else. They are also excited and cheerful. I'd say that, just like our fellows, they're spoiling for a fight, wouldn't you?'

'Yes. I suppose so, sir.' A frown crossed the boy's face. 'Sir?'

'Mmmm?' Drinkwater looked up from his journal.

'What will happen to us, sir, if this ship goes into battle?'

'Well, Mr Gillespy, that's a difficult question. We will not be allowed on deck and so, by the usages of war, will be required to stay here. Now do not look so alarmed. This is the safest place in the ship. Very few shot will penetrate this far and, although the decks above us may be raked, we shall be quite safe. Do not forget that instances of ships actually being sunk by gunfire are rare.

'So, let us examine the hypothesis of a French victory. If this is the case we shall be no worse off, for we may have extra company and that will make things much the merrier. On the other hand, assuming that it is a British victory, which circumstances, I might add, I have not the slightest reason to doubt, then we shall find ourselves liberated. Even if the ship is not taken we shall almost certainly be exchanged. We shall not be the first officers present in an enemy ship when that ship is attacked by our friends.' He smiled as reassuringly as he could. 'Be of good heart, Mr Gillespy. You may well have something to tell your grandchildren ere long.'

Gillespy nodded. 'You said that to me before, sir, when the French squadron got out of Rochefort.'

'Did I? I had forgotten.' The captain took up his pen again and bent over his journal.

This remark made Gillespy realise the great distance that separated them. He found it difficult to relate to this man who had shown him such kindness after the harshness of Lord Walmsley. In his first days on board *Antigone* it had seemed impossible that the captain who stood so sternly immobile on the quarterdeck could actually have children of his own. Gillespy could not imagine him as a father. Then he was made aware from the comments of the crew that Drinkwater had done something rather special in getting them out of Mount's Bay and from that moment the boy made it his business to study him. The attentions paid him by the captain had been repaid by a dog-like devotion. Even captivity had seemed tolerable and not at all frightening in the company of Captain Drinkwater. But bereft of that presence, Gillespy had felt all the terrors conceivable to a lonely and imaginative mind. He had implored Quilhampton to request he be allowed to join the captain.

Quilhampton acceded to the boy's request, aware that their captors were in any event likely to separate him and the midshipmen from Drinkwater. In due course Drinkwater would probably be exchanged and Gillespy might have a better chance with the captain. He and Frey would have to rely upon their own resources. James Quilhampton was determined not to remain long in captivity. Let the Combined Fleet sail, as everyone said they would, and he would make an attempt to escape, for the thought of Catriona spurred him on.

Now Gillespy waited patiently for Drinkwater to stop writing notes, watching the men of the *Bucentaure* who messed in the orlop coming below for their midday meal. He listened to their conversation, recognising a word or phrase here and there, and recalling some of the French his Domine had caned into him in Edinburgh all those months ago.

'I think, sir,' he said after a while in a confidential whisper, 'the wind has failed . . . They are laughing at one of the Spanish officers who must have come on board . . . I cannot make out his name . . . Grav . . . something.'

'Gravina?'

'Yes, yes that is it. Do you know what "*mañana*" means sir, in Spanish?'

'Er, "tomorrow", I believe, Mr Gillespy, why?'

'And "*al mar*" must be something to do with the sea; because that fellow there, with the bright bandana and the ear-rings, he keeps throwing his arm in the air and declaiming "*mañana al mar*".' He frowned again, 'I suppose he's imitating this Spanish officer.'

'That is most perceptive of you, Mr Gillespy. If you are right then Gravina has been aboard and announced "tomorrow to sea".' Drinkwater paused reflectively, 'Let us hope to God that you are right.'

He smiled again, encouraging the boy, yet aware that they might not survive the next few days, that ships might not be easily sunk by gunfire but ordinary fire, if it took them, might blow them apart as it had *L'Orient* at Abukir. Staring at the fire-screens round the entrances to the powder magazines, Drinkwater felt the sweat of pure fear prickle his back. Down here they would be caught like rats in a trap.

Towards evening Lieutenant Guillet came to see them. His neck linen was grubby and he looked tired after an active day, but he was courteous enough to apologise for ignoring them and clearly in optimistic spirits.

'Your duty has the greater call upon you than we do, Lieutenant,' said Drinkwater calmly.

'You are permitted 'alf-an-hour on deck, *Capitaine*. And you also,' he added to Gillespy, 'and then I am to take you to the General.'

Drinkwater saw Gillespy frown. 'Admiral Villeneuve, Mr Gillespy. Recall how I told you the French and Spanish use the terms interchangeably.'

The boy nodded and they followed Guillet on deck. The contrast with the previous day was startling. Amidships *Bucentaure*'s boat had been hoisted on the booms. All the ropes were coiled away on their pins and aloft the robands of the harbour stow had been cast off the sails. A light breeze was again stirring from the eastward. Some of the ships had moved, warped down nearer the islets at the entrance of the harbour. The air of expectancy hanging over the fleet after the exertions of the day was almost tangible. The inactivity would now begin to pray on men's minds, and until the order was given to weigh, every man in that vast armada, some twenty thousand souls, would withdraw inside himself to consult the oracles in his heart as to his future in this world.

Drinkwater felt an odd and quite inexplicable lightness of spirit. Whenever the *Bucentaure* cleared for action he knew he too would be a victim to fear, but for the moment he felt strangely elated. He was no longer in any doubt that in the next day or so there was going to be a battle.

After his exercise period, Drinkwater was taken to Villeneuve's cabin. There was no secrecy about the interview; it was conducted in the presence of several other high-ranking officers among whom Drinkwater recognised Flag-Captain Magendie and Villeneuve's Chief-of-Staff, Captain Prigny. Another officer was in Rear-Admiral's uniform. He wore a silver belt around his waist and an air of permanent exasperation.

'*Contre-Amiral* Magon . . . *Capitaine de frégate* Drinkwater Charles . . .'

Magon bowed imperceptibly and regarded Drinkwater with

intense dislike. Drinkwater felt he attracted more than his fair share of malice and was not long in discovering that Magon disapproved of Villeneuve's holding Drinkwater on his flagship. Drinkwater's knowledge of French was poor, but Magon's powers of dramatic and expressive gesture were eloquent.

Villeneuve was mastering his anger and humiliation with difficulty and Drinkwater glimpsed something of the problems he suffered in his tenure of command of the Combined Fleet. Eventually Magon ceased his diatribe, turned in disgust and affected to ignore the rest of the proceedings by staring fixedly out of the stern windows.

'Captain Drinkwater informs me, gentlemen,' Villeneuve said in English, 'that Nelson's attack will be as I outlined to you in my standing orders leaving Toulon. If you wish to question him further he is at your disposal . . .'

Drinkwater opened his mouth to protest that he had done nothing so dishonourable as to reveal Lord Nelson's plan of attack but, seeing the difficulties Villeneuve was under, he shut his mouth again.

'*Excuse, Capitaine, mais,* er, 'ow are you certain Nelson will make this attack, eh?' Captain Magendie asked. ''Ave you seen 'is orders to 'is *escadre*?'

'No, *m'sieur*.' It was beyond his power and the limit of his honour to help Villeneuve now.

A silence hung in the cabin and Drinkwater met Villeneuve's eyes. Whatever his defects as a leader, the man possessed personal courage of a high order. Alone of all his officers, Drinkwater thought, Villeneuve was the one man who knew what lay in wait for them beyond the mole of Cadiz.

Drinkwater woke with a start. The *Bucentaure* was alive with shouts and cries, the squeal of pipes and the *rantan* of a snare drum two decks above. For a second Drinkwater thought the ship was on fire and then he heard, or rather felt through the fabric of the ship, two hundred pairs of feet begin to stamp around the capstan. But it was to be a false alarm, although when he went on deck that evening there were fewer ships in the road. The wind had again dropped and Guillet was in a bad temper, his exertions of the previous day seemingly for nothing.

'Some of your ships got out, Lieutenant,' remarked Drinkwater, indicating the absence of a few of their neighbours of the previous night.

'Nine, *Capitaine,* now anchored off Rota.'

Drinkwater looked aloft at Villeneuve's flag and then at the sky, unconsciously rubbing his shoulder as he did so. 'You will have an easterly wind in the morning, I think.' He turned to Gillespy. 'What is tomorrow, Mr Gillespy. Sunday, ain't it?'

'Yes, sir, Sunday, the twentieth . . .'

'Well, Mr Gillespy, you must remark it . . . What is that in French, Lieutenant, in your new calendar, eh?

'Le vingt-huitième Vendémiare, An Quatorze . . .'

'What have Nelson's frigates been doing today, Lieutenant? Will you tell us that?'

Guillet grinned. 'Not coming into the 'arbour, *Capitaine.* Yesterday we send boats down to the entrance. Your frigate *Euryalus,* she does not come so close, and today with our ships going to Rota she does not engage.'

'That should not surprise you, Lieutenant Guillet. It is her business to watch.' Drinkwater added drily, 'And Nelson? What of him?'

'We 'ave not seen your Nelson, *Capitaine,*' Guillet's tone was almost sneering.

On his way below, Drinkwater realised that Lieutenant de Vaisseau Guillet did not fear Nelson and that the Combined Fleet would sail with confidence. If Guillet thought that, then it was probable that many of the junior officers thought the same. 'Do you also find,' Villeneuve had asked, 'young men always know best?' Drinkwater re-entered his cabin. He stretched himself on the cot, his hands behind his head, and stared unseeing at the low deck beams above. The strange sense of elation and excitement remained.

The following morning there was no doubt about their departure. Even in the orlop the slap of waves upon the hull indicated a wind, and soon the movement of the deck indicated *Bucentaure* was getting under way. Slowly the slap of waves became a hiss and bubbling rush of water. The angle of heel increased and the whole fabric of the ship responded.

'We're turning,' Drinkwater muttered, as Gillespy came anxiously to his doorway. The two remained immobile, the usual courtesies of the morning forgotten, their eyes staring, unwanted sensors in the gloom of the orlop, while their other faculties told them what was happening. A bump and thump came from forward and above.

'Anchor fished, catted and lashed against the fore-chains . . . We must be . . . yes, starboard tack, 'tis a north-easterly wind then . . . Ah, we're fetching out of the lee of the Mole . . .'

The *Bucentaure* began to pitch, gently at first and then settling down to the regularity of the Atlantic swells as they rolled in from the west.

'We're clear of San Sebastian now,' Drinkwater whispered, trying to visualise the scene. Outside the door the sentry staggered, the movement unfamiliar to him.

Gillespy giggled and Drinkwater grinned at him, as much to see the boy in good spirits as at the lack of sea-legs on the part of the soldier. After about an hour of progress the angle of the deck altered and the ship began a different motion.

'What is it, sir?'

'We are hove-to. Waiting for the other ships to come out.'

Evidence of this hiatus came a few minutes later when men came down to their messes for breakfast. *Bucentaure's* company had divided into their sea-watches. The battleship was leading the Combined Fleet to sea.

It was afternoon before they were allowed to emerge from the orlop. Lieutenant Guillet appeared. 'You please to come on deck now, *Capitaine*.' There was the undeniable gleam of triumph in his eyes. 'The Combined Fleet is at sea, and there is no sight of your Nelson.'

Drinkwater ascended the companion ladders through the gun-decks. Men looked at him curiously, sharing the same elation as Guillet. Drinkwater's finely tuned sensibilities could detect high morale when he encountered it. Their worst fears had not materialised. But what interested him more was the weather when he finally reached the rail in the windward gangway. The wind had gone to the south-west, it was overcast and drizzling.

'*Voila, Capitaine* Drinkwater!' Guillet extended an arm that swept around the *Bucentaure* in a gesture that embraced forty ships, adding with a fierce pride, '*C'est magnifique*!'

The Combined Fleet lumbered to the southward, topsails reefed, yards braced sharp up on the starboard tack, in five columns, the colours of their hulls faded in the drizzle.

'The *Corps de Bataille*,' Guillet indicated proprietorially, pointing ahead, 'it is led by Vice-Admiral de Alava in the *Santa Ana*, we are in the centre and Rear-Admiral Dumanoir commands the rear in the *Formidable* . . .'

'And Gravina?'

'Ah, the Captain-General leads the *Corps de Réserve* with Magon as his support.'

'And you steer south, Lieutenant . . . for the Mediterranean I presume.'

Guillet shrugged dismissively, 'Per'aps.'

'And you will be lucky with the wind. I think it will be veering very soon to the north-west.' Drinkwater pointed to a patch of blue sky from which the grey cumulus drew back.

'Where is Nelson, *Capitaine*?' Guillet asked with a grin. 'Eh?'

'When the weather clears, Lieutenant, you may well find out.' Drinkwater fervently hoped he was right.

He was not permitted to see the horizon to windward swept of the drizzle to become sharp and clear against the sudden lightening of the sky. It was four o'clock in the afternoon, as the bells of the battleships sounded their four double-chimes that marked the change of watch, when the wind hauled aft. The limit of the visible horizon extended abruptly many miles to the west. From the mastheads of the French and Spanish men-o'-war the six grey topsails of two British frigates could be seen as they lay hull down over the horizon. They were Nelson's watch-dogs.

It had been dark for several hours when Guillet reappeared, demanding Drinkwater's immediate attendance upon the quarterdeck. Wrapping his cloak around him he followed the French officer, emerging on deck in the dim glow of the binnacle. The wind had freshened a little and ahead of them they could see the battle lanterns of the next ship. Casting a glow over the afterdeck, their own lanterns shone, together with Villeneuve's command lantern in the mizen top. These points of light only emphasised the blackness of the night to Drinkwater as he stumbled on the unfamiliar deck. But a few minutes later he could pick out details and see that the great arch of the sky was studded with stars.

'*Capitaine* Drinkwater, *mon amiral* . . .'

'Ah, Captain . . .' Villeneuve addressed him. 'I do not wish to dishonour you, but what do you interpret from those signals to the west?' He held out a night-glass and Drinkwater was aware of his anxiety. It was clearly Villeneuve's besetting sin in the eyes of his subordinates.

He could see nothing at first and then he focused the telescope and saw pin-points of light and the graceful arc of a rocket trail. 'British frigates signalling, sir.' That much must be obvious to Villeneuve.

But he was saved from further embarrassment by a burst of rockets shooting aloft from the direction of the *Principe de Asturias*. From the sudden flurry of activity and the repetition of the Spanish admiral's name, Drinkwater gathered Gravina was signalling the presence of enemy ships even closer than the two cruisers Drinkwater could see on the horizon. *Bucentaure*'s quarterdeck came to sudden and furious activity. Her own rockets roared skywards in pairs and the order was given to go to general quarters and clear for action. Other admirals in the Combined Fleet set up their night signals. The repeating frigates to leeward joined in a visual spectacle better suited to a victory parade than the escape of a hunted fleet, Drinkwater thought, as he was hustled below.

'*Branle-bas-de-combat!*' officers were roaring at the hatchways and the drummers were beating the *rantan* opening the *Générale*. The *Bucentaure* burst into a noisy and spontaneous life, lent a nightmare quality as her people surged on deck and to their stations in the gun-decks, lowering the bulkheads that obstructed the long batteries of heavy artillery that gleamed dully from the fitful lights of the swinging battle lanterns. Drinkwater did not fight the tide of humanity but waited, observing the activity. The noise was deafening, but otherwise the men knew their places and, although not as fast as the ruthlessly trained crew of a British seventy-four, *Bucentaure*'s eighty cannon were soon ready for action. Drinkwater made his way below.

The messing area of the orlop that formed a tiny square of courtyard outside his and the other warrant officers' cabins had been transformed. A number of chests had been pulled into its centre and covered with a piece of sail. A separate chest supported the instrument cases of the *Bucentaure*'s two surgeons. The senior of these two men, Charles Masson, had treated Drinkwater with some consideration and addressed him in English, which he spoke quite well. Drinkwater had come to like the man and, as he retired to his cabin in search of Gillespy, he nodded at him.

'It has come to the time of battle, then, *m'sieur*?' Masson tested the edge of a curette and looked up at the English captain standing stooped and cock-headed under the low beams.

'Soon, now, I think, M'sieur Masson, soon . . .'

Chapter Twenty-One *21 October 1805*

Trafalgar

Nathaniel Drinkwater lay unsleeping through the long October night. He was tormented by the thought of the hours to come, of how he might have been preparing the *Thunderer* for action. Alone, without the necessity of reassuring the now sleeping Gillespy or the disturbance of *Bucentaure*'s people who stood at their quarters throughout the small hours, he reflected on his ill-fortune. Such a mischance as his capture had happened in a trice to sea-officers; it was one of the perils of the profession; but this reflection did not make it any easier to bear as he lay inactive in a borrowed cot aboard the enemy flagship. There was nothing he could do except await the outcome of events.

Even these were by no means certain. Gravina's signals of the previous evening had obviously been those of panic. No British cruisers had come close, but those distant rockets seen by Drinkwater meant that the Combined Fleet was being shadowed. The response of the French and Spanish admirals in throwing out rocket signals themselves had undoubtedly attracted the attention of Blackwood's watch-dogs. Connecting Blackwood's Inshore Squadron with the main fleet, Nelson would have look-out ships at intervals, and these would pass on Blackwood's messages. God grant that Nelson had seen them and that he would come up before Villeneuve slipped through the Gut of Gibraltar and into the Mediterranean.

Drinkwater did not like to contemplate too closely what might happen to himself. He had to summon up all his reserves of fortitude and rehearse for his own comfort all the argument he had put to little Gillespy as guaranteeing their safety. But they did not reassure him. The worst aspect of his plight was his inability to influence events. Never in his life had he been so passive. The sea-service had placed a continual series of demands upon his skill and experience so that, although he was a victim of events, he had always had a chance of fighting back. To perish in the attempt was one thing; to be annihilated without being able to lift a finger struck him as being particularly hard to bear.

Some time in the night the *Bucentaure*'s company were stood down from their stations. Drinkwater heard them come below and his gloom increased. To a man used from boyhood to living on board ship he had no difficulty in gauging their mood. They were grim, filled with a mixture of anxiety and hope. They were also unusually subdued and few settled to sleep. Drinkwater tried to judge the course that the *Bucentaure* was sailing on. He could feel a low ground swell gently lifting and rolling the ship. That would not significantly have altered its direction since he had observed it the previous evening. He felt it coming up almost abeam, but lifting the starboard quarter first: Villeneuve was edging away towards the Strait.

He must have slept, for he was startled by the drums again rappelling the *Générale* and the petty officers crying *'Branle-bas-de-combat!'* at the hatchways. The orlop emptied of men and then others came down, the sinister denizens of this area of perpetual night: Surgeon Masson, his assistants and mates. Shortly after this a light and playful rattle of a snare drum and the tweeting of fifes could be heard. Cries of *'Vive le Commandant!'* and *'Vive l'Empereur!'* were shouted by *Bucentaure*'s company as Villeneuve and his suite toured the ship. A sentry came half-way down the orlop ladder and announced something to the surgeon.

'What is the news, M'sieur Masson?' Drinkwater asked.

'One of our frigates has signalled the enemy is in sight.'

'Ah . . . d'you hear that, Mr Gillespy?'

'Yes, sir.' The boy was pale, but he managed a brave smile. 'Do you think that will be the *Euryalus*, sir, or the main body of the fleet?'

'To be candid, Mr Gillespy, I do not know.'

The boy nodded and swallowed. 'Do you know, sir, that *Euryalus* was slain in a wood when gathering intelligence for the Trojans?'

'No, Mr Gillespy, I'm afraid I did not know that.' The arcane fact surprised Drinkwater and then he reflected that the boy might make a better academic than a sea-officer.

'The Trojans were defeated, sir . . .' Gillespy pointed out, as if seeking some parallel with present events.

'Come, sir, that is no way to talk . . . Why, what of Antigone? Who the devil was she?'

'The daughter of Oedipus and Jocasta, sir. She buried the body of her brother after her uncle had ordered it to be left exposed and he had her bricked up behind a wall . . .'

'Enough of that, Mr Gillespy.' He fell silent. It was true that his own *Antigone* might as well be bricked up, stuck, as she was, with Louis off Gibraltar. If the Combined Fleet got through the Strait unmolested it would come upon the lone *Antigone* cruising to the eastward watching the eastern horizon for Salcedo! He groaned aloud, 'Oh, God damn it!'

'Are you all right, sir? Gillespy came forward solicitiously, but drew back at the sight of the captain's set face.

'Perfectly, Mr Gillespy,' Drinkwater said grimly, 'I am damning my ill-fortune.'

'I'm hungry, sir,' Gillespy said after a little, but this feeble appeal was lost in a sudden canting of the *Bucentaure*. Drinkwater strained to hear orders on deck but it was impossible as the hull creaked about them and the constant wash of the sea beyond the ship's side shut out any noise from the upper deck.

'We're wearing . . . God damn it, we're wearing, Mr Gillespy . . . yes, yes certainly we are . . . wait . . . see, we're steady again . . .' He gauged the way the hull reacted to the swell. It rolled them from the other side now, the larboard side. They were heading north and the rush of water past the hull was much less than it had been the day before. Either they had reduced sail or the wind had dropped significantly.

'What does it mean, sir?'

'I don't know,' snapped Drinkwater, trying to answer that very question himself. 'Either that Louis has appeared ahead of the Combined Fleet, or that Villeneuve has abandoned his intention and wishes to return to Cadiz . . . in which case I judge that the answer to your question is that our friends have sighted the main body of Lord Nelson's fleet.' As he spoke, Drinkwater's voice increased in strength with mounting conviction.

'By God!' he added, knowing Villeneuve's vacillation, 'that *must* be the explanation.' He smiled at the boy. 'I think you *will* have something to tell your grandchildren, my boy!'

Half an hour later Lieutenant Guillet appeared. He wore full dress uniform and was formally polite.

'*Capitaine* Drinkwater, I am ordered by His Excellency Vice-Admiral Villeneuve to remind you of your parole and the courtesy done you by permitting you to keep your sword. It is also necessary that I ask you that you will do nothing during the action to prejudice this ship. Without these assurances I 'ave orders to confine you in irons.' It was a rehearsed speech and he could see the hand of Magendie as well as the courtliness of Villeneuve.

'Lieutenant Guillet, it would dishonour both myself and my country if I was not to conform to your request. I assure you that both myself and my midshipman will do nothing to interfere with the *Bucentaure*. Will you convey my compliments to His Excellency and I thank you for your kind attentions to us and wish you good fortune in the hours ahead.'

They exchanged bows and Guillet departed. The forenoon dragged on. Drinkwater wrote in his journal and comforted the starving Gillespy. A strange silence hung over the groaning fabric of the warship, permeating down through her decks and hatchways. Even the men awaiting the arrival of the wounded in the orlop talked among themselves in whispers. About mid-morning they heard a muffled shout, drowned immediately in a terrific rumbling sound that startled them after the long and heavy silence.

'Running out the guns,' Drinkwater explained to Gillespy.

'*Capitaine*, will you come to the deck at once . . .' It was Guillet, his appearance hurried and breathless.

Drinkwater rose and put on his hat. He turned to Gillespy. 'Remain here, Mr Gillespy. You are in no circumstances to leave the orlop.'

'Aye, aye, sir.'

Drinkwater followed Guillet up through the lower gun-deck. It was flooded by shafts of sunshine coming in through the open gunports. Every cannon was run out and the crews squatted expectantly round them, one or two peering through at the approaching British. Lieutenants and *aspirants* paced along their divisions and a murmur ran up and down the guns. Guillet and Drinkwater emerged on deck and Guillet led him directly to where Villeneuve, Magendie and Prigny were staring westwards. His heart beating furiously, Drinkwater followed the direction of their telescopes.

Under a sky of blue and over an almost calm sea furrowed by a ponderous swell from the westward, the British fleet came down on the Combined Fleet in two loose groups, prevented from getting into any regular formation by the lightness of the westerly breeze. Drinkwater looked briefly round him to see the Franco-Spanish ships in almost as much disorder. The decision to wear, though two hours old, had thrown them into a confusion from which it would take them some time to recover. Instead of a single line with the frigates to leeward and Gravina's crucial detachment slightly to weather, the whole armada was a loose crescent, bowed away from the advancing British towards the distant blue outline of Cape Trafalgar on the horizon. The line had vast gaps in it, astern of the *Bucentaure* for instance, and in places the ships had bunched two and three abreast.

He turned his attention to the British again at the same time as Villeneuve lowered his glass and noticed his arrival. 'Ah, Captain Drinkwater. I desire your opinion as to the leading ships . . .' He handed Drinkwater his glass.

Drinkwater focused the telescope and the image leapt into the lenses with unbelievable clarity. The two groups of British ships were led by three-deckers. These ships were going to receive the brunt of the fire of several broadsides before they could retaliate and Drinkwater sensed a certain elation amongst the officers on *Bucentaure's* quarterdeck. They came on like a row of skittles, one behind the other. Knock the end one over and it would take them all down.

As he watched, flags soared up the mastheads and out to the yardarms of the leading British ships. Between the two groups he could see the frigates *Naiad, Euryalus, Siruis* and *Phoebe,* a cutter and schooner, standing by to repeat signals or tow a wounded battleship out of the line.

'Well, Captain?' Villeneuve was reminding him he was a prisoner and had been asked a question. He looked again at the leading ships. They had every stitch of sail set, their studding sails winged out on the booms, their slack sheets trailing in the water. The swell made the great ships pitch gently as they came on, their hulls black and yellow barred, their decorated figureheads bright with paintwork. The southern group was further advanced than the northern column. He closed the telescope with a snap.

'The southern column is led by *Royal Sovereign*, Your Excellency, flagship of Vice-Admiral Collingwood . . .'

'And Nelson?' Villeneuve's eagerness betrayed his anxiety.

'There, sir,' Drinkwater pointed with Villeneuve's telescope, the brass instrument gleaming in the sunshine, 'there is *Victory*, leading the northern column and bearing the flag of Lord Nelson.'

Villeneuve's hand was extended for his glass, but his eyes never left the black and yellow hull of *Victory*. As Drinkwater watched, the ship astern of *Victory* seemed to edge out of line, as if making to overtake. Then he saw her sails shake and she disappeared from view behind the flagship again. 'She seems to be supported by the *Téméraire*,' he added, 'of ninety-eight guns.'

Bucentaure's officers studied the menacing approach of the silent British ships. All along her own decks animated chatter had broken out. He noticed there was no check put to this and the men seemed in high spirits now that action was inevitable. Aware that at any moment he would be ordered below, he again looked round. The gap astern was a yawning invitation to the British, and Drinkwater's practised eye soon reckoned that *Victory* was heading for that gap. Collingwood, he judged, would strike the allied line well astern of the *Bucentaure*, somewhere about the position of the funereal black hull of the Spanish 112-gun *Santa Ana* with her scarlet figurehead of the saint. Ahead of the *Bucentaure* the mighty *Santissima Trinidad*, with her hull of red and white ribbands, seemed to wait placidly for the onslaught of the heretic fleet, a great wooden cross hanging over her stern beneath the red and gold ensign of Spain.

'Nelson attacks as I said he would, Captain,' Villeneuve remarked in English. And added, as his glass raked the following ships crowding down astern of their leaders, 'It is not that Nelson leads, but that every captain thinks *he* is Nelson . . .' Then, in his own tongue and in a tone of anguish he said, '*Où est Gravinar*?'

Drinkwater realised the import of the remark, forgotten in the excitement of watching the British fleet approach. By wearing to the northward, Villeneuve had reversed his order of sailing. The van was led by Dumanoir now. Instead of commanding a detached squadron to windward, Gravina was tailing on the end of the immense line. Villeneuve's counterstroke was destroyed!

Drinkwater's eyes met those of the French Commander-in-Chief, then Villeneuve looked away; Magendie was speaking impatiently to him and at that moment smoke belched from a ship well astern of *Bucentaure.* The rolling concussion of a broadside came over the water towards them as white plumes rose around the *Royal Sovereign*. Collingwood had shifted his flag from the sluggish *Dreadnought to* the swift and newly coppered *Royal Sovereign* as soon as she had come out from England. Now that speed carried her into battle ahead of her consorts and her chief. Soon other ships were trying the range along with the *Fougeuex*, smoke and flame belched from the side of the *Santa Ana*, and still the *Royal Sovereign* came on, her guns silent, her defiance expressed by the hoisting of additional colours in her rigging.

Drinkwater turned his attention to the other column. Much nearer now, *Victory* could be seen clearly, her lower fore-sheets trailing in the water as the lightness of the breeze wafted her down on the waiting *Bucentaure.*

Magendie barked something and Guillet tugged at Drinkwater's sleeve. He followed Guillet to the companionway. As he left the deck he heard the bells of several ships strike the quadruple double ring of noon.

'Tirez!'

As Drinkwater passed over the gun-deck, Lieutenant Fournier gave the order to one of *Bucentaure*'s 24-pounder cannon. It rumbled inboard with the recoil after the explosion of discharge, snatching at its breeching while its crew ministered to it, stuffing sponge, cartridge wad and ball into its smoking muzzle. The lieutenant leaned forward, peering through the gun-port to see where the ranging shot had fallen, and Drinkwater knew he was aiming at *Victory.* The first coils of white powder smoke drifted innocently around the beams of the deck above and its acrid smell was pungent.

Drinkwater descended into the orlop and made his way back, where he was greeted by a ring of expectant faces. Masson and his staff as well as Gillespy awaited news from the upper world.

'M'sieur Masson, the allied fleets of France and Spain are being attacked by a British fleet under Lord Nelson . . .'

He heard the name 'Nelson' repeated as men looked at one another, and then all hell broke loose above them.

For the next hours the world was an immensity of noise. The

stygian darkness of the orlop, pitifully lit with its faint lanterns whose flames struggled in the foul air, became in its own way an extension of hell. But it was the aural senses that suffered the worst assault. Despite twenty-six years in the Royal Navy, Nathaniel Drinkwater had never before experienced the ear-splitting horror of a sustained action in a ship larger than a frigate; never been subjected to the rolling waves of blasting concussion that reverberated in the confined space of a gun-deck and down into the orlop below. The guns belching their lethal projectiles leapt back on their carriages with an increasing eagerness as they heated up. They became like things with a life of their own. The shouts of their captains and the *aspirants* and officers who controlled them became nothing more than howls of servitude as the iron monsters spat smoke, fire and iron into the enemy. The stench of powder permeated the orlop, itself full of shuddering air, its shadows atremble from the vibrating lantern hooks as the *Bucentaure* flexed and quivered in response to her own violence. This was the moment for which she had been called into being, to resist force with force and pit iron against iron in a ruthless carnage of cacophonous death.

Initially the men stationed in the orlop had nothing to do. The surgeon and his mates waited for the first of the wounded to come down, the gunner and his staff peered from their shot and powder rooms, waiting for the first of the boys requiring more cartridges and shot. So far *Bucentaure* had shivered only from the discharge of her own guns. In his imagination Drinkwater saw *Victory* looming ever larger as she made for that yawning gap astern of the French flagship. He tried to recall the two ships that were trying to fill it and thought that they should have been the *Neptune* and the Spanish *San Leandro*, but they were both to leeward, he remembered, and only Lucas in the *Redoubtable* was in direct line astern of the *Bucentaure*. Drinkwater felt a sympathy for Villeneuve. Gravina had let him down and now he went almost unsupported into action with a ship heavier than his own. *Bucentaure* was a new ship and *Victory* fifty years old, but the added elevation of her third gun-deck would make her a formidable opponent.

And then Drinkwater heard the most terrible sound of his life. The concussion was felt through the entire body rather than heard with the ears alone, a distant noise above the thunder of *Bucentaure's* cannon, a strange mixture of sounds that had about it the tinkle of imploding glass and the noise of a million bees driving down wind on the back of a hurricane. The whole of *Bucentaure* trembled, men standing were jerked slightly and the bees were followed by the whoosh and crash, the splintering, jarring shock of impact, as musket balls and double- and triple-shotted guns raked the whole length of the *Bucentaure*. It was over in a few seconds as *Victory* crossed their stern, pouring the pent-up fury of her hitherto silent guns through the *Bucentaure's* stern galleries and along her gun-decks, knocking men over like ninepins. It took cannon off their carriages too, for above their heads they heard the crash of guns hitting the deck, but by this time the orlop had its own terrible part to play.

As the first wave of that raking broadside receded, Drinkwater released Gillespy whom he found himself clasping protectively. He could not stand idle and tore off his coat as the first wounded were stretched upon the canvas of the operating 'table'.

'Come, Mr Gillespy, come; let us do something in the name of humanity to say we were not idle when brave men did their duty.'

Ghostly pale, Gillespy came forward and held the arm of a man while Masson excised a splinter from his shoulder and shoved him roughly aside. It took four men to hold some of the wounded who were filling the space like a human flood so that for a second Drinkwater imagined they might drown under the press of bloody bodies that seemed to inundate them. Men screamed or whimpered or stared hollow-eyed. Pain robbed them of the last protest as their lives drained out into the stinking bilge beneath them.

'It is important we operate fast,' Masson shouted, the sweat pouring from him as he wiped a smear of blood across his forehead. 'Not him, Captain, he is too much gone . . . this man . . . ah, a leg . . . we must cut here . . .' The knife bit into the flesh, its passage marked by a line of blood, and Masson's practised wrist took the incision right around the limb, inclining the point towards the upper thigh.

'If I am quick, he is in shock . . . see how little his arteries bleed, they have closed, and I can do no more damage than his wound . . .' Masson nodded to the bunch of bleeding rags that had once been a leg. As he spoke his deft fingers tied thread around the blood vessels and then he picked up his saw, thrust it deep into the mess and quickly cut through the femur. He drew the skin together and swiftly sutured it. 'Do you know, Captain,' he bawled conversationally as he nodded and the wounded man was removed to be replaced by another, 'that the Russians and Prussians simply cut through, tie the ligatures and draw the flesh together, leaving the bone almost at the extremity of the amputation and the skin tight as a drum . . .' Masson glanced at his next patient, caught the eye of his assistant and made a winding motion with one finger. The assistant brought a roll of linen bandage and the great welling wound in the stomach was bound, the white quickly staining red. The man was moved to a corner, to lean against a great futtock and bleed out his life.

Drinkwater looked round. The wooden tubs were full of amputated limbs and still men arrived and were ministered to by Masson as he hacked and sawed, bound and bandaged. The surgeon was awash in blood and the foul air of the orlop was thick with the stink of it. Above their head *Bucentaure* was raked again, and then again at intervals as, following *Victory*, *Téméraire* and then the British *Neptune* crossed her stern.

Another body appeared under the glimmer of the lanterns and Masson looked at his assistant busy amputating the arm of a negro. He called some instructions and then shouted at Drinkwater, 'Assistance, Captain. This one we will have to hold!' Masson tore the blood-soaked shirt off the frail body of the boy, a powder monkey or some such.

'Hold him, Captain! He is fully conscious! They are always difficult!'

The white body arched as Masson began his curettage. 'We may save him, it's a fragment from a ball, perhaps it burst when it hit a gun, but it is deep. Hold him!' There was demonic strength in the tiny body and it wailed pitifully. Drinkwater looked at the face. It was Gillespy.

'Dear God . . .' The boy was staring up at him, his eyes huge and dark and filled with tears. Blood seeped from his mouth and Drinkwater was aware that he was biting his lip. Masson's mate had seen it and as Gillespy opened his mouth to scream, he rammed a pad of leather into it. Masson wrestled bloodily with the fragment, up to his wrist in the boy's abdomen until Drinkwater found himself shouting at the boy to faint.

'He will not stand the shock . . .' Drinkwater could see Masson was struggling. '*Merde*!' The surgeon shook his head. 'I cannot waste time . . . he is finished . . .'

They dragged Gillespy aside and Drinkwater picked him up. He made for the cot in his cabin, but it was already occupied and, as gently as he could, Drinkwater laid the boy down in a dark corner and knelt beside him.

'There, there, Mr Gillespy . . .' He felt desperately inadequate, unable even to give the midshipman water. He could not understand how it had happened. The boy had been helping them . . . and then Drinkwater recollected, he had withdrawn, his hand over his mouth as though about to vomit. He looked at Gillespy. He had spat the leather pad out and his mouth moved. Drinkwater bent to hear him.

'The . . . the pain has all gone, sir . . . I went on deck, sir . . . to see for myself. I wanted to see something . . . to tell my grandchildren . . . disobeyed you . . .' Gillespy's voice faded into an incoherent gurgle. Drinkwater knew from the blood that suddenly erupted from his mouth that he was dead.

Another broadside raked *Bucentaure* and Drinkwater laid the body down and straightened up. He was trembling all over, his head was splitting from the noise, the damnable, thunderous, everlasting bloody noise. He stumbled over the recumbent bodies of the wounded and dying. Reaching into the cabin he had occupied, he picked up his sword and made for the ladder of the lower gun-deck. Nobody stopped him and he was suddenly aware that *Bucentaure's* guns had been silent for some time, that the continued bombardment was the echo in his belaboured head.

The lower gun-deck was a shambles. Swept from end to end by the successive broadsides of British battleships, fully half its guns were dismounted, their carriages smashed. The decks were ploughed up by shot, the furrows lined by spikes of wood like petrified grass. Men writhed or lay still in heaps, their bodies shattered into bloody mounds of flesh, brilliant hued and lit by light flooding in through the pulverised and dismantled stern. Drinkwater could not see a single man on his feet throughout the whole space. He made for the ladder to the upper deck and emerged into a smoke-stifled daylight.

Drinkwater stared around him. *Bucentaure* was dismasted, the stumps of her three masts incongruous, their shattered wreckage hanging all about her decks, over her guns and waist where a vain attempt was being made to get a boat out. A man was shouting from the poop. It was Villeneuve.

'Le Bucentaure *a rempli sa tâche: la mienne n'est pas encore achevée.'*

Amidships a lieutenant gestured it was impossible to get a boat in the water. Villeneuve turned away and nodded at a smoke-begrimed man whom Drinkwater realised was Magendie. All together there were only a handful of men on *Bucentaure*'s deck. Magendie waved his arm and shouted something. Drinkwater was aware of the masts and sails of ships all around them, towering over their naked decks, and in the thick grey smoke the brilliant points of fire told where the iron rain still poured into *Bucentaure*. It was quite impossible to tell friend from foe and Drinkwater stood bemused, sheltered by the wreckage of the mainmast which had fallen in a great heap of broken spars and rope and canvas.

A wraith of smoke dragged across *Bucentaure*'s after-deck and Drinkwater saw Villeneuve again. He had been wounded and he stood looking forward over the wreckage of his ship. 'A Villeneuve died with Roland at the Pass of Roncesvalles,' Drinkwater remembered him saying as, behind him, the great tricolour came fluttering down on deck.

Bucentaure had struck her colours.

Chapter Twenty-Two *21–22 October 1805*

Surrender and Storm

Drinkwater stood dazed. At times the surrounding smoke cleared and he caught brief glimpses of other ships. On their starboard quarter a British seventy-four was slowly turning – it had been she that had last raked *Bucentaure* – and, to windward, yet another was looming towards them. Beneath his feet the deck rolled and Drinkwater came to his senses, instinct telling him that the swell was building up all the time. He turned. Ahead of them another British battleship was swinging, presumably she too had raked *Bucentaure*, though now she was ranging up to leeward of the *Santissima Trinidad*. And still from the weather side British battleships were coming into action! Drinkwater felt his blood run chill.

'God!' he muttered to himself, 'what a magnificent bloody risk Nelson took!' And he found himself shaking again, his vision blurred, as around the shattered *Bucentaure* the thunder of battle continued to reverberate. Then suddenly a double report sounded from *Bucentaure*'s own cannon. Two guns on the starboard quarter barked a continued defiance at the British ship that had just raked them. Drinkwater saw splinters dance from her hull and an officer point and shout, clearly outraged by such conduct after striking. He saw muzzles run out and the yellow and scarlet stab of flame. The shot tore over his head and, with a crash, what was left of the *Bucentaure*'s foremast came down. The two quarter-guns fell silent.

Drinkwater clambered aft. No one stopped him. Men slumped wounded or exhausted around the guns, their faces drained of expression. *Bucentaure*'s company had been shattered into its individual fragments of humanity. Pain and defeat had done their work: she was incapable of further resistance. He hesitated to climb to the poop. This was not his moment, and yet he wished to offer Villeneuve some comfort. On her after-deck officers were waving white handkerchiefs at the British battleship. He turned away below. It was not his business to accept *Bucentaure*'s surrender. He reached the lower gun-deck. Running forward from aft came a party of British seamen led by two midshipmen.

'Come, Mr Hicks, we've a damned Frog here!'

Drinkwater turned at the familiar voice. The young officer was partially silhouetted against the light from the shattered stern, but his drawn sword gleamed and from the rapidity of his advance Drinkwater took alarm. His hand went to his own hanger, whipping out the blade.

'Stand still, God damn you!' he roared. 'I'm a British officer!'

'Good God!'

Recognition came to the two men at the same time.

'Captain Drinkwater, sir . . . I, er, I beg your pardon . . .'

'Mr Walmsley . . . you and your men can put up your weapons. *Bucentaure* is finished.'

'So I see . . .' Walmsley looked round him, his face draining of colour as his eyes fell on an entire gun crew who had lost their heads. Alongside them lay Lieutenant Guillet. He had been cut in half.

'Oh Christ!' Lord Walmsley put his hand to his mouth and the vomit spurted between his fingers.

'I was a prisoner of the French admiral, gentlemen. I am obliged to you for my liberty,' Drinkwater said, affecting not to notice Walmsley's confusion.

'Midshipman William Hicks, sir, of the *Conqueror,* Captain Israel Pellew.' The second midshipman introduced himself, then turned as more men came aboard led by a marine officer. 'This is Captain James Atcherley, sir, of the same ship.'

The ridiculous little ceremony was performed and the scarlet-coated Atcherley was acquainted with the fact that Captain Drinkwater, despite his coatless appearance and blood-stained shirt, was a British officer.

'Come, sir, I will take you to the admiral.' They clambered onto the upper deck and Drinkwater stood aside to allow Atcherley to precede him onto the poop.

'No, no, it is your task, Captain,' Drinkwater said as Atcherley demurred. 'He speaks good English.'

He followed the marine officer. Villeneuve lowered the glass through which he had been studying some distant event and turned towards the knot of British officers.

'To whom have I the honour of surrendering?' Villeneuve asked.

Atcherley stepped forward: 'To Captain Pellew of the *Conqueror*.'

'I am glad to have struck to the fortunate Sir Edward Pellew.'

'It is his brother, sir,' said Atcherley.

'His brother! What! Are there two of them? *Hélas*!'

Atcherley refused the proffered sword. Captain Magendie shrugged. *'Fortune de la guerre.* I am now three times a prisoner of you British.'

'I shall secure the ship's magazines, sir,' Atcherley said. 'You shall retain your swords until able to surrender them to someone of sufficient rank –' he turned – 'unless Captain Drinkwater would receive them?'

Drinkwater shook his head. 'No Captain Atcherley. I have in no way contributed to today's work and am bound by my word to Admiral Villeneuve. Do you do as you suggest.' He acknowledged the tiny bow made in his direction by Villeneuve.

'In that case, sir,' said Atcherley, addressing the French officers, 'I should be obliged if you would descend to the boat.' He looked round. The *Conqueror* had disappeared in the smoke, joining in the mêlée round the huge *Santissima Trinidad* that had not yet struck to her many enemies.

'I shall convey you to *Mars*, sir,' he nodded at the next British ship looming up on the quarter. Atcherley turned to Drinkwater. 'Will you come, sir?'

Drinkwater shook his head. 'Not yet, Captain Atcherley. I have some effects to gather up.' He had no desire to witness Villeneuve's final humiliation.

'Very well, sir . . . come, gentlemen . . .'

Villeneuve turned to Drinkwater. 'Captain, we fought well. I hope you will not forget that.'

'Never, sir.' Drinkwater was moved by the nobility of the defeated admiral.

Villeneuve stared at the north. 'Dumanoir wore but then turned away,' he said with quiet resignation. 'See, there, the van is deserting me.' Without another word Villeneuve followed Magendie from the deck.

Drinkwater found himself almost alone upon *Bucentaure*'s poop. A few seamen and petty officers sat or squatted, resting their heads upon their crossed arms in attitudes of dejection.

Exhausted, concussed and hungry, they had given up. Drinkwater watched Villeneuve, Magendie and Prigny pulled away to the *Mars* in *Conqueror*'s cutter. Lord Walmsley sat in the stern, his hand on the tiller. Drinkwater leaned on the rail. Despite *Bucentaure*'s surrender the battle still raged about her. He watched Dumanoir's unscathed ships standing away to the north, feeling an immense and traitorous sympathy for the unfortunate Villeneuve. It occurred to him to seek the other part of Villeneuve's miscarried strategy and he looked southward to identify Gravina. But astern the battle continued, a vast milling mêlée of ships, their flanks belching fire and destruction, their masts and yards continuing to fall amid clouds of grey powder smoke. Ahead too, the hounds were closing round the *Santissima Trinidad*, and one of Dumanoir's squadron, the Spanish *Neptuno*, had been cut off and taken. Away to the north a dense column of black smoke billowed up from an unidentifiable ship on fire.

He looked for the British frigates. Astern he could see the schooner *Pickle* and the trim little cutter *Entreprenante*. Then he caught sight of *Euryalus*, obeying the conventions of formal war, her guns unemployed as she towed what Drinkwater thought at first was a prize but then realised was the *Royal Sovereign*, Collingwood's dismasted flagship.

'God's bones,' he muttered to himself, aware that this was a day the like of which he hoped he would never see again. The shattered hulls of ships lay all around, British, French and Spanish. Some still bore their own colours; none that he could see bore the British colours underneath the Spanish or French, although he could distinguish several British prizes. Masts and yards, sails and great heaps of rigging lay over their sides and trailed in the oily water while the whole mass rolled and ground together on the swell that rolled impassively from the west.

'Wind,' he muttered, 'there will be a wind soon,' and the thought sent him below, in search of his few belongings among the shambles.

He found he could retrieve only his journal, coat, hat and glass. He and one of Atcherley's marines brought up the body of Gillespy. Drinkwater wrapped the body in his own cloak and found a couple of shot left in the upper deck garlands. They bound the boy about with loose line and lifted the sad little bundle onto the rail. Had Drinkwater not agreed to Gillespy accompanying him on the *Bucentaure* he would be alive now, listening in Cadiz to the distant thunder of the guns in company with Frey and Quilhampton. The marine took off his shako and Drinkwater recited the familiar words of the Anglican prayer of committal. Then they rolled Gillespy into the water.

'He is in good company,' he murmured to himself, but his voice was drowned in a vast explosion. To the north the ship that had taken fire, the French *Achille,* blew apart as the fire reached her magazine. The blast rolled over the sea and hammered their already wounded ear-drums, bringing with it the first hint of a freshening breeze.

Captain Atcherley's prize crew consisted of less than half a dozen men, besides himself. They had locked the private cabins of Villeneuve and his senior officers, asked for and obtained the parole of those remaining officers capable of posing a threat, and locked the magazines and spirit rooms. Following Drinkwater's advice, some food was found and served out to all, irrespective of nationality. As the battle began to die out around them, Masson came on deck. His clothes were completely soaked in blood, his pale face smudged with gore and drawn with exhaustion.

'Did you notice,' he said to Drinkwater, 'how the raking fire mostly took off men's heads? It is curious, is it not, Captain?'

Drinkwater looked at him, seeing the results of terrible strain. Masson sniffed and said, 'Thank you for your assistance.'

'It was nothing. I could not stand idle.' Drinkwater paused, not wishing to seem to patronise defeated men. 'They were brave men,' he said simply.

Masson nodded. 'That is their only epitaph.' The surgeon slumped down between two guns and within a minute had fallen fast asleep.

Atcherley joined Drinkwater on the poop, watching the last of the fighting.

'My God, they have made a mess of us, by heaven!' exclaimed Atcherley when he saw the damage to the masts of the British ships. 'If the wind gets up we'll be caught on a dead lee shore.'

'I believe it will get up, Captain Atcherley, and we would do well to take some precautions.' Drinkwater was staring through his glass.

'Is that *Victory*? She is a wreck, look . . .' He handed the glass to Atcherley.

'Yes . . . and Collingwood's flag is down from the *Royal Sovereign*'s masthead . . .'

The two men looked at one another. There was little left of *Royal Sovereign*'s masts, but they had seen Collingwood's flag there ten minutes ago, atop the stump of the foremast with a British ensign hoisted to the broken stump of the main. Had Collingwood been killed? And then they saw the blue square go up to the masthead of the *Euryalus*.

'He has shifted his flag to the frigate,' said Atcherley betraying a sense of relief.

'But why?' asked Drinkwater. 'Surely Nelson would not permit that?'

But further conjecture was distracted by a movement to the south-east. They could see ships making sail, running clear of the pall of smoke. Drinkwater trained his glass. He knew the leading vessel; it was Gravina's flagship.

'God's bones!' Drinkwater watched as the *Principe de Asturias* led some ten or eleven ships out of the Allied line, making all possible sail in the direction of Cadiz. The Spanish grandee had finally deserted his chief, Drinkwater thought, not knowing that Gravina lay below with a shattered arm, nor that his second, Rear-Admiral Magon, galled by a dozen musket balls, had finally been cut in two by a round shot. At the time it seemed like the final betrayal of Villeneuve.

Under their stern passed a British launch, commanded by a master's mate and engaged in carrying prize crews about the shattered remnants of the Combined Fleet. Atcherley stared at her as she made her way amongst the floating wreckage of the great ships of three nations that lay wallowing upon the heaving sea.

'Good God, sir, I believe those fellows to be crying!'

Drinkwater levelled his glass on the straining oarsmen. There could be no mistake. He could see awful grimaces upon the faces of several men, and streaked patches where tears had washed the powder soot from their cheeks. 'Good God!'

'Boat 'hoy!' Atcherley hailed.

The elderly master's mate called his men to stop pulling and looked up at the two officers standing under the British ensign hoisted over the French.

'What ship's that?'

'The French admiral, *Bucentaure*,' called Atcherley, proudly adding, 'prize to the *Conqueror*. What is the matter with your men?'

'Matter? Have ye not heard the news?'

'News? What news beyond that of victory?'

'Victory? Ha!' The mate spat over the side. 'Why, Nelson's dead . . . d'you hear? Nelson's dead . . .'

The wind began to rise at sunset when *Conqueror* beat up to reclaim her prize, ranging to weather of her. Pellew sent a boat with a lieutenant and more men to augment Atcherley's pathetic prize crew. Drinkwater scrambled up onto *Bucentaure*'s rail and hailed Pellew.

'Have the kindness, sir, to report Captain Drinkwater as having rejoined the fleet. I was taken off Tarifa and held a prisoner aboard this ship!'

'Ah!' cried Pellew waving his hat in acknowledgement. 'We wondered where you had got to, Drinkwater. Stockham won't be complaining! He drove the *Prince of the Asturias* off the *Revenge*! We've seventeen prizes but lost Lord Nelson!'

'I heard. A bad day for England!'

'Indeed. Will you look after *Bucentaure* then? 'Tis coming on to blow!'

'She is much damaged but we shall do our best!'

'Splendid. I shall take you in tow!' Pellew waved his hat and jumped down onto his own deck. His lieutenant, Richard Spear, touched his hat to Drinkwater.

'I have orders to receive a line, sir.'

'Carry on, sir, and be quick about it . . . Who the devil is Stockham, d'you know Mr Atcherley?'

'John Stockham, sir? Yes, he's first luff of the *Thunderer*. He'll get his step in rank for this day's work.'

'I expect so,' said Drinkwater flatly, moving towards the compass in order to determine their position. In the last light of day Cape Trafalgar was a dark smudge on the eastward horizon to leeward.

Astern of the *Conqueror* the *Bucentaure* dragged and snubbed at the hemp cable. The wind backed round to south-south-west and increased to gale force by midnight. British and French alike laboured for two hours to haul an undamaged cable out of the hold and forward, onto an anchor. In the blackness of the howling night they were briefly aware of other ships; of the soaring arcs of rockets signalling distress; of the proximity of wounded leviathans in a similar plight to themselves. But many of these wallowed helplessly untowed, their mastless hulks rolling in the troughs of the seas which quickly built up to roll the broken ship closer to the shallows off the cape. From *Euryalus* Collingwood had thrown out the night signal to wear. Those ships which were able complied, but most simply lay a-hull, broached to and waiting for the dawn.

Short of sleep and starved of adequate food, Drinkwater nevertheless spent the night on deck, directing the labours of his strange crew in their efforts to save the *Bucentaure* from the violence of the gale. Atcherley and Spear deferred to him naturally; the French were familiar with him and he had earned their respect, if not their trust, from his exertions at the side of Masson during the battle. While *Conqueror* inched them to windward, away from the shoals off Cape Trafalgar, they cutaway the rigging and wreckage of *Bucentaure*'s masts. But her battered hull continued to ship water which drained to her bilges, sinking her deeper and deeper into the water. Of her huge crew and the many soldiers on board – something not far short of eight hundred men – scarcely ten score were on their feet at the end of the action. Many of these fell exhausted at the pumps.

Daylight revealed a fearful sight. Ahead of them, her reefed topsails straining under the continued violence of the gale that had now become a storm, Pellew's ship tugged and strained at the towrope, jerking it tight until the water was squeezed out of the lay of the rope. *Bucentaure* would move forward and the rope would dip into a wave, then come tight again as she dragged back, jerking the stern of *Conqueror* and making her difficult to handle. But by comparison they were fortunate. There were other ships in tow, British and Allied, all struggling to survive the smashing grey seas as they rolled eastwards, streaked white with spume and driving them inexorably to leeward. Already the unfortunate were amongst the shoals and shallows of the coast.

All day they were witness to the tragedy as men who had escaped the fire of British cannon were dashed to their deaths on the rocks and beaches of the Spanish coast. As darkness came on again the wind began to veer, allowing Pellew to make a more southerly course. But *Bucentaure*'s people were becoming increasingly feeble and their efforts to keep the water from pouring into her largely failed. Spirits rose, however, on the morning of the 23rd, for the wind dropped and the sky cleared a little as it veered into the northwest. Drinkwater was below eating a mess of what passed for porridge when Spear burst in.

'Sir! There are enemy ships under way. They seem to be making some sort of an effort to retake prizes!'

Drinkwater followed the worried officer on deck and trained his glass to the north-east. He could see the blue-green line of the coast and the pale smudge that was Cadiz.

'There, sir!'

'I have them.' He counted the topsails: 'Four line-of-battle ships, five frigates and two brigs!'

Had Gravina remembered his obligation to Villeneuve, Drinkwater wondered? But there were more pressing considerations.

'Get forrard, Mr Spear, and signal *Conqueror* that the enemy is in sight!'

Drinkwater spent the next two hours in considerable anxiety. The strange ships were coming up fast, all apparently undamaged in the battle. He recognised the French *Neptune* and the Spanish *Rayo*.

Spear came scrambling aft with the news that Pellew had seen the approaching enemy and intended casting loose the tow. There was nothing Drinkwater could do except watch *Conqueror* make sail and stand to windward, to join the nine other British warships able to manoeuvre and work themselves between the enemy and the majority of the prizes.

Bucentaure began to roll and wallow to leeward, continuing to ship water. On deck Drinkwater watched the approach of the enemy, the leading ship with a commodore's broad pendant at her masthead. It was not Gravina but one of the more enterprising of the escaped French captains who was leading this bold sortie. The leading ship was a French eighty, and she bore down on *Bucentaure* as the stricken vessel drifted away from the protection of the ten British line-of-battle ships. As she luffed to windward of them they read her name: *Indomptable*.

The appearance of the Franco-Spanish squadron revived the crew of the *Bucentaure*. One of her lieutenants requested that Drinkwater released them from their parole and he had little alternative but to agree. A few moments later, boats from *Indomptable* were alongside and the *Bucentaure*'s lieutenant was representing the impossibility of saving the former French flagship. *'Elle est finie,'* Drinkwater heard him say, and they began to take out of the *Bucentaure* all her crew, including the wounded. For an hour and a half the boats of the *Indomptable* ferried men from the *Bucentaure* with great difficulty. The sea was still running high and damage was done to the boats and to their human cargo. Drinkwater summoned Atcherley and Spear.

'Gentlemen,' he said, 'I believe the French to be abandoning the ship. If we remain we have still an anchor and cable. We might yet keep her a prize. It is only a slender chance, but I do not wish to be retaken prisoner just yet.'

The two officers nodded agreement. 'Volunteers only, then,' added Drinkwater as the French lieutenant approached.

'It is now you come to boats, *Capitaine*.'

'*Non, mon ami*. We stay, perhaps we save the ship.'

The lieutenant appeared to consider this for some moments and then shrugged.

'Ver' well. I too will stay.'

So a handful of men remained aboard the *Bucentaure* as the Allied squadron made sail, refusing battle with the ten British ships. Drinkwater watched them hauling off their retaken ships, the Spanish *Neptuno* and the great black bulk of the *Santa Ana*, the latter towed by a brig, scraps of sails and the Spanish ensign rehoisted on what remained of her masts. Hardly had *Indomptable* taken in her boats than the wind backed suddenly and increased with tremendous strength from the west-southwest. Immediately *Bucentaure*'s leeway increased and as the afternoon wore on the pale smudge of Cadiz grew swiftly larger and more distinct. They could see details: the towers of the partly rebuilt cathedral, the belfry of the Carmelite convent, the lighthouse at San Sebastian and, along the great bight of Cadiz Bay from beyond Rota in the north to the Castle of St Peter to the southward, the wrecked hulks of the Combined Fleet being pounded to matchwood in the breakers.

As they drove ashore, Drinkwater had soundings taken, and at about three in the afternoon he had the anchor let go in a last attempt to save the ship. The fluke bit and *Bucentaure* snubbed round at the extremity of the cable to pitch head to sea as the wind blew again with storm force. They could see the British ships in the offing and around them some of the vessels that had sailed from Cadiz that morning. They had run for the shelter of the harbour as the wind began to blow, but several had not made it and had been forced to anchor like themselves.

Bucentaure's anchor held for an hour before the cable parted. Drinkwater called all her people on deck and they stood helplessly in the waist as the great ship drove again to leeward, beam on to the sea, rolling heavily as ton after ton of water poured on board. The rocks of Cape San Sebastian loomed towards them.

'Call all your men together, Mr Spear,' Drinkwater said quietly as the *Bucentaure* rose on the back of a huge wave. The heavy swell, enlarged by the violence of the storm, increased its height as its forward momentum was sapped by the rising sea-bed. Its lower layers were slowed and its upper surface tore onwards, rolling and toppling with its own instability, bearing the huge bulk of the *Bucentaure* upon its collapsing back.

In a roar of white water, as the spray whipped across her canting deck, the ship struck, her whole hull juddering with the impact. Water foamed all about her, thundering and tearing over the reef beyond the *Bucentaure*. Then it was receding, pouring off the exposed rocks as the trough sucked out and the stricken battleship lolled over. Suddenly she began to lift again as the next breaker took her, a white-flecked avalanche of water that rose above her splintered rail.

'Hold on!' shouted Drinkwater, and the urgency of the cry communicated itself to British and French alike. Then it broke over them, intensely cold, driving the breath from their bodies and tearing them from their handholds. Drinkwater felt the pain in his shoulder muscles as the cold and the strain attacked them. He clung to an eyebolt, holding his breath as the red lights danced before his eyes and his lungs forced him to inhale. He gasped, swallowing water, and then he was in air again and, unbelievably, *Bucentaure* was moving beneath them. He struggled upright and stared about him. Not fifty yards away the little bluff of Cap San Sebastian rushed past. Beneath its lighthouse crowds of people watched the death throes of the ship. *Bucentaure* had torn free, carried over the reef at a tangent to the little peninsula of the cape. He looked about the deck. There were less men than there had been. God alone knew how many had been swept into the sea by that monstrous wave.

For twenty minutes the ship drifted to leeward, into slightly calmer water. But every moment she sank lower and, half an hour later, had stuck fast upon the Puercas Reef. Drinkwater looked around him, knowing the long travail was over at last. In the dusk, boats were approaching from a French frigate anchored in the *Grande Rade* with the remnants of Gravina's escaped detachment. He turned to Spear and Atcherley. They were both shivering from cold and wet.

'Well, gentlemen, it seems we are not to perish, although we have lost your prize.'

Atcherley nodded. 'In the circumstances, sir, it is enough.' The marine officer looked at the closing boats with resignation.

'I suppose we must be made prisoners now,' said Spear dejectedly.

'Yes, I suppose so,' replied Drinkwater shortly, aware of the dreadful ache in his right shoulder and that beneath his feet *Bucentaure* was going to pieces.

Chapter Twenty-Three *November–December 1805*

Gibraltar

'Were you received by the Governor-General at Cadiz, Captain?' asked Vice-Admiral Collingwood, leaning from his chair to pat the head of a small terrier by his side.

'The Marquis of Solana granted me several interviews, sir, and treated all the British prize crews with the utmost consideration.'

Collingwood nodded. 'I am very pleased to hear it.' Collingwood's broad Northumbrian accent struck a homely note to Drinkwater's ears after his captivity.

'Your decision to return the Spanish wounded and the expedition with which it was done undoubtedly obtained our release, sir. I must make known my personal thanks to you.'

'It is no matter,' Collingwood said wearily. 'Did you obtain any knowledge of the state of the ships still in Cadiz?'

Drinkwater nodded. 'Yes, sir. Admiral Rosily arrived to find his command reduced to a handful of frigates. Those ships which escaped the action off Trafalgar were almost all destroyed in their attempt to retake the prizes on the twenty-third last. Although they got both the *Neptuno* and *Santa Ana* back into port, both are very badly damaged. However, it cost them the loss of the *Indomptable* which went ashore off Rota and was lost with her company and most of the poor fellows off the *Bucentaure*. The *San Francisco* parted her cables and drove on the rocks at Santa Catalina. As you know, the *Rayo* and *Monarca* were wrecked after their action with *Leviathan* and *Donegal*. I believe Gravina's *Principe de Asturias* to be the only ship of force fit for sea now left in Cadiz.'

'And Gravina? Do you know the state of his health, Captain?'

'Not precisely, sir, but he was severely wounded and it was said that he may yet lose an arm . . . May I ask the fate of Admiral Villeneuve, sir?'

'Villeneuve? Ah, yes, I see from your report that you made his acquaintance while in Cadiz. He was sent home a prisoner in the *Euryalus*. What manner of man did you judge him?'

'Personally courageous, sir, if a little lacking in resolve. But he was a perceptive and able seaman, well fitted to judge the weight of opposition against him. I do not believe he was ever in doubt as to the outcome of an action, although he entertained some hopes of eluding you . . .'

'Eluding us?' Collingwood raised an incredulous eyebrow.

'Yes, sir. And he had devised a method of counter-attacking, for he knew precisely by what method Lord Nelson would make his own attack.'

'How so?'

Drinkwater explained the function of the reserve squadron to bear down upon the spearhead of Nelson's advance.

'A bold plan,' said Collingwood when he had finished, 'and you say Villeneuve had argued the manner of our own attack?'

'Yes, sir. I believe that his fleet might have had more success had the wind been stronger and Gravina been able to hold the weather position.'

'Hmmm. As it was, they put up a stout and gallant defence. Admiral Villeneuve seems a well-bred man and I believe a very good officer. He has nothing in his manner of the offensive vapouring and boasting which we, perhaps too often, attribute to Frenchmen.'

'The Spaniards are less tolerant, sir,' Drinkwater said. 'The French were not well received in Cadiz after the battle. There was bad blood between them before the action. I believe relations were much worse afterwards.'

Collingwood nodded. 'You will have heard that a squadron under Sir Richard Strachan caught Dumanoir's four ships and took them on the third.'

'Then the enemy is utterly beaten,' said Drinkwater, perceiving properly the magnitude of the victory for the first time.

'Carthage is destroyed,' Collingwood said with quiet satisfaction, 'It would have pleased Lord Nelson . . .' The admiral fell silent.

Drinkwater also sat quietly. He did not wish to intrude upon Collingwood's grief for his dead friend. In the few hours he had been at Gibraltar since the *Donegal* landed him from Cadiz, Drinkwater had learned of the grim reaction within the British fleet to the death of Nelson. At first men exhausted with battle had sat and wept, but now the sense of purpose with which the little one-armed admiral had inspired his fleet had been replaced. Instead there was a strange, dry-eyed emotion, affecting all ranks, that prevented any levity or triumphant crowing over a beaten foe. This strange reticence affected Drinkwater now, as he sat in the great cabin of HMS *Queen*, to which Collingwood had shifted his flag, and waited for the new Commander-in-Chief to continue the interview. The little terrier raised its head and licked its master's hand.

'Yes, Captain Drinkwater,' said Collingwood at last, 'we have gained a great victory, but at a terrible cost . . . terrible!' He sighed and then pulled himself together. 'Perhaps we can go home soon . . . eh, Captain, home . . . but not before we've cornered Allemand and blockaded Salcedo in Cartegena, eh? Which brings me to you.' Collingwood paused and referred to some papers on his desk. 'We have lost not only Lord Nelson but several post-captains. I am endeavouring to have the Admiralty make promotions among the most deserving officers; many distinguished themselves. Quilliam, first of the *Victory*, for instance, and Stockham of the *Thunderer* . . .' He fixed his tired eyes upon Drinkwater.

Drinkwater wondered how much of Collingwood's exhaustion was due to his constant battle to placate and oblige people of all stations in his extensive and responsible command. He leaned forward.

'I understand perfectly, sir. Stockham has earned and deserves his captaincy.'

Collingwood smiled. 'Thank you, Captain. No doubt the Admiralty will find him a frigate in due course, but you see my dilemma.'

'Perfectly, sir. I shall be happy to return to the *Antigone*.'

'That will not be possible. I have sent her in quest of Allemand. Louis put a commander into her and, for the moment, you will have to undertake other duties.'

'Very well, sir.' Drinkwater had no time to digest the implications of this news beyond realising that a stranger was using his cabin and that poor Rogers would be put out.

Collingwood continued: 'I am putting you in command of the *Swiftsure*, prize, Captain Drinkwater. It should give you a measure of satisfaction that she was once a British ship of the line. I believe you returned from Cadiz with three other prisoners from your own frigate?'

'Yes, sir, Lieutenant Quilhampton and Midshipman Frey, and my man Tregembo.'

'Very well. They will do for a beginning and I shall arrange for a detachment from the fleet to join you forthwith.' Collingwood paused to consider something. 'We shall have to rename her, Captain Drinkwater. We already have a *Swiftsure*. We shall call her *Irresistible* . . . I will have a commission drawn up for you and until your frigate comes in with news of Allemand you will find your talents in great demand.'

Drinkwater rose. 'It is an apt name, sir,' he said smiling, 'one that I think even our late enemies might have approved . . .' He paused as Collingwood frowned. 'The Dons were much impressed by the spectacle of British ships continuing the blockade of Cadiz even after the battle. I apprehend the enemy expected us to have suffered too severe a blow.'

'We did, my dear sir, in the loss of our chief, but to have withdrawn the blockade would not have been consistent with his memory.' Collingwood's words of dismissal were poignant with grief for his fallen friend.

Drinkwater sat in the dimly lit cabin of the *Irresistible* and read the sheaf of orders that had come aboard earlier that evening. Outside the battered hulk of the ship, the wind whined in from the Atlantic, moving them gently even within the shelter of the breakwater, so that the shot-torn fabric of the ship groaned abominably. He laid down the formal effusion of praise from both Houses of Parliament that he had been instructed to read to the assembled ship's company tomorrow morning. It was full of the usual pompous Parliamentary cant. There was a notice that Vice-Admiral Collingwood was elevated to the peerage and a list of confirmed promotions that would bring joy to half the ships that crammed Gibraltar Bay, making good the damage inflicted by the Combined Fleet and the great gale.

Drinkwater was acutely conscious that he would not be part of the ritual. He knew that, in his heart, he would live to regret not being instrumental in an event which was epochal. Yet he was far from being alone. Apart from Quilhampton and Frey, there was not a man in Admiral Louis's squadron that was not mortified to have been sitting in Gibraltar Bay when Lord Nelson was dying off Cape Trafalgar. They could not reconcile themselves to their ill-luck. At least, Drinkwater consoled himself, he had been a witness to the battle. It did not occur to him that he had in any way contributed to the saving of a single life by his assisting Masson in the cockpit of the *Bucentaure*. His mind shied away from any contemplation of that terrible place, unwilling to burden itself with the responsibility of poor Gillespy's death. He knew that remorse would eventually compel him to face his part in the boy's fate, but events pressed him too closely in the refitting of *Irresistible* for him to relax yet. Once they sailed, he knew, reaction would set in; for the moment, he was glad to have something constructive to do and to know that neither Quilhampton nor Frey had come to any harm.

A knock at his cabin door broke into his train of thought and he was glad of the interruption. 'Enter!'

Drinkwater looked up from the pool of lamp-light illuminating the litter of papers upon the table.

'Yes. Who is it?' The light from the lamp blinded him to the darkness elsewhere in the cabin. The white patches of a midshipman's collar caught the reflected light and suddenly he saw that it was Lord Walmsley who stepped out of the shadows. Drinkwater frowned. 'What the devil d'you want?' he asked sharply.

'I beg pardon, sir, but may I speak with you?'

Drinkwater stared coldly at the young man. Since his brief, unexpected appearance on the *Bucentaure*, Drinkwater had given Walmsley no further thought.

'Well, Mr Walmsley?'

'I . . . I, er, wished to apologise, sir . . .' Walmsley bit his lip, 'to apologise, sir, and ask if you would accept me back . . .'

Drinkwater studied the midshipman. He sensed, rather than saw, a change in him. Perhaps it was the lamp-light illuminating his face, but he seemed somehow older. Drinkwater knitted his brow, recalling that Walmsley had killed Waller. He dismissed his momentary sympathy.

'I placed you on board *Canopus*, Mr Walmsley, under Rear-Admiral Louis. The next thing I know is that you are on *Conqueror*. Then you come here wearing sack-cloth and ashes. It will not do, sir. No, it really will not do.' Drinkwater leaned forward in dismissal of the midshipman, but Walmsley persisted.

'Sir, I beg you give me a hearing.'

Drinkwater looked up again, sighed and said, 'Go on.'

Walmsley swallowed and Drinkwater saw that his face was devoid of arrogance. He seemed chastened by something.

'Admiral Louis had me transferred, sir. I was put on board *Conqueror* . . .'

'Why?' Drinkwater broke in sharply.

Walmsley hesitated. 'The admiral said . . .'

'Said what?'

Walmsley was trembling, containing himself with a great effort: 'That my character was not fit, sir. That I should be broke like a horse before I could be made a seaman . . .' Walmsley hung his head, unable to go on. A silence filled the cabin.

'How old are you?'

'Nineteen, sir.'

'And Captain Pellew, what was his opinion of you?'

Walmsley mastered his emotion. The confession had clearly cost him a great deal, but it was over now. 'Captain Pellew had given me no marks of his confidence, sir. My present position is not tolerable.'

'And why have you suddenly decided to petition me, sir? Do you consider me to be *easy*?' Drinkwater raised his voice.

'No, sir. But the events of recent weeks have persuaded me that I should better learn my business from you, sir.'

'Do you have a sudden desire to learn your business, Mr Walmsley? I had not noticed your zeal commend you before.'

'No, sir . . . but the events of recent weeks, sir . . . I am . . . I can offer no explanation beyond saying that the battle has had a profound effect upon me. So many good fellows going . . . the sight of so many dead . . .'

It struck Drinkwater that the young man was sincere. He remembered him vomiting over the shambles of the *Bucentaure*'s gun-deck and supposed the battle might have had some redeeming effect upon Walmsley's character. Whether reformed or not, Walmsley watched by a vigilant Drinkwater might be better than Walmsley abusing his rank and privileges with men who had fought with such gallantry off Cape Trafalgar.

'Very well, Mr Walmsley,' Drinkwater reached for a clean sheet of paper, 'I will write to Captain Pellew on your behalf.'

Chapter Twenty-Four *April 1806*

The Martyr of Rennes

'So you finally came home in a frigate?' Lord Dungarth looked at his single dinner guest through a haze of blue tobacco smoke.

'Aye, my Lord, only to miss *Antigone* sent in convoy with the West India fleet, and then go down with the damned marsh ague . . .'

Dungarth looked at Drinkwater's face, cocked at its curious angle and pale from the effects of the recent fever. It had not been the home coming Drinkwater had dreamed of, but Elizabeth had cosseted him back to full health.

'I have been languishing in bed for six weeks.'

'Well I am glad that you could come in answer to my summons, Nathaniel.' He passed the decanter across the polished table. 'I have a commission for you before you rejoin your ship.'

Drinkwater returned the decanter after refilling his glass. He nodded. 'I am fit enough, my Lord, to be employed on any service. Besides,' he added with his old grin, 'I am obliged to your Lordship . . . personally.'

'Ah, yes. Your brother.' Dungarth blew a reflective ring of tobacco smoke at the ceiling. 'He was at Austerlitz, you know. His report of the confusion on the Pratzen Heights made gloomy reading.'

'God bless my soul . . . at Austerlitz.' The news of Napoleon's great victory over the combined forces of Austria and Russia, following so hard upon the surrender of another Austrian army at Ulm, seemed to have off-set the hard-won achievements of Trafalgar, destroying at a stroke Pitt's carefully erected alliance of the Third Coalition.

'Aye, Austerlitz. It killed Pitt as surely as Trafalgar killed Nelson.'

Both men remained silent for a moment and Drinkwater thought of the tired young man with the loose stockings.

'It was the one thing Pitt dreaded, you know, a great French victory . . . and at the expense of three armies.' Dungarth shook his head. The victory over the Russo-Austrian army had taken place on the first anniversary of Napoleon's coronation as Emperor and had had all the impact of a fatal blow to British foreign policy. Worn out with responsibility and disappointment, Pitt had died just over a month later.

'I believe,' Dungarth continued with the air of a man choosing his words carefully, 'that Pitt foresaw the destruction of Napoleon himself as the only way to achieve lasting peace in Europe.'

'Is that why he sent Camelford to attempt his murder?'

Dungarth nodded. 'I think so. It was done without approval; a private arrangement. Perhaps Pitt could not face the future if Napoleon destroyed an allied army. Pitt chose badly by selecting Camelford, but I imagine the strength of family obligation seemed enough at the time; besides, Pitt was out of office.' Dungarth sipped his port.

'The attempt was not secret, though. I recall D'Auvergne and Cornwallis both alluding to the fact that something was in the wind,' said Drinkwater, intrigued.

'No, it was not kept secret enough, a fact from which Napoleon has made a great deal of capital. D'Auvergne shipped Camelford into France from Jersey, and Cornwallis knew of the plan, on a private basis, you understand. Billy-go-tight no more likes blockading than does poor Collingwood now left to hold the Mediterranean.' Dungarth refilled his glass.

'Poor Collingwood talked of coming home,' remarked Drinkwater, taking the decanter.

'He will be disappointed, I fear. Pitt was right, I think: almost anything was acceptable to end this damnable war, so that he and Cornwallis and Collingwood and all of us could go home and enjoy an honourable retirement.'

'And Camelford's death,' asked Drinkwater, '*was* that an act fomented by French agents?'

Dungarth filled his glass again. 'To be honest I do not know. Camelford was a rake-hell and a philanderer. What he got up to on his own account I have no idea.' Dungarth sipped his port and then changed the subject. 'I understand you met our old friend Santhonax at Cadiz?'

Drinkwater recounted the circumstances of their meeting. 'I

suppose that, had Santhonax not recognised my name on the *Guarda Costa* report, I might still be rotting in a cell at Tarifa.'

'Or on your way to a French dépot like Verdun.'

'I was surprised he departed suddenly before the action.'

'I believe he too was at Austerlitz, though on the winning side.' Dungarth's smile was ironic. 'Napoleon recalled several officers from Cadiz. We received reports that they passed through Madrid. I think the Emperor's summons may have saved you from a fate worse than a cell at Tarifa or even Verdun.'

'A fact of which I am profoundly sensible,' Drinkwater replied. 'Now what of this new service, my Lord?'

The ironic look returned to Dungarth's face. 'A duty I think you will not refuse, Nathaniel. I have a post-chaise calling for you in an hour. You are to proceed to Reading and then to Rye where a lugger awaits you.'

'A lugger?'

'A cartel, Nathaniel. You will pick up a prisoner at Reading. He has been exchanged for four post-captains.'

Drinkwater remembered Quilhampton's multiplication table of exchange. He frowned. 'An admiral, my Lord?'

'Precisely, Nathaniel. Vice-Admiral Pierre de Villeneuve. He wishes to avoid Paris and he mentioned you specifically.'

'You are awake, sir?' Drinkwater looked at Villeneuve opposite, his face lit by the flickering oil-lamp set in the chaise's buttoned-velvet side.

Admiral Villeneuve nodded. 'Yes, Captain, I am awake.'

'We do not have far to go now,' said Drinkwater. The pace of the chaise was smooth and fast as it crossed the levels surrounding Rye. A lightening in the east told of coming daylight and Drinkwater was anxious to have his charge below decks before sunrise.

'You are aware that I wish to be landed at Morlaix?' Villeneuve's tone was anxious, even supplicating.

'Indeed yes, sir. I have specific instructions to that effect,' Drinkwater replied tactfully. Then he added, 'You have nothing to fear, sir. I am here to see you safe ashore.'

Villeneuve made as though to speak, then thought better of it. After a silence he asked, 'Have you seen your wife, Captain?'

'Yes.' Drinkwater did not add that he had been prostrated by fever and that Elizabeth had born his delirium with her customary fortitude.

'You are fortunate. I hope that I may soon see my own. If . . .' he began, then again stopped and changed the subject. 'I recall,' he said with a firmer tone to his voice, 'that we spoke of destiny. Do you remember?'

'Yes, I do.'

'I was present at the funeral of Lord Nelson, Captain. Do you not think that remarkable?'

'No more than the man whose interment you honoured, sir.'

Villeneuve's sigh was audible. He said something to himself in French. 'Do you think we were disgraced, Captain?'

'No, sir. Lord Nelson's death was proof that you defended your flag to the utmost. I myself was witness to it.'

'It was a terrible responsibility. Not the defeat – I believe victory was earned by you British – but the decision to sail . . . to set honour against safety and to let honour win . . . terrible . . .'

'If it is any consolation, sir, I do not think that Lord Nelson intended leaving you unmolested in Cadiz. I believe it was his intention to attack you in Cadiz itself if necessary.'

Villeneuve smiled sadly. 'That is kind of you, Captain. But the decision to send many brave men to their deaths was mine, and mine alone. I must bear that burden.'

Villeneuve fell silent again and Drinkwater began to pay attention to their approach to Rye. Then, as the chaise slowed, Villeneuve said suddenly, '*You* played your part, Captain, you and Santhonax and Admiral Rosily who was already coming to replace me . . .'

'*I* sir? How was that?'

But the chaise jerked to a stop, the door was flung open and the opportunity to elaborate lost. They descended onto a strip of windswept wooden-piled quay and Drinkwater was occupied with the business of producing his documents and securing his charge aboard the cartel-lugger *Union*. An hour later, as the lugger crossed Rye bar, he went below to find something to eat and renew his talk with Villeneuve. But the French admiral had rolled himself in a cloak and gone to sleep.

They enjoyed a swift passage down Channel, being brought-to twice by small and suspicious British cruisers. They crossed the

Channel from the Isle of Wight and raised the Channel Islands where a British frigate challenged them. Drinkwater was able to keep the identity of their passenger secret as he had been ordered and, making certain that he had the passport from the French commissioner for prisoners in London, he ordered the lugger off for the Breton coast and the port of Morlaix. During the passage Villeneuve made no attempt to renew their discussion. The presence of other people, the cramped quarters and the approaching coast of France caused him to withdraw inside himself. Drinkwater respected his desire for his own company. It was after they had raised Cap Frehel and were coasting westwards, that Villeneuve called for pen and paper. When he had finished writing he addressed Drinkwater.

'Captain, I know you to be a man of honour. I admired your ability before you had the misfortune to become a prisoner, when I watched your frigate run up into Cadiz Road. Colonel Santhonax only reinforced my opinion of you. You came to me as an example of many . . . a specimen of the *esprit* of the British fleet . . . everywhere I was surrounded by suspicion, dislike, lack of cooperation. You understand?'

Drinkwater nodded but remained silent as Villeneuve went on. 'For many years I have felt myself fated, Captain. They called my escape from Abukir lucky, but,' he shrugged, 'for myself it was dishonourable. It was necessary that I expiate for that dishonour. You persuaded me that to fight Nelson, to be beaten by Nelson, would be no dishonour. I would be fighting men of *your* quality, Captain, and it is to *you* as one of Nelson's officers that I entrust this paper. Should anything befall me, Captain, I beg you to make known its contents to your Admiralty.'

'Your Excellency,' said Drinkwater, much moved by this speech and unconsciously reverting to the form of address he had used when this unfortunate man commanded the Combined Fleet, 'I assure you that you will be landed in perfect safety . . .'

'Of that I too am certain, Captain. But my Imperial master is unlikely to receive me with the same hospitality shown by my late enemies. You know he has servants willing to express his displeasure.'

For a moment Drinkwater did not understand, and then he remembered Santhonax, and the allegations of the murder of John Wesley Wright in the Temple. Drinkwater picked up the letter and thrust it into his breast pocket. 'I am sure, sir, that you will find happiness with your wife.'

'It is a strong condemnation of the Emperor Napoleon and of the impossible demands he has put upon his admirals, captains and seamen,' said Lord Dungarth as he laid down Villeneuve's paper and looked at Drinkwater. 'This is dated the sixth of April. He wrote it on board the cartel?'

'And gave it to me for personal delivery to the Admiralty in the event of anything untoward occurring to him. He seemed intent on making his way south to his estate and joining his wife. I cannot believe he took his own life.'

Dungarth shook his head and picked up another paper from his desk. It seemed to be in cipher and beneath the queer letters someone had written a decoding. 'I have received various reports, mainly public announcements after the post-mortem which, I might add, was held with indecent haste. Also some gossip from the usual waterfront sources. He wrote to the Minister of Marine, Decrès, from Morlaix, also to some captains he proposed calling as witnesses at the enquiry he knew would judge his conduct. They were Infernet and Lucas, who had both been lionised by the Emperor at St Cloud. He received no reply, travelled to Rennes and arrived on the seventeenth. Witnesses at the post-mortem conveniently said he was depressed. Hardly remarkable, one would have thought. Then, on the morning of the twenty-second of April his body was found with six knife wounds in the heart. The body was undressed, face upwards. One witness said face down, but this conflicting evidence seems to have been ignored. Evidence of suicide was supported by the discovery of a letter to his wife and his telescope and speaking trumpet labelled to Infernet and Lucas. Ah, and the door was locked on the inside . . . that is no very great achievement for a man of Santhonax's abilities . . .'

'Santhonax?'

Dungarth nodded. 'He arrived in town the previous evening, Nathaniel. In view of the fact that he was at the post-mortem, I regard that as a most remarkable coincidence, don't you? And consider: Villeneuve is alleged to have stabbed himself six times in the heart. *Six*, Nathaniel, *six*! Is that consistent with the man you knew, or indeed for any man committing suicide?'

Drinkwater shook his head. 'I think not.'

'No, nor I,' said Dungarth vehemently. 'I wish to God we could pay Santhonax in like coin, by God I do.'

The eyes of both men met. Drinkwater recalled Dungarth passing up an opportunity to shoot both Santhonax and his wife Hortense as Camelford had advised. Perhaps if Camelford had succeeded in his mission neither he, nor Villeneuve, nor little Gillespy would be dead. 'I think Villeneuve anticipated some such end, my Lord,' Drinkwater said solemnly. 'I think he felt it his destiny.'

'Poor devil,' said Dungarth, his hazel eyes glittering intensely. 'Trafalgar notwithstanding, Nathaniel, this damnable war is not yet over.'

'No, not yet.'

'And that bastard Santhonax has yet to get his just deserts . . .'

Author's Note

In using the Trafalgar campaign as a basis for a novel I have not consciously meddled with history. All the major events actually took place and many of the characters existed. I have used a novelist's freedom in interpreting the actions of some of these, such as Camelford, who remains an enigma to this day. As for the others, I have used their written or recorded words or opinions to preserve historical accuracy.

There is no doubt that Napoleon's intention to invade Great Britain some time between 1803 and 1805 was very real indeed. That he swung his army away from the Channel to defeat Austria and Russia does not diminish that intent; it merely illustrates his disillusion with his admirals, an understandable desire to secure his rear after the formation of the Third Coalition, and the strategic adaptability of his genius.

A great deal has been written about Trafalgar and its consequences. Perhaps the most lamentable of these is an improper appreciation of our opponents. It was this reflection that attracted me to the character of Pierre de Villeneuve, the noble turned republican, whose abilities have been entirely eclipsed by the apotheosis of Nelson. It was Villeneuve's prescience that made him the 'coward' his contemporaries took him for. Ten months before the battle, Villeneuve outlined the precise method by which Nelson would attack. Realising this and the comparative qualities of the two fleets, Villeneuve was astute enough to foresee the likely outcome of action, notwithstanding his plan for a counter-attack. Of his personal courage or that of his fleet, there is no doubt. I hope I have done justice to their shades.

None of these assertions detract from the British achievement; quite the contrary. The Battle of Trafalgar remains the completest example of annihilation of a battlefleet until the Japanese attack on

Pearl Harbor. Nevertheless there were grave misgivings about Nelson's ideas of how a blockade ought to be conducted, and these were freely expressed at the time. History vindicated Nelson, but contemporary opinion was not always so kind, and French officers like Santhonax wanted to exploit what was held to be a weakness.

Napoleon always disclaimed any part in the death of John Wesley Wright and profoundly regretted that of D'Enghien. Between denial and admission lie a number of other mysterious deaths, particularly that of Pierre de Villeneuve. Despite the official verdict of suicide, I find it inconceivable that Villeneuve stabbed his own heart six times and I have laid the blame elsewhere. As to Villeneuve's curious letter of denunciation, one authority states that such a document of unproven origin came to light among the papers of a British diplomat employed at the time. It seemed to me that it might have formed some part of those supplementary revelations of unrecorded history which the adventures of Nathaniel Drinkwater have exposed.